TUMBLEWEEDS

*Four Inspirational Love Stories
with a Pioneer Spirit*

NORENE MORRIS

BARBOUR
PUBLISHING, INC.
Uhrichsville, Ohio

NORENE MORRIS
Norene Morris is a mother, grandmother, and great-grandmother who lives in northeastern Ohio. She claims to have been born with a pencil in her hand and has written since her girlhood, but her first published book was *Cottonwood Dreams* in 1993. Since then she has continued the beloved stories of the Langdon family in three additional books that were well-loved by the **Heartsong Presents** series readership. Norene believes romance and real love are inseparable, and she hopes her characters live and talk in such a way that they communicate the Father's "good news."

COTTONWOOD
DREAMS

Chapter 1

Mary Lou Mackey hung her dish towel on its hook and retied the ribbon that bound her long, brown hair on the nape of her neck. Her head turned toward the sound of hoofbeats—Missy coming in at full gallop.

Jenny Wimbley flapped Missy's reins over the rail and ran for the cabin. "Tom wants you to meet him in the cottonwood grove right away. Says it's real important," she announced.

"I can't." Mary Lou's heart sank. "I can't leave Mama alone. She was sick last night. Pa had to get Doc Gray."

The two girls crossed to the bedroom. Ellen Mackey lay asleep, a tiny doll almost lost in the feather tick. Chestnut hair framed her pale, porcelain face. A hint of a smile curved her lips.

Jenny pushed Mary Lou toward the door. "She's sleeping. Go on. I'll stay with your mama."

Jenny sat down in the rocking chair and poked into the large basket on the floor beside it. "I'll just sit here and knit," she whispered. " 'Twill keep my hands busy. Take Missy and you won't have to saddle Dulcie."

Mary Lou lingered over Mama. She had been sleeping quietly for the past couple of hours. Jenny would be there. "I won't be long," she promised.

Mary Lou dug her heels into Missy's side to spur her on. The Kansas wind tore her ribbon free and released her hair to trail out behind her like a young colt's tail.

When she neared Point Lane, Mary Lou's heart beat in time with the steady pounding of Missy's hooves. The harvest dance was a week away and Tom had asked her to go with him. She smiled thinking of Tom's long legs and big feet on the dance floor. Could he possibly keep them untangled? Things felt so different when she was with Tom. She would have to ask Mama if these feelings were real love. Mama would know—she loved Pa.

She rounded the bend on Point Lane. Tom and Tinder waited in the shade of the cottonwoods. Mary Lou pulled Missy to a halt and dismounted in a cloud of dust swirls. Tom quickly erased the distance between them and took her into his arms.

His kiss lingered, long and sweet. Mary Lou clung to him, relishing the strength of his embrace and the smell of scrub soap, horse, and leather. She tightened her arms around his neck, and he swung her around and around. It felt exhilarating. Their gazes met, and they laughed. This had to be real love. Mary Lou could picture herself as Tom's wife, raising his children. Her thoughts shocked her. She blushed and hid her face in his neck. Tom had not told her he loved her. But he had never acted this way either, like she was his. Maybe today.

Tom set Mary Lou on her feet. He raised her hands to his lips and kissed them. His laughter faded. The blue eyes riveted on hers looked serious. "Mary Lou," he spoke her name softly, almost reverently, then shifted his gaze to Tinder, saddled and loaded. "I have to leave this afternoon. To go back to Texas."

Right on cue, the sun sneaked behind a cloud.

"I don't understand. I thought we'd planned to go to the harvest dance. Why?"

Tom stopped her words with a kiss and led her to the fallen log where they had sat two days before and talked about the dance. Facing him, Mary Lou read deep sadness in his eyes. Something was wrong.

"It's sooner than I hoped. The cattle are railed, and I have to report back with the money." He labored over each word.

We haven't made any plans, her heart protested. *We need time to know each other.* Mary Lou opened her mouth, but her dry, tight throat stopped her voice. *Tom leaving?* Uneasy, she waited for him to say the words she longed to hear.

Tom didn't speak. His gaze roamed her face. He smoothed his hands over her loose hair and kissed her lips as if planting them firmly in his mind.

Mary Lou's stubborn heart refused to accept that she wouldn't see him tomorrow, or the day after, or maybe for several months. How she would miss his curly red hair, the tanned smoothness of his fresh-shaven cheeks, and the eyes that drew her into their shimmering blue depths. Just knowing he was near made everything come alive.

"It's just. . . ," Tom paused and looked beyond her, "the drive is over. A cowboy moves with the cattle."

What did he mean?

"I'll write you," Tom added and laughed stiffly. "Being postmistress, you'll get my letter special delivery."

He had to be keeping something from her. Had she done something to offend him? Worse, had she misinterpreted his intentions? Today he had been bold, yet the next minute far away.

Mary Lou cleared her throat and smiled. "I'll write you, too. I memorized your address from the letters you mailed your mother." She laughed half-heartedly and shook her finger at him like a schoolmarm. "That's what you get for courting the postmistress."

Tom didn't laugh. He brushed her forehead with his lips and moved in search of her mouth. She raised her face and he captured her lips, sending a rush of bewildering, frightening feelings surging through her. Suddenly, he picked her up in his arms, carried her to Missy, and swung her into the saddle.

"I. . . ," he began, but didn't finish. His long legs swallowed the space between him and Tinder. He mounted, waved, and rode off at a dead run.

Mary Lou watched the cloud of dust blur the image of the man she loved. Suddenly, Mama and Jenny invaded her thoughts. She reluctantly swung Missy in the direction of home and nudged her into a gallop.

When Missy slowed to take the turn in the lane to the cabin, Mary Lou spotted Doc Gray's buggy. A knot tightened in her stomach. *Mama?* Mary Lou slid to the ground and ran. She rushed through the door and collided with her father.

"Where have you been?" He added a rough oath.

Pa cursing? She had never heard him swear. Mama did not allow it. The fury in Pa's face paralyzed Mary Lou. He grabbed her by the shoulders and shook her. His fingers bit in, stabbing with pain.

"You met that cowboy, didn't you?" he accused. "You left your mama to die alone. You're no daughter of mine."

"Buck! Stop it!" Doc Gray jumped at the man and pried his hands from Mary Lou's shoulders. "Let go of her! Let go!"

Mary Lou dropped to the floor, too stunned to cry out.

The two men scuffled, and Buck shoved Doc toward the fireplace. By the time Doc got his balance, Buck had limped into the bedroom with Ellen and slammed the door.

Suddenly, words came out of the air and hit Mary Lou. "You left your mama to die alone."

"Mama?" She staggered to the bedroom door and opened it partway, then felt it slammed shut against her.

"Stay out of here!" Buck hollered. "You had to see your cowboy. Now your mama is dead."

A cumbersome wagon rumbled noisily into the yard carrying Tibby Bradford and Henrietta Wimbley. Mary Lou ran into Aunt Tibby's arms.

Tibby looked from one person to another. "Is it true?"

"Mama's dead, Aunt Tibby," Mary Lou sobbed. "I didn't know; I didn't know. . . ." Mary Lou clung to her aunt.

Tibby held Mary Lou close and kissed her wet cheeks. "Where's your Pa?" she asked softly.

"In the bedroom with Ellen," Doc said. "He won't let anyone else in."

Tibby transferred Mary Lou into Henrietta's arms and knocked on the bedroom door. "Buck? It's Tibby. I want to see my sister."

"Keep out, I told you. Everybody keep out," Buck's gruff voice replied.

Doc Gray left to get Henrietta's husband, Big Jon Wimbley. If it became necessary to bodily remove Buck, Big Jon was the man to do it. His six feet six inches, broad shoulders, and vise-like grip had steadied the thinking of many men in Venture.

Tibby knocked on the door again, harder. "Let me in, Buck. I have to see Ellen." She wiggled the latch.

The door slowly opened. Buck's hoarse voice warned, "Just you, Tibby."

Tibby slipped through the opening and the door closed. Mary Lou ran sobbing to the door and pounded on it with her fists. "Pa, let me see Mama. Please. I've got to see Mama."

She turned in agony to Jenny. "I shouldn't have gone. What happened after I left?"

"There was no hurt. Your mama just went to sleep and never woke up," Jenny answered. "I was right there beside her knittin'. I heard her take a deep breath, then give a big sigh. That must have been when she went home to Jesus. She died peaceful, Mary Lou. That's God's blessin'."

Two voices rose and fell in the bedroom. Everyone strained to hear. When Big Jon stomped across the porch, the voices stilled. Big Jon spoke with his wife and daughter first, then crossed to the door and walked in. Three voices raised, lowered, then quieted. The door opened. Without a word, Buck hobbled outside, climbed into his buggy, and rattled off.

Aunt Tibby came out to Mary Lou, put an arm around her, and took her in to see her mother. The distraught girl moved mechanically to Ellen's bedside and stared down at her. She lay peacefully sleeping just as Mary Lou had left her.

"No." The word rose up in disbelief. "No," she repeated. "Mama. Oh, Mama, don't leave me." She dropped across her mother's body. Its stiffness shocked her. "I'm sorry, Mama. I should have been here. Forgive me, Mama."

Tibby lifted Mary Lou from the body. They sat on either side of the bed, holding Ellen's hands, mourning their loss. Henrietta finally came in and insisted they leave. She guided them to the rocking chairs beside the fireplace and placed steaming cups of coffee in their hands.

Mary Lou sipped and stared. Nothing felt real. *Mama dead? Impossible!* She got up and started for the bedroom. Henrietta intercepted her.

"It's good to cry, Child. God gave us tears to wash away the hurt."

In the comfort of Henrietta's arms, Mary Lou clung, dry-eyed and numb. Tom was gone. Mama lay dead. Pa had disowned her. *Dear Lord, what reason can You give me to go on living? Help me, God, help me!*

Chapter 2

Mary Lou clutched her mother's shawl close in a vain attempt to protect her shivering body from the September rain. Her bonnet drooped, and a small waterfall cascaded from its brim.

Pastor Miles fingered the worn edge of Ellen Mackey's Bible and opened to a ribbon-marked page. Big Jon stood behind him with an umbrella to protect both Pastor and Bible.

It had poured steadily since early morning. Tall prairie grass squished underfoot as friends crowded around the open grave. The women wrapped themselves in large shawls, big enough to cover a wide-eyed child or two huddling in their skirts. Men stood hunched with necks shoved into their shoulders to keep the water from running down their necks.

Pastor lifted the Bible higher out of the rain. His rich voice spoke familiar comfort. " 'Let not your heart be troubled: Ye believe in God, believe also in Me. In My Father's house are many mansions: If it were not so, I would have told you' " (John 14:1–2).

Mary Lou drank the words into her parched heart. Her mother had read them to her often.

Pastor continued. " 'I go to prepare a place for you. And if I go and prepare a place for you, I will come again, and receive you unto Myself; that where I am, there ye may be also' " (John 14:2–3).

Oh, Mama, Mary Lou cried inside. *Don't leave me.*

"Father, into Thy hands we commit the spirit of Ellen Lisbeth Mackey. Have mercy upon her soul."

Shovels dug into the dirt piled high at the back of the grave. Soaked clods drummed the handmade coffin. One by one, the neighbors filed past the Mackeys to express sympathy and support, then hastened to the lineup of buggies, where dripping horses waited.

Tibby, held in her husband's arms, stared into the open grave, eyes flooded with the loss of her sister and best friend. Buck and Mary Lou stood rooted, watching rivulets of water spill into the grave. Pastor Miles gently took Ellen's Bible from under his coat and placed it in Buck's hands. "If you need me. . . ," he said. Buck nodded and stuffed the Bible inside his coat.

11

Mary Lou watched her father. His jaw flexed repeatedly. One tear squeezed out the corner of his eye. Abruptly, he stared at Mary Lou. She saw his eyes fill with hate. *He blames me for Mama's death!* Mary Lou shivered more from her father's coldness than the chilling rain. She raised her arm to touch him. "Pa?"

He jerked away, grabbed his shovel, and joined the men at the grave. Mary Lou watched dirt fill the hole, each thundering shovelful building a wall between her and Mama. Finally, silence.

Mary Lou's father hung on his shovel over the grave for a long moment. Then he lumbered to his buggy, using the shovel as a staff. Mary Lou watched him haul himself into the seat, give a slap of the reins to Morgan, and slowly move away. She covered her face with her hands.

The wide expanse of Kansas sky hung its swollen clouds low and wept. Mary Lou dropped to her knees beside her mother's grave, mindless of the mud. "Mama, he hasn't spoken to me yet. Pa's mad at me 'cause I went to see Tom. But you were asleep, Mama. . .just asleep."

She felt a pair of familiar arms and looked up into Jenny's concerned face. "Oh, Jenny, what am I going to do?"

Jenny pulled her to her feet. "Mary Lou, Honey, it's rainin'. You'll catch your death out here. Your mama isn't here, anyway. She's in heaven with the Lord. Come on. Let's get you home."

"Pa left me." Mary Lou let Jenny pull her along. "Jenny, Mama's dead."

"Why, Mary Lou, you're talkin' like a heathen! If anyone believed in heaven, your mama did, and that's where she is. And your mama's still with you in all the sweet memories you have of her."

Big Jon towered like a silent giant, watching the scene. Without a word, he gathered Mary Lou into his massive arms. The grief-stricken girl collapsed against his chest, absorbing the tender father-love she needed so desperately. With Jenny at his heels, Big Jon carried Mary Lou to the Wimbley wagon that had brought Ellen's body to the cemetery.

In Mary Lou's small bedroom, Jenny peeled off her friend's wet clothes, pulled a flannel nightgown over her shivering body, and tucked her into bed.

"Just settle some. I'm goin' to make hot tea to warm us up." Jenny gathered Mary Lou's wet clothes and left.

Mary Lou lay with open, unseeing eyes. The words hammered in her head. *Mama is dead. Mama is gone.* Tears ran down into her ears. The thought of her beautiful Mama out there in that cold, wet grave, alone. . . . *Not alone, My child, she's with Me.*

Mary Lou sat up. "I need her, Lord," she cried aloud. "Lord, help me!"

Jenny bounded through the door and threw her arms around Mary Lou. "He is, Honey, and we can count on Him. Look at me. When my mama and pa died in that wagon accident, God gave me not only a new mama and papa but ten new brothers and sisters."

The two girls clung to each other and sobbed, longing for their mothers. When their sobs subsided, Jenny pushed Mary Lou down and tucked a second pillow under her head. "The tea'll be ready. I'll be right back."

They were sipping their tea when Buck stuck his head in.

Jenny rose, and Mary Lou held her breath. "Pa?"

He stared blankly at the two girls, then withdrew without a word.

"I guess I better be goin'." Jenny said.

"He hasn't said one word to me since she died. Jenny, was it my fault?"

"Of course not! Your mama was a lot sicker than anybody knew. Talk to Doc Gray. He'll tell you." Jenny leaned over, kissed Mary Lou on the cheek, and gathered the cups. "What you need is some sleep. Thank God for givin' you such a good mama, then pray you'll be able to help your pa. He's grievin' now, but your pa loves you. You'll see."

Alone, relaxed by the tea, Mary Lou let herself sink into the softness of the feather tick. The thought of Pa hurting swelled her heart with sadness and fresh love for him. *Lord, how are we ever going to live without Mama?*

Warmth and exhaustion crept in. Mary Lou slept.

When Mary Lou opened her eyes, her father stood at the foot of her bed. Abruptly, he turned and walked out.

Mary Lou flung back the covers and jumped out of bed. *Why hadn't Mama. . . .* The surge of energy drained, leaving a horrible emptiness. "Mama," she whispered. Hot tears flowed while she dressed. By habit she pulled up the bed covers and hurried out.

Pa sat in his chair by the fireplace staring into the flames. Mary Lou yearned to throw herself into his arms. Maybe together they could ease the void of Mama being gone.

A knock on the door startled Mary Lou. She opened it to four smiling faces. Henrietta, Jenny, Young Jon, and Miriam Wimbley, their hands full of dishes, trailed across the room.

"Brought your supper and enough to tide you over a day," Henrietta explained. "Jenny, Miriam, set the table. It's ready to eat."

Mary Lou sighed in relief.

Henrietta busied everyone with preparation. "Mary Lou, get a big spoon to dish out the chicken and dumplin's. Come to the table, Buck. Big Jon will be along in a minute."

Buck grunted.

Undaunted, Henrietta hustled about, lifting the lid off the tureen and releasing the savory aroma of cooked chicken.

Another knock announced Big Jon. Placing his hand on Buck's shoulder, he said, "Come on, old man. My woman makes the best chicken and dumplin's in these parts."

"I'm not hungry," Buck mumbled.

"Well, you may not be but your body is. Come on."

Buck capitulated and limped to his place at the head of the table. Big Jon sat down beside Henrietta, and the others filed in. Mary Lou hesitated, then slid into her mother's place opposite her father.

Big Jon folded his hands on the edge of the table. All heads bowed. His voice boomed out thanks to God for the food, the land, and company present. Mary Lou's eyes grew hot. Mama had always said grace. Now who would do it?

Big Jon expertly ladled steaming chicken surrounded by potatoes, carrots, and fat dumplings. Henrietta passed the fried cabbage and a large wooden tray of homemade bread, followed by a white crock of freshly churned butter.

Mary Lou swallowed the best she could. She watched Pa clean up his plate and mop gravy with his bread. He was hungry. Was that why he had come to her room—to tell her it was suppertime? Why didn't he say so?

Jenny and Miriam served huge pieces of warm apple pie. Between bites, Big Jon told the latest news he had heard at the train station about some women creating a stir axing saloons.

"They're gatherin' women together to form unions of some kind against Demon Rum. I hear Tibby Bradford is recruiting women in Venture." Big Jon laughed. "Nate better stop her or he'll be surrounded by a bigger storm than usual."

When everyone finished, the women rose, cleared the table, and washed the dishes. The men returned to the fireplace and discussed opportunities the Kansas Pacific Railroad could bring to Venture.

Henrietta swung her shawl around her shoulders and motioned for the girls to get theirs. They stepped out into the coolness of the back porch. The drizzling rain had stopped.

"Here," Jenny guided Mary Lou to Ellen's rocking chair. Mary Lou slid slowly into it and closed her eyes. Memories of her mother's presence soothed her.

Henrietta began. "Now, my dear, if you need anythin' at all, you know where we are. We've always considered you part of our family."

"Your mama worried about you when she knew she didn't have long to live," Henrietta continued. "She made Tibby and me promise we would look after you. It's hard for fathers to care for girls."

Amazed, Mary Lou rose from her chair. "You mean Mama knew she

14

was going to die? Why didn't she tell me? Why didn't somebody tell me?"

"She wouldn't let us. She kept prayin' she would live long enough to see you married, but it came too soon."

Mary Lou staggered. *Had everyone known but her? Mama, why didn't you tell me?*

Henrietta encircled Mary Lou with her arms. "Your mama had such faith. She even hoped to hold her first grandchild. Doc kept tellin' her she had to get more rest. Of all people, a doctor should know that homesteadin' women don't get time to rest."

Mary Lou looked up into Henrietta's face. Such kind eyes. They twinkled like Mama's. Prairie life was hard, but like Mama, Henrietta never lost her joy and hope. Fresh guilt swamped Mary Lou. She had never suspected Mama was so sick. The salty fountain broke and Henrietta held her close. Jenny and Miriam put their arms around them both and they cried together in their loss.

"Now," Henrietta said and loosed the girls, "we must dry our tears, set a spell, and enjoy the evening as if Ellen were here."

They sat down again. Mary Lou looked around at the simple wooden porch that Mama had made her sanctuary. Every nice evening after dinner, she had settled in her rocking chair with her Bible and read until it was too dark to see. She had called it "God's Time." Not even Pa's berating had moved her. Finally, Pa let her be. This was where Mama and Mary Lou talked of woman things.

Mama had spoken often about the wonder of God's love and read Scripture aloud. Mary Lou loved to hear her. The words came alive in a way they never did when Mary Lou read them herself.

On one of those evenings, Mary Lou had given her heart to Jesus. Ellen had put her arms around Mary Lou and squeezed her breathless. "I am so happy," she had cried. "Now I will never lose you. We both belong to Jesus because He's in our hearts."

Pa had stepped out on the porch at that moment and they had bubbled their new-found joy to him. He had shrugged and walked back into the house, mumbling something about women's foolishness.

Henrietta rose. "It's time we're on our way." She and Big Jon swept their family out, loaded with clean dishes.

When the door closed, Mary Lou turned and looked at her father. "Pa," she began, "I want to talk to you."

Without a word, Buck rose, hobbled out the door, and headed for the barn. Morgan nickered.

Minutes later, Mary Lou stood at the window and watched the horse and buggy emerge, carrying Pa to town. Trembling, she dropped into her father's chair beside the dying fire. Stillness seeped through the cabin walls and enveloped her with fear. She got up, threw herself against the door, and locked it. Fighting panic, she grabbed the lamp and sought the comfort of her own bed. *Dear Lord. . . .*

Chapter 3

Mary Lou rolled over and stared at the beams in the ceiling. A chill shuddered through her body, even though warm rays of morning sun rested on her legs. Tired. She was so tired. With great effort, she sat up.

Mama. The ache and longing returned.

She listened to the familiar morning symphony of the prairie: the eerie wail of a coyote giving up the night, the swish of the wind through prairie grass, the distant bark of a prairie dog as he poked his nose out of his hole.

Pa? She rose and opened her bedroom door. His chair was empty. She crossed to her parents' bedroom and knocked. Silence. She opened the door and peeked in. The bed was empty.

Probably in the barn. It wouldn't be the first time her father had come home late, flopped into a hay pile, and slept. Her mother had protested, but Pa had laughed and said that as a boy he had slept more often in a haystack than in a bed.

Mary Lou grabbed her bonnet on her way out the door. The sun was high and hot, but the sweet prairie air was fresh and warm. Both barn doors were wide open, and Pa's buggy was gone. Her heart sank. He must have stayed in the back rooms at the store.

Dulcie nickered.

Dulcie. Her poor horse had not been watered or fed. She released Dulcie from the stall and laid her head against the animal's warm, soft hair. "I'm sorry."

Dulcie gave a low whinny of sympathy.

Mary Lou grabbed a bucket and filled it from the well. Dulcie followed like a shadow, then eagerly dipped her nose and drank.

A dust cloud signaled a visitor. Mary Lou shaded her eyes. It looked like one of Uncle Nate's wagons. She threw an armful of hay to Dulcie and ran to meet her aunt.

Tibby expertly pulled the horses to a quick halt, jumped down, and held Mary Lou at arm's length. A backlog of grief welled up, and they clung to each other and cried until Tibby broke away.

"Heavens!" she sniffed. "We'll drown in our own tears." Aunt Tibby, ever efficient, carried a wealth of hankies in her pockets. The two women dried their eyes and faced each other with a smile.

"Ellen's probably frowning at us. Stafford girls are made of strong stuff." Tibby threw her head back and laughed. "We learned that from Mother. Think how courageous your grandmother was to live with Grandfather Stafford for thirty years."

Mary Lou took a deep breath. "I'm sorry."

"Nothing to be sorry for. A time of grieving is a necessary comfort. But life goes on, and Ellen is in a better place. She's with Jesus, well and smiling and probably singing in the heavenly choir!" Tibby settled her shoulders with a big sigh. "You should have heard your mama sing in the choir back home."

Lost in their own memories, Mary Lou and her aunt walked arm in arm toward the cabin. It soothed them to work at tasks that spoke of Ellen. Bread dough was soon made, slapped into fat rounds, and covered with warmed flannel to rise quicker.

They packed Ellen's clothes in a trunk. "These will all fit you and are yours now. After a bit you'll wear them proudly." Tibby cupped Mary Lou's face in her hands. "You are as beautiful as your mother, inside as well as out. Ellen taught you well."

Tibby walked to the fireplace and redistributed the burning cow chips. They burst into flame then settled to a steady hot fire. She peered into an iron kettle, dumped grits into the simmering water, and stirred vigorously. At the coffee mill, she ground roasted beans and poured them into a pot. "What time this morning did your pa leave?"

Mary Lou hung her head. "He left last night."

Tibby gasped. "You mean you were here alone all night? What's the matter with that man?"

"He's grieving, Aunt Tibby. He'll come around." That's what Mama had always said. But she and Mama had waited through ten years for him to come around. Ever since the accident, Pa had been a different man. And now he had disowned her. Did he not need her? With Mama gone, she desperately needed him.

"But he shouldn't leave you alone, especially now." Tibby was incensed. "Maybe your uncle Nate can straighten out his thinking." As if reading Mary Lou's thoughts, she added, "Disowning you was a result of despair at Ellen's death. He'll get over that. But leaving you out here alone at night isn't manly."

A clatter of hoofbeats pounded to a stop outside.

Jenny Wimbley wafted in with the tantalizing aroma of fresh-baked bread. Her basket held two brown-crusted loaves, fresh butter, and some vegetables. Suddenly Mary Lou was hungry.

Aunt Tibby lifted three cups from the shelf, filled them with coffee, and brought them to the table.

"Let's set a spell," she said. "We've been working long enough." She peeked in the basket and held up a loaf. "Mmmmm. Thank your ma. Our bread isn't ready yet."

Tibby sliced bread while Mary Lou brought a jar of her mother's prairie glove apple jelly and placed it on the table. A stir of the grits revealed they were not cooked.

The three sat at the table and sipped coffee. Normally, Jenny would have filled the silence with a stream of chatter. Today, her eyes flickered from Mary Lou to Tibby.

Each was absorbed in her own thoughts, comforted by the covenant that bound prairie women in their need for companionship and survival. Every mother taught her daughter the myriad tasks that would consume her days. Even the very young learned their primary task in this enormous land was to plant a home and sink deep roots for their family.

Jenny offered, "Ma said not to worry about supper. You and your pa can come for supper, or if you want, I could bring it here."

"Thank your ma," Tibby answered, "but Mary Lou is coming to stay with us."

Mary Lou shook her head. "No, I'm staying here. Home has to be here when Pa comes." She was afraid to stay alone, but more afraid of failing Pa if she did not. He needed her. She needed him. Eventually, they would talk.

Tibby drained her coffee cup and carried it to the sink table. "I must be heading home." She placed her hand on Mary Lou's shoulder. "If you change your mind, come." She was gone as quickly as she had come.

Mary Lou and Jenny continued the round of chores. Normally when they were together, words tumbled over each other. Today, Mary Lou had a difficult time with casual chitchat. It seemed meaningless.

After Jenny left, Mary Lou milked the cows and lowered the milk cans into the well to keep the milk cool. She fixed herself a light supper of dried beef, some of Henrietta's vegetables, bread, and tea. After eating, she rounded up soiled clothing to launder in the morning. A sudden tiredness enveloped her.

She walked absently around the cabin touching Mama's things. Tears flowed freely down her cheeks. Then Mama's face filled her mind. Smiling. Always smiling. Even the tears she had cried were tears of joy.

Mary Lou's gaze wandered around the room and rested on Mama's Bible on the shelf Pa'd built for Mama's books. She crossed the room, picked it up, and carried it out to the back porch. She ran her hand over her mother's empty chair and sat down. This Bible was hers now. She turned it lovingly in her hands. She noticed something she had never seen before—the faint imprint of Mama's hand around the outside binding. Slowly, Mary Lou shaped her fingers into Mama's handprint. They matched perfectly. She hugged the book to her breast. Silently, Mary Lou prayed, *Help me find the comfort and wisdom Mama gained from this book.*

She fluttered its pages. The Bible fell open to a well-used, tear-stained page marked with a faded blue ribbon. Verse 5 of Psalm 30 was circled in pencil: "For His anger endureth but a moment; in His favor is life: weeping may endure for a night, but joy cometh in the morning."

Mary Lou looked out over her beloved prairie. A calming peace gently held her, sensitizing her to the beauty she so often took for granted. The sun slowly climbed into bed and drew the sunset over the horizon like a flaming orange comforter.

Uninvited, Tom invaded her thoughts. His abrupt departure had left her disappointed. Yet she clung to the feeling there had been something he had wanted to tell her. And could not. Did it have to do with Laura? He had mentioned her so casually, but just how did Laura fit into his life?

Mary Lou's anger flared. If Laura meant something to Tom, he was no gentleman to hold Mary Lou in his arms and kiss her! Pa had warned her about cowboys. If anyone knew about them, Pa did. Her mind whirled for an answer. She found none, but her stubborn heart persisted in hoping that when Tom wrote, he would explain.

"Silly thing." She scolded her heart sternly and shut her eyes against the descending nightfall. The minute her eyes closed, Tom's image formed. He stood leaning against Tinder and smiling in a wry way that made Mary Lou feel as if he knew her innermost secrets. She opened her eyes quickly, flushed with the memory that she had made a fool of herself.

Night shadows crept in, hunting a resting place. Her eyes focused sharply as the shadows took ghostly shapes, then changed and reshaped again. Apprehension threw fear around her like a cloak. Chirping crickets sang noisily and crescendoed into a screaming accompaniment to the night howling choir of gray wolves. Mary Lou had heard stories about gray wolves. When food was scarce, they dared to scratch on the doors and windows of the cabins. One time when a neighbor was in town, the wolves had gotten in and torn the cabin apart in their search for food.

She strained to hear Pa's buggy. Her ears sifted through the cacophony of sound, but nothing resembled the clop of a horse or the rattle of a buggy.

With false bravado, she stood abruptly and scolded aloud. "You're a big girl now and have heard and seen this all before." *But not alone!*

Chapter 4

The sun yawned, stretched, and climbed over the eastern horizon. The town of Venture slept, except for a few stray dogs scrounging for something to fill their empty stomachs. A rider entered the west end of Center Street and the dogs sprang clear of the horse's hooves.

Mary Lou gave Dulcie her head and the pony quietly made her way to the store for the first time in two weeks. Usually Mary Lou rode in with her father, but since Ellen's death, he had returned to the cabin only once—the day of the funeral. She guessed she would find him in the rooms at the back of the store. They were as much home to him as the cabin. Yes, his buggy stood there and Morgan nickered to her from the lean-to.

She dismounted, tied Dulcie, and paused at the back door wondering whether her father would open it if she knocked. Her stomach twisted into knots. As much as she wanted to see Pa and talk with him, she couldn't face another rejection. She shook her head and continued along the side of the store to the front door.

At the front corner, she paused to look up and down the street. Venture resembled most other towns in northeastern Kansas. Mary Lou stepped up on the warped timber planks nailed together to resemble a sidewalk in front of the store. Old wooden posts and crooked tree limbs at the street's edge did their best to stand straight for hitching posts and rails.

Mary Lou thought back. She had lived half her life in Schineberg's Grocery. Buck had taken a long time to change the name of his business to Mackey's General Store out of respect to the man who had willed it to him. Ellen had run the post office, so Mary Lou had spent hours looking out the front window. She had watched frame structures rise on both sides of Center Street.

Across the street, Glenn Farrell walked out of Mrs. Barton's Boarding House. He waved and grinned. "Good morning, Mary Lou," he called and ran to catch up with her. He unlocked the store door and stepped aside to let her pass. "You planning on staying awhile today?"

"Yes, I'll be coming in every day now. I'm sorry I put the whole load on you, Glenn, but with Mama. . ." She welled up with tears. Just when she seemed to have things under control, a mention of Mama swallowed her in grief. But she had to get back to the post office. She couldn't expect Glenn to do her work, and she needed to be busy—too busy to think.

An early customer came at that moment and approached Glenn. "Thank you, Lord," Mary Lou breathed. She was not in the mood to talk. She even sighed a thanks that the post office was as she expected—in chaos. Piles of unsorted mail lay stacked on shelves, the counter, even on the chair. She checked their mailbox. Nothing from Tom.

Glenn poked his head in and mumbled excuses for not getting the mail sorted. "I'd better check at the stage depot and get this week's bag." He vanished.

"I'll do it," she called after him, but the door banged. Looking out the window at Glenn's retreating back, Mary Lou relived the day Tom Langdon had first sauntered across the street, tall and lean in chaps and clinking spurs. He had opened the door and brought in a burst of energy that filled the room.

"Mornin', Ma'am," he had drawled. "How much to mail this letter?"

Mary Lou had looked at the bold handwriting. "Mrs. Zachary Langdon, Harness, Texas," she had read aloud.

"My mother." He had grinned and pointed to the address. His fingers had brushed her hand.

Color had risen on Mary Lou's cheeks. She moved to the stamp box. "Three cents, please," she said. *What's the matter?* she scolded herself. *A handsome cowboy walks in, and you fall apart. Ridiculous!*

She also remembered the day the address on his letters changed to "Miss Laura Shepard." Tom had said he was sending them to Laura to be sure his mother got his mail. Now she wondered. *Was that why he left? Was that why he had never said he loved me?*

Her gaze caught Glenn returning with the mailbag. Sunlight highlighted his straight blond hair, and the wind rumpled it every time he smoothed it.

Glenn bumped through the door and dropped the mailbag on the chair. Mary Lou rescued the pile of old mail before the bag fell. The store bell jangled. Glenn looked apologetic and hurried to a customer.

Mary Lou was grateful for the small alcove that housed the post office at the front corner of the store. Pa had built it there because the window provided better light. *Pa,* she thought, *I must see Pa.* She walked out of the door and into Ida Hensley.

"Oh, my dear," Ida said, "I'm so sorry about your mama. Anythin' I can do, just let me know. I've been prayin' for you." She patted Mary Lou on the shoulder.

"Thank you, Mrs. Hensley. You're very kind."

"I 'spect your Pa is grievin' terrible. He must miss Ellen."

"Yes, we do. I'm on my way to see Pa now. Thank you, Mrs. Hensley."

Mary Lou hurried to the back. She knew their neighbor meant well, but Mary Lou could not talk about Mama's death. It hurt too much.

The two rooms across the back of the store had been the home of Jacob Schineberg and his wife, Naomi, former owners. When Naomi gave birth to their only son, she and the baby both died, leaving Jacob alone.

Then Buck had had his accident. He had been too proud to take charity, so Jacob had talked Buck into staying with him to help in the store. He had cared for Buck like a son until Buck had gotten back on his feet. Then he had taught Buck to run the store.

A couple years later, a wagonload of barrels had toppled onto Jacob. Before he died, Jacob had willed the store to Buck in front of a dozen witnesses.

At the door of the back room, Mary Lou stood, her hand poised to knock. They had to resolve this. She couldn't go on not talking. "Pa?" she called and tapped the door. Silence. She tapped again. "Pa, are you there?" Not a sound.

Her tears ran unchecked. He still had not forgiven her. Her own guilt returned, even though Doc Gray had told her Mama had been sick for years.

"It was only a matter of time," he had said. "She would have died if you'd been at her side. I told her to get more rest. She wouldn't listen."

Sorrowfully, Mary Lou went back to the post office. Sun streamed through the window. She wiped her tears and took a handful of letters out of the bag.

Her heart quickened. Maybe there would be one from Tom. As the piles grew smaller, her heart grew heavy.

"Mr. William Owen Mackey," the envelope read. "From Mrs. Lars Thurston."

Mary Lou ran to the back room and knocked again. "Pa, there's a letter for you from Aunt Nelda."

She heard stirrings. The door opened. The smell of whiskey preceded Pa's head. He appeared unshaven, his eyes bloodshot. He took the letter from Mary Lou's hand and tore it open. After reading it quickly, he handed it back and closed the door.

Mary Lou heaved a sigh and turned away. Like her, Pa felt lost without Mama. He had never treated her like this before. When she was little, he would pick her up and throw her into the air. Mary Lou hadn't been the least bit afraid. Pa had always caught her in his big arms and tickled her till she begged to be put down. Later, Pa had taught her to love horses, to handle them with respect, and to ride like the wind.

Nothing was the same now. Mama had been the joy of their family, always encouraging them. *Oh, Mama, I miss you so much.* She walked back to the post office, sat down, and opened the letter.

> *Dear Brother Owen,*
>
> *I was so sorry to learn of your Ellen's death, and my heart aches for you. As you know, I lost my Lars last winter, and life has been hard. I am staying with a good family who treat me well. I cook, clean, and help with the children. They pay me some, so I have a little money. But it's not the same as family.*
>
> *I have not been able to get you out of my mind. I know how much work there is to be done in a home, and you have the store as well. Mary Lou is young, and I am sure I could help by keeping house and cooking for you both. I would not expect any pay.*
>
> *Please let me know before the cold weather sets in.*
>
> > *Your loving sister,*
> > *Nelda*

Mary Lou put down the letter. "Thank you, Lord, for Aunt Nelda," she said. She took a deep breath and knocked again on the back room door.

"Pa, I read Aunt Nelda's letter, and I want to know what to write back." Mary Lou waited, praying the door would open.

Finally, there was scuffling within and the door opened. Mary Lou's father tried to focus his glassy eyes on her.

"Oh, Pa." She swallowed hard. "What shall I tell Aunt Nelda?" She fought the urge to fling herself into his arms. For the moment, it was enough that he looked at her.

"Tell her to come," he said thickly. "She'll be a help to you."

Mary Lou stepped forward. "Pa?"

He closed the door.

Mary Lou's voice lifted in prayer. "He spoke to me! Thank You, Lord, for answering my prayer. Please help him find You. Mama prayed for that. He needs You now more than ever."

Mary Lou went back to the post office with a lighter step. She could feel Mama smiling down at them from heaven. Mary Lou looked up—and smiled back.

Chapter 5

Tom Langdon slowed Tinder to a walk. An hour ago he had crossed out of Oklahoma Indian Territory into the Texas panhandle. He would be home for supper.

It had been a long ride. The first fifty miles he had ridden like a madman to put space between himself and Mary Lou, fighting the desire to turn back and claim the woman he loved. His heart twinged at the sight of every cottonwood.

Approaching a stream, Tom dismounted, tied Tinder to a tree, and banged the dust from himself with his hat. He fell flat on his stomach and slaked his thirst. Then he dunked his whole head in the cool water and rubbed away the trail grime.

"I don't want no cowboy marryin' my daughter. You're a wanderlust bunch. I know. I was one."

Buck had never given Tom a chance to say his intentions were honorable and that he was not just a cowboy. He had refused to listen to anything Tom had to say.

Tom knew Mary Lou loved him. He prayed she could wait until he received his inheritance in the Circle Z. Even then, his brother Doug would fight him all the way. Until things were settled, Tom had nothing to offer but his love. That was not enough for Buck. Mary Lou's confused face hung in Tom's mind. He flinched. How else could he have honored his promise to Buck Mackey? It had to be a flat cutoff. He regretted telling Mary Lou he would write. He pictured her sorting the mail for the letter that would never come.

The cowhands jawed about Buck to Tom. He had been on his way to becoming a big man in those parts, had bought land and cattle to go into ranching. Buck had worked as head man for Nate Bradford.

One hot summer night, Buck had been riding the range on his black stallion, Morgan, when a nest of rattlers had spooked his horse. The big black had skittered, reared, and thrown Buck. His left foot had tangled in the stirrup, and Morgan had dragged him, seriously injuring his back and left leg. As a result, he was unable to ride a horse.

Tom felt for Buck. Settling for a buggy after riding the range would be death. Tom couldn't remember learning to ride. His earliest memory was being astride Big Diamond with his father, Zachary Langdon. He missed his dad. Things at the ranch would be different if he were still alive.

Tom loosened Tinder and moved him to the stream. The horse submerged his nose for a long drink, then moved into a shaggy grass patch to stock up. Tom dropped to the ground on his back and flopped his arms over his eyes to shade the sun. He would give Tinder a little more rest.

The moment he closed his eyes, Mary Lou's heart-shaped face filled his mind. In his arms she felt like a little girl. But nineteen was no little girl. She was a woman—the woman he wanted to marry.

Tom wondered what his mother would say. Allena Langdon had her own ideas about who her sons should marry. Except Zachary, his oldest brother. Zack hated ranching and had left for Massachusetts to study law right after their father had died. Allena had given up on Zack but made no secret of her wishes for Doug and Tom. Marlena Kincaid for Doug, and Laura Shepard for Tom. Tom had agreed—until he met Mary Lou.

He wondered what to do when he got home. Doug would strut out, grab the money, and dismiss him like one of the cowhands. There had never been words between them, but Tom knew Doug wanted the ranch.

Tom, like his father, loved every blade of grass on the ranch. Land was not a thing; it was a living entity and would remain after every Langdon returned to dust. As a young boy, Tom dreamed of teaching his sons to ride and of someday, like his father, giving them their heritage.

In five months, according to his father's will, one quarter of the Circle Z would be his. For Doug, a day of reckoning.

Tinder whinnied.

Tom got up and grabbed his hat. This time he would fight for what was his and go back to Buck as a rancher. He whistled for Tinder. The horse chomped one last mouthful and pranced to his side. Tom angled his hat, mounted, and headed south.

Tinder tossed his head and sniffed the air when they neared the Circle Z. Tom leaned forward and patted his neck. "You're as glad to get home as I am." The thought of a bath, a hot meal, and a soft bed made him relax the reins and let Tinder go. They went through the Circle Z arch at full gallop.

The cowboys had not arrived yet. They had given him a hard time when he had told them he was traveling alone, but he had needed thinking time.

"Tom. You're home!"

Tom turned toward the shout, slid off Tinder, and ran to Nelson, who was hobbling on his crutches as fast as he could. When they met, Nelson

26

flung his crutches and threw himself into Tom's arms. They pounded each other on the back, laughing and talking at once.

Allena Langdon hurried through the ranch house door to greet her son. Tom waved and picked up Nelson's crutches. Arm in arm, the two boys walked to meet their mother.

"I'm glad you're back, Son." His mother hugged both sons and sighed. "My prayers are answered."

Tom teased, "Aren't you the one who always says 'prayer and worry don't mix'?"

His mother laughed. "I know. But you boys are all I have." She linked her arm around the other side of Nelson and the three walked back to the house.

"Where's Doug?" Tom asked. "I thought he would be waiting at the door for the money."

"Now, Tom. Doug takes his responsibilities seriously. He's in town. The cattle ranchers are having a meeting about the new Kansas law that forbids Texas cattle to be driven across their state to the railroads because of Texas ticks. Everyone's up in arms."

Funny. Tom had not heard a word about that when he was in Kansas. He would write Nate Bradford.

They were just finishing dinner when Doug stormed in. As usual, half the clothes he wore were Tom's. The boots had to be too small, but they did not affect Doug's strut. Tom noticed he was wearing his own pants. His middle had grown. Must have spent too many nights in town.

"What'd you hear about this business of not allowing us to drive cattle across Kansas?" Without taking a breath, Doug put his hand out. "I'll take the money."

"It's still in my saddlebag."

"Still in your saddlebag! That's a pretty careless way to handle money. It's a good thing I'm boss around here."

"I'll get it." Tom ambled to the hall chair where his saddlebag was waiting, Doug at his heels.

Doug snatched the bag out of Tom's hands and pulled out the money bags. "Is it all here?"

"Everything but cowboy pay and my share."

"Your share! I get it all to pay the bills."

"Now you won't have to pay me."

Doug's eyes narrowed. "I pay you like I pay the rest of the hands around here."

"You forget, Brother, I'm not a hand. I own part of this ranch."

"Not yet, you don't." Doug glared at Tom and stomped off to the ranch office.

Welcome home. Tom smiled, surprised at his inner calmness. When his father had died, Tom had been seventeen. Zack, twenty-three, should have taken over, but he had said he had waited long enough. Within a year he had packed his books and headed east to study law.

Doug, just turned twenty-one, had taken over the ranch and run it as he pleased. He was heavy-handed, and they had lost a couple of good men, but most stayed. When Doug had treated Tom like one of the hired help, the cowboys had rallied and trained him. Without them, the ranch would have folded. They were good, hard-working men. Tom respected them.

Tom was Doug's only contender to run the ranch. Zack had bowed out and Nelson could not physically handle it. Tom itched to look at the books, but he needed a reason. Doug kept them locked up. *Zack!* He would contact Zack and find out his legal rights. In the meantime, he would keep his eyes open and be patient.

Tom returned to the dining room, kissed his mother, and rumpled Nelson's hair. "All I need is a bed. Don't be surprised if I sleep for a week. Good night."

His head had scarcely touched the pillow when a longing ache filled him. *Mary Lou.* He closed his eyes, and her sad, puzzled face stared at him. Tomorrow he would throw himself into work and try to forget.

The next morning, Tom rose early and saddled the black stallion Victor, to give Tinder a rest. As tired as he had felt yesterday, he couldn't wait to look over the land his father had worked and died for.

The cattle spread as far as he could see. They would be the next drive, and he couldn't decide whether to ride with them. It all depended on how things turned out with Doug. He would get a letter off to Zack.

Victor snorted and danced. Tom patted his neck. "You're ready for a wild ride, aren't you? All right, boy, let's go."

Man and horse merged with wind and land. Victor stretched his legs to their utmost, and Tom clung like a burr. This was life, the life he loved—the heritage he hoped to share with Mary Lou.

The corral came into view. Men and animals stirred from their night's rest. Smitty waved his hat high over his head. Tom slowed and veered Victor in his direction.

"When'd ya get back?" Smitty hollered.

Tom reined Victor and dismounted. "Yesterday, about suppertime. When did you boys get in?"

"During the night. After we left Oklahoma Territory, we just kept comin'. Anxious to git home."

"Funny, I didn't hear you come in."

"We was quiet. Didn't want to stir up nothin'."

28

Tom walked Victor beside Smitty and caught up on news of the ride home. Tom liked Smitty. He had been around a long time.

Jess, the cook, filled the air with scents of breakfast, and the cowboys emerged unshaven, sleepy, and hungry. Tom would have joined them, but his mother and Nelson would be waiting for him. After some joshing, Tom made his way up to the ranch house.

Allena sat in her place at the dining room table. "I couldn't believe you went for a ride this morning after your long trip home," she said when Tom came in.

"I just wanted to look the place over," Tom answered.

"How'd you find things?"

"Lookin' good." Tom replied. "Dad would be pleased. Doug still sleeping?"

"No, he went off to town right after you left." His mother passed a plate of fragrant sourdough biscuits.

Tom laughed. "Is there anything that goes on around here you don't know about?"

"No," she answered matter-of-factly.

Nelson fidgeted and blurted, "Tell me about the drive, Tom. You're gonna take me with you sometime, aren't ya?"

"Mother will have to decide if you're strong enough to take it," Tom answered. "It's a grueling ride, Nelson. I don't know if you could stay in the saddle as long as you'd have to."

Nelson, crushed, bent over his steak and eggs.

His mother laid her hand on Nelson's arm. "Son, God doesn't give the same job to everyone. Look at the beautiful pictures you draw and paint. I don't see anyone else around here doing that."

Nelson regarded his mother, unconvinced.

"And there's plenty of work you can do on the ranch. Someone has to stay home and watch things," Allena added to comfort her son.

"But Doug doesn't let me do anything," Nelson protested. "Every time he finds me with the cowboys, he sends me back to the house."

Tom said, "I'll talk to him and see if I can't get him to agree on certain jobs for you."

Nelson brightened and dove into his breakfast.

The ensuing silence hung heavy. Tom had the feeling his mother wanted to discuss something.

Allena cleared her throat. "You're going to be twenty-one soon, Tom, and some legal things need to be settled. I've written Zack and told him that he should come back and take care of everything lawful and proper."

Tom grinned. His mother had shown concern about the way Doug handled things now and then, but she had always kept the peace. He was relieved to know she felt the same uneasiness he was feeling.

"I'm glad you wrote Zack, Mom. I've a hunch we're going to need him."

Footsteps on the porch announced the arrival of a blond-haired wisp of a girl who came in as if she lived there. Tom rose, and Laura Shepard ran and threw her arms around him. "It's about time you came back. I thought you'd found yourself a girl up there."

He hoped he had. "It was a big drive and took lots of time." But not enough time to tell Mary Lou he loved her. He sat back down.

Laura took the chair beside him and received the plate of food Allena passed to her. She fell on it like a starved animal.

Tom cast a brief glance at Laura. A Texas beauty, born and bred with a heart for Texas. At one time he had taken for granted Laura would be his wife. But compared with Mary Lou, Laura still had growing up to do.

She turned to Tom and bumped his arm. "You got back in time for the hoedown next Saturday at Schroeder's barn." She hooked his gaze. "Gonna take me?"

"Sure," Tom answered quickly and grinned. "It's time I got some Texas hayseed in my hair."

The conversation turned to the usual ranch and neighbor talk, but it was not the same. For Tom, everything sounded different. *Yep. It is biding time.*

Chapter 6

The westbound stagecoach lumbered into Center Street, stirring up a thick cloud of dust. People came running from all directions.

Mary Lou stepped out of the store and hurried to meet Aunt Nelda. Jake, one of Nate Bradford's cowboys, waited in a buckboard to transport Nelda's luggage to the cabin.

Mary Lou wondered if her father would come out. She had told him Nelda would arrive that day, but if he had heard, he had not answered. Surely he would welcome his own sister!

Her heart leaped. Pa leaned against one of the roof poles. She curbed the urge to run to him. Instead, she walked over. Their gaze met for a second as they turned to the passengers alighting from the coach.

Aunt Nelda gathered her skirts, grabbed an offered hand to step down, and threw herself into Buck's arms. "I'm sure glad that's over. My back would have snapped had we gone another five miles." She looked for her luggage and watched Jake pile it in the buckboard. Then she turned to Buck and patted his arm.

Mary Lou interpreted a world of feeling in that small gesture. Aunt Nelda was Pa's favorite of two sisters and four brothers. He hadn't seen any of them for years. But Aunt Nelda kept in touch. Pa had told Mary Lou once that Nelda was the only one of his family who cared a hoot about him.

Nelda swung around and appraised Mary Lou. "An' lookee here! Why Mary Lou, you've grown into a pretty young lady." To Buck, she grinned. "I bet these town boys are doing so much buzzing around her you're having heart failure."

Mary Lou blushed. Buck mumbled something she didn't catch, hobbled toward his buggy, and climbed in. Before Mary Lou could help Aunt Nelda into the buggy, the energetic woman hoisted herself up. Jake stretched his arm to hand Mary Lou up to the seat beside him on the buckboard.

The two women would share Mary Lou's room. Buck had sent a new bed home from the store. Jake carried in Nelda's luggage, and in no time she had her belongings neatly in place. With Mary Lou's help, she perused the kitchen supplies, and a soup pot soon bubbled away on the stove.

Pa unhitched Morgan from the buggy, came in, and sat down in his chair by the fireplace. Mary Lou sent a grateful prayer heavenward. Pa was going to stay at the cabin! They would be family again.

Days flew by. Aunt Nelda sang hymns and moved constantly. "Would you mind if I was to change your kitchen around a bit for my convenience?" she asked Mary Lou one day.

"Of course not, Aunt Nelda. You do most of the cooking. Make it easy for yourself." Mary Lou felt comforted by Nelda's thoughtfulness.

A harmonious warmth filled the cabin. Buck came home every evening, and after Mary Lou went to bed, she heard her father and aunt talk for hours. Mornings, he and Mary Lou rode to town together except when she didn't stay all day. Then she rode Dulcie. Although they didn't talk the way they used to, the tension had eased.

December blew in with a mild snowstorm that heightened enthusiasm for Christmas. The Kansas Pacific kept bringing more people and merchandise from the East. It was a prosperous time, and the busyness eased the pain of Ellen's absence at Christmas.

Everything changed. Aunt Nelda baked her brother's favorites. He ate heartily, lost his haggard look, and stopped drinking. Mary Lou thanked God for Aunt Nelda.

With Christmas two weeks away, the store had buzzed all morning with customers buying and trading. Women brought eggs, vegetables, prairie chickens, anything they could trade. Most families kept a small flock of sheep, and some traded their carded wool and items they had woven on their looms to buy shoes, boots, coats, and Christmas gifts for their families.

By noon, the customers had thinned out. Glenn joined Mary Lou in folding and straightening bolts of colorful calico. "Too bad we can't have Christmas every week. It sure helps business."

Mary Lou laughed. "Then I'd never get the mail sorted."

"I like having you work in the store here—with me," Glenn said quietly.

Mary Lou's stomach tightened. She had never thought of Glenn as a suitor. She seldom thought of Glenn at all. Pa had hired him to run the store and he did a good job. Mama, Pa, and Tom consumed her thoughts. Two months had crawled by. Still no letter from Tom. A gnawing thought tried to invade her mind. She had dismissed it before. Now it broke through. *Tom does not love you.* The blue of the calico in her hands grew misty. *If he loved you, he would have written. Perhaps I should write to him. Maybe something has happened.*

"No," she said aloud and glanced quickly to see if Glenn had heard.

Glenn peered over a bolt halfway to the shelf. "What did you say?"

"Uh. . .nothing." She sent him a half smile and smoothed the cloth with shaking fingers. She glanced again. Handsome, tall, always neatly dressed,

Glenn was a gentleman in every sense.

He patted the last bolt and moved decisively along the counter to Mary Lou. He searched her face. "I wondered if you would go with me to the church service and party afterward on Christmas Eve."

Taken by surprise, Mary Lou said quickly, "Oh, no. I don't think it would be seemly—it's too soon after Mama's. . ." She couldn't say it.

Glenn didn't move. He cleared his throat. "If you'll pardon my saying so, Mary Lou, I don't see why it wouldn't be proper. We could go to the service and stay at the party a little while. We'd only be sitting and eating and watching the children when Santa Claus comes."

Glenn's gaze disarmed her. She had never given a thought to the Christmas party, and she had never missed one. Uneasy, she moved to the end of the counter, picked up the scissors, and hung them on a hook.

Glenn followed her. "I remember your mama always enjoyed those church parties. I don't think it would show any disrespect for you to go—with me," he added.

She glanced into Glenn's pleading face. The intensity of his look unnerved her. "I'll speak to Aunt Nelda about it."

Mary Lou escaped to the post office. She dug into the half-sorted mailbag for a fistful of letters and forced her mind to concentrate as she stuffed them into their boxes. She ran her hand around the bottom of the bag for the last few letters.

"Mrs. Henrietta Wimbley," she read and put it in the Wimbley box. Henrietta's mother wrote regularly.

"Mr. Nate Bradford." Her heart flipped. She read it again, slowly. "Mr. Nate Bradford." That was Tom's handwriting! She flipped the letter to the back. To the front. Nothing. *Why is it addressed to Uncle Nate? Why not me?* She peered into the bag to see if she had missed hers. Empty.

Mary Lou slumped into the chair and stared at the letter. Hot tears returned. Tom was toying with her just as he had done last summer, making her think he loved her.

Anger flamed, and she shot to her feet. Not anger at Tom. At herself. How he must have laughed as he rode away. And she had let him hold her in his arms and kiss her. Worse, she had liked it, even thought of having his children! She shuddered with shame. She had never allowed any boy in Venture to be so bold.

The letter burned in her hand. She threw it on the counter, and a whirlwind couldn't have blown the post office into order any quicker. She locked the stamp box and took it to the safe. Without a break in her step, she grabbed the letter, fled to the back room, changed into riding clothes, and marched out the door to saddle Dulcie.

Glenn ran after her. "Are you going home?"

"Got a special letter to deliver to Uncle Nate. See you tomorrow."

Crestfallen, Glenn watched her saddle Dulcie. "Don't forget about the Christmas party."

"I won't." She mounted Dulcie and urged her into a gallop. Hoofbeats almost drowned out his "Could you tell me tomorrow?" She didn't answer.

Normally, the pristine snow would have conveyed God's beauty to Mary Lou's soul. She rode blind. Her eyes stung, her heart pounded, and she felt angry enough to explode.

Dulcie's frosty breath curled from her nostrils as she worked hard through the snow. She reached the Bradford ranch. One of the cowboys came running and took Dulcie. Mary Lou slid off and raced to the cabin door.

A smiling Aunt Tibby pulled her to the fireplace and rubbed warmth into her hands. The kitchen smelled of fresh bread and roasting meat. Mary Lou could use the peace of this friendly kitchen.

"Gracious, Mary Lou, it's too cold to be out riding. You should ride with your pa with hot stones at your feet."

"Is Uncle Nate here?"

"He's out in the barn inspecting our new colt. He'll be in shortly."

"A letter came for him, and I thought it might be something important." Mary Lou gave the letter to Aunt Tibby.

Tibby laid it casually on the table. "I'm glad you came. I've been wanting to talk to you about W.C.T.U."

Mary Lou frowned. "W-C-T-U? What's that?"

"It's the Women's Christian Temperance Union. I'd like you to come to a meeting next Tuesday. The women of Venture are going to have their say, or Mac Ludden and his saloon are going to lead this town straight to hell."

"Have you heard Pa stopped drinking?"

Tibby nodded. "I'm glad. Buck's not a drinking man. I like Nelda. She has backbone, and I bet Buck jumped to her tune when he was a young boy. Ellen would be pleased." She leaned forward. "I've been worried about you."

"About me? What for?" Mary Lou gazed into the flames, fearing her eyes would betray her. Aunt Tibby, like her mother, could usually guess what she was thinking. "It's much better since Aunt Nelda came."

"That's not what I mean. I'm talking about that young cowboy you swooned over last September."

Mary Lou's eyes blazed. "What do you mean swooned?" Words stuck in her throat.

Tibby patted her hand. "Honey, any woman can tell when another woman's in love. You sparkled like a firefly every time he came into view."

Mary Lou stood defenseless. She stared into the fire, fumbling to contain herself.

"Have you heard from him since he left?"

"No." It barely came out.

"Do you wish you had?"

The thought of Tom's brazen arms around her and his stolen kisses stiffened her resolve. "It was just a summer friendship. Like Pa says, cowboys are a wanderlust bunch and not for marrying."

"Your mama married one. And he's a good man. You didn't know your pa before his accident. He was magnificent. He knew horseflesh like no other man in these parts. I didn't blame Ellen for falling in love with him. And Uncle Nate was a cowboy. Honey, most cowboys are just young men doing a tough job. A lot of them end up good, strong men—and make marvelous husbands."

"Well." Mary Lou swallowed hard. "Tom did his job and went home." She lifted her chin and smiled. "And that is that."

Stomping feet ended the conversation. The door opened and Nate blew in looking like a snowman. "It's gonna blow up a good one if this keeps up." A wide grin brightened his face. "That colt is the prettiest little filly you ever saw. She's got a diamond shape right in the middle of her forehead." He hung up his coat and huddled in front of the fire.

Mary Lou could stand it no longer. She picked up the letter and handed it to Nate. "This came today. Thought it might be something important."

Nate ripped it open. "Why it's from Tom Langdon, that young cowboy you were sweet on last summer."

Did everybody know? Mary Lou bit her lip to keep her mouth shut.

"He says the Texas ranchers are up in arms about the quarantine forbidding Texas Longhorns to cross the Kansas borders during the warm months." Nate looked up from the letter. "I'm not surprised. But those Texans aren't considering how many of our cattle die from Texas fever. Their longhorns are immune, but they drop those ticks on the ground and infect our cattle. Joe Edel said he lost almost a third of his animals last year, and he's not the only one. We Kansans can't sit back and lose our stock. Nope, the legislature did the right thing, whether Texas likes it or not."

Mary Lou blurted, "Does he say anything else?"

"Nope. Just says he would like an answer as soon as possible." He flipped the letter over and shook his head. "That's all."

Mary Lou's last hope drained. If he had only added one line in the letter to tell her. . .what? That he didn't love her and their wonderful times together meant nothing? She felt betrayed.

"Aunt Tibby," she asked, "do you think it would be improper for me to go to the Christmas church service and party with Glenn Farrell? It's so soon after Mama died, I didn't know—"

"I certainly don't, and your mother would be the first one to say 'Go.' Ellen wouldn't have missed it. You know how she enjoyed being with God's people every time she could. I agree with her. You don't honor the dead with your denial of living."

Mary Lou smiled. She would ask Aunt Nelda and Pa, and then give Glenn his answer.

Chapter 7

Christmas Eve was perfect. Snowflakes floated from a windless blue-black sky and settled into soft mounds. Church windows beckoned sleighs and buggies from east and west. The air reverberated with laughter and greetings of parishioners. Bundled in his coat and hat, Pastor Miles stood at the door and welcomed everyone.

Big Jon, Henrietta, and their twelve children filed past, each carrying a log, which they neatly piled in the corner. Big Jon stuffed his into the stove and poked at the fire until it flared and spread warmth in the room.

In a rented buggy, Glenn and Mary Lou rolled to the side of the church. Glenn tied the reins and hopped out, pleasure reflected in every movement. His hands encircled Mary Lou's tiny waist, and he lifted her down into the ankle-deep snow.

Nate, Tibby, and Nelda drove in and pulled their buggy alongside. "Wait!" Tibby called. "Help us carry some of this food in." They trooped to the door, fumbled for a free hand to greet Pastor, then deposited their baskets along the wall of food tables.

Chairs filled quickly. The room murmured with congenial conversation. Finally, Pastor Miles stepped to the platform. The hum of voices quieted.

"Welcome, friends and neighbors." His face beamed from behind the pulpit. "We gather on this night to celebrate the birth of our Lord Jesus Christ, God incarnate, Who came to earth to rescue His people from sin. Let's open our service with prayerful hearts and receive God's great gift by reciting John 3:16 and 17." He raised his arms.

Everyone stood and spoke words most had learned as a child.

" 'For God so loved the world, that He gave His only begotten Son, that whosoever believeth in Him should not perish, but have everlasting life. For God sent not His Son into the world to condemn the world; but that the world through Him might be saved.' "

The congregation sat down.

Pastor fluttered the pages of his Bible to the Gospel of Luke and read from chapter 2: " 'And Joseph also went up from Galilee. . . .' "

Young Jon Wimbley and Clarissa Jordan, dressed as Joseph and Mary, walked slowly down the aisle carrying Alexander Walford as the Baby Jesus.

Other children clothed as angels and shepherds followed. At the front, they turned, wearing shy smiles.

" 'And she brought forth her firstborn son—' "

A baby cried out.

" 'And all they that heard it wondered at those things which were told them by the shepherds.' " Pastor folded his hands and bowed his head.

Someone started to sing, "Away in a manger, no crib for a bed," and was soon joined by others. The singing flowed reverently into "Silent Night, Holy Night."

Joseph, Mary carrying Baby Jesus, the angels, and the shepherds returned up the aisle. The singing voices faded.

Pastor Miles said, "Let us pray." Thankfulness lifted heavenward and settled a benediction of peace upon everyone.

At the "Amen," someone moved a chair. The room sprang into activity. Men and boys moved tables and placed chairs. Women uncovered dried fruit, cakes, cookies, pies, and candy. Each family brought their own place settings and tables were soon set. Pastor Miles had filled the huge coffeepot on top of the pot-belly stove with water before the service. When Sarah George had arrived, she had added coffee. The aroma whet healthy appetites. Families quickly settled into places.

Although Mary Lou missed Mama, she relaxed. She loved these people. Mama had said they were the best. Sudden peace flooded her.

"Mary Lou, can I get you something?" Glenn asked for the third time.

"No, thank you." She smiled and patted the chair beside her. He perched on the edge and talked incessantly.

"Listen!" Clarissa shouted. Everyone quieted. Bells could be heard in the distance. They grew louder. Children squealed and jumped up and down.

Suddenly, the door burst open. With a shout, a snowy Santa Claus stomped in. He set his lumpy bag in the middle of the room. The children quieted immediately, stared with wide eyes, and waited. When Santa called their names, they came forward timidly to receive packages wrapped in newspaper or brown paper—carved wooden horses for the boys, rag dolls for the girls, and a new pair of mittens for every child.

Mary Lou laughed with the children. She remembered her own young excitement waiting for her name to be called. She watched each eager face, and a new awareness of passing the simple joys of tradition to children hung in her mind.

As suddenly as he had appeared, Santa Claus vanished for another year, and the party ended. Glenn helped Mary Lou into the buggy, draped the blanket over her knees, and placed warm stones at her feet. He talked as he drove, but Mary Lou didn't hear. Her thoughts were on other

38

nights when she, Pa, and Mama had snuggled under a blanket in Pa's buggy, ridden home, and trimmed a little tree with strings of popcorn, cranberries, and colored ribbons.

"Mary Lou?" Glenn's voice pulled her to the present.

"Forgive me, Glenn. I was thinking about Christmas when Mama was here."

Glenn ducked his head, embarrassed. "I guess I've been talking too much." After a long silence he said quietly, "There are lots of things I'd like to say to you."

A fleeting thought of Tom passed through Mary Lou's mind. If he had only said he loved her, she could hang on. But. . . . She turned her full attention to Glenn. His eyes filled with hope.

It had stopped snowing. Glenn slowed the horse to a walk. "I don't want to rush you, Mary Lou, but I'd like to be. . .your. . .uh. . .beau."

Mary Lou's heart twinged. She shushed it. "Thank you, Glenn. Perhaps, but not right now. . . ."

Glenn's face lit with surprise. He smiled broadly, sat up straighter. "I understand. It's too soon after your mama's—" He didn't say it. His thoughtfulness touched her.

The cabin came into view curtained by a fine sifting snow. Nelda and Pa were waiting to trim the tree, so Mary Lou hurried inside.

Later, lying in bed, Mary Lou pushed Tom out of her thoughts and tried to replace him with Glenn. Her heart objected. She tried to envision Glenn's warm, eager face. Nothing. Regardless, the next time Glenn asked, she would accept. She would be twenty next month. She drifted off to sleep walking beside Tom in the cottonwood grove.

Trade slowed in January, a relief because the store was jumbled from Christmas. Mary Lou and Glenn checked stock, cleaned shelves, and scrubbed everywhere. By the middle of February, the store was clean, neat, and well-stocked.

That morning, they had put away a new shipment from the East. Glenn had hung shiny lanterns on spikes pounded in the wooden beam that stretched the length of the store. He looked around, obviously pleased at the result. Mary Lou climbed up and down a ladder carrying lamp chimneys to the top shelf where they would be safe. Glenn hurried to help her down. When she reached bottom, he grabbed her other hand and pulled her to face him. "Mary Lou?"

She knew what was coming.

"This may not be the right time to ask, but. . ." He swallowed hard. "Would you. . .could you accept me as your steady beau?"

Her heart didn't give the least recognition of this life-changing moment. Wasn't a girl supposed to be elated, ecstatic, or something?

Glenn's gaze never left her face.

She plunged. "Yes, Glenn." She had dreamed of this moment all her life, wondering what it would be like to be courted by a handsome young man. Her heart remained silent.

Glenn reached out as if to take her in his arms, hesitated, then took her hand and raised it to his lips. "Thank you, Mary Lou," he said humbly. "Would you go to supper with me at Mrs. Barton's tomorrow night? She cooks a special supper for anyone who has a birthday."

Mary Lou warmed. "Is tomorrow your birthday?"

Glenn nodded. "Twenty-six. Time I was getting—"

"I'd be delighted to go," she answered quickly.

"Supper is promptly at five. We could go from here." Glenn dipped his head. "If you don't mind, I'll be talking to your father about us. I'll also ask if we can leave an hour early tomorrow."

Us. We. Glenn and me. That is how it is to be. Mary Lou's heart finally responded. It beat on its chamber walls like a butterfly she had once caught and put in a jar. It had hammered its wings incessantly against the glass. She had felt so sorry for it, she had let it go.

Mary Lou nodded and headed for the post office. She was sorting the mail when a buggy rattled to a halt at the hitching post. Aunt Tibby climbed out and hurried in.

"You're just the one I want to see. We're having a meeting tomorrow at the church to form a W.C.T.U. I'd like you and Jenny to round up as many young women as you can. It's at two o'clock."

"Will we be through by four? I have a supper invitation at five."

Tibby's eyebrows went up. "With whom?"

"Glenn. It's his birthday. Mrs. Barton cooks a special supper and lets the boarder have a guest. Glenn asked me."

"That's nice." Tibby searched Mary Lou's face. "It is nice, isn't it?"

Mary Lou reached for more letters. "My life is here, and Glenn is just about the best catch in Venture."

Tibby nodded. "Glenn is a nice boy."

"Boy? Twenty-six is a bit more than a boy."

Tibby turned to go into the store. "I need some quilting thread. Did any come in the new shipment?"

Tibby bought her thread, then peered around for Glenn. She took Mary Lou's hand and pulled her out to her buggy. "If you want to," she whispered, "we could have a surprise birthday party. Have Glenn bring you to the ranch after dinner. Tell Jenny to round up everyone."

Mary Lou smiled. Leave it to Aunt Tibby to jump in. It would be fun to surprise Glenn. He had no family there, nor had she ever heard him mention one.

Tibby climbed into her buggy. "I'm going to the church. We're quilting this afternoon." She slapped the reins. The horses gave a tug and the wagon rolled. "Don't forget," she called over her shoulder. "Mention the meeting to all the women you see. Got to get prepared for the next fall cattle drive. When it's not safe for a woman to walk the streets of her own town, something had better be done."

Mary Lou watched the buggy bounce up Center Street. Aunt Tibby and her mother were so different, yet so alike. Mary Lou went back into the store and put the mail away. Enough for today. If she went home now, she would have time to wash her hair. What dress should she wear? The blue one? It was the last dress Mama had made—and Tom's favorite. He had said it matched her eyes. She shook her head. Forget Tom. The mailbox had been empty again today. No, she would wear her gray dress and the white lace collar. It made her look older. She would save the blue.

Pa came through the back door. "Mary Lou, are you ready to go home?"

"Yes, Pa. I'm ready."

Chapter 8

Mary Lou tossed the last letter into its box and sighed. No message from Tom. She told herself it was a futile hope, but her heart paid no attention, and she eagerly searched each mailbag.

The window framed a green haze of burgeoning prairie grass persistently edging the ruts on Center Street. Balmy air swept in the open door and shooed out the musty odors of winter. A familiar horse came on a fast trot. Jenny Wimbley dismounted and tied Missy to the rail. Mary Lou glanced at the clock. One-thirty! Where had the morning gone?

Jenny hustled into the post office out of breath. "I didn't know whether we'd get here or not. We washed all mornin'."

"Your ma coming to the meeting?"

"Yep, wouldn't miss it. Says it's high time somebody did something to get decent laws in Venture. Pa laughed and told her not to forget her knittin'."

Mary Lou smoothed her dress. "Uncle Nate says it's foolishness, but he knows Aunt Tibby. Once a bee starts buzzing in her bonnet, look out!"

Their laugh subsided into a rare awkward silence.

Jenny blurted, "Mary Lou, are you serious about accepting Glenn as a suitor?"

"Yes, Jenny, but it won't make any difference between us."

"It always makes a difference. My sister Sybil changed when she and Charlie became betrothed."

"I'm not betrothed, Jenny." She inwardly shuddered.

"You will be. Everybody knows Glenn is smitten with you."

"He hasn't told me yet."

"He will. What am I going to do when you get married?"

Mary Lou threw her arms around her friend. "If Glenn and I marry, it won't change a thing between you and me. Look at your ma and Mama. They were best friends in good and bad times. It'll be the same with us." Mary Lou reached for her shawl. "Come on, we'd better get to the church."

From east and west, the ladies of Venture headed toward the church yard. Mary Lou and Jenny joined the flow entering the building, spotted two chairs in the second row, and slid into them. Amiable chatter drifted out the church door and windows. Several men cast curious glances and moved on about their business.

Aunt Tibby and Henrietta sat at a table in front, engrossed in conversation with a woman Mary Lou had never seen. At the small organ, Mary Wescott pumped out one hymn after another.

Suddenly, Tibby rapped her knuckles on the table, stood up, and cleared her throat.

The room quieted.

"Good afternoon, ladies. Let's all stand and pray."

The ladies stood, their heads bowed. Tibby tilted her face toward heaven. "Our Father," she began, "we know You have seen the wickedness in our town, and we are ashamed to have waited so long to ask for Thy help to drive this evil from our midst. Now it's tearing at the fabric of our families. Alcoholic spirits are brewed in the cauldrons of hell. They take the minds of men, women, even our children. God, bless our gathering and help us find a way to drive this plague from us. In Jesus' name we pray. Amen."

Mary Wescott played an introduction and the women sang "Yield Not to Temptation." Then they sat down and gave Tibby their full attention.

"All of you know why we're here. It's time decent people took hold of this town instead of letting men like Mac Ludden dictate the law. As women and mothers, it's our duty to demand Venture be cleaned up. We must demand the men make this town a safe place."

Effie Jackson shot her arm up. "We know all that, Tibby, but what can we do about it? It's up to the men."

Sarah George rose and shook her head in dismay. "But the men aren't doing anything about it."

Tibby nodded. "Ladies, that's why we're here. There is something we can do. Sitting beside me is Amanda Way. She is a Methodist and Quaker preacher."

The ladies applauded.

Tibby continued. "She recently moved to Kansas from Indiana where she organized their first women's suffrage movement in the 1850s. She is continuing her fight for temperance and suffrage and has organized the National Women's Christian Temperance Union of Kansas. She travels to encourage women to unite and fight for prohibition. That's why she's here today—to help us form that union. Ladies, please welcome Amanda Way."

Amanda stood to speak. The ladies applauded and gave her their full attention.

"Christian sisters, your presence is a testimony that you recognize women should have a say in what goes on in your town. Women are one-half the population of America, but we have no opportunity to determine the laws we live under. The best place to begin is to fight for temperance. The evils of alcohol ruin more people's lives than all the wars this country has fought."

The women nodded agreement.

Amanda pointed to Sarah George. "Like what was said, 'The men aren't doing anything about it. Why should they? Things are going the way they want them. Saloons and gambling flourish because men get rich. The only way to stop them is to make it against the law to manufacture or sell intoxicants. Unfortunately we have no votes. But we are not powerless. We can join together and rally 'round those men who see the need not only for prohibition but also for another vital issue. My dear ladies, that issue is the voting privilege for women."

There was a noticeable intake of breath. Some women nodded. Others shook their heads.

"Ladies, please don't shake your heads. We have the right to be more than chattel. We need the right to acquire and possess property and have equal rights to the custody of our children. Our men often get shot out from under us. Where are we then? Cast back upon our sons or charity. Today we are asking you to join together to fight for prohibition."

"What could we do?" called a voice from the back of the room.

"We can be at the next election to hand out literature to voters who haven't made up their minds. We can influence how people vote for prohibition. When the law passes, we can demand that our town officials follow the law."

The women sat transfixed by the audacity of what they heard.

"First we pledge ourselves to our task. Then, for the sake of our children, we fight against the evils we abhor. Maybe not today, but—God helping us—we will win!"

As one body, the group rose, banging hands together in very unladylike fashion. A buzz of general agreement washed over the room.

Tibby rapped her knuckles on the table several times before the women settled into their seats. "Thank you, Amanda. Ladies, here on the table is a paper for us to sign, pledging ourselves to this task until it's accomplished. Next week, we'll meet to make solid plans to attack the evils in Venture."

Mary Wescott pumped up the organ, and the strains of "Onward Christian Soldiers" poured forth. The women rose and sang with fervor. Tibby closed with prayer and the women swarmed to the table. All but a timid few placed their signatures on the paper with W.C.T.U. in large letters across the top. The Women's Christian Temperance Union of Kansas was born.

Women gathered in groups talking to Amanda, Tibby, and Henrietta. Mary Lou and Jenny listened, then slowly walked back to the store discussing the meeting. Mary Lou remembered Mama had detested alcoholic spirits and had refused them from the doctor when she fell ill. "To use God's grain and precious food for such brew," she said, "is a slap on the face of God."

After Jenny left, Mary Lou went to the back room to find Pa. He had gone home.

Glenn came to meet her. "What was your meeting all about?"

"We've formed a Women's Christian Temperance Union to stop the drinking and shooting in Venture."

Glenn looked puzzled but smiled and reached out to detain her. "I have something important to ask you."

"Oh?" From his attentiveness lately, Mary Lou suspected what lay ahead. The bigger question was: *Am I ready for it?* They had gone to church together every Sunday since Christmas. He frequently visited their home and chatted with Aunt Nelda and Pa. Nelda considered him a very nice young man. But—

"We've been keeping company for three months, Mary Lou. I've been wondering what your answer would be if I. . ." He cleared his throat. "If I asked you to marry me."

Mary Lou searched for the answer in her heart. Glenn—her husband? Glenn's gaze held her, pleading for an answer.

Suddenly Tom took shape, his eyes filled with love. Mary Lou shook herself mentally. The time for daydreaming was over. Mama had always said, "A bird in the hand is worth two in the bush." Did that fit here?

Glenn cupped her face tenderly in his hands. "Mary Lou, I love you. I want you to be my wife."

Those were the words she had longed to hear. The voice was different, but Glenn honored her with living truth. Had Tom been truthful, he would never have told her he would write when he had not intended to.

Mary Lou looked into Glenn's eyes. They radiated love, patience, and respect. Glenn was different from the coarse men who came into the store. Mama had called him a gentleman. Glenn loved her. What more could she ask?

"Mary Lou? Did you hear me?"

"Yes."

"Do you have any love at all for me?"

Desperately Mary Lou searched her heart. Did she love him? She liked and admired him. Enough to marry him? "Yes, I do, Glenn. I'll be happy to be your wife." She waited for the earth to shake or her heart to pound. Nothing.

Glenn grabbed her hands. "Then I may ask your pa for permission?"

"Yes."

Delighted surprise covered Glenn's face. Very slowly he put his arms around her and pulled her close. Mary Lou lifted her face. His soft lips caressed her trembling ones. It was a sweet, living kiss, nothing like Tom's. Tom's sweet kisses held a fierce urgency.

Glenn released her and smiled. "I've been dreaming of this moment for months, long before Christmas. You've made me the happiest man in Venture." He threw his arms out wide. "In the whole world!" His arms encircled her waist. "I love you, Mary Lou. I'll love you forever."

Without even thinking, she said, "I love you, too, Glenn."

"Your father went home about an hour ago. I'll get a horse from the livery and ride home with you. I want to ask your father formally for your hand in marriage. I talked after Christmas about it, but he was not too. . . ," he sought for a proper word, "too talkative."

Mary Lou felt warmed by his words. Of all things, Glenn's patient consideration endeared him to her. "He's much better since Aunt Nelda came. It was hard for him when Mama died."

"Yes." He stood looking at her, then said, "I'll saddle Dulcie."

Mary Lou turned Dulcie into the lane. Glenn followed, and they dismounted at the barn. They walked toward the cabin, Glenn's warm hand holding Mary Lou's.

After supper, Glenn accompanied Pa to do chores. Dishes finished, Nelda dug into her mending basket. Mary Lou sat staring into the fire.

"He asked you, didn't he?"

Mary Lou smiled. How on earth Aunt Nelda knew so many things, she couldn't fathom. "Yes."

After a long pause, Nelda looked up from her garment. "Well, aren't you going to tell me what you said?"

"I said yes."

"That's what you want?" Nelda resumed sewing. "What about Tom?"

Mary Lou stiffened. "What about Tom? Aunt Nelda, when a man doesn't love you, the best thing to do is forget him. In all this time, he hasn't written. He's shown beyond a doubt that I mean nothing to him." She stared into the fire.

"Glenn is loving and kind and treats me like a man treats a woman he loves. He'll make a good husband and. . ." She was going to say the father of their children but stopped, remembering that moment in Tom's arms.

Nelda looked up. "And?"

"And I love him."

"That's what I wanted to hear. Marriage is serious business. Children are a big responsibility. None of it should be entered into lightly. Besides, he knows the Lord Jesus. Does Tom?"

She didn't know! He participated in church activities, but did he know the Lord? *Oh, Lord, forgive me. I never even thought about Tom knowing You.* How foolish she had been. To marry a non-Christian would have broken Mama's heart. Mary Lou relaxed with a sense of peace.

Nelda laid aside her sewing and kissed her. "My dear child, I feel the same as if you were my own daughter, the daughter I never had. I'm happy if you're happy."

Mary Lou clung to her aunt. "Thank you, Aunt Nelda. The Lord sent the best substitute for Mama He could find when He sent you to us. I feel like your daughter." Even saying that, she could almost sense Mama's blessing in the room. True to His Word, God had provided for her and then restored Pa. Her heart swelled with thankfulness.

Pa and Glenn stomped their feet outside the door. When they came in, Glenn immediately walked to Mary Lou's side. "Your father has accepted me as his future son-in-law. I'm proud to be in the family." He reached into his pocket for a small case and took out a sparkling gold locket. He hung it around Mary Lou's neck and kissed her. His arm around her, he grinned and nodded. "Now, it's official."

Mary Lou felt her cheeks flush.

Glenn took her hand and pulled her outside. The sky, studded with stars, stretched from one dark blue horizon to the other. He kissed her again. "I'll see you tomorrow. I love you," he said. Riding off, Glenn waved back and blew her a kiss.

Mary Lou went in with the brilliance of the stars in her eyes. Nelda glanced up from her sewing and smiled.

For the first time since Mama died, Mary Lou felt happy. She kissed Aunt Nelda's cheek and went to her bedroom to think and pray. It had been a momentous day.

Chapter 9

I
t had been a mild winter. Smitty, Tom, and the boys had used it to mend and build new fences for the corrals. Even the ranch house boasted a new fence.

About the middle of January, snow began to fall in earnest. An icy wind blew down from the north and turned feathery flakes into a stinging blizzard. Outside, animals huddled to share their warmth. Inside, fireplaces in the ranch house and the bunkhouse stove consumed cow chips and wood almost faster than they could be supplied.

Riding the range, Tom, Smitty, and the cowboys located herds of half frozen cattle that looked like snow mounds on stilts. Texas cattle were not accustomed to such weather. If they lay down, their legs froze.

Tom called to Smitty, "I don't think we'll fare too bad if it quits by tomorrow. Let's go home." Tom swung Tinder, who needed little encouragement to pick up speed when he sensed he was going toward home.

"Animals are pretty tough," Smitty hollered. "After all, they was here long 'fore we came and there's still more of them than there are of us. But my old joints sure could stand a hot cup of coffee and some of Jess's potluck stew."

Tom hunched his shoulders and wondered if Mary Lou was warm. The storm probably had crossed Kansas as it traveled south. The thought of her created a lonesome ache. Their parting haunted him. He had handled it badly. But his senses remembered everything: the softness of her lithe body as he swung her around in his arms; her warm response to his kisses; her long, soft hair; her trust. . . That is what worried him most—that he had lost her trust. Regardless, he refused to give up. He loved her.

ひ

Back in the ranch house, Allena stood at the kitchen window watching the falling snow. Earlier, a snow curtain had obliterated the bunkhouse. Now she could see a clear outline of it. Movement caught her eye. A horse and rider approached the house and came to a halt outside the door. The animal paused. The rider slid off and tumbled into a heap. The horse shook itself and lumbered to the barn.

Allena and her housekeeper, Hattie, grabbed their shawls and tied them over their heads. A blast of icy air hit them as they opened the door. They half lifted, half dragged the man through the door, laid him on the floor, and removed the scarf tied around his face. The man's eyes were glued shut by frosty lashes.

"Doug!" Allena gasped. His hat was frozen to his head, and his ears resembled frosted white shells. Hattie hurriedly filled a wash basin with snow, and Allena gently held the snow against Doug's ears to encourage slow defrosting. Hattie ran for blankets.

Doug groaned and tried to open his eyes. Allena wiped away the melting frost and was finally able to remove his hat. Slowly, Doug's eyes opened, stared blankly, and then closed.

Hattie poured a cup of coffee from one of the large pots hugging the fireplace and set it aside to cool before they gave it to Doug.

"I hope Jess has plenty of hot coffee ready for the men when they come in," Allena said.

Hattie nodded. "Knowin' him, he will."

The women draped warmed blankets over Doug. He groaned and settled down.

Allena peered out the window. Again snow obliterated the bunkhouse, corrals, and barn. She squinted in an attempt to see through it. Was she mistaken or was there movement around the barn? The men were back! She breathed a sigh of relief.

At the kitchen door, Tom slapped the snow from his hat and jacket and stomped his feet before entering. He swung the door open. His mother was on her knees bending over someone lying on floor.

At the sight of Tom, Allena sighed in relief. "I'm glad you're home. It's Doug—half-frozen."

Tom bent over his brother and rubbed him to encourage stimulation. His hand moved over a lump in Doug's vest pocket. He reached in and withdrew a set of keys. The office keys? How many times he had tried to find them. He slipped them into his shirt pocket and looked at Doug, who would probably be asleep for awhile. Tom seized the moment and headed for the ranch office.

He opened the door to a mess—papers piled everywhere under a thick layer of dust. If Doug's bookkeeping was as slovenly as his office, no wonder the ranch had not shown the profits he thought there should be.

Quickly, Tom flipped through papers piled high on each side of the desk. He tried not to disturb them too much. It would be better if Doug didn't know he had gained access.

Tom found an entry ledger in the first desk drawer he opened. He flipped its pages slowly, noting sporadic records of the past year. He recognized money he had given Doug from the cattle drive. He laid the ledger on the chair and tried several keys in the safe lock. The fourth key slid in easily and Tom swung the door open wide.

Ledgers and folded legal papers were shoved here, there, anywhere. Tom glanced through paper after paper. There was a fair amount of money in a green metal box. Tom thought it better to leave it untouched. Doug had an uncanny memory when it came to money. Any missing would be a dead giveaway. It was to Tom's advantage to keep his search a secret until the right time.

Not wanting to push his luck, Tom didn't look through everything and tried to leave things as he found them. He was sure Doug wouldn't be able to tell if things had been moved. About to swing the safe door shut, he spied something shiny on the bottom of the safe. Keys. He brought them up beside the set in his hand, and compared them. A duplicate set! Tom smiled at his good fortune and tucked the extra keys in his pocket.

Before he left the office, Tom glanced around to see that it looked the same as when he came in. The small changes in the piles of papers wouldn't show, but something nagged him. He grinned. The piles were too neat! He messed them up. After picking up the ledger, he locked the door and left. On the way to the kitchen, Tom slipped the ledger behind a chair in the main room.

In the kitchen, Doug showed signs of returning consciousness. Tom adjusted the blankets covering his brother, and in one smooth movement slid the keys into the vest pocket where he had found them. He turned to his mother. "I'm starved," he said.

Hattie hustled and in minutes placed a steaming dish of stew with dumplings under Tom's nose. He dove in and ate heartily. The hot food conquered the cold that had gripped his bones all day.

Doug stirred, and Allena moved immediately to his side. Dazed and shivering, he opened his eyes and struggled to a sitting position.

Hattie wrapped his hands around the warm coffee cup she had poured earlier. He sipped and sipped, finally stopped shaking, and then described his ride home from Harness.

"Why on earth did you start home in this blizzard in the first place?" Allena asked.

" 'Most everyone else had gone. No reason to stay. I didn't think it was bad until I was more than halfway home, so I just kept on coming. I should have stayed in town."

"I'm glad you didn't. Families need to be together when storms of any kind come," his mother said quietly.

If Doug heard what his mother said, he gave no response. He ate half a bowl of Hattie's stew then, with Tom's help, staggered to his room.

Tom returned to the kitchen and kissed his mother on her cheek. "If you don't mind, Mother, I think I'll hit the hay. It's been a long, cold day."

"I don't blame you. Hattie put a couple extra quilts on your bed."

"Thanks, Hattie," Tom called as he left. He picked up the ledger he had hidden in the main room and carried it to his room. Later, propped up in bed, he turned its pages not knowing quite what to look for. When his father was alive, family financial discussions hadn't interested him. But next month he would become a quarter owner of the Circle Z.

His next thought was of Mary Lou. Hopefully by next year at this time, Mary Lou would be his wife. He imagined her there, in the same room, for him to hold and love. He closed the ledger, slid it under his pillow, and sank into a deep sleep.

Dazzling sun woke Tom. Dazed, he sat up and looked out the window. *It stopped snowing!* He hurriedly dressed, started for the door, and stopped. *The ledger!* He tucked it into his shirt and opened the door. The hall was empty. If Doug were awake, his booming voice would be audible. At the office door, Tom slipped the key in then locked it behind him. He had his hand on the desk drawer when he heard Doug's heavy tread in the hall.

Is he coming to the office? In desperation, Tom looked for a place to hide. *Father's big leather chair!* He squeezed tightly into the corner behind it.

The key turned in the lock and Doug banged in.

Tom didn't dare look. If Doug saw him, he would play a game of cat and mouse. For some reason, Doug relished making people squirm. Doug pulled out a drawer, slammed it shut, and left, locking the door behind him.

Afraid to move, Tom waited a few moments before he peeked out. The office was empty. He climbed from behind the chair, put the ledger in the drawer where he had found it, and quietly unlocked the door. Opening it slowly, he slipped into the hall and locked the door. He went back to his bedroom to calm down, then came out as if he were just getting up.

Tom's mother and Hattie had set the kitchen table. They didn't want to waste wood firing the dining room fireplace. Allena smiled at her handsome, red-headed son. "Good morning. And it is. It's quit snowing." She glanced out the window. "I'm not fond of snow, but I have to admit it's beautiful. God transforms everything into a display of His beauty."

"Sermon over, Mother." Doug strode across the kitchen and sat down at the table. His ears, cheeks, and nose were fiery red. So was his spirit. He didn't try to conceal the anger that twisted his face. "You need to work on goodie boy here." He thumbed at Tom. "He's an outright thief."

Dumfounded, Allena stared from one son to the other. The obvious hatred on Doug's face resurfaced a fear she had carried since they were small boys. Doug, constantly angry, had fought anything and anyone, especially Tom.

Doug sneered. "Did you hear me? Your perfect son is a thief. He stole the office keys out of my vest pocket last night and stole a ledger from my desk."

Allena looked askance from one son to the other.

Tom recognized the spot he was in, but he told the truth. "Yes, I found the keys in your pocket. You won't give them to me, so I took them to find out for myself what's going on at this ranch. I have a right to know."

Doug leaped to his feet and stumbled halfway across the room, his fists clenched.

Allena ran and stood in front of Tom. "No! Douglas Langdon, I forbid you to fight. Your father, here in spirit, forbids you to fight. The time for little-boy squabbles is over—"

Doug glared at his mother. "This is no little-boy squabble. I'm talking about your son entering my office and stealing the entry ledger. Ask him about that!"

Allena turned to Tom, eyebrows raised. .

Tom hated the pain he saw in his mother's eyes. "Yes, I did take the keys from his pocket. I went into the office and looked around, but I don't have the ledger, and that's the truth."

Doug laughed. He started for the office, punching in his vest pocket for the keys.

Allena and Tom followed.

A smirk on his face, Doug swung the door open and stepped back to let his mother enter. Allena's eyes grew wide. "Douglas! This place is a mess. How would you know anything was missing?"

Doug ignored her, marched to the desk, and paused, a triumphant look on his face. He yanked a drawer open. "Look for yourself."

The ledger lay at a crooked angle. Allena and Tom stared at the book, then gazed at Doug. Allena stepped forward and lifted if from the drawer. "Is this what you're looking for, Doug?"

He grabbed it and flicked through pages. Suspicion clouded his face. "Yes, but I came to work on it this morning and it was not here."

Tom smiled. "Are you sure you looked in the right drawer?"

Doug stared knives at Tom.

I have thrown him off balance, Tom thought. *Now if I can just keep it that way.* He shrugged his shoulders and walked out of the office. "I'm hungry."

"Yes, the food will be getting cold. Hattie will have our ears." Allena preceded her sons to the kitchen. Doug, confused, closed in behind Tom and growled, "That ledger was not in the drawer when I went in this morning.

I know you were in there."

His voice rose. "But don't think this gives you any hold on the ranch. Mark my words—this whole ranch will be mine!" He marched down the hall to his room.

"Douglas!" Allena started after him.

Tom grabbed her arm. "Mother, let him cool off." He pulled her to face him. "This is a man's fight, not two little boys." His mother's stunned stare betrayed how vulnerable she was. He put his arms around her and pulled her to him. She was trembling.

Tom had won for the moment. Now he would have to be doubly alert. Doug would seize any opportunity to best him. Tom's stomach growled. He turned his mother toward the kitchen. The smell of bacon, ham, home-baked bread, and flapjacks whet his appetite and spurred his feet. "I'm starving."

Hattie had set the table for three. Tom and Allena sat down. Allena patted the third chair. "Join us, Hattie. I hate empty chairs." She smiled and bowed her head. "Tom, say grace, please."

Tom thanked God for His care, for their family, home, and land. Within, he prayed, *Thank You, Father. That was a narrow escape. You know I'm going to need all the help I can get. Thy will be done.*

Chapter 10

The early morning air blew clean and clear. A red glow in the east promised a warm spring day. Circle Z buzzed with activity.

Tom, astride Tinder, tied Victor to the back of Allena's buggy. He touched his hat to Nelson, whose face radiated his excitement at driving his mother to the stage station.

On the buckboard, Smitty sat with his elbows resting on his knees, the reins hanging limp in his hands. He squinted up at the sun and resettled his hat on top of his eyebrows.

Allena emerged from the ranch house issuing orders to Hattie. She hurried to her buggy and climbed in beside Nelson. The horses moved, and she settled back to read aloud from her Bible after they got rolling.

It took two hours to get to the stage station. Tom spotted a dustball way ahead—probably the stage. He reckoned they would just about meet coming into the station.

Tom leaned to Nelson and hollered. "Let's pick it up and beat that stage in."

Nelson grinned, slapped the reins, and took off. He pulled to a stop in the station yard with the westbound stagecoach still a mile up the road. He scooted out of the buggy onto his feet and crutches and stared admiringly as the stage driver handled the team of six snorting horses.

The first four passengers out of the stagecoach went into the station for something to eat. A tall, broad man in a stylish eastern suit stepped out and assisted an elegantly dressed young lady from the coach. She looked up and immediately opened her parasol.

Allena was out of the buggy. "Zack!" she cried and flung her arms around her eldest son. Everyone talked at once. After the boisterous greeting, Zack turned to the beautiful woman who stood slightly behind him and pulled her to his side. "Mom, Tom, Nelson, I'd like you to meet my wife, Darcy."

After an awkward pause, Allena gently embraced her first daughter-in-law. "Well! This is quite a surprise, a delightful one." She held Darcy at arm's length. "My dear, you are lovely."

Darcy smiled and stood with her head high.

Tom came forward, took her hands in his, and bowed. "How did Zack keep you a secret?" He turned to his brother. "I thought you went east to become a lawyer."

Darcy sent an adoring glance to Zack. "He did, and he's a good one. My father wanted to take him into his law firm, but Zack wants to set up his own firm in Texas." Darcy tossed her head and laughed. "I'm going to try and talk him out of it."

Three mouths dropped open in surprise. Zack? The brother who never wanted any part of Texas?

Zack shrugged. "I know what you're thinking. When I left, I never wanted to return except to visit. But it's mighty crowded in the East. You probably won't believe it, but I hankered after these wide, open spaces." He laughed and looked around. "Where's Doug?"

"He had some business to attend to in town and said he would see you at the ranch." Allena sounded apologetic.

Tom waved to Smitty, who came over to give Zack a handshake. "You sure have growed up to be a big man. One look at you, I thought you was your father standin' there."

Zachary Langdon's namesake grinned and said, "I know. Every time I look in the mirror it's a shock to see Father looking back."

"Then your father must have been a handsome, magnificent man." Darcy slipped her arm through her husband's.

"He was," Nelson shifted himself to the other side of Zack.

Darcy leaned across and touched Nelson's cheek, smiled sweetly, then surveyed the rest of the family with cool eyes.

Tom asked, "Would you like a drink of water before we start back? It'll be a long, warm ride."

Darcy surveyed the scene with disgust. "Oh, no thank you. I'll wait until we get. . .home?"

Tom swung onto Tinder's saddle and led Victor to Zack. "Come on, mount up. Let's go home."

Zack inspected Victor. "Not Diamond?"

"No, but next thing to it. He's Diamond's son. Remember the colt with a mind of his own who tossed you?" Tom grinned.

"Diamond's colt! He's as regal as his father." Zack helped his mother and Darcy into the buggy, mounted, and swung Nelson up behind him. Victor danced around under double weight, then tossed his head ready to go.

Allena gave the horse's back a slap and turned the buggy westward. Darcy sat rod-straight, her gloved hands clenched in her lap, her chin in the air. When they faced west, she grabbed her parasol and struggled to find a way to shield herself from the sun.

The men on horseback fell in behind to keep the dust off the ladies.

Smitty, luggage loaded in the buckboard, moved into last place, a knowing grin on his face.

When the caravan passed under the Circle Z arch, Hattie stood on the porch peering. Allena waved and Hattie scurried indoors. The buggy pulled to a stop in front of the low, rambling, adobe ranch. Allena tied the reins and got out.

Darcy stared, unbelieving. "This is home?"

"Yes, my dear, and a good one. Won't you come in? Hattie has supper prepared. I'm sure you must be as ready for it as we are." Allena stepped to the porch without a backward glance and Hattie met her at the door.

Zack assisted his wife into the house, came back out, and joined Tom riding toward the barn. Several cowboys came around the barn and spotted Zack. They pumped his hand, talked a bit, and finally took the horses to unsaddle.

Zack slapped Victor's flank when he handed him over. "This is what I've missed. Any fancy horse back east would be hard put to match that stallion."

The brothers walked toward the ranch. "Good to have you home, Zack, but Darcy sure surprised us. How come you didn't tell us you were married?"

Zack grinned. "I thought of it, but knowing Ma, this was the easiest way. Darcy's a city girl. Ma thinks the only wives for Texas men are Texas girls."

"How long have you been married?"

"About two months. When I got Ma's letter, I knew I had to come home. Figured Doug might try and pull something. There's a hate in Doug I never understood. Father saw it too and it worried him."

"Did I hear Darcy right? You plan to set up practice here?"

Zack sighed. "Yes. Boston is exciting but it's mighty crowded." He laughed. "When I left, Ma said, 'Once a Texas boy, always a Texas boy.' I didn't believe her. But when Darcy's father asked me to join his firm, I got to thinking. There are lots of lawyers in the East. I'd just be one of them. Out this way, there are few. That's what made up my mind. I hope to set up a law firm of my own in Harness.

"Darcy isn't happy about it. At first, she didn't understand how I could refuse her father. We'd be set for life! I thought she was going to break our betrothal. Finally, after she knew I was serious, she insisted we be married right away so she could come with me. We had our fancy wedding, went to the Carolinas to visit her sister for a month's honeymoon, then started west."

Tom thought of mentioning Mary Lou but decided to wait. They had reached the porch. Zack and Tom washed and hurried to the dining room. Allena was in her place, but Darcy wasn't there.

Allena explained, "She was tired and ordered Smitty to take her things

to your room. She demanded a bath immediately to get the filth off her."
Allena raised her eyebrows. "Did she bring a personal maid?"

Tom, surprised at his mother's tone, suppressed a smile. The shock must
have been more than she let on. Zack departed immediately to his room.

Hattie popped her head in and out waiting for Allena's signal to serve.
Finally Allena motioned. "Hattie, please go to Zack's room and tell him dinner needs to be served."

Hattie hurried out.

Nelson broke the silence. "Zack and I talked. Says he aims to be a big
lawyer in Texas." He bobbed his head decisively. "He will, too." Nelson
beamed with confidence Tom hadn't seen in a long time. For Nelson, Father
had been the world's greatest man. He had been eleven when Father died.
When Zack left, he had lost his second father.

Zack returned to the dining room alone, Hattie right behind him.
"Mother, would it be too much trouble to have Hattie take Darcy's dinner
to our room? The trip has been long and she's very tired."

"Of course," Allena said. "Hattie, bring our food to the table, then put
Darcy's dinner on a tray and take it to her."

"Yessum." Hattie disappeared.

Zack took his seat. Unless they had had company, it had remained
empty during his absence. His father's place opposite Allena was always
empty. "Now it's the Lord's place," she had said. A framed picture, embroidered by Allena's mother, hung on the wall between the windows: "Jesus,
Ever Present Guest in Our Home."

"Zack, would you say the blessing, please?" Allena asked.

He said a short prayer he had learned as a boy. Tom listened and won-
dered. Zack had given his life to Jesus Christ. So had Doug. Was Darcy a
Christian? She acted spoiled. Tom asked forgiveness for the thought. *She is
Zack's wife and it is obvious Zack loves her. Everything must be new and strange.*
A sudden longing filled him. It would be the same with Mary Lou. Texas
was a world apart from Boston or Venture.

"Tom?"

He roused to the dish of potatoes held out to him. "I'm sorry. I was daydreaming." He served himself and passed them to Zack.

Hattie came in and whispered to Allena.

"Zack, Hattie says Darcy wants to see you."

Noticeably embarrassed, Zack excused himself.

A horse thundered into the yard and a dusty Doug strutted into the dining room. His mother's eyes sent him to the wash basin in the back kitchen.

"Zack here?" he asked as he sat down.

"He's up with his new wife," Allena explained.

"New wife! Zack married? Well, that old book boy is spicier then he looks." Doug obviously didn't notice his mother's frown as she passed the steak plate. "Well, wha-d-ya know." His face creased with a secret grin.

All ate in silence until Nelson blurted, "Zack's going to stay and be a lawyer here."

Doug looked up from his plate, his mouth full.

Did Tom imagine it, or did a look of fear flash in Doug's face?

Doug gulped and sneered. "Small town boy makes good and comes home to swagger. Doesn't Zack know that lawyers don't get paid much in Texas?"

"Texas needs good lawyers. Maybe with a good one," Tom emphasized, "we could scare out the land speculators." He looked for Doug's reaction. Doug just ate ravenously.

Zack came in, greeted Doug, and sat down.

"Everything all right?" Allena asked. "I can appreciate how grueling the long ride across Texas can be. I'm surprised you didn't come as far as you could by train, then take the stage."

Doug looked up from his dinner. "So our big brother has himself a wife. Congratulations. I'm anxious to see who'd have you. Where's she from?"

"Boston."

"And she married a Texas rancher?"

"No, she married a Boston lawyer."

Tom sensed the rising tension. He didn't blame Zack. Doug's sarcasm was hard to handle. Allena broke the ensuing silence with a question about Zack's years in law school. Finally she pushed back her chair and rose. The men stood.

"I agree with Darcy. It's been a long day. Good night, my sons. It's good to have you all home again. Don't forget your prayers," she reminded as she left the room.

Tom and Zack smiled. Their mother had reminded them to say their prayers every night as long as they could remember.

"How come you didn't accept the offer Darcy's father made?" Tom asked. "You'd have probably become rich."

"I didn't feel at home there. While I was getting my law degree, it was fine, but I knew where I belonged." He sipped his cup of coffee. "Fill me in with what's going on here at the ranch."

Doug bristled. "You think you're gonna come back after four years of shoving the work over on me and take over? Think again, Brother. You walked away when you had the opportunity. Now this ranch is mine."

Zack's jaw tightened. Tom couldn't see Zack's eyes, but he knew they contained the steel determination of their father's.

"Then you need help," Zack said. "The payments I received dropped considerably in the last two years. This is the best ranch in these parts and with the demand for beef, you should be thriving."

Doug rose abruptly. His chair clattered to the floor. "This ranch is as good now as it ever was."

Zack never moved. "I agree. But the money is sifting away somewhere. This isn't the same place I left. The barn and corral are in need of repair."

Doug leaped at Zack, eyes blazing. "Who are you to walk in here and criticize me? I've spent these past four years working harder than you ever worked. You're not going to stroll in here and take over." He swung toward Tom. "Nor is your birthday going to change things. This ranch is mine!" Doug stomped out.

Tom and Zack sat silent.

"Something's wrong," Zack said. "I'm used to his anger, but he's like a snorting longhorn under attack. We've got to watch those horns. They're dangerous."

Tom nodded. "I've a hunch it has to do with land speculators. I've been wondering if Doug has been selling off some of the land. We could ask the cowboys if they've seen anything."

"I've seen some men come with Doug and ride out to the range," Nelson offered.

"Did you recognize any of them?" Zack asked.

"No, but they wore Eastern clothes."

Zack sighed. "Well we can't do anything tonight. I need to see the books. Have you seen them?" he asked Tom.

"No. Doug keeps the office door locked. As far as he's concerned, I'm just one of the hands."

"Figures. We'll start tomorrow. I'll go into town to the land office and see what activity I can find." He pushed back his chair. "Right now, I'm tired and I have a wife waiting for me, so I'll see you in the morning."

Hattie peeked into the dining room.

Tom waved her in. "Come in, Hattie, you can clear. We're leaving." He went to bed and slept sounder than he had in months. Zack was back.

ʊ

Tom and Zack left early. Long after the sun rose, Allena rapped on Zack's bedroom door. The door opened a crack. A tousled Darcy peered through. She had been crying.

"Did you rest well, my dear?"

Darcy's child-like eyes hardened. "Yes."

"The men will be in for breakfast in half an hour. I thought you'd like to join us."

"How do I wash?"

"Hattie will bring you warm water for the basin on the stand."

"Thank you," Darcy said and closed the door.

An hour later deep voices announced Tom and Zack were back. Everyone was seated at the breakfast table when Darcy entered, her nut-brown hair fashionably pinned on top of her head. Her simple blue dress had a white lace collar. The men stood as she swished into her seat beside Zack.

All but Doug sat down. He walked around the table with a big smile on his face and kissed Darcy's hand. "So you're the beauty I've been hearing about." He turned to Zack. "I have to admit, you sure can pick 'em."

Zack stood. "Darcy, this is my younger brother, Doug."

"Welcome to the Circle Z." Doug made a magnificent sweep of his hand. "I'll be glad to show you around while Zack's busy at his law office."

"Zack, Doug, sit down, please. The food is getting cold. Tom, would you say the blessing?" Allena bowed her head.

"Dear Father," Tom prayed, "we thank You that our whole family is gathered at this table and for Darcy, our new member. We thank You for this day and ask Your help in our work. We ask Your blessing on this food so bountifully given. In Jesus' name. . . ."

Everyone except Darcy said, "Amen."

After the food was passed and everyone was eating, Allena said, "Zack, I think it would be nice if you gave Darcy a tour of some of the ranch to get her better acquainted." She turned to Darcy. "You do ride?"

"Of course." Darcy sat up straighter. "My father had some of the finest animals in Boston. I've ridden since I was a little girl."

"Good." Allena looked at Zack.

Tom smiled. His mother gave directions without people realizing they were being ordered about. He glanced at Darcy. She looked different this morning. Simple and sweet. No wonder his brother loved her.

He turned to Zack. "We'll be heading out tomorrow on the roundup. You want to try riding with us?" Tom grinned. "After four years of being a city slicker, figured you might not be up to—"

"Hold it, little brother. Once a Texas boy, always a Texas boy. Remember?"

"Then eat hearty. Jess's grub isn't half as good as Hattie's."

No one noticed Darcy stiffen. "Zack! I thought you were going to show me the ranch!"

"Nelson and I will do that," Allena said.

Darcy gave Allena an injured look. "I want Zack to show me. And I want to go to the roundup. Do they dance the Virginia Reel?"

Every face went blank, trying hard to suppress smiles.

Zack turned to Darcy. "A roundup isn't a dance. It's gathering the cattle that have roamed all winter and finding the new calves. We could be gone eight or ten days."

Darcy pushed back her chair, rose, and spit out, "Excuse me!" She flounced out, Zack at her heels.

Everyone else thought, *Poor Zack,* but Tom envied him, married to the girl he loved. The next day Tom would come into his quarter of the ranch. His hopes were pinned on the fall cattle drive. He would stop at Venture and hopefully bring his bride back home with him.

Chapter 11

T he post office door banged open. Mary Lou looked up from sorting mail. Jenny plunged through, breathless.

"He's here! He's come back."

Smiling, Mary Lou asked, "Who's 'he'?"

"Tom Langdon." Jenny's eyes shone.

The letter on its way to the top pigeonhole stopped midair. Mary Lou's mind rushed to the last time she had seen Tom—under the cottonwoods. Without closing her eyes, she felt the press of his hands on her shoulders, the sensation of being drawn into his arms. Other than being with Mama, it was the only place she had ever felt at home.

Jenny slapped the counter. "Well, aren't you gonna say somethin'? You just gonna stand there and poke mail? He's over at the livery."

Mary Lou completed the first letter's journey and started another on its way. She needed to gather her scattered reserves. "It's nice to hear he's back," she said, surprised at the calmness in her voice.

"Mary Lou Mackey, are you pretendin' to me he don't mean nothin' to you? I know better. You've been moonin' around here since he left."

Evidently she had not concealed her feelings as well as she thought. So many times Mary Lou had smothered the longing for one look at that lanky, red-headed cowboy.

"Cowboys rarely settle" had been Pa's comment. But that wasn't true. Pa had settled with Mama. Uncle Nate had married Aunt Tibby. Mary Lou's dream was to be a rancher's wife and own a big spread like Aunt Tibby and Uncle Nate.

"Mary Lou, I declare, you are exasperatin'. I bring you the best news in the world and you just stand there."

"For heaven's sake, Jenny, what do you expect me to do—run out and throw myself into the arms of a man who doesn't love me?"

"Well! I thought you'd be so glad to see him nothin' could get in your way." Jenny stopped Mary Lou's arm and peeked over it. "You can't fool me. I know you love him."

Mary Lou spun around. "Jenny! Watch what you're saying. I'm betrothed to Glenn and he might hear you." Her disobedient heart struggled to wiggle from her tight control.

"Glenn. Oh pooh. You may be betrothed, but you don't love him." Jenny faced Mary Lou. "This is Jenny, Honey. You might fool everybody else, but you don't fool me."

Mary Lou didn't dare look at Jenny. She was too angry at herself for the longing that invaded her.

Relentless, Jenny pressed on. "You'll never be happy. I won't be able to stand by and take that, and neither will you!"

Dear Jenny who knew her too well. From that first day when the Wimbley family wagon rolled into the old Martindale homestead, they had been inseparable. Jenny was three and Mary Lou four. They had grown closer than sisters. Mary Lou should have known better than to try to disguise her feelings from her dearest friend. Jenny's gaze pinned her. "Well?"

"There's nothing I can do about it. Tom doesn't love me, and I like Glenn—"

"Like is not good enough." Jenny snapped. "Not for marriage." Jenny grabbed Mary Lou's shoulders and forced her to regard the determination in her eyes. "I'm serious. If you try to marry Glenn, when the preacher asks if there's anyone who knows why these two shouldn't be wed, I'll tell. So help me, I will."

Jenny shook Mary Lou and everything fell apart. The mail in her hands spilled to the floor. Until that moment, Mary Lou had willed herself to accept the neat little package her life was tied in. She and Glenn would be married in two weeks and inherit the store, Pa's wedding gift. Even the townspeople had nodded approval. They all awaited the happy event.

Mary Lou stooped to pick up the mail. Jenny bent to help.

Tom. Here. She had to see him. She shook her head. It wouldn't be right. She was betrothed. Anyway, he hadn't sent one letter. Where was her pride? *Tom is here!* A fresh lasso tightened around her heart and her body came alive.

"Mary Lou? You all right?"

Mary Lou glanced up into Jenny's concerned face. She threw her arms around Jenny. "Thank you, Dear Heart. What would I ever do without you?"

The door opened again and Glenn came in, his blond hair disheveled, a strange look on his face. He breathed like he had been running.

"Miss Jenny, if you please?" Glenn held the door open and waved his arm toward the opening. "I would like to speak to my intended about something personal. If you wish, I'll escort you—"

"I'll go myself, thank you." Jenny swung around to Mary Lou. "Intended," she mimicked and made a face. "I'll see you later." She snapped her skirt around the counter and slammed the door behind her.

Glenn shifted from one foot to the other. "I suppose Jenny told you."

"Told me what?" Mary Lou turned to stuff the last few envelopes into their boxes. She willed her hands to be steady, thankful for the task. It kept her back to Glenn.

"Now, Mary Lou, I saw her turn and come running over here as soon as she saw him."

"Are you referring to Tom Langdon?"

"Yes." Curt, clipped, unlike Glenn.

"Jenny told me." She tried to sound disinterested but didn't dare look at him.

"I thought when he left he was never coming back."

"This is a free country." She shrugged. "He's a cowboy and they drive cattle to the railroad. That's his job." She finished the mail and turned to him. He looked troubled, defiant—an expression she had never seen before. "Did the new railroad shipment come?" she asked to change the subject.

Glenn shifted uneasily, then softened. "Yes, the men are unloading the wagon. You staying today?"

"No." Mary Lou busied herself putting away postal supplies. "There's a W.C.T.U. meeting at the church this afternoon."

"What do you ladies do at your meeting?" Glenn took a deep breath and relaxed.

"We're trying to find a way to close Ludden's saloon. It's not safe at night for the people who live in town. I don't know how they put up with all the noise and shooting that goes on."

Glenn smirked. "You just said this was a free country. Those men mean no harm to the ladies of our town."

"Maybe that's true when they're sober, but they become unpredictable when they're liquored up."

Glenn laughed. "You ladies have your little meeting. But I doubt you'll have much effect on Mac Ludden. He's a rich man and does a lot for this town."

"That's another thing. Mac Ludden is taking money families need. The good Lord knows there's never enough of it."

"Come on, Mary Lou, the men visit the saloon on their own. Mac Ludden has nothing to do with it."

"Nothing to do with it!" She glared, glad for an excuse to challenge him. "Venture is a different town when the cattle drive arrives. Gamblers, speculators, outlaws, barmaids, and those. . .women invade this town like grasshoppers."

Glenn raised his eyebrows. "We all make money during the cattle drive, including your father's store."

"The cattle drives also bring trouble." Her anger mounted. "I'm glad I don't live in town when all that shooting starts. Some of them don't even aim. When they're drunk they just shoot for the fun of it." Mary Lou grabbed her shawl and hurried out to the stalls.

Glenn followed. "You better watch that you ladies don't get into more than you can handle."

She couldn't suppress her fury. "Then why don't you men do something about it? Would you like your son going to school drunk?" She felt her face crimson. "If it were just the men it would be different, but this affects the women and children." She concentrated on saddling Dulcie.

Glenn leaned against the stall. "It's just I don't want you ladies to get hurt."

She swung and faced him. "That's exactly what I'm saying! The whole town gives in to Mac Ludden's clientele and the cattle drives. Seems to me it should be the other way around. They should give in to our town's law and order."

"Just what do you women plan to do?"

"We don't know yet, but the best thing for Venture would be to get that saloon out of town." She felt the back of her neck prickle. *That's it! Get the saloon out of town!*

"Good-bye, Glenn, see you tomorrow." She rode off on Dulcie and didn't look back.

At the church, Mary Lou tied Dulcie beside Missy. Jenny waved from the front. Mary Lou talked to Aunt Tibby, then joined Jenny and the younger women in the first two rows.

Tibby rapped the table and stood. "Ladies, may I have your attention please?"

Conversation stopped, all eyes on Tibby.

Tibby opened the meeting with prayer. The women sang "O God Our Help in Ages Past" and sat down.

Tibby's face reflected good news. "Today one of our young ladies proposed an idea. She suggested that we get the saloon out of town."

"How you goin' to manage that?" a skeptical voice called out. "Problem is, we're too close to Abilene. It might be easier to move the town."

The ladies laughed.

Sarah George stood. "We certainly need law and order in town. It's gotten so we have to get to the town pump before suppertime. With the saloon in the center and the town pump at the east end, I have to walk right through it all."

Tibby rapped for order. "Ladies. We all know why it should be done. Let's concentrate on how to do it. Any suggestions?"

There was a momentary lull.

"Let's ask Mr. Ludden to move the saloon," came the young, timid voice of Miriam Wimbley.

The ladies laughed.

"Don't laugh." Henrietta stood, eyes shooting sparks. "Some of the men agree with us. Big Jon said many times he wished the saloon stood someplace else. Trying to raise seven curious sons with temptation in the center of town is impossible. Other fathers must feel the same. Why can't the saloon be made to conduct its business outside the town limit? That would free the town and keep the ruckus in one area." Henrietta sat down.

The room was quiet.

From the sea of puzzled faces, Bertha Leggett hesitantly rose. "I know we're new homesteaders in Venture, but we have four, fine Christian sons and want to keep them that way. Psalm 101:3 says, 'I will set no wicked thing before mine eyes.' We need to remove as much temptation as possible from our children. My husband feels like Big Jon. I think we should find out how many men are on our side. It's a difficult task for us alone."

The room hummed with a murmur of agreement.

Tibby rapped again. "All right, there's our task this week. We'll meet next week after we talk to our men. Thank you for coming, ladies. Remember, together we can do more than we think. Let us adjourn with prayer."

The ladies bowed, then hurried out with fear, courage, and determination in their eyes.

At the supper table, Nelda and Mary Lou told Buck about the meeting and asked his opinion.

"I think you women are in over your heads. Mac will never voluntarily move that saloon. It would mean building a new place." Buck shook his head. "You'd better look for another way."

Neither Nelda nor Mary Lou missed Buck's tolerant half smile.

I bet this is the way all the men will react, Mary Lou thought. *Lord, what can we do to make these men recognize the evil right before their eyes?*

Next morning when Mary Lou arrived at the store, she found Glenn arranging barrels of New Orleans molasses, vinegar, flour, salt pork, and white and brown sugar. He came to meet her.

"Good morning." He held Mary Lou in his arms. She accepted his embrace, but her heart hurt. She steeled herself to keep from pushing him away.

"We finally got the white dishes and those steel knives and pewter forks and spoons. I thought they might look good over there." He pointed to a shelf under the lamp chimneys. "And the new dress goods came in."

Halfway through the morning Mary Lou asked, "Can you think of a way we could get the saloon moved out of town?"

Glenn looked up startled, then grinned. "You ladies thinking of moving the saloon? That I must see."

Rankled, Mary Lou snapped, "I didn't ask your opinion. I asked if you could think of a way we could do it."

Glenn laughed. "Whoever thought up that wild idea?"

Mary Lou lifted her chin. "I did."

Glenn gulped. "You did!" He shook his head. "There's no way. Mac'll veto that."

Mary Lou bristled. "Well, it won't do any harm to ask him."

"I don't want you mixed up with Mac Ludden."

"You don't want me mixed up! Then you better do something. Either you men do something, or we women will."

Glenn softened. "Mac's in business same as we are. How would you like Mac to tell us to move out of town? You ladies don't know how business works. You compete where you can, but you don't order another man out."

"Not even if he's in the devil's business?" Mary Lou demanded.

Glenn laughed. "Come on, Mary Lou, you're out of place."

"Out of place! And just where is my place?" Her temper rose. "You're just like all the other men."

"Now, Mary Lou—"

She didn't stay to hear more. Men never took women seriously. Well, the women of Venture would show them—and soon!

Chapter 12

Dulcie picked her way home through the rippling prairie grass, her reins slack. Mary Lou rode oblivious to her surroundings. Her heart was engaged in a battle. She fought the urge to see Tom. If he loved her, he would have written. Too late, anyway. Betrothed to Glenn, the door had closed.

"God doesn't close doors. He opens them. God is our Father and wants us to have every good and perfect gift." How often Mama's wise words rang in her mind. *Oh, Mama, I wish you were here.*

A dust cloud revealed a rider up ahead.

Mary Lou nudged Dulcie into a trot. Daydreaming wouldn't help Aunt Nelda sew white lace on her wedding dress.

The rider slowed, then turned. Her heart recognized Tom before her mind allowed it. The gap closed. Her hungry eyes feasted on the tall, slim cowboy she had longed for since he rode away. She stopped.

Tinder trotted toward her until the two horses were nose to nose. Tom removed his hat. Red hair, curled tight from the dampness under his hat, glistened bronze in the sun. "Hello, Mary Lou. I've been wanting to see you."

His voice sounded more beautiful then any of the songbirds Mary Lou had heard that spring. "Hello, Tom. How's Texas?" She couldn't think of anything else to say.

"Fine." Tom's gaze clung to her face. "But my heart's been in Venture."

Mary Lou stiffened. "I'd never have known it."

"I'm sorry, Mary Lou. I wanted to write, but under the circumstances, I didn't dare."

All her hurt spilled out. "Didn't dare write? You wrote to Uncle Nate."

"There are a lot of things I couldn't say before, but now I can—like I love you, Mary Lou."

Why had he not said it before—or written it and erased the ache of the past year?

"I do love you, Mary Lou, but I didn't have the right to tell you before."

"What gives you the right to say it now? I'm betrothed to Glenn."

Tom ran his hands around the brim of his hat. "I know. But now I have something to offer and can ask your father. Your pa thought I was just a

68

cowboy last fall. At that time, I couldn't tell him any different."

"What are you now that makes the difference?" Her curiosity and Tom's presence held her like a magnet.

"When I asked your pa if I could marry you—"

"You asked Pa if you could marry me? You never told me you loved me. You never asked me if I loved you. Yet you asked Pa if you could marry me?" She swung Dulcie's head and jabbed her sides hard. Dulcie took off like a shot.

"Mary Lou! Wait!"

The audacity of that man! She loosed the reins and let Dulcie gallop home. Hurt and disappointment spilled with her tears. When the cabin came in sight, she eased up and slowed Dulcie. She couldn't go into the cabin in this condition. She would have too much explaining to do. Still, when she reached the cabin and slid off Dulcie, she barged through the door in tears.

Nelda turned from her pie dough and caught the distraught girl in her arms. When sobs subsided, she pushed Mary Lou into a chair and pulled up her rocker. "I take it you've seen Tom."

Mary Lou sniffed. "He—he told me he loved me!"

Nelda smiled and patted Mary Lou's hands. "Well, now, isn't that the very thing you've wanted to know?"

"No."

"No?" Nelda sat back and shook her head.

"He asked Pa to marry me without even telling me he loved me."

Nelda smiled. "Is that all? I thought it was something serious."

Mary Lou raised a shocked face. "What do you mean? He should have told me first. Am I a horse to be auctioned off?"

"Mary Lou, you're being ridiculous. Did you let Tom explain why he didn't ask you first?"

Mary Lou stared in disbelief.

"Did you give him time to tell you that when he asked your father, Buck said a cowboy was the last man he wanted his daughter to marry? Now, evidently he has something to offer and has come to ask your pa's permission."

"I don't know what you're talking about," Mary Lou wailed.

"That's obvious. You didn't give Tom a chance. What must the poor man think?"

Was Aunt Nelda on Tom's side? "Have you talked with Tom?"

"Yes. He came here to see you. He didn't think it would be proper to go to the store. I think Tom was very considerate of Glenn. Tom's a gentleman."

"He's a cowboy."

"Cowboys can't be gentlemen?"

"I thought—"

"That's the trouble, Mary Lou, you didn't think. At least not with your heart. Can you imagine how Tom feels" He comes back to see you and you verbally smack his face and run. Is that the response of a lady?" Nelda went back to her pie dough.

Mary Lou shrank into the chair. She had acted abominably, so taken with her own feelings she never thought of Tom's. "What am I going to do, Aunt Nelda?"

"You're going to be what every Christian should be—completely honest." Nelda crimped the pie crust with her fingers. "There's one important question: Are you in love with Tom or Glenn? Decide that and you'll know what to do."

Mary Lou thought of Glenn. He loved her and would be a good husband. To break their betrothal would hurt him terribly. She really didn't know much about Tom. How could she make an honest decision?

Nelda slipped a pie in the baker and placed hot coals in the recessed well of the iron lid. "Perhaps we'd better wait to put lace on your wedding dress—at least until you make up your mind."

The rumbling of Buck's buggy announced his arrival. Mary Lou went to the window and watched her father hobble toward the cabin. He looked tired. Life's spark in Pa died with Mama. His love and respect for Mary Lou seemed to have died, also. She and Pa talked, but never about Mama. Would he ever forgive her?

Buck dropped into his place and vacantly watched Mary Lou and Nelda put supper on the table. "Barney Alden's pretty mad," he said. "Last night a shot went through the front window of the land office."

"Don't blame him," Nelda said. "It'll take a month or more to get new glass. The one who shot it should have to pay for it."

Buck shrugged. "Nobody knows who did it."

Nelda brought plates of steaming prairie chicken and corn pudding to the table. Mary Lou sliced bread, opened a jar of prairie globe apple jelly, and sat down.

They bowed while Nelda said grace.

Mary Lou spread a piece of bread with jelly. "Aunt Tibby went to Mac Ludden today and told him the W.C.T.U. ladies felt he should move the saloon out of town."

Buck gulped. "Tibby's crazy. She's going to get her nose pinched if she keeps it where it doesn't belong."

"Good for Tibby," Nelda said.

"You women better pull in your horns. Somebody's going to get hurt."

A horse galloped into the yard. Matthew Wimbley slid off and dashed breathlessly through the door. "Mr. Mackey, Pa wants you to come right away. Georgie's been shot." Tears ran down his dusty face.

Buck swung in his chair. "Come here, Son. Tell me what happened."

Matthew pulled a bandanna from his pocket, wiped his face, and blew his nose. "Georgie and Sam were goin' rabbit huntin' tomorrow and needed some shot, so they rode in to your store. Just as they mounted their ponies to come him, some shootin' started in the street and Georgie got shot in the back."

Buck grabbed his cane. "Where's your pa?"

"At Doc Gray's with Georgie."

"Come help me hitch up. Then go home and tell your ma not to worry." Buck, Morgan, and the buggy soon thundered out of the barn toward town. Mary Lou and Nelda saddled Dulcie and Jewel and followed Matthew to the Wimbley farm.

Henrietta, dry eyed, sat outside the door watching the road, her bewildered children gathered round. Nelda dismounted and pulled Henrietta into her arms. Mary Lou hugged Jenny and the other children, too numb and wide-eyed for words.

Two hours later, Big Jon carried his son into the cabin and laid him gently on a bed. Henrietta leaned over Georgie, smoothed her hands over his quiet face, and kissed him. Brothers and sisters crowded around, their faces filled with fear and disbelief.

Big Jon stood at the side of the bed, taking deep breaths to assuage the agony mirrored in his face.

Four-year-old Caroline looked up at the faces above her. "Is Georgie dead?"

Big Jon picked her up. "Yes, Child, he's gone home to be with Jesus."

The younger children edged closer to their mother and father and stared.

Sam pinched his lips together and said with hateful determination, "I'm gonna shoot whoever shot Georgie."

Young Jon turned. "If you don't, I will."

"You'll do nothing of the kind," Big Jon ordered. "Remember Romans 12:19: 'Vengeance is mine, I will repay, saith the Lord.' "

One by one the children went timidly to look at Georgie. Caroline touched him. "He still feels like Georgie. But he needs a blanket. He's cold."

Henrietta knelt beside her son and began unbuttoning his shirt. Nelda joined her, unbuttoned Georgie's shoes, and slipped them off.

Big Jon took Caroline and Sam by the hand and moved the other children outside ahead of him.

Mary Lou and Jenny watched the two older women undress Georgie. They left the bandage Doc Gray had placed over the wound and washed and redressed him in his Sunday suit. When they were done, Henrietta rocked him and wept. Then she laid him down tenderly, kissed him, and knelt beside the bed. She stroked his face and her tears ran free. Jenny slipped to her knees beside her mother and stared at Georgie, her cheeks wet.

Mary Lou lifted a cup from the shelf, filled it with steaming coffee, and offered it to Henrietta. She shook her head. Mary Lou took it outside to Big Jon.

The children were full of questions. Mary Lou marveled at this giant of a man whose son had just been shot. He sat answering questions from his eleven children, trying to assure them of God's goodness.

"Papa, Georgie never got to grow up," Caroline said.

"I don't know how God will use this for good, but as Christians, we believe that God loves us. Even when we don't understand, we have faith that God will make it right." Big Jon soothed each child with his hand and smiled. "And Georgie is the first one of us to see Jesus."

Mary Lou had a hard time accepting those answers. The same agony she felt at her mother's death crowded her chest. She felt the family's loss. Mama had called God "the God of all comfort" and explained that the comfort we received was given so we could comfort others in trouble. Now Mary Lou knew what that verse meant, and how Henrietta and Big Jon and their children felt. "Help me, Lord, to give the comfort Mama would give if she were here," she whispered.

A tear-stained Jenny came out from the cabin. Mary Lou slipped to her side and hugged her. "Oh God," she prayed, "ease the pain of my dear friend and her family."

A buggy and wagon rattled into the yard. Mary Lou recognized Uncle Nate and Aunt Tibby and Sarah George with baskets and pans of food. Pastor Miles talked a lot about being a Christian family. Mary Lou's heart swelled with love. *Thank you, Father.*

She noticed Pa sitting in his buggy down the road, hunched over. Did Georgie's death bring back the hurt of Mama's death to him? Mary Lou walked out. His pained eyes locked with hers for a second. "Pa, come and eat," she urged.

He shook his head. "I'll eat at home. Tell Big Jon I'll see him later." He swung the buggy around and trotted off.

He is thinking of Mama. Mary Lou ached afresh.

It was dark by the time they finished the meal and cleaned up. Sarah George and Nelda planned to stay the night and sleep in Sarah's wagon. Tibby and Nate took their leave. Mary Lou rode Dulcie alongside.

"I want you to round up as many W.C.T.U. women as you can, and we'll meet at the church tomorrow morning after the funeral," Aunt Tibby said. "If any husbands want to come, they're welcome. We've got to do something."

They rode silently until Mary Lou turned in the lane to her home and waved good night.

One lantern burning low on the table welcomed Mary Lou. The cabin was quiet; the door to Buck's bedroom was closed. Mary Lou went into her room and shut the door.

God doesn't close doors, he opens them. . . .

"Oh God, open the door between Pa and me so I can talk with him about Tom and Glenn. I don't know what to do. I need his help." Mary Lou sobbed into her pillow. *Does life ever turn out the way we want it?* She cried for Mama, for Pa, for her disappointment in Tom, for little Georgie, for. . .

Eons later, sleep finally came.

Chapter 13

Townspeople and homesteaders attended the funeral of young Georgie the next morning and came away thoughtful. A long procession wended its way to the meeting called by Nate and Tibby Bradford. Chairs filled quickly. Latecomers leaned against the walls. Men gave their seats to the ladies.

Nate Bradford faced his neighbors. "Folks, we know why we're here. The death of young Georgie has made us realize something must be done to stop senseless shooting and killing. We've been without a sheriff since Duke Williams got shot last year. We need to find a new sheriff."

Murmurs of assent swept the room.

"There's only one man in this town who qualifies for the job, 'n' that's Big Jon," Jeremy Halderan called from the back.

Big Jon shook his head.

The same homesteader shoved his way to Big Jon's side and slapped him on the shoulder. "Here's our man to create law and order in this town."

A number of men rose in agreement. "Big Jon for Sheriff," one shouted.

Big Jon slowly rose. The room quieted. The men sat down.

After a significant pause, Big Jon faced the people. "I'm not your man. I won't carry a gun. I'm a homesteader and a father. I'm as eager as you are—more so—for better law and order in Venture. But I'm a Christian. I can't kill a man, even if he is my enemy. If there is to be a sheriff in this town, I feel the good Lord will make one available. But I'm not that man." He sat down beside Henrietta.

Nate stepped into the silence. "A campaign for sheriff is not why we're here. We're here to take immediate action about the saloon. First we need to talk with Mac. I want several men to go with me—immediately."

Big Jon raised his hand. So did Buck; Henry George, who lived in town; and Martin Clay, a farmer south of Venture.

Nate nodded. "Thank you. Let's go." They followed Nate out the church to the saloon.

Half an hour passed. An impatient hum reflected the people's restlessness. They had crops to hoe, animals to tend, tasks waiting at home. A few men got up and left.

"They're comin'," a man called from outside.

Mac Ludden walked briskly with the men, talking and nodding. When they approached the church, everyone scurried inside.

Mac strode down the aisle of the church and greeted Pastor Miles. "May I speak to my neighbors?" he asked and turned without waiting for an answer. His fancy vest spread tightly across his ample middle. "I am indeed sorrowed at the accident that killed little Georgie. There was an argument and two men met in the street." He smiled. "I'm sorry one of them had such poor aim."

Henrietta stood abruptly. "If men are so irresponsible with their guns, they shouldn't wear them."

"Madam, I agree with you. I've arranged to have the men who come into my place of business check their guns at the door. If they want to fight, it'll have to be with their fists. At least, it won't hurt anyone but the fellow who gets a bloody nose." His broad smile faded before sullen faces.

"We've heard your agreement in the company of these people, Mac, and it'll be considered binding," Nate said. "Is it agreeable to everyone present?" Affirmative murmurs rippled the room.

"Then it's settled. We'll have no more drunken shootings in the streets of Venture," Nate turned to Mac. "Agreed?"

"Agreed," Mac said soundly. "Venture is my town, too. Whatever's good for the town is good for me and my business." He pushed his way out through the people, handing jovial greetings as he went.

The crowd dispersed in all directions. The nights quieted. Guns remained silent.

A week later, Mary Lou carried the mailbag to the stage station and stacked it with other parcels in the corner.

Two shots rang out.

The station agent and Mary Lou ducked to the floor, then cautiously rose and peeked out the window. Two of Mac's boys were hustling a couple of men back into the saloon. Townspeople who had flattened against a wall or dropped to the ground scurried indoors.

On her way home, Mary Lou stopped at the Bradford ranch to tell Tibby.

"I knew it!" she exclaimed. "I don't trust that Mac Ludden any farther than I can throw a buffalo. That's it!" She grabbed Mary Lou's shoulder and guided her toward the door. "You and Jenny round up as many women as you can. Spread the word that the W.C.T.U. will meet at the church this afternoon. The men have had their chance. Now it's our turn!"

Shortly after noon, the church filled with questioning women. Tibby marched in, followed by Henrietta, Sarah George, and even Maggie Bartlett, who ran the boardinghouse. Everyone sat down but Tibby.

"Ladies, we're here to put an end to needless shooting in this town. Any agreement made with Mac Ludden is not worth the breath to speak it. The men tried, but Mac needs something stronger than a gentleman's agreement. Now it's our turn."

"My Barney didn't want me to come," Hallie Crompton began. "He said the men will speak to Mac again. But I came anyway."

Tibby smiled. "Glad to see everyone here. Before doing anything, we must decide where we're aiming."

"If the saloon suddenly burned down, couldn't we keep them from building a new one in town?" The voice came from a tall stocky woman who, with two daughters, farmed her own land. Her husband and son had been killed in a Center Street shootout.

Maggie Bartlett jumped up. "You can't do that! You'd jeopardize my boardinghouse next door. I've heard some W.C.T.U women go into saloons to pray and talk to those poor, deluded customers."

"Deluded customers? People are where they want to be most times," said buxom Petula Hilary in the back row. Her husband appeared and disappeared periodically. "The only way to change things is to get rid of the saloon." Petula propped her fists on her hips.

"I heard a train passenger talking about a group of W.C.T.U. women who smashed a saloon with axes and hatchets." The tall woman swung a good wallop into the air with a pretend hatchet and sat down. The women laughed and tension eased.

Tibby called for order. "These are all good suggestions. Do we agree that our number one aim is to get the saloon out of town?"

The women agreed fervently.

"How do you move a saloon?" a small woman asked.

"Well!" Petula responded. "If we can't move it, can't we smash everything so they can't use it?"

Sarah George applauded. "That's a good idea."

The ladies buzzed their assent and dissent.

A small woman raised her hand. "I think we ought to talk to our men once more." Her timid eyes darted to the women on either side.

"I agree. But if mine doesn't do something, I won't talk to him for a month. I've dodged bullets on my way to the town pump once too often," Bessie Campbell announced.

Town women nodded with understanding. The room lulled.

"I won't talk to mine either." Petula giggled. "He'll probably enjoy the peace and quiet."

Everyone laughed.

Tibby clapped for attention. "Is it agreed that we talk to our husbands tonight? If they put us off, tomorrow we go into the saloon with axes and hatchets. I'm sure Buck has lots of them in the store. We'll borrow and return them after we're done. Tonight, talk to your men, but don't tell them what we plan to do."

"And if they refuse to act, we won't talk to them until they get that saloon out of town." All heads turned toward Sarah George.

"That's not a bad idea," chimed in Bessie. "We've got to do something drastic."

"Not talking! That's drastic, all right."

"I don't think I could do it," the small woman responded.

"Ladies," Tibby interrupted, "it's time for us to get on home. Before we leave, let's pray for guidance. Pray about it at home. Remember, we are the Women's *Christian* Temperance Union. We'll meet same time tomorrow, hopefully with the Lord's blessing and a plan of what to do—or not to do. Let's pray.

"Father," Tibby began, "we know that doing the right thing is important in our witness of Thee. Search our hearts, Lord, bring us into unity with Thy will, and let us be brave and courageous to carry it out, whatever the cost. Amen."

After a momentary silence, the women dispersed.

Early the next afternoon, a determined group of eighteen women faced Tibby. Tibby prayed. A hush followed. "Well, ladies, what comments did you get from your men?"

"Big Jon is concerned for our safety."

"My Barney says there is nothing we women can do."

Hallie glanced around. "My husband said our twin boys learn to be strong when they face challenging situations. He feels we women are hollerin' down a rain barrel."

Mary Lou watched faces clench and backs stiffen.

"Hollerin' down a rain barrel, are we?" Sarah replied. "I'd say we've taken our heads out of the sand. Tibby, what did Nate say?"

"Nate talked to Mac about the shots. Mac said a couple fellows grabbed their guns out of the holsters on the wall and ran into the street to settle their differences. His boys took care of them. Now Mac's put his barkeep, Wade Parker, in charge when he's gone so it won't happen again."

Petula spoke with disgust. "Any barkeep I ever knew was too busy dishin' out booze to be a gatekeeper at the same time. That's just another of Mac's empty promises."

The room lay quiet as a millpond. The seriousness of what they were considering quivered in the room.

"I say we get our axes and hatchets," Hallie said finally.

Tibby searched their faces. "Are we agreed that we smash the saloon and put Mac out of business?"

"Yes," the women responded.

"Once we start, there's no turning back," Henrietta cautioned.

"It's time to quit talkin' and do it." Petula looked around at the women. "Or are we just goin' to talk and do nothin' like the men? If so, I should've brought my mendin'."

"Then it's agreed. First we proceed to Buck's store and borrow the axes and hatchets." Tibby looked at Mary Lou. "Is that all right with you?"

Mary Lou nodded. She had been fighting anger all morning. When she had tried to discuss the saloon with Pa, he had sneered. "That's no job for women. We men'll talk to Mac again." Mary Lou stuck her chin in the air. "The axes are in a barrel by the overalls, and the hatchets are a little to the left in a wooden crate."

Tibby rose. "All right. We'll get our tools, go directly to the saloon, and break everything we meet. Don't stop for anythin'! If a man interferes, holler, and we'll come at him with our weapons. When we're finished, take the axes and hatchets back to the store, put them where you found them, and meet back at the church."

"Nope!" Hallie shook her head. "Mac's just goin' to fix the place up again and be back in business in a week. All we're goin' to have is trouble with our husbands. What'll we have gained?"

"Then let's not talk to our men. You can't have a fight when one person doesn't talk." Bessie pointed out. "Let them holler, threaten, whatever, but we won't talk to them until the saloon is out of town."

"Bessie, can you keep from talking to your husband day and night?" one woman asked.

"I can do anythin' I have to. So can you. If you couldn't, you wouldn't be tryin' to make a sod house a home with snakes falling from the ceiling in the middle of the supper table. How many times have you spent blisterin' days under a hot sun nursin' a crop out of dry cracked ground until the rains came? We can do anything it takes to make this land ours. One man and his saloon will be easier than any normal day's livin'."

"She's right. I can do it," called Petula.

"Me, too." "Me, too."

Bessie began singing "Onward Christian Soldiers."

The women joined hands, swung their arms in rhythm, and sang with vigor. Then they stood silent, eyes on Tibby.

Tibby straightened her shoulders and spoke. "After we smash the saloon, we won't speak to the men until the saloon is moved to the outskirts of town. Agreed?"

In unison, the women answered, "Agreed."

Tibby started for the door and raised her eyes heavenward. "May God go with us."

As one body, the eighteen women marched into Mackey's Mercantile. Without a word, each lady grabbed an ax or hatchet. Aghast, customers watched them storm down the street into Ludden's saloon.

"Mary Lou!" Glenn called and followed her into the street. He stood transfixed when she lifted her hatchet and crashed it through the glass window of the saloon.

The sound of tearing wood and shattering glass echoed into Center Street. Astonished men poured into the street, cursing and yelling.

Inside, flying hatchets whacked chairs. Several women attacked the bar's polished walnut surface. It splintered under the onslaught of their wild, swinging axes.

Henrietta picked up a mug and sailed it into the huge mirror behind the bar, which shattered glass everywhere. She chopped the table it had been sitting on until it collapsed into a pile of splinters.

The women, surprisingly silent, thundered their energy through swinging arms. Their fury echoed and re-echoed into Center Street. One smirky fellow waltzed into the saloon and came flying back out, chased by Petula's swinging ax.

Townspeople stuck their heads out their doors and cheered. Next door, Bartlett's boarders peered out windows and doors but stayed inside.

One of the men from the livery shouted to the station agent. "Why doesn't somebody stop those crazy women?"

"But they are ladies," he called back.

"Ladies?" the man shouted. "They sure ain't actin' it."

Like a swarm of marauding bees, the women devastated the saloon. Then heads high, they returned to the store, replaced their weapons, and retreated to the church.

A triumphant, breathless Tibby faced the women. "Well done!" she shouted. "Now our job is to get as many women as we can to join in the silence. I know some were afraid to come today or couldn't get here, but they agree with what we're doing. I'm sure they'll join us in the silence."

"Those who don't, we won't speak to them," Bessie stated emphatically.

Henrietta shook her head. "No, that wouldn't be Christian. And it would divide us. We must stick together no matter what. We need their support even if they couldn't in good conscience join us today."

Petula gave a decisive nod. "That's right. We gotta stick together."

"Then pass the word," Tibby cried. "Silence until the saloon is moved outside the town limits. And pray a lot!" she added. The women bowed and Henrietta closed in prayer.

Chapter 14

The news of the W.C.T.U. axing the saloon spread like prairie fire, but when the women closed their mouths, a tornado struck. Homes became battlegrounds. Energetic, docile wives became fortresses of maddening silence.

At first the men laughed. What woman could keep her mouth shut? Flabbergasted when a week dragged by, the men turned into mad prairie dogs, barking at everyone.

Mary Lou left a written notice to Glenn in the cash drawer of the store: *Under the circumstances, our wedding will be postponed until the matter of the saloon is settled.*

Usually a model of gentlemanly deportment, Glenn stormed through the store shouting, "Mary Lou, our wedding is certainly more important than some silly whim you women have about that saloon."

Mary Lou busied herself sorting the mail. She was afraid in a moment of anger she might discredit her vow of silence.

Glenn faced her indignantly. "Don't you think our wedding is more important?"

She smiled sweetly and clenched her jaws.

Glenn fumed back into the store.

Movement outside the window caught her eye. *Tom.* Her heart came alive. He tied Tinder to the rail and moved out of sight. What did he want? She reminded herself that she was betrothed and had dismissed Tom from her life. The store bell jangled his entry and her capricious heart jumped for joy.

Tom stepped into the post office, removed his Stetson, and stood watching her poke letters into the pigeon holes.

Mary Lou's neck prickled. Her stomach churned. Why had she not stayed home?

Tom's spurs clinked as he moved to the counter. "Has any mail come in for me or my men?"

Head high, Mary Lou whisked his mail from one of the extra boxes in the bottom corner. There were several letters, one addressed in a distinguished handwriting. She put it on top and handed the letters to him.

"Good," Tom exclaimed. "One from my brother Zack." He shuffled through the rest, looked up quickly, and captured her gaze.

Mary Lou sank into those clear pools of blue.

"Does this silence ban apply to me too? I'm just an innocent bystander from Texas." His mouth spread into a grin.

He seemed taller than she had remembered, his shoulders broader. The magnetism she had felt the first day he walked into the post office danced up her spine.

Glenn came in and stood beside Tom. "The ladies aren't talking to the men after their silly episode last week," he said to Tom. Glenn frowned at Mary Lou. "I couldn't believe that Mary Lou would be a part of such unladylike behavior."

How dare he! Mary Lou squashed a cap on a retort that rumbled like a powerful geyser ready to explode. *Men! Do they ever understand how a woman thinks or feels? Why don't they both go away and leave me alone?*

Tom and Glenn blocked the doorway and stared at her. She grabbed another handful of mail and turned her back on them.

Glenn looked indignantly at Tom. "If I hadn't seen it myself, I'd never have believed our Venture women would act so. Mac is furious!"

Mac! Glenn was concerned for Mac? She had had enough. Mary Lou stuck all the mail in one of the boxes, reached for her bonnet, and walked to the door. Would the gentlemen step aside and let a lady pass?

Tom moved first. "I'd best get along." He touched his fingers in a salute to Glenn. His gaze brushed hers. "Bye, Mary Lou."

The door jangled and she heard him ride off. Her heart foundered.

"Mary Lou, I beg you to stop this foolishness," Glenn pleaded.

Foolishness! When women do something it is foolishness. Why could men shoot at each other's feet and roar with laughter while a victim dodged bullets? Or on the slightest provocation march into the street and kill each other—or a sweet, innocent young boy. Tears welled. Mary Lou stretched to her full height but lowered her eyelids lest they betray her intense anger. She would be as stubborn as he.

Glenn did not move.

Did he plan to physically detain her? Fresh resolve shot up her spine and squelched a desire to defend herself. Her Christian sisters must be finding it equally hard—more so for those who dealt with a husband. Glenn was not her husband yet, but lately he had issued orders as if he owned her.

"Ye have not because ye ask not." The verse Mama had often quoted steadied her. *Lord, give us strength to do what we must.* The prayer subsided her inner churning. She faced Glenn and gazed at him with steeled determination.

Under no circumstances would she allow him to make her break her silence.

"I can see we aren't getting anywhere." Glenn's voice betrayed an undercurrent of anger. Shoulders back, head erect, he strode into the store.

Mary Lou seized the moment and escaped. Outside town, she slowed Dulcie to a walk. She needed thinking time and found her animal friend comforting.

Rapid hoofbeats from behind overtook her and Tom galloped up.

Mary Lou's first thought was to jab Dulcie in the flanks, but her feet wouldn't move. Instead, her disloyal heart hammered in joyous surprise. She took a quick breath to steady herself. A glance at Tom recalled the handsome angle of his jaw, his broad muscular shoulders, his ease in the saddle.

Tom slowed Tinder's pace to Dulcie's and the two mounts fell in step as if they were hitched.

"Please don't run away this time, Mary Lou," Tom pleaded. "I must talk with you."

Aunt Nelda's scathing words about her inconsiderate behavior to Tom shamed Mary Lou into polite composure. The *clip-clop* of the horses' hooves calmed her fluttering heart. They had ridden together like this last summer.

"When I left you in the cottonwoods. . ." He paused. "With all my heart, Mary Lou, I wanted to tell you I loved you. Your pa gave me no right to say it. I tried to tell him about my inheritance. He wouldn't listen. I asked his permission to ask you to marry me. That made him angry. He said no daughter of his would ever marry a cowboy. That's all I was then. Last month I inherited my quarter of our family ranch in Texas."

A Texas rancher! Her spirit soared and reached for her dream—to be a rancher's wife like Aunt Tibby. She thanked God for the vow of silence that forced her to be quiet and listen. In all honesty, Tom was still a stranger. Last year there had seemed no need to know. Now she had much to learn.

"I have three brothers and we own the ranch together," Tom continued. "My father died five years ago. My oldest brother, Zack, should have taken charge, but he was determined to be a lawyer, so he went east to study law. Doug, second in line, took over. I have a younger brother, Nelson, whose legs never grew strong enough to hold him. But he's a wonderful boy, you'll like him."

Three brothers? She had always longed for an older brother. Mary Lou glued her gaze on her reins. She dared not look up.

"I'd have told you all this last year, but your pa forbade me to see you. Trouble was, I couldn't leave without saying good-bye. Jenny offered to take a message to you." He leaned toward her. "Please understand, Mary Lou, riding away from you was the hardest thing I ever did."

It was as hard for Tom to leave me as for me to let him go, Mary Lou thought. What manly fortitude Tom had displayed. As a gentleman, he had honored her father's wishes. She had never guessed that at the moment of their parting, he had risked losing the woman he loved.

A whirl of joy danced in her head! *I'm the woman Tom loves.* What beautiful words! They healed the hurt of confusion, abrupt departure, no letters. Mary Lou gazed squarely into Tom's eyes. They mirrored the pain in his voice. She opened her mouth—the vow! She couldn't betray silence. Like magnets, their gazes clung. Could hers speak for her? Would they say what her lips could not?

Tom held her gaze tenderly, as a gift. Finally, he lowered his head and splintered the fragile connection.

Mary Lou felt bereft. The vow towered between them, a wall she could not scale. It wasn't the only wall. Another, even more formidable stood higher than wider—Glenn.

As if he read her thoughts, Tom said, "I know you're betrothed to Glenn, and I have no right to say some of the things I'm saying. But I had to make you understand I wasn't dishonest with you. A vow to your father sealed my lips. I could hardly live until this fall's cattle drive and prayed you'd wait. I'd hoped—to marry you and. . ." Tom reached for her hand. His gaze held her face, memorizing, then lifted her hand to his lips.

The touch of his lips on her fingers sent a thousand shivers through her body, dissolving the vast vestige of anger. The gate swung open. Fresh love rushed in and answered her question! She loved Tom.

Suddenly, her soul washed with guilt. *Glenn!* Her betrothed, her constant comfort when Mama died and Pa had been too deep in his grief and anger to care. In hard moments, Glenn had been at her side. He had kept her from drowning in the loneliness of Mama's absence and Pa's rejection. How could she brush him aside?

She liked Glenn—no, she loved him, but with a different kind of love than what she felt for Tom. Her mind tried to slam the door on the dreams she and Tom might have shared. Her fickle heart strained to keep the door open. Something in her throbbing chest bowed its head and died to the way she wanted it, but Mama had taught her as a little girl that nobody gets everything they want.

They rode slowly together, Tom and Tinder, Mary Lou and Dulcie. It seemed so right. *Oh, Lord,* her spirit cried out, *help me to know Your will in this matter. Either way, someone gets hurt.*

Tom's voice broke into her thoughts. "If anything should change—" He stopped the horses and looked at her.

Oh, God, what do I do? Tom has nothing to do with all this. But I cannot break silence. I cannot!

After a charged pause, Tom said, "I'll be here for another week—" His words hung in the air. He smiled and patted her hand. "I admire you, Mary Lou, for sticking to your guns." He nudged Tinder. Mary Lou's and Tom's fingers clung until Tinder pulled them apart and moved into a slow canter.

Again Mary Lou watched a cloud of dust blur the image of the man she loved. Her mind strayed to the cottonwood grove. She remembered Tom's last tender kiss, the strength of his arms when he had gathered her up and swung her onto Missy. His face had been tense, his eyes clouded. He had said only one word, "I."

Her heart took a giant leap. He had tried to tell her—but his lips were sealed then as hers were now! She watched the bobbing figures move farther and farther away. *Oh, Tom, forgive me.*

Dulcie stamped one foot and tossed her mane. Impervious to her prompting, Mary Lou remained adrift in a sea of rippling prairie grass that waved farewell to her dreams. Unconsciously her heels pressed into Dulcie's flanks, and the horse moved into a trot for home. "I wish I could talk with Pa," Mary Lou said aloud. *The vow!* Mary Lou pressed Dulcie's sides harder, and the animal eagerly galloped home.

Nelda and Aunt Tibby sat at the table sipping cups of tea when Mary Lou entered the cabin. "I'm glad you're both here. I have to talk with somebody. I didn't know it would be so hard not to talk to the men."

"Be thankful you don't have a husband or a brother. Nate and Buck haven't been gentlemen of valor lately," Tibby commented.

Mary Lou poured herself a cup of tea and told them of her morning with Glenn and Tom. "Tom caught up with me on the way home and—"

"You mean you stood still long enough to let the poor boy explain a few things?" Nelda grinned.

I deserved that, Mary Lou thought. "Yes. Pa told him he didn't want his daughter marrying a cowboy. I don't understand. Pa was a cowboy." She shook her head. "He still blames me for Mama's death. Is he going to hold it against me all my life?" Fight as she might, tears came.

Aunt Nelda pressed a handkerchief into Mary Lou's hand, and Aunt Tibby put her arm around her.

"Your pa knows there are cowboys and there are cowboys," Aunt Tibby said. "What else did Tom say?"

Mary Lou's voice quavered. "He said he had planned to take me back as his wife this time." Suppressed sobs broke and Mary Lou covered her face with her hands.

"For someone who's betrothed to another man, you sure are weepy,"

Aunt Nelda said quietly.

Mary Lou nodded. "Mama always said God gave us tears to wash away the hurt."

"What else did Tom say?" Tibby asked.

Mary Lou mopped her tears. "That he's twenty-one, has inherited a quarter of the family ranch, has three brothers. . . . The problem was, now he could talk, but I could not."

"You didn't break silence?"

Mary Lou shot a disappointed glance at Aunt Tibby. "Of course not!"

"Good girl." Tibby smiled.

"But what am I going to do?"

Nelda placed her cup on the table and leaned forward. "Who do you love? Tom or Glenn?"

Mary Lou shook her head. "Glenn has been so wonderful to me. I know he loves me. I don't want to hurt him or. . ." Her voice trailed off.

The two older women eyed each other knowingly.

"The question is: Which one do you love?" Tibby countered.

"I love both of them." Mary Lou felt silly saying it.

"That may be," Nelda said. "But you're only allowed one husband. Until you decide, there isn't much anyone can do for you."

Aunt Nelda was right. So was Jenny: "Like is not enough."

Tibby said suddenly, "Your uncle Nate said the men had a meeting with Mac. He agreed to move the saloon out of town if the townspeople help build it."

Nelda sniffed. "That seems wrong to me. If we're against it, we're against it. Building a saloon is a travesty. What are people going to think of the W.C.T.U. if we allow that?"

Tibby shrugged her shoulders. "Who cares? There's always someone to complain if he gets his toes stepped on. Venture's problem right now is to get rid of the saloon's disruption to the townspeople and town business. Amanda says our main thrust is for prohibition and the passing of a law that prohibits the making and selling of alcohol. Cutting off the source of supply will eliminate the saloons."

"But to build a new saloon? Even help supply some of the lumber?" Nelda shook her head. "Seems like condoning."

"I think it's just the first step for the town to get some control. Nate said they'll fence the east end of the town-limit line and put a curfew on crossing it. That'll free the townspeople from all the noise and shenanigans underfoot. They can walk to the town pump or come to Buck's Mercantile and post office in peace." Tibby rose and gathered the cups. "I gotta scoot to get supper ready."

"How long will it take to build it?" Mary Lou asked.

"Taking the usable wood from the old saloon and everyone adding some, they could have sides and roof on in a couple weeks. Big Jon says that if Mac wants a fancy place, he's responsible for the fancyin'."

Two weeks? Tom would be gone by then. The bloom of the day withered.

Chapter 15

Mary Lou watched a steady train of wagons pass the post office window. For two days, buckboards and wagons loaded with logs had rattled through Center Street toward the town line. Buck had donated kegs of nails, and Mary Lou could hear axes splitting logs and shakes.

But the women were absent. Mac kept several large pots of coffee brewing. Maggie and women boarders at Bartlett's Boarding House made and sent over pies. At noon, the W.C.T.U. ladies brought dinner and served it silently in the church yard to anyone who came to eat. Promptly at one, they cleaned up and went home.

Glenn avoided Mary Lou. He had only been out to visit once since the saloon episode, then said it was of no use if she wouldn't talk to him. She hadn't seen Tom either. Someone mentioned the cowboys were driving the herd on to Abilene.

By the end of the first week, the new saloon stood solid on its feet, the roof shakes in place. The battered bar was repaired and polished, but even the best kerosene rubbing could not hide its wounds. The women had done a thorough job on the chairs and tables. The salvageable few were nailed, wired together, and pressed into service until new furniture arrived from the East. Mac bellowed like a wild bull till the men threatened to stop work if he didn't tone down. They pounded at fever pitch toward the day they would finish—not for Mac, but to end the vexing silence of their women.

Sixteen days after the smashing, a makeshift saloon opened for business in a brand new building, and the men went home.

"I wonder whether it's been worth it all?" Nelda said to Mary Lou as they gathered cow and buffalo chips. "Kind of makes our work of no effect."

"Aunt Tibby said we accomplished what we set out to do. She talked to Amanda who says now we'll work on the deeper issues of prohibition and women's suffrage and hope to get John P. St. John elected governor. He promises to push the legislature to pass an amendment to stop the manufacture of intoxicants."

Nelda laughed. "That should knock some of the strut out of Mac Ludden."

They pushed the loaded wheelbarrow to the lean-to at the side of the barn.

Buck eyed the two of them when they hurried in. "Well, ladies." He grinned. "You won. The saloon is finished. Now I expect some talking." He looked from one to the other, awaiting any word from either one.

Nelda and Mary Lou nodded to one another. Neither spoke. Mary Lou left for the barn, saddled Dulcie, and rode off. Nelda, Mary Lou, and Henrietta had agreed to check with each other before they said a word. Jake Benson came home on the fifth day and told his wife they had finished with the building. She believed him and talked, much to her chagrin. After that, women made arrangements to contact each other and verify the saloon was built before they opened their mouths.

Dulcie's hooves pounded dry ground. Jenny waved from the door until Mary Lou got close then ran to meet her.

"Pa came home and said the saloon is finished. Did your Pa say the same?" Mary Lou called.

"Pa ain't here yet," Jenny said.

Henrietta stood in the door and shaded her eyes to look across the fields. If Big Jon were two miles away, a dust cloud would announce his coming.

"When did Buck come home?" Henrietta asked.

"Just now. He said the saloon is finished, so now it's time to talk. I'm checking to see if it's true."

"I'm sure Big Jon wouldn't pull any tricks, and I feel guilty doubting him. But the men haven't been themselves since this all started." Henrietta laughed. "Neither have we. I know he'll be as glad as I am it's over." She scanned the horizon again.

Jenny grabbed Mary Lou and pulled her to the shady side of the house. "Now what? Will you and Glenn get married right away or have you decided to marry Tom?"

Mary Lou panicked.

"Come on, Mary Lou," Jenny coaxed. "You're gonna tell me, aren't you?"

Mary Lou shook her head. She was ashamed to admit that she couldn't make up her mind. Was it possible for a girl to love two men at the same time?

"Don't tell me you still don't know!" Jenny threw her hands up in the air. "That's not bein' fair. It has to be one or the other."

"I think the decision's been made for me." Mary Lou's heart bowed. "Tom's gone back to Texas."

"He went to Abilene with the cattle. He'll be back." Jenny nodded reassuringly.

"But he said he would only be here a week. It's been two weeks, Jenny.

I couldn't talk. What must he think?"

She tried to hide her disappointment. "I don't think Tom will be back. It must be the Lord's will I marry Glenn."

Jenny put her arm around her and they walked toward the well. "Which one do you love?"

She had to share her dilemma with Jenny. "I love them both."

Jenny's mouth dropped open. "Can't be, Mary Lou. Like my ma says, God has a husband in mind for each of us. I asked her once how I'd know the man for me. She said if I loved him, I would know without a doubt and be eager to follow God's will. So Mary Lou, choose you this day who you want for your husband."

They laughed together—like old times. Jenny had been right. Her engagement to Glenn had changed things. They didn't see each other as often or go off to the cottonwood grove for little picnics like they used to.

"Besides that," Jenny continued with her hands on her hips, "it ain't fair for you to have two when the rest of us have a hard time findin' one." Jenny chuckled, then her chocolate eyes darkened. She leaned forward, suddenly serious. "Mary Lou, are you marryin' Glenn thinkin' it'll mend fences between you and your pa?"

"Oh, no, Jenny," the answer popped out. But was she?

Big Jon galloped into the yard on his chestnut stallion followed by a dust cloud that enveloped them all. He leaped from the saddle and hollered, "Henrietta, the building's finished. Come here woman, I want to hear your voice tell me you love me!"

Henrietta flew across the yard and landed in his arms. They looked into each other's faces and talked intimately, then strolled arm in arm toward their children pouring out of the cabin.

Henrietta looked up at Big Jon with an impish grin. "Do you have any idea how hard it was for me not to talk to you? I almost burst."

Big Jon guffawed then leaned and kissed her right in front of the children and Mary Lou. When released Henrietta laughed and called, "Come on children, supper's ready. Mary Lou, you goin' to join us?"

"No, thank you, Mrs. Wimbley. Aunt Nelda has supper ready and isn't talking till I get back. I came to check and see if the building was really finished." She mounted Dulcie and trotted off.

Almost home, Mary Lou spotted an exuberant Glenn galloping to meet her. All smiles, he swung his horse to trot beside her. "The silence is over, Mary Lou. The saloon's finished. Mac opened today and served everybody free of charge—as a thank you, he said. Now we can talk and get married."

The silence that had been such a nuisance now seemed golden. Mary Lou cleared her throat. "Glenn," she began, "I still have things to do, put the lace on my dress, and—"

"How long's that going to take?" Glenn grabbed her saddle horn and stopped Dulcie. "Mary Lou, look at me."

Mary Lou steeled her gaze to be as noncommittal as possible.

"Mary Lou, I love you and want to marry you. I seem to have the feeling you aren't of the same mind."

His forthright abruptness tied her tongue. What could she say? "Glenn, I think we should postpone it for a bit—"

"Postpone it! What for?"

"I'm just not ready yet. Everything has been so upsetting and—"

Glenn laughed. "Oh, darling, I'm sorry. This whole business has been an awful ordeal for you, too, hasn't it? I haven't been very pleasant. But it's over and you're just having those nervous symptoms every bride has. I admit, this is new for me, too. . . ."

Amid a constant stream of Glenn's plans, they rode to the barn and tied their horses. As Mary Lou slid from Dulcie's back, Glenn caught her and kissed her.

Walking to the cabin, Glenn chattered about the wedding arrangements he had already made. "I figure all could be ready in two days."

Two days? Mary Lou felt numb. Try as she might to avoid the facts, her choice was closing in on her. The cowboys and Tom had gone to Abilene, Jenny had said. *But that was over two weeks ago. Tom said he would be here only a week. What was it Mama often said?* "A bird in the hand. . ."

Aunt Nelda invited Glenn to supper and he eagerly accepted.

Two days. Mary Lou felt leaden.

Glenn would find Pastor Miles and tell him to come. . .she and Aunt Nelda would put the lace collar on the blue dress. . .they would pick bouquets of prairie flowers to decorate the Bradford parlor and for Mary Lou to carry. . .Aunt Tibby would renew preparations for a big wedding party at the Bar-B Ranch. . .a sign on the store door would say they were closed for the wedding. . .they would invite everybody.

Mary Lou thought of yesterday. She and Aunt Nelda had spent the day in town cleaning the back rooms of the store so she could set up housekeeping until Glenn arranged for their house to be built—a town house rather than a cabin on the outskirts as Mary Lou had hoped. She loved the openness of the prairie, the quiet, the wind that blew through her hair and gave her a sense of life. But Glenn said a house in town would be more convenient, and he didn't have time or money to keep up a cabin and a house.

Just before Glenn left, he told Mary Lou he had a house already picked out. Mary Lou curdled when he told her he could buy the old saloon cheap.

"It's a good, strong building with an upstairs." He had already checked on some men to help him change it into their home.

Aunt Nelda sat in her rocker, listened, and searched Mary Lou with penetrating eyes.

When Glenn finally left, Mary Lou went to her room, dry-eyed and wide awake. She slid into the little wooden rocker Pa had made for her when she was eight. *Was God telling her that her dream of being a rancher's wife was not His will?* Pa acted pleased. He had approved of Glenn from the beginning. She heaved a resigned sigh. Maybe her marriage to Glenn would clear the gulf between them.

Her tiny room suddenly became very dear. So much of Mama remained. Mary Lou's gaze lifted to the print feed-bag curtains. She helped Mama make them—the first real sewing she had ever done. Mama had said every girl should know how to make a running stitch, a back stitch, and an overcast stitch. She had learned all three when they had made the curtains.

Mary Lou ran her hand over the oak chest. It had been in Mama's bedroom in Toledo, Ohio, when she was a young girl. Grandmother Stafford brought it when she visited Aunt Tibby and Mama after Grandfather Stafford died. Mama and Grandma looked alike, both small, dainty women with pretty faces and an abundance of curly chestnut hair. But Mama laughed a lot and her eyes looked happy. Grandmother's were always sad.

They had tried to make Grandmother live with Aunt Tibby, but she got so homesick, she finally returned to Ohio. Not long after, she died.

Mary Lou undressed, climbed into bed, and closed her eyes, hoping to sleep. She could not. She returned to her rocking chair and picked up the sock she was knitting, but her hands finally dropped into her lap and she rested. Her head against the back of the chair, she dozed off and dreamed she saw Tom on Tinder riding toward her but never getting any nearer.

The endless night tried to outreach the faint glimmers of dawn creeping into the corners of the room. Mary Lou finally climbed into bed and cried for what might have been. In an agonized whisper she said, "Good-bye, Tom."

That morning, Mary Lou dragged from bed an hour later than usual. Aunt Nelda had water heating to wash clothes. Mary Lou dressed quickly and hurried out. If Aunt Nelda noticed the deep hollows under her eyes, she didn't let on, but Mary Lou was disturbingly aware of her scrutiny.

She picked up the basket of sheets and draped one over the line. A rider pounded toward her. She squinted through the morning haze. It was Jenny! Was something wrong at Wimbleys?

Jenny slid off Missy and marched angrily to Mary Lou. "I thought as your best friend and bridesmaid you'd tell me."

Confused, Mary Lou asked, "Tell you what?"

"That you're marrying Glenn tomorrow at ten-thirty!"

Mary Lou gasped. "But I just made up my mind last night. I haven't even told Glenn. How did you know?"

"Glenn is telling it all over town—and inviting everybody."

Chapter 16

A shudder spiraled up Mary Lou's spine. Tomorrow? 10:30 A.M.? Without conferring with her?

Jenny faced her, eyes smoldering under pinched brows. She spun and marched away.

"Jenny! Wait." Mary Lou caught the back of Jenny's calico dress and hung on. "I didn't know, honest. It's as much a surprise to me as you. Ten-thirty? What a horrible hour."

Jenny swung around, her expression disbelieving.

"It's true, Jenny," Mary Lou pleaded. "He said we could be married in two days, but believe me, Glenn's gone ahead and chosen the day without consulting me."

"Well, you'd better do some consulting about something or you're going to be a married woman in twenty-four hours."

How could Glenn do such a thing?

A familiar arm crept around her shoulders. "Mary Lou, I'm sorry. I was so hurt. I'd thought you'd chosen someone else for bridesmaid. What're you goin' to do?"

Mary Lou's confused mind reeled. Then rising fury began its course until she felt so angry she took deep, quivering breaths to calm herself. She straightened her shoulders and headed for the barn to saddle Dulcie, Jenny close behind. Her fingers trembled as she saddled and mounted. Mary Lou looked down at Jenny. "I'm going to see Glenn and demand an explanation."

"You'd better put a muzzle on him first or you're going to have most of the town in church tomorrow waitin' for a weddin'."

Mary Lou pressed Dulcie into a fast gallop. By the time they reached town, Mary Lou was breathless and the stalwart animal had worked herself into a lather. Mary Lou slid the saddle off Dulcie's back, rubbed her down, threw a blanket over her, and hurried into the back room. Voices of customers halted her. She didn't want to make a scene, but if necessary, she would. One customer could relay news faster than wildfire.

The store quieted and she peeked in. Old Mr. Kennard stood leaning on his cane, leisurely talking with Glenn. Resolutely, Mary Lou stepped up the two steps into the store.

Glenn's face brightened at the sight of her. Mr. Kennard grinned and pointed his cane.

"Lookee who's here! Ain't this here the bride?" He chortled good naturedly and nodded his head. "Be seein' ya at yer weddin' tomorree." He straightened. "I'd best be leavin' you two lovebirds." He knowingly patted Glenn on the shoulder, thumped across the floor, and went out the door chuckling.

The minute he disappeared, Glenn crossed the floor to take Mary Lou in his arms. Mary Lou refused his embrace, turned her back, and retraced the two steps into the back room.

Glenn followed. "I was not expecting you, Dear. I planned on coming out to see you. I didn't think you believed the old superstition that it's bad luck for the groom to see the bride before the wedding."

Mary Lou spun, fanning smoldering coals of anger. "Glenn, I can't believe what I hear. This morning Jenny came all upset, angry because she thought I'd changed bridesmaids. She heard you telling everyone the wedding is going to be tomorrow at ten-thirty, and I hadn't informed her."

Glenn nodded. His cheeks dented with a grin. "That's right."

If she had not been bred a lady, she would have wiped that silly smile off his face with a resounding slap. She steadied her voice. "I'd like to know when we planned the day or time? Or when you asked me if the choice would be suitable?" Her nails dug into the palms of her hands. "How could you make all the arrangements without considering me?"

"Why, I've been telling you what I was going to do." He shook his head, amazed at her outburst.

"I never heard any plans for tomorrow at ten-thirty. Ten-thirty! What kind of a time is that to be married?" She barely controlled the rage rolling through her.

"Well, it was the best day—"

"For whom? I thought the bride had some say. I told you I wanted to postpone things a bit, that I couldn't be ready. Now, I won't be ready. Have your wedding tomorrow, I won't be there!" Mary Lou ran into the lean-to and began to resaddle Dulcie.

Glenn stepped behind her. "Now, Mary Lou. . ." His voice was tempered as if cajoling a child. "I was coming out as soon as I could leave the store to tell you the plans."

Mary Lou stopped abruptly and faced him. Her eyes snapped defiance. "How kind of you to visit me the afternoon before my wedding and inform me I'm to be married tomorrow. Did it occur to you it might not be suitable for me?" She put her foot in the stirrup.

Glenn grabbed her waist and held her. "I'm sorry. I just found out this morning it's the only time Pastor Miles could be in Venture until he comes for church week. It's ten-thirty because he has a burial in the afternoon and needs time to get there."

Mary Lou opened her mouth in shock, closed it in frustration, shoved Glenn's arms away, and walked Dulcie through the door. Outside, she turned, eyes blazing. "As of this minute, Mr. Farrell, I'm postponing the wedding indefinitely." She mounted and rode off without a backward look. She did not care if she ever married anyone.

Mary Lou trotted Dulcie up Center Street, ignoring the pleased glances and waves. Unconsciously, she guided Dulcie to the cottonwood grove at Point Lane. In the flickering shade, she slid to the ground and paced, hugging herself to keep from falling apart. "Oh, Mama," she cried aloud. "Loving Tom was painful but loving Glenn is exasperating! Isn't it better not to love at all?"

She shook her head. How could she believe that after knowing Mama? On the wall over Mama's rocking chair hung a picture she had embroidered when she was a little girl in Ohio. "God is love," it proclaimed. Mama had said love was the most important thing in heaven and on earth. Mama had given hers unconditionally to everyone. *That is what I need to learn*, Mary Lou realized.

Far above a hawk hung suspended, then dived to the ground and snatched up a wiggly, brown prairie mouse with his mighty talons. Mary Lou gasped in sympathy for the tiny, helpless thing. She sank on the old log, cradled her head in her arms and sobbed. "Mama." She felt numbed by the day's assault. Waves of anger, shame, frustration, and futility washed over her.

Dulcie whinnied.

"Oh, God," Mary Lou cried, "I don't know what to do. I put myself completely into Your hands. I can't do it alone anymore."

Slowly, beginning at her shoulders, the heavy weight she had carried since Mama's death slid down her body and puddled on the ground at her feet. The warm Kansas breeze floated by and caressed her face. A permeating sense of peace birthed a depth of love she had never felt before.

Mary Lou's thoughts leaped to joyous memories of Mama's picnic lunches under the cottonwoods—simple bread and jelly sandwiches and apple hand pies. How carefree she had been in those days. On this very log, she had discovered a different kind of love with Tom—and lost it. Or had she?

Mama's laughter whispered through the trees. "No matter what happens to His children," she had always said, "God takes it and weaves it into strength, courage, wisdom, and freedom to do His will. Remember James 1:2–3: 'Count it all joy when ye fall into divers temptations; knowing this, that the trying of your faith worketh patience.' "

Faith and patience. Mary Lou needed large doses of both. Her trust in men stood at low ebb, yet loving Pa couldn't have been easy for Mama. Bitter and frustrated over his accident, sometimes Pa withdrew. Still Mama loved and encouraged him until the mood passed.

Mary Lou stretched her arms toward heaven. "Oh, Father," she cried aloud. "Forgive me for forgetting what Mama taught me, for being so hateful to Glenn, for insulting Tom because I thought he had insulted me. Help me to grow up into a godly woman like Mama." She took a deep breath and relaxed as it released. She had a lot of fences to mend.

Mary Lou walked to Dulcie and circled her arms around her horse's neck. "Come on, friend, let's go home," she whispered and mounted her horse.

Aunt Nelda peered from the doorway when Dulcie trotted in. She walked to the barn as Mary Lou dismounted. "I've been worried about you," she said. "What did you find out?"

"That everything was exactly as Jenny said. I've called the whole thing off."

Aunt Nelda's face showed shock, then amusement. "It doesn't hurt to put these men in their places once in awhile." They linked arms and walked silently to the cabin.

Nelda brought out two plates of sandwiches, said grace, and leaned forward. "Tell me what happened."

Mary Lou related the unnerving details of the morning but omitted what had happened at Point Lane. That belonged to her and Jesus. She gazed at her aunt who spoke lovingly of "my Lars." Like Mama, Aunt Nelda loved freely and unconditionally. Mary Lou's world steadied itself.

That afternoon Glenn apologetically arrived to discuss the wedding. Mary Lou's new heart regarded Glenn with forgiveness. Before he left, they planned their wedding to be held at the Bar-B Ranch in one week at two o'clock in the afternoon.

Aunt Tibby and Nate promised a big wedding celebration after the ceremony. This also gave time for Nelda and Mary Lou to finish preparing the back rooms at the store and sew the lace on Mary Lou's dress.

The next day, Henrietta, Jenny, and Caroline stopped for a visit on their way back from town. Mary Lou and Jenny escaped and walked to the small stream not far from the cabin.

"How come you changed your mind so quick?" Jenny asked. "I thought you were so mad at Glenn you'd never marry him."

"I was." Mary Lou didn't know whether to tell Jenny about her enlightening time at Point Lane. "I guess the good Lord drove the anger out of my heart and put in love."

Jenny wrinkled her brows but didn't pursue it. "One of these days, I'm goin' to find some fella who'll marry me," Jenny said solemnly, then laughed. "But it better be soon or I'll be an old maid. There are only two men in

Venture I even considered. You got one of them."

Surprised, Mary Lou asked, "Glenn?"

"Yep. At one time I considered him a pretty good catch. But when he chose you, I picked out Wilbur George."

Mary Lou pictured tall, dark-haired young Will who worked part-time in the store and laughed. "I guess I can't think of you ever being serious—even about marriage."

Jenny giggled and made a face. "Aren't most girls? My real hope was to find someone like Big Jon. Even though he's not my real father, Papa Jon became my ideal the day he found Matthew and me."

Jenny didn't often talk about the wagon accident that had killed her parents. Mary Lou encouraged her. "Do you ever wonder what your real papa and mama were like?"

"I remember Mama had long hair like mine. She used to let me brush it. Usually it was braided and wrapped around her head. Papa called her Angel, but her real name was Angela. Papa was tall like Big Jon, but skinny."

She lowered her head, then looked up with misty eyes. "The day Big Jon and Henrietta found us, I was so scared. Matthew cried and cried. I didn't know what to do to make him stop. Henrietta just took him to their wagon, nursed him, and he quit crying. Samuel was six months old, too. Henrietta said it was like having twins."

Mary Lou seldom saw Jenny so pensive.

"My pa was a soldier—from Virginia, I think. I sort of remember our house 'cause it had an upstairs with a banister, and Pa used to hold me as I slid down. Matthew was born there."

What would it have been like to grow up without Mama and Pa? Mary Lou sensed a blessing she had taken for granted.

The dinner bell rang, and Jenny and Mary Lou wandered back to the cabin.

Alone at night in her bed, Mary Lou couldn't escape thoughts of Tom. *I wonder what it would have been like to be Tom's wife.* Even though he had confessed his love, his absence and silence said volumes. His tender kisses on her fingers tugged at her heart. She shook her head. *What kind of thinking is this for a woman to be married shortly? Where is he?* She couldn't silence the question.

"I love Glenn. He loves me. My girlish days of dreaming about handsome cowboys are over. It's time I grew up," she reminded herself and deliberately placed a period on her past.

"Father, I accept Your will for my life. Thank You for the family and friends You've given me. Now, bless Pa, Aunt Nelda, Aunt Tibby, Uncle Nate, Jenny, the Wimbleys, Tom. . ." Mary Lou sank into dreamless sleep.

Chapter 17

Tom halted on Tinder and looked back at the fifteen hundred Texas longhorns that stretched north on the Chisholm Trail. Smitty, the trail boss, scouted forward for water and pasture. Jess had driven the chuck wagon ahead to start the noon meal.

They were on the last leg of the journey to Abilene. There the cattle would be loaded and shipped to Chicago, headquarters of the beef industry.

The sky promised rain, but the hot, muggy day dragged on interminably. Tom pulled his bandanna, used it to mop his face, and retied it around his neck. The usually exciting trail drive had grown tiresome. The Chisholm Trail, two hundred miles wide and six hundred miles long, seemed twice that length.

He had been restless to get to Venture to see Mary Lou. When they had met on the prairie, her loveliness had locked her in his heart forever. He had feasted his eyes on her sweet, expressive face and those wisps of chestnut hair that defied confinement and curled at her small ears. Try as he might, he could not dislodge her from his mind. Had he let her slip away? Had she lost what Tom thought was love for him because he never wrote? That crazy vow of silence had denied him answers. Yet he couldn't shake a nagging urge to go back to Venture right after the cattle were railed.

Smitty galloped up. "Chuck wagon up ahead. Better get these cows milled so's we can eat."

Tom nodded and rode the line to pass the word to the boys. It didn't take long to work the cows into a circle. Riding back to his watch, Tom's mind again filled with Mary Lou. She rode well, knew animals. . .would make a perfect rancher's wife. *Whoa!* Plain foolish to harbor such thoughts of a girl betrothed to another man. But how could he stop loving her? He took off his hat, wiped the sweat off the inner band, and shoved it back on.

What else could he have done? When they last met, had he read love in her eyes? Or had he imagined what he wanted to see when he kissed her fingers. . .?

The day he and Jess had gone to Mackey's for supplies before heading north to Abilene had been a disappointment. On the outskirts of town, they had passed a crew of Venture men industriously building the new saloon.

When they had entered the store, Tom had gone directly to the post office to mail letters to Zack and his mother. Behind the counter had stood a tall, dark-haired young man who had stamped his letters and handed him a letter from Zack. He had tucked it into his pocket for later. Tom's desperate need to see Mary Lou again had been denied.

Glenn had come into the post office and eyed Tom suspiciously. All business, he had said, "Did Will get your mail for you?"

Tom had nodded, patted the letter in his pocket, and joined Jess in the store. Glenn had tailed them, wrapping and stacking as Tom and Jess had picked out supplies.

Back in the saddle, Tom figured it would take a few days to close the deal. He would pay the cowboys, then head back to Venture while they let off steam. He had mentioned that in his letter to Zack. Tom and Zack had discussed the trail drive the night before Tom had left Texas. Tom had also told Zack about Mary Lou.

"Marry the girl you love," Zack had advised. "I did, and even though others find her difficult, I know how sweet she can be. Don't be surprised if you have to fight to get the woman you love."

Those words had strengthened Tom's resolve to straighten things out. With Zack home, he had been content to leave his mother and Nelson.

That last night, Zack had also explained how the use of guns in the West alarmed Darcy. The western lack of refinement whirled her in a critical storm most of the time, much to his mother's distress.

"What Darcy needs is the Lord's direction. Until she recognizes someone else is more important than herself and her Eastern ways, she'll be unhappy," Allena had proclaimed. "Evidently Darcy wasn't brought up to put God first. Our duty is to love her because she's Zack's wife; he loves her and God has placed her in our family. When some of that Eastern veneer rubs off, we'll find a fine, spirited young woman. Maybe then, she'll see her need for a Savior."

Tom's mother was usually right.

An orange belt settled on the hips of the horizon. Facing it, Smitty squatted beside Tom and sipped a cup of coffee before supper. "Tomorrow, we'll make it into Abilene. I reckon there's some plans runnin' in your head. Care to tell me what?"

Tom grinned. Smitty substituted as a clucking mother hen to all the cowboys, as adept at reading men as animals. They were out of earshot of the other cowboys, so Tom answered. "Yeah, I have a few. One might surprise you."

"I doubt it, if it concerns a young woman in Venture."

Tom laughed. "I should've known I couldn't get anything past you.

Trouble is, she got herself betrothed to someone else last winter. I saw her when we stopped in Venture, but it was when the women weren't talking to the men over that saloon episode, so nothing got settled. I think she still loves me, but," Tom shook his head, "I'm not sure."

"Aw, any man can tell if a woman loves him. All he has to do is kiss her."

Tom raised his eyebrows and punched Smitty's arm. "You old coot! What makes you so smart about women?"

Smitty grinned. "Since we're tellin' secrets, I was married once. 'Twas before I started workin' fer your pa. She died birthin' our son too early. Poor little fella didn't have enough strength to breathe proper and died a day after his ma." Smitty hastily swallowed some coffee.

"I'm sorry, Smitty. You'd have made a great father. Now I understand why you treat the cowhands like a bunch of your kids."

Smitty recovered and looked up grinning. "They are a bunch of kids— you included." He slapped Tom on the shoulder.

Jess banged a spoon on the bottom of a frying pan. "Come and git it or I'll throw it in the creek. A good meal waitin' ain't fit to eat," he hollered.

Half the cowboys gathered, more than ready for supper. The herd mingled quietly while the hands ate their beans, cornbread, steak, and scalding coffee in shifts. One by one, they left to relieve the other half of the crew so they could come into camp. After the usual joshing, singing, and spouting cowboy ballads, those not on duty crawled into their bedrolls to get some sleep before the next watch.

Tom slipped out of his tarp at two o'clock in the morning and rode out to relieve Cooney. An endless expanse of blue-black sky peacefully blanketed the herd and bedded down Tom's turmoil. How long would it take the men to build the saloon? Tom smiled as he thought of those determined women. The men probably gave them a rough time at home. Glenn made it obvious he wasn't pleased with Mary Lou. Tom admired her. She had Texas spirit.

That is why he had to know who Mary Lou loved. If she still wanted to marry Glenn, Tom would ride out.

The next day, Tom and Smitty watched their Texas longhorns prodded into railroad cattle cars. Their ears rang with shouts and bawling cattle.

Tom stuffed the money inside his shirt. They had made a good profit. He jotted figures down on a piece of paper and stuffed it in beside the money. In his letter, Zack had written that the ranch books looked all right. But that was no proof. Zack and Tom had agreed to make up their own set of books. There was a leak somewhere. Eventually, Zack said, he would find it. When he did, they would face Doug, settle their differences, and hopefully run the Circle-Z together. For their mother's sake, Tom hoped they would be able to solve the problem peacefully.

The day after they railed the cows, Tom rode to Venture. He decided to see Mary Lou's Aunt Nelda first. Maybe it was unfair to involve her, but he had talked to her before and found her understanding. She reminded him of his mother, a faith-filled Christian woman with wisdom to see through surface nonsense.

Tom turned down the lane to Buck's cabin. Would Mary Lou be there? He hoped not, even though he ached to see her. The cabin looked deserted. He dismounted and discovered Nelda grinning in the doorway. "You didn't come a hair too soon," she called and turned back into the cabin.

Tom followed her.

"Sit down, Tom," Nelda said. "Mary Lou isn't here. She's at Tibby's. They're getting ready for the wedding tomorrow."

Tom's heart plunged.

"I'm glad you came back. Everything's beginning to get out of hand. First, I want to know just what your intentions are."

Nelda has an abrupt way of catching a fellow off guard, Tom thought. "I love Mary Lou and would like to marry her. Unfortunately, it looks as if I've lost my case."

"Nothing is too late till after it's done." Nelda poured Tom a cup of coffee. "Now, what are you going to do about it?"

Tom frowned and shook his head. "What can I do about it? Glenn was Mary Lou's choice."

"Was he?"

"Well, she's betrothed to him."

After a long silence, Nelda said quietly, "Do you love Mary Lou?"

Tom smiled. Nelda never minced words. He looked her straight in the eye. "Yes, I do."

"Enough to marry her?"

Tom nodded. "Yes." What was Nelda driving at?

"Are you ready to fight for the girl you love?"

Zack's words! Tom hedged. "It's just that I don't want to interfere—"

"Don't want to interfere! What kind of a weak-spined answer is that?" This woman could punch! "Before I do anything I have to ask Mary Lou if she loves me."

"She does, but she hasn't admitted it yet."

Hope leaped in his chest. *Bless this interfering old lady's heart!* "That's why I'm back. I could not get her answer when you women were silent."

"Then we'll go to Tibby's and you'll get your answer. If you'll help me saddle Jewel, we'll get things settled now."

Tom loved this woman. Invincible—ready for any challenge. *Thank*

God for strong women like her. Tom suddenly remembered something his father had said one night. "Women are nesters—this wild country's only stability. Without women, the West would remain a sprawling, brawling, uncivilized land of men." Tom rose from his chair and followed Nelda to the barn.

Tibby's housekeeper met them at the door. "They's gone ta town. We needs more supplies," she said, wiping her hands on her apron.

Tom's heart fell into his boots. Every hope seemed to get trampled.

Nelda walked in and sat down. "We'll wait. Sit down, Tom, and tell me something about your family and Texas."

As he talked, Nelda nodded and smiled.

A single set of hoofbeats came to the front porch, then Tibby kicked the door with her foot. Tom jumped to open it. She came in with her arms full, emptied them on the table, and stared at him. "Oh, you're the other horse," she said. "I recognized Jewel."

Tom stood, not quite sure of her meaning. "I came to see Mary Lou."

Tibby darted a glance at Nelda. "You must be Tom. Well, I'm glad to finally get a look at you. You've made my niece a very unhappy girl."

Tom didn't know whether to leave or stay. He shifted uneasily.

"Young man, why didn't you include a note to Mary Lou in the letter you wrote to my husband? That girl was heartbroken. I was glad when Glenn paid attention to her. After her mother's death and your neglect, he was just what she needed."

Tom feared to open his mouth.

Then Tibby smiled. "I had to get that out of my system. You being here, I'm assuming you have some honorable intentions."

Tom grinned broadly. "Yes, Ma'am!" With these two women on his side, how could he help but win?

Chapter 18

Dulcie padded her way into town, reflecting her rider's reluctance. Mary Lou's insides gnawed with increasing apprehension. Something was wrong.

Her feelings toward Glenn bothered her most. Were all brides as timid as she felt? She remembered Lucy Thompson who ran away the day before her wedding and hid in an empty soddy for over a week until her father found her. Now Mary Lou understood why.

Tom bounced in and out of her thoughts. The memory of their last meeting reached into her soul and evoked longing she thought she had put away. But he was gone. Her only regret was they hadn't been able to talk.

Mary Lou scolded herself for letting such thoughts pervade her mind. Once married, they would disappear. She closed her eyes and lifted her face to the warm sun. Mama had told her to pray when things didn't seem right, and God would give her peace. *Father,* she prayed, *I want to do the right thing. Getting married is a big step. Help me.* Her heart warmed and she relaxed.

At the edge of town she noticed a changed Venture. The absence of the saloon brought peaceful days as well as nights. Residents walked about town with a new sense of freedom and order. Sarah George, out early, waved from the town well.

Mary Lou waved back and turned into the small alley at the side of the store. Entering the housekeeping rooms, she bristled. To think that Glenn would consider the saloon building for their new home! Given a choice, she would have taken any small cabin in the fresh openness of the prairie. Some days even the post office and store gave her claustrophobia.

Glenn habitually allowed customers in before the store opened. "Every sale counts," he said. Three browsed this morning. Mary Lou hurried through with a breezy "Good morning" and sought the solitude of the post office. Two mailbags leaned against the counter. She softened. Glenn, always thoughtful, made sure she never carried the bags to or from the station.

Glenn stuck his head in the door. "Good morning, Dear. One more day and you'll be Mrs. Glenn Farrell." His knowing smile sent crimson to her cheeks.

She pushed down panic and smiled. "Good morning."

Glenn disappeared to continue his jovial chatter with the customers. Mary Lou immediately dug into the mailbags, sorting letters and stuffing them into their respective boxes. Out of habit, she read the sender's name just before she tucked it into the box.

Mr. Thomas Langdon from Laura Shepard. Her heart stopped. The sudden stab of jealousy surprised her. That name dragged old memories of Tom using Laura's address last year to send letters to his mother. She stuffed the letter quickly into Tom's box. Dissatisfied, she removed it and studied the handwriting. Sprawly, definitely feminine. What was Laura like? Pretty? Tom never mentioned her other than his explanation that he wanted to make sure his mother got his letters. But did he love her?

All morning Mary Lou plodded, her mind busy with speculations about Laura, wonder about Tom, and interruptions by Glenn. At noon, she gathered her belongings and headed for the back rooms.

"Leaving already?" Glenn followed her and put his arms around her. The tenderness of his touch and the love pouring from his eyes soothed her fears. When he kissed her, she couldn't help comparing it with Tom's kiss. Ashamed of her fickle thoughts, she pecked him on the cheek, patted his face, and left.

Perky, blue cornflowers parted as she rode through the prairie. This was where she felt at home. She dismounted and gathered flowers for Aunt Nelda while Dulcie nibbled on clumps of grass.

When she approached the cabin, she noticed a horse tied to the hitching rail. Tinder? She stayed herself from leaping off her horse and running to the cabin by trotting Dulcie leisurely to the barn. Then, fingers shaking, she slipped off Dulcie's saddle, commanding herself to be calm.

A beaming Aunt Nelda met her at the door with a big hug for the cornflowers. "Somebody to see you," she whispered, leading her to Tom. "Look who's here."

Mary Lou wavered between wanting to run and aching to stay. She stretched out her hand toward Tom. "Glad to see you again before you go back to Texas." Her heart trembled at his touch.

Tom cupped her hand in both his big ones. "Hello, Mary Lou. I had to see you again." He grinned and added, "To hear your voice."

Her crazy heart responded to a rising surge of emotion. Why didn't she feel like this around Glenn? Did she imagine it, or did Tom release her hand reluctantly as she pulled away?

"I've got dinner ready, so wash up to eat. I invited Tom to stay. We won't wait for Owen. He just left for town."

Mary Lou noticed Tom's quizzical frown. "Owen Mackey is Pa's full name. Aunt Nelda is the only one who uses it."

In no time, dinner was spread invitingly on the table.

"Tom, would you say grace?" Aunt Nelda asked.

"Yes, Ma'am." He bowed his head.

No one seemed to notice Mary Lou's surprised intake of breath.

"Our Father, we give thanks for the blessing of this home, its welcome for me. We're thankful not only for the food on the table but also for Your provision of eternal life. Teach us to number our days and serve You well. In Jesus' name, Amen."

Listening to Tom pray, Mary Lou held her breath. *He's a Christian!* Her whole being responded with a joy she had trouble concealing. She ate little, her gaze fixed on Tom's animated face. He talked of home, his mother, three brothers, and the ranch. Hearing the drawl of his voice made her come alive. He never mentioned Laura.

All too soon, he rose to leave. "Have to get back," he said. "Smitty and the crew are camped outside Venture."

Nelda suddenly busied herself cleaning up the table, noisily rattling dishes and pans.

Mary Lou walked outside with Tom. They took Tinder to the water trough for a drink. Tom surveyed the sky, the barn, the grove of walnut trees.

"Nelson would have a great time painting this. He says he gets tired of painting sagebrush, cactus, and tumbleweeds. He's quite good at it. Mother says it's God's special gift to him since his legs never grew strong."

Tom's mother sounded like Mama. Concerned, Mary Lou asked, "How crippled is he?" The word was out without thinking.

Tom grinned. "He gets around pretty good. He can ride a horse, drive Mother's buggy, and moves mighty fast on his crutches. He's a great boy."

Without warning, Tom turned Mary Lou so she faced him. Mary Lou fought a desire to feel his arms around her.

After an awkward pause, Tom said softly, "Before I go, I have to find out one thing." His eyes searched her face. "Mary Lou, do you have any love for me?"

Her heart hammered against her chest demanding to be recognized. "Why, yes, Tom." The minute the words escaped, she knew she had to grab them back. "I've enjoyed having you for a friend." She turned from his gaze.

"Just say you love Glenn and I'll ride out of your life. But I have to know."

Did she love Tom? Did she love Glenn? She smiled. "Why," she sputtered hoping for understanding, "I love you both."

Tom studied her, then smiled. "Well, there's still hope for me."

What a ridiculous thing for him to say the day before her wedding! Slowly she lifted her gaze to Tom's earnest face, read love in his eyes, and felt it reach for her. All doubt vanished. *Tom loved her!* She longed to slip into the comfort of his arms, But Glenn's invisible presence held her steadfast.

Tom turned to Tinder, checked the saddle straps, and remarked lightly, "If I'm still in town—" Suddenly, he swung around, pulled her into his arms, lifted her chin, and kissed her.

Her whole being soared. She slid her arms around his neck. This was the way it should be. Unguarded, complete, giving. Tom released her slowly, his eyes clinging to her face. Mary Lou trembled, not only from the impact of his kiss, but the realization that she had betrayed Glenn. Undaunted, her heart kept reaching, stretching for what she could be—Tom's wife. Ironically, for the first time, Glenn's face formed in her mind. She wilted.

"Forgive me, Mary Lou. I shouldn't have done that. But for what I have to do, I had to be sure." He swung into the saddle, touched his hat, and trotted off.

Mary Lou felt abandoned. Had to be sure? Of what? That she loved him? Yes, she loved him. She raised her finger tips to her lips. The walnut trees rustled then stilled. She walked shakily back to the cabin.

Nelda, settled in her rocker mending, looked up when Mary Lou came in. "He's a nice young man. I like him." She poked her needle into a good-sized hole in the heel of Buck's heavy sock.

"Yes, he is," Mary Lou answered. Did that voice belong to her? She tried to escape her aunt's probing eyes. "Even though I love Tom, I can't hurt Glenn. It would be cruel. His love and kindness saved me when Mama died and Pa. . . Glenn loves me, Aunt Nelda. I can't just—"

"So, you finally know which one you love?" she held up her hand to stave off Mary Lou's comment. "And you're willing to give up Tom and marry Glenn?"

"I have to."

"That doesn't make sense, Child. You don't have to marry anyone."

Mary Lou shook her head. "I really don't know Tom that well. I know Glenn. No matter what decision I make, I'll hurt one or the other." Mary Lou's shoulders raised and lowered in a final sigh. "And Tom got a letter today from Laura Shepard, his girl in Texas. She must be accepted by his family, Tom wrote letters to his mother through her."

"It's true some men have girls at both ends of the trail, but that has nothing to do with you. No one should marry out of pity." Nelda's darning needle wove furiously back and forth.

"It's too late, Aunt Nelda. My wedding's tomorrow. Things have gone too far to stop them, and Pa approves of Glenn—"

"Your Pa isn't the one marrying him. He won't have to live with him and be his wife." Nelda dropped her mending into her lap. "There's only one reason to marry a man—and that is you love him so much you can't live without him. When I met Lars, there wasn't anyone else I could have married."

"Aunt Nelda, do you have something against my marrying Glenn?"

"Against him personally, no. It's you. I think you're tryin' to tie up too many ends—brotherly love for Glenn plus a duty to your father."

"Like is not enough!" Jenny had cried when Mary Lou first told her of her betrothal. If she could see it. . .

"Any girl who marries a man she doesn't love is eventually miserable." Nelda finished her last sock. "I've said my say." She stuffed her needle in the spool of darning thread, shoved it into her basket, and carried it to the shelf.

Mary Lou inhaled deeply to shift the dead weight that had returned to her chest and shook her head. "Pa wouldn't accept Tom."

"You're not thinking straight. Your Pa will have to accept your choice, just like your grandfather Stafford had to accept Tibby's and Ellen's decisions. He lost two daughters and a granddaughter by never forgiving them.

"I remember the letter Owen wrote me after he met your mother. Ellen was a real lady. His biggest worry was that he couldn't be her kind of gentleman. He loved being a cowboy. My advice was that if they loved each other, they could survive anything. And they did. Owen's accident, your mother's ill health, losing two baby sons. Nothing conquered the love they had. That's why your pa is so devastated at her death. He's lost half of himself.

"That's the kind of love your pa should want for you. It's the only kind that lasts and makes for happiness. Read again what God says about marriage. There's only one other decision to make that's greater—the accepting of the Lord Jesus Christ as Savior."

Suddenly, Mary Lou felt tired and confused. Her mind boggled at Nelda's defense. And she knew her aunt was right. She rose and kissed her aunt. "Thank you, Aunt Nelda for being honest—and for loving me so much. I'm going to bed." She gave her aunt a hug. "I want to get up early so I can look my best tomorrow." She passed over the determined look on Nelda's face. She needed to be alone on her last night as Mary Lou Mackey.

In her room, she sank into her mother's rocker. *Mama,* she cried within. There was no answer. She laid her head back and closed her eyes. Her chest ached. Her heart cried dry tears. Where was God? In the cottonwood grove when her heart found a new depth of His love, she thought she would never again have to go through this kind of agony.

Don't worry, My child, everything is going to be all right.

Mary Lou's spirit responded. She got ready for bed, climbed in, and lay staring at her wedding dress hanging on the way. "Thy will be done," she prayed, "not mine."

107

Chapter 19

Mary Lou stirred, stretched, and caught the sun peeking through her window. Her wedding day. She rose, bathed, and dressed, ignoring an unexplainable heaviness.

Her wedding dress monopolized the room—the blue dress Mama had made. Mary Lou and Aunt Nelda had added a fresh lace collar and cuffs and a slight bustle on the back—Aunt Nelda's idea, for style.

Mary Lou fingered her dress, each handmade stitch neat and even, the darts on the bodice sharp and shapely. Her favorite color, blue. "Like the color of your eyes," Tom had said.

Determinedly, Mary Lou tossed her head and flung the thought away. She had best not think of Tom. She had had her chance; she had made her choice. By suppertime, she would be Mrs. Glenn Farrell. Maybe then Pa would look on her favorably. She wrapped her dress in a sheet for transport to Aunt Tibby's, buttoned her shoes, and opened the door.

Aunt Nelda looked up from biscuit dough with a cheery smile. "Good morning. You look rested, and you'll be a beautiful bride."

Mary Lou flushed and hurried about setting the table. By the time Buck appeared, breakfast was ready and they sat down.

Aunt Nelda bowed her head. "Our Father, thank You for another day to accomplish the tasks You set before us. We ask Your blessing on Mary Lou and . . . ," she hesitated, the quickly continued, "and her new husband. Thy will be done. Thank You for the bounty before us. In Jesus' name, Amen."

Nelda dished up fried cornmeal mush with butter and maple syrup and poured steaming cups of coffee. Between sips, she talked excitedly about preparations Tibby had made for the wedding. They had spent all week cooking and baking.

The Bar-B ranch house had grown from its original cabin to a series of rooms. Then Nate had added a whole wing with an upstairs. Tibby, as usual, had all details arranged. Mary Lou would walk down the stairs, meet her father at the bottom, and walk into the parlor where Pastor Miles would perform the ceremony. Mary Wescott had offered to play hymns on Tibby's small organ. Venture townspeople and neighboring homesteaders for miles around had been invited.

Mary Lou looked at the clock. Seven-thirty. She left for the barn to do morning animal chores for the last time. Tomorrow she would be a townswoman. When she reached Dulcie, she put her arms around her and leaned her cheek against her warm neck. "I can tell you the truth." Mary Lou swallowed tears. "I wish it were Tom and I'd be a rancher's wife." She stroked the animal's neck. "At least I'll have you."

Dulcie nickered and tossed her head.

Mary Lou rubbed the horse's forelock, slid her hand down the smooth hair of Dulcie's face, and nuzzled her velvety nose with the palm of her hand.

Suddenly, she had to ride. Blanket and saddle went on quickly. She mounted and they flew out the barn door into the morning wind. Mary Lou automatically reined Dulcie toward Point Lane. She desperately needed the peace of the Lord she had found the other day.

A rider moved through the cottonwoods. *Tom? What is he doing here?*

He trotted up, a grin on his face. "I found out one thing this morning," he said brightly. "God answers prayers. For some reason, I had to come here."

Had God's Holy Spirit prompted her to come as an answer to Tom's prayers? Mary Lou gazed at Tom. "Until the other day when you said grace, I didn't know you were a Christian."

"You don't know my mother," Tom smiled and added, "or my father. Jesus became my Savior when I was four. My mother didn't believe a child had to wait until he was grown. You'd like Mother." He lowered his gaze to his saddle horn. "Even as a little boy, I made up my mind to marry a Christian woman just like her."

"I hear most little boys want to marry someone like their mother." Mary Lou fought to keep her voice casual.

"Guess so." He looked straight into her eyes. "Today's the day."

She glanced away. "Yes."

The cottonwoods couldn't soothe her. Tom's nearness provoked feelings that disturbed her, feelings not easily dismissed. She swung Dulcie's head. "I'd better get back. Lots of things to do. I just had to take a last morning ride—"

"As Mary Lou Mackey?" Tom finished.

She looked directly at him. "Yes." How did he know? She wanted to stay, but didn't dare. "I must be going. Good-bye, Tom." She swung Dulcie's head and jabbed her flanks.

"See you at the wedding."

She halted and turned. "You're staying?"

"For a couple more days. Smitty and the boys have started back. I have some business to attend to."

Mary Lou forced a smile. Words eluded her. She pushed Dulcie into a trot but couldn't keep from looking back. Tom sat watching her every move. Her heart pounded its protest, but she only waved. "Let's go," she ordered Dulcie. By the time she reached home, she had gained control.

Mary Lou, Nelda, and Buck squeezed into his buggy at one o'clock to go to Tibby's. The Bar-B ranch house buzzed with a festive air. Vases of jaunty cornflowers and blue grass bowered the parlor, and the dining room overflowed with wedding supper preparations.

Mary Lou hugged her aunt. "It's beautiful, Aunt Tibby. Thank you. Mama would love it."

Tibby cupped Mary Lou's face in her hands and smiled knowingly. "Yes she would. But I bet she knows."

Mary Lou walked slowly upstairs to the bedroom. She opened the door. Her dress greeted her from a peg on the wall. Tibby had insisted she send someone for it so it wouldn't get crushed between the three of them in Buck's buggy. She sat down on the bed and smiled. *I hope you see it all, Mama.* She remembered a wedding she and Mama had attended when she was sixteen. Mama had turned to her and said, "When your time comes, you'll be a beautiful bride and bless some young man with a good Christian wife."

Please, God, bless our marriage. Help me to love my husband. That struck Mary Lou as an odd prayer moments before her wedding.

Aunt Nelda hurried in to help her into her dress and fix her hair. Small cornflowers were snuggled into the braid over her head. A whole bouquet of them stood in a vase, ready for her to carry when she walked down the stairs.

At two o'clock, Mary Lou was ready and heard a soft knock at the door. When she opened it, there stood her father. "Pa?" He had climbed all those stairs to see her! "Come in."

Her father looked as she remembered him when she was a little girl. Some of the pain had gone from his face. He was handsome in a dark suit with a string tie. This was how he must have looked to Mama when she fell in love with him. Mary Lou didn't blame her.

Buck gazed at his daughter. Slowly, he leaned his cane against the door and held out both hands. Mary Lou placed hers in them. He spread their arms, smiled, and shook his head. "You look just like—and as beautiful as—your mama."

Had he forgiven her at last? Mary Lou breathed a sigh of relief and walked into his arms. A long-awaited peace settled over her. "Pa," she said softly as he held her. "I do love you, Pa."

Buck awkwardly released her and nodded. "Yes." He ran his hands down his string tie. "Be as happy as your mama and me."

Mary Lou hadn't heard that tone in his voice for a long time. "Thank you, Pa." This time, her tears fell for happiness.

Buck retrieved his cane. "I'd best be gettin' downstairs."

Was that a mist she saw in her father's eyes? *Thank you, Lord, for Pa's blessing.*

The sound of the organ's familiar hymns floated up the stairs along with Nelda and Tibby. "It's time," Tibby hugged her. "My, you do resemble your mama. I remember the day she married your father. I don't believe I've ever seen two people more in love." She laughed. "Except your uncle Nate and me."

Nelda held Mary Lou in her arms lightly to keep from crushing her dress. "You ready?"

Mary Lou reached for her flowers and took a deep breath. "Yes."

Her two aunts scurried out.

Mary Lou settled her bouquet in her arm and slowly stepped down each step, her knees shaking. At the bottom, Pa looked up, smiled, and nodded. Smiling faces of friends and neighbors greeted her. Pastor Miles and Glenn waited in the parlor. When she reached the bottom step, her father tucked her arm into his.

Her father released her when they reached Glenn. Mary Lou turned a fleeting glance at Glenn and caught a seriousness in his eyes. Was he as nervous as she? She turned to Jenny and handed her the flowers. Jenny looked stricken. She felt Glenn's touch. He lifted her hand to his lips and kissed it, sending color to her cheeks.

The organ music stopped.

Pastor Miles cleared his throat and began. "Dearly beloved, we have gathered together to join this man and this woman in holy matrimony." He cast his gaze over those attending. "If there is anyone who deems this marriage should not take place, speak now or forever hold your peace."

The room stayed silent. Someone coughed.

"I do."

Mary Lou gasped. *Jenny? Oh, no!* But—it was not Jenny's voice!

"I do," the voice repeated.

Glenn? She faced him in disbelief. *Spurned at the altar?*

A strained smile twisted Glenn's face. Guests, at first silent, recovered. They buzzed and stretched to see what was going on. An astonished Pastor Miles looked from Glenn to Mary Lou, demanding an explanation.

Glenn turned to Mary Lou and gently took her hands in his. "Forgive me, Mary Lou, I shouldn't have waited until now." He bowed his head. "I kept hoping." He looked into her incredulous face. "But we can't be married. You aren't in love with me—at least not enough to marry me."

She fought for meaning in what he was saying. She had agreed to marry him, had she not? "Glenn, why—"

Glenn grasped her arm firmly and propelled her past the crowd of gaping neighbors. Aunt Tibby recovered and led them into Nate's office. Mary Lou heard the thump of her father's cane.

Jenny rushed up and put an arm around her. "Mary Lou, I'm sorry. He said it before I had a chance."

"Before you?" She stared into Jenny's agonized face. She turned to Glenn—to her father. The light of love she had seen in his eyes upstairs had twisted into a scowl. Mary Lou covered her face.

In the office, Pastor Miles stepped forward. "Will someone please tell me the reason this wedding has been made a travesty?"

Nelda spoke up. "It's probably my fault as much as anyone's, but it didn't turn out the way we'd planned. Jenny was supposed to object to the marriage."

Mary Lou swung to Jenny. Betrayed by her best friend? The knot in her chest threatened to suffocate her.

"It's my fault, too." Tibby said. "We thought this was the only way to keep Mary Lou from marrying Glenn when she's in love with someone else."

Mary Lou wished she could die. Glenn shook his head and put a protective arm around her. "None of you have anything to do with this, and I have no idea what you're all talking about. This is solely my doing." Glenn turned to Mary Lou. "Last night," he said softly, "I saw you say good-bye to Tom."

Mary Lou's hands flew to her crimson face. She looked for a way to flee, but she was surrounded with dismayed faces.

"I love you, Mary Lou," Glenn continued, with the kindest look Mary Lou had ever seen on his face. "But after I saw you and Tom together, I knew you really loved him. No matter how much I loved you, I'd never be able to make you happy."

Buck, furious, faced Glenn. "Do you mean you refuse to marry my daughter?"

"Yes, Sir. Because I love her and want her to be happy. You should want the same."

If Mary Lou had been the fainting kind, she would have swooned. Instead, her embarrassment gave way to anger. Everyone except her had decided what was best for her life. Didn't anyone care how she felt? She had heard enough.

"Wait a minute!" she burst out. "Don't I have anything to say about this?" Everyone turned to her as if she had appeared from nowhere.

Bang! The door slammed against the wall. Tibby walked in, followed by Tom.

Chapter 20

"Now!" Tibby shouted. "Let's get this matter cleared up."

Mary Lou swayed. Would it ever stop? Never could she have imagined her special day would turn into the worst day of her life. And Tom?

Nelda slipped a concerned arm around Mary Lou. "This girl deserves an explanation from all of us. She's in shock. Now that I look at it, it was a sneaky, backhanded way to handle things." Nelda kissed Mary Lou on the cheek. "Dear child, I'm sorry we've put you through this."

Tibby nodded. "Forgive us, Mary Lou. But Nelda and I were watching you being pushed into making the biggest mistake of your life." Tibby shook her head. "At the time we planned it, it seemed a good, simple way to correct things, but it's turned out to be the worst." Tibby folded the stunned girl in her arms. "Your uncle Nate keeps telling me I can't run the world. Can you ever forgive us two old busybodies? Our honest concern was for your happiness."

The rising anger in Mary Lou subsided. These dear ones loved her more than she deserved and had gone to extreme lengths so that she could marry the man she loved.

Tibby continued. "The plan was to have Jenny protest the wedding. That would give time to get a few lives straightened out—or so we thought. After we got you and Tom to admit your love for each other, Tom would take Glenn's place. But when Glenn stopped the wedding—"

Glenn broke in. "I didn't know of your plan. I only knew what I had to do." He turned to Mary Lou. "I've known for some time you loved me only as a friend. I hoped it would grow into more than that. That's why I waited so long. Then I saw for myself—you love Tom. Forgive me for hangin' on till the last minute." Glenn hung his head. "I should have told you before the wedding. Instead, I mortified you before family and friends. I'm sorry."

Mary Lou smiled at the young man who loved her enough to give her up. Through all the confusion, Mary Lou suddenly remembered Mama quoting Psalm 37:4: "Delight thyself also in the Lord; and He shall give thee the desires of thine heart." Was God giving her a fresh opportunity to marry the man she loved?

Mary Lou found her voice. "If anyone is at fault, it's me. Until this moment, I never realized how selfish I was. For me to say I loved both Glenn and Tom was cruel and dishonest. The truth is, I love Glenn—"

Mouths dropped open and shoulders slumped.

"As I'd love the brother I never had." She looked deep into Glenn's troubled eyes. "I've never loved you more than I do right now. I'd have been lost without your caring after Mama died. I'll always love you for that." She reached around her neck and unhooked the locket he had given her. "Here, this belongs to your bride-to-be." She placed the locket in the palm of his hand.

Glenn raised Mary Lou's hand to his lips. "Thank you." His open smile released her.

Buck leaned against the window, scowling. Mary Lou ached for him. Upstairs, she had had her old pa back, the loving father she had known as a child. She had thought he had forgiven her. What could she say to him now?

Suddenly Tom moved across the room to Mary Lou and turned to the others. "This has to stop. Can't you all see what you're doing to her?"

Mary Lou slowly faced him. "But I can't marry you either, Tom."

Disbelieving silence blanketed the room. Mary Lou smiled up into Tom's stricken face and shook her head. "I can't marry you—because you've never asked me."

Tom's eyes filled with relief. A sly grin spread across his ruddy face. He nodded, took her hands in his, and pulled her to face him. "So I haven't. But there's something I don't know either. I've never heard you say you loved me—only me."

All restraints dissolved. "Oh, Tom, I've loved you since the first day you walked into the post office."

Tom stood erect. "Mary Lou Mackey, I love you with all my heart. Will you do me the honor of becoming this cowboy-rancher's wife?"

Love flooded her being. Mary Lou offered both hands. "Yes, Tom, I want very much to be your wife."

All anguish disappeared as he locked her in his stalwart arms and kissed her. She slid her arms around his neck and boldly kissed him back, regardless of the audience. She was tired of pretending.

The approving family watched with relieved smiles spread across their faces.

A familiar *thump, thump, thump* reverberated across the room. Tom clasped Mary Lou's hand and pulled her with him to her father. "Mr. Mackey."

Buck paid no attention.

Tom and Mary Lou caught up with him at the door, and Tom took hold of his arm. Buck stopped, eyes cast down.

"Mr. Mackey, I ask you again for permission to marry Mary Lou."

Buck ignored him, walked out, climbed into his buggy, and rode off, waving a tail of dust.

Nelda called them back. "Mary Lou, I know your mama would disagree with your father. Her first thought would be for your happiness. Owen's felt like a cheated man since his accident. The loss of Ellen didn't help. Losing his daughter is another blow. He's forgotten how desperately in love he was with your mother.

"Sometimes things repeat themselves. Your grandfather Stafford denied Owen permission to marry Ellen, but your mother married him because she loved him. She was never sorry. She forgave and prayed for her father till the day she died. Forgive him, Mary Lou, and pray for him. I don't think he realizes he's making you and Tom suffer same as he and Ellen did."

Mary Lou looked into Tom's concerned face. Tom had done what he should. Now the decision was hers. She faced him. "Tom, if you'll have me without my father's blessing, I'd like very much to become your wife."

Tom beamed. "Have you!" He enclosed her in his arm and turned to Tibby. "Do you think we could still have this wedding?"

"I don't see why not, and you could stay with us till you're ready to head for Texas." Tibby cleared her throat. "Well, now," she smiled broadly. "We have lots of guests who are probably wondering what happened to the wedding. Some have come a far piece to enjoy this event. Let's go out and start over."

She swung the office door wide and marched out to the parlor. "Get ready for the wedding, folks. Thank you for your patience. We had to change a few things." She ignored the questioning stares and clapped her hands. "Mary, let's have some proper music."

Mary Wescott lifted her hands to the organ keys and familiar hymns again filled the room.

Tom crossed to Glenn. They spoke for a few moments, Glenn nodded, and they shook hands. Pastor Miles hustled Tom to the parlor. Glenn followed and stood at Tom's right. More than a few eyebrows raised, then faces broke into smiles.

Before she left, Jenny threw her arms around Mary Lou. "I'll miss you but I'm happy for you," she whispered, eyes swimming. She started off, then spun around. "I'm still your bridesmaid, aren't I?" Jenny giggled and left.

Nelda and Tibby smoothed Mary Lou's dress, then beamed in approval. Mary Lou kissed each one. These dear women. They had fought hard for her happiness.

Just before Mary Lou started through the door, Tibby handed her the wilting bouquet of cornflowers. Mary Lou walked forward and stopped. She would have to walk alone. She glanced desperately at Aunt Nelda.

"Don't fret yourself. You're marrying the man you love. If Owen isn't happy about it, that's his problem, not yours. Now, go—with God's blessing."

Mary Lou took a wobbly step. Gently, a strong arm slipped through hers. Uncle Nate steadied her, led her forward, placed her beside Tom, and stepped back. The music slowly faded.

Pastor Miles cleared his throat and began again. "Dearly beloved, we are gathered together to join," he hesitated a second, "this man and this woman in the bonds of holy matrimony." Nervously, he paused. "If there is . . .anyone. . .who deems this marriage should not take place, speak now or forever hold your peace."

The room held its breath.

Pastor Miles drew a relieved sigh and hurried on. "God has given us one of the most sacred unions on this earth when He ordained the marriage of man and woman, and it should never be entered into lightly. It is not unlike the union of His Holy Spirit with His people. God is spirit and those who worship Him must worship Him in spirit and truth. And God sent his Son, Jesus, to be joined with His bride, the church.

"In like manner, the true joining of this man and woman is in spirit as well as heart." He turned to Tom. "Thomas Langdon, do you take Mary Lou Elizabeth Mackey to be your lawfully wedded wife, to cherish her, honor and protect her. . .?"

Mary Lou could hardly contain her happiness. She closed her eyes and drank deeply of the joy that coursed through her.

"Will you answer 'I do'?"

Tom's gaze never left her face. He reached for her hand. "I do." he said.

Pastor turned to Mary Lou. "And do you, Mary Lou Elizabeth Mackey, take Thomas Langdon to be your lawfully wedded husband, to cherish, honor, and obey, and to cleave unto him until death you do part?"

Mary Lou's heart guided her answer. "I do," she said quietly.

Pastor folded the couple's hands between his. "I now pronounce you man and wife, in the name of the Father, Son, and the Holy Ghost. May God bless you, my children."

Mary Lou walked into the arms of her husband. Tom kissed her gently and whispered in her ear. "Thank God. My wife at last." They turned arm in arm to greet a swarm of well wishers.

Maggie Bartlett squeezed Mary Lou's hands. "My, this is a surprise. I was lookin' forward to havin' you and Glenn as next door neighbors. I figured you'd spruce up that old saloon. Sure would make my place look better."

Mary Lou had forgotten that! She smiled. "Thank you. I'm sure someone else will buy it and fix it up."

Sarah George circled Mary Lou with one arm, patted Tom on the shoulder, and leaned confidentially toward Mary Lou. "You married the right one. You never were meant to be a town girl."

Tom smiled broadly. "I'll see to that."

Mary Lou turned to a tap on the shoulder. Ida Hensley's long, sad face moaned, "What's your poor pa goin' to do with both you and your ma gone?"

Henrietta moved protectively between Ida and Mary Lou. "Buck'll do fine. He has his sister Nelda to look after him." Henrietta hugged Mary Lou. "But I'm going to miss you terribly. You're like one of my own." She turned to Tom. "When are you leaving?"

"In four days."

"Oh!" Mary Lou gasped.

"I'm sorry, Dear, but I have to get back," Tom pleaded, then laughed. "This wedding is still full of surprises."

When the last guest left, Tibby gave a sigh and ushered Tom and Mary Lou to an upstairs bedroom. She stood in the doorway, smiling. "It was worth it all," she said and closed the door.

The next four days flew by quickly. Nate gave Mary Lou and Tom a buckboard and a western team as a wedding present to carry Mary Lou's belongings to Texas. Nelda and Tibby fluttered over Mary Lou, pouring out guidance for her new life as a wife. Mary Lou hoped she would remember all their good wisdom.

The three women packed everything carefully under canvas in the buckboard, including Mama's rocking chair padded with Mama's quilts.

"A daughter should have her mother's quilts," Aunt Nelda insisted. "We have enough left, and I've got lots of old clothes to make some more."

"Can't send you off to your mother-in-law like some poor relation." Tibby said. She wrapped a lamp globe and tucked it carefully into a basket.

Jenny visited often. They talked and talked, storing up a lifetime of memories before they parted. They reminisced about the hours they had spent as little girls roaming their beloved prairie on foot between the two cabins.

Every day, Mary Lou rode into Venture to the store to see Pa. Glenn said he came in late and left early. "He gave me half-interest in the store if I moved out of the boardinghouse into the back rooms to run the store. He's a great man, Mary Lou."

"I know. My mama married him. I hope I see him before I go, but if I don't, please tell him I'll always love him and that someday, I hope he'll forgive me."

Mary Lou glanced into the post office where she had spent most of her life. In spite of her sadness, she couldn't resist the freedom and joy she felt. She was now a rancher's wife!

Chapter 21

Only one day remained before their departure.

Mary Lou planned to spend it with Aunt Tibby, her second mother. Mama had willingly shared Mary Lou with her sister since Tibby had no children of her own. In the last year of Mama's illness, Aunt Tibby had come every day to relieve Mary Lou of some of the burden. They had grown much closer.

Mary Lou stepped into her aunt's familiar kitchen, received a welcoming hug and was suddenly struck by an attack of homesickness. The homey fragrance of bread fostered memories of happy times shared when Mama was alive. Mary Lou expected to yearn for Kansas after they got to Texas. But now? While she was still surrounded by the people and land she loved?

What sparked her sudden emotion was the table. Aunt Tibby's good china was neatly set for a special tea party, and her aunt's arms held her longer than usual. "Don't tell me we're having a special tea party all by ourselves?" Mary Lou asked lightly.

Tibby smiled. "Yes. I'm reminding you to have tea parties with your children."

Mary Lou laughed. "Gracious, Aunt Tibby, aren't you rushing things a bit?"

Her aunt's expression gave her away. She had always planned to join Ellen in being "grandmother" to Mary Lou's children. It hurt to realize that distance would keep her children from getting to know their loving, energetic great-aunt.

Tibby picked up the teapot. "Sit down. Henrietta and Jenny will be here later, but we'll sip a chattin' cup before they come. I need to talk to you anyway."

They sat and Tibby poured.

Special tea parties had begun when Mary Lou was a little girl. Whenever they were together at either home, Mama and Aunt Tibby always had made time for a pot of tea and a lot of talk.

One day, Ellen and Tibby had been at the table, engrossed in their conversation. Three-year-old Mary Lou had climbed on a chair, gotten a cup from the shelf, and carried it to her mother. Then she had shoved a chair to the table and joined the tea party.

Aunt Tibby had taken the hint. Laughing, she had prepared a special cup of tea for Mary Lou. Much later, Mary Lou had discovered that her cup of tea was a small amount of tea doctored with lots of milk and sugar.

It was during winter special teas that Aunt Tibby had taught Mary Lou and Jenny to tat. At first the thread had resembled a tangle of knots. Gradually, both girls had grown proficient.

The next Christmas, Mary Lou had presented a tatted collar and cuff set to her mother and Aunt Tibby and had even sent a set to Grandmother Stafford.

"And don't worry about your father."

Mary Lou jolted back to the present.

"It's ironic," Tibby continued. "Your mother and I went through the same thing. I remember when Nate asked Father for permission to marry me. Father forbade it! When we went counter to his wishes, he refused to speak to us, even to bid me good-bye. Mother was in tears. But I loved Nate and couldn't bear to have him leave without me. We got married, bid my mother good-bye, and left for Kansas. I was homesick and missed your mama, so I wrote, asking her to visit. Father was aghast! His daughter travelling on stage coaches to that uncivilized country! But Ellen must have read "homesick" between the lines. She came anyway. And she fell in love with a cowboy and married him at our house.

"Father disowned us both. He never allowed Mother to speak about us or even mention our names in front of him. He carried that unforgiving spirit to his grave." Tibby slowly sipped tea, staring into memories Mary Lou knew nothing of.

"All this made Mother's life miserable. By cutting himself off, Father cut Mother off too. Your mother and I prayed. We wrote letters telling how happy we were and what wonderful things we were doing, but neither Father or Mother answered."

"How could Grandfather act like that?" Mary Lou interjected. "He was a Christian and so faithful in church."

"The church had his body, but Jesus never had his heart," Tibby replied.

Suddenly Tibby got up, rummaged in a chest, and returned with two packages of faded letters tied together with frayed ribbon. She handed them to her niece.

Mary Lou turned them over and looked up in surprise. One set was addressed in Aunt Tibby's bold strokes, the other in her mother's neat script. "They' aren't opened!"

Aunt Tibby's lips formed a hurt smile. "No. They are yours to read. If nothing else, they are the history of our lives after we left Ohio and married cowboys." Tibby emphasized the last word. "Mother gave them to us when we attended Father's funeral. She said when they were delivered, he threw them in the rubbish but she retrieved and hid them."

Mary Lou frowned. "But why didn't Grandmother open them?"

"We asked her the same thing. She said she feared she might mention something from them and betray herself."

"But Grandfather died before she did. Why didn't she read them then?"

"By that time, Mother couldn't see. She didn't want anyone else to read them to her." Tibby sat swishing the remaining tea in her cup. "If she had, she would have known I lost my only child, Ellen lost two baby boys, and you were born. Having been a teacher herself, Mother was very proud when Ellen became a teacher. She never knew Ellen continued her teaching by having school in your cabin for you and seven neighbor children."

It was unbelievable! Why hadn't Mama told her some of this? Had she been too much a baby to tell it? A child? Yes, a happy child because Mama wanted it so. Now Mary Lou understood why Mama was so concerned about Pa and his moody, reclusive ways. She had been through rejection from her own father and wanted to shield her child from the hurt she had experienced.

"The sad thing is," Tibby went on, "Father not only cheated himself, but he robbed his wife of the joy of her children and grandchildren."

Mary Lou sat amazed that anyone would act as Grandfather. "But Pa won't. . ."

Tibby shook her head. "It doesn't make any difference what your pa does or doesn't do. That's between him and God. It's what you do I'm concerned about."

Dazed, Mary Lou shook her head. "Mama never said a word."

"That's because your mother was a loving God-fearing woman. She forgave Father and Mother completely. She never embraced the hurt, anger, and disappointment like I did.

" 'That's all past,' Ellen kept telling me. 'God gives a new day, every day, and tells us we aren't to hang on to yesterday or make big plans for tomorrow. Our most serious work is to find and follow the will of God each day.' "

How many times Mary Lou had heard Mama say that same thing!

Tibby shook her head. "I wasn't so inclined. I was angry—no—furious with Father. It took years before I finally admitted Ellen was right. She told me hating, holding grudges, unloving retaliations aren't of God. Her loving, forgiving example taught me to forgive Father and Mother. Then God was able to lift the terrible, hate-filled weight from my life. I thank Ellen for that."

Mary Lou's understanding opened to a number of things she had wondered about. Mama had shielded her from her own father's anger over the accident that had changed him from a loving father and husband to a resentful stranger. And she had surrounded Mary Lou with love and happy times. Even in her illness, love had radiated from her face and words. *Oh God, help me learn to love and forgive Pa like Mama did.*

Tibby's and Mary Lou's gazes held, relaying a new understanding, not between aunt and niece but between woman and woman.

Tibby rose and poured boiling water into a fresh pot of tea just as Henrietta and Jenny rode in. Everyone shared a cup, then Jenny and Mary Lou excused themselves, stepped outside, and walked toward the stream.

"When are you leaving?" Jenny asked.

"Tom wants to leave tomorrow."

"Oh."

For two girls who had spent their lives tumbling over each other's words, Mary Lou and Jenny were suddenly tongue-tied. They walked hand in hand, as they often did. Big Jon had jokingly told them when they were little to hang on so they wouldn't lose each other in the tall grass and flowers. They had believed him. Those early days hadn't only clasped their hands, but also their hearts.

Jenny giggled. "After you go, I'm going to let Glenn catch me."

"Then you'll have to slow down. Glenn likes things done in order."

"I do too! Guess that makes me the right wife for him."

"You'll make him a good wife, Jenny. You'll make what he needs—a home and a bright, loving spot in his life."

"Oh, I almost forgot," Jenny said suddenly. "Last night Glenn asked me if I wanted to be the new postmistress!"

"Wonderful!"

"He won't have to run very far to catch me, will he?"

Their steps carried them back to the Bar-B Ranch. In the distance, they saw a rider coming. Mary Lou turned to Jenny, determined not to cry. "Dear friend, I'm going to miss you so much."

"Aw, you'll have Tom."

"And you'll have Glenn."

By the time they reached the porch, Henrietta was waiting to leave. Last hugs round, then Jenny mounted Missy and rode off with Henrietta.

Mary Lou watched Tom ride toward her. He sat a saddle well, tall and straight. Her heart overflowed with love.

When he reached her, he dropped to the ground, took her into his arms, and kissed her. Tibby, watching from the door, smiled.

Chapter 22

That night as Tom and Mary Lou climbed into their comfortable bed at Aunt Tibby's, Tom informed Mary Lou that Smitty and the boys had already left. He grinned. "I told Smitty we were married and swore him to secrecy."

"You did? Did he make any comment about it?"

"Yep, he asked me if you were a pretty lady."

Mary Lou lifted her chin and asked, "And what did you say?"

Tom pulled her into his arms, his eyes reading her face. "I said "Nope—"

Mary Lou opened her mouth in a quick intake of breath.

Tom grinned. "I said you were a beautiful lady."

"Thank you, Sir," Mary Lou answered demurely. "If I were out of bed I'd curtsy." Instead, she snuggled into his embrace.

The next morning, Mary Lou lay wide awake, watching a morning sunbeam across the back of Tom's curly, red hair. A thousand thoughts tumbled in her mind. She was going to a new life, new home, new family. Even a new state! She had never been to Texas but had heard it was a rough and tumble place. Yet Tom lived there. He was a gentleman and from what he had said about his family, they seemed much the same as any she knew in Kansas. Why was it then that most news was bad, when surprising and wonderful things were happening all around?

Mama had always said, "God's goodness is around us in far greater quantity than all the evil put together. It's just that we aren't looking." Good was all Mama had ever seen.

When Pa had left home after his accident and lived with Jacob Shineberg at the back of the store, Mama had cooked meals and taken them to the store for both Pa and Jacob to eat. Jacob had been delighted and had eaten with relish. "Good! Good! Just like my Frau used to make."

While Mama was there, she had gathered both men's soiled clothes, taken them back to the cabin, washed them, and returned them.

Mama. She had to see Mama before she went so far away.

Tom stirred. Still asleep, he reached for Mary Lou. She moved into his arms—into her safe place where she felt loved and protected. What was it Pastor Miles had said? "The true joining of a man and woman is in the spirit and heart."

The back of Mary Lou's neck tingled. As much as she loved Kansas, thoughts of going anywhere with Tom filled her with anticipation. She could appreciate the Bible story of Ruth who left her own country to go with Naomi. Pastor had also said, "Forsaking all others." Mama had done it. So had Aunt Tibby.

Tom peeked through one eye and drawled, "Y'all ready to leave this morning?"

She raised up on one elbow and smiled. "Yes, I am." She rumpled his hair and kissed him. "But there's one thing I want to do before we go."

"What's that?"

"Say good-bye to Mama."

He nodded with understanding, picked up her hand, and kissed her fingers. "We can ride out there after breakfast."

Mary Lou prayed he would understand what she was about to ask. "Tom, I'd—I'd like to just walk out there alone, if you don't mind."

Tom's tender gaze caressed her face. "I'll watch for you and meet you on the way back. After all that's happened, I'm almost afraid to let you out of my sight."

They laughed and climbed out of bed.

The early morning air was crisp, but the sun spread a warm glow over Mary Lou's head and promised a perfect day. She set out toward the family cemetery, across dewy prairie grass that wet the bottom three inches of her skirt.

The ever-constant Kansas wind tugged gently at her hair, and she reached back, loosened her ribbon, and let her hair blow free. Her eyes etched deeper into her heart this land that had been her playground and the only home she had ever known.

Mary Lou stood tall above the flowers, but could remember walking among them when their colorful faces had brushed against her nose. She bent and picked a bouquet for Mama. When she was little, she had gathered wild flowers almost every day because Mama loved them and set them around the cabin.

Mary Lou pulled the cemetery gate open. Four people were buried in the little plot. In one corner, lay Mama and two baby sons, both of whom died in infancy. Mary Lou's only memory of them was that they had cried a lot and Mama had carried them in her arms most of the time. The only time she had ever seen Pa cry was when he lost the sons he had always wanted.

In the opposite corner was a small grave with a bouquet of fresh wild flowers stuck into a quart canning jar that was buried to its neck. During snowy months, the jar held dried weeds and flowers Tibby gathered during the summer.

This grave held the only child of Aunt Tibby and Uncle Nate, a baby girl. Her first name, Elizabeth, was whittled into the small wooden cross. *Elizabeth.* Aunt Tibby, Mama, and Mary Lou also carried the name Elizabeth in honor of a great grandmother.

Mama's grave was overgrown again with weeds. The wooden cross Pa had made was almost hidden. Mary Lou knelt and pulled the weeds, her eyes battling tears that made small damp spots on the ground at her knees.

She sniffed. "Mama, you always said there were two kinds of tears, one for sorrow and one for joy. I'm crying both. I miss you so, and Pa won't speak to me. He didn't want me to marry Tom. But I love Tom, Mama, and he loves me. Oh, Mama, I know you'd love him. I did what you told me. I looked for a gentle man."

She lifted her face heavenward. "I know you're glad for me, but Pa. . ."

Mary Lou laid the flowers on the grave. The wind's gentle warmth enfolded her and reminded her of the night on Mama's porch when she had accepted Jesus as Savior. Mama had cupped her face and lifted it to her own. "Now I will never lose you," she had said. "We both belong to Jesus because He's in our hearts."

Mary Lou turned and saw Tom standing a short way off. She waved high over her head and he ran toward her. When they met, they clung to each other, then walked back to the ranch.

Horses, buggies, and buckboards were waiting. It seemed like everyone had come, the friends and neighbors of a lifetime.

Nelda brought bread, a crock of butter, and a couple jars of prairie apple jelly. "To remind you where you came from," she said and tucked in a pan of sourdough starter, with enough flour to last till they got to Harness.

Tibby brought a big basket with "something to eat on the way" and tucked it under the front seat.

Big Jon, Henrietta, and all eleven children came to say good-bye. They brought ground coffee, dried beef, and bread pudding with dried apples. Other neighbors brought gifts to "set them up." The buckboard groaned.

A subdued Jenny leaned against the wagon fighting tears. Glenn stood at her side, concerned.

Henrietta hugged Mary Lou and shoved a brown-wrapped package into her hands. "We want you to have this."

Mary Lou unfolded the paper to reveal a beautiful crocheted tablecloth. She gasped, knowing the hours and days of work it took to make it.

Henrietta nodded. "It's too fancy for us and I'll have time enough to make another for Jenny when she's married."

Mary Lou's chest tightened. She couldn't imagine living without these dear people who had been her life. She hugged them all again and hurried to the buckboard.

Tom shook hands with Nate and Big Jon, men he had come to respect. Big Jon reminded him of his father, strong and gentle at the same time. Tom helped Mary Lou into the buckboard and picked up the reins. He glanced into the distance, hoping to spot Buck's buggy for Mary Lou's sake.

"Thank you, Aunt Nelda and Aunt Tibby," he said. "Without you, this day would never have come. Pray us home."

The two women nodded, mopping tears and noses with their handkerchiefs. At last, everyone stepped back.

Tom gave a slap of the reins and called to the horses. The wagon slowly rolled forward.

"Good-bye. God bless you." Mary Lou waved and watched her friends grow smaller. She strained her eyes for her father, her heart heavy. Yet she couldn't suppress the exhilaration bubbling inside. Beside her sat her husband, the man she truly loved. She had pinched herself all week to make sure it was true. Was it possible to be happy and sad at the same time?

The wagon rumbled past Point Lane. Mary Lou spied a buggy among the cottonwoods. It was Pa.

Tom halted the horses. Mary Lou waved and called, "Bye, Pa."

Buck started to raise one hand, then jerked it back to the reins. Tom swung the wagon toward the grove, but Buck abruptly turned into the trees and disappeared.

Tom stopped. Mary Lou stood, waved, and called. "Bye, Pa. I love you. We'll be back to visit." She blew him a kiss and sat down aching with disappointment.

Tom slapped the reins and turned the wagon south. Tinder and Dulcie, tied to the wagon, tossed their heads and trotted alongside. The cottonwood trees in Point Lane waved their fluttery green hands.

Mary Lou turned to the handsome young man beside her. Her heart swelled in gratitude. *Thank you, Father.* She settled into the seat, adjusted her bonnet, and set her eyes toward Texas, leaving behind her girlish cottonwood dreams for the reality of love.

RAINBOW
HARVEST

To my rainbow harvest,
Sharleen, Paula, and Allen

Chapter 1

Tom Langdon pulled his wagon to a stop at the edge of the Red River. "This is where we cross. It's fairly shallow here. The bottom's bumpy, so hold on. Better steady Dulcie. Tinder's used to it, but it might frighten her."

Tom eased the front wheels into the water. The wheels sank into the reddish-brown clay. Mary Lou grabbed her seat with one hand, pulled the rope tied to Dulcie with the other, and coaxed her wild-eyed horse to enter. Dulcie's nostrils flared, her front hoofs dug into the mud, and she backed from the water.

"Come on, Dulcie, you're all right. Nothing to be afraid of. Easy, girl." Mary Lou wasn't quite sure who she was encouraging, her horse or herself. She pulled hard on the rope that tied Dulcie to the wobbly wagon and forced her into the water that slowly crept halfway up the wheels.

Dulcie laid her ears back and followed the familiar voice.

Mary Lou glanced admiringly at her fearless new husband. Feet braced, he maneuvered the struggling team and swaying wagon across the river. When wheels rolled onto the other side, Tinder and Dulcie splashed past the wagon to dry land. Mary Lou heaved a relieved sigh and smiled at Tom.

He leaped to the ground and lifted Mary Lou down to soothe Dulcie. Tinder trotted to Tom and nuzzled his arm. "Good boy! You're getting to be an old hand at this." Tom inspected the dripping wagon and team, handed Mary Lou back up into her seat, climbed aboard, and flipped the reins around his knee. He pulled her to him and kissed her. "Well, Mrs. Langdon. Welcome to Texas!"

His enfolding arms brought instant calm. Mary Lou warmed in her husband's gaze, returned his kiss, then adjusted her bonnet to shield her face from the late afternoon sun. Ahead, a distant copse of trees enticed her with its fan of precious shade.

"Crossing the river means we're close to home." Tom patted Mary Lou's hand and pointed to the trees. "They're about two miles away. We can rest and get some shade." Mary Lou heaved a sigh and smiled gratefully.

"If we pushed, we could make it home by nightfall," he added.

Panic rose in Mary Lou's throat. Her lips parted for a quick intake of breath. Tom's home—the place she eagerly anticipated seeing, yet feared. A bubbling undercurrent of excitement overrode momentary alarm and flooded her mind with indescribable joy. Home—where she and Tom would begin their life together.

All the way from Kansas, Tom had proudly described the Circle Z until Mary Lou's mind pictured a rambling adobe ranch, horse and cattle barns, corrals, bunkhouse, amiable cowboys, and the majestic beauty of the surrounding land. Hearing him talk about his father's fierce love of the land, Mary Lou recognized Tom had inherited that love. He spoke with purpose and pride, eager to get home and show it to her.

"There's a fair-sized stream winding in those trees—a good place to camp for the night, rest, and clean up. What do you think?"

"I'd like that." Mary Lou relaxed. "Maybe I could wash my hair. Meeting your family tomorrow, I'd like to look my best."

Tom leaned over and kissed her again. "All they're going to see is the beautiful bride I brought home. After they get to know you, they'll love you as I do."

Mary Lou hoped so.

Lying awake beside Tom, long after her husband's breathing told her he slept, Mary Lou prayed for her new family. In her mind, they'd become life-and-blood people.

Tom spoke of his mother with loving admiration—called her a strong Christian woman. And Nelson. Mary Lou could hardly wait to meet Tom's youngest brother and see his beautiful paintings. Tom held an obvious pride in his oldest brother Zachary. She wondered about Zack's new wife, Darcy. Tom hadn't said much except that she was from the East and wasn't too happy with ranch life. He'd spoken briefly of his older brother, Doug. "He needs lots of prayer," was all he had said. Not knowing exactly what to pray for, Mary Lou simply lifted Doug's name to God.

Her heart tugged her back home to her father. She couldn't help grieving at his disapproval of Tom and his refusal to come and say good-bye when they left. As always, the memory of Mama's sweet spirit reminded Mary Lou of God's willingness to listen to His children's problems. *Lord,* Mary Lou prayed, *I thought Pa'd forgiven me, but marrying Tom made him angry again. I don't know what to do anymore. It would all be so different if Mama were still alive.*

"If your father isn't happy about it, that's his problem, not yours. Now, go—with God's blessing." Aunt Tibby's parting words echoed in Mary Lou's mind and soothed her.

This would be Tom and Mary Lou's last night alone under the dark, friendly sky that kindly provided a blanket of twinkling stars and a warm quiet breeze. As much as she looked forward to the comforts of the ranch, Mary Lou cherished this time when they belonged only to each other. Hereafter, they would be surrounded by Tom's family.

Wide awake, Mary Lou gazed into her husband's sleeping face, his copper-crowned head cradled on one arm. He looked as vulnerable as a small boy, but at their wedding Tom had proved himself a true Christian gentleman, even to Glenn. The two men had shaken hands and parted friends, even though Mary Lou had almost married Glenn.

Tom stirred, opened dreamy eyes, and caught Mary Lou's loving gaze. His mouth bent into a sleepy grin. "Come here, Wife," he said huskily and gathered her into his arms.

Wife! The new truth permeated her innermost being. Home would always be wherever Tom was. She snuggled closer and surrendered mind and body to loving him.

U

The dusty buckboard rattled under the Circle Z arch around one o'clock. Nelson, behind an easel on the porch, grabbed his crutches and stood, cautious and curious.

Tom waved and hollered, "Nelson, it's me."

Nelson spun on one crutch, called through the open door, and bounced along at a surprising speed toward the approaching wagon. In the doorway, a woman appeared, paused, then came running.

When they met, Tom jumped out and threw his arms around his mother and brother, then lifted Mary Lou to his side. Nelson's winsome face beamed with expectancy.

Mary Lou took to Nelson immediately, just as Tom had said she would. She smiled at his mother and steadied herself against Tom's shoulder, apprehension fluttering her stomach.

Mrs. Langdon stood tall and regal. The sun sparked silver highlights on her crown of red-bronze hair.

Tom put his arms around Mary Lou. "Mother, this is Mary Lou—Langdon."

Allena Langdon's eyes widened in surprise and stared. *Oh, Lord, let her accept me,* Mary Lou prayed.

Allena regarded her new daughter-in-law with raised brows, then stepped forward graciously, clasped Mary Lou's shoulders with firm, gentle hands, and planted a kiss on her cheek. "Now I know why Tom was so eager to leave on this year's cattle drive." She turned to her grinning son. "I should have known you'd find yourself a beauty."

Tom grinned. "Was I that obvious?"

"I knew there was something you weren't telling me." She turned to Mary Lou and held out both hands. "Welcome home, Mrs. Langdon."

Mrs. Langdon! Mary Lou's heart flooded with gratitude to this kind woman whose eyes sparkled clear and honest like Mama's. "Thank you. I'm glad to be—home."

Allena's arm encircled Mary Lou's small waist. "You must be tired, Child. That's a long, hard trip. Come with me and we'll see what we can do to Tom's room to make it proper for a bride. Hattie can make us some tea and rustle up something to eat."

They stepped inside the ranch house door. Its coolness surprised Mary Lou. They walked through a spacious and airy main room with an Indian blanket hanging on one wall and small rugs of similar design scattered on the floor in front of rugged furniture. Simple. Homey. She gazed with delight at the intensely alive Texas landscapes that dominated the walls. At any moment, she expected balls of tumbleweed to escape their confining frames and bounce into the room. Had Nelson painted these?

Down the hall at the far end of the house, Tom's room held a large bed, a bureau, and a washstand. More Indian rugs dotted the floor. A breeze fluttered homespun curtains at the windows.

"The men will unload the wagon. Until they come, you and I can get acquainted." Allena sat on the bed and patted for Mary Lou to sit beside her.

Mary Lou's heart pounded in her ears. She'd never felt more alone. She wasn't afraid of Tom's mother—her tender greeting had erased that. Could she live up to be the wife Mrs. Langdon wanted for her son?

"Tell me about yourself and your family," her mother-in-law asked. Mary Lou described her father's general store and how she and her mother had worked in the post office. Her words stopped when she spoke of Mama's death. A gentle hand grasped her shoulder. Another lifted her chin.

Allena Langdon reached into her apron pocket and gently daubed Mary Lou's moist eyes with a hankie that carried the fragrance of fresh wind.

Mary Lou sniffed, swallowed, and continued. "That's why I became postmistress and how I met Tom. Every day he came either to post a letter or to pick up mail for his men."

Allena nodded and smiled. "You're shedding light on a lot of my questions. I'd never received as many letters from Tom on any previous cattle drive. Tom is a Texas boy at heart and loves his ranch. I just thought he was homesick."

Mary Lou closed her eyes. Her mind filled with delicious remembering. "I loved him the first day he walked into the post office and our hands brushed when he handed me a letter."

Allena's face spread with pleasant surprise. "Same as Tom's father and me. Zachary asked me to dance a square with him at a barn dance when I was fourteen. When our hands touched it was magic." Allena's voice faded and her gaze hung on a faraway memory.

"You must have loved him very much," Mary Lou said softly.

"He was my life—the only man I'll ever love. He gave me four sons and enough good years for a lifetime." Allena gathered within herself, lost in memories. "When Zachary died, I transferred my love to them."

Surprisingly, Allena laughed. "Sometimes I'm too much mother hen for their liking, but I'll let go when they each find their love." She paused, then commented aloud, as if to herself. "But I have Nelson. I hope he can marry someday. If not, we have our painting."

So that's where Nelson inherited his talent. Being alone with her new mother-in-law these few moments sent tingling excitement through Mary Lou. Had God moved again to give her not only the blessing of a good husband, but a new mother and brothers and sister as well?

Mary Lou continued the story of her betrothal to Glenn. "After Mama died, Glenn was gentle and caring. His attentions eased my pain, especially when I received no letters from Tom. I finally gave up ever seeing Tom again. Glenn and I worked together in the store. I still love him as a friend, but I wanted Tom for my husband."

Allena laughed. "So that's why Tom wrote letters and tore them up!"

Mary Lou's heart leaped. Tom had told her he had wanted to write but didn't dare. One by one, things settled into place and made sense. She laughed. "Poor Tom. When he came back I was betrothed and couldn't talk to him because we women in Venture had formed a Women's Christian Temperance Union, had smashed the saloon, and weren't speaking to the men until they moved the saloon to the outskirts of town."

"Good for you! You've got spunk. A rancher's wife needs the strength of two women to survive Texas."

"Or Kansas."

Allena squeezed Mary Lou's hand and nodded. "I've a hunch you'll make it. Zack looks like his father, but Tom has his father's heart and needs a woman for a wife, not a little girl."

Touched, Mary Lou swallowed a lump that rose in her throat.

"You may find people around here a bit rough at first," Allena continued, "but inside most are good, kind, solid Americans trying to cut a life for themselves out of this harsh wilderness." Allena fixed her gaze on Mary Lou. "If it's not too soon, I'd be proud if you'd call me Mother."

Mary Lou relaxed. Feeling no disrespect for Mama's memory, she leaned toward Mrs. Langdon. "Thank you—Mother." The last vestige of fear of Tom's mother took wings.

When Mary Lou related the crazy confusion of the wedding, the two Mrs. Langdons laughed so hard that tears came. Until that moment, Mary Lou hadn't appreciated the humor of the situation.

The thump of boots resounded down the hall. Tom appeared in the doorway, his arms loaded. "What's going on in here?"

Allena and Mary Lou exchanged knowing glances.

"Just woman stuff," Allena said, rising to accept an armful of quilts.

Mary Lou sprang to help. They found space for Mama's dresser, rocking chair, and small table. Mary Lou unwrapped Aunt Tibby's lamp.

Allena gasped with pleasure. "Haven't seen anything this pretty since I was a little girl back in North Carolina. I have a small one of my mother's, but nothing as grand as this." Allena turned the lamp round and round.

Mary Lou inwardly thanked Aunt Tibby. "Can't send you off to your mother-in-law like a poor relation," she'd said. Her aunt had been right, as usual.

They unrolled her mother's lovely quilts and Henrietta's lace tablecloth. Allena oohed and aahed over each one and smoothed them with her hands.

Mary Lou lifted the lamp and surveyed the room. "I don't know where I'd put this in here. It's too fancy for a bedroom. Mother, could you use it in the parlor?"

Allena was jubilant. "Thank you, my dear. I've just the place for it." She flashed Tom an appreciative smile. Lamp held high, she carried it carefully out the door and disappeared.

Tom's gaze carried his love across the room. He pushed the door shut with his boot and took Mary Lou in his arms. "You'll never know how many times I've dreamed of this moment. You—here, with me—my wife." Tom held her tenderly and whispered into her hair, "I thank God for you."

His kiss ignited a flare of happiness that warmed her whole being. She relaxed. Home at last.

Shortly after everyone gathered for the noon meal, Zack's booming voice announced he and Darcy were home from Harness. He seated Darcy and spied Tom. "You're back! I wondered who that buckboard belonged to."

The brothers affectionately slapped each other on the back.

"Zack, this is Mary Lou, my wife."

Zack stared in surprise then threw back his head and roared. "Well, I'll be. Couldn't let your big brother get ahead of you, could you?" He punched Tom's arm and walked to Mary Lou and put out his hand.

Zack's firm fingers closed over hers. His blue-black head bent, and Mary Lou crimsoned when his soft lips touched the back of her hand. He glanced up and grinned. "So, you're Mary Lou. No wonder my brother was pining." Zack reached for Darcy, who rose and came to Zack's side. "Mary

Lou, meet my wife, Darcy."

Darcy gazed up at Zack then turned nonchalantly to Mary Lou, green eyes snapping a clear message: "Zack belongs to me."

Allena's mouth opened in surprise. "You knew about Mary Lou?"

Zack smacked his hands together. "For the first time in my life, Mother, I knew something before you. It's time you learned men know a lot more than we tell the ladies." Zack clasped and pumped Tom's hand. "When we talked, it seemed hopeless. I'm glad it worked out."

Allena held her hands up. "I surrender and admit my boys are grown and don't need a tagging mother anymore."

Zack released himself from Darcy, crossed the room and kissed his mother's cheek. "Mother, no one will ever take your place. You'll never be dethroned, but we're glad you've discovered your boys are now men."

Allena laughed and playfully shoved Zack toward his chair.

Mary Lou, charmed at the scene, glanced at Darcy who stood rigid, her lips tight, her dark eyes flooded with displeasure. She was beautiful—but unhappy. How sad Darcy couldn't appreciate the love and respect Zack had for his mother, Mary Lou thought. *Mama always said: Watch how a man treats his mother. Most often, he'll treat his wife the same way.*

Allena lifting a serving bowl, passed it, and picked up another. "Sit down, please. Let's eat our dinner before it gets cold."

Darcy filled her plate and between bites began talking about Mrs. Cassidy, the only dressmaker in Harness. "The clumsiest woman I've ever seen. All thumbs and poking fingers. I know she has my measurements all wrong. My waist is only nineteen inches." Darcy spread her hands around her waist and pressed her fingers into her middle. "Can you imagine? She said I measured twenty-two!" She stuffed another bite into her mouth.

Around the table with Mary Lou and Darcy sat three men and an older woman. *It's probably just as strange here for her as it is for me,* Mary Lou thought. *Maybe she needs a friend her own age.* She tucked that thought in the back of her mind and picked up her fork.

Chapter 2

Mary Lou's eyes opened slowly. She stared at the unfamiliar adobe ceiling. Beside her, Tom slept. She raised to one elbow and studied the features of his handsome, suntanned face, enthralled with the still unbelievable fact she was his wife.

He stirred, opened his eyes, and grinned. "Mornin,' Mrs. Langdon," he drawled. *Mrs. Langdon.* She loved the sound of it.

Tom squinted at the window and sat up. "Is that daylight?" He bounded out of bed and grabbed his pocket watch. "Breakfast in this house is six sharp. I should have been up and out an hour ago." Tom grabbed Mary Lou's hands and pulled her out of bed into his arms. "See what you do to me, Woman? I forget everything."

Mary Lou snuggled in to stay, but Tom released her and hurried into his clothes. She washed, slipped into a blue calico, brushed and braided her long chestnut hair, and wrapped the braid around her head. She sensed Tom watching her as she dressed and flushed at the tender amused expression on his face. When she finished, he gathered her into his arms, kissed her, and nuzzled her neck. "I love you," he whispered before he released her and swung the door open.

As usual, Allena sat in her place waiting. Tom held Mary Lou's chair, and she slipped into it. Meticulously dressed in the latest fashion, Darcy followed Zack into the dining room.

"Good morning, Darcy, Zack," Mary Lou said cheerily.

Darcy nodded slightly and slid into the chair Zack held for her.

The Langdon men had dignity and manners. Mary Lou glanced with admiration at Allena, who sat like a queen on a throne, patiently waiting for her subjects to settle.

Alert and smiling, Nelson greeted everyone.

What a dear boy. In spite of his handicap, he is undaunted. Mary Lou made an inward promise to find time to talk with him, tell him how much she loved his paintings, and see more of them.

"Tom, say grace, please." Allena bowed her head.

When Tom finished, Mary Lou gazed across the table at Doug's empty chair, curious about this brother she hadn't met. He hadn't appeared the night before for supper. Allena was visibly disturbed by his absence. During the night, Mary Lou vaguely remembered shuffling and whispering in the hall. Had that been Doug?

"Doug's late again," Zack commented.

"Doug had an early breakfast and left for Harness." Allena sipped her coffee. "Said he had some business to take care of."

A frown creased Zack's brow. "He needs to run this ranch on the ranch instead of from ten miles away." His voice betrayed his irritation. He avoided his mother's gaze. "A lot of repairs need to be done. Father would be appalled."

"I agree with you," Allena said. "I know it; Tom knows it; Smitty and the cowboys know it. Why do you think I wrote you to come home?" Like a mother hen sparring for an attacked chick, she threw a challenge. "Why don't you and Tom take the responsibility of repairs and fix what's needed with help from the boys? It's your ranch, too, you know. Doug has carried the load since your father died and you left for law school. He could use some help."

Zack leaned against the back of his chair and met his mother's indignant stare. "Doug refuses to let loose any ranch business or discuss it. He avoids us by running to town. Mother, I haven't seen one record ledger. Tom and I should have access to them as well as Doug." His jaw flexed. A knowing look passed between him and Tom. "Either he does a better job—and soon—or there'll have to be some drastic changes around here to save the ranch."

"Save the ranch?" Allena straightened and paled.

"Yes. I've checked on some land dealings and. . ." Zack leaned over his plate and stuffed a forkful of steak into his mouth.

Allena stiffened. "And?"

Zack chewed, swallowed, then met his mother's demanding gaze. "It looks as if part of the Circle Z has been sold."

"Sold! Who? When?"

"Mother, right now Doug is the only one except me with legal authority to sell any land, and I haven't been here."

Allena gasped and her eyes filled with pain. She shook her head. "Doug wouldn't!"

"I haven't solid proof yet, but at least a quarter of the land in the far south acreage may be sold."

"To whom?"

"I'm not sure. I'm guessing land speculators from the East. I've seen several in Harness. But everything is shady, and I'm having a hard time pinning down facts. No one wants to talk, especially to me. I don't have enough proof to make any accusations." Zack gazed tenderly at his mother. "I suspect

Doug is selling off the land to pay his gambling debts. He owes everybody in town."

Mary Lou watched the proud woman shrivel in her chair. Her life and pride rested in her four boys. Gambling was bad enough, but selling off their inheritance to do it was beyond belief.

Suddenly, Darcy sat indignantly erect. "Then the quarter he sold is his quarter. Why don't you just disown him?"

Allena glared in shock at her daughter-in-law. "He's my son!"

"But if he's already sold his quarter and sells more—that means he'll sell Zack's land. . . ," Darcy's voice faltered under the mortified scowl of her husband, "and Tom's. And Nelson's," she added. Wilting before five astounded faces, she sputtered, "It isn't. . .fair."

"Nor is it fair to accuse a brother when we don't know all the facts." Zack's glare pursed Darcy's lips, and she stared petulantly at him like a falsely rebuked child.

"In my search," Zack continued, "I discovered two land titles and deeds with vague descriptions of the southeast quarter of the Circle Z. There are wide discrepancies and confusing land boundaries, but they look like a blend of Langdon and Shepard property. Some of Will's cowhands were out hunting strays and reported strangers camped in two covered wagons who looked like they were settling in. Will is coming this morning, and we're going to investigate it."

Allena raised her chin. "Until we have proof, we'll discuss it no more. What if we should accuse my son and your brother when he is innocent?"

"That's what I'm counting on, Mother, that I can find the facts that will prove Doug innocent."

Mary Lou related to Allena's pain. For Mama, it had been Pa who dampened the sunshine. For Allena, her son. Did every family have a difficult member? Mary Lou's curiosity heightened about her truant brother-in-law.

Tom rose, his mother's hurt and disappointment mirrored in his eyes. "As far as we're concerned, Doug is innocent until proven guilty, and we'll treat him so." He placed his hand reassuringly on his mother's shoulder, glanced at Zack, and flashed good-bye to Mary Lou with his eyes.

Allena sternly faced her oldest son. "From now on, I want to be informed of what's going on. This is my ranch, too." Her expression mixed disappointment and anguish with stoic determination.

"All right. Tom and I have stumbled across things that don't seem right. There are too many unanswered questions. We also hate to think Doug is mixed up in anything shady, but he won't talk to us about the ranch, even when we question him.

"When Will told us what his boys discovered, we thought it wise to investigate first. It could be something simple. Someone might have mistakenly moved on what he thinks is his newly purchased land. It's happened before."

Allena nodded. "What makes you think these wagons aren't the usual stopovers partaking of western hospitality? It's not unusual. Traveling wagons stop anywhere. We've had them stop here. I've found most to be good people on their way to their lands, appreciative of the chance to rest and be friendly. I've enjoyed them. Company's rare, and they bring news from back east."

Zack agreed. "But these wagons have been there over a month. Will's cowhands told us whoever it is has erected a shed and it looks like they're digging a soddie in the side of a small knoll. Will's boys wouldn't have paid any attention to a couple wagons stopped at the stream for a week or so."

"I'd like to go see."

Zack's nostrils flared. "I'd rather you didn't. It's rough riding in that quarter, and we don't know what to expect. That's why Will is bringing all the boys he can. We're taking everyone but Tex and Jess in case—"

"In case?"

"Mother, we can't take chances. If they're poachers, we need to know. If they're not, we can extend Texas hospitality for awhile longer." Zack matched his mother's determined gaze.

No one had any appetite for breakfast.

Except Darcy.

Mary Lou remained quiet. Any comment she would make would be out of place considering her new position in the family. But the thought of riding out over the land enticed her. "I'll ride with Allena," she ventured. "Tom's been so busy. . ."

"And it'll be a good chance for Mary Lou to see some of the ranch," Allena offered.

Zack stared at his plate and stirred and restirred his coffee.

"Well then, how about if Mary Lou and I ride out a ways and then come back with Tex?" his mother coaxed.

"I want to ride, too," Darcy enjoined.

Zack stood and faced three determined women. His shoulders heaved and lowered with a resigned sigh. "All right. I'll have Tex ride and bring you back." Zack faced Darcy and anchored her with a stern expression. "On one condition. When I say you come back, you come back." He didn't wait for Darcy's answer and walked to the door. "Will said he'd be early, and we're leaving as soon as he comes. We'll wait for no one."

He turned and left, the solid thump of his boots across the kitchen placing an emphatic period on his conditions.

"Good morning, Mr. Zack," Hattie called as he passed through the kitchen. She received a slight nod of his head.

The blazing sun claimed the day and splayed its sultry rays over the Circle Z. Even though it was early, the pulsating heat kept the men wiping their foreheads and sent cows and horses in search of available shade.

Tom, Zack, Nelson, Smitty, and half the ranch cowboys emerged from the barn, ready to mount as neighboring rancher Will Shepard, his three sons, and four cowhands rode in to meet them. A beautiful young girl with flowing blond hair, riding a frisky, dappled-grey filly trotted toward the house and dismounted before Allena and Mary Lou. Allena made the introductions.

"I came to meet Tom's new wife," Laura said. "Ma said 'twas high time we paid our respects. She's been feelin' poorly. Says she'll never get used to hot Texas." She smiled at Mary Lou. "Ma's from Massachusetts." Laura plunked her hands on her hips. "So! You're the girl who stole my man."

Mary Lou's breath caught. She forced a sick smile. Then there had been something between Laura and Tom.

Laura laughed and shrugged. "Don't worry. He didn't love me. I knew it but hoped someday I'd grow up enough to make him notice me. You know how romantic young girls are about cowboys." She tossed her head. Golden curls tumbled over her shoulders and down her back. "Whew! I've got to get rid of this mop." She reached into her pocket for a ribbon and quickly tied the thick locks together at the nape of her neck.

Mary Lou stepped forward and offered her hand. "I'm glad to meet you Laura." How could Tom have ever resisted this beautiful girl?

Allena put an arm around Laura and gave her a squeeze. "This is my shared daughter. Will and her mother, Emily, bought the land west of ours six years after Zachary and I married. We had four boys; they had three: Matthew, Mark, and Luke. Finally Emily had this girl-child. She's been generous and shares her with me." Allena turned to Laura. "We plan on riding out a ways with the men, then come back before lunch. Want to ride along?"

"Sure," exclaimed Laura. Her eyes narrowed as she looked beyond them to the ranch house. "She goin', too?"

Darcy stood on the porch dressed in a fashionable Eastern riding habit. "Of course I'm going." She tossed her head and the feather plume on her hat waved back and forth.

Laura grinned and stated flatly. "You'll need that fan. You're going to bake in that outfit. There isn't much shade where we're goin'."

Mary Lou couldn't withhold a smile. Laura reminded her of Jenny, her dearest friend back in Kansas—outspoken, forthright, and alarmingly honest. Maybe. . .

Tex appeared with their horses in tow.

Zack helped Darcy mount. She followed him to ride with the men and squeezed her horse between Zack and Will.

Tom hung back and rode with Mary Lou, Laura, and his mother.

In great delight, Nelson sat proud in the middle of the cowboys and talked incessantly.

The morning air became stifling. Mary Lou wondered how Darcy stood the heat in her finery. She'd worn a long sleeved calico to protect her from the sun and was thankful for any small breeze, even a hot one.

An hour later, the men came to a halt. Darcy's demanding voice carried back to the other women. "But you have to take me back. I don't feel well." She jerked her elbow from Zack's hand.

It wasn't the sun that made Zack's face red. "I can't take you back. Tex will ride back with you and the others."

Darcy wailed, "But I'm sick!"

Allena rode forward. "Come, Darcy, it's an hour's ride back to the ranch. The heat is getting to me, too." Nose in the air, Darcy spoke as if to an audience. "Zack is taking me back."

Zack grabbed Darcy's reins and swung her homeward. "You're going home with Tex." His jaw muscles flexed for control. "I'm not going to argue with you." Zack softened and put his hand over hers. "Please, Darcy, if you aren't feeling well, you shouldn't be riding in this heat. This sun is much hotter than back east."

Darcy glared at Zack. Innately she sensed her surrounding audience, lifted her head and shoulders, and smiled sweetly. Her gloved hand raised and patted Zack's cheek. "I'll go, Darling." Her face wilted. "But don't stay too long. I don't feel well at all."

Zack touched her hand, turned, and rode to catch up with the men. Darcy stiffened, swung her horse, slapped the reins, and took off at a gallop.

Three surprised, concerned women turned and followed.

Shortly, Darcy slowed her steed to a trot.

"Probably so hot she's about to faint," Allena said and spurred Brown Beauty to catch up with her.

Mary Lou and Laura trotted side by side suppressing giggles.

Laura shook her head. "What Zack sees in her, I don't know."

"He loves her," Mary Lou answered simply. "Someday the right man will come into your life, and you'll understand."

"He has come."

Mary Lou slowed. "We're not close friends yet, but would you care to tell me?"

A secret grin highlighted Laura's face. "It's Nelson."

"Nelson!"

"What's wrong with Nelson?"

"Why—nothing."

Laura's smile faded. "You think the same as Mrs. Langdon. But Nelson is nineteen, and I'll be eighteen next month."

Mary Lou's heart claimed kin to this active, charming girl. "I don't think it's age as much as a mother's concern as to how Nelson would be able to provide for a wife. How could he take care of one?"

"What's wrong with a wife to take care of him? I could run a small ranch if I had to. I've grown up with seven boys, horses, longhorns, cowboys—"

"But Nelson's—"

"Crippled? That's only his body. He has a heart, and mind, and a beautiful spirit in that body. He's talented and could become a great artist. He could. . ." Laura dipped her head and tears ran free.

Mary Lou's surprise settled into admiration for this courageous, young girl who was ready to take on the whole world for the boy she loved. And here was her first real friend. *Thank You, Father. How can I help?*

Chapter 3

Tom and Zack trotted Tinder and Victor under the Circle Z arch and moved into a gallop toward Harness.

Mary Lou waved until they were out of sight, then walked slowly back to the house. The main rooms were empty. She wended her way to the kitchen.

Hattie Benson stood hunched over a pan of hot, soapy water, energetically scrubbing a pot.

"May I help?"

Hattie shook her head. "No, thank you, Miss Mary. I'm near done except for the few dishes on the dining table."

"I'll get them," Mary Lou said and returned to the kitchen with a tray full of dirty breakfast dishes.

"Put them on the side cupboard. I'll get to them shortly."

Mary Lou sensed faded blue eyes following her as she wandered around the ample kitchen. A huge fireplace dominated the outside wall. Hanging pans and kettles peppered the fireplace on both sides. A hand-hewn, smoothly scrubbed table stood solidly in the center of the room. Mary Lou rubbed her hand over it. "This looks like a good place to knead dough and make bread. As a new daughter-in-law, I don't know quite what I'm supposed to do."

Hattie paused in her scrubbing and beamed. "You get your orders from Mrs. Langdon, and you can do all the bakin' you want. It's a never-endin' job keepin' up with bread, biscuits, and pies for this bunch." She bobbed her head, a wide grin spread across her tanned face. "You're gonna make Mr. Tom a good wife. Any woman who likes cookin'll take good care of her man." She glanced around quickly and lowered her voice to a giggly hoarse whisper. "An' you got the best of the four. Mr. Tom, he's special."

"I think so, too," Mary Lou whispered back, and they laughed at their little secret. Even at short acquaintance, Mary Lou admired this plain, hard-working woman crowned with a wealth of silver gray hair gathered into a tight knob. "Thank you, Mrs. Benson."

"Mrs. Benson? Call me Hattie."

"Then you call me Mary Lou."

Hattie shook her head. "No, Ma'am. You're Miss Mary."

143

Allena entered the kitchen. "Here you are. I can see by Hattie's face you've gained her approval. How did you do it so quickly?"

"She told me she enjoyed making bread and biscuits, that's how," Hattie answered. "She asked me if it would be possible."

"Possible?" Allena raised her brows and nodded to her new daughter-in-law. "Welcomed! Everyone in this house has to keep a hand in somewhere." Allena laughed. "Hattie lets me come out and make bread once a week so I won't lose my touch.

"Mary Lou, how would you like to ride this morning? The boys never want me to ride alone. They're concerned something might happen like the horse stepping into a hole or being spooked and throw me. My husband and I had a few rounds of disagreement 'cause I thought it was a lot of nonsense. I've ridden since I was a little girl. But after a few accidents to people around here, I decided I'd do what he asked."

Mary Lou nodded. "My pa was an excellent horseman, but one night when he was riding the line, Morgan threw him, and he never rode a horse again. It changed our whole life. Yes, I'd love to ride out with you."

Allena linked arms with Mary Lou and called back over her shoulder, "Pack us a couple biscuits and some fruit, Hattie. My new daughter-in-law and I are going on a picnic!"

A dress rustled in the doorway. Darcy drooped against the frame like a pale, lost child.

"Would you like to ride with us, Darcy?" Allena asked. Darcy hesitated, then agreed.

Allena told Hattie to pack another biscuit. She turned to Darcy. "Get ready as soon as you can, Dear. We want to ride out and get back before it gets too hot."

Tex brought Dulcie, Allena's Brown Beauty, and a chestnut filly named Buttons and tied them to the hitching post.

Mary Lou and Allena, ready to ride, stayed in the house out of the rising heat and waited for Darcy.

After ten minutes, Allena and Mary Lou walked back to Zack and Darcy's room and knocked. No answer. After another unanswered knock, Allena opened the door.

Darcy lay half-dressed on the bed. The room reeked. Both women rushed forward.

"Ohhh," moaned Darcy. "I'm sick again. Hattie must be putting something in the food."

Allena rushed to the basin and flinched. She turned to Darcy and smiled. "Darcy—are you with child?"

Darcy sat up with a jolt. "Oh, I hope not."

"You hope not?" Allena's smile faded into a frown. "Does Zack know?"

Darcy's glazed eyes flashed. "It's Zack's fault. I don't want a baby, he does." Darcy looked down at her stomach. "I can't have a baby. It'll ruin my figure!" Suddenly, Darcy leaped from the bed and fled to the basin.

Shocked, Mary Lou stared at her. *How can she say such a thing? Not want a baby?* Mary Lou looked forward to the time when she and Tom—

"Mary Lou, please go tell Hattie to get a couple of buckets of hot, soapy water and bring them here. I must clean this room."

With Hattie in tow, Mary Lou returned, each carrying a bunch of cleaning rags and steaming buckets filled to the brim.

Allena's face was white, her lips tense.

Darcy moaned and cried on the bed.

The three women scrubbed and cleaned. When they finished, Hattie fetched a pail of fresh water and a clean basin.

Allena returned to the bed. "Darcy, if you get sick, do it in the bucket, not the basin."

Darcy wailed louder.

"Do you hear what I'm saying, Darcy?"

Darcy sat up in bed, her face twisted with rage. "I hear you. But I'm not having a baby!"

"Yes, you are, Darcy." Allena's voice sounded strained but stern. "This planted child not only belongs to you, it belongs to our family. I don't want to ever again hear you say you don't want it. Children are a gift, a heritage from the Lord. They are God's creation in His hands until they are born into ours. Like it or not, you happen to be carrying my first grandchild!" Allena moistened a cloth and mopped Darcy's sodden face.

Darcy shoved her hand away, her eyes snapping defiance. "Your first grandchild will ruin me and rob me. I'll never be the same again." She turned her back on Allena, buried her face in the pillow, and wailed.

Mary Lou listened in disbelief. Why was Darcy so angry? All the women she'd ever known rejoiced at the coming of a baby. At home in Venture, their neighbors, the Wimbleys, had ten children, and Henrietta joyously anticipated holding each new son or daughter in her arms. Her big heart and loving arms even gathered in Jenny and Matthew when she and Big Jon found a wrecked wagon, a bewildered little girl, and a crying six-month-old boy beside dead parents. Poor Darcy. She was sick and not thinking straight. She would feel differently after the sick days were past and the baby was born. Babies had a way of changing people.

The three women stepped into the hall. Allena closed the door, her face drained of color, her eyes brimming with tears.

What an awful thing for a mother to hear, Mary Lou thought.

"Do you still want to go for a short ride?" Allena asked. "We'll eliminate the picnic. I could use some fresh air."

Mary Lou nodded.

It felt good to be on Dulcie's back. For the first mile they ambled in a slow walk. Neither said a word. The persistent sun climbed the steps of the day, warming it considerably. Half an hour later, they dismounted to rest beside a small stream in the shade of a clump of beech trees.

Seated with her back braced against a tree, Allena swung to Mary Lou. "How do you feel about having a baby?"

Mary Lou leaned and touched Allena's arm. "I'll be delighted, and so will Tom."

Allena heaved a big sigh. "I thought so." Her gaze traveled the wide expanse of land before them. "This week has certainly been enlightening. First I hear I'm being robbed of my land by my own son, then my daughter-in-law tells me she rejects my first grandchild." Allena looked lovingly at Mary Lou. "I want you to know I'm thankful Tom picked a Christian wife. It looks like I'm going to need some prayer help."

Quite an admission from a strong woman, Mary Lou thought. "Mama said our strength comes from nothing within ourselves, but from the Lord."

"You'll have to tell me more about your mama. She sounds like my kind of woman." Allena laid her head back against the tree trunk and closed her eyes.

Mary Lou warmed at the thought of Mama. "She loved the Lord and He ruled her whole life," she began. "I remember Mama reading her Bible aloud to me. Every morning and evening we sat on her porch and she told and read me stories about Adam and Eve, Abraham, baby Moses, boy Samuel, and baby Jesus." Mary Lou ached in longing memory. "When Mama read the Bible, it came alive. We used to bathe and wash our hair in the stream near our cabin." She laughed. "I remember hiding behind a bush that hung out over the water, pretending I was Miriam watching baby Moses floating in his basket."

A hot breeze rustled the beech leaves overhead, and they danced a flickering ballet across the two women.

Mary Lou glanced at Allena. She sat motionless, her face relaxed. The younger woman continued. "It was on Mama's porch, at her knee, that I accepted Jesus as my Savior. I think I was about five." A press of tears checked more words.

The resting woman beside her stirred, opened her eyes, and smiled at Mary Lou. "You had a good mother." She studied Mary Lou's face for a long moment. "Do you think we could spend some time in prayer early every morning?"

Mary Lou's heart swelled with gladness. She and Mama had read Scripture and prayed every morning after Pa left for the store. "Yes, I'd like that. Mama and I. . ." The tears refused to be contained. Allena gathered Mary Lou into her arms. Young and old clung together and wept—one for a lost life and one for a life to come.

On their way back to the ranch, the two women rode silently, emotions close to the surface. The horses, sensing the release of a tight hand on the reins, headed for home and shade.

Tex came from the barn and took the horses, and the women walked leisurely to the house. Two men slowed to a trot as they rode under the Circle Z arch.

Allena paused and raised her hand to shade her eyes. "It's Doug," she exclaimed. As they drew closer she called, "Did you see Zack and Tom? They went into Harness this morning."

Doug shook his head. Both men dismounted. "We didn't come that way. We came from Abilene."

Allena frowned. "I didn't know you'd gone to Abilene."

Doug laughed and turned to his friend. "My mother still thinks I'm a little boy who has to ask his mama to come and go."

So this was Mary Lou's elusive brother-in-law. He reminded her of Mac Ludden, the owner of the saloon in Venture, whom Pa called a dandy. Dressed all in black, Doug absently fingered a golden watch fob draped across a fancy satin embroidered vest. He was handsome, but not nearly as comely as Tom or Zack. He resembled Zack, but his jaw hung loosely, separated from the rest of his face by a thin-trimmed mustache underlining a sharp nose and shifty, penetrating eyes that rang alarm signals in Mary Lou.

"Mother," Doug said sweetly and placed a kiss on her forehead. "This is Kenneth Dillard from Boston, who's interested in seeing what the wild, wild West looks like."

The dark, handsome stranger with a boyish face tucked the map he carried into his pocket, stepped forward, and with all the suavity of a gentleman, lifted Allena's fingers to his lips. "My pleasure, Madam."

Allena put her arm around Mary Lou. "Doug and Mr. Dillard, this is Mary Lou Langdon—"

"Mary Lou Langdon?" Doug's eyes widened in surprise.

"Yes, Tom's wife."

A smirk crossed Doug's face. He stepped forward quickly, reached for Mary Lou's hand, and captured her gaze. "So my little brother has grown up enough to take himself a wife." He bent his head. His lips brushed and lingered over her fingers, and he tightened his grip as she pulled her hand away. He turned to Kenneth. "My new sister-in-law from—uh—what's the

147

name of your town?"

"Venture, Kansas."

"Oh yes, east of Abilene, I believe."

"No, Sir, southwest."

Doug smirked at Kenneth. "Can you imagine my brother keeping her a secret?" He raised his brows and nodded approval. "No wonder he never said a word."

Mr. Dillard bowed over Mary Lou's hand and barely touched it to his lips. "Yes, I can. Mrs. Langdon, my pleasure," he said and stepped back beside Doug.

"Let's get inside out of this heat." Allena took Mr. Dillard's arm and Doug anchored Mary Lou's hand into the crook of his arm.

"So you're a Kansas girl. You have a sister or two, I hope."

"No, I'm sorry to say."

"So am I." Doug patted her hand.

Mary Lou's stomach churned.

"Where in Boston do you live, Mr. Dillard?" Allena asked as they settled in the parlor. "My oldest son, Zack, married a girl from Boston."

"Really? I'll be happy to meet her."

Allena turned to Mary Lou with a knowing glance. "Would you please see if Darcy is able to receive visitors?"

"Darcy?" Mr. Dillard sat up. "Could that be Darcy Whitney? I know a Thomas Whitney family in Boston. Mr. Whitney is a barrister."

Doug laughed. "Wha-da-ya-know."

Allena nodded to Mary Lou. "Tell Darcy that Mr. Kenneth Dillard is here."

Mary Lou knocked on Darcy's door. "Darcy?" No answer. Perhaps she was asleep. Mary Lou quietly opened the door.

Darcy spun from the window. Her face was swollen and red, and her hair hung in disarray. "What do you want?"

"Doug brought a visitor from Boston. He thinks he knows you."

"Boston!" Darcy brightened. "What's his name?" she demanded.

"Kenneth Dillard."

"Kenneth? Kenneth Dillard! I don't believe it." Darcy's face switched from despair to delight. "What on earth could he be doing in this god-forsaken place?" As if on wings, she flew from one wardrobe to another, grabbed dress after dress, draped them over her front, appraised her image in the standing oval mirror, and tossed them on the bed. "None of them fits anymore." Her hands flew to her hair. "Oh, what will I do with my hair?" Finally, she threw a dress on the bed and turned to Mary Lou. "Help me get dressed," she commanded and opened a bureau drawer for brush and combs.

"No!" Darcy grabbed Mary Lou's arm and shoved her to the door. "Go out and tell Kenneth I'll be there presently, then come back and help me." Darcy opened the door and shoved Mary Lou into the hall.

Mary Lou stood incensed. Darcy was treating her like a maid! Who did she think she was? Mary Lou walked briskly to the main room. *If she thinks I'm coming back, let her dress herself. I'm not going back!*

In the main room, Kenneth Dillard stood holding his lapels, gazing enthralled at the paintings on the wall. "Who painted these?"

"My youngest son, Nelson," Allena said proudly.

"How old is your son?"

"He'll be nineteen in a month."

"So young! He has great feeling for depth and perspective. I'd like to meet that young man if it's possible."

"Of course." Allena looked away from the painting when Mary Lou entered. "Is Darcy coming?"

"Yes. She was resting and will need a little time to make herself presentable. I'm going back to help her." Mary Lou couldn't believe those last words came out of her mouth.

Allena nodded her blessing to Mary Lou. "Mr. Dillard and I are going to Nelson's room to see his paintings." She led the way, chattering as they walked.

"He keeps everything in his bedroom except what hangs on our walls, which we change every so often. His room is on the end corner, so he has window lighting from two directions. Nelson will be pleased to meet you. It's a rarity around here to find someone interested in talking about paintings." Allena's voice faded as she and Mr. Dillard walked to the end of the hall into Nelson's room.

On her way back to Darcy, Mary Lou realized she hadn't seen Nelson's roomful of paintings and promised herself to do it in the morning.

Mary Lou knocked and then opened Darcy's door. She was surprised to find that Darcy had completely dressed and was combing her hair with shaking hands. Mary Lou took over. Darcy had wavy hair, soft and fine as silk. *She's beautiful,* Mary Lou thought. *Too bad it's only on the outside.*

Ten minutes later, the young women were on their way back to the main room. Before entering, Darcy paused, patted her hair, pinched her cheeks, pulled herself to fullest height, swept Mary Lou aside, and made a smiling entrance, hands extended. "My dear Kenneth, how delightful. . .to see. . ."

The room was empty.

Darcy spun to Mary Lou, her face a mask of fury. "What kind of trick. . ." Her eyes flashed embarrassment and bored holes of hate through Mary Lou.

If Darcy's behavior hadn't been so shocking, Mary Lou would have laughed. But the obvious debilitating effect the vacant room produced also revealed a fresh glimpse of her sister-in-law. Darcy was afraid. In this strange new land, nothing was familiar. The elegant lady she'd been trained to be felt out of place in Texas. Mary Lou had the advantage. Some things were different, but much was familiar. She'd been born a pioneer girl.

Mary Lou's heart begged forgiveness. *I wonder how I'd feel in Boston.* She imagined the raised brows that would greet her appearance in calico. *I'd probably be uncomfortable in Darcy's finery and act like a simpleton and say all the wrong words. Poor Darcy is insecure, homesick, afraid, and going to have her first baby.*

Love tugged open Mary Lou's heart to see the lovely girl who had yet to realize what it meant to be a woman instead of a clothes horse. Was it possible for them to someday be friends in spite of everything? *Lord, I'm going to need lots of help with this one,* Mary Lou prayed.

Nelson's excited chatter and Allena's laughter joined by Mr. Dillard floated up the hall as Darcy and Mary Lou came out of the main room.

Darcy was caught off guard only a second. Her whole demeanor changed. "Kenneth!" she called. "How wonderful to see you." She floated down the hall, a vision of tulle and chiffon, hands outstretched.

150

Chapter 4

Mary Lou formed the last loaf of dough, put it in a tin, and covered the eight pans with flannel cloth. Making bread was a satisfying job. She didn't know why; some days the need was an insatiable tyrant.

Mama had always made bread reverently. "It's the staff of life," she used to say. "It shows every Christian his need of Jesus, the Bread of Life for the believer."

Allena had read that verse during their devotion time that morning, as their weekly memory verse. When breakfast was over, Mary Lou and her mother-in-law moved into the main room, read God's Word, discussed the passage, and then finished with prayer for their family, the ranch, their neighbors, and even for the state of Texas. Mary Lou often drew in Kansas and her family back home.

Outside, Hattie passed by the kitchen window, her arms full of dirty clothes. Wash day. She spent a day each week scrubbing smelly barn pants and sweaty shirts for the cowboys. They each gladly paid her a dollar a week.

Mary Lou hurried to the door. "May I help?"

"Nope, this is my job unless you want to carry some water."

Mary Lou hauled buckets and buckets of water until the tubs were full.

Hattie then shooed her away. "Nelson asked about you. Wants you to look at the new picture he painted."

Good. Mary Lou wanted to see it.

Nelson's wheelchair stood outside his door. Mary Lou knocked.

"Come in," Nelson called and greeted her with a wide smile. Other than a low cot and a washstand, the room had no semblance of a bedroom. Canvases and pictures were everywhere, hanging on the walls or stacked against them. No wonder his wheelchair had to stay outside. In a cleared area by the window, Nelson sat on a stool in front of a large easel and canvas, his pencil poised over the sketch he was working on.

"Mind if I visit and watch you paint?"

Nelson grinned broadly. "I hoped you'd come and tell me about the prairie in Kansas. Tom says it's beautiful and would make great paintings."

"It would." Mary Lou's mind formed a picture of their cabin in Kansas, surrounded by a broad sweep of ever-swaying prairie grass. "I love the space and openness and the feeling it gives of everything being endless. There's always a breeze blowing. Sometimes it's hot, but it still cools and cleans the air."

"It's like that here," Nelson said.

"Yes, but different. The prairie grass shimmers in the heat, and when the wind blows, the prairie resembles ocean waves rolling in from the sea." Mary Lou laughed. "Tom told me you were tired of painting tumbleweeds."

She turned to the profusion of canvases elbowing for space. She pointed to one. "They might be boring to you, but these tumbleweeds look exactly like the ones I see rolling around the ranch." Mary Lou picked her way, then stooped to a stack leaning against the wall. "Do you mind?" she asked.

Nelson grinned and shook his head.

She thumbed through them and pulled one out. "Nelson, is this Diamond?"

Nelson nodded. "Does it look like him?"

"Look like him! We'd better run and get a saddle or he'll take off without us. Your father would be proud of this. Why isn't it hanging somewhere?"

Nelson rose and grabbed his crutches. In the opposite corner, he brought out canvas after canvas of an imposing man who looked like Zack. "This is my father," he said. His face glowed with pride.

Mary Lou nodded. "He and Zack do look alike."

"But Father was different. He made me feel—whole." Nelson tightened his lip and quickly turned to another stack of pictures, all of his father.

What feeling! It wouldn't have surprised Mary Lou if her father-in-law had spoken. "Your father must have been an extraordinary man."

"He was." Nelson choked up and restacked pictures.

Mary Lou bent to help him. "I know how you feel," she said softly. "I lost my mama." Their eyes met and laid bare the depth of their common suffering.

Nelson returned to his stool.

Mary Lou walked up behind him, hesitated a moment, then dared to put her arms around him. Here was the sensitive, caring brother she'd always longed for. Her heart raised in praise of God's constant provision for her.

Nelson sat still and didn't move until Mary Lou walked in front of him. He blinked tears that moistened his eyes but his mouth was smiling. He ducked his head. "Thank you, Mary Lou."

She spent an hour helping Nelson see Kansas as she had seen it. Suddenly, a thought struck her. "Have you ever thought of selling any of your paintings? I'm sure other people would find them as exciting as I do."

Nelson grinned. "That's what Mr. Dillard said." He shrugged. "But who'd want them? People around here see what I paint all the time. They don't want it hanging on their walls."

"Who knows. Texas people might like what's outside enough to enjoy it on the inside. Maybe the general store in Harness could sell a few. Tom and I plan to go back to Kansas for a visit next year. We could take a few and put them in Father's store and even take some to Abilene. There are lots of people there. How do you know if you don't try?"

A new light twinkled in Nelson's eyes, a new purpose took root.

Mary Lou left him enthusiastically back at work on his sketch. She felt restless so she walked to the corral. Dulcie nodded her head, tossing a welcome with her mane.

"Good morning, Friend. How would you like to ride?"

Dulcie whinnied and pranced. Mary Lou looked toward the barn. Tom knelt on the roof, hammering. Ladders leaned against the sides, and two cowboys climbed up and down like agile prairie dogs, carrying boards. She waved at Tom.

He wiped his face on his sleeve, waved, and immediately went back to work. Mary Lou had her answer. He was too busy to ride.

Dulcie whinnied and pranced.

"Sorry, dear girl, but you know the rules. Women don't ride alone in Texas. Between the Mexicans, Indians, and animals, Tom says it's too dangerous." Mary Lou rubbed Dulcie's face and soft nose. "Now if we were back in Kansas—"

"Mary Lou!"

Mary Lou turned toward the call.

Allena stood on the porch and motioned her back to the house.

As Mary Lou neared she saw Allena's troubled face.

"Have you seen Darcy this morning?"

Mary Lou shook her head. "I was with Nelson. Why?"

"I can't find her." Allena pursed her lips and shook her head. "I thought she was in her room, but she's not."

"She has to be here somewhere," Mary Lou said reassuringly. "Don't worry, we'll find her."

They didn't. By the time they'd searched the house and surrounding area, it was obvious Darcy had disappeared.

"Maybe she went with Zack to town this morning," Mary Lou suggested.

"Surely they would have told me." In sudden anguish Allena looked toward the corral. "Do you think that silly girl. . . ?" She ran toward the stables and hailed Tex.

Tex nodded. "Yes, Ma'am." She came this morning and told me to saddle her up a horse. I wondered but. . ." Tex shrugged his shoulders.

Allena paled. "When? What time?"

"About nine."

Allena swung toward the barn, headed for the tack room and told Tex to get their horses. Halfway there, she stopped and shaded her eyes. A horse galloped hard across the field.

"The saddle's empty!" Mary Lou cried.

Allena called Tex and pointed. "Is that the horse you saddled for Miss Darcy?"

Tex squinted and nodded. "Yes, Ma'am, that's the one."

Allena ran to the barn and told Tom. The three men scrambled down from the roof, saddled, and galloped off. Tex joined them.

Allena watched them go, shaking her head. "That girl knew she shouldn't ride alone. She's been told often enough. Sometimes I wonder what kind of upbringing she had. She does anything she pleases when Zack isn't here!"

Allena's sharp voice surprised Mary Lou. It was the first time she'd seen her mother-in-law angry. Allena had cried out in anger, but her face was pained in anguish. *Whatever possessed Darcy to do such a foolish thing? And with child! Come to think of it, nothing was said at dinner last night.* Allena, Hattie, and Mary Lou had agreed to say nothing of their discovery until Darcy had told Zack. Surely if Zack had known, he'd have announced it at supper. Could it be that Darcy hadn't told him and had ridden out with the intention of. . . ?

No. She wouldn't! But yesterday, Darcy had been so emphatic about not wanting. . . Mary Lou shook her head. Her gaze connected with Allena's. Were Allena's thoughts mirrors of her own? Would Darcy do something dangerous in hopes that the horse might slip, fall, or. . . No. She wouldn't think that of Darcy.

As soon as the men left, Allena busied with preparations to care for Darcy when she came home.

Hattie got a tub of boiling water ready. It seemed Hattie got a tub of boiling water ready for everything.

Suddenly, Allena grabbed Hattie's and Mary Lou's arms. "We must pray," she said.

The three women sank to their knees in silence, heads bowed.

Softly, Allena began to pray aloud. "Father, my child is out there alone. . . ."

Mary Lou opened her eyes and looked up at Allena. *My child.* Regardless of how Darcy acted, Allena accepted her as her child. Humbled, Mary Lou asked God's forgiveness for the thoughts she harbored of a spoiled, selfish, rude girl who seemed to consider no one but herself.

Allena's voice faded back in. "But she doesn't know You yet, Lord. Give us time to love her enough so she feels it and recognizes she is hurting herself more than anyone else. Oh, God, keep her safe. Forgive me for my selfishness in thinking only of the baby she carries. Let no harm come to either of them. Thank you, Father. In Jesus' name, Amen."

After a momentary pause, Hattie nodded. "Thy will be done."

The morning dragged on interminably. No one could concentrate. Finally, Allena took a stool and sat on the shady side of the house facing the direction the men left, furiously knitting a sock. Mary Lou sat beside her, checked clothes, mended, and sewed buttons where they were missing. Hattie rattled around in the kitchen, coming out periodically to peer, hand over eyes, into the distance.

No one said much, but Mary Lou felt surrounded by ascending prayer. *Foolish, foolish girl,* her mind repeated. But hadn't she had the same idea that morning? She'd yearned to saddle Dulcie and ride out into the wide spaces that stretched before her to enjoy the exhilarating feeling of flying with the wind. Mary Lou thanked God she hadn't.

Or had God given her the idea to ride? Like the morning of her wedding, when the urge to ride sent her to the cottonwoods and Tom was there. He had said he'd felt compelled to ride there, too. She'd been awed at what he said. "Now I know God answers prayers." Had this been God's guiding? Maybe if Mary Lou had satisfied her yearning this morning, she'd have sighted Darcy or found her.

No. Mama had always said that two wrongs never made a right. In the area of Kansas where Mary Lou had grown up, it had been comparatively safe to ride alone, but she seldom had. Her father, mother, Jenny, Aunt Nelda, or Glenn usually had accompanied her.

Here in Texas, only the bravest rode alone. Even though it seemed peaceful, marauders, without warning, regularly descended to raid and plunder. No, she had to believe she'd done the right thing. Anyway, God had Darcy in His hands whether she accepted Him as Lord or not. *What was the verse Mama always repeated? "We love Him because He first loved us"* (1 John 4:19). *Yes, God loves Darcy.*

Mary Lou closed her eyes. *Keep her safe, Father. Let no harm come to the baby. You know if Allena lost her first grandchild, it would break her heart. You know what it is to lose a son. . . .*

"Here they come!" Nelson shouted. He dropped his pencil, tucked his crutches under his arms, and moved amazingly fast across the yard.

Everyone followed and ran toward the cloud of dust and horses. Had they found her?

Tom had Darcy in his arms. Allena and Hattie caught her as Tom slid her off the saddle.

Darcy, her face smudged with dirt, was pale and semi-conscious. She whimpered, opened her eyes, slid her arms around Allena's neck, and sighed.

Tom dismounted and carried Darcy to her bedroom.

She opened her eyes and stared up at Tom. "Oh, Tom, I love you," she said, fainting in his arms.

Mary Lou's heart stopped. *I love you?* She immediately chided herself. She loved him as a brother, of course. It was Darcy's way of saying thank you. She was shaken and didn't know what she was saying.

Allena shooed everyone out of the bedroom except Hattie. "This bedroom won't hold us all. Hattie and I will find out if she's hurt and let you know."

Mary Lou felt a tinge of rejection, but as Mama always had declared, sometimes too many are no help at all. She went to find Tom.

At the barn, he stood unsaddling Tinder.

"Where did you find her?"

"About three miles south of the bog. We saw horse tracks go around the bog, so we followed them to the top of the knoll. They stopped there, then turned and went back. We found Darcy at the bottom. She either fell from her horse or the horse slipped and threw her and she rolled down. She was scared, moaning, and crying when we found her. I don't think she's hurt. She rode home in no noticeable pain."

Mary Lou shook her head. "I hope it didn't hurt the baby."

Tom swung and stared with his mouth open. "What baby?"

Mary Lou could have bitten her tongue. Now she had to tell Tom. "Yesterday, we found Darcy sick, and Mother suspects she's with child. But don't say anything yet. We don't know whether Zack knows, and Darcy should be the one to tell him."

Tom nodded. He turned back to Tinder and methodically slid off the saddle, swung it over the side of the stall, removed the saddle blanket, and absently rubbed Tinder's back. Without looking at her, he said, "Mary Lou, will you promise me something?"

"Anything, Tom."

"When you're with child, will you please tell me first?"

Mary Lou smiled and slid between Tom and Tinder. Their eyes met and held. "Mr. Langdon, you'll be the first to know." His arms encircled her, and he drew her close and kissed her tenderly. Arms around each other, they walked outside.

The men had already climbed back on the roof. Tom went up the ladder and joined them.

Mary Lou paced back and forth in front of Darcy's bedroom door. Periodically, Darcy cried out and moaned. Allena's and Hattie's voices were muted, so Mary Lou heard little.

Finally the door opened and Hattie came out.

"Is she all right?" Mary Lou asked.

"Don't seem to be hurt much, no bones broken, just scrapes, bumps, and bruises. That's all we can see."

"The baby?"

Hattie shrugged her shoulders. "Allena's been listening to see if she can hear anything."

If that baby dies, part of Allena will die with it. Dear Jesus, please. . .

Mary Lou, to calm her fears, joined Hattie in the kitchen to help with dinner. Tom came in and said he'd sent Tex to Harness for Zack.

When Allena entered the kitchen, her brows were knit with worry. "Mary Lou, would you sit with Darcy, please? I think she's asleep."

Mary Lou tiptoed into the bedroom, quietly pulled up a chair, and sat down. Darcy's face was relaxed from her usual expression of antagonism. Even with bruises and scratches, she looked beautiful. Her luxurious chestnut hair trailed across the pillow, highlighting flushed cheeks that cupped like soft rose petals on a fragile doll.

The door opened quietly. Tom peeked in, entered slowly, and stooped beside Mary Lou's chair. "She all right?" he whispered.

Mary Lou nodded. "Your mother says she couldn't find anything wrong except scrapes and bruises."

Darcy stirred and opened her eyes. "Tom?"

Tom patted Darcy's hand. "You're home, Darcy. Everything's going to be all right."

"Thank you," she said weakly. "I prayed you'd come."

Darcy had prayed Tom would come? Maybe there was hope for her yet. Then a disturbing thought gnawed at Mary Lou: Why hadn't Darcy prayed for Zack?

Tom patted Darcy's hand, kissed Mary Lou on the cheek, mouthed good-bye, and left quietly.

When Mary Lou turned back to Darcy, the young woman was staring at her.

"I'm glad you're safe and not hurt, Darcy. We were all very worried about you."

"You were?" A strange look crossed Darcy's face and relaxed into a smile.

Mary Lou patted Darcy's hand. "Yes, and we hoped nothing would happen to the baby."

Darcy withdrew her hand immediately. Her sweet smile dissolved into her usual petulant expression. "Of course," she stated flatly. "Nothing must happen to the baby." She turned and squeezed away tears that flooded her long lashes. "Not Allena's first grandchild!"

Mary Lou saw the tears and immediately regretted her reference to the baby. Her heart sank. She'd lost her. For a moment, Darcy had opened up an opportunity to talk, but Mary Lou had spoiled it. Could it be Darcy felt no one liked her, or that she was miserably homesick? How terrible that would be! Once again, Mary Lou vowed to try to befriend the beautiful, lonesome, unhappy girl.

Chapter 5

Victor's hooves pounded a dust storm. Zack leaned as he rode through the Circle Z arch to the ranch house, dropped to the ground, and ran through the front door, wild-eyed and breathless. "Where is she?"

Allena motioned with her hand. "She's—"

He brushed past his mother and Mary Lou, who both hurried down the hall behind him.

"Zack! She's all right. Shook up and bruised a bit, but not hurt."

He opened the bedroom door, rushed in, sat on the side of the bed, and reached for Darcy's hand. "Darling, it's me. Are you all right? Do you hurt anywhere?" He gently gathered her into his arms.

Darcy moaned, opened her eyes, let out a cry, and circled her arms tightly around Zack's neck.

Zack stroked her hair and cradled her like a baby. "It's all right. Doctor Mike will be here shortly." Darcy's eyes widened. "Doctor? I don't need a doctor." She sat up, anxiety dancing from one blue eye to the other.

"I didn't know how bad you were hurt or whether you'd broken any bones. I wasn't taking any chances, Darling."

"But. . . ," Darcy sputtered.

Tom came in, followed by Dr. Mike. The doctor moved briskly to his patient's side, took her hand, and fingered her pulse.

Zack stood and stepped back.

Dr. Mike smiled. "Well, young lady, I see you haven't been in Texas long enough to know you're supposed to stay on the back of the horse to ride." He laughed at his little joke.

No one else did.

He turned to the worried faces surrounding him and shooed them toward the door. "You can be sure I'll take good care of my patient. Wait outside, please."

Zack moved to the foot of the bed.

Holding Darcy's limp wrist, Dr. Mike stared at Zack. "That means you, too."

Zack hesitated, casting a despairing look at Darcy.

Dr. Mike straightened up and turned a beady eye on Zack. "And close

159

the door behind you."

Zack left.

Everyone stood in the hall and leaned against its walls.

"We could all have coffee," Allena suggested.

Heads shook no.

Zack's gaze searched his family. "How did it happen?"

No one replied.

Zack straightened. "Is something wrong? Somebody say something!"

Allena spoke. "Darcy was out riding—"

"Who with?"

"She went out alone."

"Alone!" Zack's eyes blazed. "Who saddled her horse?"

"Tex."

Zack swung and started down the hall.

Tom jumped and grabbed his arm. "Whoa! You can't blame Tex. Darcy has a way of getting. . ." Tom hesitated, obviously uncomfortable.

"Getting her own way," Zack finished. "Nobody knows that better than I do. But why didn't somebody stop her?"

Allena moved to Zack's side and placed a steadying hand on his shoulder. "None of us knew she was gone. No one saw her go out. Around lunch time we missed her. Mary Lou and I looked everywhere. We finally asked Tex if he'd seen her. He said she had insisted he saddle her a horse. We were just about saddled up to ride out and find her when Buttons came home empty. So Tom, Tex, and Bart rode out and followed the trail."

Tom picked up the story. "That good rain we had last night marked us a clear trail to Bog Hollow. The tracks walked along the edge, danced around, turned, and headed back home. We figured something must have spooked or tripped the horse and knocked Darcy off. We followed marks where she rolled down to the edge of the bog. Thank God a log stopped her and kept her from rolling into the mire. That's where we found her, lying against the log in tears, afraid to move. When I carried her home on Tinder, she didn't seem hurt."

The bedroom door opened. Dr. Mike came out smiling and shook Zack's hand.

Everyone came to attention.

"Your wife is fine. A few bumps and scrapes, but no broken bones. And I don't think the baby is harmed."

Zack's eyes widened and his mouth fell open. "Baby? What baby?"

"You didn't know? Your wife's about three months in the family way."

For the first time in his life, Zack was speechless.

Dr. Mike grinned, grabbed Zack's hand again, and pumped it briskly.

"Congratulations! Hope it's a fine boy to carry on the Langdon name."

Surprised shock dissolved into relief. A silly grin spread across Zack's face and turned on a twinkle in his eyes. "Well, wha-da-ya-know!" Zack's glazed stare moved from one family member to another. "I'm going to be a father!" he shouted and bolted through the bedroom door.

His family's happy smiles were tinged with guilt. Zack had been the last to know.

Hattie appeared at the end of the hall. "Mrs. Langdon, dinner's ready."

"Thank you, Hattie." Allena turned to Dr. Mike. "Won't you join us before you go? You have to eat. Might as well fill up at our table with us."

Dr. Mike joyfully accepted, settled himself before a heaping plate of steak, potatoes, and vegetables, and monopolized the conversation between mouthfuls, catching everyone up on the comings and goings of his territory.

"The Peabodys down at the old Wilson place are leaving. Henry never was cut out for ranching in the first place. He never liked taking care of animals—said he'd rather hunt and eat them." The doctor shoveled a mound of potatoes into his mouth. "If truth were known, I think he's afraid of them." He laughed. "Without his spunky little wife and their boys, Peabody would never have lasted this long."

Doc accepted another helping of steak and potatoes. "Too bad. Nice family. Hate to lose them. I guess Henry and Agatha are going back East, but the boys want to stay here and hire on as cowboys. All they have to do is talk their mother into it. Fred is sixteen and George is fourteen, good training age."

Allena looked at Tom. "Think we could use a couple more? I like Agatha. She's a strong, godly woman and raised those boys right. I think she'd feel better if they were settled into a job with some neighbors she knew."

Tom glanced at Zack, who nodded. "If you see them, Doc, tell them to come around," Zack said.

"I'll do that." Dr. Mike finished off his second piece of Hattie's shoofly pie and rose, patting his stomach and bowing to Allena. "Madam, it's a rare treat to have the chance to enjoy dinner with such lovely ladies."

Hattie entered with another piece of pie.

Dr. Mike held up his hand and bowed to her. "Madam, you do me honor, but my stomach objects. I compliment you. It's the best shoofly pie I've eaten, bar none."

Hattie nodded, shyly smiled, and carried the pie back to the kitchen.

"Well, I must be on my way. I suppose somebody's out trying to find me," Dr. Mike said.

Everyone stood. The men walked out with Dr. Mike.

Darcy rose, hurried to Zack, grabbed his hand, and marched out alongside him, head held high.

Silence hung heavy.

Allena looked at Hattie and Mary Lou. "Let's forget we knew and congratulate Zack as if we just heard the news."

Both nodded, and Mary Lou renewed within her promise that she would tell Tom first when the time came.

Allena returned to the table and beckoned Hattie in to clear it.

"I must say I'm concerned about Darcy. The way she smothers Zack is unnatural."

Mary Lou poured them each a cup of coffee and sat down beside Allena. "Maybe she's feels. . .uh. . .that he's the only one who loves her."

Allena's raised brows asked a question.

Mary Lou went on. "I think she feels the family hasn't accepted her."

"That's not true. I've accepted her, but she pushes me away. I know part of it is that she doesn't want to be here. She's unhappy that Zack refused her father and came back home to set up his law practice. Her heart and mind are still in Boston. She misses the social life.

"Life is so different here. Before you came, we attended Betsy Travis's wedding at the ranch east of us. I'm afraid Darcy looked more like a bride than the bride. She made people uncomfortable, and she was miserable. I've tried to treat her the same as I'd treat my own daughter if I had one, but she doesn't make it easy." Allena thoughtfully sipped her coffee. "I love her because Zack loves her. He sees a loveliness in her we haven't found yet."

"Mama always said there's good in everyone, but sometimes we have to look awfully hard to find it." Mary Lou studied Allena for a moment. Dare she be honest? She decided to chance it. "When I sat with Darcy after her accident and told her we were all worried about her, she seemed surprised and pleased. Then I mentioned we were grateful nothing happened to the baby, and she drew back into herself again. I wonder if she feels we're only concerned about the baby, not her."

Allena sat staring into her coffee cup.

Mary Lou continued. "You think maybe she feels all alone with Zack gone so much? I know I miss Tom when the work keeps him going twelve hours a day."

"Could be," Allena mused. "I've asked Darcy to do things with me, but she refuses and bluntly comments that at home, they have servants to take care of such things."

Mary Lou laughed and confessed to bristling at some of Darcy's caustic remarks. "I was thinking, it's easier for me than Darcy. Much that I do here is similar to what I've always done back home. From her comments, she's led a pampered life. It's not her fault her family lived in a big house with servants. She's been deprived of the chance to learn what we pioneer girls take for granted." Mary Lou paused to catch and assemble the jumble of thoughts tumbling in her head. "I wonder."

"Wonder? About what?"

"How I can pull Darcy into the family. I'm her age. I'm new in the family. I didn't know what a daughter-in-law was supposed to do until I asked Hattie if I could make bread." Mary Lou's new thoughts intrigued her. She faced Allena. "Mother, do you suppose I could teach Darcy to make bread?"

Allena suppressed a smile and nodded. "All you can do is try. You have my blessing."

Mary Lou began the next morning, after devotions. Darcy, as usual, left the breakfast table with Zack and walked with him to the barn to get Victor and wave him off. Most of the time, she returned to her room. Sometimes though, she walked to the wooden bench under the mesquite trees and sat and stared into the distance. This morning, Mary Lou watched her slowly walk into the house and return to her room.

Mary Lou waited for awhile, then knocked on Darcy's door.

"Who is it?"

"Mary Lou."

No answer.

Mary Lou was about to turn away when the door slowly opened. Darcy's blank face perused her sister-in-law. "What do you want?"

"I just wondered how you felt this morning."

Darcy eyed her with suspicion. "I'm all right, considering."

If I don't step in now, the door will be closed tighter the next time, Mary Lou thought. "Since we're both newcomers to this family, we ought to find time and make the effort to get to know each other better."

Darcy raised her eyebrows. "Why this sudden friendly interest?"

"Well, I'm the newest one, and at first I felt I should wait until others approached me. But when they don't. . ." Mary Lou shrugged.

For a questioning moment Darcy stared at her. Suddenly a charming smile broke her mask. She swung the door open. "Come in," she said and stepped back.

Mary Lou had been told that when Zack came home, Allena moved into one of the smaller bedrooms and gave the master bedroom with the fireplace to the newlyweds. The room was twice the size of Tom's. Two large wardrobes almost filled one wall, and a four poster bed projected into the center of the room on a multi-colored rug. Behind the door, a large washstand with a china basin and pitcher sat under an oval mirror hung on the wall. This lovely bedroom surely was equivalent to what Darcy had back east. Aunt Tibby's home had been one of the grandest in Venture, but this room was larger than any in the Bar-B ranch house. Mary Lou would be grateful for such a room.

At the moment, though, it wasn't too neat. The bed, still unmade, held several of Darcy's dresses, one draped dejectedly over the tall foot rail. Two others were thrown on a chair.

Darcy's gaze followed Mary Lou's to the strewn clothing. "I'm used to having a maid," she said bluntly, then gathered the dresses from the chair into one arm and opened the wardrobe with the other to expose dress after dress of delicate fabrics and colors, mostly blue.

"Blue must be your favorite color," Mary Lou said.

"It goes with my eyes."

Mary Lou ran her hand over the soft cloth of the pale blue and cream sateen dress draped over the bottom of the bed. "This is lovely."

"You can have it." Darcy grimaced. "It's too small for me. Since I'm carrying this baby, I don't fit anything. Mrs. Cassidy will have to make me something. Maybe she can make me some baggy clothes, since she can't make anything to fit."

"You always look lovely, even in Mrs. Cassidy's clothes."

Darcy dipped her head and narrowed her eyes. "Was there something special you wanted this morning?"

Maybe Mary Lou had stayed too long. "Like I said, I'd like us to be friends as well as sisters-in-law."

"All right." Suddenly Darcy dropped her guard. Sad eyes betrayed her unhappiness. "I could use a friend."

After that visit, it seemed that Darcy looked forward to Mary Lou's morning chats, although Mary Lou never knew exactly what reception she'd receive.

One day they began talking about their childhood homes. Darcy radiated as she described the fancy balls, horse racing, family vacations at the ocean, and the young ladies' finishing school she'd attended in Boston to learn the etiquette and social manners needed to be the mistress of a large house with servants.

"We could have had all that if Zack would have joined my father's law firm." Her voice dripped bitterness.

"Texas needs good lawyers, too."

"Exactly what Zack said." Darcy lowered her head. "When I agreed to marry him and come here, I never realized it would be so primitive." Darcy raised wistful eyes. "I wish you could see how lovely my home is in Boston. It's brick with trees all around and paths one can walk on with pretty shoes." Suddenly, Darcy's face relaxed into a totally unguarded expression and she swung toward her wardrobe. "Here," she said. "Try this on."

Amid giggles, Darcy unbuttoned Mary Lou's skirt, and it dropped to the floor with her shirtwaist. She threw two crisp petticoats over Mary Lou's head and pinned them tightly around her waist.

"At least you have a tiny waist," Darcy commented and swung a shimmering blue moiré ball gown over Mary Lou's head. She unbraided Mary Lou's long hair, describing the elaborate coiffures and styles in Boston, then swept the wealth of chestnut tresses to form a twist loosely wrapped around Mary Lou's head, deftly anchored with shell combs and a plume feather.

Darcy's whole countenance and demeanor changed to charming enthusiasm. She draped a golden necklace around Mary Lou's throat and handed her a pair of cream high-button shoes.

Donning long white gloves, Mary Lou stood staring into the mirror at a woman she'd never seen before. She felt like an elegant lady. No wonder Darcy liked to dress in these clothes. Suddenly she was struck with how much she looked like Mama in a picture taken when she was a teacher in Toledo before she married Pa. Mary Lou giggled and wished Tom could see her in this finery.

Mary Lou noticed the expression on Darcy's face was completely new, the petulance gone. The face reflected beside Mary Lou's in the mirror radiated and glowed with warmth. This must be the girl Zack saw. No wonder he loved her.

The two girls were still absorbed in their finery when the ranch bell pealed from Hattie's impatient hand.

"Oh, my goodness," Mary Lou cried, "I didn't do my job of setting the table!"

Darcy helped her out of her finery and Mary Lou slipped into her calico dress.

They hurried to the dining room. Everyone was seated. The two girls slipped into their places, smiling faces veiled with mystery.

Allena's questioning gaze traveled from one to the other and then turned to Tom. "Say grace, please."

The next morning, Mary Lou knocked on Darcy's door carrying one of her calico dresses. "I brought this dress because I didn't think you'd want to learn to bake bread in any of your lovely ones."

"Bake bread! I've never baked bread in my life, nor do I intend to."

For a moment Darcy's indignant stare dampened Mary Lou's resolve. "Oh, but it's fun and such a satisfying job. I think you'll enjoy it."

"That's a servant's job." Darcy's stare turned to outrage. "Ladies don't—"

"Yesterday you said I looked like a lady. Today am I a servant just because I have on a calico dress and make bread?"

Darcy lifted her nose in the air and closed the door.

That bedroom is Darcy's escape, Mary Lou thought. *It must be pretty lonesome to primp and read your time away.* Mary Lou knocked again and waited. Just as she turned to leave, the door opened.

The two girls gazed at each other.

Mary Lou felt Darcy's searching distrust, yet a yearning bled through her indignant mask. "You don't have to do anything," Mary Lou coaxed. "I thought you might watch while I made bread and see if you'd like to try." For a moment Mary Lou thought Darcy was going to step back and slam the door in her face.

Darcy cast a glance at the calico dress, then lifted her nose. "I'll come, but I won't wear that!"

Mary Lou felt she'd won a small opening as they walked together to the kitchen.

When they entered, Hattie looked up in surprise, but wise old bird that she was, she gave a disinterested nod and continued measuring flour for bread.

"Darcy and I are going to make bread."

Hattie's hand halted midair, poised to empty a cup of flour. It obviously took great control for her to keep her mouth shut. She bobbed her head, put the cup down, dusted the flour from her hands, and wiped them on her apron. "Good." It came out in a squeak. She cleared her throat. "Can use all the loaves you girls want to make." She hurried outside to her wash tubs.

Darcy didn't touch a thing, but she watched Mary Lou expertly check the bread recipe she didn't need, combine the flour, yeast, sugar, salt, water, and milk, beat and punch the dough, and form it into loaves.

Darcy gingerly held the bread pans while Mary Lou placed the loaves in them.

"Now, then. You can surprise Zack and tell him you and I made bread today."

Darcy's expression was, as usual, unfathomable. What went on behind those beautiful clouded eyes? She was like a wild, changeable wind: gentle, soothing, and pleasant one moment and then an unpredictable, gathering storm the next.

Thank You, Lord. We've taken the first step.

Chapter 6

Morning chores done, Mary Lou strolled to the corral and clapped her hands.

Dulcie, ears alert, whinnied, tossed her head, and came on a run.

"How about a little workout in the corral?" Mary Lou patted Dulcie's warm sleek neck and opened the gate.

Dulcie nuzzled Mary Lou's shoulder and danced behind her mistress.

Mary Lou swung the double barn doors wide and walked to Dulcie's stall, her frisky horse at her heels. She adjusted the bridle, smoothed Dulcie's blanket over her back, swung the saddle into place, pulled the girth, and tightened the cinch. Just like home. A hot breeze blew through the barn, accentuating strong straw and animal odors that gnawed strangely at Mary Lou's stomach.

In the corral, Mary Lou settled in the saddle and rode the fence line, relishing the movement. Other than when she and Tom rode in the cool of the evening, her riding had been curbed, much to her dislike. The warmth and bouncing produced a new unpleasant feeling. Her stomach grew queasy, her head felt light. She glanced up at a sun suddenly grown hot. In defense, she turned Dulcie back toward the barn, much to her horse's displeasure. It was worse inside. Pungent odors perched Mary Lou's stomach on a precarious edge. She hurriedly unsaddled Dulcie, slapped her backside, and sent her reluctantly back into the corral. Slowly, shakily, Mary Lou walked back to the house.

The kitchen felt blessedly cool. Hattie, surrounded by pie making, looked up and smiled a welcome.

Mary Lou took a deep breath. "Need some help?"

"Bread's gettin' low," Hattie answered.

Immediately, Mary Lou set about gathering bread pans, flour, and mixing bowls and took them to the table. Up to her elbows in bread dough, Mary Lou found the aroma of the bread suddenly intolerable. Without warning, her stomach flipped and she felt clammy. Her eyes refused to focus. The walls swayed! She grabbed the edge of the table.

"Hattie, I feel terrible. Can you finish this bread?"

At her side at once, Hattie guided her to the wash basin, rinsed her hands, and then applied a cold wet cloth to her forehead. "You been lookin' mighty peaked lately." Hattie's mouth arched into a wry smile. "Miss Mary, have you missed your monthly?"

Mary Lou's mind rolled over the months. She looked sheepishly at Hattie, then shivered. A delicious shiver! She dried her hands quickly and set out to find Tom. Jess, the only one around, told her Tom and some of the boys had ridden over to see Will Shepard.

Disappointed, Mary Lou returned to her bedroom and busied herself picking over her dresses. Most of them were fitted at the waist. She smiled, trying to picture herself with a full stomach. Her first baby! What would they name him? *Thomas, of course. Thomas Owen? After her father? Oh Lord, would a grandson give Pa the will to live?*

Or—delightful thought—*it could be a girl.* Sweet times she and Mama had shared flooded Mary Lou's mind, and tears welled up in her eyes. Then, she remembered. All Stafford girls carried the name Elizabeth. Her daughter must continue the line. Grandmother Stafford had been Ruthella Elizabeth, Mama had been Ellen Lisbeth, Aunt Tibby was Elizabeth Mae, she was Mary Lou Elizabeth. Which sounded better, Ellen Lizabeth—or—Lizbeth Ellen. Either way they would call her Beth. Mary Lou imagined her mother gathering a little namesake girl into her loving arms and her eyes grew moist.

Joy and anticipation flooded Mary Lou's heart to near bursting. She sighed deeply, laid both hands on her stomach, and raised her eyes. *Thank You, Father, my cup runneth over.*

She sat inside and mended. The morning dragged. Intermittent buoyancy and excitement gave way to nagging nausea. She paused often, listening for the pound of Tinder's hoofbeats, longing for Tom to come. She tried to imagine what he would say. They hadn't talked much about children.

The dinner bell bonged under Hattie's persistent hand. When all gathered, there was only Allena, Darcy, and Mary Lou. Doug and Zack were in Harness. If the work at Shepards were unfinished, Tom would eat with them.

Mary Lou squirmed to find a comfortable spot on her chair. She stared at food which held no appeal. The smell of it played havoc with her stomach. She smiled at Allena. "I'm not very hungry, Mother, just tired. If you don't mind, I think I'll go rest for a little while."

Allena's brows squinted a question, but her mouth remained closed—for which Mary Lou was thankful. She feared she wouldn't be able to keep the news from her mother-in-law if Allena asked. Above all, Mary Lou wanted to keep her promise to Tom that he would be the first to know. As for Hattie, nothing that happened in the Langdon household ever escaped that shrewd old woman, yet her loyalty to each member kept her silent.

It seemed she had just closed her eyes when the bedroom door creaked and Tom stood at the bedside. His suntanned face, creased with worry, stared at her. "You all right? Mother said—"

"I'm fine." Mary Lou smiled. *What a perfect time and place to tell him.*

"Mother said you were out riding, came in not feeling well, and didn't eat dinner. For November, the sun's unusually hot today." Tom's eyes clouded with concern.

Mary Lou tingled with excitement. *It's unkind to worry him, but I want this to be a special moment. Our first child!*

She nodded. "The sun was hot, and for the first time I didn't enjoy riding Dulcie. The bouncing, the barn odors were too much for me because. . ." She stood up, circled her arms around Tom's neck, and looked into the depths of his eyes. "Because we're going to have a baby."

Tom's eyes registered shock and surprise. Then a timid smile slowly crinkled the corners of his mouth and raced across his astonished face.

It was what she had been waiting to see.

Tom's arms circled her. He kissed her eyes, her cheeks, drank in the joy radiating in her upturned face, then captured her lips.

Mary Lou sensed a new oneness between them that she had never felt before.

"Wha-da-ya-know!" he drawled. "My big brother isn't as far ahead of me as he thinks he is!" Tom straightened up. Mary Lou's feet left the floor and he swung her around, kissing her cheeks, her eyes, her mouth. Suddenly he stopped and eased Mary Lou to the floor. Tom's gaze, suddenly serious, quizzed hers. "Am I the first to know?" His voice was husky.

"You are the first to know," Mary Lou assured him. "Except Hattie."

Tom's face fell.

Mary Lou cupped his face in her hands. "It was Hattie who told me! I almost fainted on her this morning while making bread, and she guessed right away. I went to find you and you were gone." She watched his smile return, and she stretched to reach his lips for a tender, lingering kiss.

Mary Lou settled into her husband's arms. His kisses on her mouth and cheek, his whispered love into her hair, carried warm caressing joy to every part of her body. God had joined a special part of each of them and, in eight or so months, would give them the gift of a child. She sighed contentedly. "I hope it's a boy and looks just like you."

"Or a beautiful little girl, like you." Suddenly, Tom released Mary Lou and grabbed her hand. "Come on, Woman, let's shout it to the world." He reached the door, stopped abruptly, and shook his head. "Nope. We'll calmly announce it at supper."

Much to Mary Lou's surprise, Tom waited until halfway through supper before he stood, grinned, and tapped his spoon on his cup. "I bring great news," he began.

All heads turned.

"It gives me great pleasure to announce that the Thomas Langdon family is on the increase." His eyes twinkled.

It took a minute for the family to comprehend what he had said.

Allena caught it first. She rose smiling, moved quickly around the table, and threw her arms about Tom. Then she turned and pulled Mary Lou to her feet, hugging and kissing her. She embraced her son again. "Wonderful! Now there will be two arrows in my quiver."

Darcy sat silently toying with her food, her stone face an enigma. At Allena's comment, she raised her chin and swept a haughty gaze around the table. "It looks like we're going to have a race to see who becomes the heir of the Langdon estate." She returned her gaze to her plate and placed a forkful of food in her mouth.

Silence hovered over the table, faces stunned.

An embarrassed red curtain lowered over Zack's countenance. He stared at Darcy for a moment, his face stern. "There's no race for the Langdon estate as you call it. This ranch belongs to all of us."

Darcy tossed her head. "Well, Doug is making sure he gets his share and then some."

Zack's fierce gaze pinned his wife. "That's between me, Doug, Tom, Nelson, and Mother. We'll discuss it no more, especially at the supper table." He surveyed the immobile faces of his family. "Does everyone understand that?"

Without hesitation, Tom answered, "Yes, Zack, and I agree with you."

Mary Lou's stomach churned, but not because of the baby. Why did Darcy say such things and embarrass Zack? It happened time and time again. Was she that afraid she was going to be cheated? By her own family? What kind of a family did she have in Boston that fostered such suspicion?

Darcy rose indignantly and flounced out. Silence again filled the room, broken by heaving sighs.

Zack sat with his head down, the muscles of his jaws flexing. Abruptly, he looked up. "I ask forgiveness for my wife," he said in a low voice. "She's homesick and says things without thinking."

Mary Lou remembered one of Nelson's pictures of their father. He looked exactly as Zack did now. Stern but compassionate. It must be hard for Zack to follow in his father's footsteps without the support of a strong, loving wife. Father Langdon had Allena at his side. Allena would never have said a thing like that. Mary Lou glanced at her mother-in-law. Allena's eyes reflected deep hurt—not for herself, but for the burden carried by her oldest son.

Allena picked up her fork. "Let's eat our supper. It's getting cold." She

170

turned toward the kitchen door. "Hattie, I think we need another pitcher of milk."

Hattie appeared immediately with a pitcher and removed the empty one. The table was soon empty, and Hattie cleared the dishes.

ᙁ

Early fall and winter suddenly filled the days with endless work. Harvesting and preparing enough food to feed and sustain all the people and animals on the Circle Z until spring was a momentous task.

Tom and the cowboys butchered cows and hogs, hunted antelope and buffalo, and scraped, cleaned, and hung skins in the barn to dry.

The women spent endless days preserving meat: cutting strips to dry for jerky, grinding sausage, salting and smoking hams and bacon, submerging pork and beef in barrels of congealed fat, and lining the barrels against the outer wall in the shed adjoining the kitchen. As the barrels emptied, the women rendered and clarified the fat into lard.

Darcy threw her hands up in horror and retreated to other parts of the house, but then she surprised everyone by setting the dining room table for dinner one noon.

Like a spry old mouse, Hattie, on all fours, her apron pinned into a pouch filled with vegetables, climbed up and down a ladder into the cool root cellar dug under part of the kitchen and sorted her bounty into bins and crates.

Mary Lou and Allena filled flour sacks with nuts, dried beans, potatoes, onions, and a variety of squash and handed them down to Hattie.

Even Darcy wandered into the kitchen one day and sorted vegetables, only to complain later that her hands were ruined because she couldn't wash off the dirt and stain.

During winter days, the men made and repaired wagons, harnesses, and furniture. Tom and Zack each worked with loving hands on cradles and joshed each other about whose was the better one.

In the house on cold, snowy afternoons and evenings, Allena, Mary Lou, and Hattie sat around the big kitchen fireplace rubbing animal hides into softness so that they could be cut, fit, and sewn or laced into leather jackets, leggings, hats, and fur mittens. Buffalo hides were made into rugs and sleigh robes.

One winter evening when the men had gone for a few days to check on the cattle, Allena, Mary Lou, and Hattie sat in rocking chairs around the warm kitchen fireplace making baby clothes.

"Look." Mary Lou held up a flannel dress, bonnet, and booties she'd just finished. She had crocheted a dainty edging around the neck, sleeves, and bottom hem.

Darcy, sitting close to the fire to keep warm, reached for the dress and held it up, her eyes misty. "I wish I could make something like this for my baby."

Hattie's mouth dropped open in surprise, then quickly closed into a poker face. Allena and Mary Lou glanced at each other and smiled.

"I'll help you," Mary Lou said. She walked to a chest, took out another piece of flannel, cut it into pieces for a dress, and showed Darcy how to sew the parts together.

That baby's dress opened the door for Darcy's joining the family. Much to the women's surprise, Darcy caught on fast. She appeared one afternoon with several of her dresses and cut baby clothes out of the skirts. She made one lovely sateen dress into a christening dress embroidered with minute, exquisite stitches. The other women were vocal in their praise.

"I learned all this in finishing school in Boston," Darcy confided one evening. She laughed. "I never thought I'd use it on baby clothes! It was supposed to decorate dining linens, dress collars, pillows, and pictures. I really like to do it."

A refreshing window opened into Darcy. On the men's shirts and women's shirtwaists, she made sturdy or delicate buttonholes.

"I hate to make buttonholes." Hattie squinted her nose. "I just use overcast stitches. Ain't so pretty, but they make a hole to get a button through and that's all that's needed."

Allena, charmed at the fresh insight into her daughter-in-law, gave Zack a long list of supplies—yard goods, yarn, needles, embroidery thread, and buttons—to bring back from Harness. During morning prayer time with Mary Lou, she expressed her thankfulness for Darcy's noticeable change of heart, and they prayed that someday Darcy might feel her need for a Savior and join them in morning prayers.

Chapter 7

A blood curdling scream cut through the quiet night.

Tom and Mary Lou bolted upright in bed. Tom bounded out and hopped around on one foot, then the other, getting into his pants. He grabbed a shirt and ran barefoot out the door and down the hall. Mary Lou slipped quickly into a wrapper, stuffed her feet into slippers, and hurried after him.

Another scream. It was Darcy.

They found Zack, eyes betraying panic, nervously pacing in front of the bedroom door. "Wish we could have found Dr. Mike."

Mary Lou opened the door and slid through. Darcy lay on the bed, her usual well-coiffured hair tangled and soaked with perspiration, her knuckles white from gripping and pulling the sides and head of the bed. Hattie and Allena labored between her jerking legs.

Mary Lou had never actually birthed a baby, but she had been on hand many times to receive the slippery newborn from the birthing woman to clean with oil and wrap snugly in a warmed blanket. Now that she carried a baby within her, she felt it was time she learned more about the process. If she got caught alone. . .

Mary Lou carefully watched Allena and Hattie as they pressed gently on Darcy's stomach and quietly and efficiently received the tiny head covered with black hair when it released itself from its confinement. A small body followed, caught by Hattie's waiting hands.

Allena beamed. "It's a boy!" She tied and cut the cord of her first grandson and handed him to Mary Lou, who cleaned and wrapped him and then placed the tiny baby in his grandmother's eager arms.

Allena lifted her head and closed her eyes. "Father, we thank You for this new little one whom You've given us. May we love him as You love us." Tears of joy spilled freely, her lips parted in a wide knowing smile.

"Another Zack. His grandfather would be proud." She turned and laid the tiny bundle beside Darcy. "Here's your son, Darcy."

Darcy opened her eyes. Her lips trembled as she gazed at the squirming infant beside her. She stared for a long moment, slowly raised her hand to touch him, then pulled back and turned her head, tears streaming down her face.

"You're tired, Darcy. Rest now, Dear."

The eyes of the two women met. The younger eyes were tinged with bewilderment, fear, and anger; the older flooded with love and thankfulness.

Darcy buried her face in the pillow. "Take it away," she breathed in sobs. "That baby ruined me."

Allena's face filled with anguish. She lifted her tiny grandson and cradled him in her protective arms.

Mary Lou opened the door and Zack almost fell in.

Allena met Zack and placed his baby into his arms. "Here's your son, Zack."

Zack's worry vanished as he awkwardly cupped the tiny bundle in his arms and gazed in awe. "My son," he said softly. "Zachary Thomas Langdon."

A crying moan came from the bed and erased the tender moment.

Zack frowned at his mother. "Is she—is Darcy all right?"

"She's fine, but very tired after a full night's work." Allena smiled and took the baby. "Go see for yourself."

The door closed behind him, and they heard Darcy sobbing.

Probably nestled in Zack's arms, Mary Lou thought. *That's where I would want to be.* When she turned, Tom was staring at her, a serious look on his face.

"Are you going to have to go through all that?"

Mary Lou laughed. "I don't know of any other way to have a baby, do you? Women have told me it hurts while the baby's coming, but after it's born and in their arms, they don't remember it, too awed at the fruit of their labor."

The expression on Tom's face told her he was not convinced.

He'll have to see for himself, Mary Lou thought. Arm in arm, they slowly walked to their bedroom. Tom held her tightly. Mary Lou's heart flooded with love at his overt concern and protection. Behind the closed door of their bedroom, Tom enclosed her in his arms and held her tenderly. He kissed her hair and forehead and finally sought her mouth. It was a different kiss, not of passion, but compassion.

Tom whispered in her ear. "I don't want you hurt."

Mary Lou clung to him and whispered, "But this will be a good hurt. Mama always said good hurt brings great joy."

Tom placed his hand tenderly over Mary Lou's noticeably protruding stomach. "I'm going to be a father."

Mary Lou smiled and placed her hand over his. "And me a mother." She snuggled closer.

Tom grinned sheepishly. "It's a little scary, but I think we can handle it."

The ranch bell rang impatiently. Hattie had breakfast ready.

ʊ

Over the next weeks, the household changed. Demands of a hungry baby went round the clock. Darcy stayed in bed much of the time, and although she still insisted that she didn't want a baby, Mary Lou walked in on her nursing little Zack and caught an undeniable expression of love on her face.

Zack came home earlier every day and Darcy came alive when Victor thundered to the ranch porch. Now Zack bounded into the house rather than spending time out at the barn joshing with the cowboys. Tex always took Victor to unsaddle and rub him down.

Doug was just the opposite. He stayed more and more in town. "Don't like crying babies," he said in protest one evening at the dinner table.

"That's just an excuse to avoid the ranch work and stay in town," Tom accused one night.

If real truth were spoken, Mary Lou thought, *Doug wanted to avoid talking to Zack and Tom.*

Harsh words often crossed the dinner table about the squatters on the south quarter. One night as they wrangled, Allena stood abruptly and slammed her fist on the table. "I forbid such talk! We're a disgrace to the Lord! His Word says in Romans 12:18, 'If it be possible, as much as lieth in you, live peaceably with all men.' That should mean double for brothers. I'll have no more of this until we can discuss it in love. Maybe then we'll solve problems."

She turned abruptly and left.

Her four sons watched their mother's receding back. They had never seen her so angry—nor so composed. They glanced sheepishly at each other.

Doug clattered to his feet. "I'm going to town. Mother is right. We'll never settle anything by shouting at each other."

Zack pinned Doug with a sharp gaze. "Or, running away to town."

Doug glared at his older brother. "Everyone thinks I am a bounder and a thief. No one ever sees my side. I have always been the bad kid nobody liked." Doug clenched his fists. "What reason have I to stay here? I have friends in town. They appreciate me."

"No one has accused you of anything," Zack snapped back. "You'd better look to your own conscience."

Doug's eyes narrowed to slits. His mouth parted, and he gritted his teeth and clenched his fist.

Tom jumped to his feet. "I think we'd better settle this in the barn. I'm sure Mother can hear us, and it upsets her. I'd rather upset the horses."

Doug spun on his heel. "I'm going to town." He gave them his back and slammed the door so hard the windows rattled.

Mary Lou sat watching and aching. A breach in a family was so hard to watch. Hattie peeked in warily with the coffeepot in her hand. Zack smiled and held out his cup.

"Thanks, Hattie, I need a refill."

Tom nodded and lifted his cup.

Zack sipped and shook his head. "Doug's getting doubly touchy. We must be hitting close. I'm checking out a land deal now and. . ." He pursed his lips and met Tom's gaze. "It doesn't look good. We might have less land than we think. Our southwest poachers are nothing compared with the whole eastern border of the ranch."

Tom sat up quickly he almost spilling his coffee. "You found something?"

"I hope not, but it looks suspicious. A fancy dresser was checking out our eastern border. I don't know which side of the line he bought, Spenser's or ours. I'll find out tomorrow for sure."

The two brothers sipped thoughtfully, worry lines denting their foreheads.

Darcy slid her chair back, stood, and glared at Zack. "I know I'm not supposed to have anything to say about ranch business, but if you don't get rid of him soon, none of us is going to be left with anything."

Zack's eyes narrowed, his teeth clenched. He took a deep breath and exhaled slowly. "I think we can handle it," he said calmly. He rose and moved to the back of her chair. "Are you ready to take a ride? I told Tex to hitch the buggy so we could go after supper."

Allena entered with Baby Zack in her arms and gave him to Darcy. "I think your son is hungry. He can't seem to settle."

Darcy gritted her teeth. She took him from Allena's arms. "There goes my lovely ride. All this boy ever thinks of is his stomach." She swung to Zack. "You might as well know he is the only one we'll ever have. I'm never going through this again."

Zack sagged as if he had been hit.

Mary Lou swung toward Darcy and fought the urge to shake her until her teeth rattled. Armed with an arsenal of sharp words, Darcy threw them like daggers with wanton abandon. For awhile during the winter, Mary Lou had thought Darcy had softened and changed. Mama's words gentled her spirit: "Only Jesus can tame a wild, selfish heart."

Oh Lord, Mary Lou prayed silently. *There's a sweet girl somewhere inside Darcy. I have had a few glimpses. Surely she couldn't have meant what she said. She's just—*

"I want to go home for a visit." With that abrupt announcement, Darcy turned on her heel and left the room to feed baby Zack.

Mary Lou followed Darcy to see if she could help.

Chapter 8

Except for feeding Baby Zack, Darcy paid little attention to him. She kept reminding Allena that she wanted the baby to have a wet nurse as soon as possible. "In Boston," she said, at breakfast after the men left the table, "we have nursemaids to care for babies and children so it doesn't curtail the mother's activities."

Mary Lou suppressed a smile. What activity? Other than dressing and undressing two or three times a day, eating, and going to town with Zack or on a buggy ride in the evening, Darcy kept herself to the bedroom or went on solitary walks. Darcy's congeniality and friendship with Mary Lou had cooled after Baby Zack was born.

Morning devotions with Allena over, Mary Lou returned to her bedroom and opened Mama's big chest. Many of her dresses didn't fit around her waist so she decided to pack them away and wear Mrs. Cassidy's "balloon dresses," as Darcy called them. On a rare visit to Mary Lou's room, Darcy, arms full, gladly dumped the lot on Mary Lou's bed.

"I will not be wearing these anymore." Her nose wrinkled as if they were distasteful. "You can keep them."

Mary Lou was grateful. They were much more comfortable. She had bought material to sew a couple larger dresses to accommodate her growing stomach, but now she would save the cloth and make herself a new dress for church after the baby was born.

She closed the lid of the chest and glanced out the window. What a lovely April morning! She decided to take a walk to see if there were any spring flowers in bloom. Mama had always kept a bouquet of fresh prairie flowers in the vase Grandmother Stafford had sent from Toledo. Other bouquets Mama arranged in Mason jars and set anywhere she could find a spot.

Mama's vase! Mary Lou reopened the trunk, slid her hand down inside, and felt around. She remembered Aunt Tibby rolling the vase in a blanket when they packed for Texas and snuggling it with clothes to cushion it.

Suddenly Mary Lou's hand bumped something hard. She pulled it up and removed the blanket. For the first time in a long time, tears gushed to the surface. She held the vase gently in her arms as she would have held Mama, her heart aching with the wish that Mama could be with her to see the baby born. Mama would have birthed it!

Mary Lou put the blanket back in the trunk and closed the lid. On her walk, she'd find something to put in Mama's vase.

But that wasn't the only reason she wanted to go for a walk. There was a certain place she wanted to see again.

Last night she and Tom had taken a stroll "to my favorite spot," he had said. They had stopped on a broad knoll and looked all around. The horse barns and corrals of the Circle Z were about three-quarters mile away.

"I like this place," Tom had said. "It has a good all-round view and is graded about right for a ranch house."

"A ranch house?" Mary Lou had felt exciting prickles tingle her neck. "You mean—our ranch house."

Tom had looked down at her with a silly, smug grin. "Mmm. Been thinking about it."

Mary Lou had stood on tiptoe and thrown her arms around his neck. "Oh Tom. Our own house? The main ranch house is so big, I figured we'd always live there."

"Well, there's two families plus Mother in the house now, and if Doug brings a wife and Nelson brings one, it's going to get mighty crowded." Tom had stooped down and picked her up in his arms. "Mostly I thought you might kinda like a house of your own."

Mary Lou had planted a kiss soundly on his mouth and squeezed him so hard he'd choked.

"Hold it, woman, I need to breathe."

They'd strolled back slowly in the deep twilight, full of plans. In bed, they had talked until the wee hours.

Now Mary Lou walked to the front door to go for her walk.

Darcy appeared in her morning dress.

"Going for a walk?" Mary Lou asked.

"Yes."

"Would you mind if I walked with you?"

Darcy shrugged. "If you want to."

Mary Lou stepped through the door. "It's a beautiful day. I can't stay inside."

Darcy had dressed in a delicate blue sateen with a shirred apron front that draped gracefully over her hips and met in a small bustle in the back. Mary Lou had to give her sister-in-law credit. At all costs, she fought to remain a Boston lady, even though at times it must have been difficult. In her calico, Mary Lou felt like Pioneer Jane.

The two women walked east, away from the ranch. Mary Lou decided she would wait to walk to her and Tom's special place. She breathed deeply and drank in the freshness of the spring air, almost experiencing the exhilaration of her beloved Kansas prairie wind. It was in her blood, and nothing could quite match it. Was that the way it was for Darcy? Boston must be in her blood. She must feel the same as Mary Lou felt about Venture.

"How soon will I be able to stop nursing the baby?" Darcy asked abruptly.

"It depends on the baby, mostly. And the mother. Some can be weaned around eight months, but most go a year or more."

"A year! My God, I can't stand that."

Mary Lou cringed at Darcy's careless use of God's name, but she recognized desperation in her voice. God was the one Darcy needed, but the few times Mary Lou had mentioned things Mama had said about God, Darcy had stiffened and changed the subject. "Does it bother you so much to nurse him?"

"I hate it!"

Mary Lou could see it. Darcy's nose and mouth twisted in disgust.

"You're shocked?" Darcy raised her brows and smiled.

"Well. . ." Mary Lou had to be honest. Darcy was too astute to be fooled. "Yes, but then again, no. I've been brought up with it and don't think anything of it. If I had been brought up like you, maybe I'd think like you do."

Darcy stopped.

Mary Lou turned to face her. "It's just like making bread. I helped Mama make bread from the time I was a little girl, so the feel of the dough and the greasing of the pans doesn't bother me. But it did you. You don't like to touch the dough, let alone knead and shape it. Things are a little different here in Texas for me, but for you, they are a lot different." Mary Lou shrugged her shoulders. "I guess it's just what you get used to."

Darcy's penetrating gaze searched Mary Lou's innermost being. Finally, she turned back to their walk. "There's nothing here for me," she said softly. "I don't fit in like you do."

"But you have Zack. He's here for you. You love him, don't you?"

Darcy stared at Mary Lou for a moment, then sauntered over to a fallen log under a cottonwood tree and sat down. "I loved him in Boston. He was a gentleman and moved well in our society. He fit in, he knew the other men, we had the same interests. Here, he's not Zack. He's not my Zack— not the man I fell in love with." She sniffed and pulled a dainty handkerchief from the underside of her sleeve. Tears rolled down her cheeks.

Mary Lou, speechless, had never seen this Darcy, vulnerable, hurting, miserable. Darcy had everything to live for, but she didn't recognize it. What did she want? The joy of marriage was being with the one you loved. It didn't matter where, who was around, or what you were doing. If the one you loved was happy, you were happy. If they were sad, so were you. Mary Lou loved being with Tom. It didn't matter where they lived as long as they were together.

"But Zack loves you more than anything," Mary Lou protested.

"No, he doesn't." Darcy shook her head. "If he loved me, he would have accepted the position in my father's law firm. Why did he want to be a lawyer? To potsy around in a desolate place like this when he could have become a judge someday?"

"Potsy? Is that what you think Zack is doing? Oh, Darcy. Zack is trying to bring law and order to Texas—to Harness in particular—so everyone can live in peace on their own property and not have some of the Eastern land speculators rob us blind."

"Eastern land speculators! Why Eastern? They come from all over."

Mary Lou had hit a nerve. "I didn't mean Boston particularly. I meant they come from everywhere east of Texas." Mary Lou thought she'd better change the subject. She didn't want to lose Darcy now. This was the best talk they'd ever had.

But Darcy was finished. She rose indignantly and marched toward the house.

Mary Lou followed her, but the weight she carried in her stomach slowed her down, and Darcy soon outdistanced her.

That afternoon, Laura rode in and invited everyone, cowboys and all, to a big barbecue. Darcy, to the surprise of the whole family, offered to stay home and take care of Baby Zack.

"Oh, but I want to show off my new grandson," Allena exclaimed. "Please, Darcy, come with us."

"Take him. Zack can bring him home when it's time to eat." Darcy started for the bedroom.

Zack followed her and pleaded, "Darcy, I'd like you to go with me."

"I don't like barbecues. I don't like the meat. It's too greasy and—"

"There will be lots of other things to eat."

Darcy stretched to her tallest. "Zack, I am not going!" She swung around and walked away from him.

"But Darcy. . ."

She spun back, her eyes flashing, fury mounting. "How am I supposed to say it so you'll understand. I'll say it again! Listen this time! I—am—not—going!" Her skirt snapped a period on her statement as she flounced around the chair and headed for their bedroom. "Take your son and bring him back when he needs Mama."

The family remained uncomfortably silent, wishing they could disappear rather than see Zack so humiliated. He stood stiff, nostrils flared, until

Darcy left the room. Then his shoulders crumpled and he dipped his head. No one said anything. They stood beside him, hurting with him.

"Hattie!" Allena called.

Hattie entered immediately and glanced around the room.

"Is everything packed to go?"

"Yes'm."

Allena took a deep breath. "Then let's all get going. Mary Lou, will you please get Baby Zack."

The paralyzed family snapped to attention and went their various ways to gather and assemble. Tom on Tinder and Zack on Victor took the lead. Shortly, the wagon, driven by Nelson and carrying Allena, Baby Zack, Mary Lou, Hattie, and two baskets of food to contribute to the barbecue, moved under the Circle Z arch and turned west toward the Shepard's Bar-S Ranch.

Chapter 9

Dr. Mike's faithful Betsy trotted under the Circle Z arch, headed for the hitching rail, and stopped. The doctor flopped the reins, climbed out of the buggy, and leisurely walked to the kitchen door. Hattie swung it open and greeted him with a wide, welcoming smile.

"Well, and here's my favorite girl." Dr. Mike grinned as Hattie shook her finger at him. "They say the easiest way to a man's heart is through his stomach, and your cookin' sure does touch my stomach. Someday, I'm going to ask you to marry me."

Like a flustered school girl with her first beau, Hattie ducked her head and twittered. "Oh, Dr. Mike, you're always joking."

Allena and Mary Lou entered the kitchen.

"I thought I heard your voice," Allena said. "What brings you out here? Nobody sick in this family that I know of."

Dr. Mike sat down at the kitchen table. "Now if someone was to kindly offer me a good, hot cup of coffee, I think I might have strength enough to give you an answer."

Hattie moved immediately and set a steaming cup of coffee before him, surrounded by a pitcher of cream and the sugar bowl. He dumped two spoons of sugar and a generous amount of cream in the cup, stirred, and sipped.

"Mmm. Now a couple good pieces of your homemade bread with some applesauce on it might just settle my stomach."

Everyone laughed. Hattie moved and it was done. Allena and Mary Lou joined the doctor at the table.

Allena raised her cup to her lips and gazed through the steam. "You haven't answered my question. Perhaps if you give the right answer I might invite you to stay for dinner."

Dr. Mike's head bobbed a courteous bow. "I accept." He concentrated on stirring his coffee some more, and then looked straight into Allena's eyes. "I want to talk to you about Baby Zack."

"Is there something wrong?" The words choked her.

"Darcy and Zack brought him to show him off when they were in town the other day. While there, Darcy changed his diaper and he began to cry. It wasn't a usual baby cry—it was a hurt cry—so I examined him. I noticed that the bottom half of his body swung to the left side, the left leg in particular. I asked Darcy if he usually cried when she changed him. She said, 'most times.' "

Allena's face drained of color. "But he's just new and hasn't gotten straightened out yet."

"Allena, you know better than that. Did you notice anything unusual when you birthed him?"

Allena frowned and shook her head. "He was all curled up and seemed to straighten out when I gave his bottom a smack to catch his breath."

"You didn't notice if his body swung to one side?"

Allena's lips trembled. "As far as I could tell, it was a normal birth. He came out head first, his body followed."

"That's right." Hattie nodded.

Dr. Mike looked at Mary Lou. "Did you notice any swing to the left when you cleansed him?"

Mary Lou shook her head. "Most babies are so curled up right after they are born, it's hard to tell much of anything about what they look like stretched out."

"What's wrong, Dr. Mike?" Allena's eyed darkened. "Something is wrong, isn't there?"

He picked up the coffeepot and poured another steaming cup. "I examined him, and I believe his left leg is shorter than the right one."

Disbelief flooded Allena's pale face. Not another one! That was what old Doc Lamb had told her about Nelson. Baby Zack like Nelson?

Mary Lou slipped her arm around Allena's shoulders.

"It is just the one leg. The other seems sound as a dollar. It's not as serious as Nelson's condition. But his left leg is shorter, and that'll give him a definite limp. Of course, as he grows and uses it, he could learn to walk in a way to camouflage it."

Allena sat drained, motionless.

She'll take this in stride like everything else, Mary Lou thought. *Like Mama. Sometimes things stunned Mama, but they never defeated her. Allena is the same.* Even in her short lifetime, Mary Lou had seen many pioneer women engulfed in life-threatening danger, filled with fear and foreboding, but they had stood strong and firm.

"Then if I massage his leg like I did Nelson's, will that help?"

Dr. Mike placed his hand over Allena's limp one. "The massaging you did for Nelson is why he is able to get around as well as he does. Yes, it will help a whole lot. That's why I wanted to talk to you first. Do the same, and Baby Zack might never need crutches."

Mary Lou watched her mother-in-law slump, straighten, then draw a deep breath and pull herself under control.

"Do Darcy and Zack know about this?"

"No, that's why I came today. I saw Zack in town and he told me he was coming home at noon for dinner. Says he wants to spend some time with his boy. I thought this would be the right time and place to tell them."

Allena nodded slowly.

Mary Lou ached for Allena. Her first grandchild. *O Lord, give her strength.*

Allena raised her chin and smiled. "Then the Lord has given Baby Zack a special gift that will be enhanced by any handicap."

Mary Lou's heart swelled with pride in her new mother. She sounded just like Mama. No matter what happened, Mama had always faced it squarely.

A rider pounded into the ranch yard, and Zack burst through the door grinning. "Where's my boy?" He stopped short when he saw Dr. Mike and strode over to shake his hand. "I caught you, Doc. Bet you're out here for some of Hattie's good cookin'!"

Dr. Mike smiled and gripped his hand. "And to talk to you."

Zack patted Doc on the shoulder. "I'll be right back. Gotta see my boy!" He crossed the kitchen with three long strides and then bounded down the hall.

Allena's gaze swept Dr. Mike, Mary Lou, and Hattie. Then she smiled. "Baby Zack is going to be all right. I'm going to see to it."

Zack entered carrying his son, Darcy at his heels. Mary Lou noticed Dr. Mike's lips purse and a frown dent his brow. *Would he rather have talked to Zack alone?*

Zack settled himself and his son. "Now what did you want to talk to us about?"

Dr. Mike looked from one to the other. "Darcy," he began, "remember when you were in my office and your baby cried when you changed him? I noticed then that his left leg is not quite right."

Fear leaped into Zack's eyes and filled his face.

"You mean my son isn't perfect?" Darcy asked.

"Let me tell you first what I discovered."

Zack's brows nervously moved up and down. His jaw clenched and released as Dr. Mike explained what was wrong with Baby Zack. He turned to Darcy. "If you massage him like your mother did Nelson, that will help a lot. He may have a slight limp, but he will probably learn to swing in his walk so it won't be noticeable."

Darcy's eyes grew wide and wild. "You mean Baby Zack is going to be crippled like Nelson?"

"That's not the worst thing in the world that could happen."

Everyone turned to the door where Nelson stood on his crutches, grinning. Allena rose immediately and walked to her son's side, her face pained for him.

"Mother's right. She told me that God gave me something that would compensate. I love to draw and paint. I really do. If I had been normal, I would have probably killed myself bucking broncos." His eyes twinkled as he smiled. "Now I paint them."

What a brave speech, Mary Lou inwardly cheered. Her love for her sensitive brother-in-law poured from within her toward him. Nelson's gaze turned to Mary Lou and their eyes met in mutual understanding. Mary Lou nodded. The times they had spent together had made each more sensitive to the other.

"What on earth ever made him that way?" Darcy was defensive. "My family doesn't have anyone crippled." She looked at Allena.

Darcy's sharp barb fell on dead ears. "There is no sense in searching why," Allena answered, "or who's to blame."

Mary Lou's mind kept tugging at thoughts of Darcy's ride out alone and her fall from the horse. Could that have. . . ?

Dr. Mike turned to Darcy. "Your mother worked and massaged Nelson's legs which strengthened them so he could walk with the crutches. She'll show you what she did. That will help a great deal to keep the leg stimulated and strengthen the muscles."

Darcy stared at Dr. Mike as if he were a stranger. She turned abruptly and left the room without a word. Mary Lou had an urge to follow her, but didn't. Darcy was in no reasoning mood.

Zack rose, handed Baby Zack to his mother, and followed her.

Dr. Mike pushed back his chair. "Zack told me one of your cowboys took a bad fall from a horse. I think I'll go check on him."

The three women watched him go out the door, grab his bag from the buggy, and head for the bunkhouse.

No one said a word. Hattie picked up the cups and took them to the washing table.

"Hattie, let the dishes be." Allena, holding Baby Zack close to her heart, slid off the chair to her knees.

Mary Lou and Hattie knelt beside her.

"Dear Lord in heaven, Baby Zack is Your gift to us. We know that Your love for him is far greater than ours. Now You have given us the task of caring for him to make his body stronger and to discover why You honored us by sending him to us."

Mary Lou's heart stood at attention. *Honored by a baby being crippled?*

Remembrance triggered the voice of Big Jon's prayer the day his son, Georgie, had been needlessly shot in a shootout in front of the saloon in Venture. Mary Lou had been amazed at the lack of anger in his voice. The words that giant of a man prayed, surrounded by his questioning, frightened children, would forever echo in her ears: "I don't know how God will use this for good, but as Christians, we believe that God loves us. Even when we don't understand, we have faith that God will make it right."

Allena and Mama had that same kind of holding faith—no matter what happened.

In Venture, good had come from the spark of Georgie's death. It motivated the women to ignite and smash the saloon so that their men would have to build it outside the town line.

Little Georgie was a hero of Venture just as much as any soldier who gave his life in the Civil War. He had died for his home to make it a safer, better place.

Chapter 10

A bright, new day and a fresh breeze caressed Mary Lou as she stepped outside the kitchen door. Breakfast over, her bread set to rise, she moved toward the barn to find Tom. He had mentioned the cradle was almost finished.

She felt like a clumsy, waddling goose and locked her hands under her stomach to help carry its weight. Her time must be close. For the last three days, her back had ached constantly.

The familiar smells of the barn sent her thoughts back to Kansas. Jenny's letter yesterday had bubbled with happiness about her new married life with Glenn and how Venture had changed since the saloon no longer dominated Center Street. Twinges of homesickness surfaced. Jenny had written about how Glenn had changed the store and how she loved being postmistress. Fondly Mary Lou pictured those familiar places where she and Mama had spent so much time together. Those had been good days, but now. . .

"I really would like to ride, Tom."

Mary Lou stopped. Darcy's voice? She stretched her neck, peered over the stalls, and gasped. Darcy and Tom were at the other end and Darcy had her arms around Tom's neck! His back was to her and it looked like he—

"I love you, Tom." The words echoed back from the day Tom had carried Darcy from his horse to her bedroom, the day she had ridden out alone and fallen from the horse, and he'd found her. "I prayed you would come. . . ."

"Sorry, I can't leave right now, Darcy. Maybe later." She couldn't breathe, her knees trembled and threatened to fold. *I've got to get out of here.* Wild eyes scanned the distance between where she stood and the door. Her body felt like a heavy, immovable stone. *I'll never make it.*

"Then get Tex or somebody else to go with me. In Boston, I rode every morning. Please, Tom," she coaxed, "please, I—"

Her words stopped! What was happening? Mary Lou felt like tearing back to rip Darcy's arms from around Tom's neck. She slowly pulled herself up and gazed over the stall.

Tom's hands were loosening Darcy's from around his neck. "Tex is out on the range this morning. The only one left here is Jess. You'll just have to wait until Zack comes home."

Mary Lou closed her eyes, eased out of sight, and blew out a silent sigh of relief. Tom's voice held a tolerance—and a finality.

Shame flooded her. *Oh, Tom, forgive me.* She should know Darcy by now. That girl would do anything to get her own way. Instead Mary Lou had mistrusted Tom!

The stomp of Darcy's boots echoed her displeasure. "In Boston, men are gentlemen," she tossed back as she stormed out.

Mary Lou waited a moment to compose herself before she continued on her way to Tom. When he saw her, his face lit with delight. He immediately dropped his tools and encircled her in his arms. Mary Lou dissolved in tears and clung.

Tom gently pushed her back and gazed into her face. "You all right?"

Sobbing, she nodded and tried to push a trembly smile into place.

Tom guided her to an old stool and dropped to his knees in front of her. "Darling, what's wrong?"

"Nothing's wrong. It's just me." Mary Lou threw her arms around his neck. "Forgive me, Tom."

"Forgive you? For what?"

Between sniffs and broken sentences she related to Tom what she'd seen and what she'd thought.

Tom stood, exploded into laughter, and pulled Mary Lou up into his arms. "I hope I have shown better taste in women than Darcy. Don't cry over Darcy."

"I'm not crying over her. It's me. I mistrusted you!"

Tom held her close as he could, but her stomach kept them apart. After shifting a few times, they both began laughing.

"I'm just as eager for that baby to come as you are, but for different reasons."

Mary Lou blushed. The couple wrapped arms around each other and started out of the barn.

"How about us riding out to see our place? I've got a few more ideas. Want to help me plan?"

"Oh, yes." Mary Lou watched Tom hitch Buttons to one of the buggies.

"This should be a little more comfortable. You'll have some shade. That sun is deceiving."

The road was rutted and bumpy. In truth, it couldn't boast of being a road at all. Wobbly grooves had been creased into soft wet clay from hundreds of wagon wheels and the sun had turned them into solid rock.

Tom let Buttons have her head and pick her own way.

Land stretched everywhere, dotted by thousands of longhorn cows that formed moving patches of brown and white as they grazed. Texas had grown on Mary Lou. She was beginning to see the beauty Tom talked about. He stood tall when he talked of the Circle Z, thankful to his father who had poured his life's blood into making the ranch one of the largest, most productive spreads in north-central Texas.

"Are we going to build our own barns?" Mary Lou asked as they stood on their knoll and gazed across the landscape.

"Oh, yes." Tom answered. "I intend to raise horses as well as cattle. My father's reputation for fine stallions is known even in the East. He raised the best horses in these parts, and I want to do the same."

Allena's voice echoed in Mary Lou's mind: *"Tom has his father's heart."* Mary Lou swelled with pride, joy and—"Ohhh!" She doubled over in pain and sank toward the ground.

Tom caught her in his arms and carried her to the buggy. "I think we'd better head back."

The road appeared rougher than when they came. Every bump hammered Mary Lou's back, while periodic pains stabbed her stomach. The trip lasted an eternity.

When the buggy reached the ranch, Tom bounded out and hollered for Hattie. She appeared at the door, took one look at Tom carrying Mary Lou, and disappeared.

Within seconds, Allena came.

By the time Tom carried Mary Lou into the bedroom, Hattie had the bed open and ready. She scurried out to fill her tub and boil water.

Tom helped his mother undress Mary Lou and get her into a large gown. When he was satisfied that his wife was settled, Tom pulled up the chair and sat beside her.

Pains began coming harder and more often. Mary Lou gritted her teeth and moaned. She smiled at Tom, thinking to ease the pain she saw in his anxious face.

Allena put her hand on Tom's shoulder. "Son, it would be better if you left. We women can take care of everything."

Mary Lou felt Tom's hands on her face and his kiss on her forehead. She smiled weakly. "Pretty soon, Tom, our—" Her words were cut off by a sharp pain that rhythmically brought on another and another.

"Now git." Allena took her son by the arm and led him to the door. "Things are happening fast. I don't think it will be too long. I'm surprised she was able to bump over the road." She laughed. "That's probably what started everything."

Never had Mary Lou endured such pain. Her body writhed in protest. Hattie kept wiping her face with a cool cloth.

After what seemed like hours, Allena hollered, "Now, push, Mary Lou. Push!"

Her body felt ripped in half.

"It's a boy!" Mary Lou heard Allena call out, then laughter filled the room.

A boy. Her swimming head cleared at the joyous news. She laughed with them. *A son for Tom.* Mary Lou took a deep breath. It was over.

Suddenly the hammer of pain pounded her body again. She heard Allena and Hattie talking, but the hurt mumbled their words. Mary Lou gasp as another pain tore at her, then another and another.

"Mary Lou!" Allena's voice came from a deep well.

She dragged open bleary eyes. Her mother-in-law's face was close to hers.

"Bear down again, Mary Lou. Hard. Do you hear me? Bear down again."

Again? But she was done. A fresh pain stabbed her lower parts. Would it ever be over? It didn't seem Darcy had had such a time, or was it just that Mary Lou was the one hurting this time?

"Mary Lou, stop screaming and push!"

Allena's words shattered in her head and her body convulsed, but Mary Lou pushed—and pushed. She heard a baby cry and Allena and Hattie laughing. It boggled her mind. Finally her body settled into peace and everything went black.

Chapter 11

Mary Lou forced open heavy eyelids. Blurred figures surrounding the bed evolved into shapes.

Tom stood with a baby in each arm. He leaned over, kissed her, laid a baby on each side of her, and raised up grinning. "How about this, little Mama? We have twins, a boy and a girl."

In awe, Mary Lou gazed from one small bundle to the other, then into the proud, adoring eyes of her husband. "Oh, Darling," she cried. "The Lord gave us hundredfold!" She laughed until it hurt, her gaze devouring one small pink face, then the other.

Little Tom's head was hazed with red and looked just like his father. Beth's hair was longer and the color of Mama's. *Twins!* Even seeing them, Mary Lou couldn't believe it.

Allena opened each blanket to expose tiny legs and arms. She patted Beth. "She took us by surprise. Little Tom came, and then you went into labor again and out came this tiny little girl, who screamed as if she thought we'd forgotten her." Allena leaned over and kissed Mary Lou on the forehead. "Thank you, my dear. That puts three arrows in my quiver."

Tom helped Mary Lou sit up, lifted the babies into her arms, and sat beside her with his arms around his family.

Mary Lou touched and rubbed their soft, tiny legs and hands. "I wish Mama were here to see them." She felt Tom's arm tighten around her.

Allena smiled. "And who's to say she doesn't know? I'm sure in heaven she's as pleased and happy as I am with our two beautiful grandchildren."

"Thank you, Mother."

Hattie came in with a bowl of steaming soup. "If you're going to nurse two, you'd better start eating." She handed the bowl to Tom.

Allena took the twins, while Hattie added plump pillows to help Mary Lou sit up straight to eat.

A knock sounded on the door, and Darcy peeked in. "I came to see what all the fuss is about."

Mary Lou's heart warmed. "Come in, Darcy, and look what the Lord sent!"

Darcy's lips formed a noncommittal smile.

Did Mary Lou read a longing in Darcy's dark eyes? It vanished as quickly as it came. "Won't Baby Zack, little Tom, and Beth have fun playing together?"

"I'm glad for you," Darcy said with genuine compassion.

Their eyes met. For the first time, Mary Lou felt kin to Darcy. They were both mothers. She sensed a desolate ache and longed to put her arms around Darcy as she had Nelson. Darcy dropped her gaze. A second later she looked up. The veiled Darcy was back.

Three small babies kept things buzzing day and night. Hattie tried to keep up with the baby laundry, and for the first time, she couldn't seem to keep a supply of hot water.

Tom stayed close to home as much as he could and tended to needed jobs around the barn, stables, and ranch house. Mary Lou often put the twins in baskets, and they each carried one to the barn just to be together. Tom worked steadily on a cradle for Beth, who seemed quite comfy in a makeshift bed in the bottom drawer of Mama's chest.

Darcy dressed and fed Baby Zack, but Allena did the therapy on his leg. She tried to teach Darcy, but Darcy refused to learn.

One day the young mothers sat in the rockers on either side of the fireplace in the kitchen, their babies in their laps. Hattie loved their company and usually found a job she could do sitting in her rocking chair.

She surprised them that morning by confiding, "I had a little son when I was about your age."

Mary Lou exclaimed, "Hattie! I didn't know you were ever married." Hattie sat and nodded, seemingly lost in her task of paring potatoes. Softly she spoke. "My man Jeremy was killed in the Civil War. I tried to keep our farm in Pennsylvania going for Sonny and me. When he was killed—"

Mary Lou gasped. "Killed! Oh, how old was he?"

Hattie heaved a painful sigh. "Four. I was busy working in the garden and didn't notice him wander into the woods." She dropped her hands into her lap, mindless of the knife and partially peeled potato, and stared into the painful memory.

Mary Lou sensed her anguish. "What happened?"

"I heard a bear growl, then Sonny's scream. I jumped up and ran into the woods." Hattie's voice broke.

"After a bear?" Mary Lou exclaimed. "Oh, Hattie, I would be scared to death." Neither she nor Darcy asked the next question.

Hattie gathered a corner of her apron to capture her tears. "All I found was his torn bloody clothes." Her voice grew soft and husky. "I buried them in a grave and left the farm."

"How did you ever get here from Pennsylvania?"

"I got on the first stage headin' west. Mr. Langdon was on the stage, and he kindly became my protector. After I told him my story, he said his wife had been hunting for a housekeeper and asked if I would consider the job. I came to see and stayed." Hattie peeled another potato. "I know as well as I sit here, it was God's providence."

Mary Lou's neck tingled.

Later, out in the barn, Mary Lou told Tom.

Tom nodded. "I remember when she came. I was about four or five. She was the one I always ran to when Doug would pick on me."

Mary Lou remembered her first conversation with Hattie. "Mr. Tom, he's special," she had said. Now Mary Lou knew why.

"There, it's finished." Tom gave Beth's cradle a final polish with a cloth. "Now I can concentrate on the cattle drive. Smitty and the boys have been getting things ready for that long trip to Abilene. We'll be leaving next week."

Mary Lou dreaded the thought of Tom being gone for a couple months. She knew it was impossible, but she longed to go home for a visit. The thought of seeing Aunt Nelda, Aunt Tibby, Jenny, Glenn, and her father filled her with her worst case of homesickness since she had left home. Yet she knew the twins were much too small to travel that long distance.

"Perhaps after the spring roundup next year," Tom suggested, "the twins will be old enough to travel and we can head to Kansas for a visit. How would that be?"

Mary Lou threw her arms around her dear husband, who so often seemed to sense what she thought. At times it was a little scary, but in truth, she knew love could do that. She remembered Mama and Pa before his accident broke the connection.

Chapter 12

T he day before Tom, Smitty, and the boys left on the cattle drive, Mary Lou and Hattie scrubbed over washboards all day in between the needs of the twins. For the moment, Tommy and Beth were both asleep in their cradles—a rare phenomenon.

Line after line of clean clothes fluttered in a gentle warm morning wind and dried quickly. The two women caught and pulled the dry clothes from the line, separated the baby clothes, piled them all in two laundry baskets, and carried them toward the house.

A shiny new buggy rolled into the yard and stopped at the hitching rail. Doug got out and ran around to the passenger side.

Hattie motioned with her head. "Looks like Mr. Doug bought himself a new buggy." She continued toward the kitchen door and then stopped. Mouth open, eyes wide, Hattie stared.

The same expression covered Mary Lou's face.

Brazenly hanging on Doug's arm was a girl from the saloon! Mary Lou couldn't believe it. *One of those women? Why would Doug bring her here? His mother will be shocked!*

Hattie's mouth closed into a pursed line of fury. Her eyes spit fire. Mary Lou hurriedly opened the kitchen door, and Hattie stomped through, plunking the basket on the floor. "I knew that boy had a lot of nerve, but this is too much. Shows no respect for his mother at all."

Allena entered the kitchen as the front door banged.

"We have company" was all Mary Lou could think to say.

"Good." Allena moved toward the parlor to greet them. Mary Lou followed hesitantly.

Doug strutted in, the girl slightly behind him and noticeably uneasy. He stood, a sly grin on his face, and looked at Allena. "Mother, this is my wife, Lily." He pulled the girl from behind him and thrust her forward. "Sorry we didn't have time for her to change from her wedding gown."

Allena raised to her full height and nodded slowly.

The new bride wore a short, flouncy ruffled dress and high-heeled, lacy shoes. A black Spanish fringed shawl covered her bare shoulders, the ends clutched tightly in her hands.

Thunderbolts exploded in Mary Lou's head. *Doug married her?*

Allena hesitated only a second. Irrespective of what must have been going through her mind, she graciously stepped forward and stretched both hands toward her new daughter-in-law.

"I thought since Zack and Tom surprised you with a bride, I could do no less." Doug laughed.

Allena reprimanded her son with a sharp glance, accepted Lily's hesitant hands, smiled, and placed a gentle kiss on her cheek. She turned to Doug. "When were you married?"

"This morning. We thought we better make it legal so we went to a justice of the peace."

Mary Lou watched a disturbing shadow cross Allena's face and her heart ached for her. For a Christian, marriage without clergy was no marriage at all.

Allena linked her arm through Lily's. "Come, my dear."

At Allena's touch, Lily drew herself to full height.

Mary Lou marveled at the composure and dignity her mother-in-law displayed. Three of her sons had ignored any plans she might have had for them and married absolute strangers.

"I'm sure you would feel more comfortable if you changed out of your wedding dress." Allena turned to Mary Lou. "Lily looks about your size and should fit into one of your dresses, don't you think?" Allena guided Lily toward the bedrooms.

Doug folded his arms, his mouth a twisted grin of malicious pleasure.

Mary Lou shuddered. He was enjoying the situation—had created it deliberately! For what reason? To hurt his mother? What cruel quirk chewed at him inside and fanned an inner war that made him enjoy hurting others? At home he constantly put everyone on edge and changed the whole atmosphere of the household.

Hattie must have been glued to the dining room door frame. She appeared the minute Allena and Lily left and gazed down the hall at their retreating figures. "Well, I never—"

Doug walked over and put his arm around Hattie's shoulders. "What's the matter, Hattie, don't you approve of my new wife?"

Incensed, Hattie brushed his arm off her shoulders. Doug's wry smile pulled his nose into a sneer. "You don't like me, do you, Hattie?"

"I'm a Christian. I love you, but I don't like the way you act. Shame on you, puttin' your ma in such a position. One of these days, Mr. Doug, you're goin' to get your comeuppance, and it won't be good."

Doug's face clouded into a scowl. "Dear Hattie. I always knew I was your favorite." He laughed.

"Humph!" Hattie grabbed the laundry basket, stomped outside, and banged the door against his laughter.

Mary Lou tiptoed quietly into her bedroom and slowly opened Mama's chest, hoping not to disturb the twins. They looked like soft, pink cherubs. She pushed aside her favorite blue dress that Mama had made and picked up a couple of her better calicos and a petticoat. She followed Hattie, who was carrying a pitcher of hot water to Doug's room. After placing the clothes on Doug's bed, Mary Lou and Allena stepped out into the hall.

They heard rustlings and splashing within. Shortly the door opened, and Lily stepped out in a long-skirted calico. Her face had been scrubbed till it shone, and her light brown, wavy hair was twisted into a high bun on top of her head.

Mary Lou stood in awe at the transformation. Lily was pretty!

Allena smiled and nodded. "That looks more comfortable." She swept her hand around Doug's room in its usual state of upheaval. "Forgive this room. Hattie and I will clean it and help you get settled."

As they entered the parlor, Doug struggled to carry two carpet bags through the door. His eyebrows raised at Lily, and he wrinkled his nose. "Now you look like all the women. I like you better the other way." He dropped the bags in the middle of the kitchen floor.

Lily smiled, lips trembling. A horse clattered to the post.

Tom! Mary Lou thought with relief. She watched him dismount, bang the dust off himself, and stride toward the door.

Doug greeted him with a punch on the shoulder and moved him in front of Lily. "Little brother, meet my new wife." Doug moved beside Lily, put his arm around her waist, and grinned.

Tom's eyebrow arched in surprise. "You? Married? I don't believe it!" He grinned, reached out, and returned Doug's punch. "About time you settled down."

"Who said anything about settling down?"

Tom's expression exhibited the shock they all felt. Lily's lips opened for a sharp intake of breath. Her shoulders sank for a scant second, but then her chin and shoulders squared and she smiled sweetly. "You must be Tom."

Tom nodded his head and walked toward her. He picked up Lily's hand, lightly kissed it, looked up, and smiled. "Welcome, Lily."

Lily bowed her head slightly, visibly shaken. When Tom released her fingers, she withdrew her hand and held it as if she'd been given a gift.

Darcy entered, carrying Baby Zack, and was introduced to her new sister-in-law. She assessed the young woman from head to foot, and then nodded in dismissal.

Lily brightened. "Oh." Her laugh jangled. "You have a baby! I love babies."

Doug's eyes widened, his brows lifted, and he rolled his eyes.

Darcy held the baby forward. "You can hold him if you like."

Lily hesitated a moment, darted a glance at Doug who shrugged his shoulders, then eagerly gathered the baby into her arms.

"We have two," Mary Lou said proudly. "Tom and I have twins, a boy and a girl. They are both asleep, which doesn't happen too often or last too long. If one wakes. . ."

Lily looked wistfully into Mary Lou's eyes. "How fortunate you are."

Doug snickered and made an exaggerated bow. "Now if you ladies can spare me, I've got to get back to town and meet a man coming in on the stage." He glanced at Darcy. "A friend of yours."

Darcy came to life. "Kenneth?"

Doug nodded. "He'll be here today hopefully with two other Eastern gentlemen."

"Do bring them out!" Darcy beamed. "It will be wonderful to see Kenneth again."

Doug nodded, grabbed his hat, and aimed for the door.

"Bye, Lily. See you later," he called over his shoulder. The *clip-clop* of his horse's hooves faded quickly.

Lily raised her hand in a short wave and turned her undivided attention to Baby Zack.

"I'll be out in the barn," Tom said and left.

For a strained moment, the four women regarded one another.

Hattie moved first, toward the kitchen. "I'd best be gettin' busy. I'm way behind in my work."

Allena pointed down the hall. "Let's see what we can do to make Doug's room presentable."

"I'll set the table, Hattie," Mary Lou called, carrying an armful of dinner plates into the dining room. She hovered over the table with the extra place setting, wondering where to put it. Allena sat at the end of the table and father Zachary's place was completely set, his chair in place at the opposite end. Zack, Darcy, Tom, and Mary Lou sat on Allena's right. Immediately to her left, Nelson had the end chair to facilitate him maneuvering his crutches. Doug came next.

Mary Lou set Lily's plate in the place next to Doug. That left one guest chair next to Lily, across from Mary Lou. She stared at it a long moment. *I wonder who will fill it?*

Chapter 13

Tom pulled the wagon up to the hitching rail to let Mary Lou off with the twins. They had spent the morning in their future home. Each room that took shape fulfilled something deep inside Mary Lou. Tom said as soon as the floors were in, they could prepare to move. Excitement bubbled in her heart, and she thanked God for her many blessings.

A horse thundered through the Circle Z arch. Laura, her hair stretched behind her riding the wind, came to an abrupt halt and slid to the ground, breathless, in front of Tom and Mary Lou.

"You're just the ones I want to see. I need help." Laura grabbed Tommy from Tom, and she and Mary Lou walked to the house. Tom swung the wagon toward the barn. "I'll be back," he called over his shoulder.

Allena and Lily, carrying Baby Zack, had gone to town to buy yard goods for new clothes for Lily plus a list of supplies needed by Hattie. Darcy accompanied them for a visit to the dressmaker. Kenneth Dillard fused new life into Darcy, and she spent hours eagerly making plans to return to Boston to visit her parents. Nelson clumped down the hall to greet them.

Laura ran to meet him and brazenly embraced and kissed him in front of Tom and Mary Lou. She turned smiling. "This is what I—we—want to talk to you about."

The twins had to be fed and settled for their naps before any serious conversation could take place, but soon the four adults were gathered around the table with some dinner.

Nelson blurted out the news. "Laura and I want to get married."

Neither Mary Lou nor Tom was surprised at the announcement, but they understood the younger couple's dilemma. Allena had closed her ears to their plea.

"What does Mother say?" Tom asked.

Nelson shook his head. "She says we're both too young to handle a ranch because of my legs."

Laura tossed her head like an impatient pony. "Owning a ranch isn't the only thing in the world. We could move to Harness, have a business, or something else. I'm a good cook; we could open an boardinghouse."

Nelson sipped his coffee. "I always knew I would never be a rancher.

Mother says God has something else for me, yet she keeps talking about me working a ranch. Other people earn a living without a ranch. I'm confident Laura and I can make it somehow."

He reached into his pocket and brought out a necklace made of dainty polished stones. "If I can sell my paintings to Mr. Dillard, I can sell these too."

Mary Lou turned the necklace over and over in her hands and draped it around her neck. "Nelson, this is lovely. When did you make this?"

"This spring. I saw a stone necklace hanging around the neck of an Indian girl in Harness. I gathered these stones around your place, polished them, scraped a hole through and strung them."

Mary Lou's heart ached for these two young people reaching for any straw that would enable them to have a life together. She remembered the year she yearned for Tom, not knowing whether she would ever see him again, let alone marry him. But God had answered her prayers.

She remembered her own quandary and how she had clung to Pa's arm as he led her into Aunt Tibby's parlor to be married. Her heart had wept over her lost dream, but she had resolutely resigned herself to marrying Glenn and being a town girl. Yet within that next hour, God had fulfilled her dreams of being a rancher's wife. If all the bizarre obstacles she and Tom had faced were swept away to make it possible for them to marry, then there was a way God had in mind to work out a marriage for Laura and Nelson.

"How do your folks feel about it?" Tom asked Laura.

"Father and Mother have given their blessing, but they know how Allena feels. Ma says she is too protective of Nelson, that he is a grown young man now, not her little boy." Laura's eyes glistened with tears, and she shook her head vigorously and wailed, "He can't be her little boy all his life!" Tears spilled and Laura placed her hand over her mouth. "I'm sorry—that was disrespectful."

Tom gazed at Nelson. "And how do you feel about it all?"

Nelson looked up with stars in his eyes. "I love Laura, and I'm going to marry her. We'll make it. God will show us a way. I know it." He set his face.

Silence prevailed, minds churned.

Tom's voice broke through. "Are you two prepared to live here at the ranch for awhile after you are married to satisfy Mother that you are capable of handling whatever comes?"

No answer was needed in light of the beaming smiles on two young faces.

"Then let's pray and look for what God has in mind. In the meantime," Tom grinned, "you two get ready to be married."

Hattie came through the kitchen door with a bag over her shoulder, a vegetable bounty from the garden. She glanced at four shining faces, grinned, plopped her bag on a chair, and faced them with that knowing look.

Tom laughed. "And what do you think about it, Hattie?"

She stifled a smile. "About what?"

"Don't pretend to me, Hattie. Your ears are wiggling."

"Oh, Mr. Tom."

Tom jumped up and put his arm around her shoulders. "Hattie, I want to know what you think about Nelson and Laura getting married."

"It's high time." She gazed at Nelson. "That young man needs a wife." She turned to Laura. "And he's not goin' to find a better one than you, Miss Laura."

Laura rose, rushed to Hattie, threw her arms around her, and planted a kiss on her cheek. "Tell that to Mother Langdon."

Hattie got all ruffled. "Now you children know me. I don't interfere."

Tom let loose a hearty laugh. "You and Mother interfere with everything that goes on around here and seemingly never make a decision."

"I've said my say." Hattie grabbed the washing pan, poured water into it, and began scrubbing vegetables vigorously.

"So you have." Tom touched her bouncing cheek and made her blush. "And we are all in agreement." He stood in thought and then bowed his head. "Now it's praying time."

Everybody bowed.

"Father, God," Tom began, "You know all about us, out deepest hopes and desires. And You know all about love. You displayed it for us on the cross. We ask, Father, that our personal desires not hinder You in this matter. Thy will be done. In Jesus' name, Amen."

Head still bowed, Laura added quietly, "And help us recognize Your answer when it comes, dear Lord." She sighed. "And, please—make it soon!" She lifted damp lashes and gazed at Nelson.

Nelson cradled her gaze in his. "Amen."

A howl from one twin cut through the air, accompanied quickly by the other. Mary Lou and Laura both rose and left the kitchen. Tom and Nelson walked to the barn.

In the late afternoon, Allena and Lily drove into the yard. Mary Lou and Laura ducked through lines fluttering with baby clothes and diapers and carried the twins to meet their grandmother.

"Where's Darcy?" Mary Lou asked.

"She wanted to stay in town and come home with Zack and Mr. Dillard. Zack will rent a buggy to bring them home."

Both women climbed out of Allena's buggy and grabbed a twin. Laura and Mary Lou gathered their string-tied packages, and they all walked to the house.

Allena opened the kitchen door. "Get ready, Hattie. Mr. Dillard will be here for supper."

The evening bubbled with plans. Mr. Dillard already had arrangements for he and Darcy to leave on a stage riding north the next Monday. He couldn't leave earlier—had business to finish up, he said.

The week passed quickly. Darcy went into town twice to be fitted and to check on her new dresses and hats.

Lily took care of Baby Zack and loved every minute of it. She showered him with love, and he preferred Lily to anyone else. Allena and Mary Lou were in the parlor reading the Bible for morning devotions. A sudden noise caught their attention and the flip of a rustling skirt caught their eye. Mary Lou rose and went to see who it was. As she reached the door, she saw Lily's back disappearing into the kitchen.

"It was Lily passing by," she said.

Next morning, the rustling was there again. Mary Lou rose, very quietly this time, and tiptoed to the door. When she peeked around the door frame, Lily was standing with her back to the wall, listening. Mary Lou motioned Allena to come.

Allena stepped into the hall.

Startled, Lily pressed back against the wall as if she'd been caught in a crime.

Allena smiled. "Lily, would you like to come join us in our devotions?"

Lily's smile erased uneasiness. "Yes, Ma'am. I would."

"Then come in, my dear. You're welcome."

The three women settled themselves.

"We were just finishing the last few verses of Proverbs 31."

Lily nodded and folded her hands in her lap.

Allena picked up her Bible, smoothed the page, and continued: " 'She looketh well to the ways of her household, and eateth not the bread of idleness. Her children arise up, and call her blessed; her husband also, and he praiseth her. Many daughters have done virtuously, but thou excellest them all.' "

Mary Lou spied two fat streams of tears cascading down Lily's cheeks. Her shoulders shuddered and sobs began.

Allena looked up from her reading.

Lily covered her face with her hands. "I. . .shouldn't be. . .here. I'm. . .a . . .sinful woman. I knew—when Doug married me—I. . .shouldn't have. . ." Sobs consumed her. She covered her head with her arms and slumped into a heap of misery.

Allena laid her Bible aside, looked tenderly at Mary Lou, and nodded. Mary Lou knelt beside Lily, put her arms around her, and cradled her head.

"Don't cry, Lily, you're fine now. God has given you a whole new life."

Allena's hand smoothed Lily's hair. "This is exactly where you should be, my dear. Remember the question Jesus asked the woman caught in adultery: 'Where are your accusers?'"

Lily raised her wet, agonized face.

Allena cupped it in her hands. "No one has come forth to accuse you. Neither do we, Lily. God has given us a glimpse of your true heart."

Lily's tear-stained eyes lifted in amazement and searched first Allena's face, then Mary Lou's. Lily slipped from her chair to her knees. "Oh, God, forgive me," she cried and collapsed into tears.

Allena and Mary Lou slipped to their knees beside her.

"Father," Allena began, "Your child has come home, and she accepts Your forgiveness. There is no one here to cast the first stone."

The three women knelt in silence for a few moments, then rose and hugged one another. Tears flowed freely, and each found the corner of her apron to wipe her face.

A familiar sound penetrated. Babies were crying. The women smiled and went back to work.

Chapter 14

The sun yawned, stretched, opened its eyes, and peeked into the new day. Golden fingers traveled across the land and encircled a young man and woman standing in front of an adobe shell of a house, snuggled into the ground by its new roof.

Tom slipped an arm around Mary Lou, grinned, and squeezed her waist. "I really wanted to be done and have us moved in before I left, but I couldn't make it. Tex and Bart are in charge while I'm gone, and they'll finish putting down the wooden floor. By the time I get back, they should be done and we can move in. The well and root cellar were finished yesterday."

Tom gently folded his wife in his arms and gazed into her upturned face. "It used to be I could hardly wait until the trail drive began. Now I wish it was over. It's not going to be easy being away from you and the twins. I'll probably have Smitty on my back for trying to move the cows too fast, but I intend to make this the fastest trip on record." He bent and rested his lips on hers and they melted together into a soothing, gentle kiss.

Mary Lou clung to her husband to stem the surge of loneliness that came from the mere thought of him not being near. The hollow, uncomfortable feeling she remembered when he had left her at Point Lane the day Mama died returned and stabbed her heart. She had filled one of Tom's pouches with letters to Aunt Tibby, Aunt Nelda, Jenny, and her father, and she had secretly included six letters for Tom with instructions for him to read one a week. She smiled. Knowing Tom, he would read them all at once and reread them many times. She would have done the same.

Tom pulled her inside the house. "I have to show you something."

Mary Lou saw it immediately, sitting in the middle of the kitchen floor. Their big, new, four-poster bed! Tom had worked on it every evening, but she hadn't realized it was done! She walked around it and ran her hands up and down the smooth posters. "It's beautiful!"

"And long enough for me to sleep with my feet in the bed."

They both laughed.

Mary Lou's gaze wandered around the two rooms. As soon as the floors were done, she would have Tex and Bart move the bed into the bedroom. Hopefully, with Allena and Lily's help, she could get the rugs for each side of the bed finished and the new patchwork quilt all backed and tied before Tom returned. Then after his long, tiring ride home, they could snuggle in their own bed in their new home.

Mary Lou's memory jumped back to the day she, Pa, and Mama had moved into their new cabin in Venture. "Always set up and make your beds first thing when you move into your new home," Mama had said. "Then they are ready for everyone to fall into after the hard day's work of settling." Mary Lou planned to do just that.

Tinder and Dulcie stood like two sentinels, patiently awaiting their masters. Once mounted, the horses trotted eagerly back to the ranch house.

As they approached, they spied Kenneth Dillard's rented buggy at the hitching rail. They dismounted and stopped to catch voices in vigorous discussion drifting out the parlor window.

"I know your mother and father are looking forward to seeing their only grandson," Tom and Mary Lou heard Kenneth say.

"He's too young to travel all that distance," came Allena's quick reply.

"Darcy, travel is hard enough for an adult, let alone a seven-month-old baby." Zack's voice.

To announce their coming, Tom and Mary Lou opened and closed the kitchen door with a bang.

Darcy glanced up as they entered. Baby Zack was tightly cradled in his mother's arms. "I wondered if you were coming back before we left so we could say good-bye." Darcy eyed Mary Lou. "Maybe you two can help us decide this matter. Mother and Zack won't let me take my baby home to see his grandparents."

Mary Lou couldn't believe what she heard. Darcy had told her just the day before that she had no intention of taking Baby Zack. Her mouth opened in surprise. "But I thought you said—"

"I know, I know," Darcy interrupted, "but Mother Langdon and Zack insist the trip will be too much for him." Darcy's dark eyes flashed Mary Lou a warning.

"The trip will be rather tough on the little fellow," Tom offered. "It's a long, bumpy, dusty ride between stations."

Mary Lou stared in disbelief at Darcy's mother act. Darcy hugged her baby tightly to her breast as if she never wanted to let him go. She wended slowly back and forth among Zack, Allena, and Kenneth, who leaned against the wall watching her with the hint of a wry smile on his face.

Mary Lou's confusion cleared. Darcy didn't want to take Baby Zack home with her. She had cunningly directed everything so it would look like she did. Mary Lou could almost guess what would happen. Soon Darcy would make a dramatic sacrifice. She would let her mother-in-law and husband have their own way, and she would win the battle with no one the wiser.

Darcy's dark, sad eyes gazed from one to the other. She raised Baby Zack to her shoulder, kissed and patted him, and exuded a long, trembling sigh. After a long moment, she raised moist lashes to Zack, sandwiched their son between them, and looked repentantly into her husband's face.

"Darling, I'm sorry. I'm afraid I'm being selfish." She pressed the Baby into his father's arms, lowered her head, and said softly, "Zack, you are right. The trip will be too hard on him now." She paused and looked painfully into Zack's face. "I'll wait till next time."

Mary Lou, astounded at Darcy's farce, stood grounded in one spot, her tongue glued to the roof of her mouth.

Big teardrops slipped from Darcy's eyes. She daintily reached for the lace handkerchief tucked inside her sleeve, daubed her eyes, and then stood on tiptoe and kissed Zack's cheek. "For Baby Zack's sake. I'll leave him with you. I'll tell Mother and Father they will have to wait until he is old enough to travel." She turned and walked out of the room.

Both Allena and Zack eased a visible sigh. Zack held his son close and followed Darcy. Mary Lou stifled a smile. Darcy had won, but in truth she had lost. The real winner was baby Zack—and Lily.

Kenneth informed Zack the stagecoach would arrive in Harness around six o'clock in the morning. Rather than ride out so early from the Circle Z, Kenneth suggested that they arrange for a room at the hotel in Harness for Zack and Darcy to stay overnight, so that Darcy could be rested before the long trip. Before supper, they piled Darcy's trunk and several carpetbags on the back of the buckboard.

A radiant Darcy presided at the supper table. Mary Lou couldn't keep her eyes off her. Nor could anyone else. This was a Darcy the family had never seen: gracious, charming, smiling, chattering, beautiful in behavior as well as in appearance. Now all could see the girl Zack fell in love with. *I don't blame him*, Mary Lou thought. From the look on Allena's face, her mother-in-law agreed.

Supper over, everyone gathered around the buggy and buckboard to say good-bye. Darcy, standing beside Mary Lou, turned abruptly, and their eyes met in a penetrating stare. Mary Lou perceived a softness, a winsomeness in Darcy she had sensed many times, but had never seen set free.

Darcy gently put her arms around Mary Lou and said softly, "Thank you for being my friend. I'm afraid I gave you a hard time, but I always admired you and have often wished I could be like you, Prairie Girl. I have a friend in Boston who is a lot like you, sweet and kind to everyone." Darcy ducked her head. "Even me. She talks about God like you do, as if

He is with her every minute."

Mary Lou's heart soared. Here was her chance to speak a word about God to Darcy. Without restraint, Mary Lou threw her arms around her. "He is!" Mary Lou whispered in Darcy's ear, and then pushed her back and looked into her dark, fathomless eyes. "And He will be with you always if you let Him."

Oh God, Mary Lou prayed. *Help Darcy's godly friend to bring her to the saving grace of Jesus.*

"I'm going to miss you, Darcy." Mary Lou gave her an extra squeeze. "Hurry back," she said and meant it.

Zack helped Darcy into the buggy with Kenneth, then climbed into the buckboard. As they trotted off, Darcy spotted Lily standing with Baby Zack in her arms.

Darcy waved. "Take good care of him, Lily," she called

"I will." Lily lifted Baby Zack's arm and waved it to his mother. Everyone waved until the wagons passed under the Circle Z arch.

At four o'clock the next morning, Tom climbed out of bed, gathered his clothes, leaned over for a long look at the twins in their cradles, and tiptoed to the kitchen to get dressed.

Mary Lou, already dressed, checked the twins. Their reposed pink faces spoke of angels and fluttered her heart. She dared not touch one for fear they would wake.

Tom, Smitty, and the cowboys had ridden the range for the last month rounding up the longhorns from summer pasture and heading them north. The cowboys had been on night watch for three weeks with several good cutting horses to change the mind of any feisty bull that suddenly decided he wanted to be boss and lead off a bunch of cows.

Long before sunup, Jess, the cook, had risen to make an early breakfast of beef, sourdough biscuits, gravy, potatoes, and greens for the cowboys to stock up before they left. After cleanup, Jess drove the chuck wagon out with Smitty, the trail boss, who took the lead to find grazing land up ahead. The cowboys' job was to keep the cattle together and moving.

Mary Lou and Tom had planned to say good-bye in the parlor. She sat braiding old material into a rug and put it aside when she heard Tom's step.

Other than a few night watches when Tom had been out riding the line, they had never been apart. Neither of them said much, but both dreaded this time of parting.

Their kiss was long and sweet. Tom's arms held Mary Lou extra tight, as though he wanted to hold her forever. When he released her, Mary Lou felt cast adrift.

Tom picked up her hands and planted a kiss on each palm and closed her fingers. "Keep these until I come back, and I'll redeem them."

They went outside.

"I'll tell everyone in Venture you said hello and you miss them very much," Tom said as he mounted Tinder.

Mary Lou nodded her head. She didn't dare speak. A dam of tears awaited any release. She had determined to send Tom off with smiles and waves. She stood with her arm in motion until he blended into the landscape.

A familiar cry came from the house. Tommy. A soft gurgling voice joined him. The twins were awake.

Chapter 15

A month dragged by. Mary Lou shook and spread the wet clothes on the line to dry, a never-ending job with three babies. Lily came around the side of the house carrying another full basket.

"We're going to have to string another line," Mary Lou hollered.

Lily dropped her basket, spun on her heel, and shortly emerged with more rope. She strung it between two poles and proceeded with her task of tossing and smoothing the wet clothes over the line.

A familiar horse and rider pounded through the arch. Doug reined abruptly, sending a dust swirl into the air that innocently settled on the clean wash.

Lily ran to meet him, all smiles. "You're home early."

He slid to the ground and dropped the reins. "Not for long," he said and strode in giant steps toward the door.

By the time Mary Lou and Lily walked into the kitchen, they heard Doug in the ranch office, slamming drawers and mumbling to himself. "Where is it?" he shouted.

The two women, surprised to see the office door standing open, watched Doug as he scattered papers everywhere.

"Where's what?" Mary Lou asked and knew by the fierce look on Doug's face that her question was out of order.

He opened and banged shut a couple more drawers, then swung to face Mary Lou. "My brothers have been in here, haven't they?"

"I don't know what you are talking about." Tom had told her under no circumstances to tell Doug that he and Zack had the extra set of keys. They had spent a lot of time just before Tom left looking for an important paper.

"You mean you, Tom, Zack, and my mother haven't been in here searching through these drawers while I'm gone? Don't give me that! I'm not dumb. I don't know how they do it but—"

The look of surprise on Mary Lou's face must have been a better answer than any words she could have conjured.

Doug continued to yank open and slam shut every drawer in the desk. When he found nothing, he reached into his vest pocket, took out the safe keys, and rummaged through the mess of papers inside with such vigor that they scattered all over the floor.

"What's going on here?"

The younger women stepped aside to let Allena enter.

Doug swung to his mother. "I thought I was supposed to run this ranch! I don't need any help from my brothers."

"This ranch belongs to all of us, Doug. We wonder why you don't let us share the burden of running it. It's too great a load for only one person."

Doug straightened up with a sneer. "Then help me find the land deed to the southeast corner. I must have that paper!"

Not quite knowing what the land deed looked like, all three women began sorting and folding papers into orderly piles.

Mary Lou shuddered. Chaos everywhere. The room even smelled stuffy and dusty. How could Doug know a deed was hidden in this mess of papers, let alone expect to find it?

No deed was found.

Doug shooed the women out of the office, locked it, grabbed Lily's hand, and hurried her back to the bedroom. Allena and Mary Lou turned toward the kitchen. Neither said a word.

"Will Mr. Doug be here for dinner? It's just about ready."

"I imagine so, Hattie. Mary Lou and I will set the table so we can eat before Doug goes back to town. He looks like he could stand a good meal. I wish he would take time to eat properly. He looks thinner every time I see him."

"No cookin' like home cookin'." Hattie went back to her pots.

In the past month, along with growing thinner, Doug had also become angrier and returned to his sullen ways. When he first brought Lily home, he had changed. He'd actually smiled and joked with his brothers. Lily's love had softened him.

On other days, Mary Lou didn't know how Lily put up with him. Yet, no matter what time of day or night Doug came home, Lily was there, checking to see if he had eaten or slept. She openly loved him and made him a good wife. He was so lucky to have her. Mary Lou told her so. Lily blushed and bowed her head.

The dinner bell rang for the third time with impatience and volume. "Nothin' worse than cold food," Hattie mumbled and stomped back to the kitchen.

Everyone got her message and hurried to the table. The twins and baby Zack were bibbed and tied in chairs. In the barn, high chairs were in the process of being built.

Allena said grace and began passing dishes of food. "The ranch seems to be doing better," she said cheerfully. "Tom said we have at least a thousand more head going to market this year."

"He had better get top dollar. We need it." Doug ate hurriedly and glanced around. "Where's Nelson?"

"At the Shepard's." Allena's face clouded.

Mary Lou knew Mother was troubled about Nelson and Laura. They spent a lot of time traveling back and forth between the Circle Z and the Bar-S. They were together as often as possible, open in their love for each other. Allena's only comment spoke to the neglect of Nelson's painting.

"Mother, I love my painting," Nelson had responded, "but I have something else. I need to be normal, or as normal as I can be. I want to marry Laura."

"*Oh, Lord,* Mary Lou prayed, *help Allena to remember how she loved Father Zack and how necessary it is for Nelson to be joined to the one You have chosen for him. Let her listen to her heart, Lord, remembering how it was to be young and in love.*

Mary Lou had no doubt that if it hadn't been for God's intervention through Aunt Tibby and Aunt Nelda, she and Tom would have missed each other completely and been cheated out of the best.

If Allena didn't soften, it wouldn't surprise Mary Lou if Nelson and Laura took things in their own hands, especially with the Shepards on their side. Allena's heart would break if they moved without taking her into consideration—her fourth son to take matters into his own hands in the task of choosing his wife.

Mary Lou recognized the fear clutching Allena's heart. Fear for her baby. But Laura was right. Allena's little boy no longer existed. Nelson was a young man in love.

The women had only half-finished their meal when Doug shoved his empty plate away. "I've got to get back." He turned to Lily. "I'm staying in town tonight. See you tomorrow afternoon."

Lily followed him out.

Allena and Mary Lou fed bits of mashed food to the children. A smiling Lily returned to the table, picked up a spoon, and began feeding Baby Zack. To nurse the twins, Mary Lou moved to the rocker.

Lily settled in the opposite rocking chair to give Baby Zack his bottle. When she finished, she took him outside for exercise and held his hands while the baby seriously maneuvered one high step after the other, favoring one leg. Under Allena's tutelage, Lily's massage and exercise had encouraged Baby Zack's short leg to grow half an inch, impressing Dr. Mike.

Sleepy children's faces washed, each woman rocked a baby until small eyelids drooped and closed. They tucked them quickly into bed for their naps and hurried to waiting tasks.

Mary Lou gathered her curtain material and sewing implements into a basket, saddled Dulcie, and rode to their new house. She heard rhythmic pounding of two hammers afar off. Tex and Bart had finished the floor in the bedroom and had moved the bed into the spot she had told them, the small table and chair beside it.

A light, warm breeze skipped through the open door, exhaling a breath of cool air. Mary Lou settled to cut and sew. When finished, she stretched to the top of the window to tie the curtain cord to the nails on either side.

"Mighty pretty," Tex said as he stood at the door watching.

Mary Lou nodded. "Thank you. They should cheer up the place a bit, don't you think?" She pulled the cord tighter around the nails on either side of the window. The curtains still sagged in the middle.

"Tex, could you pound me a nail in the middle so the curtains will hang straight across the top?"

"Yes ma'am." He pulled a nail from his pocket, poised it, and hammered. "How's that?"

"Perfect." Mary Lou stretched the cord, a panel on each side of the center nail. Then she and Tex anchored the cords to the frame on each side and stood back to appraise their work.

Tex hung back a moment. "Forgive me, Ma'am, for sayin' so, but watchin' you and Tom makes me kinda hanker to find me a good woman I could make my missus." He rubbed his nose and grinned. "Trouble is, I can't seem to find a woman who will put up with me."

Mary Lou smiled. "It all depends on where you are looking. There are a lot of young women around these parts who are hunting for a good steady fellow like you."

Tex's eyebrows raised in surprise. "A cowboy?"

"What's wrong with a cowboy? My pa was one." Mary Lou's heart flew back to what Pa had been like when she was a little girl. He had sat solid in the saddle and laughed all the time. His accident changed all that. Mary Lou bobbed her head.

"He was the best. My aunt Tibby told me before I married Tom that cowboys were just young men doing a very hard job. She married Uncle Nate, who was a cowboy and now owns the biggest spread in Venture."

Mary Lou grinned. "She also said they make good husbands. So you see, there's hope for you." Mary Lou smiled at the red spots growing on Tex's cheeks. "Yep, someday you'll make some lucky girl a good husband, Tex, and I'll pray she'll come."

The color heightened. Tex ducked his head. "Thank ya, Ma'am. I. . .uh . . .never heard anyone say it so good before."

Mary Lou gathered her materials into the basket. "But remember, if you want a good wife, you have to start looking in the right places." She laughed at the intrigued look on Tex's face. "Try church. We're going to build one soon. Maybe you'd like to help. Women and girls bring the noon meal."

Tex grinned and glowed.

"Lots of pretty ones, too. I'm sure you will find one who will take a shine to you. And more than likely she'd be a good cook. Things haven't changed much. The way to a man's heart. . ." Mary Lou laughed, mounted Dulcie, and rode off, leaving Tex standing with his mouth open and some things to think about.

Trotting home, a sudden pain clutched Mary Lou's heart and brought with it new discovery. With Tom gone, she felt like only half a person and found herself looking for her other half wherever she went; at their new home, in the barn, she was constantly expecting her handsome, red-headed husband to walk through the door. She missed talking with him, sharing the amazing growth of the twins. Busy as she was, each day seemed a month. The nights were forever.

Mary Lou often found herself gazing far into the horizon, hoping for a glimpse of Tom riding in on Tinder. Home for her had truly become wherever Tom was. She hungered for his embrace, the smother of his kisses, and his sweet whisperings of love. She would even enjoy the smell of hay, horses, and sweat that surrounded him when he rode hard through the Circle Z arch in a hurry to get home to see her and the twins.

Something Mama had said one night during one of their woman talks popped into her memory: "When you really love someone, they become so real and so much a part of you that you find if they are not near, part of you is gone." Mama had known. She had continued to love Pa even after the bitterness from his accident shoved his wife and daughter out of his life.

Mary Lou sighed. At least she was counting off the last days. If all went well, Tom could be home in two weeks. Another forever.

Supper chores done, babies asleep and tucked in, the women dragged their rockers outside. The wind cooled and calmed. Every so often a breeze fluttered by, touching everything. Descending twilight soothed the night with a covering of peace.

The women's chatter stalled. Their mouths at rest, they leaned their heads against the backs of their rockers, watching the sun close its eye and release its hold on the night.

Long after everyone had gone to bed, Mary Lou woke to the clamor of a horse's hooves. She sat up. *Tom?* She prepared to leap out of bed, but then sank back. Zack's voice? Then Allena's. Their muffled voices floated from. . . the office? *Zack must have the keys.*

Prickles in her neck filled Mary Lou with apprehension. Could

something be wrong? Should she go and find out? With Tom not there. . .
She strained to listen. Abruptly the talking stopped, then continued outside.
Suddenly, a horse snorted, stomped around, and took off in a gallop.

Mary Lou sat on the side of the bed, waiting to see if Allena would come.
If it were something life-shaking, Allena surely would wake her. She waited
in the quiet. Her shoulders slumped. It had been a tiring day. Her heavy eyelids refused to stay open. She gazed at the twins, motionless in their cradles.
Mary Lou lay back and never remembered pulling up the cover.

B reakfast over, Mary Lou tied a ribbon around her hair at the nape of her neck. An hour or so at the new house that morning and the curtains would be finished. Allena and Hattie had to hoe the vegetable garden, so Lily offered to care for all three babies.

By working together that evening, the four women would be able to finish the quilt. All it needed was the tying and it would be done before Tom got home. Mary Lou tucked her sewing basket handle in the crook of her arm and started for the barn. Tex usually had Dulcie all saddled and ready to go. *Yep, he would make some lucky girl a good husband.*

Halfway across the yard, Mary Lou stopped and watched an unfamiliar wagon roll slowly through the arch, Zack at the reins, Dr. Mike in the seat beside him. Two familiar saddled horses were tied behind. The looks on the men's faces shot panic into Mary Lou.

Tex, Bart, and the cowboys came out of the barn to gawk, then walked slowly to the hitching rail as the wagon bumped to a halt. Zack jumped off and walked into the house. He emerged shortly, his mother on one arm and Lily on the other.

Mary Lou's reluctant feet carried her to the wagon. Dr. Mike jumped down, and she followed him to the back. Last, Nelson came out of the house, moving as briskly as he could.

Everyone gathered at the wagon, their eyes focused on a mound underneath the canvas. Mary Lou's heart held its breath. It looked like a. . .

Dr. Mike folded back the canvas.

Allena gasped, her hands flew to her mouth. She broke from Zack's grasp and flung herself on the body of her son, sobs wrenching deep within. "No, no," she wailed. "Oh, Doug! Doug."

Lily stood transfixed, a look of utter disbelief on her face, her eyes wet and wild. Slowly she reached out and laid one hand on her mother-in-law's shoulder, the other on the leg of her husband.

Hattie rushed outside, looked into the wagon, and stepped back. She grabbed a corner of her apron to mop escaping tears, shook her head back and forth, and then voiced what everyone was thinking. "I knew it. I prayed, but I knew Mr. Doug was headin' fer a no good end."

Mary Lou's gaze searched Zack, who looked haggard and drained. "What happened?"

"Let's go inside." Zack guided his mother, and Dr. Mike put his arm around Lily to steady her.

The cowboys rolled Doug's body in the canvas and carried it to his bedroom where they unrolled it onto the bed. Bart and Tex removed his boots.

"I'll finish," Allena said. "I'll wash and dress him." Her voice sounded hollow.

"Yes, Ma'am."

"I'll help." Lily held the door open for everyone to leave.

Hattie brought a basin of hot water, soap, and some towels left the two women who loved Doug most to do the last earthly thing they could for him.

Hattie busied herself setting out spoons and cups, which she filled with hot coffee. She pushed the sugar and cream in front of Dr. Mike. Before long, everyone but the two women were around the table. The cowboys stood behind, holding their steaming cups in their hands.

At first, no one talked. But the coffee revived their broken spirits, and Zack slowly began an explanation.

"Doug made another land sale. He received the money yesterday with a promise that he would turn over the land deed by suppertime."

Mary Lou voiced her thoughts. "So, that is why Doug was in such a frenzy in the ranch office yesterday!"

Zack nodded. "I saw him leave Harness in the afternoon and then come back. One of the sheriff's boys told me that they heard the land speculators were upset when the deed didn't arrive at suppertime. They accused Doug of reneging on the deal. Doug told them he never kept important papers in town, so they insisted he go home last night. They followed him so he could get it and give it to them."

Then it was Doug, not Zack, who Mary Lou had heard late last night!

Zack wet his dry mouth with a couple swallows of coffee. "The sheriff got wind of this deal last week. We planned to pretend we knew nothing, but we got ready for the speculators when they met Doug at suppertime. Unfortunately what we didn't know was that Doug had already been given the money yesterday and had promised to have the deed by last night. That is why they followed him home, to make sure they got the deed."

Unable to hide his moist eyes, Zack bowed his head. "What Doug didn't know was that I have it. Early this summer when I finally figured out what was going on, I took all the Circle Z deeds and put them in the safe in my office in town."

Nelson sat motionless, his eyes incensed. "You mean, they waited for

Doug and shot him on his own land?"

Mary Lou could almost hear Nelson's thoughts. If he had been able, he would be out now riding wildly to find his brother's killers.

Zack said, "I don't know where he was shot. Somebody came running to my office this morning and told me my brother's horse with Doug's body tied over it had come to a halt behind the saloon. Dr. Mike declared him dead, and we brought him home." Zack drained his cup, pushed back his chair, and left for Doug's room.

Hattie sniffed loudly. "That poor boy never had a chance."

Hardly a boy, Mary Lou thought. She remembered Mama reading in Luke 12 about a foolish man who flouts God. Jesus said, "But God said unto him, 'Thou fool, this night thy soul shall be required of thee: then whose shall those things be, which thou hast provided?' "

Zack stood in the doorway. "He's ready now."

After the family left, the cowboys stood about uneasily. Hattie went around with the coffeepot again. Shortly, Zack came back.

"You can go in now." His voice broke. He cleared his throat and gulped a couple swallows of coffee. Zack's nostrils flared, his jaw flexed. "They shot him in the back."

The cowboys stiffened. Silence enveloped the room like a shroud. It was one thing for a man to be shot facing his enemy, another to be shot from behind without a chance. Even a scoundrel didn't deserve that.

Later the barn resounded with hammers pounding nails into boards to make Doug's burying box.

Emily Shepard stayed close to Allena, who sat unnaturally quiet in one of the rocking chairs beside the fireplace.

The next day, wagons from neighbors filled the yard. They brought all kinds of food and comfort. Doug was laid in his burying box on two sawhorses in the parlor. One by one, the neighbors paid their respects.

Emily Shepard stayed close to Allena, sensing her needs.

Someone came from town and said Pastor Clayburn had been notified and would be at the burying early in the afternoon as soon as he could travel to Harness.

Mary Lou ached for Tom. Doug's death would be a greater shock when he came back than if he had been there. Now they were surrounded with loving support from neighbors and friends. Tom would have to take the loss square on the chin.

The wooden box holding Doug was already on the wagon when Pastor Clayburn came. Other wagons and neighbors on horseback followed the family to the Langdon cemetery.

Zack, Tex, Bart, and Will Shepard, with Nelson following on his crutches, carried the box with Doug's body to the fresh grave in the family cemetery and lowered it in with ropes. A damp wind blew a hint of rain, creating a sense of urgency.

Everyone gathered around the open grave. Women, dressed in black, stood close to their husbands. Timid, wide-eyed children shied into their mother's wide skirts.

Pastor Clayburn opened his Bible. "Let not your heart be troubled. . ."

Does every pastor begin a funeral services with the same words? Mary Lou's heart pounded as her memory rushed her back to another fall day when she had stared down into the grave holding her mother. The vacuum returned and revived her complete sense of loss. Tears streamed down her face. She was ashamed to admit they were not for Doug.

She gazed at Allena. Was she reliving the day she had laid her husband in the next grave?

"And those who believe in the Lord Jesus Christ and live according to His Word will live again. That is God's promise."

A heaviness settled on Mary Lou. As far as she knew or could discern, Doug had never accepted Jesus Christ. She remembered Tom one time saying that when they were little, his father had been firm about them accepting Christ as Savior. Had Doug taken that step as a small boy? A young man?

Yet, how did anyone truly know if someone had accepted Jesus as Lord and Savior? Mama had always said that was between a person and God, but that we were to love people regardless, like God loves us. But if Doug had not. . .

Mary Lou gazed at Allena and shared her grief. Whether Doug was guilty or not, Allena grieved for her son. Did God grieve for his lost ones, too?

"And may God have mercy on his soul." Pastor Clayburn closed his Bible and walked to Allena's side. A restless hush followed.

Zack stepped forward and picked up the first shovel. He pushed it into the soft earth and slowly tipped it.

The sound of the dirt hitting the box exploded in Mary Lou's brain. *Mama!* Her soul cried out in the pain of remembering. She felt alone and ached for Tom's comforting arms. Slowly an unexplainable warmth enveloped her, and she rested in a wash of reassurance that death was never the end.

Allena reached for a handful of dirt and poured it slowly through her fingers into the grave. Zack handed the shovel to Nelson and stepped behind him to balance him. Allena reached for his crutches. Nelson filled the shovel with dirt and poured it into the grave. He turned to Lily and stretched forth the shovel.

Lily drew back a moment, but after a smile of encouragement from

Allena, she filled the shovel. With dry, sad eyes, she slowly poured the soil into the grave.

Everyone stood in silence. Zack put his arm around his mother's shoulders, took Lily's hand, and led them both to the buggy. Nelson followed and climbed in the driver's seat. The buggy pulled away, and Zack returned to join his neighbors.

The dirt clods fell softer and softer as Zack and his neighbors dropped each shovelful into the grave.

For the first time in his life, Douglas Langdon was at rest.

Chapter 17

Doug's death hung a pall over the ranch.

Allena worked constantly, quietly, the strain of the loss of one of her sons mirrored in her grief-stricken eyes.

Lily seemed to be in a daze but faithfully did her chores, her sweet smile reduced to a small line across pale lips. She left the ranch every morning, walking no one knew where, but always returned before Baby Zack woke. When not doing chores, she cared for the baby and couldn't hide her obvious love for him. He was the only one who could call a smile to her face.

Every morning as soon as chores were done, Allena gathered Mary Lou, Lily, and Hattie into the parlor for devotions. They searched the Bible for words of comfort they found nowhere else.

Emily and Laura Shepard came often to join them. Emily also knew the heartbreak of losing a son. Her little Timothy had been three when he had wandered into the path of an angry bull, which gored and killed him.

Gradually the overriding undercurrent concerning the marriage of Nelson and Laura surfaced. At first, it was a comment here and there. One morning it blossomed into a full-blown discussion.

"I'd like to know your objections, Allena. Laura is brokenhearted." Emily's face was firm, her eyes pained.

"Emily, we have always talked plain to each other. I love Laura and consider her as my own."

"I know that, which makes it more difficult to understand your hesitancy about Nelson and Laura's marriage."

"You know the responsibility a man takes on when he marries. Under God, he vows to care of his wife and. . ." Allena paused.

Emily finished, "And for any children they may have? Is that what bothers you?"

Allena's disturbed gaze searched Emily, then the other women. "Well, yes. I'm concerned about that, but the largest part of a man's job is to provide for his own."

"My dear friend, as Laura's mother I am naturally concerned that any young man my daughter would choose to marry would have the ability to take care of her. But I have no doubt Nelson can do that, and neither does Laura.

"Allena, you should see him work with the cowboys at our ranch. Sometimes it is hard for them to remember there is anything wrong with him. He finds his own way to handle any situation. He and Laura work together like a well-matched team of horses."

Emily shook her head. "Allena. Think back. Remember what it was like when you and Zack met and fell in love. Nelson and Laura love each other and want to get married, and no reason you have given is more important than that."

Baby cries voiced a need. Hattie and Lily rose quickly and waved their hands at Mary Lou to stay put, then slipped out quietly.

In the trapped look upon her mother-in-law's face, Mary Lou could almost read her thoughts. Shortly after Mary Lou came to Texas, Allena had told her, "When Zack died, I transferred my love to my boys." Must she desperately hang on to them to give her life meaning?

Mary Lou knew it had hurt Allena to have been left out when Zack, Tom, and Doug had chosen their wives. Was Allena grasping Nelson as her last straw?

But that was not the way love worked. Mama had said love multiplies when you give it away. Was Allena blinded to the fact that she could drive a permanent wedge between herself and Nelson if she kept him from marrying the woman he loved?

Nelson and Laura walked into the parlor. "Since you are all talking about us, don't you think it would be well if you asked us how we feel?" Nelson asked.

Looks of startled guilt crossed faces and tied tongues.

"Mother, I know you want me to be happy. You've given me full proof of that all my life. You taught me not to feel like a cripple, that I can accomplish what I want to do in spite of my legs. But I have never thought of myself as a cripple—until now. That seems to be the only thing keeping Laura and me from being married. Mother, I love Laura, but if there is some other girl you think would make me a better wife, tell me who." Nelson's voice was quiet, controlled.

Allena bowed her head.

The room waited impatiently.

When Allena raised her head to Nelson's anxious face, her eyes swam with tears, but she was smiling. "Thank you, Nelson, for asking." She kissed his cheek. "You are the first son to ask me that. You've grown into a man before my very eyes, but I refused to acknowledge it."

She stood, walked to her son, and held his face between her hands. "In truth, I am the cripple. Since your father died I've leaned hard on four strong crutches. It's time I stood up and learned to walk on my own."

Nelson started to say something, but she put her hand over his mouth.

"Let me finish. Zack told me it was time I recognized the fact that my boys are men." She turned to Laura and kissed her, took both her hands, and gave them to Nelson. "Of all the girls in the world, Laura is the only one I would choose for your wife because I know she loves you. After loving and being loved by your father, that's what I want for you."

Laura and Nelson grabbed Allena at the same time and squeezed her.

"Wait a minute," Allena gasped. "You haven't heard my one condition."

Nelson beamed. "Anything, Mother."

"That you live here at the Circle Z. Tom and Mary Lou will be moving into their own place." She paused with a sigh. "Doug's gone, and the few of us who are left are going to rattle around this ranch and get lost if you don't."

Leaning firmly on one crutch, his arm around her, Nelson gazed into Laura's eyes. Whatever communication passed between them escaped the onlookers. They turned to Allena with two wide smiles. "That suits us fine, providing we can be married next Saturday." Nelson grabbed Laura and kissed her in front of everybody.

The tension in the room lifted and bounced away on everyone's laughter.

Busy days followed. As requested, the wedding would take place at the Bar-B Ranch at twelve o'clock. Zack told Dr. Mike, which was as good as handing the news to the Pony Express. Trips were made back and forth between the two ranches. Laura's belongings began to arrive at the Circle Z, and the women scurried to find space for them in Nelson's room. Laura insisted on leaving Nelson's easel by the window for his painting. The stacks of pictures that controlled the floor space were hung everywhere. Even in the kitchen. Nelson had painted Hattie making bread.

Toward the end of the week, tantalizing aromas wafted from the kitchen. Hattie outdid herself with a huge wedding cake filled with dried fruit and nuts.

Mary Lou thanked God for answering her prayer for Nelson and Laura and joined eagerly with preparations. Yet, even amid the flurry, her constant thought was of Tom's return. She hourly searched the horizon for his familiar shape moving along in the rhythm of an easy gait astride Tinder. She rose early one day, sensing a deep feeling within that he could come at any moment.

Tex and Bart had loaded Mama's dresser, chest, and rocking chairs in the wagon, each wrapped in quilts for protection, and were ready to move them to the new house. They criss-crossed rope on the bottom of the bed to hold the mattress bag Mary Lou had made out of rough ticking fabric stuffed as firmly as she could with straw and hay. She had stuffed the under side with a layer of goose feathers so she could flop it come winter. That way, the straw would be cooler in summer, the feathers would create warmth for winter. When she could afford muslin for sheets, she would make some. For now, they would sleep between Mama's quilts.

Mary Lou smiled as the cowboys unloaded the wagon. Tucked in a large wash basin were soap and lots of flour sacks for use as dish towels, diapers, cleaning cloths, or whatever, a contribution from Hattie.

The gardens around the ranch house had grown an abundance of vegetables. The women picked almost daily. Those vegetables which could not be eaten were put into flour sacks and stored in the root cellars.

Mary Lou thanked Hattie for generously donating some of the ranch vegetables to her new home. She opened the trap door in the kitchen floor and climbed down the ladder into her new root cellar. She stacked her first vegetable bags side by side on the dirt ledge the men had carved out of the wall.

In the bedroom, she spread the quilts over the mattress, put the wash basin on the dresser with Mama's pitcher, spread a new rug on each side of the bed, and then stood back to appraise her work. Beautiful! Her heart swelled with pride. Everything was ready for Tom, whenever he came. She sighed, praying it would be soon.

"Is this the new home of Mr. and Mrs. Thomas Langdon?"

"Tom!" Mary Lou spun around and flew out of the bedroom into the arms of her husband. As his mouth pressed hungrily on hers, Mary Lou's heart pounded dizzily. She clung to Tom, relishing the feel of his body next to hers as the tight enclosure of his arms melted them together and made her feel whole again. Tom was home!

Tom slowly released her and stretched her to arm's length. His gaze roamed every inch. "I couldn't stand another day. I left Smitty and the boys yesterday and rode all night." He gathered Mary Lou into his arms, gentler this time, and touched his lips to hers again and again, drinking in their soft sweetness. When he released her, he stepped behind her, closed his arms around her, and surveyed the room. "I can't believe it. You have done wonders to this place."

Mary Lou wiggled from his arms and grabbed his hand. "Come see." She pulled him to the bedroom.

He turned an inquiring gaze from the bedroom to Mary Lou and lifted the quilts and the mattress. "Who roped it?"

"Tex. He has been a great help. In fact, this has set him thinking that maybe he ought to find himself a wife."

Tom laughed. "Wait a minute. He is too good a man to lose." His arms encircled Mary Lou again. "But I wouldn't want to deprive a man of a wife. Hope he finds a good one like I have." He kissed her soundly. "Now I would wish that on any man."

They walked into the twins' bedroom. Mary Lou had had Tex build beds right on the walls of the room. Instead of rope, Tex had constructed a solid bottom, making a box which Mary Lou filled with straw and hay. She covered the filling with ticking fabric until she could make mattress bags. In a week, Tommy and Beth would be four months old. Before long, they would learn to sit. Their cradles would be too small.

Mary Lou hugged Tom again. "Have you any idea how glad I am you are home? I missed you."

"Me too." Tom pulled her into his arms and held her.

Tinder and Dulcie nickered outside.

"Poor Tinder. I rode him hard. He needs feed and a good rest." Tom kissed Mary Lou again and pulled her toward the door. "Time to get back to the ranch."

Mary Lou didn't tell Tom about Doug. He needed to enjoy his homecoming. Zack should be the one to tell him.

Zack had just walked into the ranch kitchen with Baby Zack when Tom and Mary Lou opened the kitchen door. He stretched out his hand and smiled a welcome. "Welcome home. How was the trip?"

Tom grabbed his brother's hand. "Too long."

Zack laughed. "Makes a difference to have a family at home, doesn't it?" Zack frowned. "I didn't hear Smitty and the boys come in."

"They'll be here tomorrow. I left them at Doan's Crossing."

Lily entered the kitchen, the twins in her arms.

Tom gazed with delight, took them into his arms, and stared in amazement. "I can't believe how they have grown."

Everyone laughed.

Hattie, a platter of steak in one hand and a bowl of creamed potatoes and onions in the other, nodded. "Babies do that," she said and disappeared into the dining room.

Tom dried his hands on the towel as his mother walked into the kitchen.

"Oh, Tom." She embraced him, clung, and sobbed.

Taken by surprise Tom looked from one member of the family to the other. Then Zack told him of Doug's death.

As Tom listened, his jaw tightened and a look of fury spread across his face. "And nobody has any idea of who did it?"

"I'm sure somebody knows, but they are going to make sure I never find out."

"Dinner's getting cold," Hattie stated flatly.

The family ate and talked until the twins and Baby Zack grew restless tied in their chairs. Mary Lou and Lily untied them and took them to the kitchen to feed them their milk.

After the babies were fed, Hattie took Tommy and Beth from Mary Lou. "You and Tom just ride up to your house and leave these babies with me. I'm afraid they'll fall out of those new beds."

Bless Hattie, Mary Lou thought, with a smile at her candor.

Tom came out shortly, nodded at the arrangement, and kissed and held his son and daughter again.

They began their walk to their new home. On their way, they stopped at the cemetery and stood beside Doug's fresh grave.

"Strange. At this moment, I cannot think of a thing I have against my brother, even though I have had an inner dislike of him all my life and hated myself for it. As a Christian, I felt I should love him in spite of everything. I admit it was hard!"

"You did love him, Tom. And he loved you and Zack and Nelson and his mother as best he could. Like my pa. Mama said he still had love in his heart, but his accident made him so angry he refused to let it out, pushed us from him, and threw his life away. Doug did too.

"My real sorrow for him is that he denied himself so much by acting as he did. He baited people to hurt them and got hurt in return and wondered why. The way he talked to Lily and treated her. . ." Mary Lou shook her head. "But it is over. Now he is in God's hands, and we must forget the unpleasant memories or they will sour us. That will be our fault."

They reached their door, stood with their arms around each other, and looked up. The heavens radiated peace as myriads of tiny lights poked holes through the dense blue night sky to wink and blink at the world and soothe its spirit.

They opened the door. A whole new life stood on tiptoe before them. Tom lit a lamp. Eerie shadows danced on the walls as they undressed for bed.

Tom extinguished the lamp, and they climbed into bed. A satisfying contentment settled on Mary Lou. She turned to her husband's arms. Tom was home. So was she.

Chapter 18

Laura, dressed in blue, stepped out of the ranch door on Will Shepard's arm.

Her father led her between neighbors and friends standing by a group of beech trees decked in golden leafy gowns. He placed Laura beside Nelson. Her smile radiated joy as her sparkling eyes rested on Nelson. She held a bouquet of flowers in one arm and placed her other hand over Nelson's on his crutch.

Tom and Mary Lou took places beside them.

Pastor Clayburn cleared his throat, looked out over the assembly, and opened his Bible.

Gazing at Laura's happy face triggered the memory of the happiness Mary Lou had felt as Pa walked her through Aunt Tibby's parlor to Glenn's side. Now even thinking about it churned her stomach. Glenn's rejection of her at the altar was the most humiliating experience of her life, but she blessed him for it. It had opened the door for Tom to be her husband.

Pastor Clayburn cleared his throat. "Friends and neighbors, we are gathered together to join in holy matrimony Nelson Langdon and Laura Shepard. If there is anyone who objects to this union, speak now or forever hold your peace."

Mary Lou held her breath. Her own wedding had fallen apart after those words.

The pastor turned to Nelson. "Do you, Nelson Langdon. . ."

Mary Lou couldn't see Nelson's face, but his answer vibrated with joy. In a few moments, his dream would come to reality.

"And do you, Laura Shepard, take Nelson Langdon to be your lawfully wedded husband, to cherish, honor, and obey him, and keep yourself only unto him? If so, say I do."

"I do." Laura's gaze never left Nelson's beaming face.

"In the name of the Father, Son, and Holy Ghost, I pronounce you man and wife. Beware you let no man set you asunder." He gazed out over the people gathered. "Let us pray." He bowed his head.

"Father in heaven, in Your Word, You made the woman out of the rib of a man and joined them together. Let these two, standing before us today, be joined together by hearts of love in Jesus Christ. Amen." He turned to the newlyweds. "God bless you, my children."

Laura turned to Nelson, put her arms around him, and they sealed their vows with a kiss. Then they turned into a circle of friends who expressed good wishes and pressed presents into their hands.

To Texans, any social event, be it wedding or funeral, was an occasion to bring people together from miles around. Daily existence was monotonous, so any opportunity to meet with their neighbors became cherished time.

Will Shepard stepped in front of the food table and raised his hand. "Friends, the ladies have outdone themselves making all this good food. Eat your fill to give you strength to continue our celebration at the barn dance. Now it's time to thank the good Lord for His blessings." He bowed his head.

Hats came off. All heads bowed.

"Our Father, we ask Your blessing not only on our food, but also upon the marriage of Laura and Nelson. We thank You for good neighbors and friends to join us at this happy time. In Jesus' name, Amen."

Along the shady side of the house, long tables made from boards put on top of barrels groaned under the weight of roast beef and venison, wild turkey, and all the special dishes from the guests' gardens and kitchens. One table alone proved too small for the wedding cake and all the pumpkin and apple pies, bread pudding, fat loaves of bread, and fancy jams, so two more barrels and boards were hastily assembled.

Hattie's wedding cake was delicious. It didn't last very long. Mary Lou watched her cut a small piece and put it into her basket. She caught Hattie's eye and wiggled her finger at her.

Hattie shook her head. "'Taint for me. I'm taking it home to put under Lily's pillow. I'm worried about her. Since Doug's death, she's a different girl. Maybe this will help bring her another husband to cheer her up."

Mary Lou smiled at Hattie's solution to Lily's problem, but she, too, had been concerned about her sister-in-law. She gazed over the crowd. Poor Lily. Claretta Pearson had her cornered and was enumerating her ailments and the woes of living in this forsaken country. Claretta came from Virginia and it was all she ever talked about. Mary Lou hurried to rescue Lily.

When the guests had eaten their fill, Alvin Yeager, the fiddler, began to saw his fiddle and call for dancers. Toes tapped and feet shuffled till the dancers found their partners for five rounds of the Virginia reel. To give them a rest, Alvin played a half-dozen waltzes, and Tom led off dancing with the bride. His big feet and long legs stayed miraculously unentangled and in rhythm.

Then *stomp! Stomp! Stomp! Stomp!* Alvin changed the tempo, called for squares, and his fiddle screeched "Turkey in the Straw." Ladies and gentlemen formed squares, and in obedience to Alvin's calls, skirts swung wide, feet shuffled, and the square dancers bounced in time to clapping onlookers.

What fun!

The twins and Baby Zack got passed from arms to laps, as did other small babies, to allow their mothers freedom to join the merriment.

The stalwart sun presided over the day until a bright, silver moon rose to take its place and remind the guests it was time to board their wagons, buggies, and horses and head for home.

The bride and groom climbed into a new buggy given to them for a wedding present and, midst waves and shouts, left for Tom and Mary Lou's new house to stay for a two-day honeymoon, Mary Lou and Tom's gift to the newlyweds.

Mary Lou thought of the gift when she remembered the precious days she and Tom had spent alone together on their trip from Kansas to Texas. By the time they reached Texas, they were truly man and wife.

Riding back in the wagon to the Circle Z, where Tom, Mary Lou, and the twins would stay for the two days the newlyweds were at their home, she breathed a silent prayer of thanks for the blessing of God's gift of marriage. Never had she been happier. She glanced down at the two tired, sleeping children in her arms, then at the young man beside her who loved her and made life worth living. Never in all her cottonwood dreams could she have imagined such happiness.

The next morning, Mary Lou struggled to open her eyes. She reached for Tom. He was gone. She raised up on her elbow to check the twins. They were gone, too.

Mary Lou took the luxury of lying back down for a few minutes. The past weeks of working on the house and the work of the wedding had added up to exhaustion. Her legs refused to swing over the edge of the bed. She dozed off. When her eyelids opened again, sunlight had captured the whole room.

Mary Lou threw back the covers and sat up. The house was unusually quiet. What time was it? Without Tom's pocket watch, she had no way of knowing, but it had to be late. The sun was high.

Energy triggered within. She should be up and about! Hattie and Allena planned to get the meat hanging in the barn ready for drying. She hurried and dressed.

When Mary Lou opened the kitchen door, Hattie grinned.

"Did you get your beauty sleep?"

Mary Lou laughed. "I don't know whether I got it or not. I slept too hard to find out." She looked around. "Where are Tommy and Beth?"

"With Miz Langdon. She has all three."

"Where's Lily?" Mary Lou grinned. "Did you put the cake under her pillow?"

"I didn't have a chance. It was too late. She went to bed before I could do it." Hattie's brows knit together. "I'm a bit concerned. Lily isn't back from her walk yet."

"When did she leave?"

"As soon as she fed Baby Zack his breakfast and exercised his leg."

Mary Lou glanced outside. "It's a beautiful day. I don't blame her. I would like to go out myself and just wander. Yesterday was a big day."

Hattie's face remained troubled.

Mary Lou touched her cheek and smiled. "A little prayer might not hurt if you're so concerned. Did Allena have morning devotions yet?"

"No, she said we would wait for you."

Mary Lou went to the parlor. They were all there. Baby Zack wobbled on two hands and two knees, but nothing seemed to work together well enough to gain any ground. The twins, on their backs on a blanket, had their four arms and legs flying. Tommy threw one leg over the other, turning him on his side. One of these days, Mary Lou expected to find him over on his stomach.

"Good morning. Have you had morning devotions yet?"

"No, I have been waiting for you and Lily. Her daily walks get longer and longer. I believe she is grieving for Doug."

Mary Lou nodded. "I've noticed that. The only one who seems to give her any happiness is Baby Zack."

Hattie came in. They decided not to wait for Lily. Allena read aloud from the book of First John.

Beth grew fussy, so Mary Lou nursed her while Allena read Scripture. Beth soon fell asleep in her arms. Allena made a little bed on the floor in the corner with blankets, laid Beth in it, and then continued her reading. Then Mary Lou nursed Tommy, and shortly his eyes grew drowsy and closed. They put him in the other corner and covered both babies.

Devotions over, Allena picked up Baby Zack, and the three women tiptoed out. They went from room to room, gathering dirty clothes to take out to the wash tubs to soak.

Hattie came flying out of Lily's room. "Miz Langdon, come quick!"

Was Lily sick? Had she come back from her walk and gone to her room without them noticing her?

Lily's room was neat, orderly, and empty.

Too orderly, Mary Lou thought. Her dresses were not hanging on the wall pegs, and her comb and brush were gone from beside the basin.

"She's gone!" Hattie looked from Allena to Mary Lou. "All her stuff is gone!"

It was true. Mary Lou found the two calico dresses she had given her laying on her bed.

Hattie stayed with the babies while Allena and Mary Lou started out to find the missing girl. They went to the barn. The cowboys said Lily hadn't come for a horse. Tom and Smitty had ridden out on the range right after breakfast. It was a fruitless search. Lily was nowhere on the ranch.

As they returned to the house, Allena voiced her thoughts. "I'm afraid to say what I think, but she must have gone back to Harness." Allena sadly shook her head, her eyes clouded.

"Where would she go?" Mary Lou asked.

Allena bowed her head and said, "Probably back to where she came from. Where else could she go?"

Mary Lou shook her head. "No! I won't think that of Lily. She's a sweet girl."

"I agree with you. I admit I was shocked when Doug brought her home, but after I got to know her and learned she had been orphaned at ten and raised in an orphanage until she was sixteen, I understood that the poor girl just got swallowed up in circumstances."

Mary Lou's heart ached too much to say anything. She didn't believe Lily would go back to the brothel. How could she? Not after that morning when she had accepted Jesus as her Savior and was so repentant.

Suddenly Allena was on the move. "Put on your bonnet, Mary Lou. We are going to town."

Chapter 19

Allena and Mary Lou got to Harness about noon and parked in front of the saloon. Ignoring raised eyebrows and questioning looks, they climbed out of the buggy and walked through the front door.

The nauseating odor of whisky assaulted Mary Lou's nostrils and reminded her of the day the women of Venture went into Mac Ludden's saloon with hatchets and axes. Now she felt the same incensed anger. If an ax had been at the end of her arm, she would have smashed it through the front window the same as she had in Kansas.

Bleary-eyed, cocky men and shameless, gaudy women stared. Allena, head high with all the dignity of a matriarch, marched boldly to the highly polished oak bar. "Could you tell me, please, is Lily Langdon here?"

The barkeep lifted his eyebrows. "Lily Lang—? Why, uh. . .no, Ma'am. I ain't seen her since she. . .uh. . ."

"Thank you." Allena didn't wait for him to finish. She turned and walked decisively toward the stairs. Mary Lou caught her breath, hesitated, then followed.

A dark-haired girl with large, penetrating brown eyes standing halfway up the stairs walked down to meet Allena and shook her head. "You don't want to go up there, Ma'am. Lily isn't there."

Allena stared into her soul. "How do I know you are telling the truth?"

A wistful smile softened the girl's face. "I know Lily well, and I am telling you the truth. She isn't here. She never really belonged here."

A painted girl, hand on hip, sidled toward Allena and stood in front of her. "She married your son, Ma'am. I knew him well." Her lip curled into a sneer. Her gaze scanned the room and returned to rest on Allena. "Or didn't he bring her home?"

Allena never flinched. "Yes, he did, on the same day he married her, which makes Lily my daughter-in-law. I want no harm to come to her."

The girl raised her eyebrows and shrugged her shoulders.

During Allena's encounter, Mary Lou viewed the other girls. Some stood brazenly at the bar, others draped themselves over men as they sat at cards, one plunked herself into a man's lap. But they all had one thing in common. Sad, veiled eyes. Lily had had those eyes when she first came

230

home with Doug. It took Baby Zack to rip the veil away and reveal the deep well of love that Lily had kept locked out of sight.

"Thank you and good-day," Mary Lou heard Allena say. She followed her out the door, shutting it on the howl of laughter.

Once outside, they noticed Dr. Mike coming out of the boarding-house on the way to his buggy. He waved, leaned on a hitching post, and waited. He tipped his hat. "Good morning, Allena, Mary Lou. What brings you to town?"

"I'm looking for Lily."

Dr. Mike's eyes narrowed. "Something wrong?"

"She hasn't been herself since Doug died. This morning we found she had packed her clothes and left."

Dr. Mike pursed his lips. "Hmm. I'm sure there is some good reason."

"What reason is good enough to leave your family?"

"Maybe Lily doesn't feel like your family since Doug is gone, or the ranch reminds her too much of Doug and she thought it would be better if she got away. There are lots of reasons, Allena, some of which none of us would understand."

"Well, if in your travels you find out anything, please let me know. If you see her, tell her I still consider her my daughter-in-law. We love her, Baby Zack cries for her, and I would like her to come home where she belongs."

Dr. Mike smiled and nodded. "I'll tell her just that if I see her, and if she will come with me, I will bring her out." He tipped his hat. "Good-day, ladies."

Allena and Mary Lou both tipped their heads, said good-day, and crossed the dusty street to the general store. "Might as well get a few things since we're here. We always need more sugar, flour, and salt. And you need muslin for sheets."

As they entered Orval Picket's Mercantile, Mary Lou felt a twang of homesickness. In the center was the pot-bellied stove, chairs around it and a cuspidor beside it. Other than the placement of supplies, general stores were much the same. The back wall was lined with barrels and tubs containing pickles, tobacco, crackers, sugar, flour, and who knew what else. Above them, shelves climbed to the ceiling trying to supply every-thing anyone asked for. Built-in bins contained coffee, tea, dried peas, fruit, rice, and oatmeal.

Mary Lou sniffed. There were spice drawers nearby. The aroma of pep-per, cinnamon, cloves, and other spices permeated the air. She closed her eyes and breathed deeply. The sounds and smells transported Mary Lou back to her father's store in Kansas.

Along a side wall stood four iron cookstoves. She walked over to one and ran her hand over the hard, black surface. She could picture it sitting in her new kitchen. What luxury it would be to be able to set pans of food on top of the stove to cook instead of standing in front of a hot fireplace on a summer's day stirring a pot hanging on the swingarm. She opened the oven door. *Oh, to be able to bake bread in an oven like this. Someday. . . .*

With the help of one of the young boys in the store, they carried their purchases to the buggy and climbed in.

Allena picked up the reins but didn't move. "I feel as if there is somewhere else we should ask questions."

"What about the boardinghouse? Lily will have to stay some place."

"Dr. Mike surely would have said something."

"Maybe she is there but he didn't see her. He is gone a lot."

They climbed back out of the buggy and went down the street to Jenny Wagner's boardinghouse.

"Yes, she was here trying to find a job, but I don't need any more cooks or house maids," Jenny told them.

"Did she say where she might be going?" Mary Lou asked.

Jenny slowly shook her head. "No, she just looked real sad and left. I felt sorry for her, but there was nothing I could do except offer her a meal, which she refused."

Allena turned to go, then hesitated. "Jenny, do me a favor."

"Yes'm?"

"I would appreciate it—if you see Lily or hear anything about her—if you would tell Dr. Mike so he could get word to me. If she comes back again or you see her anywhere, offer her a job, any job, then let me know. I'll come and get her and repay you any money you have paid her."

Jenny lowered her head and stood uneasy. "Pardon me, Ma'am, for saying so, but. . .did you. . .did you check. . .uh, the saloon? Upstairs?"

Allena pulled herself to her full height and looked Jenny straight in the eye. "Yes, I did. She has not been there. She is not that kind of girl anymore. She is my daughter-in-law and a Christian."

Jenny's face registered shocked surprise. "Oh, yes, Ma'am. If I see her, I'll do as you say, Mrs. Langdon."

Allena walked from the boardinghouse with all the poise and dignity of a true lady. Like Mama.

Buttons seemed to take his time on the way home. It didn't matter. Mary Lou and Allena were absorbed in their own thoughts.

Mary Lou was praying for Lily's safety and had no doubt her mother-in-law was doing the same. Things were different for Lily now; she belonged to God. That was it! She was God's child. He would protect her.

Mary Lou's prayers turned into praise rather than worried pleas, thankful for all He had done for Lily already. She even praised God for Doug bringing Lily out of a life of ill repute. For the first time, Mary Lou prayed with a proper attitude for Doug. Without realizing it, he had done a good thing.

It was almost suppertime when the buggy turned under the Circle-Z arch. Hattie came out the door and peered under her hand, searching to see if Lily was with them. When the buggy stopped, she shook her head. "You didn't find her?"

"No." Allena climbed out of the buggy.

Hattie raised her eyes. "Oh, God, take care of our Lily."

In the days that followed, the family noticed a change in Baby Zack. He was restless, didn't sleep well, and cried a lot.

"Is he sick?" Zack asked his mother one night when nothing seemed to settle him.

"No. I think he misses Lily."

Zack sat and stared into the fireplace. "He needs his mother to come home."

"Did Darcy say anything about coming home in the letter you received the other day?"

"She said she would like to stay and celebrate Christmas with her family once more."

Mary Lou could tell by the set of Zack's jaw that Darcy being away so long bothered him. Over two months. In every letter Zack received, Darcy wrote of some special reason for her to stay: her mother's birthday, her best friend's marriage, her father's illness.

"Maybe he misses the twins since we moved. Maybe if we took him home with us to be with the twins. . ." Mary Lou offered.

Zack turned pained eyes to Mary Lou. "It might help. The poor little fellow is deserted."

Laura and Nelson walked in and surprised everyone. Contentment shone on two happy faces. "What little fellow is deserted?" Laura asked. "Baby Zack? Where's Lily?"

Mary Lou and Allena told of their visit to Harness.

"I'll be glad to help take care of him."

Mary Lou laughed. "Thanks, Laura. Two is trouble but three. . ."

"Is one too many at any age," Allena added.

Long after everyone had gone to bed, Zack and Tom sat in front of the fireplace talking about the ranch and the changes to be made now that they would run it together.

Two of the deeds written up for land deals were not legal, so Doug's debts were not honored.

"By law," Zack said, "after a man is dead, his family is not liable for his gambling debts."

In practice, anyone who didn't pay a gambling debt might have to pay for it later with his life. And both brothers knew it.

Chapter 20

Allena lifted Baby Zack out of the wooden tub of bath water, wrapped him in a blanket, and laid him on his back on the kitchen table. His lips puckered, then opened to make way for a protesting scream.

Left in the tub, Tommy and Beth squealed with delight, banged their hands on the surface of the water, and soaked Mary Lou, Laura, and the floor. They joined Baby Zack on the kitchen table to be dried and dressed.

Allena massaged her grandson's little legs straight, held them together, and smiled. "I do believe the short leg is growing."

She sat the baby on his bottom, measured his legs in a sitting position, grinned, and gave him a bear hug. "One of these days, dear baby, you will run like the wind." She kissed the top of his head.

"Since you massage his legs four times a day, Mother, show me how to do it. I could do it a couple times and give you a rest."

"Thank you, Laura. It is really very simple." Allena laid Baby Zack on his back and worked her fingers in kneading fashion up and down along his whole leg into his back. He quieted as soon as her hands touched him.

"Knead gently, but firmly to stimulate the blood to come into his legs, Dr. Mike says. Then rub your hands up and down his leg, around his legs, and massage his little feet. Press your fingers gently under each toe and rub so the toe stands at attention. Then do it again, several times. He'll fuss when he has had enough."

Laura shook her head in amazement. "Where did you learn how to do this? Who taught you?"

"God." Allena smiled at Laura's skeptical expression. "Desperate mothers try desperate measures. I figured if God made our bodies, as the Good Book says, then He certainly would tell us how to take care of them. Dr. Mike was very interested in what I was doing. Now he says if I hadn't worked with Nelson's legs, the muscles would have shriveled and Nelson would have been confined to a chair. At least he's mobile."

Mary Lou dried the sturdy, kicking legs of Tommy and praised God for His blessings.

"Then one day," Allena continued, "when Nelson was about three, my Zack came in from the barn carrying a tiny set of crutches he had made and taught Nelson to use them. Nelson, delighted, worked, and struggled, falling more often than walking. Some days it broke my heart to watch him struggle to drag one foot after the other between those crutches. But his little heart was bigger and more determined than my faith.

"To our amazement, he finally mastered them by placing a crutch as a balance beside one leg, then swinging the balance from one leg and crutch to the other, strengthening his shoulders and arms as well. He may not walk as you or I, but he gets around to wherever he needs to go."

Allena smiled at the one strong leg of her grandson kicking the air and the other stretching to match it. She tickled his tummy, nuzzling his nose with hers. "And that's all legs are for, isn't it?" She kissed his forehead.

Again, Mary Lou's admiration for her mother-in-law grew. Like Mama, she had captured an open secret from God to learn from Him what to do, especially in dire times of need. "God told me" had been the answer Mama had given Pa many times.

℧

Days flew by, chewing precious time from the month of December. Needles hurriedly assembled garments, and hammer blows resounded from the barn in preparation for Christmas Day. Hattie spent the last week preparing special food.

Mary Lou's thoughts carried her back to Kansas, their little church in Venture, and the Christmas party on Christmas Eve. Her childhood remembrance of that event created an intense desire for the opportunity to build a treasure of memories for her own children—an anchor to let them know where they came from and a vision of where they were going. Perhaps, next year when the church was built. . .

Two days before Christmas, Tom appeared at the door with a pine tree. He had pounded some boards on the bottom of the trunk so it would stand up.

"It's wonderful!" Mary Lou held back the urge to throw her arms around him, too shy with everyone present.

Mary Lou and Laura used ribbons of all colors and tied them into bows to trim the tree. They bought some popcorn from an Indian, strung red holly berries and popped corn on thread, and draped it around the tree.

All was ready by three o'clock Christmas Eve. The Shepards came in two wagons. Will, Emily, Luke, and John in one, Matthew and Mark with their wives in the second. Each came in, arms full of food and presents.

The men gathered in the parlor around the fireplace and discussed their ranches and plans for the future. The women hustled an early supper to the table, surrounded with babies in new high chairs.

The long-standing neighborliness and friendship of the Shepard and Langdon families reminded Mary Lou so much of home. Will, as father, played Santa Claus. He dug into a big, mysterious bag and pulled out one present after another wrapped in brown paper or newspaper with red and white store string.

A tiny white dress for Beth from Emily, a cloth doll from her grandmother, and a fancy bib from Laura and Nelson. Wooden blocks, a toy wagon, and carved horses for the little boys. New bonnets and handkerchiefs with tatted edges for the ladies. Mary Lou's shirts for Zack, Tom, and Nelson—there seemed no bottom to Santa's bag!

When all the presents were opened, Tom took Mary Lou's hand and led her outside to a wagon standing just beyond the hitching post. He hopped up onto the wagon bed and pulled Mary Lou up beside him. A horse blanket covered something. Grinning, Tom yanked the horse blanket off the top.

Mary Lou's mouth dropped open. Her beautiful, black iron cookstove! She ran her hands over it again. This time, it belonged to her!

"And it is all ready to be taken home after dinner and hooked up to the stovepipe!" Tom threw the blanket over the stove again, leaped down, and held his arms out for Mary Lou.

She jumped into his arms. A swelling of love almost smothered her. "It is the very one I wanted. How did you know?"

"You don't ask Santa Claus how he knows such things. It is his business to know." Tom held her close and whispered in her ear. "I never tell anyone Santa's secrets."

Hattie came out the kitchen door, went over to the bell, and rang it with gusto.

Smitty and the cowboys came from the bunkhouse, all clean and shaved, and joined the two families for Christmas supper.

Zack rose from his chair and stuck his thumbs in his vest pockets. "As I look about, I cannot help but think this is what we are all working for and what Christmas is all about. Peace on earth and good will to men. And we understand a little better this year how much we need God's peace.

"We think of our brother," Zack lowered his head and swallowed hard, "who is missed around this table." He choked up and turned to Tom. "Will you say grace, please?" Zack sat down.

Tom stood quietly. "Father, we thank You for the gift of a Savior born that night long ago to save us from our sins. Thank You for our families and friends and these cowboys who work hard with us." He paused. "We thank You for this bounty of food before us and ask You to bless it in Jesus' name. Amen."

Dusk descended early. After a merry day and a delicious Christmas supper, the Shepards climbed aboard their wagons with their gifts and were waved on their way. Later, Tom and Mary Lou boarded their wagon and started home, followed by Tex and Bart on horseback to help put the stove in place.

Mary Lou sat beside Tom, a drowsy, blanket-wrapped twin in each arm. She gazed up at the dark winter sky spattered with tiny stars faithfully maintaining their vigil. What must it have been like for the shepherds that special night when that bright star led them to Jesus in Bethlehem? They probably never knew the significance of their faithful visit.

She pulled the blanket tighter around her babies. "And she wrapped him in swaddling clothes and laid him in a manger." For the first time, Mary Lou realized how Mary must have felt for the safety of her son. And Joseph, who had the burden of their care and safety, just like Tom. The importance of each detail in the beloved Christmas story flooded her with deeper understanding.

The wagon rolled to a stop in front of their house. Tom took the twins, and Tex helped Mary Lou down from the wagon. By the time the twins were tucked in their beds and Mary Lou came out into the kitchen, the stove stood in place. The men were hooking up the stovepipe. As soon as it was finished, Tex and Bart called "Merry Christmas" and rode off.

Tom took her in his arms and said in a deep, throaty voice, "Merry Christmas, Darling." He bent his head until his lips touched hers.

Mama said heaven was much more than anyone dreamed of, Mary Lou thought. *Could it possibly be much better than this?*

Chapter 21

Allena, Hattie, and Laura came to visit Mary Lou three days after Christmas to see how the stove worked, so they planned to eat supper together.

The women brought their own dishes since Mary Lou didn't have enough to serve everyone. They also brought their food in pans to cook on the top of her cookstove. Hattie brought dry biscuit makings to mix with water later and bake in the oven.

They were all impressed with the five-gallon water vat on the side of the stove where water could be stored and kept hot all the time. Hattie got a fire started in the fire pit, commenting about the small pieces of wood that could be used and how easy it was to carry them. She kept picking up the circular lids with the handle to see how the fire was burning, like some child with a new toy.

Mary Lou had a hard time keeping Tom's surprise to herself. Tom had told her that when he bought her stove, he had ordered one for his mother and Hattie.

For Mary Lou, it was a joy to have company for supper in their new home. As they ate, they decided to make it a habit to have supper at Tom and Mary Lou's every Saturday evening.

By April, the days warmed up and stirred homeward thoughts in Mary Lou's mind. The morning Tom rode out on the spring roundup, he kissed her, held her in his arms, and said, "As soon as the roundup is over, we will begin the trip to Kansas. Will you be ready?"

Ready! She had been waiting for those words. Mary Lou enveloped Tom in a smothering hug and lingering kiss. For the first time, she waved him off gladly.

From then on, Kansas and home was all Mary Lou thought about. Her mind buzzed with ideas of how to travel with the twins, what needs they would have, how long it would take.

Allena's concern for the babies was the daily exposure to the hot sun or rain. Tom solved that problem by soaking thin pieces of wood in water and then bending and tying them until they dried in a curved shape. He used the shaped wood as stays covered with canvas to form a shelter in the back of the wagon, making it look like a miniature Conestoga.

Mary Lou packed two wooden buckets to scoop water from rivers or ponds. Tom strapped a water barrel on the side of the wagon between the wheels.

Dr. Mike stopped by one day to check the babies.

Hattie smiled. "That's what he says he comes for, but I think his stomach is crying out for a good, home-cooked meal."

Dr. Mike's appetite proved her right.

"Have you any news of Lily?" Allena asked.

"There are rumors she left town with some man, but no one seemed to know who or where or why. It's just a rumor, and Allena, you know you can't count on everything you hear. It has been going around, so by now it's probably far from the truth."

Allena shook her head. "That can't be true. Somehow I can't believe that of Lily."

Mary Lou didn't either—unless Lily had backslidden.

A couple days later, Zack came home in the middle of the day for dinner, which he hadn't done since Baby Zack was a newborn. The family soon found out why. He had received a letter from Darcy with another offer from her father of a position in his law office.

"I can read between the lines," Zack said sadly at the dinner table. "She doesn't want to come back here to live, so the offer is an enticement for me to go back to Boston." His jaw tightened as he read parts of the letter to his family.

The news came as no surprise to Mary Lou. In each of Darcy's letters, she had given reasons why she needed to stay in Boston a little longer. Mary Lou had pushed her thought aside and never voiced what she had sensed all along. Darcy had never intended to come back.

"This Zack isn't the Zack I married," she had said.

But what about Baby Zack? Doesn't every mother love her own baby? Evidently not. Mary Lou remembered at the baby's birth when Allena laid Darcy's newborn son in her arms. "Take it away!" Darcy had cried. It! Was that all her baby was to her? Darcy had rejected both son and father.

Tom returned from the spring roundup and preparations for going to Kansas became the daily chore. Mary Lou gathered her bags of dried vegetables and meat. Allena gave her a metal tin for flour, and they made a batch of sourdough starter so Mary Lou could fry bread in a frying pan over an open fire.

The excitement of seeing Pa, Aunt Nelda, Aunt Tibby, and Jenny made Mary Lou yearn to push each day ahead of itself.

Laura rode in one morning before they planned to leave. "That wagon's not going to hold much more," she commented.

"That's what Tom said this morning. Yet I have a feeling I'm forgetting something, but I can't remember what." Staring at Laura, Nelson came to mind. "Nelson's paintings! I have forgotten Nelson's paintings!"

"I wondered whether you remembered," Nelson said when they went to see him. "Thought maybe you didn't have room."

"We'll make room!"

Nelson had already selected pictures he thought were particularly good. Those of Father Zack and Victor he refused to part with. Mary Lou didn't blame him. They were priceless.

There were many pictures of tumbleweeds. They selected the best of those. Choosing the best of the cowboy paintings was difficult. They shifted them from the "go" pile to the "stay" pile several times until they felt they had culled the best. One exceptional painting of Smitty holding Diamond, Nelson refused to part with. By the time they finished, they had sifted out the best portraits and landscapes and had enough variety to make them interesting.

Allena brought muslin bags she had made to protect them.

"I'm sure there will be some place in Pa's store where he can hang them," Mary Lou said. "We will take some to Abilene. There are lots of people there." She pointed to Nelson's signature. "Did you have that on there before?"

"No, Mr. Dillard told me that every artist signs his work, and he showed me how when he was here the last time. It took me awhile to sign them all, but I did." Nelson looked up with a satisfied grin.

"We did," Laura corrected.

Nelson laughed. "She's right. It gave her an excuse to go through all my things and clean the room. So, while she was handling every picture, she brought them to me to sign." Nelson's gaze crossed the room and caressed her. "Otherwise, it would have taken me forever and I would never have known which I signed and which I didn't."

There were fourteen pictures. Laura and Mary Lou slipped each one in a muslin bag and then bunched paintings of like sizes together and tied them with small rope.

The day of departure finally came.

"I want to start about five-thirty in the morning," Tom said. "That will get us across the Red River and hopefully well up into Indian territory before nightfall."

Good-byes are always hard. Hugs, choked tears, and kisses were given as if it were the last time. In the back of every mind, though no one said so, it could be. Crossing through Indian territory was sometimes safe and sometimes not. Most Indians were friendly and curious. Some were not. Just like white men.

241

Allena and Hattie each held a twin until the last minute. Reluctantly they handed them up to Mary Lou, who settled one in each arm. Tom had built the seat back taller so the twins could sit between their parents and not fall back into the wagon.

Finally Tom slapped the reins on the horses' backs, the wagon creaked, and the wheels slowly rolled forward.

Mary Lou couldn't wave for risk of losing a twin. One quick look back was enough. All three women were crying. Zack stood waving his arm. Nelson stood tall and smiled.

Mary Lou turned her face to her husband. The wagon was rolling now and he glanced into her eyes.

"Mrs. Langdon, you keep praying, and I'll keep driving, and we'll get there in good shape."

Excitement and fear fought in Mary Lou's stomach. She didn't remember being this afraid when they had come from Kansas. The ecstasy of being Tom's wife precluded everything.

Her mind shot home. An old fear revived. Had Pa forgiven her? Would he accept Tom now? Would he speak to her at all?

Pray for yourselves and your father as you go. God is with you. That's what Mama would have advised. Mary Lou's frantic heart eased. Her eyes rested on Tom's capable hands, tightly gripped over the reins. She glanced at the babies in her arms.

The sun fanned forth golden spears that flooded their way with sunshine.

"This is the day the Lord has made. Let us rejoice and be glad in it," Mary Lou said and turned a smiling face to Tom.

"And we will do just that."

PIONEER
LEGACY

Chapter 1

Tom veered the wagon into a cluster of Siberian elm trees for relief and protection from the hot June sun. Tommy and Beth had been a cranky handful for Mary Lou the last hour, and a rear wagon wheel had begun to wiggle precariously a couple miles back.

Tom jumped from the wagon, patted each horse's face as he rounded the front of the team, stretched his arms for the twins, swung them to the ground, then reached for Mary Lou.

Mary Lou leaned her waist into Tom's hands and jumped. The ground felt restfully solid after their jostling ride all morning. Gratefully accepting the welcome shade, she slid her bonnet off her head and tousled her hair, relishing even a hot breeze through it.

Tom continued to the wheel, ran his hands over it and stooped to inspect it. "Looks like I'm going to have to tighten this wheel before we go on. That will delay us a bit. Too bad it couldn't have held out till we got to the river. Now, we will barely make Red River Station by suppertime and will have to wait until morning to cross over into the Nations."

"The Nations? Where is that?" Mary Lou had heard of it but never really knew where it was.

"It's Indian Territory on the other side of the Red River. Texas laws don't apply. We may meet a few Indians."

Mary Lou knew Kansas Indians but—

"Don't worry, I know sign language, and Mother gave me some cloth, beads, and feathers to give them if we get stopped. They don't bother people like they used to. I remember one cattle drive with Father and Smitty. An Indian rode into camp with one finger raised demanding a dollar a head to cross over his tribal lands. Father refused to pay it. The Indians stampeded the herd, cut off six cows and drove them off. I was only fourteen, but I remember that we had one wild time gaining control of that herd."

Sharp fingers of fear scratched at Mary Lou's stomach. She didn't remember being afraid when she and Tom made the trip to Texas from Kansas. All she could recall was the overwhelming love she felt for her new husband and the consuming thoughts of meeting Tom's family. This time was different—the twins. . . . She shook her head to dispel a disturbing uneasiness. She needed to get busy. "Will I have time to make something to eat?"

Tom nodded and grinned. "Ma'am, my stomach sure would appreciate it." His admiring eyes danced love across the space between them. Suddenly, he rose from the wheel, and his feet followed his gaze. Tom took Mary Lou into his arms and captured her lips for a long, sweet kiss. "Been wanting to do that all morning," he said in her ear and hugged her close.

Mary Lou relaxed in his embrace, her body's tiredness eased. Tom's arms always had a soothing effect. Her arms pressed him closer while her heart pounded its thanks to God for His gift of a good, loving husband. Suddenly an unnatural quietness invaded the loving moment and struck fear into her heart. "The twins. . ."

They turned in time to see Beth disappearing into the high grass that surrounded them. Mary Lou hurried to pick her up. Tom checked the drag marks on the dusty ground and followed them into grass higher than his knees.

Her heart pounding, Mary Lou watched Tom search the tall grass. He walked slowly, parting the grass with his left hand, the right poised at his holster.

"Tommy. Where are you, Son? Come to papa," he called softly.

Suddenly, Tom whisked his pistol from its holster and shot into the grass. Tommy screamed.

Mary Lou's mind exploded with the shot! *Tom shot*— "Tommy," she screamed. Her stunned body refused to move.

Tom bent into the grass and raised up with Tommy in his arms.

"Oh, Tom," she screamed, tears of relief flooded her cheeks. "Why did you shoot?"

Tom poked his gun back into the grass and came up with a dead rattlesnake draped over it. "I had to shoot. This fellow was curling up for business. If Tommy had moved or if I had reached for him, the snake would have struck."

Mary Lou threw herself and Beth against her husband and son. Tom's free arm wound around her in comfort. Tommy squirmed in the tight embrace and hollered.

Tom and Mary Lou discovered they had to keep a closer eye on their little son who was delighted with his new mobility. His crawl on one knee and one leg sped him across a floor or ground as fast as Mary Lou could walk. Any little movement sparked Tommy's curiosity and lured him off to investigate. One day he picked up a bee, put it in his mouth, made a wry face, and quickly spit out the startled insect before it had a chance to use its weapon.

Beth, enthralled and fascinated by her brother's busyness, followed him everywhere and did everything he did.

Tom plopped Tommy beside him on the ground, and he watched with avid interest as his father built a fire. Tom carried the boy to sit beside him while he worked on the wheel and kept him immobile by handing him tools. Tom ruffled Tommy's hair and grinned as he retrieved a wrench from his son. "Gotta make a rancher out of you, Young-un, and this is where you start—learning how to fix things."

Beth crawled over and sat with the men.

Mary Lou cooked and fed each twin mash with egg, then nursed them to settle them down. They hadn't slept much during the morning. Hopefully, they would bed down for a nap in the kiddie coop Tom had made behind the front seat of the wagon and give everybody a rest.

Tom paused in his repairs long enough to eat beef jerky, a couple pieces of Hattie's homemade bread, and a delicious apple hand pie.

Tucked at the bottom of Hattie's basket, Mary Lou found biscuits, smoked ham, and a large jar of canned peaches. *Bless her,* she thought to herself. Mary Lou repacked the basket and put it near the back of the wagon where she could easily retrieve it for supper.

Tom checked the other wheels. "Good as new," he said, climbed aboard, and handed Mary Lou up into the wagon seat beside him. "Glad we are heading north. Won't have to face that sun."

Nevertheless, a hot afternoon dragged on. Fortunately, the wagon rolled in and around the ruts of the trail and rocked the twins to sleep.

Mary Lou asked, "Any idea how long it will take us to get home?"

"We can only go about four to five miles an hour. Probably a good week to get to Venture after we cross the river. We should reach Red River Station before suppertime, sleep on this side and cross over in the morning. That way, the wagon will be dry to bed down tonight, and we will be able to dry out as we travel tomorrow."

Tom sensed Mary Lou's uneasiness about crossing. He reached over and patted her hand. "The water will be a little high at this time of the year because of the swell of spring rains, but there will be plenty of help from the cowboys at the station to get us across safely." He glanced at his wife and grinned. "So don't worry, little mama."

She returned a half-brave smile. It amazed her how often Tom read her mind. She watched her strong, confident husband seated beside her, feet braced, reins loose, but firm in his hands.

In their nearly two years as man and wife, Tom had more than displayed his ability to handle every situation they had faced and proved that his uppermost thought was always for his family, not only her and the twins, but his mother, his brothers, and even the housekeeper Hattie, who treated him like the son she had lost.

Big Jon Wimbley rose in Mary Lou's mind; he was a giant of a man in soul as well as in stature and was her measure of a true family man. In her growing years, after Pa's accident, he gathered her in with his own twelve and became her substitute father. When Mama died, Big Jon gave her the comfort and consolation her own father, in his grief, denied her. Mary Lou's conscience twinged. It was unfair to measure Pa against Big Jon. She felt like a traitor, yet looked forward to seeing Big Jon more than she did her father.

Weeks before they began their trip to Kansas, the hurtful question nagged. What kind of a reception would Pa give her when they arrived? She had written faithfully every month, but had never received an answer. The only letters she received were from Aunt Nelda, Aunt Tibby, and Jenny. Not even a small note from Pa at Christmastime about the socks she had knitted for him. Aunt Nelda wrote that since he had given the back rooms of the store to Glenn, Pa seemed glad to come home most nights. Mary Lou prayed that her time away had softened his anger so they could talk, and that he had forgiven her for marrying a cowboy. Hopefully, he had learned the truth that she had not neglected Mama.

Mama. In Mary Lou's reasoning mind, three years should have eased the ache of Mama's death but her heart told her it hadn't. In times alone, even surrounded with the joy and abundance of her life with Tom, his family, and the twins, she longingly envisioned Mama sitting in her rocker with Tommy and Beth in her arms, her face beaming with pride and joy as she cradled her grandbabies. The vision never failed to provoke a spontaneous rush of tears. If possible, she missed Mama even more. She needed Mama to teach her how she gleaned such strengthening wisdom from the Bible for every situation and how to be a good mother. Slowly, Mary Lou made discoveries of her own with the help of underlined passages and word meanings written in the margins in Mama's precise schoolteacher script. They called Mary Lou's attention to a gem she probably would have missed. Mama's Bible lay safely tucked in her carpetbag with her clothes. She would get it out in the morning, and perhaps when the twins napped, she would read aloud to Tom; and they would mull over God's encouraging words as they traveled.

The rhythmic *clip, clop* of the horses hooves hitting the hard trail accelerated Mary Lou's excitement at the thought of seeing her two aunts. She could envision them when they saw the twins. They would be ecstatic!

Suddenly, in the distance, a swishing sound rose and grew louder as they travelled.

Tom looked at Mary Lou and grinned. "Well, it won't be long now. That's the Red River you hear."

Mary Lou squelched a rising apprehension and watched a small speck on the horizon grow into a rough border town squatted on the approaching shore. Streamside trees held grotesque tangles of driftwood in their branches betraying the magnitude of past floods. A short distance from the shore at one side of the buildings was a rude cemetery of bizarre crosses leaning haphazardly over graves of men who had been killed or drowned during cattle crossings.

Tom pulled the team to a halt. "Red River Station," he called and perused the river. "Oh, that's not bad. We'll float across easily. I even think the wheels might touch."

Float across! In a loaded wagon? Mary Lou lifted her eyes. *I need lots more faith, Lord!*

Two cowboys appeared from the side of a building.

"Tom!" one of them hollered, yanked off his hat and waved it vigorously over his head. "You goin' over now or waitin' 'til morning?"

Tom waved back. "Ho, Lannie! We'll cross tomorrow. You and Shade going to be here in the morning?"

"Yep, we'll be here." The cowboys followed the wagon as Tom pulled it off to the side of the buildings. When the wagon stopped, the twins woke and clamored to get out of the kiddie coop.

Lannie's eyebrows raised. "Well, whatdaya know! These here your young-uns?"

"Yep," Tom said with noticeable pride as he climbed into the back and handed Beth down to Lannie. She was not quite sure she wanted to leave her papa.

Lannie took her and held her high in the air. "Well, I'll be," he said, "She's gonna be as purty as her ma one of these days."

It was Mary Lou's turn to swell with pride.

Tom filled Shade's outstretched arms with a wary Tommy who squinted dubious brows at his receiver.

Shade laughed. "This boy's a real bruiser. He'll make some kind of tough cowboy when he hits thirteen."

Mary Lou marveled that Lannie and Shade seemed so at home with her babies but she couldn't quite picture Tommy as a cowboy, yet.

"I'm hoping he will make a great rancher like his grandfather," Tom said.

Or like his father, Mary Lou thought. Her heart swelled, and she prayed that Tommy would not only look like, but act like Tom. Tommy's present escapades sometimes planted small seeds of doubt. But then, she hadn't known Tom as a little boy. She smiled. She had a hunch he had been as rambunctious as his busy, little son.

Finally, Lannie and Shade handed the twins back to their parents. Mary Lou noticed several rain barrels along the side of the main building. The two with dippers hung on nails above were obviously for drinking. The other three spaced separately were for washing. Tom held the twins while Mary Lou washed the surface grime from their hands and faces and dried them on her apron. Tantalizing smells wafted beneath her nose. Suddenly, Mary Lou was ravenous.

Inside, the building was dim. The walls were papered with newsprint, put there mainly for warmth, but still readable where it wasn't covered with maps, a post card here and there, cattle breeding charts, various photographs, old calendar pictures, and even demure pinups.

Tom seated Mary Lou at a table. Immediately, a stocky woman, accompanied by smells from the kitchen, emerged with long, well-used strips of cloth to tie Beth and Tommy into their chairs. Mary Lou smiled. "Thank you. They are used to that. Until their father made high chairs for Christmas, we did exactly what you are doing."

The woman's merry eyes spoke her welcome. She clucked both babies' chins. "Don't get many wee ones here. 'Tis a pleasure to see them. They twins?"

Mary Lou nodded and smiled again. The woman's voice was soft, lilting and almost gentle, a surprise coming from someone who must have spent most of her life around boisterous cowboys and cattlemen. "Yes, this is Beth, and this is Tommy."

The twins stared wide-eyed as the woman moved around their chairs and tied them in. She patted the top of Tommy's head and smoothed her hand over Beth's curls, then returned to stand beside Mary Lou. "We have beef, pork, fried potatoes, sourdough biscuits, cowboy beans, and vinegar pie."

Tom ordered some of each, Mary Lou took beef, sourdough biscuits, a piece of vinegar pie, and an order of mashed cowboy beans for the twins.

As they ate, cowboys stopped at the table for a few words with Tom. They were a jolly, sociable bunch of surprisingly young men. It wasn't easy to tell their ages. Yet, Mary Lou guessed which ones were twelve to fourteen. They were boisterous and strutted around pretending to be older.

When Tom finished eating, he told Mary Lou he wanted to talk to Lannie and Shade about plans to cross the river in the morning. He picked up his tin cup of coffee and joined them.

Mary Lou finished feeding the twins, glancing at Tom now and then. She could tell from their motions that he and the boys were discussing details of the crossing. Then, they laughingly began to josh Tom. From a word she heard now and then and through their motions, Mary Lou surmised they wanted Tom to come back to the station with them after he settled his family. Tom shook his head, rose and returned to Mary Lou.

Tom moved the wagon away from the buildings under a tree for privacy. Tired, cranky twins finally settled in the kiddie coop for the night. Mary Lou and Tom snuggled together in blankets under the wagon and listened to the cowboys songs and laughter from the big building at the far end.

"Would you rather be over in the other building having a good time with the cowboys or—" She never finished her sentence. Tom's mouth closed over hers. Talking ceased.

Chapter 2

Tom slowly slipped from their blanket bed under the wagon, stood up, stretched, appraised the day, and climbed into dew-damp clothes.

It was early. The sun, its eye only half open, had not emanated enough heat to dispel the sleepy morning mist that blinked and sparkled on blades of prairie grass in answer to the sun's wake-up call. Even the brown river water flowed drowsily, soothed by a calm night.

Good, Tom thought, *it will make crossing the river easier for everyone.* As he rounded the other side of the wagon, he paused, stood, and gazed at his beautiful, sleeping wife. Long, chestnut waves spilled casually around her shoulders. He loved to touch those soft, silky strands and watch her braid and unbraid her hair. He knelt on one knee beside her and pushed stray locks from her pug nose. He loved that, too. When she laughed, it wiggled bunny fashion.

"Papa, papa," came a call from the wagon.

Tom grinned. Mary Lou always spoke to the children about their "papa," and Tommy within the last week discovered the word connected him with his father. The call tugged at Tom's heart. He reached into the wagon and lifted his son from the kiddie coop. Beth sat rubbing her eyes, then stretched her arms forward. He deposited them one by one on the ground, and they crawled to their mother under the wagon. Tom went to feed and water Buttermilk and Babe.

Their call woke Mary Lou, then she felt them as they nuzzled her. She sat up amazed. She hadn't felt Tom slip from her side. He had decided last night they would have breakfast in the station so she wouldn't have to pack and unpack to prepare a morning meal. Her body evidently seized the opportunity to rest, its first chance to release itself from all the preparations and work of the trip. She rose, dressed quickly, and nursed the twins. Tom draped their bedding over the seat of the wagon, hoping the sun would dry out some of the night's dampness. On their way to breakfast, they paused to splash water on their hands and faces before they went into the station.

"Good morning," welcomed the same cheery woman from last night. She tied the twins in their chairs and patted their heads.

The menu was much the same as supper the night before, flapjacks, steak, and fried potatoes, but thick, steamy oatmeal was added to the breakfast menu. The parents shared their oatmeal with the twins.

Mary Lou sensed an urgency in Tom. They ate quickly and hurried back to the wagon to get ready to cross the river.

Only the twins were content with the moment. They sat on the ground playing with stones. Tommy popped one in his mouth then spit it out. Beth, watching him, did the same, made a face, opened her mouth, and it rolled off her tongue to the ground.

Tom hitched the team and moved the wagon to the edge of the river. On the other side, Lannie, Shade, and three cowboys on horseback appeared and waved.

Mary Lou picked up the twins and followed the wagon. Tom helped her into the seat and knotted a long rope around her waist. He took a shorter rope, looped it through the one tied around Mary Lou's middle, then tied a twin at each end so they were tied to their mother.

Tommy squalled and squirmed to get loose.

"Be still, Son!" Tom's stern tone caught Tommy's attention. Two pairs of intensely blue eyes met and challenged. The boy's squalling quieted, his lip receded, and he stuck his thumb in his mouth, his gaze still anchored on his father. A second later he pulled out his thumb and his face exploded into a wide grin that squiggled his tiny nose. Tom stroked Tommy's chin, patted the top of his head, and smiled. "Be a good little man, Son. We have to take care of our women." He gathered the rope connected to the twins and looked seriously into Mary Lou's eyes. "Hang on to both of these with one hand and the wagon with the other." Tom turned, hollered, captured Lannie's attention, and threw the other end of the rope tied to Mary Lou.

Lannie caught it and knotted it over his saddle horn. The cowboys shouted back and forth to Tom, coordinating signals, then one by one they threw Tom the loop end of four lariats across the river.

Tom caught and tied them to the four corners of the wagon. His heart swelled with admiration at the determination he saw in his wife's eyes. "They will have control of all four sides of the wagon to keep it from floating downstream and will pull us right over," he said with a teasing grin. "Still scared?"

Mary Lou nodded. "I have to be honest. I'll be glad when we are safely on the other side."

Tom's eyes spoke agreement. He adjusted the twins in her lap so she could put one arm around the front of them. "Concentrate on hanging onto the wagon with one hand, hug the twins, and keep a grip on the ropes they are tied to. "Don't panic if you fall off into the water. Lannie will be watching you and if that happens, he will immediately pull you and the twins to shore. Don't worry about the twins. Just don't let go of their rope. I'll keep

Buttermilk and Babe going, and we'll be over in no time."

For the first time in Mary Lou's life, two hands were not enough.

With a quick leap, Tom seated himself beside her and flicked the reins, braced his feet, and yelled, "Come on, Buttermilk. Let's go, Babe!"

Mary Lou watched the snorting, stomping horses as they gingerly responded to the guiding shouts of Tom and the cowboys. She felt the wagon ease down the sloping shore and heard the water begin its hungry rush around it. As the wheels left the ground, the current grabbed them greed-ily, as if to swallow them whole. For a scary moment, the river took command. Then four rhythmic, determined jerks assured Mary Lou that it was Tom and the cowboys who had control, not the river.

The twins quieted, aware of a new sensation. Tommy's eyes grew wide. He twisted his head and looked up at his father as Tom shouted encouragement to the horses. His little body stiffened, he opened his mouth, and babbled in concert with his father.

Suddenly, the ropes became taut and Mary Lou felt they were afloat. She hugged her babies tighter in her arm. "Children, this is your first boat ride." She forced a laugh and felt them relax. She glanced down at the water crawling onto the floor of the wagon and could picture it swishing around their supplies and steeled herself for the drying-out job awaiting her as soon as the wheels reached the other side.

"We've got 'em!" a cowboy shouted.

Buttermilk and Babe clambered for footing. Mary Lou felt the front wagon wheels claw at the land and the rear wheels obediently follow. The tilt cascaded water from underneath as the rear wheels climbed onto land. They made it! A deep sigh rose in Mary Lou, then expelled in thanks to God, silently thanking the Lord for good, solid ground. They were safe on the other side.

Three cowboys leaped into the wagon, unloaded and inspected everything, and helped Tom sort out the bottom layer of wet things. The cowboys resembled washerwomen as they hung and spread dripping large and small canvases on bushes and tree limbs to dry.

Mary Lou was surprised so much had been spared. Nelson's pictures on top were perfectly safe. Bedding and clothing were all dry. Tom had packed well.

Before the boys left, they built a good fire, Tom put the coffeepot on, and Mary Lou handed out the best she had, Hattie's apple hand pies. They scarfed them down quickly, then sat around, their tin cups of coffee in hand, talking trail drives, cattle, and the problem of barbed wire fences cutting up the open range.

"The worst is them sheep. They close-crop the grasses and don't leave no feed fer the cattle." Shade swilled his coffee, reached for the pot, and filled his cup. He scrunched his nose. "And besides, they smell bad."

"Well, it ain't much worse than a fightin' farmer who wants to move in and plow up the land. If'n it keeps up like this with sheep and them Eastern money bags buying up the land, we won't have no ranchin' room left."

Mary Lou couldn't understand the problem with sheep. Mama always kept a dozen or so. They supplied wool and meat. Lamb chops had always been her favorite.

The cowboys finished the pot of coffee, shouted hearty farewells, mounted their horses, and crossed the river back into Texas. Tom and Mary Lou packed up, draped the damp canvases from the bushes over the top of the wagon for the sun to dry, took their seats, and continued their journey. By late afternoon, they were deep into Indian Territory.

Mary Lou smiled at the contented babbling of the twins as they played in the kiddie coop.

Tom pointed to specks on the horizon. "Indians," he said.

Mary Lou nodded. She had never felt a fear of Indians when she was growing up on the Kansas prairie. Other than keeping an eye out for rattlesnakes, she and Jenny used to play hide and seek in the tall grass and had roamed their beautiful playground unafraid. Indians had never bothered them. The Plains Indians had usually been friendly. Mama had told Mary Lou that in the first years of 1860 when she was newly married to Pa, she had welcomed squaws and their children into their cabin. Pa objected. "Mothers are the same all over the world," Mama told him. "We get together to talk about our children." But those women had also taught Mama a lot about preservation of food, cleaning animal skins, and how to make them supple for clothing and robes.

True, there were times when they had been a nuisance. They had no sense of property. Especially, young Indian men. They were like little boys who felt perfectly free to walk into any cabin and pick up whatever took their fancy. If they had chosen something Mama didn't want to part with, the sweet way was to offer them something other than what they had taken, then bargain with them as she would a child.

Pa had always grumbled Mama was too soft on them.

"They are God's children," she had exclaimed, "and He loves them as much as He does us." For Mama, there was nothing in the whole world that God's love did not touch. "God saw everything he had made, and, behold, it was very good." Mary Lou sighed deeply. Mama had made it sound so simple.

Tom reached over and patted her hand. "Give me one guess, and I'll say you are thinking of your mama."

Mary Lou turned to his touch and drank in the love pouring from his gaze. "Tom, sometimes you scare me! It amazes me how you read my mind."

"Not true." Tom grinned. "I can tell by the look on your face whether your mind is in Kansas or Texas."

The twins squealed behind her. She checked the kiddie coop to see what they were doing. Tommy was sticking a finger through a knothole on one of the barrels, then jerking it back and hugging it to his stomach. Beth did the same. Their baby giggles made her think of tinkling bells.

The specks in the distance grew into real, live, Indians. They were probably a half a mile or so away.

The warm day and joggling wagon lulled Mary Lou into her reminiscence again, and she remembered the day an Indian had staggered through the cabin door and fell face down on the floor. Immediately, Mama had dropped to his side to attend to his wounds. She rolled him over and saw he had been attacked and mauled by an animal and had fainted from loss of blood.

At Mama's insistence, Pa had reluctantly fixed him a bed in the back shed. Pa wanted him out in the barn. Mama refused to have it so.

"If you insist on caring for him, why not out in the barn?" Pa had asked. "Ellen, there are good and bad Indians." Pa knew. He had ridden the plains as a young cowboy before his accident and had been in constant contact with them.

"But I can't keep my eye on him in the barn. I need to know when he needs help to show him that God loves him. The only way he can learn is if someone who loves God, loves him."

Pa gave in. He couldn't fight God, he said.

However, in 1878, when Mary Lou was eighteen, she remembered how it frightened everyone when the Northern Cheyenne escaped from their reservation at Fort Reno in western Kansas. Pa had said they were dissatisfied with poor living conditions and inadequate food rations supplied by the government. Chief Dull Knife and his discontented warriors took their squaws and children and plundered and murdered homesteaders in their drive north through western Kansas toward their homeland in the Dakotas.

When they heard of it, Mary Lou had asked Mama, "Why do people do such terrible things?"

"Because they don't know that God loves them and will care for their needs. Jesus died on the cross for the sin of all the terrible things people do. He was God telling everyone 'I love you. Let Me teach you how to love Me and each other.' " As always Mama had quoted from her Bible. "For God so loved the world that he gave his only begotten son that whosoever—" Remembering, Mary Lou smiled. Her magnanimous mama had paused and

255

looked into Mary Lou's eyes. "And that 'whosoever' includes Indians." A decisive nod stamped a period on her final statement.

Tom's hand pressed over hers. "You are in Kansas again."

Mary Lou nodded and they laughed. They were smiling when the Indians approached them.

Tom held his hand up in sign of welcome, and the Indians responded with nods and raised hands. Tom made a few motions, and the Indians nodded again.

Tommy babbled from the kiddie coop.

"My son," Tom signed.

The Indians smiled wide, nodded, and nudged their horses to peer into the coop.

Tom retrieved the twins and the Indians looked from one to the other. "Twins," Tom said and held up two fingers. "Two at one time," he said, straightened his shoulders, smiled, and proudly pointed to himself.

The Indians caught on and beamed, commented back and forth to each other, pointed to Tom, smiled, nodded, and held up two fingers. Tom held up his hand and climbed into the back of the wagon for a small leather bag. He opened the top, reached his hand into it, and brought out some beads. "Beads," Tom said.

Four eyes brightened.

Tom dumped the beads back into the bag and held it out. The bigger Indian took them, poured some into his hand, showed his partner, spoke in his native tongue, then said, "Beads."

Tom nodded, gave them a salute from his hat brim, picked up the reins, and slapped them across the backs of his team.

The big Indian stuffed the bag into his tunic and swung his horse as the wagon began to move.

Tom grinned at Mary Lou. "Just a couple friendly Indians out for a ride. That was one of Mother's little tricks. She taught us boys the best way to show you were friendly was to give them decorations for their clothing."

Mary Lou settled back. They still had a long way to go.

Chapter 3

Z ack leaned forward, looked out the train window, and gave a sigh of relief. Surroundings were beginning to look familiar as the train rumbled through the outskirts of Boston. He straightened in his seat and rolled his shoulders a couple of times to ease the stiff stabbing fingers that poked his back. The ride from Texas had been interesting and exciting, but exhausting.

Of all the new modes of transportation sprouting up in America, Zack was most impressed with the new railroad systems that linked the East and West with hundreds of miles of track. Trains were smelly and noisy but a vast improvement in speed and comfort over horseback or stagecoach. And trains were changing everything, even ranching. The long cattle drives up the Chisholm Trail were now being herded to the nearest railroad, loaded into cattle cars, and shipped to Eastern markets hungry for beef. He, Tom, and Smitty had been talking about the changes necessary in the Circle Z to keep it profitable, but Tom said he already had in mind what he wanted to do: raise prize stallions like Father Zachary.

The train had *clickety-clacked* across Arkansas, Mississippi, Alabama, and Georgia, then turned north along the Atlantic seacoast. Zack had marveled at the expanse of cotton fields in the South. Since the invention of the cotton gin, cotton was now the leading product of the entire South. Even eastern Texas had cotton fever and grew it as a viable crop. Zack gazed out the train window. America was changing everywhere.

The train blew its whistle, slowed, huffed, and puffed its way toward the station platform which bustled with people waiting for passengers to disembark and make room for the next travelers.

Zack reached for his valise from the shelf above his seat and noticed his dust-laden sleeves. His coat and muddy boots were no better. *I'll stop at the hotel and clean up.* Darcy frowned on unkempt men.

His heart quickened at the thought of her being so near. His arms ached to hold her. It had been almost three months. He sighed and hoped this visit had soothed her homesickness and she would be ready and content to go home to take up their life in Texas with their son.

Zack smiled inwardly, anticipating her reaction to the surprise he had waiting for her back home—a new ranch house. He had wanted it to be farther along when he brought Darcy home from Boston, but the windows he ordered from the East had not arrived and that held up inside finishing work. Could that have been part of what had bothered Darcy, not having a home of her own? She always talked proudly about her family home in Boston. Zack understood that. He was right proud of the Circle Z. But three families in one ranch house was more like a boardinghouse and left little privacy except for their bedroom. He had heard that most women yearned for a home of their own. Most men did, too. A spread gave a man a solid, anchored feeling of belonging. Now he understood why his father had expressed such feeling for the land. It added substance to a man.

Zack could hardly wait to show the new ranch to Darcy. He had picked an area on the western side of the Circle Z. Tom and Mary Lou's ranch lay south of the main house. It was commonly understood that Nelson would inherit the main ranch house and that Mother would remain there. Had he lived, Doug's share would have been east. Zack would only need a house and a horse barn since he planned to be a lawyer. What a spread the Circle Z would be—four families and all the children! Baby Zack emerged in his mind and a lonesome ache tugged at his heart for his son.

The train came to a screeching, hissing stop. Zack picked up his carpetbag and moved along behind other passengers on their way out. When he stepped on the platform, he glanced about for a carriage that could take him to the hotel to bathe and get rid of his travel grime and Western clothing.

U

The elegant gentleman who emerged from the hotel and hailed a carriage bore little resemblance to the man who had entered. Zack rehearsed a scene he had anticipated in his mind. Darcy would probably be in the rose garden at this time of day. He could already feel her in his arms. Memory breathed the fragrance of sweet rose water and felt the soft touch of her lips on his. He hoped that first kiss would communicate how much he had missed her while they had been apart.

The carriage pulled up in front of an impressive, brick house surrounded by tall maple trees that cupped their leaves overhead into a huge, green umbrella. A black, iron fence stood guard. Neat, brick walks would round the sides of the graceful house to the back.

Zack twisted the doorbell and heard it ring within. It seemed forever until the door opened.

Sylvia greeted him with wide surprise. "Mr. Langdon! Land sakes!" She swung the door open. Zack removed his hat, placed it in Sylvia's waiting hand, and walked into the spacious, polished hall, a hub for numerous doors around its walls.

"It's good to see you again, Sylvia." He glanced around. "Where is Mrs. Langdon?"

"Um, she's not here, Sir. She went for a carriage ride this afternoon. It is such a lovely day. . . ." Sylvia's wan smile belied her bright eyes. "Come this way, Sir," she said and crossed to the parlor.

Zack followed her across the shiny floor. Their footsteps echoed up the handsome, winding staircase that climbed to the second floor.

Sylvia opened the parlor door and stood aside to let Zack pass.

"Emery will take your bag to you room, Sir. Miss Darcy should be home soon. They left before dinner." Her smile vanished as she turned to leave.

Zack seated himself in one of the large lounge chairs beside the fire-place. Everything looked the same. His gaze roamed the room. Zack could understand why Darcy loved this house. It had elegance. Luxurious lace curtains and draperies hung on long windows that almost reached from the ceiling to the floor, flooding the room with light. Each chair had a table companion draped to the floor with a brocade cloth and a large painted globe lamp perched on its top. Circle Z was in another world.

Impatient, Zack rose and walked to the window that faced the front porch. Roses stretched thorny fingers and clambered up trellises to bathe in the sun. Inside the fence, peony bushes drooped their large, colorful heads. Maybe if he could duplicate the porches on the new ranch, it might make Darcy feel more at home. He glanced around to see what else could be copied.

A roan horse pulling a shay pranced to a stop in front of the ornate iron fence. A young man quickly jumped out his side and hurried around to a lady in a large picture hat who shut her parasol and turned to be assisted from her seat.

It was Darcy!

The solicitous young man gently held her hand, then her elbow, and helped her to the ground. He must have said something that delighted her, because she tossed her head and laughed.

The movement was too familiar. Zack remembered how coquettish she had been with him. His insides churned, but the joy of seeing her overrode it. He heard Sylvia scurry to open the front door.

Zack eagerly turned from the window.

Darcy's tinkling laughter filled the hall. "Thank you, Charles, Dear. What a delightful afternoon in the country."

Darcy's voice dripped sweetness. Her heels clicked across the wooden floor toward the parlor.

"Uh—Miss Darcy," the young man called.

She stopped, swung, and turned beguiling eyes on Charles.

Charles cleared his throat. "Miss Darcy, I would be most honored if you would allow me to escort you to the Sweetheart Ball this Friday evening." Charles moved to her side. "That is, of course, unless you are already spoken for."

Zack cleared his throat and stepped into the hall. "Yes, Charles, she *is* already spoken for."

Darcy spun and froze.

Zack walked to his wife and embraced her. "Darling," he said and kissed her cheek. His left arm around Darcy, Zack extended his right hand to the startled young man and smiled. "I'm Zack Langdon, Mrs. Langdon's husband."

Charles's eyes shot open. Unnerved, he looked first at Darcy, then at Zack, and gingerly shook the offered hand before him.

Immediately, Darcy seized the situation and turned to Zack. "Darling." She slipped from his arm, planted a soft kiss on his cheek, and smiled up into Zack's face. "I want you to meet Charles Pearce. He has been such a gracious gentleman and escorted me on a few outings so I wouldn't be so lonely."

The men shook hands.

Charles, a surface smile on his face, began backing toward the door, his hat in both hands. He nodded quickly to Darcy. "Thank you for a delightful afternoon, Darcy—" He swallowed. "I mean—Mrs. Langdon." He bumped into the doorframe which cracked his smile into an embarrassed grin. "Nice to meet you, Sir," he said and turned in hasty retreat across the porch, down the walk, and through the wrought-iron gate. He climbed through his buggy from the passenger side, grabbed the reins, and snapped them. The roan responded with a leap and flopped Charles abruptly into his seat, and they sped away.

Zack turned to Darcy to demand an explanation but the words stuck in his throat. His heart betrayed him. He reached and drew her into his arms. Love hunger flooded his body in response to her nearness. He closed his eyes and held her to allay the loneliness he had fought in her absence. His momentary anger evaporated with the familiar fragrance that floated around her.

Darcy let Zack hold her, then relaxed, brushed a kiss across his mouth, pushed him away, and leisurely pulled off her gloves as she swished into the parlor and casually dropped them on one of the tables. "My dear, why—why didn't you let me know you were coming? I—I would have come to meet you. Did you come by train? It must have taken days of dreary travel. Are you tired, Dear? Hungry?" She turned, gazed at him for a long moment while her mouth formed a sweet smile.

Zack's gaze met hers with outrage, but again his desire for her love hammered at his chest and ensnared him.

Slowly, Darcy moved into his arms and melted him with a kiss.

Zack succumbed to his need for her, pressed her close, and returned her kiss. As always, she captivated him and won.

Chapter 4

Emery, the butler, entered the parlor. "Dinner is served, Madam."
The men rose, escorted the ladies to the dining room and seated them.

Zack glanced at Thomas Whitney, his distinguished father-in-law who presided at his dinner table with the same confident assurance that commanded his law firm. Zack truly admired the man. He had been a forceful instrument in Zack's becoming a lawyer, which had been his dream as long as he could remember.

At the opposite end of the elegant table of fine china and shining silverware sat Sarah Whitney, a small, pretty woman who gestured and nodded commands to the servants as they moved quietly to serve each person.

Thomas tucked his white linen napkin into his neck to cover his cravat. "Glad to see you at our table again, my boy. I've missed you. I still think you ought to reconsider and come back east to be a barrister with my firm."

Zack shook his head and smiled. "Thank you, Sir. You do me great honor, but what would I do with my own law practice in Texas? Its shaky legs are just settling on solid ground. I have the mammoth job and challenge to be part of bringing law and order to the West."

Darcy shot Zack a frown, then turned and smiled sweetly at her father. "Tell him now, Father."

Zack gazed from one pair of telling eyes to the other and almost read their faces. *Wonder what juicy offer they have cooked up this time to make it attractive for me to become a part of Whitney and Marcus.* Zack had travelled halfway to Boston with a fellow lawyer who told him shocking news. The elder Joshua Marcus, partner of Whitney and Marcus, had been shot a month ago. Knowing Thomas, he would relish being in full charge.

Thomas frowned at his daughter.

Zack knew that frown. She had stepped ahead of him, and Thomas never knowingly followed anyone. An excellent barrister, a demanding boss, but he was fair and seemingly enjoyed teaching Zack. Their relationship had been good.

"In your travels, I suppose you heard my firm is standing on only one leg at this moment." Thomas lifted his chin, looked down his glasses at

Zack, and cleared his throat. "I have decided to offer you the partnership. Whitney and Langdon! How does that sound to you, my boy?"

Zack hated being referred to as "my boy." Thomas did that to everyone. It accomplished its purpose and kept everyone in line. A smile crossed Zack's face but his heart sank to his feet. From the contrived looks and grins on Thomas's and Darcy's faces, Zack surmised his father-in-law had stretched to pacify his daughter. Zack had seen that same resigned expression at the end of a few courtroom sessions where Whitney and Marcus had lost the case.

Darcy reached over and seized Zack's hand. "It would be wonderful, Darling, and I have found a lovely English Tudor house not too far from here that would be perfect for us."

"Does it have a fenced-in yard for Baby Zack?" Zack asked. His words shattered in the air.

"Why—yes—of course, Dear." Darcy forced the words through her teeth and smiled.

"I can hardly wait to see my first grandson," Sarah injected. "I ache to hold him while he is still a baby."

"He's a fine lovable boy, Mother Whitney. And his leg is growing nicely. He will probably be walking and will run to his mother when we get home." Zack smiled at his wife.

Darcy's eyes narrowed.

"Oh, did the baby fall and hurt his leg? I didn't hear about that. How serious was the injury?" Sarah asked.

"No, Mother, he was born with one leg shorter than the other. My mother knew how to massage it so it has almost grown as long as the other one. My brother Nelson was born with both legs weak and one shorter than the other. Mother massaged his legs, and Dr. Mike said she did better than any nurse. Nelson has grown strong enough to move everywhere on crutches and is even married!"

"Your mother must be a dedicated, loving woman," Sarah commented.

"She is." Zack took a deep breath, pinned his gaze on Darcy, and smiled. "I have a big surprise for you, too, my dear." *Might as well lay everything out on the table.* Zack gazed lovingly at Darcy. "Our new ranch house is raised, roofed, and ready for the windows. I was hoping it would be much farther along and almost finished when you came home. I ordered large windows like these from the East—" Zack pointed to the long graceful windows facing him, "but they haven't arrived yet. I thought they would make you feel more at home."

Darcy's clouded eyes concealed her thoughts. Suddenly, she brightened. "But, Darling," her voice carried a sweet warning. "If you are a partner in father's law firm, we won't be needing a house in Texas."

Zack's heart sank. He should have guessed. This whole scene had been spelled out in advance—the answer cut-and-dried before he had even been asked. He glanced at his father-in-law who sat ramrod straight behind a masked expression he had taught Zack to use to conceal his thoughts—a basic lawyer pose to buffalo his opponent. He could see through the whole ruse. Darcy had seized the opportunity of Joshua's death to twist her father's arm to arrange the offer. But Thomas Whitney had taught Zack well. He read his father-in-law's cues, which betrayed the exuberant, smooth voice. There was no doubt in Zack's mind that Thomas would gladly wiggle out from under this offer if he could.

Zack watched Darcy's face and read her obvious thoughts blazoned in a victorious I-am-going-to-win look. It tore him in half.

"Zack, are you going to accept my offer to become a partner in my firm or aren't you?"

Zack looked up from his dumpling and faced his father-in-law. He took a deep breath. "No, Sir."

A pair of gray, shaggy eyebrows raised in disbelief.

Zack searched for the right words. "You do me honor in your offer, Father. I know it is a great opportunity. I thank you for even considering me." He paused, aware of bristling emotions. "My mother told me when I left Texas to come here to study law that 'once a Texas boy, always a Texas boy.' I didn't believe her then. I do now." He laid his fork on the table. "Sir, I see my job in Texas as very important also. I want to help tame an unlawful territory into law-abiding working communities like you have here in the East. We have to find some way to help Americans, Mexicans, and Indians establish laws so we can all live on the land in peace. People are moving west. The government recently made it lawful for settlers to buy up land the railroads didn't use and towns are springing up all around them. But they are boom towns and need law and order. I find it exciting to be a part of taming anarchy by establishing law in those places." His gaze dropped to his dumpling, and he sensed their disbelieving stares.

No one said anything.

Suddenly, Darcy rose, pushed back her chair, and faced Zack.

Zack shifted to rise from his chair, but a very unladylike thrust from Darcy shoved him back into it.

Two red angry flames fired Darcy's cheeks, her mouth withdrew into a line that almost cancelled out her lips.

"Well, I am *not* going to live with Mexicans, Indians, nor Texans!" Darcy jerked her skirt around the chair and stomped out, her angry face set as if in stone. Her heels resounded like exploding cannon balls in the hallway, then she ran up the stairs.

Zack rose and bounded up after her two steps at a time.

Darcy slammed their bedroom door shut in his face.

He was angry at himself. That was no way to tell her. Surely, she understood as his wife that it should be up to him to determine where they would live. It had to be where he could make a good living. Zack shook his head. *Weak point!* He could make a better living here as part of the firm. But everything inside him shrivelled at the thought of accepting a partnership in a law firm in Boston.

His thoughts circled round and round. He tried to open the door. It was locked. He knocked hard to dislodge his anger and hurt. He must speak with Darcy. They could never settle anything if they didn't talk about it. Yet it angered him that Darcy and her father had tried to manipulate him. This whole scene could have been avoided if they had consulted him, given him some input at the beginning, then asked him. He knocked again—again—

Abruptly, the door swung wide. Darcy turned her back and swished to the fireplace. "We might as well get this over with," she said to the mantel, then turned and faced him.

"Darcy—" Zack began.

She shook her head. "No! I've heard what *you* are going to do. Now *I'm* going to tell you what *I'm* going to do," she snapped. Her eyes were cold and angry; her hands clenched like white claws in front of her.

Zack stepped toward her. "Darling, let's—"

"Don't 'darling' me. You have known all along how I hate ranch life. It is dirty, ugly, uncomfortable, and uncivilized. I will not live like that. I was raised to be a lady, and I cannot be a lady there."

Zack stiffened. "Then what do you call my mother? I call her a lady!"

"Don't pull your lawyer stuff on me! I will not—do you hear me?—*not* go back to Texas. Either you take Father's offer and stay here, or we will no longer be man and wife!"

Her words thrust through him like a heavy beam and snatched his breath. Zack stared at her belligerent face. "What on earth do you mean by that?"

"Exactly what I said. A man and wife are supposed to live together and share in marriage. In this marriage, I am the one who has to give up everything! There is no life for me in Texas."

Zack knew it had been very hard for Darcy on the ranch. He had felt so helpless, yet had tried his best. "That's part of the problem, Darcy, you expect me to stay here, give up the important work I am doing, and be a puppet to your father."

Darcy shook her head vigorously. "We did not say 'puppet,' we said 'partner!' Zack, you will still be a lawyer, either in Boston or Texas. Don't you understand? You will still be who you are—a lawyer—doing what you love to do. I will be nothing in Texas. I would shudder to have to do all that horrible work with food your mother and Mary Lou had to do. I could not do it. I will not do it!"

We. I. An unsurmountable wall of hurt rose between them.

Suddenly, Darcy softened and took a step toward him, her arms stretched. "Zack. . .Darling. . .don't you understand there are men in Boston who would jump through hoops at the chance of being a partner with my father? I cannot believe you don't understand what a privilege has been offered you. You should be grateful that my father even considered you. He has many other men he could have chosen, men far better qualified than you—"

"Wait a minute. Let's get this straight. I'm beginning to catch on that this whole matter has nothing to do with me."

Darcy turned her back to Zack.

Zack grabbed her elbow and swung her around to face him. "How long did it take you to get your father to agree with you? I know your father, and I don't believe this was his idea at all. I think he is happy I refused. You demanded he offer it to me. Didn't you?"

Darcy jerked to free herself from his hold.

Zack grabbed both her arms and made her face him. "Didn't you!"

Darcy twisted angrily in his grasp and turned her face away.

He pulled her tight against him and held her still. "*Didn't you?*"

Darcy refused to acknowledge him.

Angry as he was, her closeness triggered his love-hungry body and mind to consider what she was asking. *Oh God!* he cried within. *We have to resolve this. We have a son to consider.* He steeled himself to calm down. In all his life, he had never felt so helpless. His barrister training had taught him self-control, but he felt undone, as if parts of him were flying everywhere.

Darcy held herself rigid, ignoring him.

"Darcy—Darling—I love you. A man is supposed to plan for his wife and provide for her. I plan to make money in Texas, I have already built a beautiful ranch home. After the windows are put in, you can have it decorated any way you want. If you want it to look like this house, we can order everything you like from the East and it will be just as beautiful as here, and you can be a lady." Zack felt her relax and leaned to press his lips on hers—

Darcy jerked free, walked to the fireplace, and stood with her back to him.

Zack fought his desire to follow her and enfold her in his arms and kiss away her anger. They were both too overwrought. They needed calming time.

Suddenly, Darcy swung, faced him, and stretched to her fullest height.

265

Rage flashed from wide eyes filled with fury.

From the very first day they met, Zack had felt this fierceness in Darcy. She loved life! She was magnificent, beautiful, charming, a delightful companion. His anger at her slackened as he remembered how their relationship and love grew. They had been deliciously happy in Boston after they were married. Their honeymoon with her sister in Georgia on the way to Texas was all he could have asked for. But when they got to Texas the transplant had been like placing a blooming flower into dry ground. He watched her shrivel and withdraw, and he hurt for her. Yet he still felt that if she had given herself half a chance, her natural zest for life would have overcome even Texas.

Darcy took a deep breath. "Zack, I'm only going to say this once." Her voice was controlled, hard, brittle. "No matter what you do, I am staying here in Boston. This is my life. I want no other." She bent her head and lifted her fist to her quivering mouth. Abruptly, she jerked her head up and gazed into Zack's eyes. "Now—now I know. We should never have been married in the first place."

Never—? Stunned, Zack stared at Darcy in disbelief.

Darcy softened and hurried on. "But you were different when you lived here. I truly loved you."

Zack flinched. "What do you mean, 'loved'?"

"You are not the same man I married. I loved and married a Boston lawyer and intended to live here, where I can live in the style that is my custom." Darcy looked beyond him. In a voice cold and brittle, she spit out the words that blew him apart. "Zack, unless you take that partnership from my father, I will no longer be your wife. I will have my father arrange for a divorce."

Divorce! The word exploded in his head! A divorce was a disgrace, a failure. His wooden mouth choked out, "You wouldn't!"

"I will!" She stood straight, chin up. Her eyes bore accusing holes through him.

Zack watched determination set her face. "But, Darcy, I love you, you love me—"

"No, I don't. I don't want to be your wife anymore."

"What about our son?"

Darcy threw her head back and laughed. "That was the worst thing that ever happened to me. I hated it. I will never have another child."

Zack sagged. *She hated having our son?* A ragged memory surfaced from those first moments when Baby Zack was born. His beaming mother had brought his new son to him. He remembered the intense father-pride he had felt as he awkwardly cradled this tiny child made up of part of him and part of Darcy. He had stood in the doorway and watched his mother return the baby to Darcy. *"Take it away,"* she had screamed.

"But Darcy—"

"But Darcy—but Darcy! Can't you think of anything else to say?" Her eyes narrowed into slits. "Get out of my sight!" she hissed. "I never want to see you again. My father will arrange everything. Now *get out!*" she screamed.

Zack stood numb. He felt his heart crumble into pieces.

Darcy moved towards him, only to shove him aside, walk out, spit out her words, and throw them back over her shoulder. "I suggest you get the next train back to your wonderful Texas where you belong!" At the top of the stairs, she turned. "And you can keep your crippled son. I don't want him."

The winning blow. Zack watched her walk out of his life and felt his life blood drain from him. His love for her demanded that he run after her, but his body refused the command. She had made it very clear. He felt paralyzed, his ears remained alert to hear the clatter of her heels on the staircase finally fade away.

Slowly awareness returned. Zack turned and stared vacantly around the room, seeing nothing. Finally, after what seemed like forever, his body voluntarily bent to pull his valise from under the bed. He hadn't even had time to unpack it. Just as well. Time to go home. Home to Texas. . .and their son. *No. My son.*

Chapter 5

Mary Lou took a deep breath and inhaled the Kansas spring air, relishing the sweet smell of the prairie.

Tom turned to her and grinned. "Getting anxious?"

"Oh, yes!" This last day's trip had seemed endless even though Tom had made good, steady time. Mary Lou glanced back, surprised to find the twins curled together, sound asleep. "I think those poor babies feel they are resigned to live forever in that kiddie coop. You were a genius, Tom. It has given them a place to play and sleep. What would we have ever done without it?"

Tom leaned and kissed her cheek. It had been a long, hard, slow ride for Mary Lou and the twins. Cattle drives, even though they were about the same distance and more arduous, were never monotonous.

Mary Lou clasped her hands and stretched them out in front of her to relieve her backache, then shook her head and smiled. "I can hardly wait to show everyone the twins. I have a feeling they will be spoiled rotten by the time Aunt Tibby, Aunt Nelda, and everyone else passes them around. Oh, how I wish Mama. . ."

Tom put his arm around Mary Lou and pulled her close. "I don't think loving attention spoils younguns. If that were the case, we both should be rotten by now." He gave her a squeeze and a sideways glance. "I give you a lot of loving attention. Do you feel spoiled?"

Mary Lou blushed. "Spoiled? If I am, I love it!"

Tom slowed the horses, wrapped the reins around his knee, and pulled her into his arms, his azure eyes serious. "I love you more than my own life, Mary Lou. Before I met you, I didn't know what real love and happiness were." His kiss was long and tender.

Mary Lou clung to him. If anyone had ever told her a person could love someone as much as she loved Tom and the babies, she wouldn't have believed there was that kind or that much love in the world. A sudden rush of hot tears rolled down her cheeks, and she sniffed.

Tom looked at her in surprise. "Crying? What did I say to make you cry?"

Mary Lou batted wet lashes and smiled. "Oh, you know me. I always cry when I'm happy."

Tom grinned and snuggled her within his arm.

"Papa."

Mary Lou and Tom turned. Their son's penetrating eyes stared into theirs.

Tommy grinned. "Papa," he began, then his tongue tumbled out gibberish that included an almost recognizable word here and there. His wide blue eyes stared question marks.

"Yes, Son, and I pray someday you'll find a woman who will love you like your mama loves me." Tom turned a pair of identical blue eyes toward Mary Lou and received a "thank you" from hers.

Beth let out a wail as she bumped her head on the side of the kiddie coop. Mary Lou reached into her pocket and retrieved a small piece of sugar candy Hattie had tucked into a food basket. Tommy's hand shot up for his piece.

Tom spurred the horses to a leisurely trot.

Mary Lou's gaze roamed familiar terrain. They were getting close. First, they would pass Petula Hilary's place, then Jeremy Halderan's farm, then the Martin Clay homestead. Mary Lou hated just to ride by and wave, but she wanted to show the twins to the family first. Her old neighbors would understand.

Petula stood at her well, pulling the rope to raise her bucket. She paused, shaded her eyes with one hand, then raised it in a wide overhead wave.

Mary Lou waved back. "I am surprised Petula recognizes this wagon. Let's keep going, I'll see her later. I am anxious to get home."

Tom gave a slap of the reins to signal Buttercup and Babe to step it up.

Mary Lou squinted at a small figure way out in a wheat field guiding a plow being slowly dragged through the dirt. "For goodness sake, Nellie's still alive. That old bag of horse bones has pulled Jeremy Halderan's plow as long as I can remember. Jeremy treats that mare as if she were his mother."

"It's real easy to get attached to an animal," Tom said. "Father felt the same way about Diamond. Mother often said Father loved that big stallion more than he did her. Every inch of that animal shouted power, yet he could be as soft and gentle as a kitten. I remember the day Father first swung me up on Diamond's back all alone. He put the reins in my hands, and I think that horse sensed I couldn't have controlled him if I'd tried, 'cause he stood motionless as if he cradled a baby. As for me, I sat tall and felt like a big man."

Mary Lou warmed. Whenever Tom allowed her a peek into his life before she knew him, she tucked the golden memory in a special place in her heart until she could write it down in the memory book Mama gave her on her sixteenth birthday. Some day, things would be reversed. It would be Tom putting their boy on Tinder to create a memory for his son. Mary Lou sighed. Good memories are so important. Mama knew the value of them and had sprinkled her generously with too many to count or remember.

The Martin Clay homestead looked deserted. Probably everyone was out in a field somewhere.

As the landscape said "home," Mary Lou stretched her neck and caught her first glimpse of the speck on the horizon that would become Pa's cabin. The wagon's pace eked an eternity before it closed the gap and allowed the cabin to grow into recognizable size. Memory helpfully rushed in and put Mary Lou on Dulcie's back to relive the feel of flying in a wind that had torn at her hair, snatched her ribbons, and whirled them skyward. She peeked at the twins. Beth raised questioning eyes. Her little fingers gripped the wooden bars of the coop and she swayed with the faster roll of the wagon.

"I wish I had time to clean the twins up a bit," she said to Tom. Yet, she was sure no one would pay the least bit of attention to their tousled hair or soiled, wrinkled clothes, considering their trip. Her heart began to pound. She stretched her neck to see if the barn door was open or closed. Was Pa home? Had he forgiven her? She inwardly called, *Can You still reach his heart?*

Tom pulled on the reins. Buttermilk and Babe slowed to a plod. They were near the end of their journey.

The door of the cabin flew open and Aunt Nelda ran out, fanning her apron and shouting, "Tom! Mary Lou! Thank God you got here safely!"

Tom jumped out of the wagon and walked around to receive the twins from their confinement.

Mary Lou lifted the top of the kiddie coop. The twins had pulled themselves expectantly to a standing position. Mary Lou scooped out Beth, handed her to Tom, who transferred his daughter into the eager waiting arms of her great aunt.

Nelda hugged her close and kissed the baby on both cheeks. "Land sakes! This must be Beth! She is beautiful and looks just like your mama." She shifted Beth and stretched out her other arm for her nephew as Mary Lou handed him down to Tom.

Tommy's wide eyes surveyed his great aunt only a second, then he turned abruptly and wrapped himself around his father.

Nelda laughed. "That's all right, Sonny, we'll get well acquainted before you go back home."

Tom helped Mary Lou to the ground.

Mary Lou ran to her aunt who threw her arms around her. Beth pushed back, looked with surprise at the woman holding them, then turned and wrapped her arms around her mother's neck.

Everyone walked toward the cabin, over-talking each other's words.

"I sure had a hard time all week keeping my mind on my work. Today, I figured you had to be close if you left Texas at the time you told me in your last letter."

Mary Lou's gaze toured the cabin, barn, and fields, then turned questioning eyes to her aunt. "Is. . .is Pa home?"

Nelda smiled tenderly. "No, Child. He and Glenn had a big stock shipment come in today, but he promised to come home as early as he can for supper."

Suddenly, Tommy stretched out his arms to Nelda. As she reached for him, Beth reached out toward her, too.

Aunt Nelda laughed. "I figured they would come around soon." She perched Beth on one arm and held out her other arm to Tommy. "Come on, young man. I've got two arms and this one is aching to hold you."

They trailed into the cabin and Mary Lou's home hunger feasted on this dear place, her true home. As they walked through the door a quiet peace enveloped her.

Aunt Nelda had made few changes. Mama's bookshelf Pa had built on the wall still held her books. Mary Lou would love to take them home with her to teach her children when they were old enough. Mama used them when she taught Mary Lou and the neighboring homestead children as well. Her gaze touched everywhere, and Mary Lou's heart rejoiced with the comfort of being surrounded with Mama's things.

Nelda bent to put the twins on the floor. "Whew! They are two armfuls," she said and plopped down on the floor with them.

Mary Lou and Tom laughed when the twins both tried to clamber into her lap and almost bowled their great aunt over.

"And how's Aunt Tibby and Nate? Is she still stirring up the world?" Tom asked. He picked up Tommy and untangled his fingers from Aunt Nelda's hair. He laughed. "Are you sure you did the right thing when you switched grooms at our wedding?" Beth snuggled into Nelda's lap.

"Absolutely! Without our female meddling, you wouldn't have married this girl of your dreams, and I wouldn't be hugging these babies." Nelda teased.

They laughed, then Nelda wanted to hear all about their life in Texas and their new ranch house.

"Oh, you would love it, Aunt Nelda. It has five rooms!"

"My goodness, I'd like to see it sometime."

"There will always be room for you in our home," Tom said.

"Oh, I mean to visit. My home is here with my brother. He and I are the only ones left in our family as far as we know."

With quick efficiency, the table was set, the children fed, nursed, and put on the floor with a ball of yarn Nelda gave them to play with. It lasted until Tommy was so tangled in it, he had to be rescued before he strangled himself.

Supper pots hung ready and waiting.

Mary Lou set four places at the table and only half listened to Tom and Aunt Nelda's joshing. Her ears were tuned for the familiar sound and rhythm of a well-remembered *clip-clop*. When it reached her ears, she could sit no longer, so she rose and stood in the cabin doorway. About a half mile away a dust-cloud tail swirled behind a dear, familiar buggy. *Oh Lord,* her heart cried to God. *Let him receive me again as his daughter. May he have forgiven and forgotten my defiance and accept Tom as his son-in-law. And the babies, will he accept them?*

Mary Lou felt Tom's presence behind her. His arms folded around her waist to steady her trembling.

Pa made his usual loop around the cabin and into the barn.

Mary Lou looked up at Tom. No words needed to be said. He let her go. She slowly stepped out the door, walked around the cabin to the barn.

As she walked in, he had already unhitched Morgan from the buggy and was guiding him out the barn door to the water trough. Their eyes met as he passed her, but he continued his chore. Mary Lou walked to the trough and stood beside it. When Morgan dipped his head, their gazes met and clung.

"Hello, Pa," Mary Lou said. A rising lump closed her throat.

"Hello, Daughter," Buck answered, "good to see you."

Four words, but each one was studded with diamonds. *Good to see you.* Did that mean—?

Her father hobbled beside Morgan as he swung him around and went back to the barn. He loosened and pulled the harness, held on to the stall, and threw the leather rigging up over a hook with one hand.

Mary Lou had always admired the way Pa managed in spite of his injury. She slid a hand over the horse's ears and warm neck, glancing now and then at her father. Their gazes brushed several times.

Her father never had been a man of many words. Mama always said Pa was a doer, not a talker.

"How was your trip?"

Mary Lou smiled. "Long, Pa."

Buck nodded. "It's a fer piece." He grabbed his cane and started toward the door.

Mary Lou walked beside him. Evidently he had had his say. She managed to keep her welling tears beneath the surface. It was not the right time. Too many fences to mend.

Tom stood and reached out his hand as Buck entered the room. The men's looks met and challenged.

Mary Lou held her breath and prayed.

"Owen, you still owe them your blessing." Nelda never wasted words, but her voice was soft, firm, and, as usual, to the point.

That caught Buck's attention. His gaze moved from his sister, to his daughter.

Tom stood erect, his hand still extended.

Mary Lou could almost sense the battle going on within both her husband and father. She knew Tom would stand the breech.

Tommy crawled across the floor, sat down, and looked up at his grandfather. Their eyes locked and suddenly Tommy opened his mouth and poured out a stream of gibberish.

Buck bent and smiled at the baby at his feet, then looked up, first at Mary Lou, then at Tom.

"That is your grandson, Buck." Nelda picked him up and pointed to Beth on the floor. "Twins! Owen, you are a blessed man."

Buck's eyes returned to his son-in-law, who stood with his hand still outstretched. He stepped forward and clasped Tom's hand. In a husky voice, he said, "Thank you."

Beth, sitting alone on the floor, folded her little neck back so she could look up at the giants who surrounded her and let out a wail.

Mary Lou scooped up her daughter and turned to her father. "And this is Beth, Pa, your granddaughter."

Buck's eyes widened. He stared for a long second then turned to Mary Lou. "Beth? She looks like—" His words stopped.

"Her grandmother, Ellen." Nelda finished his statement. "Come, Owen, and sit down." Buck hobbled to his chair by the fireplace. Nelda placed his grandson in his lap when he sat down.

"Beth?" Buck's voice was noticeably shaken.

"Yes, Pa. We named her Allena Elizabeth after Tom's mother and Mama." Mary Lou placed her daughter on her father's other knee, and he stared at her with misty eyes.

It was a holy moment. A peace washed over Mary Lou. *Mama, you are here. I can feel you smiling.*

Mary Lou dropped to her knees in front of her father and two children. "What do you think of your twin grandchildren, Pa?"

Buck looked from one to the other. When he lifted his head, his eyes glistened. "I wish your mama could see them."

"Pa, she's in heaven. She knows."

Pa looked into Mary Lou's face for a long hushed moment. "I wish I

273

could believe that."

Mary Lou's heart sang. As small a hope as it was, Mary Lou accepted it and was thankful. *Dear God, give Pa time to find You.*

The twins squirmed, and Tom stepped over to catch Tommy as he slid from Buck's knee to the floor. Beth wiggled after him with the help of her father.

"Well, now, is everyone ready for something to eat? That rabbit stew ought to be just about right."

The room broke into busyness.

Tom got chairs and tied the twins into them.

Aunt Nelda tied brand new large bibs she had made around their necks.

Mary Lou dished up large soup bowls of rabbit stew and put one at each place at the table.

Finally, they all settled.

Nelda looked to Mary Lou, then to Tom. "Would you say the blessing, please, Tom?"

Tom bowed his head and everyone followed except Buck. His face was a mask, but the angry wrinkles in his forehead were noticeably shallower.

"Our heavenly Father," Tom began, "we thank You for Your wisdom to place us each into this family and ask Your blessing on each one gathered around this table. We thank You for healing wounds that only You can heal, for opening our hearts and pouring love into them so we can give it to each other. Forgive us our trespasses and bless this food in Jesus' name. Amen."

When Mary Lou raised her head, she looked straight into Tom's eyes. She hoped her gaze conveyed her thanks for the love and respect Tom had showed her pa. But she should have known.

Nelda picked up a plate of sourdough biscuits and handed them to her brother. "Here you are, Owen. I made these especially for you."

It was obvious to everyone that Buck had been noticeably moved by all that had happened. There was a touch of softness Mary Lou had only seen when Pa was around Mama. *There has to be a lot of love bottled up in Pa.* She looked at the twins as Nelda shoved spoonfuls of mashed vegetables from the stew into their mouths. A sudden realization swept over Mary Lou. Had Aunt Nelda ever had any children of her own? She realized she had never asked nor had she ever heard her aunt mention any.

Mary Lou sighed. *Life's mysteries grow deeper as I grow older.* For the second time in her life since Mama died, Mary Lou sensed an acute awareness of the heartache of people all around her, suffering in ways of which she was totally unaware. Yet Aunt Nelda always seemed strong, unperturbed.

Mary Lou and Tom were so happy. They had two beautiful children. Why was it life was so full for some but not for others? She had no answer.

Something Mama said brushed through her mind. "No matter how long we live, life's mysteries increase instead of decrease, and we will never understand fully. We see through the glass darkly, the Bible says. That is why the Bible teaches and stresses that we need to learn to live by faith. No one will ever know it all."

She looked at Pa in faith. Was she imagining it, or did he look different? Had it happened before she came, or tonight, when God graced the family with His peace. *Whatever. Thank You, Jesus.*

Chapter 6

Your pa is going with us to Tibby's?"

Mary Lou nodded and her heart raised thankful praise to a God who could use two little babies to turn a stubborn man around and mold him into a devoted grandfather.

Nelda's face registered the pleasant surprise Mary Lou felt.

Mary Lou, Nelda, and the twins joined Tom and Pa in the barn. Pa had Morgan already hitched to the buggy. Tom had saddled Buttermilk and Aunt Nelda's Jewel. Mary Lou mounted Jewel. What a treat to sit in a saddle after the long wagon trip!

"Now you two just ride on ahead," Nelda called. She climbed into the buggy with Buck and held out her arms.

Tom set the twins on Aunt Nelda's lap.

A desperate wail erupted from Tommy. The little boy wiggled in Nelda's arm and reached for his mother.

Tom mounted Buttermilk. "Here, hand him up to me. I rode half the state of Texas with my father on Diamond's back till I was big enough for a horse of my own. Come on, Son."

Tommy's tears shut off as Tom settled his son in front of him. A twinkling, satisfied grin spread across his little face, and he grabbed the saddle horn.

"Let's get going," Nelda called. "Word has probably reached your aunt Tibby from somewhere that you have arrived. She will have my scalp if I don't get you over to see her soon. Like me, she has been anxiously waiting for days."

And I can hardly wait to see Aunt Tibby, Mary Lou thought. She patted Aunt Nelda's sweet mare on her neck, gave her a nudge to get moving, and trotted up beside Tom.

"You two go ahead," Buck called. He swung the buggy around and as they started off, Beth wiggled in Nelda's lap, cried out and stretched her arms toward her mother.

Nelda waved them on. "Go on ahead," Nelda called. "I think I can handle one little girl." She snuggled Beth in her arms and talked and pointed as they rode away.

276

It felt good to be straddled across the back of a horse. Mary Lou would choose horseback over a wagon any day. Her old sense of freedom seized her, but she restrained herself from dashing off across the prairie to satisfy it. She heard Tom talking to Tommy as she caught up to him.

Tommy, eyes wide, settled happily with his father, stuck his little arm in the air, pointed, and babbled his observations.

"That young man has discovered how to get his own way," Mary Lou remarked.

"Oh, Mama, your son has to get used to a horse as soon as he can. He will spend most of his life on the back of one."

True. Mary Lou's heart ached afresh for her father who had to give up that great freedom. *What a horseman he was! If it hadn't been for the accident, Pa would be so different.* Mary Lou glanced back at the buggy. Aunt Nelda pointed up at something and had Beth's undivided attention.

When the Bradford ranch tipped the horizon, Mary Lou became as eager as her children. Aunt Tibby thought like Mama, except Mama's softness contrasted with her aunt's forthrightness. Mary Lou admired women like Mama and Aunt Tibby. What a job it had been to settle the wilderness in their time, and Mary Lou heard it now was so civilized that some women even had their well water piped into a kitchen sink with a pump. Perhaps, after she and Tom returned, they could check and see if it could be done in her kitchen. What a help that would be! Water inside the house!

As they neared the Bar-B Ranch, cowboys poured from the barn and surrounded them. Aunt Tibby banged out the front door, waving her arms. "Thought you would never get here," she hollered.

Mary Lou slid from Jewel, dropped into Aunt Tibby's arms, and allowed her ribs to be squeezed until they hurt.

"Good gracious, Child, I've been looking for you for days."

Tibby turned to Tom on Buttermilk and stretched up her arms. "This has to be Tommy." She clapped her hands. "Come on, young man. Come to your aunt Tibby and let me get a good look at you."

Tom lowered his son into Tibby's arms.

"Well! You are the spittin' image of your handsome father, you lucky young man." Tibby hugged and swung the surprised boy around. She pointed. "See? Your grandpa Mackey is coming." Tibby turned to Tom and Mary Lou. "How did Buck receive the twins? He should be one proud grandpa!"

Mary Lou nodded. "Overwhelmed might be a better way to describe him." She hugged her aunt and son.

Tibby held Tommy up in front of her so she could get a good look at him.

Tommy stared and puckered his tiny brows.

"Shucks, I think you are better lookin' than your father!" Tibby teasingly grinned at Tom, kissed Tommy's cheek, and snuggled him. "Tom, someday you are going to have your hands full chasing away all the pretty girls—"

Tom slide off Buttermilk and lifted both hands in the air. "Wait a minute. I have all the girls I can handle. I am in no hurry for him to grow up and multiply my problems."

Tommy reached for his father.

Tibby hugged him, then plunked him in Tom's arms.

Tibby spun and enfolded Mary Lou again and said quietly in her ear, "You have no idea how much I have missed you! When you left, your mama seemed to leave with you."

Mary Lou hugged her aunt. "I know." They clung in their need for each other, then separated and watched Pa circle his buggy to the hitching post.

Tibby hurried to Nelda's side of the buggy with a welcoming smile for her little great-niece.

Beth stared at another stranger and started to cry as Tibby lifted her into her arms.

"Hello, Beth. Come see me." Tears immediately filled Tibby's eyes and rolled unashamedly down her cheeks. She hugged the little girl close. "She looks just like Ellen," she said in a choked voice to Nelda.

Nelda nodded. "Yes. Owen noticed it, too."

The women walked to the Bar-B ranch house, trying to catch up on the news all at once for the past year in Kansas and Texas. The men headed for the stables.

Sudden movement in the doorway caught Mary Lou's eye. A little girl peeked around the frame, batting wide fearful eyes. When Tibby stepped on the porch, the little girl opened the door and ran to Tibby's side.

Tibby transferred Beth to Mary Lou, bent over, hugged the child, then took her hand and turned to face everyone. Undeniable delight sparked Aunt Tibby's eyes. "This is my new little daughter." Tibby glanced at Mary Lou and smiled. "I can see you are stunned. No more than I! The Lord sent me this child three weeks ago."

A daughter? Aunt Tibby? Mary Lou's mind whirled.

The smug look on Nelda's face revealed she had been sworn to secrecy to give Tibby her moment of triumph.

The girl ducked behind Tibby's skirt, peeked out shyly, then drew back.

Tibby pulled her from behind. "Come, Dear, and meet your family." She stood the girl in front of her and crossed her arms protectively over her shoulders. "This is Snow Flower, my new daughter."

Snow Flower's intense frightened eyes and hair were almost black, her skin light brown.

Aunt Tibby took Snow Flower's hand. "Come inside and I will tell you about her."

Aunt Tibby's kitchen kindled memories. Mary Lou had always felt at home here. The kettle on the stove busily bubbled its readiness. Tibby made tea and they settled around the table which displayed two heaping plates of tempting sugar cookies, one with raisins and one without for the babies. Beth and Tommy were each tied in a chair and given a cookie.

Snow Flower clung to Tibby, a questioning look on her face.

"Where did you get her, Aunt Tibby? She looks Indian."

"She is Indian. Caroline Wimbley found her wandering alone on the prairie. And you know Henrietta and children. She gathered her in and was going to keep her till someone came for her, but I asked Henrietta if I could keep her till then. Big Jon said she probably became lost from her tribe when they were on the move. As far as we can figure, she must be three or four years old."

"Lost from a tribe?" Mary Lou shook her head. "Mama always said the Indians took very good care of their children. She surely knows her tribe. Did you ask her?"

"Oh, yes. But she doesn't speak or hear. At first I thought she couldn't understand. Then, one day, we were out in the garden. I clapped and called her name but she never looked up, turned around, or anything." The little girl stood gazing up at her new mother. Tibby cupped her upturned face in her hands, bent over, and kissed her on the forehead.

Mary Lou asked, "How did you know her name?"

"I named her. Caroline said when she found her, she was carrying a handful of snow flowers. I thought Snow Flower would be an appropriate name for her."

Snow Flower snuggled closer, her dark eyes fixed on her new mother. She darted shy glances at Mary Lou.

"What if someone comes for her?" Mary Lou asked.

"Then I will have to give her up. But until that time—" Tibby smiled into Snow Flower's upturned face, "I figured the good Lord sent her to me and has given me the blessing of being her mother even though it may be only a little while." Tibby put her arm around the child. "For now, she is mine."

Tommy and Beth squirmed to get on the floor.

Snow Flower's eyes followed them as they crawled toward each other. Suddenly, she left Tibby's side, sat down on the floor, folded her legs under her, and looked at them. The twins crawled and sat beside her. Snow Flower touched each one on the head, then sat motionless while Tommy climbed and grasped her shoulder for balance, intrigued with a new playmate.

Tibby turned to Mary Lou. "Now, tell me about your new house."

Mary Lou described the ranch, adding their plans for its future to make it a vital, joint part of the Circle Z.

Mary Lou asked, "Tell me about Jenny and Glenn. Jenny's letters sound so happy and busy."

Tibby nodded. "They are good together, Mary Lou. Jenny has made a comfortable little home at the back of the store. Glenn is talking of adding more rooms on the back to give them a full kitchen downstairs, and adding bedrooms upstairs to make a real home. Jenny is full of ideas and seems content."

Mary Lou laughed. "Jenny told me she never did want to be a farm woman. I agree, they need more rooms than just those two behind the store. I remember the shrinking feeling I had when Glenn and I were engaged, and he announced to me those two rooms would be our home. The very thought smothered me. I wanted to be a rancher's wife. And I am—thanks to you two." Mary Lou blew a kiss to her aunts.

Nelda smiled. "God has a way of working things out far better than our best intentions. Jenny enjoys working in the store as well doing the post office."

Mary Lou relaxed. A longing to see her dearest friend nagged at her heart. It would be impossible to go to Venture today—tomorrow perhaps?

The women sat, reminiscing between jumps to retrieve Tommy as he struck out on new adventures. Then Tommy took a sudden shine to Aunt Tibby, who was delighted. She carried him around, talked, and named to him the different things in the kitchen. Beth watched their every move.

Mary Lou's gaze travelled the room—her second home when she was a little girl. A mood of nostalgia swept over her. Funny how a look, a word, a house, a land could lift up memories and make them become doubly precious. She gazed at her dear family. *I have to capture as many memories as I can to take home with me.*

Mary Lou related the events of the past year: the birth of Baby Zack, Nelson and Laura's wedding, the birth of the twins, Doug and Lily's marriage, Doug's untimely death, and Lily's disappearance.

Her aunts doubled with laughter as Mary Lou told of trying to befriend Darcy and teach a city girl to be a rancher's wife. "Before we left, Zack left for Boston to bring Darcy home from a visit to her parents. They will probably be there when we return." Mary Lou spoke fondly in praise of Allena and Hattie.

"It is a busy household, believe me. I love them all, but Tom and I are glad we are in our own place."

Mary Lou got up and walked to Aunt Tibby's stove. Hers at home was just about the same. Mary Lou felt proud. Tibby and Nelda were interested and pleased when Mary Lou told them about their new ranch. A sudden burst of pride in Tom and their accomplishments welled up as she spoke of them.

The twins became fussy. No wonder. It had been a big day for them.

"I think we had better put these babies to bed," Aunt Tibby commented. Stomping boots announced the men's return.

Mary Lou's heart swelled with unbounded joy when she saw her pa and Tom walking and talking slowly behind Nate and a couple cowboys. Tears surged for release. *If only*—the words struck in her throat. How many times Mama had cautioned her. *Never say "if only this would happen—" or "if only that—" it's a weak crutch. Instead of wishful thinking,* Mama always said, *pray!* Mary Lou's heart rose with a new sense of loss. Being home had freshened her longing for Mama. *Father,* she prayed, *I miss Mama so.*

A sudden explosive thought grabbed Mary Lou's mind. *If Mama were alive, she would be here with Pa, and I would be in Texas with Tom. We would be apart! More so.* Now, Mary Lou sensed Mama's presence wherever she went. *How strange are the ways of God!*

Chapter 7

Beth's whimpering wakened Mary Lou. She looked at the clock. Six already? She quietly slipped out of bed, into her wrapper, and picked up Beth. Father and son stirred. She softly touched Tom's arm so he would think she was still beside him. Mary Lou wanted him to get all the extra sleep possible. He needed it.

She stooped for the pair of slippers Aunt Nelda had made and given her yesterday. She had forgotten to bring her own. Mary Lou smiled. Mama would have commented, "But my God supplieth our every need."

Beth cooed and nuzzled against her mother. Mary Lou shushed her and tiptoed out of the room, coaxed by the aroma of fresh coffee.

Aunt Nelda, as usual, had risen before everyone. "Best time to keep from being interrupted in my morning prayers," she had once told Mary Lou.

Nelda looked up from her Bible that lay open in her lap and smiled apologetically. "I heard Beth and would have gotten her so you could sleep, but figured I would create too much fuss and wake the whole household." She closed her Bible, laid it on the table, rose, and reached for Beth.

Mary Lou shook her head. "Let me change and nurse her first, then she will play quietly. She is altogether a different little girl when she is not around her busy brother."

"Aren't most women different when they are around men?"

Mary Lou nodded. "I guess we are. I never thought about it before." She smiled at her aunt. "You are a wise bird."

Nelda nodded. "A wise *old* bird."

Mary Lou shook her head. "I never think of you as 'old,' Aunt Nelda. I've seen days when you ran circles around me and other younger women."

"Result of good training. My mother was a worker and expected everyone else to keep up with her. I hated it when I was young but was thankful after I married Lars. I declare, I was the envy of the neighborhood wives. Had my wash hanging out on the line first thing Monday morning before the other women were out of bed." Nelda laughed. "It became my prideful fetish 'cause it made the other women look up to me. Or, so I thought." Nelda chuckled and shook her head. "Isn't it silly how hard we work when we are young to blow ourselves up to look good, only to find out when we are older it was a waste of our precious time?"

Mary Lou laughed. "Could it be when we are young we don't have very much to offer? I know when I worked with Mama, I tired out long before she did and breathed a sigh of relief when we finished. Mama took a deep breath and began another job!"

Nelda sipped her steaming coffee. "Some wise soul said life is what we are alive to." She nodded. "Makes sense. I sure have known a lot of people who were never alive to work!"

They laughed—like old times.

Nelda set a cup of coffee on the table beside Mary Lou while she nursed Beth, then pulled up the other rocker and eased into it with her own hot cup and sipped. "Now, tell me about your new home. I hope a time will come when your pa and I can visit."

Mary Lou's heart skipped a beat. "Oh, Aunt Nelda, do you think Pa would be able to stand a trip to Texas to see us? He would love it. Tom is breeding horses. Mama said that was what Pa set his heart to do before his accident. Tom has a special mare in foal now." Mary Lou tried to imagine Pa in their barn. "I think Pa would feel at home on the Circle Z."

Nelda nodded her head. "If there is a way to go by train, I think Owen could handle it, but never by wagon. Riding to and fro in the buggy to Venture some days troubles his back." Nelda smiled, leaned, and patted Mary Lou's knee. "I'll see what I can do. A visit might settle his mind. He would see you happy and contented, then be right proud he has Tom as a son-in-law."

What a dear woman, bless her. Not a selfish bone in her whole body. If anyone can persuade Pa, it will be Aunt Nelda. In only a day's time, Mary Lou had noticed many changes in Pa. For one, he talked. After Mama's death he had spoken few words to anyone. To see him so open and pleased with his grandchildren made Mary Lou's heart sing. There hadn't been any formal I-forgive-you's said between them, yet her heart told her Pa had forgiven her. Actions sometimes say what words cannot.

Beth sat quietly playing on the floor, intrigued by a string of buttons Nelda had strung for her to play with. "She might as well get the feel of woman stuff," was Aunt Nelda's comment when she gave them to her.

Breakfast smells gradually coaxed two drowsy men to appear. Tom carried his sleepy-eyed son into the kitchen. "It is a first. I had to wake up Tommy! I didn't dare leave him alone cause I knew when he awakened he would find things to do where there are none." Tom sat Tommy on the floor beside his sister, who was absorbed in her buttons.

Tommy proved his father right. In the short time it took the women to put breakfast on the table, Tom refereed both son and daughter and had to separate them in a do-or-die fight over the buttons. Finally, Tom tied them both into chairs and placed Beth's chair beside her mother and Tommy's chair by him on opposite sides of the breakfast table.

Buck came in and took his place. Mary Lou's heart rejoiced as Pa bowed his head while Tom said grace.

Today they planned to go to Venture. By the time everyone was ready to leave, Tom had completely emptied the wagon except for Nelson's pictures and the kiddie coop.

Bumping along in the wagon surrounded by her beloved prairie, Mary Lou took an imaginary fast ride to town on Dulcie's back. She used to make it in twenty minutes. In the buggy and wagon, it took twice that time. She thought of Dulcie in Texas and wondered, *Do horses get homesick or nostalgic? Had she come, would Dulcie have felt she was home?* Mary Lou naïvely believed she would.

Tom followed far enough behind for the buggy dust to dissipate before it reached the wagon.

Tommy fussed to be in the kiddie coop to play rather than being confined to his mother's lap. Mary Lou opened the lid and put him in to play with his toy horses, resettled herself on the seat, felt her body relax, and feasted her eyes on her dear homeland. The prairie grass had grown over knee high already. She remembered one day when she was little, she and Pa had walked through grass higher than her head. Like something alive, it had slapped at her face and frightened her even though she had hold of Pa's hand. She had screamed and cried until Pa picked her up and carried her home. When older, she and Jenny used to hide in it.

Tom had told her Texas had similar prairies in the south eastern part. "I'll show you sometime," he had promised.

She squinted at the broken outline of Venture ahead on the horizon and wondered if it had changed much in the almost two years she had been gone. It didn't matter. Venture would always be the same to her. It sheltered precious memories.

As the wheels chewed up the distance and rolled into the west end of Center Street, Mary Lou waved to people she recognized. Neighbors and friends who had peopled her whole life came walking, running, smiling, and greeting them as Pa and Tom pulled the buggy and wagon to a halt in front of Mackey's Mercantile.

But it was soon obvious the star attractions were the twins.

A beaming Sarah George grabbed hold of the wagon as soon as it stopped. "Land sakes! Is this our little Mary Lou with a baby in her lap? Why I remember when. . ."

One after another came up and said "Hello," "Glad you came to visit,"

"We have missed you. . . ."

Dear people, almost like family. They had come to know her, and she them, as they came to the post office twice a week to get their mail. Mama had worked three days each week and at first carried Mary Lou in a wicker basket and set it on the floor by the window so she could see the birds, clouds, and sky. Her first real memory of involvement in the actual work had made her feel very important. Mama had stood her on a chair beside her and gave her the mail to hand over the counter to waiting customers while Mama searched the boxes. She knew all the townspeople's names by heart before she ever read them.

She and Mama had worked together fifteen years. When Mama's illness kept her home, Mary Lou had assumed the job of postmistress. Now these dear familiar faces, smiling and welcoming her— She fought the intrusion of a waterfall within and scolded herself. *No! Don't you dare cry!*

Jenny bounded out the front store door, waving her arms in the air. "Mary Lou Langdon! You goin' to stay in that wagon all day?"

"Jenny!" She looked beautiful! Mary Lou passed Tommy down to Tom who gave her arm leverage as she jumped to the ground.

On her way to Jenny, old friends and neighbors smiled, said, "Welcome home," "Good to see you again," and patted her shoulders and arms. Finally, the two girls came face to face smiling. Jenny propelled Mary Lou to the store. As soon as they were inside, Jenny's arms wrapped around her and squeezed hard. "Oh," she sighed, "how I have missed you."

They clung for a moment.

"Me, too," were all the words Mary Lou could squeeze out.

The store looked wonderful. Mary Lou identified Jenny's artful touch on the neat, clean shelves, shining bowls, lamp chimneys, and orderly dress good shelves. She perused the merchandise and observed that Glenn had expanded their stock to include many new items Pa never carried. More furniture, kitchen stoves, one similar to her own at home. Mary Lou took a deep breath and turned her head to the spice boxes that still permeated the front corner of the store with their pungent fragrances.

Glenn strode forward and took both of Mary Lou's hands in his. "It's good to see you, Mary Lou. How have you been?" His soft brown eyes spoke love for a dear friend.

"I'm fine. And you—Glenn you look so happy. It was glad news when we heard you and Jenny were married." She had wondered how she would feel when she and Glenn met.

Glenn's gaze searched the room till he found Jenny.

Mary Lou sighed, and a long-held burden broke loose and floated away. Glenn loved Jenny! It spoke from his eyes and shined in his face when he looked at her. Mary Lou relaxed. They had both done the right thing.

People crowded the store. Buck and Nelda sat proud, holding wide-eyed, transfixed twins, overwhelmed by so many strange people.

Gradually, as Mary Lou wandered around the store, her feet turned toward her special place, the post office.

Jenny saw her and followed.

Mary Lou stepped behind the counter. It looked much the same as—no, that was the picture she carried in her mind. Her eyes opened to the present, and she discovered changes everywhere. Counters and the pigeon hole boxes had been moved, the large safe stood firmly in the far corner. *How convenient*, she thought, remembering how she had to carry her stamps and money all the way through the store to the back rooms where Pa had kept the safe.

Mary Lou turned and smiled at her dear friend who stood beaming with anticipation of Mary Lou's approval. "Quite an improvement, Jenny. You have made it much more efficient."

"Glenn says that if Venture keeps growing, he wants to enlarge the store. He's already ordered kitchen chairs from Chicago he saw in an order catalog to begin a small furniture section. I don't know where he expects to find room. Every available space is stuffed already." Jenny laughed. "But knowing Glenn, he will find it. Sometimes I think some of his ideas are way over his head, but we have doubled the business and with all the new people coming in and. . ."

Mama? Mary Lou's mind called. Silence.

All of a sudden, Mary Lou didn't want to look at or hear any more. Priceless memories labored to shift and reshape to accommodate the present. *Mama? I don't feel you here anymore. I don't even feel* me *here!*

Mary Lou turned to leave. She felt as if something precious was in danger of being snatched from her and that if she lost it, she would be destitute without it. She turned and walked out.

Jenny followed her back into the store. "Come see the back rooms, Mary Lou. The curtains you and Aunt Nelda made are still there."

True, Aunt Nelda's perky curtains hung at the windows, but Mary Lou delighted in Jenny's imaginative hand everywhere. How charming! Jenny had done so much with so little.

Mary Lou's spirits lifted. She stretched her arms wide and twirled in appreciation. "Jenny, you have done wonders to this place. And did I hear right, you plan to build on the back and make a real house with an honest-to-goodness kitchen and upstairs bedrooms?" Mary Lou hugged Jenny. "I'm happy for you. Dear friend, you have earned it!"

Jenny beamed and returned her hug.

They walked back into the store. Mary Lou checked the twins. Tommy stepped lively between two young boys, and Beth stood shakily between two little girls. Obviously, they were being well watched and entertained.

She looked for Tom. He had Nelson's pictures on display. Glenn and a group of men nodded in lively conversation. Mary Lou told Aunt Nelda that she and Jenny wanted to take a peek at the new pews in the church.

Nelda nodded her head and shooed them off with a wave of her hand.

Like chattering magpies, the young women walked toward the church, stumbling over each other's words, trying to relate at once everything that had happened since they had last seen each other. They giggled at everything, the same as they used to. Yet there hung between them a strangeness, a barrier that had never been there before.

Mary Lou sensed Jenny felt it too. She could tell by the jumpy way Jenny talked. Of course, they had been apart for a long time, and there were so many new and different areas of change in each other's lives they each knew nothing of. . .and—

Suddenly, Mary Lou remembered Jenny's concern when her older sister got engaged and married. Jenny had said she felt as if she had lost her.

The girls reached the church, quietly opened the door, walked in, and stood together in the silence.

Memories whirled. Mary Lou's heart settled to rest as her gaze anchored on the new pew in the place where she and Mama always sat with an empty space beside them for someone new or visiting. Mary Lou inwardly knew Mama prayed that Pa would fill that place. He never did.

The big, fat, pot-bellied stove, the pulpit—all still the same. A tingling warmth ruffled Mary Lou's heart to alert her. *Mama is here.*

Her mind mentally produced highlights of her life in this sanctuary: the special honor given her when she was fourteen and chosen to be Mary, the mother of Jesus, in the Christmas pageant; high-pitched children's voices at the joyous celebration afterward when Santa stomped in with his bag of gifts, one for every girl and boy. For years Mary Lou had wondered how Santa always knew exactly how many girls and boys there were, knew all their names, handed out the exact amount of toys, and left with an empty bag.

She glanced out the window into the church yard that recalled Fourth of July picnics, and how she and Jenny always won all the running races 'cause they always ran the prairie.

Her gaze returned to the pulpit where every Sunday, Mama and Mary Lou had given serious attention to Pastor Miles as he moved back and forth waving his arms and hands through stirring sermons that took Mary Lou awhile to appreciate and now, which she was ashamed to admit, she remembered very little.

Her mind shifted to the day she was thrust into womanhood as Aunt Tibby and the women of the W.C.T.U., with faith and purpose, smashed the saloon. The exhilaration of that day vanished two weeks later in the humiliation of her wedding at the Bar-B Ranch. *I'm glad my wedding was not here,* Mary Lou mused. The unbelievable events of her wedding had made it the worst and the best day of her life.

As if reading her thoughts, Jenny's voice broke through her reverie.

"I'll never forget the day of your wedding, Mary Lou. I felt so bad that I was in on the plan to stop your wedding to Glenn. But I knew you really loved Tom, and in honest friendship, I couldn't let you marry Glenn. That's why I promised your aunt Tibby I would speak. Worst thing was, I told you I would do that very thing, remember? You liked Glenn, you said, but remember I said like isn't good enough for marriage."

Mary Lou nodded. "How well I remember and naturally, I thought of you first, then suddenly realized it wasn't your voice. Then Glenn spoke and acted like the gentleman he is."

Both women got lost in momentary reverie.

Jenny broke the silence, her voice pained. "But the bad thing was, I always sort of felt our friendship was never the same after that, Mary Lou."

Mary Lou put her arms around her dearest friend. "No, Jenny, God had His hand on all our lives. He knew my heart. He knew I loved Tom. Feeling as I did, it would have been wrong for me to marry Glenn. Besides," Mary Lou smiled, "you told me that you were sweet on Glenn, so everything worked out for the best."

Jenny heaved a big sigh, then they giggled, just like old times.

"But that's not all of it, Jenny. Remember the time you told me that things were never the same between you and your sister after she was married. That has happened to us. But it doesn't mean it is bad and will harm our friendship. We had a special little-girl friendship. Everyone doesn't have one. You had lost your mother and father and I was an only child. God put us together in His plan so we could teach each other what friendship really is. All is blessing from God, Jenny. He gave us the opportunity to truly love someone who wasn't part of our family. When we grew up, we knew what real love truly meant. Mama always said a real friend accepts the other person's faults, good and bad, always believes the best and would rather give than get. She also told me Jesus was my best Friend. 'I have called you friends.' She also told me that to be accepted as a true friend was the highest compliment anyone could ever pay me." Mary Lou smiled and watched Jenny's face break into a broad smile of relief.

The old familiar tingling teased Mary Lou's neck to announce a new discovery. *A husband and wife should be best friends. Why is it,* Mary Lou thought, *whenever you try to help someone else understand you get a better understanding for yourself?*

Jenny slowly walked toward Mary Lou and looked at her. "I never thought of it that way, Mary Lou. You are right. Our friendship isn't ever going to be the same way it was. We were children then. Now we're women. It will be even better." Jenny put her hands on Mary Lou's shoulders and gazed into her dear friend's eyes, smiled, and nodded. "You know what, Mary Lou? You sound just like your mama."

The statement took Mary Lou's breath away. *Me, like Mama?* "Oh, Jenny." She gently took Jenny's face in her hands and kissed her cheek. "That is the most wonderful compliment anyone has ever given me."

They left the church with eyes sparkling. The old, relaxed, teasing chatter returned with a fresh knowing that the bonds of true friendship can never be broken.

Chapter 8

Tibby Bradford and Snow Flower joined the other wagons and buggies in front of Mackey's Mercantile. Snow Flower jumped out of the buggy and tied the line to the hitching post.

On her way back from the church, Mary Lou waved to Aunt Tibby who waved back and waited on the boardwalk with Snow Flower.

Mary Lou greeted her aunt with a kiss on the cheek. "I didn't know you were coming to town today, Aunt Tibby."

"Well, I figured if I am going to see very much of you, I'll have to follow you wherever." She put her arm around her niece.

Snow Flower ran to Mary Lou's other side, slipped her hand into Mary Lou's, looked up, and smiled. Her dark eyes spoke her welcome.

"She likes you," Tibby said.

"I like her, too, and I'm happy for you, Aunt Tibby. You finally got your girl."

"Why, Tibby Bradford! How are you?"

Mary Lou turned to the voice. It belonged to a tall, thin woman draped in a tiny-flowered, ill-fitting calico dress. *She must be someone new in Venture.* Mary Lou had never seen her before.

"Hello, Mabel. May I introduce you to my niece, Mary Lou Langdon? This is Buck's daughter. She, her husband, and family live in Texas and are visiting us for a couple weeks."

"Oh, you must be the one who used to work in the post office and had such an awful wedding." Mabel waved a limp wrist. "We just moved here from Virginia. My man wanted to come west but our money ran out when we got to Kansas, so I guess I am stuck here, but I—"

"It is nice to meet you, Mabel." Mary Lou struggled for composure. "I hope you grow to like Kansas after you are here awhile. I was born here. I think it is a lovely place to live."

Mabel shrugged her shoulders. "A woman goes where her man goes whether she likes it or not." Mabel leaned over and stared at Snow Flower standing behind Mary Lou.

Aunt Tibby reached for Snow Flower's hand and moved aside a couple steps. Mabel grinned and nodded. "Oh, is this the child I've heard about?"

Tibby's eyebrows lifted. "I don't know. What did you hear?"

Snow Flower ducked behind Tibby.

"Well," Mabel began hesitantly, "I heard you had taken someone in to work for you. Is it the custom in Kansas to have Indian girls work as servants? I could use one."

Aunt Tibby stretched to full indignant height. "I am sorry, Mabel, you have been misinformed. Snow Flower is not my servant, she is my adopted daughter." Tibby suppressed a smile as Mabel's eyes widened and her mouth dropped open.

Mabel's disbelieving gaze bounced from child to Tibby and she gasped, "But—she's—an—Indian."

Tibby slipped a protective arm around Snow Flower. "Yes." She stroked the child's cheek and smiled into her upturned face. "And isn't she a lovely one?"

"But—but—you got her dressed like a little girl!"

Tibby's brows shot up. "Of course. Because that is what she is—a little girl!"

Mabel's disconcerted gaze darted back and forth. Her mouth opened for a weak "Yes" and stretched into a limp smile.

Tibby moved toward the store. "Nice to see you again, Mabel, but please excuse us. I must hurry to my errands." Tibby grabbed Snow Flower's hand and walked in the store. Mary Lou and Jenny hurried behind her, discreetly trying to keep their faces straight.

Tom crossed to Mary Lou the minute she entered the store. Beth lay drooped in Aunt Nelda's arms, sound asleep. Tommy had wrapped his little arms around his father's leg and hung on, his eyes wide and starey.

"Are you ready to leave? I think it's time we got these two back to the cabin." Tom grinned. "It has been a busy morning."

"Tom, would you mind if Mary Lou rode home with me so we can visit a bit?" Tibby asked. "I have a few things to get at the store and will send her home later."

Tom nodded. "That is what we are here for, visiting."

Tommy laid his head on Mary Lou's shoulder while Tom climbed into the wagon, then Tom lifted his exhausted son into the kiddie coop, straightened his hat, waved, and slapped the reins.

Pa and Nelda followed, in the buggy, Beth sound asleep in Nelda's lap.

When Mary Lou re-entered the store, Glenn stood on a ladder hanging Nelson's pictures on a side wall.

I wish Nelson could see them displayed, she thought.

Customers commented favorably and one seemed very interested in Mary Lou's favorite: a lean cowboy, in chaps, who sat tall in the saddle and reminded her of Tom. Perhaps knowing people were interested in his paintings would give Nelson a new incentive to keep on. Since he and

Laura had married, Allena showed concern that Nelson spent so little time at his art.

On their way home before they turned south, Tom planned to go east to Abilene to take the rest of Nelson's paintings to Silas Jamison's big general store. Glenn told Tom he would keep a check on them and return the money to Nelson by mail.

"Now I will finally get a chance to talk to you," Aunt Tibby said as they climbed into her buggy.

Snow Flower sat between them and laid her head in Tibby's lap. The rocking of the buggy quickly lulled her to sleep.

"I want to hear all about Tom's family. A letter isn't the same. I gather your mother-in-law is a solid Christian woman."

"She is and has been wonderful to me from the moment I met her. But she has had one jolt after another. All three sons brought home wives and thrust them on her unannounced. When Zack came home from Boston, he brought Darcy. Then Tom came home with me. Allena graciously accepted us and treats us as one of her own. She is a loving lady, a strong woman, so nothing throws her off balance for long.

"The big jolt came a few months later when Doug brought one of the saloon girls home as his wife. He had married her before a judge in Harness the night before. She was dressed in their usual short flouncy dress, black stockings, and high lace shoes. Doug laughingly called it her 'wedding dress.' Allena stood stunned for only a moment and ignored her son's disrespect. Instead of showing disappointment in her wayward son, her heart reached out to Lily, who put up a brave front and stood obviously nervous and uncomfortable. She ordered Hattie to get a pitcher of warm water, told me to loan Lily one of my dresses, so she could get out of her 'wedding dress,' then guided Lily to Doug's room and told her to wash and change and make herself comfortable.

"Lily returned to the kitchen looking like a different person. With all the paint washed off her face, decent clothes, and her beautiful hair piled on top of her head, her whole demeanor changed. She was beautiful! Doug said he liked her the other way.

"Lily fell in love with Baby Zack, much to Darcy's delight. Lily took complete care of him and adored him. He thrived. Darcy pretty much ignored him and treated Lily like some hired nursemaid.

"Then without saying a word, two weeks after Doug was shot, Lily disappeared, and we haven't seen nor heard from her since. We were all heartbroken and still cannot understand why she left. She had been a good wife to Doug, even though he was rude and uncouth to her."

"Humph," Tibby grunted. "Too many men find themselves a good wife, then treat her like dirt." She shrugged her shoulders. "But I guess it's no different than when a good man gets stuck with a lazy, good-for-nothing for a wife."

Mary Lou chastised herself for thinking of Darcy.

"Well," she continued, "at least we know Lily is God's girl. Before we built our own house, Allena and I had devotions every morning in the parlor. One day we noticed movement outside the door and discovered Lily standing in the hallway listening. Allena asked her to join us. That week the study we had selected was Proverbs 31. Allena calls it 'God's mirror of a beautiful woman.'"

Tibby smiled and nodded. "How like our Lord to arrange that."

"Yes, and that chapter dissolved Lily into tears, she repented of her past life, accepted Jesus as her Lord and Savior and daily, God noticeably released Lily's dormant inner beauty. Doug also noticed the change, disapproved, and spent more time in Harness.

Tibby stroked Snow Flower's long black hair. "Does Lily have parents somewhere?"

Mary Lou shook her head. "Mother and I asked her about them. Lily told us she doesn't remember her parents. She thinks her grandmother cared for her, but she died and that was when she became a bound child. She was sold two times before she was fourteen; then the man who owned her sold her to a fellow who came by in a wagon filled with young girls Lily's age and transported them from one house of ill repute to another."

Tibby slowly shook her head back and forth. "That poor girl. I've heard of the practice of selling both children and old people who are destitute on auction blocks like slaves. The children bring good prices 'cause they are strong and can work, but the older people are sold to the lowest bidder for their keep for a year for what work they can do."

Aunt Tibby's brows pinched together. She shook her head. "Selling any people, especially young vulnerable children, is sinful and against God's will. The Bible makes it very clear what will happen to anyone who harms a child, even in the womb. Jesus says in Matthew 18:6: 'whoso shall offend one of these little ones which believe in me, it were better for him that a millstone were hanged about his neck, and that he were drowned in the depth of the sea.' And I abhor the sinful traffic in young girls and women for the saloons. One day, we women will be able to vote, then we'll see a change."

Tibby looked down at Snow Flower, whose head was nestled in her lap. "I wonder what would have happened to this sweet child if those hucksters had found her. When we discovered that she was unable to hear or speak, the good Lord told me He had sent this little girl to Nate and me to love and fill the childless void in our hearts. Nate and the cowhands adore her." Tibby bent and kissed Snow Flower on the forehead.

Mary Lou gave high praise of Hattie then and tried to give her aunt a word picture of her new ranch house and how wonderful it felt to have a home of her own.

"Do you like it better in Texas than Kansas?" Aunt Tibby asked.

Mary Lou had to think a moment. "Not really. Different states are—different. Our home, Tom, and the children being there is what makes it a special place for me."

The Bar-B Ranch came into view. Nate came out of the barn with one of the cowboys who took the horse and buggy.

"You ladies have a good time in town?" Nate asked. He lifted Snow Flower to the ground, smiled, and smoothed his hand over her long, straight hair.

"Wonderful!" Tibby called, turned, and motioned to Mary Lou. "I'm hoping you have time to come in for a short tea party."

The special embroidered cloth, three good china cups, saucers, and Grandmother Stafford's teapot were taken from the shelf and swept Mary Lou into a wave of nostalgia as she set the table. There had always been at least three places, Aunt Tibby, Mama, and Mary Lou. Now it was Aunt Tibby, Snow Flower, and herself. She swallowed a lump that tried hard to stick in her throat.

Aunt Tibby set a plate of her special individual fruitcakes on the table. *I'm glad that some things don't change*, Mary Lou thought.

"Did Nelda tell you we are having a barbecue tomorrow? We thought instead of you having to visit everywhere, everyone could come here to see you."

Mary Lou sighed in relief. "That will be wonderful." She and Tom had discussed how they would spread their time to see everyone.

Aunt Tibby sent a scribbled note with Snow Flower to the barn that Mary Lou would need a horse to ride back to Buck's.

They carried the dishes to the wash table. Tibby suddenly turned and gently cupped Mary Lou's face with her hands and kissed her cheeks. "The older you get, the more you remind me of your dear mama. You are a lot like her, you know."

The comment took Mary Lou's breath. Aunt Tibby was the second person today who had told her she reminded them of Mama. Joy exploded in her innermost being. "Thank you, Aunt Tibby," was all she could say through her choked-up throat. It made her proud yet humble. To follow in Mama's footsteps. . . Her heart swelled with thanksgiving to God. She kissed Aunt Tibby, mounted, and headed for home.

The ride home was exhilarating. It would have been better if she had been on Dulcie's back, but. . . As she neared Pa's cabin, a sudden strange feeling of inner detachment loosed her spirit and sent her mind soaring to Texas. She missed Allena, Zack, Laura, Nelson. . .their new home.

The next morning, Nelda and Mary Lou cooked and packed food for the barbecue and planned to leave at before ten o'clock.

"Tibby told me she wanted us there first to greet everyone," Nelda grinned. "Get ready, 'cause it sounds like she has invited everyone in the state!"

Shortly after they arrived at the Bar-B, Mary Lou recognized a familiar wagonful coming from the west. Tom and Mary Lou each held a twin, who waved their little hands at the children as the wagon came in, and they all waved back and giggled.

Big Jon pulled the wagon to a halt, jumped down, walked around, and helped Henrietta to the ground. The older children, one by one, jumped and helped the little ones to the ground, and they formed a long line behind their mother and father in front of Tom and Mary Lou.

Henrietta swept Mary Lou into her arms in a motherly squeeze that brought tears to both their eyes, then pushed her at arm's length to take a good look at her. "You have matured, my dear. It becomes you." Hastily she took the twins, one in each arm, before they could object. "And these babies!" She kissed each one. "My, my, wouldn't Ellen be proud. They are beautiful."

Next thing Mary Lou knew, a pair of burly arms swept her off her feet. Big Jon! How many times those arms had been her solace and substitute for Pa's. Her heart swelled with gratitude and love for this man—a true man of God. Mary Lou also knew that she hadn't been the only recipient of his largess. Big Jon eased her down on her feet and held her an arm's length away. "Look at you! Happiness shouts from every corner of your face." His kind, brown eyes bathed her with his blessing. "I'm glad," he said softly.

Mary Lou's tears refused to stay contained. They poured down her cheeks unashamedly as she drank in the welcome and affection of this dear man. "Thank you, Big Jon," she sputtered.

He stepped aside to expose his brood.

Mary Lou couldn't get over how the ten little Wimbley children had grown. Little! Young Jon stood tall as a man, almost to his father's shoulder. Miriam, a young lady of fifteen, and. . .

One by one, each child shyly gave her smiling hugs. Caroline, almost six, threw her arms around Mary Lou's legs and looked up. "Where did you go so long? You never come over to our house anymore. Where did you get the babies?"

Mary Lou and Tom laughed. "God sent them." Mary Lou swept the child into her arms and looked at Big Jon. "Thank goodness she hasn't changed. Still the same little continuous question box."

Caroline backed off and looked seriously into Mary Lou's face and nodded. "Oh, God's gonna send you lots more, I betcha."

Big Jon reached for Tommy, then scooped Beth into his other arm. "I can't believe my eyes. Two dear babies, how blessed you both are."

All smiles, Tom and Mary Lou basked in their children's shadows.

One by one the families came, in wagons, buggies, on horseback from town, ranch, and farm.

The men sat and tended the roasting steer, suspended and sizzling over the pit while engaged in a rousing discussion of farming and ranching. As usual they came to an impasse. The farmers objected to the cattle over-running their planted fields. The cattle ranchers complained of the shrinking grassland for grazing because of the plow.

Everyone wanted to hold the twins. Tommy and Beth were passed around and stepped high between children until they were exhausted. Mary Lou finally took them inside and nursed them. She laid them sound asleep on a blanket on the floor of Aunt Tibby's downstairs bedroom and returned to the party.

Eating, talking, and joshing went on all afternoon, but the food never seemed to diminish. For these hard-working pioneers, any social event in the company of neighbors was a joyous time.

As the sun took aim at the horizon, one by one, the wagons of dear friends and neighbors departed amid waves and shouts of good-bye. When the last wagon left, everyone began the cleanup.

The Wimbleys and Jenny and Glenn stayed to help and were the last to go.

Later, in the upstairs Bradford bedroom where Mary Lou and Tom had spent their first night as man and wife, they covered their tired, sleeping son and daughter on their double comforter floor bed. Mary Lou lifted her mind and heart in thanksgiving for all the dear families who had peopled her life for as long as she could remember. What memories flooded back in seeing them.

She knelt at the bedside, said her prayers, then climbed into bed and Tom's arms.

He held and kissed her. "Have you had your visit? Are you about ready to start home?"

Mary Lou's mind travelled to Texas to their lovely new ranch house. Oh, but it had felt so good to be home.

"We should be leaving fairly soon. My mare will foal in a couple months, but she was mighty big when I left home. She must be carrying a big stallion, which could spell trouble. Smitty can handle everything, but I'd like to be there."

Mary Lou raised on her elbow, cupped Tom's head with her arm, and kissed him. "Anytime you say, Tom."

Mary Lou's heart wavered. This was home. Yet— She thought of their ranch, her new stove, the rolling land, Allena, Hattie. . . The last thing she remembered was the feel of Tom's soft lips kissing her forehead.

Chapter 9

Tom rolled the dripping wagon out of the Red River onto the Texas side of the Red River Station. Lannie, Shade, and Pete gave a holler, wound up the ropes and brought them to Tom.

"Thanks, boys, much obliged," Tom said. "Can I buy you some grub in the station?"

All three shook their heads. "Naw, we ate before ya come. 'Twern't no trouble. Anytime." They each touched their hat brims, bowed their heads to Mary Lou, then headed for the big red barn that housed the station.

Tom climbed down to check Babe and Buttermilk. Their heads hung low. Tom had driven them hard every day since they had left Abilene where they had dropped off Nelson's paintings, then headed down the old Chisholm Trail. He figured he wouldn't be meeting many herds at this time of the year.

They entered the station and the same cheerful lady who had waited on them before looked up and smiled big. "Well, now, if'n it ain't them beautiful twin babies back again." She nodded to Tom and Mary Lou. "Glad to see ya. Did ya have a good trip?" She straightened and wiped off a table. "Here, set yourselves down, and I'll get some rags to tie in them twins."

Unfortunately, the menu hadn't changed, but it was hot and surprisingly tasty. Better than trail food.

Back in the wagon, it didn't take the twins long to settle in the kiddie coop.

Tom and Mary Lou rested on a blanket and leaned their backs against a wagon wheel to give the wagon time to dry off.

Mary Lou laughed. "I've done less in the last week than I do in one day at home, but I don't remember ever being this tired since we built our house." Her heart suddenly reached for that little ranch house on top of a knoll. "It will be good to get home."

Tom nodded. "Sure will."

The next morning both Tom and Mary Lou were up and gone early. They didn't eat breakfast at the station. Tom built a small fire, Mary Lou made coffee, and they munched on sourdough biscuits. She nursed the twins, put them in the kiddie coop, and they both lay down. *Good little travelers*, Mary Lou thought.

The warm morning sun climbed until it was overhead and hot. Tom kept a steady pace. It would take the best part of the day to get home.

"Do you want to go straight home, or stop off at the big house before we go on?" Tom asked Mary Lou.

Even though her first thought led to their house, she, as well as Tom, knew everyone would be on the lookout for them, every day, expecting them "any time" and be disappointed if they passed by.

Mary Lou shook her head. "We'd better stop at the big house. I hope there is some supper left over."

"Don't worry," Tom said. "With Hattie around. . ."

Tom rode under the Circle Z arch shortly after suppertime and pulled into the ranch yard.

The wheels hadn't even rolled to a stop when Allena, Hattie, and Laura were out the door and running beside the wagon.

"Oh, thank the Lord you are here safe and sound. Our prayers are answered," Allena called.

The wagon groaned to a stop. Tom reached back into the kiddie coop for the twins. Allena's arms, already outstretched, grabbed Tommy, hugged him, and passed him to Laura. Beth ended up in Hattie's arms while Allena clasped Mary Lou and her son in her arms. "Thank God! Thank God!" she whispered. She pushed them back and looked at them with glistening eyes and swallowed hard. "How did you find everyone at home?" she asked Mary Lou.

"Wonderful."

"Good! And your Pa?"

Tom laughed. "The twins won his heart. It seems he has forgiven Mary Lou, and I've been accepted as his son-in-law. But," Tom gazed into his mother's eyes, "Buck is really a great man. We talked and I think his problem is that he misses his wife, and his cowboy spirit is languishing in a buggy. I feel for him."

Mary Lou was touched and rushed her love and thanks to Tom through her gaze.

Allena nodded slowly. "I can understand that," she said. "Maybe some day he may be able to come this way." She turned and walked toward the ranch house. "Have you eaten yet?"

"Yes, but if it's Hattie's cookin', I'll eat again," Tom answered.

One word about food and Hattie was on her way to the kitchen. Soon heaping plates of beef stew, vegetables, and cinnamon cream pie appeared, as if by magic.

Shortly, Nelson arrived home from the Shepards, and joined them in pie and coffee.

"I have been getting Father Will's ledgers in order," Nelson remarked. "Did Zack tell you he put me in charge of the Circle Z ledgers and accounts?"

Tom nodded his head in approval. "He said you were getting very good at it. And you better start a ledger of your own. I brought home good news and—" Tom reached in his pocket, pulled out a roll of greenbacks, picked up Nelson's hand, and plunked them into it. "This is from the sale of some of your pictures from Mackey's."

Nelson's mouth opened in amazement. "You sold some!"

"Yes, and as fast as they went, you had better get busy! This is only for what Glenn sold the past couple weeks while we were there. On the way home, we went to Abilene and left ten at Silas Jamison's General Store. Glenn said he would keep track of them and send you the money.

Laura jumped from her place, dropped to her knees beside Nelson, and looked up into her husband's incredulous face. "Nelson, I knew it! We all knew they were good."

THUMP! Tommy let out a scream. He had pulled himself up on a chair, then let go and fallen backwards.

Mary Lou cradled him in her arms to quiet him. She looked into his unhappy face and said, "I think we had better finish our journey and take our family home." She sighed. "And that includes me!" Mary Lou glanced across the table at Beth slumped half asleep in Allena's arms. "It has been a long, wonderful month. Time to go home."

Mary Lou climbed up on the wagon seat and was handed a twin for each arm. Suddenly, every muscle in her body complained. The seat felt like a hard rock, her back threatened to break, and the twins had never seemed so heavy.

Thank goodness Tom had fixed the rough road to their ranch that she remembered so well traveling over the day the twins were born. There was still room for improvement, though.

As they approached their ranch house, her heart swelled with pride in Tom and Tex's handiwork. But the poor thing looked dark, forsaken, and lonely. Well—it wouldn't be for long!

Tom stopped the wagon in front of the house and unloaded their clothes bags and opened the door. Mary Lou carried in the weary twins. She walked to the water crock, lifted the lid, and smiled. Bless whoever had thoughtfully filled it. *What do people do without a thoughtful, loving family? They miss a lot of the tender loving touches of life.* She washed her sleepy babies and laid them gently into their own beds, then undressed, washed, pulled her nightgown over her head, loosed her hair, and brushed it.

Tom came in from the barn in just his pants. He had used the barn water barrels to bathe. His red hair glistened with drops of water. Without stopping, he dropped his clothes on a chair, walked across the kitchen, took Mary Lou in his arms, and kissed her. "I've been wanting to do that all day."

Mary Lou laughed. "You always say that!"

" 'Cause it's true. I only feel like half a person when you aren't in my arms." His vivid, blue eyes spoke his desire. They blew out the lamps and climbed into their own bed.

∪

Mary Lou opened her eyes and turned over. Tom lay asleep beside her. Usually he was gone early for chores. Mary Lou resisted snuggling against his back. He'd earned a late morning's rest. Last night even the twins had curled up with no resistance.

She slowly slipped out of bed, grabbed her clothes, and tiptoed out. Surprisingly, the twins didn't stir.

Quietly, she made a fire in the stove, put the coffeepot on, stepped to the door, and swung it open.

An early red-pink border edged the horizon and highlighted a pale, morning sky. Wispy, white clouds floated like veils over an upper haze of soft blue. Her heart rose in praise and prayer to God for His provision of an abundant, beautiful earth.

Mary Lou folded her arms across her breast and hugged the peaceful, delicious feeling of being home, then suddenly felt like a traitor. She had just come from home: Kansas, Pa, Aunt Nelda, Aunt Tibby and Uncle Nate, Jenny, Big Jon, Henrietta, and teary good-byes. Yet standing here, basking in the soft light of a new day in the doorway of her own house, things began to reshape.

Her gaze roamed the roll of the Texas landscape and rested on their new barn in process when they left. Was it finished? Mary Lou's spirit again raised in praise. Tex must have completed it while they were gone, bless his heart. Had Tom noticed it when he took the wagon to the barn last night? He must have. *Why didn't he tell me?*

Her gaze threaded through the morning mist to the roof of the new house Zack had built for Darcy. She turned her head north to the main ranch house and watched wisps of telltale smoke announce that Hattie was up and cooking breakfast.

She felt Tom's arms fold around her and turned her cheek to his kiss.

He snuggled his head beside hers. "I am glad we are home."

"So am I," Mary Lou admitted. Ambivalent feelings bounced around her heart in search of a landing place.

Tom gazed across the land. "Getting rather impressive, isn't it? Best sight of all is that finished barn. Tex never lets any grass grow under his feet.

I know he wants a ranch of his own someday, but I am selfish enough to hope it is not too soon."

"I think if we could find him a good wife, he might settle down around here somewhere," Mary Lou remarked. "That man wants a home of his own. His roaming cowboy days are over. He is looking to settle."

"If that is true, I would give him a piece of land to keep him on the Circle Z."

A small speck of a figure on horseback emerged from the Circle Z barn and headed in their direction.

"I bet you it's Mother!" Tom said grinning. "She has to check to see if everything is all right. Hattie has probably instructed her to bring us back for breakfast."

Mary Lou nodded and laughed. "I will gratefully accept. I had better see to the twins." She turned and sent a smirky little smile back at Tom. "Now we'll find out what sort of prophet you are." She laughed and left.

Mary Lou found the twins hanging over the side rail of the bed. Tommy grinned. It looked as if he had figured a way to the floor. One leg over, he hung in balance.

"Well, you two look bright-eyed and bushy-tailed this morning." Mary Lou lifted, kissed each one, and sat them on the floor. Tired as she had been when she put them to bed the night before, she had taken time to find clothes in their chests for them to wear for this morning. She dressed them quickly. The oncoming hoofbeats halted at the door, and Mary Lou heard Tom greet his mother. She grinned. He *was* a prophet!

The next moment Allena was at her side. "Where are my babies?" she cried and swept them both into her arms and bounced kisses off both their cheeks. Allena sat on the floor, gathered Beth and Tommy into her arms, and hugged and squeezed them till Tommy wiggled free and crawled over to his father. Beth laid back in her grandmother's arms and giggled as Allena tickled her stomach. She paused and looked up. "Hattie gave me instructions to make sure you came to the main house. She has been in the kitchen hard at work since before daylight."

"Oh, Mother, I accept!" Mary Lou responded. "And thanks to whoever filled the water crock. I'm glad to be home, but not quite ready to dive in."

To their surprise, Tex appeared leading Tinder and Dulcie all saddled for Tom and Mary Lou. "Welcome home. Glad to see you made it safe and sound. I'm invited for breakfast, let's go."

Tom settled Beth at the front of Mary Lou and Tommy in front of him and trotted up beside Tex. "Looks like you finished the barn."

"Yep. One of these days I am going to build my own."

"Yep," Tom said and grinned. "And I'm gonna help you build it."

Hattie met them all at the door and swung it wide open. "Breakfast is all ready."

Mary Lou and Allena put the twins into their high chairs.

Everyone took their place, quiet settled, and everyone bowed their heads.

"Father," Tom began, "we thank You for the gift of a new day filled with Your mercy and bounty. We pray to live so our lives are a witness to Your love and providence. In Jesus Name—"

Everyone said, "Amen."

In the middle of breakfast, Zack emerged from the bedrooms and joined them. He talked and ate, but Mary Lou sensed something had happened. A restraint surrounded him.

"Did Darcy come home with you?" Tom finally asked Zack.

Zack bowed his head for a second. "Darcy is not coming back." He quickly forked a piece of bacon into his mouth. Tom stared at his brother. "Does that mean you won't be here at the ranch—that you are going back to—?"

Zack shook his head. "No." He paused, then spoke quickly. "Darcy will not leave Boston. She is divorcing me."

"Divorce!"

The ugly word screeched and dangled in the air.

Tom winced at the pain in Zack's eyes.

Zack fought emotion as he recounted his trip to Boston. "The basic truth is I don't want to be a Boston lawyer under any circumstances, and Darcy won't live in Texas with me." Zack's gaze held Tom's eyes a long moment before he lowered it.

Mary Lou voiced her thoughts. "But—what about Baby Zack?"

Sadness fleeted across Zack's face, and she wished she hadn't asked the question.

"She—she doesn't want him. Baby Zack is mine alone."

A sad, quiet hush hovered over the table.

"I am sorry, Brother," Tom said softly.

Mary Lou thought of her pa and how difficult it had been for him to lose Mama. She glanced at Zack. His eyes were focused on his plate. It would be the same with Zack. Like Pa, time would give Zack the blessing of remembering all the good things. It was the same whether you lose your loved one by divorce or death. They go and you learn to cope. When Mama died and left her and Pa. . .

No!—her heart suddenly cried out. *It's not the same! When Pa lost Mama he still had the nourishment of her love in his heart and the memory of their life together. Darcy had stripped Zack of her love and hadn't only rejected him but denied their child a mother's love as well! Oh, Darcy, do you realize what you have given up for your party life in Boston?*

Zack glanced fleetingly at his mother then dropped his gaze to his plate. In a husky, pain-filled voice he asked, "Figure out and tell me what purpose God has in this mess, Mother." His jaws clenched and released. His gaze darted back to his mother's face with an instant apology for his disrespect.

Allena's return gaze bathed her son with loving forgiveness. "Our Father has one," she answered, "but at the moment, our hearts are too full of hurt and our eyes too full of tears to recognize it." Allena drew a deep breath and let it out slowly. "When something first happens, we seldom understand why God allows it to happen to us. I am sure that Joseph in the Bible spent many hours wondering why his brothers hated him so much that they stripped him and sold him to Egyptian traders, who in turn sold him as a slave. Yet, because of his integrity and trust in God, Joseph concentrated on being an excellent slave, which caught his master's attention, and he made Joseph master over all his affairs."

Allena paused. "You know this story as well as I do, Zack."

Without looking up, Zack slowly nodded his head.

After a moment, she went on. "We think Joseph had suffered enough at other people's hands. Not so. Then his master's wife accused him of insulting her. Though innocent, Joseph landed in prison. But he excelled there also. Soon he was in charge again, and God gave him power to help two prisoners attain their freedom, and they promised to help him gain his.

"Unfortunately, once free, they promptly forgot all about him."

Zack stared intently at his mother.

Allena cradled his gaze. "This has always been one of your favorite Bible stories, Zack, even as a little boy."

Zack nodded slowly.

Allena continued. "Son, through all those events, Joseph had no way of knowing that God was positioning him to be the savior of the whole country of Egypt during the horrible famine that stretched even into his homeland of Canaan. God gave Joseph power not only to save his own family from starvation but to arrange for a reunion for family forgiveness in Egypt." Allena reached and placed her hand over her son's. "But remember, all these blessings covered one act of jealous spite, which God completely swallowed in His love."

The familiar kitchen gathered unto itself the spirit of a cathedral.

"Zack, don't ask God 'why' or wonder that He allows such things to happen. In His timing, you will live to see the 'why' and understand." Allena rose, walked to Zack's chair, and laid consoling hands on his shoulders.

Zack looked up. "Thanks, Mother, I needed that." He rose, put his arms around her, and held her while she released tears that ran down her cheeks in sympathy for her firstborn. After Zack left, the talk around the table remained subdued for a while.

Allena and Hattie wanted to hear all about Tom and Mary Lou's trip, so Hattie poured more coffee and they sat and talked.

Finally, Tom rose and reached for Tommy. Mary Lou rose—

"Why not leave the twins with us?" Allena said. "We haven't seen them for so long we'll have to get reacquainted. The Lord knew what He was doing when He made children resilient. I've learned that while they are young, all they need is love and care, and next to parents, grandmothers are rather good at that."

Tom asked suddenly, "By the way, where is Baby Zack?"

"Nelson and Laura took him with them to spend the night at Shepards'. Emily says since Laura married Nelson and all her children are gone, it is too quiet. Laura took Baby Zack along because Zack is having such a difficult time. She thought it might give him a rest. They should be home sometime this afternoon."

Tom and Mary Lou mounted their horses, waved, and trotted off.

"How about we take a little ride around the ranch so I can catch up on what has been done and be boss again? Riding around in wagons and buggies never has been my first choice. I will take Tinder's back, any day."

Mary Lou smiled. "Would you believe I was thinking the same thing! Dulcie must have wondered what happened to me. I feel as if I have neglected a good friend."

Mounted, they headed for Zack's house to see its progress. What would he do with it now? *Unfinished. . .like his life right now.* Mary Lou's heart went out to him in sympathy and love.

The land had shed some of her youthful spring caprice and settled down to its more mature summer work. Long, soft puffs of air teased Mary Lou's hair. She had piled it in a bun on top of her head and resisted the urge to drop it.

Tom and Mary Lou trotted alongside, each aware of a sense of freedom they had not had for awhile. Moments of aloneness were rare since they'd had the twins.

Tom pointed to a grove of cottonwood trees and grinned. "Be a nice place to rest for awhile and spoon a little," he said. Mary Lou blushed.

The shade and privacy offered a luxury they both needed. They tethered the horses and sat down beside the narrow stream that quietly played water music over pebbles and stones that washed their faces as the water rippled by.

Tom laid his hat aside and untied Mary Lou's bonnet. He reached back and released the hairpins from her luxurious chestnut hair and watched it tumble down her back. They laid back on a soft bed of grass in the shade and relaxed. Tom held her in his arms and kissed her eyes, nose, and lips. "I knew you were my girl the first day I walked into the post office."

Mary Lou laughed. "My first look at you was the day I watched you cross Center Street and come into the post office. You never knew how I scolded myself for the feelings you evoked in me as you touched my hand when I handed you your mail."

"Ummm. You never told me about that. All I remember is a girl with a tiny waist and the most beautiful face I had ever seen that I couldn't forget. Without realizing it, I had chosen the girl I wanted for a wife."

Neither mentioned how close they had come to losing one another.

The sun travelled past the clump of trees, poked its warm piercing rays into the precious shade and frightened it away.

They watered the horses and walked awhile, talking and sharing the precious secrets that lovers store in their minds and hearts.

Tom stopped, leaned, and kissed her. "We can see Zack's house another day. I have a hunch I should get back to my mare. Smitty says she shows all the signs to foal, but she is too early, and all is not quite normal." Tom shook his head. "She probably knows better than we do, but judging from the size of her, it is going to be a big one and could give her trouble."

As they approached the main ranch barn Tex hurried out with a worried look.

"Something wrong?" Tom asked.

"Yeah, Smitty thinks you may have a new colt before morning."

"Go on, Tom," Mary Lou said. "I'll stay here at Mother's with the twins for awhile, then go on home. You go take care of your little mama. I'll be praying all goes well."

Tom nodded, grinned, and swung Tinder toward his barn.

Tex took Dulcie, and Mary Lou walked toward the ranch house to see her own babies.

———

Chapter 10

Hattie finished the breakfast dishes, wiped her hands on her apron, and met Allena as she entered the kitchen carrying two baskets.

"Would you be interested in going to Harness this morning, Hattie?"

"Yes, Ma'am. I was hopin' we'd go someday soon. Our flour supply is runnin' low, and I need a new pair of shoes." Hattie glanced at her feet. "These I got hurt my toes somethin' awful, and they're too gone for mendin'."

"Well, Jess plans to drive into Harness this morning after supplies. I thought we would check to see what we need and go with him."

"Sugar and flour is gettin' low and—" Hattie's voice followed her into the storeroom and got lost.

"Make a list," Allena called. "I'll check with Laura and see if she needs anything."

Laura walked into the kitchen carrying Baby Zack. "Did I hear my name?"

Allena leaned and kissed the baby's cheek. "Good morning, sweet boy," she said and was rewarded by a two-tooth grin. "Jess is driving the big wagon to get supplies for the bunkhouse larder. We are going to town with him. Anything you need?"

Laura slowly shook her head. "No, nothing I can think of. I would just as soon stay here and take care of Baby Zack." Laura squeezed and nuzzled him till he laughed.

"Good morning," Mary Lou called as she entered the kitchen, carrying Tommy in her arms and Beth like a papoose on her back. She leaned over and deposited Tommy on the floor. "Whew! That walk from our house gets longer every day."

"It is not the walk; it's the weight of those twins," Allena said and relieved Mary Lou of her papoose.

"You're right. I'll be glad when they are both on their own two feet."

Allena smirked. "One of these days I will remind you that you said that." They all laughed.

"We are riding into town with Jess for supplies. You want to go along?"

"Oh, yes; I need flour, sugar, and yeast." Mary Lou looked down at her clothes and shook her head. "Oh, I'm really not dressed to go to town."

"We are the same size," Laura said. "Change into something I have, and I will keep the twins. Baby Zack will love having somebody to play with."

Clothes changed, lists made, the three women climbed into the two-seater wagon and were on their way. As Jess swung the team around and headed toward Harness, Mary Lou waved to her children. Tommy and Baby Zack had attention only for each other. Beth watched her mother pull away, stuck out a lip, and wrinkled her face into a cry.

As they pulled out, Hattie called to Laura, "Don't forget to bake the bread when it's raised."

Laura nodded and turned to the children.

The day, delightfully warm, relaxed the passengers. The steady *clip-clop* of the horses' hooves had a hypnotizing affect. Even Allena rode silent.

Just before they reached town, Mary Lou pointed to the newly built church. "Oh, my! Look how the church has grown while we have been gone. The roof is on and the windows are in. It looks beautiful."

"Yes, doesn't it?" Allena smiled and caressed a memory.

The original church had been built by Father Zack, who often preached on Sundays when the travelling preacher couldn't make it. When the preacher moved westward, Father Zack preached every Sunday. One cold winter Sunday, a couple of years after Father Zack died, someone forgot to close the stove damper. The stove overheated and exploded, igniting the wooden wall behind it, and the church burned to the ground, scorching the trees surrounding it. Fortunately, one of the church families returning home from Harness spotted the fire. They saved as much as they could, ten of the precious hymnbooks and, fortunately, were able to carry out the beautiful hand hewn pulpit that had been crafted by Father Zachary with only its base injured from the blaze. It now sat repaired and wrapped in a large quilt in Allena's bedroom awaiting the first Sunday service in the new church. Then it would be brought into the new building and set in its rightful place by Zack and Tom. Tom, Nelson, Tex, and devoted community members had worked faithfully on the rebuilding as their time permitted. But church families still gathered together every Sunday morning at one neighboring ranch or another to worship.

"It is not the same to have church at home," Allena said to Mary Lou, "but the Bible tells us we must 'not forsake the assembling of ourselves together.' "

Mary Lou nodded. Mama had felt the same way. She had always loved to be with fellow Christians. "It impoverishes oneself soul to deny oneself the blessing of worship with fellow believers," Mama had said.

Jess kept a steady pace and made good time to Harness. For the early hour of the day, the town bustled with people. Jess maneuvered the wagon as close to Orval Picket's Mercantile as he could.

Mary Lou, Allena, and Jess each left their list with Orval's wife, Martha, to fill. Hattie sat down in the chair beside shelves filled with shoeboxes and tried on shoes. Mary Lou searched the dress goods for some sturdy cloth to make dresses for the twins. They were growing so fast their dresses already touched the tops of their new high-laced shoes. Tommy now occasionally managed to stabilize both feet square on the floor and stood, his arms held high for balance, a self-satisfied grin on his little face.

Sudden wild shouting outside the store alerted everyone.

Jess immediately turned and ran outside. Everyone followed. A laboring horse carrying an excited man pounded through the center of town while the man shouted for Dr. Mike. In seconds, the doctor hurried through the door of the boardinghouse with his bag. "Somebody hitch up my buggy. Quick!" He turned to the breathless man. "Tell me what happened."

The man spoke between gasps. "Gustave Zigwald—who lives in the old Humphrey place—his two boys came told me—their father—gored by a bull—"

Dr. Mike spun to Allena. "I need you as my nurse." To Mary Lou and Hattie he said, "There are children and a sick mother to care for." He turned to the messenger. "You stay and lead the ladies to the farm."

Dr. Mike hustled Allena into his buggy and was gone.

Jess swung the wagon around and a couple of men quickly assisted Mary Lou and Hattie into it. Jess followed the messenger as he took off ahead of them.

After what seemed like hours, in reality only thirty minutes, the women spotted Dr. Mike's buggy in front of a dilapidated barn. They hurried in, followed a man's moans and Dr. Mike's voice.

"Allena, hold this blanket and press."

At his command, Allena dropped to the doctor's side, replaced his hands with hers, and pressed on a blanket wadded in the middle of the man's stomach.

The man lay sprawled on a blood-stained, hay-covered floor. His breathing was shallow. One leg jerked spasmodically.

The doctor moved Allena's hands for a second, lifted the blanket to expose an ugly, gaping hole gouged through the middle of his stomach. The doctor tried futilely to capture and halt the persistent flow of blood.

All of a sudden, the man convulsed into coughing, then gasped for his last breath.

Dr. Mike fingered his pulse, released it, then slowly crossed Gustave's hands over his chest. He reached for the man's hat, placed it beside him, and stood helplessly staring down at his patient. "That bull's pointed horn punctured his heart. He was a good, strong, independent man. It's a miracle he was alive when we got here." He slipped a horse blanket from its drape on the stall and covered the man. He looked at Hattie and Mary Lou. "Go see Gustave's wife and two boys."

As they emerged from the barn, Hattie and Mary Lou saw two wide-eyed little boys standing in the doorway of the cabin. The older boy stretched his neck and looked beyond them for his father, then reached immediately for his brother, put his arm around his shoulder, and drew him close.

Hattie placed her hand on the older boy's head. "We have come to help your mama. Show me where she is so I can see if she needs anything."

The boy stared at her seriously for a moment, then swung and walked through a door beyond the fireplace. Hattie followed him.

Mary Lou bent over and lifted the little boy's hand. "Can you show me where there is some water?"

His large, bewildered eyes searched her for a moment, then he turned and walked to a bucket on a table with a tin cup sitting beside it.

"Thank you." Mary Lou looked around the room. "Does your mama have any coffee?"

He frowned, then shook his head.

"Tea?"

He walked to a shelf and pointed up.

Mary Lou found two small cans. She opened one and released the pungent odor of sassafras. The other can was empty. She found a teapot, poured hot water from the hanging kettle in the fireplace, and made tea. As she hunted for sugar, she noticed everything was neat and clean.

The door opened and Dr. Mike walked in with drooped shoulders, and Allena's pained expression must have signaled the boys something had happened.

The older boy straightened up and looked beyond them. "Where's my papa?"

"Papa?" The smaller boy began to cry and moved closer to his big brother.

Dr. Mike's knees bent, he gathered a boy in each arm and looked from one bewildered face to the other. "Lars. Wilmot. You remember your papa talking about Jesus, don't you?"

The boys nodded their heads.

"Your papa has gone to live with Jesus in heaven and tell him what good boys you are."

Wilmot's face clouded and tears etched two clean streaks down both cheeks.

Dr. Mike drew him close. "You are both going to have to be brave little men and take care of your mama." He turned to Lars. "You are the man of the house now, and it's going to be up to you to take care of your little brother."

Lars straightened his shoulders, squeezed his trembling lips together, and nodded.

Mary Lou crumbled inside. *What will happen to this family now?*

Dr. Mike stood up, a hand on each boy's shoulder. "How is Zelda?"

"I don't know. She hasn't moved much since we came except for a bad coughing spell and she coughed up blood. Her breathing is quiet now."

Mary Lou followed Dr. Mike and the boys into the stark, neat, clean bedroom.

Gustave must have been a tidy man to keep such a good house, Mary Lou thought.

A wan, emaciated figure of a woman lay motionless on the bed.

Dr. Mike bent over Zelda, took her pulse, and gently returned her hand to her side.

Suddenly a strong, healthy cry of a baby cut through the quiet.

"A baby?" Dr. Mike looked at the boys. "Where is the baby? Show me."

Both boys ran out into the main cabin to a box on the floor in the corner near the fireplace and pointed.

The three women followed.

Dr. Mike reached into a box and lifted a small blanket-wrapped baby into his arms. He turned with serious, questioning eyes. "Where is the baby's mother?"

Lars swung his arm in a wide sweep. "Out pickin' greens."

Dr. Mike shook his head. "Boys, whose baby is this?"

"She's mine!"

That voice!

Allena, Mary Lou, and Hattie all spun at once. Their mouths dropped open and hung, speechless.

Lily dropped her basket of greens and vegetables, crossed the room and relieved Dr. Mike of her crying child. She cuddled the baby to her, straightened its blankets, swayed back and forth, then she looked up at Allena and smiled.

Chapter 11

She is mine." Lily's lips trembled. Her eyes sought Allena's. "Mine—and Doug's."

The incredulity of the moment paralyzed everyone and defied speech.

Allena's face grew radiant. She hurried across the room, enfolded Lily and her granddaughter in her arms and allowed her stored tears to spill down her cheeks.

Joy leaped in Mary Lou's heart and carried a prayer to heaven. *Thank You, Father. Thank You for Mother's sake.*

Lily handed the baby to Allena who gazed into its tiny face, then into her daughter-in-law's eyes. A questioning smile crossed her lips. "Have you named her yet?"

Lily nodded. "Genevieve Allena."

Allena beamed, then her brows posed a question. "Who was Genevieve in your life?"

"My grandmother, the only mother I ever knew—except you."

Dr. Mike turned to the boys. "When did Lily get here?"

Lars shrugged his shoulders. "She comes and helps Ma."

Allena's mouth dropped open in disbelief. "You mean you have been here —this close—all this time and you didn't—?"

Lily shook her head. "Oh no!" Lily pulled out a chair. "Come, sit down at the table and I'll explain everything." She smiled at Mary Lou. "I see you found the tea. Good."

"Not for me, Lily," Dr. Mike said. "I haven't had the chance to tell you that Gustave is out in the barn, dead."

Lily gasped a sharp intake of breath. "Gustave dead?" She bent, cupped her forehead in her hand and pursed her lips. "I bet it was that cantankerous old bull he wouldn't get rid of! Zelda always said that crazy animal would get him someday."

Dr. Mike nodded. "He did. Looked like the bull turned on him when he entered the stall, gored him, and ran. From what I could make out, the point of the bull's horn pierced his heart."

Lily's eyes misted, she glanced at the boys and shook her head. "Oh my, what will this poor family do without him?"

Dr. Mike picked us his bag. "Leave his body where it is for the time being. It's covered in the closed stall. I'll tell the townspeople. Someone will come and help you prepare him for buryin'."

"All I really need is someone to help dig the grave and say a few good words on his behalf. Zelda is too sick. . ."

Dr. Mike nodded and grabbed his bag. He cupped his hand under the chin of each wide-eyed boy. "Take care of your mama and help Lily." He strode to the door and left.

Lily moved into the bedroom to check on Zelda.

Mary Lou placed cups and spoons around the table ready to serve tea.

Lily returned to the table, poured tea, sat down, and smiled at everyone. Her gaze asked patience from the three pairs of unbelieving, questioning eyes that followed her every move.

"Lily, where did you go when you left us?" Allena asked.

"Back to Harness where I came from."

Allena sucked in a short, quick breath.

Lily answered Allena's question before she asked it. "Oh, no, Mother." She shook her head. "I couldn't go back to the life I had before I married Doug." Lily stared lovingly at Allena. "I assure you, Mother, I have been with no man since my husband. Doug is the father of Genevieve. I went to the only person I could trust, Glenna, who took me under her wing the first day I was brought to the saloon. I was seventeen and terrified. The first thing she said to me was that I didn't belong there. I knew it. I didn't want to be there, but I had no choice. I was bound to the man who brought me."

A heavy silence pressed the room.

Lily took a deep breath and continued. "Doug had never paid any attention to me, then one evening, he jokingly told me he was going to marry me. No man had ever mentioned marriage to me before. But the more I thought about it, the more I realized that it could be my escape from the life I hated. Because once I was married I would belong to my husband by law, and all the man who owned me could do was ask Doug to pay my price.

"Then one night Doug asked me again. I thought he was joking so I said 'yes.' He took my arm and led me out of the saloon just as I was. Doug woke up the judge, he married us, and in the morning, he piled me into his buggy and drove to the Circle Z. Mother, I don't know whether you can understand this or not, but for the first time in my whole life, I felt free." Lily gazed from Allena to Mary Lou. "I fully expected Doug's family to completely reject me and order me out, so I began planning how and when I could leave, and where I could go."

"Lily, did you have any love for my son at all?"

"Yes, after we were married, I believe I did. At first, from some of the things he said and did, I thought he married me for spite. For some reason, he seemed like a driven man and quickly angered. Yet, once in awhile he'd show me his loving side. If it hadn't been for that, I would have left long before I did.

"But what floored me the most, you all accepted me and treated me like family. It made me suspicious.

"Then one day out of curiosity, I wondered where you and Mary Lou disappeared every morning after breakfast. So, I followed you to the parlor, stood outside the door, and listened to you during your morning prayer time and when you prayed for the family, you included *me*. I felt terrible 'cause I realized I was using all of you for my convenience same as Doug had used me." Lily bowed her head. "After Doug's death, I knew I couldn't stay. Without Doug, I didn't belong."

"Did not belong!" Allena stared in disbelief. "Lily, the Lord allowed us to read your heart and showed us what kind of girl you really are. We love you, Lily. When Jesus saved you, you became part of God's family and our family. We were devastated when you left and even went to the saloon to find you, but one of the girls told us you weren't there."

"That was Glenna, and she told you the truth. I wasn't there when you came. When I left the Circle Z, I wandered and slept in the woods, then stumbled across Gustave's barn and hid here until he discovered me. Zelda's illness hadn't yet put her to bed, so I worked for my keep for a few weeks. My morning sickness told Zelda I carried a child. I had suspected it, but refused to think about it. What would I do with a baby? I stayed here and helped Zelda for a month, then went to see Glenna. Two weeks later, she found someone about forty miles away who needed a nursemaid for their children and hid me until she could find a way to get me out of town."

Lily's eyes filled with tears. "When Glenna told me you two had come to that house to find me, I couldn't believe it! You knew what I had been. Why. . . ?"

Allena shook her head. "Lily, we aren't interested in what you *have* been. You are no longer that girl. We came for the Lily you became the day you asked God to forgive you. You aren't that old girl anymore, you are a new creature in Christ, Lily, and you were a model daughter-in-law and loved my son, who was very difficult to love." Allena paused. "Forgive me, Lily, but I must ask. Did you know you were with child when you left?"

Lily shook her head. "No, I wasn't aware of it when I left the Circle Z. I just stayed here until I heard from Glenna, then left."

Mary Lou rose and replenished the tea.

Sudden choking and coughing from the other room raised Lily from her chair, and she sped to the bedroom.

Allena sat staring into her teacup. "Who is going to take care of this family?"

"Lily, probably." Mary Lou almost sensed Allena's mind churning and surmised she would want her new granddaughter and Lily at home—

Allena rose and went into the bedroom with Lily.

Mary Lou poured some hot water into a small basin of cool water, washed the dishes, and strained her ears to hear the words Lily and Allena quietly spoke in the bedroom.

"I must ask you what you have in mind, Lily," she heard Allena ask.

A long pause preceded Lily's answer. "I know what I feel I should do, but—"

Silence.

"What *should* you do, Lily? What is God saying to you in your mind and heart?"

Mary Lou's ears stretched to capture their soft words.

When Lily spoke, her voice betrayed inner turmoil and pain. "Dr. Mike said Zelda is too sick to leave alone. And the boys? How could they manage? Lars is five and tended the animals when his father was gone. But Wilmot is only three, a sweet little boy and a good helper. They are both good boys. Gustave taught them well—"

Mary Lou stopped washing the dishes.

"But it is out of the question that they could tend their mother—and—they are too young to be alone—and—" Lily kept talking to avoid the obvious answer. Her voice faded into a whisper.

Mary Lou also knew the answer. She knew Lily felt obligated to stay and care for Zelda and the boys.

Silence cloistered the room, only to be shattered by Zelda who convulsed into a siege of coughing and cried out, "Gott. . .halp me! Oh. . . Fodder Gott. . .halp me."

Allena suddenly leaned and spoke softly into Zelda's ear.

Zelda sucked in a gasp of air and released it in a "Yesssss."

Footsteps and someone knocking on the door roused Mary Lou from her eavesdropping. It was Jess.

" 'Scuse me, ma'am, but with the ride back and all—it's gettin' close to noon—I gotta cook dinner for the boys. Is Miz Langdon ready to leave yet?"

"I'll see." Mary Lou crossed the kitchen to the bedroom. Before she reached it, Allena emerged.

"Yes, Jess, I know. I want you to take Hattie and Mary Lou with you and go back to the ranch. I am staying until Gustave is buried, which should be tomorrow. Then—"

Lily stepped out of the bedrooms with Genevieve in her arms and stood beside Allena.

Jess stared, mouth open.

Allena laughed. "You can close your mouth, Jess. It really is Lily you see."

Lily nodded and smiled. "Hello, Jess, it's me."

Jess's gaze moved back to Allena. "Y—yes, Ma'am. It's just I was surprised—"

"We, too, Jess."

He bobbed his head and consciously forced his attention to Allena and a wide grin spread across his face. "Yes, Ma'am!"

Allena nodded. "But now, I want you, Hattie, and Mary Lou to go on home with the supplies. Lily and I must stay here and do what we can. Tell Tom where we are, about Mr. Zigwald's death, and that we will stay here till after the burying tomorrow. If he can't come himself, tell him to send two wagons and bring lots of quilts and pillows. He can take them off the beds, if he needs to. Tell him Mrs. Zigwald is very sick and is willing to come home with me so we can nurse her back to health. We are also bringing her two little boys."

Jess nodded. "Yes, Ma'am."

As the ranch wagon rattled away, Allena turned to Lily and smiled. "Don't you think it might be a good idea for us to see to gathering Zelda's and the boy's clothing together, so we will be all ready tomorrow when Dr. Mike sends someone out to help with Gustave's funeral? Then when Tom comes, we will be all ready to move to the Circle Z."

Lily melted into tears, stumbled forward, and threw herself into Allena's arms and sobbed.

Genevieve, squeezed between them, protested her tight quarters and squalled.

The two mothers burst into laughter, backed away, and mingled their tears with their daughter and granddaughter on her soft, pink wet cheeks.

Chapter 12

A late afternoon sun descended its steps toward the western horizon when two packed wagons slowly rolled under the Circle Z arch, carrying precious cargo.

The kitchen door flew open, and the whole family poured out.

Mary Lou, Tom and the twins, Hattie, Zack holding his son, Laura, and Nelson all stood with welcoming grins.

The first wagon stopped. Tex leaped from the driver's seat and ran around to assist Allena.

In one sweeping motion, Allena laid Genevieve in Tex's arms, placed her hand on his shoulder, her foot on the hub of the wagon wheel, and jumped to the ground.

Tex held the baby gingerly out in front of him.

Amused, Allena laughed. "She won't bite you, Tex."

Tex reddened. "I know, Ma'am, but I never held such a little one before."

"Well, you had better get used to it. This ranch is beginning to blossom with them." She relieved Tex of his charge, and he moved to the other wagon and helped Lily descend.

"Thank you, Tex." She smiled and watched him as he lifted each boy to the ground.

Lars and Wilmot immediately plastered themselves to Lily.

Zack carried Zelda into Allena's bedroom. The minute he laid her down, a coughing spell seized her. Finally, exhausted, the poor woman sank back on the pillows and focused blurred, grateful eyes on Allena. "Gott—bless you," she said in a forced whisper and slowly closed her eyes.

Lily had taken Genevieve, Lars, and Wilmot into her old bedroom, so Mary Lou carried her twins, followed by a tottering Baby Zack, into the room to meet their new playmates. "My, how your family has grown. With only one bed, Lily, where is everyone going to sleep?"

Lily shook her head and laughed. "Lots of room. I'll make the boys a bed with blankets on the floor. That is where they have slept most of their lives anyway. Maybe later we can make them a real bed. Genevieve sleeps with me."

Baby Zack walked forward, stood in front of Lily, and stared up at her. When he caught Lily's eye, she looked at him and smiled.

"Baby Zack?" she said in a shaky voice and stooped to her knees. "Do you remember Lily?" Tears dampened Lily's lashes and she stretched her arms for him.

Baby Zack's two-and-a-half-year-old questioning eyes stared at her for a minute, then he hesitantly walked into her arms.

Lily sat down on the floor, tears streaming down her face, and rocked him. "Oh, Baby, how I have missed you."

"Ma-ma?" came a tiny voice from deep within.

Lily looked up at Mary Lou through her tears and laughed. "I don't know whether that means he remembers me or not."

Lars and Wilmot circled them, then sat down on the floor beside Lily.

Tom knocked on the door, peeked in, and grinned. "Room enough for a man in here?"

Lily raised her tear-filled eyes. "Absolutely!" her shaky voice answered, "—if you want to sit on the floor."

Mary Lou reached to take Baby Zack, but he clung to Lily's neck and wouldn't let go.

Tom helped Lily to her feet and put his arms around them both in a brotherly hug. "I'm glad you're home, Lily. We have all missed you." He tickled Baby Zack in the neck. He ducked his face into Lily's shoulder. "Especially this fellow."

Mary Lou's heart alerted her to one of life's special moments, and she tucked it away in her heart's room for remembrance of priceless memories.

Tom leaned over Genevieve who stared back at him with the wide, dark eyes of his brother. "She has Doug's eyes," he said softly.

Lily nodded. "I've noticed that, too."

Tom squatted in front of the boys who looked like they were ready to run. He held out his hand. "Hello, there, cowboys. My name is Tom Langdon, what's yours?"

The boys backed up. Wilmot slid behind Lily and hid his face in her skirt. Lars leaned against her and bravely stared. Lily unglued Lars and Wilmot from her side and touched their heads. "This is Lars and Wilmot Zigwald."

Tom smiled and nodded his head. "It's all right, fellas. We'll shake hands tomorrow." He rose quickly and grinned. "Father always said he should have built a double-sized ranch—one side for us to live in, and the other half for Mother's strays."

Just like Mama, Mary Lou thought.

"I'm proud to be one of her strays," Lily said softly. "There is no way you could imagine how thankful I am to be here."

Tom glanced at Mary Lou and grinned. "We found that out this spring as we traveled; there really is no other place quite like home." He turned to Mary Lou. "Is there?"

Mary Lou's head nodded agreement, and she tried to stretch home from Texas to Kansas. This time she didn't get very far.

A galloping horse and rider pounded into the yard. "Tom! Tom! Quick! Get to your barn right away."

Tom rushed out the door, jumped on Tinder, and was gone.

Lily looked concered. "Something wrong?"

Mary Lou shook her head. "I hope not. He and Smitty have been nursing Tom's favorite mare who is too early to foal. I hope nothing happens to that colt. Poor Annie. Tom says it is going to be a big one and has hopes it will be the first of many of his champion stallions. He wants to breed them like Father Zachary." Mary Lou laughed. "Having babies seems to be the same whether it is human or animal. Birthing is an anxious waiting game." She remembered the day the twins were born. Poor Annie. Mary Lou lifted a prayer for her.

Leaving Genevieve asleep in the middle of the bed surrounded by pillows, Mary Lou picked up Beth under one arm and Tommy under the other; Lily carried Baby Zack, held Wilmot's hand, and called to Lars to come. Lars stretched to his full manly height and walked beside her.

They trooped to the kitchen, tantalized by the familiar smells of Hattie's cooking and, all of a sudden, realized how hungry they were.

"How's Zelda?" Lily asked Allena.

"Sleeping quietly. The trip was a big ordeal for her. Rest is the medicine she needs right now."

Hattie worked, as usual, like two people. She sliced cold beef, stirred her pot of bean porridge hanging on the fireplace as she passed by on the way to slice up two whole loaves of bread. Each woman as she entered the kitchen assumed a chore: set and reset the table as the number constantly changed, open a quart jar of pickled beets, stir the fried apples and onions, mash the potatoes, cut the raisin pies. When all was ready, Baby Zack followed Lily on her way out to ring the dinner bell.

Zack rode in, dismounted, and tied his horse to the hitching post.

"Supper's ready," Lily called to him.

"Good! I'm ready," Zack said. He picked up Baby Zack and positioned the rope between him and Lily, and they rang the bell, to the little fellow's delight.

Mary Lou saw a glow in Lily's eyes and a smile on her face as she walked through the door with Zack and his son.

If Lily missed the mention of Darcy's name in the usual course of conversation, Mary Lou felt relieved she had not asked about her. She would learn soon enough.

A horse and rider clattered into the yard. Tex burst through the door and waved his hat over his head. "Miz Langdon!" He looked to Mary Lou and Allena. "Tom sent me down to getcha both. You gotta see this. Annie just gave birth to a colt *and* a filly! Come quick!"

The impact of the news hung a moment for comprehension, then prodded everyone into action.

Supper forgotten, Mary Lou mounted Victor, and Zack mounted behind her.

Allena called to one of the cowboys for Brown Beauty—"Bareback!"

When Mary Lou ran into their barn, Tom stood in the stall, his arms around Annie's neck, stroking her, softly talking to her, his face filled with awe.

On the floor of the stall, in the hay, were two dark-brown, struggling animals that didn't even seem to be aware of anything except the fact that they needed to get up. Each tried, but their wobbly, uncooperative legs could not manage the right angles, and each time, they toppled back to the floor.

Mary Lou gazed in wonder. "Oh, Tom, they are beautiful. I have never seen twin foals before."

Tom's pride couldn't be contained. He swooped Mary Lou into his arms, twirled her, and sent her skirts flying; then, he kissed her in front of everyone! "The Lord did it again, Mary Lou! Gave us a hundredfold! I was too stupid to see it. I had my mind set on one." Tom tucked Mary Lou into the crook of his arm and grinned. "Whatdaya know! The Lord sent a colt for Tommy and a filly for Beth."

Smitty stood at the back of the stall with a satisfied grin propped by weary lines of hard labor. "I have been around horses all my life, and this is the first time I have seen twin foals born, let alone a colt and filly." His eyes beamed the contentment of a job well done.

Mary Lou gazed at Annie's babies, smoothed her soft neck, and felt a kinship. "You and I have something in common, Annie. I know exactly how you feel."

Everyone laughed.

Annie stood, her head hung low, periodically nuzzling, licking, and whinnying to the helpless, struggling, brown things at her feet.

An overwhelming sense of the almighty greatness of God enveloped Mary Lou. *The spark that is brought to life through birth is beyond our comprehension,* she mused. *Life is so common. It is everywhere, in sky, in sea, in land, in us, until we regard it lightly and live in frippery as if it will last forever.*

Suddenly, a recall from one of Pastor Miles sermons rose from deep within Mary Lou. *"Live each day as if it is the only day you have to live. Appreciate and use each moment because you will never be able to live it again."*

Allena smiled broadly and looked wistfully at Tom. "Wouldn't your father have been proud?"

Tom looked into her eyes. "Mother, I think he is."

Zack rached his arm across Tom's shoulders and gave him a solid pat.

Watching the three, Mary Lou warmed at the love and appreciation between this woman, her sons, and the proud lingering memory of father and husband. She had admired it before. And today, Mary Lou viewed an even deeper glimpse into Mother's magnanimous heart. With no hesitation, in one day, she had gathered in a desperate family, had given unlimited love and acceptance to a confused daughter-in-law who blessed her with the little baby girl she had always longed for. She had also gathered into her large heart two little fatherless boys to love and watch grow as she had her own four sons.

Mary Lou smiled, remembering how Allena hesitated to relinquish her tender baby, Nelson, her special talented child into whom she had poured her own artistic life. With fresh insight, Mary Lou realized the shock of having three of her four sons dump three unknown wives, whom she had graciously accepted, on her.

What a woman! Same breed as Mama. *Oh Lord, You have surrounded me with models of godly women. Not only Mama and Mother, but Aunt Nelda, Aunt Tibby, Henrietta. I want to be one of their number. May I bless my husband and children with my life as these strong God-fearing women have blessed me.*

Chapter 13

Mary Lou climbed out of the wagon and lifted the twins to the ground. They both clung to a wagon wheel for balance, then she led a twin in each hand, and they tottered to the kitchen door. Baby Zack squealed as the twins wobbled in.

"Good morning, Hattie, how is Zelda?" Mary Lou asked.

Hattie shook her head. "We thought we lost her last night, then she rallied. Miz Langdon says it'll be a miracle if she lasts the day. She hasn't said a word, eaten anythin', or opened her eyes for two days. Poor dear, her breathin' grows more shallow with each breath. Allena's with her now."

Allena's head appeared in the kitchen doorway. "Zelda is calling for Lily and the boys," she said and disappeared.

Hattie hurried outside, called the boys, and they came running from the barn, followed by Lily.

Lily guided Lars and Wilmot to their mother's bedside and stood with her arm around each one.

Lars, wide-eyed, gazed at his mother.

Wilmot darted frightened eyes, first at his mother, then at Lily, then at Lars.

Allena leaned near Zelda's face. "Zelda? Lars and Wilmot are here with Lily to see you."

Zelda slowly turned her head and blessed her boys with a weak loving smile. "Lars—take—care—of—your—little—brother." She gasped for breath between each word.

"Yes, Mama," Lars said and wiped his wet face on his sleeve.

Lily lifted and held each boy so he could kiss his mother's cheek.

Zelda's shaky hand raised, caressed, and blessed each one. "Good—sons—my—boys—"

Lily leaned over Zelda. "Yes, Zelda, and don't worry, I'll take good care of the boys. You just rest now and get better."

Zelda's blurred eyes searched for Lily, found her, and smiled faintly. She blinked a slow greeting with her eyes, stared at Lily, inhaled, and released a deep breath with her thanks. "Dankë." Peace settled on her face and her breathing ceased.

Allena picked up her wrist, felt the pulse at her neck for a moment, then shook her head. "She's gone. Her suffering is finished. Zelda has gone to be with her 'Gott.'"

The boys clung fearfully to Lily. She stooped, enclosed a boy in each arm, and gently laid her cheek against each one. "Boys, your mama has gone to be with Jesus and your papa, but I promised your mama I'd take care of you. You are my boys now."

A reverent quiet embraced the room as each woman prayed for Zelda's departed soul and her two orphaned boys.

Tex offered to ride into Harness, inform Dr. Mike and help dig a grave beside Gustave. Lars clung to Tex and pleaded to go with him. Finally, Lily gave permission and they rode off, Lars' legs stretched across the saddle, his back pressed against Tex's broad chest.

Tom and a couple of the cowboys made a burying box, and by late afternoon, the funeral procession slowly began Zelda's last ride.

Hattie stayed at home to care for the twins and Baby Zack. When they all returned, a hot supper was ready and waiting.

The family gathered around the table. Lars and Wilmot stood back until Lily sat, then each boy gingerly slid into a chair on either side of her.

Tom stood, bowed his head. A hallowed quietness descended on all. "Our Father, we thank You for this day and all it has brought forth. In times like these, You make us all more aware of how dependent we are upon You and appreciate what a gift You give us in every person's life. We ask Your blessing not only upon this meal, but upon each life seated at this table. May we honor You daily with our living." He paused as if he would continue, then finished with a quiet, "Amen."

Later, in bed in their own house, Mary Lou lay awake long after Tom's breathing had relaxed into the slow cadence of sleep. The funeral had rekindled memories of Mama and a fresh realization of how fragile life really is. All the way home, each person had ridden subdued. Even Lars and Wilmot had seemed caught in the finality of the moment when they had stood beside the graves of both parents, barely aware of the seriousness of the occasion. Wilmot had clung to Lily's and Lar's hands, Lars had held Wilmot's hand and clung to Tex, their eyes darting silent questions from the graves of their parents to the faces of their new family around them. They had timidly followed directions and tossed their shovelful of dirt upon the box that held their mother. Now, in retrospect, Mary Lou felt it seemed almost callous to have ridden home, sat down immediately to a good meal, and discussed the general activities of the day and those planned for tomorrow as normally as if death had never visited.

No matter what—life goes on! The thought shimmered in Mary Lou's mind. Mama? Or was it God Himself who called her to attention? In after-thought, Mary Lou sensed its great truth. In all circumstances, life is on-going, surges past death, and moves on without a backward look.

Mary Lou lay in reveries, remembering a day when Mama told her how God made the trees and flowers. Mama had said their only real reason for living was to produce seed peculiar to the parent plant. At the end of their season, plants released their seeds to fall into the arms of Mother Earth who nurtured each seed in its propensity to grow into the likeness of the former life. Mary Lou remembered how precious corn and wheat seeds were to the homesteaders in Kansas. Seeds were considered golden treasure, sustenance to the life of all families.

Is this what life is all about? Spending your life for the next generation? She thought of Allena who insisted that at her dinner table, Tommy, Beth, and Baby Zack's high chairs be placed at the corners on either side of her so she could nurture these little extensions of her sons, Tom and Zack.

Yes, Lord, no matter what, life does move on. Mary Lou turned over in bed, reached her arm around her husband and cuddled his back. He stirred and wrapped her arm in his. Mary Lou lifted a prayer of thanksgiving and praise to her Father in heaven and slept.

The rays of the morning sun teased her eyes awake. Tom was gone. She dressed hurriedly and peeked in at the twins. Beth say playing with her rag doll, Tommy lay under his bed pulling out the straw in the mattress.

Mary Lou poured oatmeal and water into a pan and set it on the stove to cook, set the table, and grabbed a hand of each twin.

"Come on, childen, let's see where your father is."

They started the slow walk to the barn. Tommy's balance had grown to the point where he insisted on trying to run and usually ended up in a heap. He kept twisting his little hand from his mother's to venture out on his own. When they reached the barn, he wiggled free, ran through the barn door, fell flat on his face, and screamed.

Tom appeared, leading Tinder, stopped, picked up his son, and straddled him over Tinder's back. The tolerant animal swung his head around, nick-ered at his passenger, and followed Tom to the corral door. Tom retrieved his teary, smiling son and released Tinder into the corral.

The family moved to Annie's stall. Like their own twins after they were born, Annie's babies took a lot of care. Especially now. They walked back and forth under their mother's stomach and tried to nurse constantly.

Tom grabbed the colt, pulled him away, and guided the filly to its mother. "He's a glutton. He'd starve his sister if I didn't interfere."

Tommy squealed with delight when Mary Lou guided his hand to pet the colt. Beth mimicked her brother, stretched her hand, touched the soft warm hair, withdrew her hand, and wrinkled her nose.

Tom smoothed his hands over the colt's back and rump. "He has great form, strong chest and neck. Even from his small start, he is going to be a fair-sized animal." Tom nodded toward the filly. "And she is going to grow into a sleek, trim young lady." He came out of the stall and picked up Tommy.

Mary Lou picked up Beth and they walked from the barn toward the ranch house for breakfast.

"Have any idea what we can name these critters?" Tom asked.

"No, but the names will come. What were you going to name just one?" Mary Lou asked.

"Uh—kind of thinking—Valiant."

"I like that." Just before they reached the ranch house, Mary Lou laughed. "What about Adam and Eve?"

Tom threw back his head and roared. "I like that! Adam and Eve it is!"

The smell of the oatmeal tweaked their hunger as they entered the kitchen.

Tom sniffed the air. "I'm ready!"

Mary Lou dished out the oatmeal, fried bacon and eggs, sliced bread, and sat down. Tom said grace.

"When do you think the church will be done?" Mary Lou asked.

"It is done for all practical purposes. Will Shepard had some of his boys working on new benches yesterday. I think Mother is hoping we can hold the first church service within the next couple of weeks. After breakfast, let's ride down and talk to Mother."

Chapter 14

Z ack walked out the ranch door and waved as Tom guided the buggy into the yard. "Was on my way up to see you!"

Tom reined the horses, jumped out, and lifted the twins from Mary Lou's lap to the ground.

"Mother and I were talking about having the first church service this coming Sunday. Think the church is ready enough?"

Tom nodded his head. "I don't see why not. Still some finishing to do, but not enough to keep from having church."

Allena came out the kitchen door and stooped, opened her arms wide, and the twins waddled across the yard into her arms. She hooked one under each arm, hung them on her hip, and swung around and around. The twins tinkling laughter matched hers. She set them on their feet, and they clung dizzily to her skirts.

"How about us taking the pulpit to the church this afternoon and setting it up?" Zack asked his mother.

"No." Allena said. "That pulpit doesn't enter the church until the first congregation is there to see it brought in."

By the determination in their mother's face, both boys knew no argument would be considered.

"We will drive it there the day it is to be taken in," Allena announced. "When it enters the church, it should be carried to its rightful place and set permanently."

Zack nodded. "I see your point. All right, we will aim to have the inside of the church finished, and we will get the pulpit on the wagon and take it next Sunday."

"And keep it wrapped in the quilt." Allena led the twins to the kitchen door.

During the week, the ladies of the church, Emily Shepard, Allena, Mary Lou, Lily, and many of the surrounding ranch wives, cleaned furiously, banishing the dust and building debris, and set the benches in place, ready for Sunday. By dinnertime, they were finished and unpacked huge baskets of food for both themselves and the men at work on the outside finishing.

Zack, Tom, and Nelson had rubbed the pulpit to a high sheen and lifted it into a wagon, safely wrapped in Allena's quilt and clean horse blankets, and parked it in the barn overnight. By Sunday, the drivers of the wagons were ready, dressed in their best clothes, with directions from Allena that whoever drove had to go to church and could participate in the church picnic planned for after the service.

Sunday morning, Mary Lou slipped out of their ranch door early and tramped through damp range grass to a place where she'd spotted wild flowers profusely in bloom. She gathered a huge bouquet to take to church. Yesterday, she had opened Mama's trunk, lifted out one of Mama's special vases and packed it carefully in one of her picnic baskets. She carried the bouquet into the cabin. Tom and the twins were waiting for her.

"Where did you go so early?" Tom asked when she entered the ranch door.

She lifted her bouquet. "I thought it would be nice to have some fresh flowers in front of the pulpit for the first Sunday. Mama always took flowers in a vase to church when they were in bloom."

Tom pulled her into his arms and kissed her. "From what I've been told about your mama, you grow more like her every day."

The words brought tears to Mary Lou's eyes. More than anyone else, Mary Lou had hoped to be the sweet, loving wife and mother her mama had been to her and Pa. She also wanted to transfer to her children the inner joy of love and appreciation of God's world that Mama had given to her.

Sunday morning dawned, and the sun sprayed its warm rays across the sparkling dew and whisked it away in a vapor.

Buggies, wagons, and men and women on horseback made their way to the church for its anointing day. By the time the pulpit was to be brought in, the benches were full. Some wise souls had even brought milking stools for their children, and set them along the side walls to leave the center aisle clear.

In the left front corner stood a shining new organ donated by the Shepard family after they found out the new schoolteacher could play one. No one had seen her yet. Old Anna Whitney, the former schoolteacher, who had to quit because of poor eyesight, offered to board her free so she could have a companion in her old age.

The churchyard of Harness Valley Church, as it had been named, began to fill with wagons, buggies, and saddled horses.

Allena and family had been given the first two rows on the right side of the church. The Shepard family sat left front.

A sudden hush followed a tall, elegant lady in a blue dress and hat who gracefully walked down the center aisle to the front.

Emily Shepard rose, greeted her, and turned to Allena. "Ruthella, I want you to meet my dear friend and closest neighbor, Allena Langdon."

Allena rose in anticipation.

Emily beamed. "This is Miss Ruthella Truesdale, our new school teacher from Virginia."

"My dear, it is a pleasure to meet you," Allena said.

Miss Truesdale bowed her head in greeting. "I've heard many good things about you, Mrs. Langdon. I'm happy to meet you."

Allena smiled and turned to her family stretched out along the bench and introduced each one. When she introduced Lily and the two boys, the teacher's eyebrows raised.

Smiling at Lars, she said, "Do I see a young man who might become one of my students?" she asked.

"Yes, he will," Allena answered. "He's Lars Zigwald."

Miss Truesdale smiled at Lars and his gaze darted from side to side, then he stared down at the shiny toes of his shoes.

"Emily, if Miss Truesdale is not sitting with you, I would be glad to have her join us. We seem to have more space available on our bench than you do."

Emily laughed and looked at her family's two full benches with only one space left for her next to Will. "I agree." She turned to Miss Truesdale.

Miss Truesdale nodded. "Thank you, Mrs. Langdon. Now if you will excuse me, I do believe it is time to begin service." As she walked to the organ, one of the Shepard boys scurried behind to man the organ pump. Soon the sweet notes of "To God be the Glory," filled the room. When she played it a second time, the whole congregation lifted their voices in a hearty song.

Everyone on the Langdon bench shifted to leave room for Tom next to Mary Lou. Allena moved and left two spaces at the end of the bench at the center aisle, one next to her for Miss Truesdale to sit during the sermon, and the end seat for Zack after he and Tom brought down the pulpit.

Will Shepard rose, stood before the congregation. The buzzing murmur faded. "Friends, neighbors, it seems right and proper, before we bring in the pulpit, that we all stand and thank the good Lord for this new church."

Feet shuffled and everyone rose.

Will bowed his head. "Our Father, we're much obliged to You for this fine new church. The men have done a good job buildin', and we praise God for each one and their willin' work. Thank You for Miss Truesdale to play the organ. And now, Lord, we want to place the last piece of furniture, the pulpit, all that is left of our old church, and we thank You for the good memory and preachin' of Your man, Zachary Langdon, who made this pulpit and fed our souls every Sunday morning with Your Word until he went home to be with You. And we thank Ya, Lord, for his son and our friend, Tom, who will carry on in his father's footsteps and explain Your Word to us. May this church become a holy place that honors You. Amen." Will stepped forward and sat down on the end bench space next to his wife, Emily.

Zack and Tom carried Father Zachary's pupit down the center aisle and placed it in its proper place.

Mary Lou set her vase of flowers on the floor in front of the pulpit.

Zack sat down on the end of the bench, while Tom stepped to his mother who gave him the large pulpit Bible. Tom carried it to its place and slowly turned its pages to his text.

Before Tom began his preaching, Miss Truesdale slid quietly into her place between Allena and Zack on the bench.

Tom's message began in the first chapter of Genesis. "The first verse tells us the earth was without form and void, and God made all things new. . ."

The congregation sat in hushed attention while Tom told of God's work of creation and the creation of man and woman. "And God gave us the strength to create our good life out of His earth, here in the state of Texas. Now, in this church, we used the abilities He gave us to make a house in which to worship Him. All our God asks of us is that we obey His laws in the Bible so He can spread His blessing among us as we work together in love and peace. Yes, we all contributed with our abilities, hands, effort, energy, and devotion. But may we never forget that this building is only a man-made wooden building until we, God's people, who are His church on this earth, walk through those doors. Then it becomes "Church." May God favor us with His blessing."

Miss Truesdale resumed her place at the organ and the congregation lustily sang "Oh God, Our Help in Ages Past."

After a short prayer of dismissal, the parishioners poured out of the church, and in no time at all, the men had rolled barrels off their wagons, set them up, and laid boards across them for serving tables. As fast as the men laid them, the ladies covered the boards with beef, fish, and fowl, pies, cakes, puddings, and an endless variety of fresh fruits, vegetables, pickles, and peculiar specialties.

Clean, old blankets and quilts dotted the ground, filled with nibbling, chatting neighbors and friends. The children ate on the run in their delight to be with all the playmates. Lars and Wilmot stood off to one side and watched while Zack and Lily joined in helping some of the children play "London Bridge Is Falling Down." Lily finally coaxed Lars and Wilmot to join in and was rewarded by two little boys who suddenly remembered how to laugh.

Chapter 15

Summer passed quickly, consumed with caring for land, crops, animals, and children.

Tex walked into Tom's barn to put Annie and the twin foals out into the small corral. He hung on the fence and grinned at them as they awkwardly sprawled their long, front spindle-legs to enable their noses to reach the ground and nibble grass.

Movement way down at the main ranch house caught Tex's eye, and he smiled. Lars raced toward him ahead of Lily. Wilmot and Baby Zack walked beside her as fast as their short legs allowed. Tex waved and Lily waved back.

Lars arrived breathless and spewed a stream of chatter that gave no chance for Tex to say a word.

Tex took his hand, and they walked backed to meet Lily and the other boys.

By the time Lily reached the barn, she was puffing. "For the life of me, I can't imagine how Mary Lou manages carrying those twins back and forth from the main house." Her gaze turned to Tex. "The boys wanted to see the baby horses, and it's such a beautiful morning I couldn't resist a walk with them."

Tex resisted the urge to assist Lily under her elbow, but when she approached, he settled for a walk at her side.

The boys skipped ahead and hung through the lower rails on the corral, giggling and pointing to the "baby horses."

Lily and Tex rested their elbows on the top, leaned, and watched the foals feebly jump after their mother as she ran to stretch and exercise her legs.

Lars looked up at Tex. "Can I ride that baby horse?"

Tex grinned. "Not yet. He's too little to hold you."

Lars shook his head. "I'm not very big."

"Well, he has to be a grown-up horse before even a little boy can ride him."

"When I grow up, then will that baby horse be big enough for me to ride him?" Lars asked.

"Oh, yes," Tex grinned and tousled the boy's hair.

Lars climbed on the second rail, hung on to Tex, stood tall, and looked

Tex in the eye. "I'm gonna be a cowboy when I grow up."

"All right, Boy, and I'll teach ya." Tex turned and grinned at Lily as she joined him. "That is—if I'm around here that long."

Lily's mouth opened in shock. "You planning on leaving?"

"Well, I've been saving my money so's I can buy a piece of land of my own." He side-glanced Lily. "I've always had a hankerin' to run my own place."

"Don't most men?" Lily asked.

"Maybe so, but I know some cowboys lot older'n me who can't shake the wanderin' dust out of their feet."

Lily and Tex both leaned on the rail and stared straight ahead.

"Well," Lily began softly, "I've known a few women, too, who aren't much interested in taking on the work of a man and family."

Lars looked up at Lily. "Wilmot and me are your family, ain't we, Lily?"

Lily tapped each boy's shoulder and grinned. "You certainly are, and I'm glad."

"Is Baby Zack your family, too, like us?"

"Well, sort of, but he really belongs to Zack."

Tex shifted his feet, his eyes riveted straight ahead.

Lily shot a quick glance at Tex. "Well, come on boys. Let's see what Mary Lou and the twins are doing, then we have to go back down and help Mother and Hattie work the vegetable garden."

Tex turned his full gaze on Lily. "Yeah, and I guess I'd better get to my chores."

Both headed opposite directions.

Lars hung back. "I want to go with you, Tex."

Lily grabbed Lars's hand and pulled him with her. "Tex has work to do, Lars."

Tex swung around. "Oh, Lars can come with me, if he wants. Maybe learn a thing or two."

Lily's gaze met Tex's. "Sure he's no bother?"

"No, Ma'am! I enjoy his company."

Lily gave Lars a pat on the back to push him toward Tex. "I know he enjoys yours. Talks about you all the time."

"Yeah?"

Lily nodded. "Says he's gonna be a cowboy, just like you."

Tex's face reddened. He turned and motioned his arm. "Come on, Boy."

Lars ran to Tex and began a ceaseless barrage of chatter that only faded as Lily walked to see Mary Lou.

Lily peeked in the open door. "Hello! Mary Lou?" No answer broke the stillness, so she led Wilmot and Baby Zack around the house and spotted

Mary Lou, hoe in hand, working a row of vegatables.

Lily laughed. "Those poor plants don't stand a chance with the help you've got."

When Tommy saw Wilmot, he squealed and ran willy-nilly across vulnerable rows of tender vegetable plants.

Mary Lou straightened up, wiped the moisture off her forehead with her sleeve, placed her hands on her hips, and surveyed her garden being trampled by her twins. She dropped her hoe, grabbed them, and hung one on each hip and wound her way up between the rows. "I guess I'm pushing it. Tommy does more pickin' than he does plantin'." She grinned at Lily. "Someday, and soon, I hope."

They laughed and walked to the shady side of the house. Mary Lou sighed. "Glad you came. I'm ready to set a spell."

The twins immediately each took one of Wilmot's hands and waddled beside him. Baby Zack fell in line. Tommy babbled a stream of gibberish, but Wilmot seemed to understand and put a word in here and there.

Mary Lou and Lily fixed cold vinegar-sugar tea for everyone. Wilmot took a sip, scrunched up his face, and went "Yaack." The women laughed and gave him a plain cup of water.

Lily stared into her cup, then suddenly looked up at Mary Lou. "Has Tex said anything to you about leaving?"

Mary Lou searched Lily with an intensified gaze. "Yes. In fact, when we were building this house, Tex helped me put up the curtain ropes in the bedroom. I gathered from his comments, he has a hankering to find a wife and settle down."

Lily's brows raised. "Oh? Did he mention any particular one?"

"No, he just said he'd like to settle down, but couldn't find a good woman. I told him the best place to find one was in church."

Lily laughed. "He must not be very interested, or else he's given up. I don't see him in church every Sunday."

"Maybe he's found her." Mary Lou noticed a shadow cross Lily's face and smiled.

They chatted and sipped and kept the children corraled.

Lily rose and heaved a deep sigh. "Well, I'd best get back. Genevieve will need a feeding. That's the one thing Mother can't do. She does everything else for her."

Mary Lou caught a tone of hurt in Lily's voice. "Does that bother you, Lily?"

"Sometimes." Lily's smile held a touch of sadness. "I know Mother is trying to take some of the load of the three children off me, but I want Genevieve to grow up knowing *I'm* her mother." Lily shook her head. "I'm

331

sorry, I sound very ungrateful."

"No, you don't. It is only natural for a mother to want to care for her own baby. It's nice to have some time off, but they are still your babies, and others don't have the same thing in mind for them that you do."

Lily heaved a big sigh and smiled. "Thanks. I've been feeling guilty 'cause I resent it every time Genevieve cries and Mother beats me to her."

"I think Mother is trying to help you and has no idea that you feel this way. Having two active boys thrust on you with such a small baby can be a hardship. She thinks she is helping."

Tears welled in Lily's eyes. "I'm sorry, I feel like I'm being unthankful. And I'm not. I am so happy to be home with the only family I have ever had, I guess I am a bit jealous and holding on too tight. You are such a sharing bunch. I've never had much to share, so you're going to have to teach me how!"

Mary Lou laughed. "Oh, you'll learn. That's what a family is, a sharing bunch, in everything! If we didn't share the work, we'd drop from overload."

Lily rose, drained her glass, and set it on the table. "I'd best get going. Thanks." She patted Mary Lou's hand.

Mary Lou rose and they both stood and observed the children at play. Their squeals, giggles, and constant activity were a joy to watch.

Lily stepped out the door. "Wilmot, get hold of Baby Zack's hand. Time to go home."

Mary Lou stood by her house and watched Lily fade to about half size, then gathered her own two and went determinedly back to her garden.

Chapter 16

Tom and Zack waved good-bye to Allena and rode off into the early mist of a hazy Texas morning on their way, at their mother's insistence, to check out the school building and see what repairs were needed, if any.

"It suited Anna Whitney, but I'm sure the new teacher will bring a lot of good ideas from her teaching experience in Virginia," had been their mother's comment.

So Zack had volunteered to consult with Miss Truesdale and supervise whatever repairs might be needed to enhance the school.

"Since you were schooled in the East, you will know better what we need here and don't forget your son will soon be a student there."

Zack had seen Eastern schools and agreed that much could be done to make better schools in Texas. Even state legislators were slowly realizing the growing interest Texans were expressing for the education of their children.

The schoolhouse was about five miles past the church. In comparison, the condition of the schoolhouse was noticeably lacking. Surrounding ranch families had expressed cooperation in their support of a better school. Those with children of school age had each promised to pay one dollar a month per pupil to the new teacher, Miss Ruthella Truesdale.

Tom and Zack trotted into the school yard and noticed a sidesaddled horse standing patiently ground-reined at one corner. As they dismounted, Miss Truesdale appeared in the open doorway.

"Good morning, sirs." She smiled, looking very different from the elegant lady who had played the organ in church the day before. Today, she wore a dark skirt and a shirt waist with the long sleeves rolled halfway up her arm, which she quickly brushed down and buttoned the cuffs.

Both men doffed their hats.

"Good morning, Miss Truesdale," Zack said.

Tom nodded. "Miss Truesdale."

"We are glad to find you here," Zack said. "We came to see what needs to be done to the school before it starts."

A wide smile spread across Miss Truesdale's face, revealing a row of very white, even teeth. "Oh, thank you. I just arrived myself and was standing in

333

the middle of the classroom wondering where to start! Come in, gentlemen."

The clunk of the men's boot heels disturbed the quiet and the dust in a room that had obvious need of repairs.

"I wondered whom I would be responsible to, and where I could express my needs for my classroom," Miss Truesdale said.

Zack dropped his head, then lifted it with a grin. "I guess I'm sort of expected by the parents and my mother to see that you are situated. It will be my pleasure, Ma'am."

Miss Truesdale nodded her head and swung around. "I see we do not have desks of any sort, just benches. Would it be at all possible to have long desks made along these two walls with benches for the older children so they can rest their arms to write properly? The benches are fine for the younger children at first." She moved to the opposite wall, turned, and waved her arm across the large blackboard. "I'm pleased with this. It is a wonderful aid to teaching and children dearly love to write on it. It also gives them good practice since much of the time there is usually a dearth of writing paper."

Zack reached into his vest pocket and drew out a small notebook.

"And I wondered if there would be any objection if I allowed Miss Whitney to come in as she has strength and can teach special subjects. It will not cost the parents. We can both manage on the salary expressed." Miss Truesdale smiled. "You know, once a teacher, always a teacher."

Zack nodded and smiled. "The teaching of the children is your responsibility, Miss Truesdale. I'm sure Miss Whitney will be a great help to you. I was taught by her. In fact, my brothers and most of the folks who grew up here were taught by her. It was in deference to her that this schoolhouse was built by Will Shepard. She made a special trip to his ranch twice a week to teach him to read and write. Her failing health is the only reason we put out a call for a new teacher. I'm sure it would be hard for her to just sit by after all her faithful years of work."

Miss Truesdale nodded her head. "Thank you. She will also be teaching me because the school where I taught was much more structured, and I can see the variety and scope of work is much greater here. I accept the challenge."

Zack followed Miss Truesdale around the room, making jottings in his little book of her needs and comments. Before Tom and Zack left, Miss Whitney limped in, leaning heavily on her cane.

"My, my, look who's here," she said. A pleasant glow filled her face. She patted Zack's sleeve and turned to Miss Truesdale. "Here is my best pupil, Ruthella. No one ever studied harder than he did. He wanted to be a lawyer and despite all the obstacles, he did it." Miss Whitney patted Zack's arm again and smiled up into his face. "But it pleases me and I'm proud that after all that good education and opportunity you had in the East, you decided to come back home and use your knowledge for the benefit of Texas."

Miss Truesdale's eyebrows raised. She smiled and nodded to Zack.

Zack grinned. "Once a Texas boy, always a Texas boy, my mother says, and I proved her right."

They all laughed and Miss Whitney bobbed her head.

"How many children will be enrolling from your family?" Miss Truesdale asked.

"This year, a boy named Lars. He isn't one of our family, actually. Sort of adopted. But give us a few years, and you will have Wilmot, his brother, my son, and Tom's twins.

Miss Whitney nodded and looked up into Zack's face. "Oh, yes, and I haven't seen Darcy for some time. Is she still back East visiting her family?"

Zack's face became a mask. "Yes, Ma'am." He didn't elaborate and turned to Tom. "Anything else you wanted to look at, repairs or something?"

Tom shook his head. He had a few questions, but sensed his brother's need to leave. They could be discussed elsewhere.

A slight twinge of Miss Truesdale's brows stated a question, then her face broadened with a smile and she made no comment. "I will be happy to meet all your children," she said cordially.

Tom and Zack mounted and left Miss Truesdale waving in the doorway where they found her.

At the road, Tom and Zack parted company, Zack off to Harness and Tom back to the ranch.

Tom and Tinder rode under the Circle Z arch and stopped at the main ranch house.

His mother came out the door, stood, and waited until he rode up beside her. She patted Tinder's neck and looked up. "Well? What did you think of Miss Truesdale?"

"She is a fine woman, and I think she will make an excellent teacher for my children," Tom said and grinned. "She sweet-talked Zack into some new desks and benches, and asked if Miss Whitney could help her in the classroom."

"Wonderful. My heart identifies with a woman being put out to pasture."

Tom frowned. "You—out to pasture?" He laughed. "I don't think I'll ever live to see that day."

Allena grinned. She hoped she would never see it either.

"Mary Lou here?" Tom asked.

"No, Lily just came home from there."

Tom swung Tinder. "That's where I better head for."

Allena nodded and watched her son trot off, then turned toward the sound of squealing children.

Tom rode to the corral first to check on Annie and her foals. She was thin. Smitty had brought an old mare work horse from the main ranch as a wet nurse. He should be able to wean those colts next month.

He laughed aloud as he watched Adam dart and dash everywhere and nowhere. Yesterday, he'd noticed that neither the colt nor the filly could walk under their mother's stomach anymore. Eve was noticeably smaller and trimmer. *Pretty little thing,* Tom thought. *I'm surprised Nelson hasn't been out here with his easel painting those two.*

He rode Tinder back to the barn, took off his saddle, and turned him out to pasture.

Walking toward the house, the tantalizing smell of food made him realize that he was hungry. When he opened the door, he found a frazzled wife with his daughter in tears. Tommy had just spilled a pitcher of milk and pulled Beth's hair.

Mary Lou looked up from the stove and pushed back a few wisps of hair that had lost their anchor and grinned at Tom. "Mama never told me there would be days like this. But then, all she had was one sweet little girl!"

Tom laughed and picked up his mischievous son. Beth put both arms around one of his legs and looked up expectantly.

Tom put both children in their high chairs, tying Tommy in his.

"Well—tell me about the new teacher. Was she at the school? Did she know you were coming? How does she like the schoolhouse?"

"Whoa! She was at the school. She didn't know we were coming and she is a very lovely, gracious lady, and one who knows exactly what she wants. Zack has a list of what she needs and wants, plus she wants Miss Whitney to be able to help her when she is able."

"That's wonderful! I felt for that dear lady having to move out of the position she has held in this community for so long."

Mary Lou placed the last bowl on the table, sat down, and bowed her head. Tommy took his cup, ducked his chin into his chest, and looked out of the tops of wide eyes.

Tom cupped his hand on his son's head. "Good boy," he said, bowed his own head and said grace.

Chapter 17

Tex watched from a bunkhouse window as Zack and Lily mounted and rode off toward the west. The only thing he knew in that direction within short riding distance was Zack's house.

Into his mind flashed a scene he'd watched from the barn of Zack riding in, dismounting, walking to meet Lily and Baby Zack; then, with Baby Zack between them, the three laughing as they rang the dinner bell. Tex's mind churned. *Zack and Lily. . .Darcy gone. . .Baby Zack needs a ma. . .*

Tex stared after the fading figures. After all, they are brother and sister-in-law. Maybe he just needs her advice about something at the house. Yet, Tex couldn't seem to convice himself of anything. The two figures grew smaller. He seethed inside with intense jealousy, an entirely new experience.

A horse and rider galloped from Zack's house. Tex squinted. *Looks like Pete.* His face spread with a wide grin. *Bet he's up there workin'.* Pete had told Tex he'd been helpin' Zack. As Tex watched, Pete met them, they talked, then all three rode to the house. Tex smiled, heaved a big sigh, and walked back into the horse barn and furiously cleaned stalls.

What is wrong with me? Tex jawed himself. Disturbing new feelings churned inside him. He had never felt this way before. Maybe it was time for him to move on. Not that he wanted to. He liked working for the Langdons. Good, honest, family people, and he appreciated the fact that Tom treated him like a good friend. Of all the ranches he'd worked, the Circle Z topped them all.

"Tex? Are you in here?"

"Yes, Ma'am." He walked through the barn to Mrs. Langdon.

"Has Zack said anything to you yet about building desks at the school?"

"Yes, Ma'am."

"Would you have time to work at the school today? Miss Truesdale said she would like to have the desks made as soon as possible 'cause of the mess involved. She needs them finished so she can clean and set up the schoolroom to get ready for school next month. You finished with your work here?"

"Just about."

"Well, I'll have Hattie pack you a basket of food for dinner, enough for you, Miss Truesdale, and Miss Whitney, too. Tell the ladies a couple things

337

will need to be heated. By the time you get your wagon loaded with the wood and tools, we'll have it ready." She turned and walked toward the house, then turned suddenly. "Oh, and Tex?"

"Yes, Ma'am?"

"Why don't you take Lars? He's almost six. He's old enough to fetch for you. Besides, I think he needs to become acquainted with his new teacher. Maybe if he gets to know her, he might be a little more eager to go to school. This morning he told me he's not going, 'cause he's going to be a cowboy, just like you." Allena couldn't contain her smile.

Tex ducked his head but it didn't conceal his satisfied grin. "Well, Ma'am, we'll have to see 'bout that!"

Within an hour, Tex had his chores done, the wagon loaded with wood, and tools waiting in front of the main house.

The door bounced open, out flew Lars, his face beaming. He climbed on the wagon hub and scrambled onto the seat beside Tex. "Tommy's mama said I'm going to be your fetch boy!"

Tex laughed. "That's right. Do you promise to work real hard and do what I tell ya?" Tex yanked Lars's cowboy hat down over his eyes.

"Yep." Lars laughed and righted his hat.

Allena and Hattie came out, each with a basket, and Tex put the baskets in a space he had saved for them.

"Thank ya, Ma'am." Tex nodded and swung the team toward the Circle Z arch. In what seemed like no time at all, they bumped across the school yard. Tex leaped from his seat.

Lars prepared to jump like Tex, changed his mind, scrambled down over the wheel, and stood at Tex's side. He glanced up at Tex who removed his hat when the lady came out of the schoolhouse door.

"Take off your hat, Boy, in the presence of a lady," Tex said softly.

Lars shot a quick look at Tex, removed his hat, held it in his hand in front of him like Tex, stood up straight beside him, and watched the lady come out the door and walk toward them.

"Good afternoon, gentlemen. You must be Tex. Mr. Zack Langdon stopped by this morning on his way to Harness and told me you might be able to come today." She looked down at Lars and smiled. "And who is this young man?"

"This is Lars Zigwald, and he will be your pupil when school starts next month."

"Oh, so you are the boy from the Langdons who will be starting school this year?"

"No, Ma'am. I'm going to be a cowboy like Tex." He looked up at his idol.

Tex frowned down at Lars, shifted his feet, and looked up in apology to Miss Truesdale. "Yes, he is, Ma'am. He don't quite understand 'bout school yet."

Miss Truesdale smiled and nodded. "I see." She turned and walked back toward the school. "Come in, gentlemen, and I'll show you what needs to be done."

After dinner, halfway through the afternoon, the wood had been sawed to fit, and Tex, with Lars fetchin', had the big desk started on the long wall.

Miss Truesdale came in periodically and gave forth constant praise. She watched Lars for awhile, then suddenly asked, "Lars, don't you think if you are going to be a cowboy like Tex and have to build barns and maybe schoolhouses, you had better learn your numbers so you can count and measure like him?"

Lars shot a quick glance at Tex. "Did you go to school when you were like me, Tex?"

Tex shot a desperate glance at Miss Truesdale, who gave him a reassuring nod.

Miss Truesdale laid her hand on the top of Lars's head. "Now Tex must have had schooling of some kind to learn his numbers like he knows them, wouldn't he, Lars?"

Lars looked from Miss Truesdale to Tex and thought for a minute. "Did some teacher learn you your numbers?" he asked Tex.

Miss Truesdale cupped Lars's chin in her hand and turned his face up to her. "Now think, Lars. Somebody had to teach him." She looked up and smiled at Tex. "Didn't they, Tex?"

"Yes, Ma'am. Why—uh—somebody did teach me my numbers." He looked down into Lars's face. "And somebody's got to teach you yours."

Lars questioning eyes focused on Miss Truesdale's teacher-face. "Did somebody teach you your numbers, Ma'am?"

Very seriously, Miss Truesdale nodded her head. "Aboslutely! I learned them in school."

"If I come to school, will you teach me numbers?"

Miss Truesdale nodded her head decisively. "Yes, Lars, I certainly will."

Tex's gaze spoke his thanks. "I'll see what Tom and Miz Langdon have for me tomorrow. When I get a chance, Lars and I will be back to build the rest."

Lars stood straight. "Yes, Ma'am. We'll come."

Tex unloaded most of the wood from the wagon and put it inside the school to keep dry.

"I am so pleased, gentlemen. I can see we are going to be finished in plenty of time before the first day at school. I thank you for your good work."

" 'Tis a pleasure, Ma'am. It won't take too long to finish the small wall.

Since I have the measures, I can finish the benches in my spare time at the ranch." Tex hoisted Lars onto his seat.

Miss Truesdale stood in the door and waved as they drove off.

Anna Whitney walked around the schoolhouse and watched them go. "That cowboy is a good young man, but what you need is a learned gentleman," she said and glanced up at Ruthella.

Ruthella's mouth dropped open, then spread into a smile. "Anna Whitney! Do I sense a little matchmaking?"

"I'm just saying he's a very nice young man for a cowboy, but not for you. I had a nice talk with Allena Langdon the other day when she stopped by the day you went to town. I asked her about Zack's wife, and she told me that Darcy will not live in Texas and has had her lawyer father arrange a quiet divorce."

Ruthella's mouth flew open. "Zack is a divorced man?"

"Yes, but it isn't his fault. I've known Zack Langdon all his life. He was the best student I ever had, a very intelligent young man. I must admit I had a hard time liking Darcy and still don't understand what he saw in her, or how the Langdon family put up with her. She was too uppity and seldom spoke to people here. She showed me with her snooty ways that she thought us beneath her. They had one little boy who is crippled in one leg. When Baby Zack was born, Darcy was so upset about that she didn't want anything to do with him. If you want to hear my say, I think he's better off without her. She was the wrong wife for such a fine man as Zack Langdon."

Miss Truesdale didn't say a word, but her brows drew together in thought.

"And Zack's more your level, Ruthella, and the best catch for you around here."

Ruthella laughed and shook her head. "Anna Whitney! You are an old cupid. I'm not even thinking of getting married, especially to a divorced man. I am a schoolteacher. I have to be an upstanding example to my students."

Anna shook her head. "I thought like you once. I'm sorry I didn't accept the nice young man who loved me. If I had, I wouldn't now be old and alone, and I could be enjoying the blessing of my children in my old age." Anna rose and thumped after her cane to the door and turned. "Well, my dear, you think about it. My opportunity to marry a good, loving man came only once. My refusal of his loving offer was the biggest mistake of my life." Anna thumped out.

Ruthella sat down on a bench. Her mind pictured the tall and handsome dark-haired man who had sat in church on the end of the bench beside her. Zack had manners, and Ruthella liked a well-mannered man. When she had come from the organ, he had risen, waited until she was seated, then sat down beside her.

She remembered his neat, trim appearance when he had stopped on his way to town yesterday to tell her Tex would be doing the building. She ducked her head and smiled, remembering her heart had beat a little faster in his presence.

She gasped an intake of breath. *Ruthella Truesdale!* She chastised herself within. *Come to your senses.* She stood and hurried across the floor and out the schoolhouse door, banging it behind her. *God, forgive me for indulging in such foolish thinking.*

She slowed as she neared the little cabin behind the schoolhouse. Anna's pathetic, wistful confession pierced her heart. *I could be like her some day.* Something shriveled inside her. *No! No!* her heart protested. She walked into the cabin and straight to her room to hide her welling tears.

Chapter 18

The whole family gathered for supper.

"Emily Shepard and I have been talking about having a big harvest barbeque here at the Circle Z," Allena announced as they sat around the table enjoying Hattie's mincemeat pie and coffee.

Tom nodded. "Sounds like a good idea to me. It's been a good year. The ranchers have worked hard. We need to gather in fellowship and thanks for God's bounty."

Family discussion bounced back and forth across the supper table and finally settled for the first Saturday in October.

The following week, Hattie and Lily volunteered to stay home and care for all the children while Allena and Mary Lou took the day to visit surrounding ranches. They found everyone enthusiastic and delighted. Allena told Zack to stop at the school and invite Miss Truesdale and Anna, also to check and see if Dr. Mike could make it, or leave a note telling him about it if he wasn't there.

Two days before the barbeque found Mary Lou busy at her cookstove. Lily had come early in the morning and took Tommy and Beth to the main house to play. As she watched them toddle toward the main ranch, Mary Lou stretched, relaxed in the released feeling without them—free to work.

She laid her hand on the stove and held it there until she counted to twenty. The warmth told her practiced hand the oven was ready so she slid three risen loaves of bread inside to bake. A big pot of beef stew for supper simmered on the top.

She walked to the new chicken coop Tom had built between the house and her vegetable garden, close enough for her to care for her chickens, but also far enough to release them into the vegetable garden to help Mary Lou keep ahead of the bugs. She smiled. *Everything on a ranch has to earn its keep.* She caught three old hens, chopped off their heads, removed the entrails, and kept the liver, heart, and gizzard to make giblets in the gravy, then hung the chickens by their feet on a high line to drain. She'd wash and pluck them later and put them into a stew pot.

She worked steadily all day. By the middle of the afternoon, she had made shells for pumpkin pies. She had two pumpkins perched outside the kitchen door next to the chairs where she and Tom sat. Hopefully, they could get the pumpkin all ready to put in the pie shells to bake first thing in the morning. Spread everywhere were freshly-baked cookies and bread, two large pans of chicken pie awaiting tender biscuit dough tops, and their allotted time in the oven. She even had enough buttermilk from her freshly-made butter to make cottage cheese.

About three in the afternoon, she glanced around the kitchen, then at the clock and smiled. How much she had accomplished without the twins! She washed her face, put on a clean apron, smoothed her hair, and began her walk down to the main ranch house to get her children. From afar, she watched Lily cross from the house to the barn. *The children must be asleep.* She waved.

∪

Lily paused, waved at Mary Lou, then proceeded to the barn for Lars. Poor Tex. She wondered how he worked with that boy under his feet most of the time. Tex was a good, patient man. He would make a great father. She could hear voices across the stalls.

As they came into view, Lars stood beside Tex, barely giving him room to breathe. "Lars! Step back and give Tex room to work."

Tex turned and greeted her with a warm, welcoming smile.

"Don't you get a little weary of Lars tagging after you all the time?"

Tex shook his head and grinned. "No. He's good company and learns fast. A cowboy's life is a lonely life. . ." He glanced into Lily's eyes.

The longing she saw in his eyes took her by surprise. She tried to avert her eyes, but they refused to move. Was that tenderness she saw in his face? Or—could it be—love?

Tex broke their gaze and quickly busied himself cinching the saddle, picked Lars up and swung him onto the horse's back. "Lars and I were going to take a riding lesson. Want me to saddle you up a horse so's you can ride with us?"

"Just a minute," she said, "I'll see if they can spare me. We have a houseful of children." Had Lily seen a wisp of pleading in his gaze or was she misreading him because she wanted it that way? She turned and hustled across the yard and disappeared through the ranch door. Almost as fast as she went in, she reappeared and hurried back to the barn.

"Mother says I need a rest and to take a ride with you and Lars, and it will give you a rest as well. She said you've been working very hard lately."

Tex saddled another horse, handed the reins to Lily, mounted his own, grabbed the reins of Lars's horse and put him between them.

They rode to the chatter of Lars asking questions about everything they passed, he saw, or he thought about. All of a sudden, he quieted. Both Lily and Tex looked at him to see if something was wrong. Their eyes met across the top of the boy's head.

Lars looked first at Tex, then at Lily. "Lily, why don't you marry Tex so he can be my pa?"

Silence reverberated the air.

After a long moment, Lily laughed. "Lars, I think it's time for you to stop talking and listen. You cannot talk all the time. It's polite to allow others to speak as well as you."

Tex pulled his and Lars horse to a halt.

Lily rode ahead, stopped suddenly, turned, and was swallowed by Tex's questioning gaze.

Tex laughed and ducked his head. "Well, Fella," he said and turned his eyes to Lily. "That ain't the way it's done, Lars. First, you have to find out if the girl you want to marry wants to marry you."

"Sure she does!" Lars answered.

Tex turned a stern look at Lars. "Be quiet, Boy." He glanced at Lily and his face reddened.

Time hung awaiting.

"Well, Lars," Lily began hesitantly, "a girl first has to know whether a man is in love with her or not."

Lars looked at Lily. "Are you in love with Tex, Lily?"

"Lars!" Lily ducked her head then raised up laughing, two very red spots flooding her cheeks.

Tex moved his mount up beside Lily. "I'd like to know the answer to that myself."

The tender look in his eyes warmed Lily's heart. "What would you do, Tex, if I said 'yes'?" She drank in the love he poured from his eyes. "Do you realize if you married me you would not only get Lars but Wilmot and Genevieve as well?"

Tex, beaming, slipped from his horse, hauled Lars to the ground, walked over to Lily, and held up his arms.

Lily slid off the horse into them. Tex gazed at her a moment, then pressed his hungry lips over hers. "I'll take anything if I can have you for my wife."

Lily closed her eyes and tasted the sweetness of his mouth on hers and felt his heart pounding his love. For the first time in her life she felt completely comfortable in a man's arms. This was where she belonged. His arms encircling her were more wonderful than she had ever dreamed.

Lars stared up at them. His little brows bent into a frown as they kissed.

344

Suddenly, his eyes brightened and his mouth stretched into a wide grin. "Does that mean you are married, and Tex is my Pa?"

Tex smiled at Lily, and they turned to the boy. "Almost!"

Tex swung Lars up on his horse, grabbed the lines of the other two, put his arm around Lily, and they walked back to the barn.

☊

The day of the barbecue dawned warm and sunny. A perfect day. The men busied themselves setting up saw horses, boards, and benches. In a clear spot at the end of the barn closest to the house, Jess and several of the cowboys already had the steer strung up on the spit. The acrid odor of the animal's seared flesh permeated the air.

Wagons, horses, and buggies of neighbors, including the Shepards, pulled into the space at the end of the barn. Each family carried armfuls of food with tempting aromas to a long row of sawhorse tables and deposited their donations to the feast. A festive mood took hold with back-slapping, joshing camaraderie among the men, organizing chatter among the women, and wide-eyed excitement of the children playing nonsense games.

Crops, cattle, hunting, windmills, and the impact of the railroads were thrashed over, argued over, and laughed over. Yet a spirit of optimism pervaded the conversations, generated by everyone's fierce love of Texas.

Come late afternoon, one by one the neighbors reboarded their wagons, pulled out with hearty good-byes, and wended their ways toward home. Some had a good hour's ride compounded by cranky, exhausted children who had run themselves ragged, by an exhilaration of excess of playmates. It had been a joyous day.

Zack cleared his throat. "There is some business the family needs to discuss about the ranch. Can we go into the office for a short meeting?"

Zack seated his mother in Father Zack's big leather chair and faced his brothers. "Mother and I have been talking about Lily. We feel that, since she was Doug's wife and Genevieve is Doug's child, some inheritance should be arranged. Mother suggested we give Doug's share of the ranch to Genevieve, and with Tex and Lily contemplating marriage, we thought to give them an interest in the land if Tex works it, with the stipulation that at Tex and Lily's deaths, the land reverts back to Langdon property and will belong exclusively to Genevieve."

A silence of churning minds and a short discussion brought all family members into agreement. They returned to the dining room table, and Tom went out to the barn to get Tex.

When they returned, Zack laid the offer on the table.

Lily stared first at Zack, then Allena, stunned.

"Well, Tex," Tom grinned. "You always said you wanted your own spread."

Both Tex and Lily were speechless.

After more discussion, Zack said, "Then I'll draw up the papers, and after they are signed and presented to the judge and the clerk, it will be done."

Lily glanced around the family with tear-filled eyes. "God bless you. You're more family than I ever hoped for. Thank you." Her tears allowed no more words. She gazed at Tex.

His eyes were shining and moved from Zack to Allena to Nelson and finally rested on Tom. In a choked voice, he said, "Thank you good people. I'll work hard to help you make the Circle Z the best ranch in Texas."

Everyone laughed.

Zack scanned the faces at the table. "Then all is in agreement. I'll see to it on Monday."

There were hugs all around.

Hattie shooed Mary Lou away from the piles of food. "Don't fuss with this. Someone will bring it up to the house tomorrow morning."

"Better yet," Allena interrupted, "just plan to eat here every meal so we can use up this cooked food."

"Sounds good to me," Mary Lou said. "Thank you, Mother."

Tex hooked up one of the buggies for Tom to take his family home. Tom patted him on the shoulder. "Thanks, Tex, see you in the morning. You can help me fight with Adam and Eve. Time to separate them from their mother."

Tex nodded.

Tom gave a slap with the reins.

Tommy whimpered through his thumb and Beth's head wobbled in sleep on the way home. Both Tom and Mary Lou undressed, washed, and rolled them into bed both sound asleep.

It had been a memorable day.

Tom went out to the barn to do chores and check the animals.

Mary Lou pumped some cold water and made vinegar-ginger tea.

If she hadn't been so tired, she would have walked to the barn. Instead, she sat down on one of the chairs in the front of their house and watched the sinking sun cling tenaciously to the edge of the horizon.

She thought of the glow Lily's face when Zack announced about the land division. *Brave man that Tex! He's not only marrying Lily, he's marrying a whole family!*

Thank You, dear God. Why is it we don't fully realize that our best interest is in Your precious will? You want to give Your children a thousand times more than they want to receive.

An old familiar warmth washed over Mary Lou. She looked up and smiled. Mama? "I'm still praying for Pa to accept the Lord Jesus as his Savior, Mama. God never gives up on anyone and neither will I," Mary Lou whispered softly.

Tom emerged from the barn and walked through the shadowy twilight.

Mary Lou slid out of her reverie, suddenly aware of the tears on her lashes and cheeks. She glanced up at Tom standing in front of her and smiled. His brows squinted a question.

"Looked like you were in another world, my dear. Welcome back." He bent over and squinted into her eyes. "It is too dark for me to see but was that your Kansas or your mama look?"

Mary Lou stood up, slipped her arms around her husband, and gazed into those clear, blue pools she fell into when she met him. She slowly shook her head. "It was neither this time." Mary Lou smiled. "It was my Texas look."

Tom's brows raised, then a knowing grin creased his tanned face. "Welcome home, Mrs. Langdon."

A HEART
FOR HOME

To our Father, God,
Who placed us in families
To teach us to love.

Chapter 1

T ommy! Come back here!" Breathless, Mary Lou stopped when she saw Tom emerge from one of the corrals. To keep an eye on her son, Tommy, was a full time job and to keep him occupied for any length of time with anything was nearly impossible. His sturdy legs beat double time to his mother's. He was almost to the point where he could outdistance her.

"Tommy! Obey your mother!" Tom's stern voice called from the barn door.

Tommy stopped in his tracks, darted a glance from one parent to the other, drooped his head, turned, and walked slowly back to his mother.

Mary Lou smiled and stretched out her hand when he reached her. "You're a good boy. Come help me plant the potatoes. Then you can go out to the barn and work with your father."

Tommy grabbed her hand and hopped along at his mother's side with a wide grin plastered across his eager little face. Tom and Mary Lou recognized the necessity of keeping two-year-old Tommy busy at useful tasks to teach him that life wasn't one big field to play in, with him in charge. His quick mind changed course by the moment, and his feet followed blindly where his mind directed.

"One of these days, he'll mesh the two together," Tom had assured Mary Lou on one particularly exasperating day.

Mary Lou sighed. *Yes, he will.* She recalled her adjustment to a whole new way of living as Tom's wife in her husband's big family. Her family had only been she, Pa, and Mama. Mostly Mama. Pa had spent most of his time riding Morgan out on the range and then later working in the store.

Mary Lou couldn't contain her smile as Tommy bobbed up and down beside her singing "Jesus Loves Me." They moved surprisingly fast along the rows of potatoes. When they plopped the last potato in the ground, Tommy turned and looked expectantly at his mother.

"We done?" Tommy stood poised to run.

Mary Lou surveyed the neat rows and smiled at the eagerness of her son. She leaned and kissed his cheek. "Yes, we are!"

Tommy turned and shot off like a bullet. "I'm coming, Papa!" he shouted and seemingly flew to the barn.

Mary Lou watched her energetic son with pride. He had the exuberant energy and exactness of Tom, but to keep that energy focused was a major task. Any little bug or movement that captured his imagination was enough to coax him off course.

Tom appeared at the barn door and stood grinning as Tommy raced toward him. He waved overhead to Mary Lou, clamped his hand over his son's shoulder, and guided him into the barn.

Mary Lou waved back, heaved a sigh, and turned to her garden. Her small daughter, twin to Tommy, sat patiently between the bean rows, picking all the flowers from the middle of the rows and carefully placing them in her basket. The fact that they were generally known as weeds didn't daunt her enthusiasm. Beth picked another, squashed its blossom against her nose, smiled, then carefully added it to her basket of treasures.

Amused by her dainty daughter's actions, Mary Lou shook her head in amazement. No, it wasn't her imagination. Every day Beth *did* grow to look more like Mama. Thick, soft, chestnut curls bounced round her shoulders. One of Mary Lou's fond memories as a young girl was taking all the hairpins out of Mama's luxurious, wavy brown hair and watching it tumble down Mama's back. Then Mary Lou would brush and brush—

"Come, Beth," she called. She walked back to the cabin and washed her hands as she passed the pump. In the kitchen, she picked up the basket filled with half the cookies she had baked that morning with the dubious help of the twins. The shapes were interesting, the sizes not uniform, and they had a strong cinnamon taste, but she was sure they would disappear regardless.

Beth gathered herself and her flower basket then ran as fast as her little legs could travel over the irregular ground. She fell once, spilling her basket, lay in a surprised heap for a second then, undaunted, picked herself up, brushed her knees, and retrieved her scattered weed-flowers. She placed each one carefully into her basket and continued, mindless of the trail of weeds that escaped as she balanced her load and walked.

Mary Lou waited for her at the pump, washed Beth's hands and face, and dried her with her apron. Together they headed down the road to the main ranch, Beth chattering and skipping beside her mother like a frisky little puppy out for a morning romp. As they entered the gate, they saw Hattie moving up and down over her scrub board at the side of the house.

Hattie looked up suddenly. " 'Bout time you came for a visit. We was wonderin' if you still lived up there!"

Mary Lou nodded and laughed. "Yes, but there is just as much work to do up there as there is down here, only you have four women to do it."

Hattie nodded sharply. "Just proves the old adage 'A man may work from sun to sun but a woman's work is never done," she said in singsong.

"Might as well get used to it. But I wouldn't trade places with any one of them men with having to work from sunup to sundown to take care of their families—all them animals and crops plus doin' the buildin' and all the other work they do around here plus helpin' their neighbors." Hattie wrung the rinse water out of another pair of overalls and slapped them over the line to punctuate her observations.

Mary Lou caught a sparkle of tears. Hattie's husband must have been a good man. Sometimes when Hattie played with Tommy or the other boys, Mary Lou wondered if she was thinking of her own little four-year-old son who had been killed by a bear. She walked over and put her hand on Hattie's shoulder. "Has anyone told you lately that we all thank God that He chose us for your second family?"

Hattie looked up, eyes sparkling over a warm smile and slowly nodded. "Don't have to. You all show it, and I have thanked the good Lord everyday of my life since I came here."

Mary Lou leaned over and kissed Hattie's wet cheek.

Beth raised her face for a kiss, too.

Hattie gathered the child in her arms, kissed her on both cheeks and forehead, squeezed her in a snuggle, set her back on her feet, then turned to her washtub.

As Mary Lou and Beth entered the ranch kitchen, Allena walked in from the hall. "Gamma!" Beth squealed and made a running dash to her grandmother.

"Here's my Bethie!" Allena cried and scooped her up into her arms, basket and all. "I was hoping you would come visit me today."

Beth responded with a squeal and stretched forth her basket of remaining treasures.

Allena feigned surprise. "For me?"

Beth giggled and nodded vigorously.

"They are beautiful. Thank you, Beth." Allena leaned over and set the basket with its tousled weeds in the middle of the kitchen table. "There!" she said. "Aren't they lovely?"

Mary Lou smiled. "Only a grandmother would do something like that. No wonder children like to visit Grandma."

Allena smiled and whispered, "Don't tell anyone, but grandmothers are notorious manipulators when it comes to their grandchildren's attention."

Lily walked into the kitchen, followed by Genevieve, who tottered in, toppled to the floor, then determinedly pushed herself back onto her feet and stood, weaving precariously, a triumphant grin spread across her delighted little face.

"She's walking!" Mary Lou cried.

Lily laughed. "If you can call it that. At this point it is an up-and-down business." Lily turned to Beth and stretched her arms wide. "And here's our sweet little Beth! Come give Aunt Lily a big hug."

Beth obliged then pushed her away and turned to Genevieve. "Geevie," she cried and gave Genevieve a hug that toppled them both. They sat stunned for a moment then everyone laughed. Suddenly they realized they had done something to capture everyone's attention. They beamed, pushed themselves up on their feet, and gleefully plopped to the floor again amidst the laughter.

Allena clapped her hands. "There is nothing as delightful as children. When my four boys were growing up, I could hardly wait until they were grown young men. But my grandchildren are growing up too fast! Sometimes nothing seems to be the way it ought to be." Allena nodded her head and smiled. "I think the good Lord in heaven often laughs not only at the children but us grown-ups as well. To Him we must act like silly children much of the time."

Everyone nodded agreement.

Mary Lou turned to Lily. "I really came to find out about your wedding. How is everything by now?"

"Well, Mother and I just finished my dress. I think I'm about as ready as I can be. Now it's up to the men to take time out for us to get married!"

"Have you set the day?" Mary Lou asked.

Lily nodded. "In between finishing our house and the fall roundup." She smiled and blushed. "That way we can get away from the three kids for a week."

The women burst into laughter.

Mary Lou threw her arms around Lily. "Sounds a little like a cart before the horse, but I agree! Tex is going to make a wonderful father for your darling little girl and those two sweet boys you have taken into your heart and home. Anyway, one thing we do thank Doug for, may his soul rest in peace, is the blessing of bringing you into this family."

Lily's eyes softened and became moist. " 'Tis I who am blessed." She batted tears from her eyes, bowed her head, and said no more.

Allena slid her arm around her shoulders. "And God blessed me with a daughter, a granddaughter, and two more dear little boys in my old age. It takes most of us a good many years to discover that God has a way of making wrong things right, even though sometimes it takes us a long time to recognize His help."

The women were suddenly quiet.

The children looked up in wonderment. It was a hallowed moment.

Chapter 2

Tom Langdon nudged Tinder toward the steep, treacherous trail up the north side of Langdon Mountain, which stood almost in the center of the family ranchland. It was small compared to the mountains to the west, stony and dangerous underfoot, but it commanded the best overall view of the Circle Z Ranch. Tom gave Tinder his head and let him pick and climb at his own speed.

Finally, the wary, sure-footed animal scrambled onto the smooth top of the mountain that looked as if a slice had been cut off the top to make a surprisingly smooth, sloping tabletop almost as flat as the plain below.

Tom dismounted and stroked and patted his panting horse. "Good boy, Tinder." He dropped the reins to the ground and stood surveying the expanse above and below, drinking in the breathtaking magnificence of the sky and land he loved. It had been worth the climb. How many times he and his tall, stately father had stood on this very spot, dreaming up the vision. Tom almost heard his father's resonant voice. *Take care of the land, Son, and it will take care of you.* Tom now viewed the truth of his father's statement. The land now cared for not only one but four families.

The Circle Z Ranch and range spread as far as Tom could see. Standing in the midst of it, Tom's whole being surged with fresh awareness of the depth of his father's love and satisfaction in the land. During those times he and his father had scanned the land from the top of Langdon Mountain, Tom now recognized that his father had deliberately imbedded in him a deep sense of pride, contentment, and the joy of ownership.

A quiet humility swept over Tom as his father's words flooded his mind. "God plants every man somewhere then coaxes and enables him to rise above the ordinary. Make sure, my son, that as you rise you remember whose son you are."

The first time his father had spoken thus Tom thought his father meant his son—Tom. Now he understood his father had meant Tom as a son of God.

Tom raised his eyes toward heaven. "God help me," he said aloud. "I want to honor You through Your gift of this land to my family. I pray to always be as honest and honorable in all my ways as my earthly father—" Tom bowed his head. "And my heavenly Father," he added softly.

A peaceful serenity enfolded Tom. He felt held in the arms of the whole scene while sky, land, and air poured energy into his soul and accelerated his spirit with a new sense of unexpected joy and anticipation. His body surged with new vigor, and his heart soared upward in a silent pulsing of gratitude to God.

Tom gazed across the whole Langdon spread and surveyed it with a new eyes. It stretched out on all four sides of him and beyond what he could see.

To the north, the main ranch rambled expansively. Heat waves shimmered in the glaring afternoon sun from the roofs of its several large barns, corrals, stables, and the squat, sprawling ranch house. Nelson would be there now in the ranch office going over the books.

Marriage to Laura had fired Nelson with such confidence he had surprised even himself and had discovered within an acute business sense and innate knack for bookkeeping. Therefore, Zack put him in complete charge of the business side of the ranch, and his mother's long, fearful concern for her youngest son gave way to pride and open confidence and fostered a deep love and respect for her feisty daughter-in-law, Laura. Yes, the main ranch was in good hands.

Tom slowly turned south toward his own ranch with its growing barns and buildings. In another year, his spread would almost equal the main ranch in size. A satisfied smile settled on Tom's face as he savored the joy of ownership and success in breeding two prize stallions that rivaled the best in the East. His father would have been proud. It also gave him confidence he was moving in the right direction in his aim toward his father's reputation as a breeder of prize stallions.

Time and scene faded and a quiet humility settled over Tom. His father's voice seemed to echo in the wind. "If a man's life crop is small he evidently hasn't been a very good farmer." Only now Tom intuitively understood what his father had meant and knew he would be right proud if he saw his Circle Z now.

Tom turned to the west and felt a wave of sadness as he looked as Zack's beautiful house that stood halted and as empty as the shell of his marriage. When the first shock of impending divorce papers had arrived in the mail from Darcy's father, Zack would have lost all incentive to live if it hadn't been for Baby Zack. Tom watched his older brother withdraw even from his own family. He and Zack had always shared their successes or hurts, but now no one or nothing seemed to penetrate Zack's deep pain at Darcy's rejection.

At first, his brother had taken Baby Zack on long walks or horseback rides. Then abruptly he had cooped himself up in his office at Harness for weeks. Finally, he went to Boston in the middle of a snowstorm to talk to Darcy, but neither his wife nor her father gave him audience. When Zack returned home, his pain had hung like a heavy, dark cloud over the whole family. Tom had ached for him so. The whole family had prayed.

Finally, Tom's gaze turned to the land in the east that had belonged to his dead brother, Doug. It had been deeded over to his only daughter, Genevieve. From where Tom stood now it looked as if a swarm of busy ants scrambled over a partially finished house that had seemingly sprouted overnight on top of a small rise on the land. Tom grinned. It had taken a determined shove from six-year-old Lars plus constant coaxing from that persistent boy before Tex had finally gathered up enough courage to ask Lily to marry him. Now Lars proudly declared to everyone, "Tex is gonna be my pa!" Tom even noticed a new, softened look about Lily.

Tom grinned. "Yep," he said aloud, "Mother is right. Love does have a way of overcoming the worst obstacles."

Now all the women were in a flurry of sewing, cleaning, baking, buzzing, and busying themselves with whatever it was women seem to have to do to get ready for a wedding.

Even nose-to-the-grindstone Smitty had been generous in allowing several of the cowhands free time to help Tex build his new ranch house. It almost seemed to have mushroomed overnight! " 'Course," the cowboys had joked at Tex, "we're only helpin' to get rid o' ya out of the bunkhouse so's there'll be some grub left fer the rest of us ta eat fer a change."

Tex took their joshing in good fun. He knew none of the boys meant a word of it. If the truth were known, Tex guessed they were a bit jealous of his good fortune, but they would never have let on.

So, in no time at all a shell of four walls and a roof stood perched on top of a good-sized root cellar. A well had been dug, and Tex assured Lily of a good supply of water.

"A roof over my head and a well with water are the only two things I really need to start with," Lily had commented to Tex. "The good Lord will provide the rest as we need it."

Movement at his own ranch caught Tom's eye, and he whistled for Tinder. Mary Lou must be back home. The obedient horse trotted to his master's side and stood. Tom rubbed his forelock, patted Tinder's neck, mounted, reined him toward the path at the edge of the top, then trustingly gave him his head to seek his own footholds and choose his way back down.

When they finally reached level ground, man and animal seemed to be of the same mind to get home. At Tom's prompting Tinder broke into a frisky gallop and hightailed it toward the barn and a drink of water. Tom saw the small form of his wife emerge from the cabin door, look in his direction, then turn and walk back into the cabin.

∪

Mary Lou opened the oven door, grabbed a couple of hot pads to remove the baked bread from the oven, and tipped the loaves out of their pans onto the wooden racks Tom had made for her last Christmas. She rubbed the crusty, fragrant loaves with a light coating of bacon grease then covered them with a cloth to soften the crust. She pulled her hanky out of her apron pocket, mopped her brow, and gladly stepped outside to catch a breath of cooler air. She faced the mountain, shaded her squinty eyes with her hands, searched for the tiny speck of her husband, and spotted him halfway down the mountainside.

She ran her hands over her hair to smooth its straying locks and sat down on her "restin' chair" as Tom called the old kitchen chair just outside her kitchen door. All was ready. Chicken stew simmered on her stove, awaiting dumplings. Mary Lou sighed. She'd just set a spell and seize the reward of a few precious moments at home by herself. There would be plenty of time after Tom got home to go down and get the twins from the main ranch. They always protested coming home at any time and much preferred being left at the main ranch to play with their cousins. Mary Lou grinned. They were now probably eating supper at their grandmother's table. She sighed and settled. It had been a long day—a long week of solid work. She and Tom could do with a quiet supper at home. Tom's face had looked strained and tired at breakfast that morning. Even the night's sleep had not erased the strain lines from his face. On top of the daily work of the ranch and helping to finish Tex and Lily's home, Tom was also deep in plans to build a new framed house for his own family.

Mary Lou looked forward to having more bedrooms and a dining room. She knew it would be such a help to be able to keep a table dressed and ready for company, as Allena did at the main ranch. Besides, she needed her kitchen table to work on. Tom and the cowboys promised Tex they would finish Tex and Lily's house so they and the children could get settled in after the wedding. Then the men would come and work on their house.

Mary Lou's gaze followed the moving speck of Tom and Tinder as they made their cautious descent toward the bottom of the mountain. She knew exactly when Tinder found his footing on level ground. From a snail's pace, he moved with a burst of speed and turned toward home.

She raised her eyes to the late afternoon sun. The quiet moment suddenly swelled her heart with love toward her heavenly Father for His gifts of a good, loving husband, two healthy children, a home, and a large loving family. Never in her wildest dreams could she have imagined her life to become what it had. Tears welled and spilled. Her heart and spirit soared her thanks to God for His love and kindness to her. Then it was almost as if The Lord received her praise then returned it to rest on her with a blessing of peace. "My cup runneth over," she said aloud and looked up. "Thank You, Father."

When Tom was near enough and she knew he could see her, she stood out a ways from the cabin and waved her arms over her head. Tom removed his Stetson and circled it high in answer; then Tinder broke into a full gallop.

By rights, instead of resting, she should have gone to get the twins. But there were so few times when she and Tom were alone during the day. She selfishly decided to snatch another hour so she and Tom could have a quiet supper together. Then they would both go to the main ranch for the twins.

Chapter 3

A few weeks later as Tom approached the barn he heard a roar of laughter from the cowboys inside. Suddenly Tex hoofed it out the door, his face the color of a ripe tomato. He looked mighty mad.

"What's up, Tex?"

"Nothin'."

"If it's the cowboys joshin' you, don't pay attention to them. They're jealous that it isn't one of them that's getting married next week." Tom fell in step with Tex as he hustled toward the corral. "Wanna take a ride and cool off?"

A quick, sharp nod spoke Tex's consent.

They saddled their mounts in silence, and the routine job of saddling his horse seemed to calm Tex. His jaw relaxed, and he glanced sideways at Tom now and again. A half-grin finally crossed his face.

They rode off at a smooth, easy trot until the barns were out of sight then slowed to a walk.

"I never was good at joshin'," Tex commented. "When I was growin' up, my pa didn't allow no foolishness—"

Tom laughed. "Aw, Tex, don't let them get to you. In one week they will be green-eyed, watching you head home to your own place with a nice home-cooked meal and a pretty woman awaitin'—and don't let them tell you any different. Come on, Tex, they're just trying to get a rise out of you."

Tex grinned. "Well, they did."

The men turned their horse in the direction of the new house being erected on the land straight ahead.

"The roof will be finished tomorrow, and Lily wants to start moving some stuff in already. But—there's so much more to do." The tone of Tex's voice bespoke bewildered confusion.

Tom laughed. "Tex, you gotta learn that a woman has to settle. We men are used to sleeping on the ground with a saddle for a pillow and a blanket wrapped around us to keep warm. My father told me women like it to be soft and smell clean and soaplike. Mother calls it 'nesting.'"

Embarrassed, Tex ducked his head, nodded, and grinned.

They rode together in silence, watching Tex and Lily's new home loom closer and closer.

Tom thought back to when he and Mary Lou were married. It certainly hadn't been the usual wedding! Before it all ended happily ever after, he remembered wondering whether he or Glenn would end up as her husband. Tom grinned. He understood all too well the anxiety Tex was going through. Even in a normal wedding, a man taking on a wife was a big step.

"You have a mother and father someplace, Tex? I've never heard you mention them. I'm sure they would like to know you are marrying a good woman."

The *clip-clop* of the horses' hooves filled the silence for a short piece, then, voice husky, Tex said, "My pa was killed in the Civil War and my ma in an Indian attack when we was comin' west with the wagon train. I was only seven then so the family we was ridin' with just took me in. They was good folks. They treated me kindly, just like their own."

Tom's eyes widened and he suppressed a grin. That was the longest speech Tom had ever heard Tex make since he'd hired him. "Soon as I was eleven I hooked up with some cowpunchers, and they learned me the tricks. Been on my own ever since."

"So that's why you're such a good cowhand! I know I'm right proud to have you a part of the Circle Z."

Tex shot an appreciative glance at Tom, ducked his head, and grinned in embarrassment. "Yeah, I like it, too."

They plodded along in silence. Tom turned toward Tex. "I don't know about you, but my stomach's telling me the women will probably have dinner about ready." Tom said. "Let's find out."

They swung their horses, called a "tch," and headed them toward the new ranch house. The animal's hooves pounded the ground in rythmic cadence as the new house grew larger and larger.

Lily stepped out the open doorway, shaded her eyes with her hands, then suddenly waved both arms over her head.

The men pressed their mounts into a moderate gallop till they reached the new sturdy hitching rail, dismounted, and flopped their reins around it.

Lars came running out the door to Tex. "Where you been? Lily wouldn't let me go find you."

"I was working at the ranch, Lars. Did you help Lily with chores around here, like I told ya?"

"Yes, he did," Lily answered. "He carried water and chopped some wood and—"

Tex smiled and tousled the boy's hair. "You're going to be some good, big, strong cowpuncher come one of these days."

Lars stretched taller and straightened his shoulders. His face beamed and he followed Tex around the house.

Lily greeted Tom. "Mary Lou came today, and thanks to her we have the wedding all planned." She smiled and lowered her eyelids.

Tom looked at the pretty woman standing in front of him, and his mind harkened back to the day his brother, Doug, had brought Lily home as his wife. She had been dressed in the revealing clothes all the saloon girls wore. Many people who knew her then would be hard put to recognize the beautiful woman before him today. Tom marveled at what God and the love of a family had done for this one soul.

His gaze caught hers.

Lily smiled, then lowered her eyes.

Was she remembering, too? Was he embarrassing her? "Well, Lily," he asked expectantly, "when did you decide the wedding day will be?"

"Mother said we could probably figure a week or so, and that Tex had better see to the legal fixings." Lily blushed.

Did Tom imagine it or had he heard Tex gulp?

"My dress is all ready, and Hattie has even begun some of the cooking." Suddenly, Lily shot an anxious look toward Tex. "Did you tend to all the legal papers today?"

Tex turned and shot a desperate look of "help!" to Tom.

Tom laughed and patted Tex on the back. "Don't worry, Lily. You women take care of the wedding and home fussin', and we men will have all the right papers to make it legal."

Lily flushed and gazed at her feet. "I'm sorry." Harking back to Lily's marriage to Doug, it was only natural Lily would have some anxiety. Even though dead, Tom's brother Doug stamped even this marriage with his usual unpleasant mark.

Movement turned Tom's head. A wagon was leaving the main ranch. Even though it was too far away to see clearly, he figured Jeff, the bunkhouse cook, was at the reins of the chuck wagon, probably driving up with dinner for everyone. He turned to Tex. "Seems we got here right on time. Here comes dinner."

The gentle *clop, clop* of a horse's hooves caught Tom's attention. Tom hurried to lift Mary Lou from her horse.

All work ceased. Everyone washed up and hunted for a seat. There were only two chairs made, so the men settled long boards across wooden horses and nail kegs. By the time the chuck wagon arrived, all were ready and stood waiting. Everyone dished up from the wagon, and the makeshift benches were soon filled.

Tom helped his mother and the children get settled, then sat Tex at the head of his first dinner table in his own home and sat down beside him.

Tex stared straight ahead, his face flushed, then he turned desperate eyes to Tom.

Tom read their message, grinned, and glanced around at the expectant faces. "Well, now, I can't think of a better time to put a blessing on this house than right now. Let's bow our heads."

A hush fell as all heads bowed.

Tom raised his face to heaven. "Father God, we thank Thee for Thy blessings of home and family. We thank Thee for the blessing of this land You gave to my father for his family to use as their home on this earth. Now we ask Thy blessing upon this new home and the new family it will shelter. Thank You for this good food prepared for us. May it make us strong in Thy service. In Jesus' name, Amen."

Everyone looked up and Tom noticed a sparkle of tears in his mother's eyes as they rested upon him.

She blinked, smiled, and nodded her approval.

Tom grinned in return. A tender memory surfaced of his father's dignity and command even at a dinner table. Father had always said grace, but every so often he would call on one of the boys to do it. In turn they had each squirmed and sputtered but gradually learned to pray at the table. Only seventeen at the time of his father's death, Tom had been still too young to appreciate what an important role a man and father plays in a family.

Suddenly Tom sensed the tremendous loss his mother must have felt when his father died, so much so that she had never allowed anyone to sit in his chair or take his place at the dinner table, a visible reminder of his absence.

Zack had said grace until he left to go east to study law. Doug had always refused to say grace or wasn't home, so it had filtered down to Tom. Funny, Tom had never thought about it before. Now as he watched his mother shift into her role as gracious hostess, even at a makeshift, wooden table in a half-built house, a rush of love and respect for her flooded him. As always she sat with an endearing, cheerful smile, a concern for her family's needs always uppermost in her mind. *O God*, Tom prayed, *give my mother a double blessing.*

"Tom! Don't you want any of these potatoes?" Mary Lou asked for what must have been the second time.

Tom snapped back to the present and grabbed the pan of browned potatoes stretched toward him. He dumped several spoonfuls on his plate and passed them to Tex. Their eyes met in a new understanding.

Chapter 4

T he twins took off at a run ahead of Mary Lou as they neared the main ranch house.

Suddenly the ranch kitchen door swung open and Lily marched out wearing a face like a storm cloud. She stopped abruptly when she saw the twins, scooped up each one as they reached her, swung them in a high circle, then replaced them on the ground.

They squealed and made a giggling beeline for the kitchen door. Like a little gentleman, after much training from his father, Tommy opened the door for Beth to go through, followed her in, and ran to Baby Zack.

Lily, her face like a mask, walked briskly toward Mary Lou. When they met, Lily linked her arm through Mary Lou's. "Want to go for a walk?" Lily's eyes pleaded, her lips trembled, and the irritation in her voice told Mary Lou she needed not only to walk off some steam but to talk it out as well.

Mary Lou pointed toward the clump of Texas umbrella trees. "Why don't you go out there and sit in the shade and cool off a bit? I'll be ready to set a spell as soon as I say hello to Mother and Hattie." She squeezed Lily's hand for assurance as she left her.

Mary Lou entered the kitchen and immediately guessed Lily's problem. Allena was busy bathing and dressing Genevieve.

Hattie, with hanging floury hands, bent over Beth, who had evidently thrown her arms around Hattie's skirts to give her a hug. Tommy already had his arm around Baby Zack's shoulders. Both were eyeing two little wooden toy horses Wilmot was playing with; Tex had carved them for him.

"Hello," Mary Lou called as she entered. "Just what you need, a couple of more children."

"The more the better," Allena said. "Now I understand what my grandmother used to mean when my brother and I came to visit. She used to call us the "joys of her life.'" She made a wide sweep with her arm. "Now these are my joys."

Mary Lou stood beside Allena as she washed and splashed with Genevieve. "Looks like you're busy right now; I met Lily as I came in. I need to ask her a couple questions about the wedding and see how our bride-to-be is holding up."

"Not too well," Allena commented. She lifted Genevieve out of the bath pan and enfolded her in a large flannel blanket.

Mary Lou smiled. "Shucks, all brides are allowed the jitters. I know I had them. Heavens! It's the biggest step any woman ever takes." Mary Lou bent over and kissed the sweet baby Genevieve, who wiggled impatiently while her grandmother rubbed her dry.

Hattie glanced from one to the other like the wise old bird she was but never opened her mouth.

Mary Lou found Lily sitting on the ground with her back leaning against a tree trunk that sheltered her from the hot sun with its dense shade of motionless leaves. She sensed Lily's distress, dropped to her knees, lifted Lily's downturned face, and smiled. Lily pinned an intense, troubled look on Mary Lou but didn't speak.

Mary Lou sat down beside her. *She's very angry about something.* It was written on her face and confirmed by the rigid set of her body, arms crossed tight in containment.

"Was Grandmother bathing *her* baby granddaughter?" Lily spit out the words.

Mary Lou heard Lily's irritation, felt her hurt. "Yes."

"Sometimes I wonder whose baby Genevieve is. Hers or mine."

So it had finally come to the boiling point. Mary Lou had expected it long before this and had admired Lily's generosity and patience in sharing her little daughter with her grandmother. Ever since Lily and Genevieve had been found, Mary Lou had noticed a growing tension between her mother-in-law and sister-in-law.

She understood Allena's joy in caring for her precious granddaughter after having longed for a baby girl all the while she raised four boys.

Mary Lou also recalled Allena's delight in Laura before she and Nelson announced their intention to be married. It had been difficult for the family to understand Allena's vigorous opposition to Laura and Nelson's marriage. Though Nelson's body was not strong, his spirit had displayed vigorous strength. He had stood adamant and informed his mother that if Laura wasn't welcomed as his wife on the Circle Z then they would live elsewhere.

To be honest, even Mary Lou had seriously questioned the wisdom of their marriage, but both she and Tom had supported Nelson and Laura because they loved each other and their love would surmount the obstacles. It had taken some strong talk to finally convince Allena that marriage would be a good thing for both of them.

To Allena's credit, after their first year she had acknowledged that Laura had given Nelson what she could never have given him. His manhood.

Lily suddenly covered her face with her hands, bowed her head, and let the tears roll. Her shoulders rose and fell with whimpering sobs.

Mary Lou slid an arm around her and sat quietly patting her shoulder, waiting for her to cry it out. What was it about women? Sometimes the only thing that relieved any situation was a good cry. Mama used to say tears were a blessing from God that gathered up all our hurts and washed them away.

Lily's sobs gradually subsided. She glanced up into Mary Lou's face and smiled through her embarrassment. "Just like some little child who runs to Mama with her hurts," she sniffed.

Mary Lou grinned, gave her an extra squeeze, pulled a handkerchief out of her apron pocket, and handed it to Lily. "I am a mama. In your case, I'm the handy substitute." She lifted Lily's face and looked into her teary eyes. "But after you and Tex are married, you'll find your most comforting place will be in your husband's arms. At least that is the way it has been for me." Mary Lou hadn't thought about that before but it was true. Early in their marriage Tom's arms became not only Mary Lou's place of love but of rest and peace also.

Suddenly an old memory crossed Mary Lou's mind. Even as child, she had never remembered any time ever seeing her father hold her mother in his arms! *Oh, Mama. How did you stand it? Pa was gone so much of the time...but even when he was there. . .* The precious love she shared with Tom overwhelmed her heart. She gazed into Lily's teary eyes and tried to spill some of her overflow of love into the agony of Lily's sadness.

Lily daubed her tears with Mary Lou's handkerchief and smiled feebly. "In all my life, I don't remember anyone's arms being there for me except for all the wrong reasons, so maybe I don't really know what I'm looking for."

Mary Lou laughed. "Oh, Lily, you are just having bride jitters. Lord willin', you will have the love you seek when you marry Tex. He worships the ground you walk on." Mary Lou laid her hand across Lily's. "Lily, forget about your past. Your past doesn't mean anything to him. It is truly past. Forget it! Tex loves you as you are, and you're the woman who loves him. That's what it takes to make a marriage, Lily, two people deeply in love, accepting and loving each other as they are, regardless of what they may have been. It won't work any other way."

Lily slowly nodded then glanced up, a new light of understanding shining in her misty eyes. She smiled and wiped away her tears. "I'm going to make Tex the best wife in the world."

Mary Lou nodded and gave Lily a reassuring pat. "I know you will. I'm happy for Tex, too, 'cause I remember the day a young cowboy named Tex helped me hang curtain rods when Tom and I were finishing up our cabin. I thanked him for his help and the good job he did. He smiled and wistfully spoke with yearning of wanting a wife and his own spread someday just like

Tom's. Just from the way he said it, I felt he would make some sweet, loving woman a good husband and began praying she would come."

Mary Lou cupped Lily's face in her hands. "You are that woman, Lily."

"Me!" Lily covered her face and shook her head. But—"

"No buts. Just love him. That's what he wants and needs. Let him know you love him. Tell him every day." Mary Lou laughed. "Lily, if you can't see the love pouring from that cowboy's eyes when he looks at you, you are blind! It has to be love with a lot of courage in Tex's heart to take on the job of not only caring for the woman he loves but to immediately assume a ready-made family of a baby and two orphan boys! Lily, you are a blessed woman!"

Lily stared at Mary Lou through her tears and slowly nodded acceptance of a new discovery. "Yes, I am," she said softly. Her lips parted in amazement. "I am!" She raised her eyes toward heaven. "Thank You, Lord, for giving me a family. Now I'm counting on You to help me to become the woman You want me to be."

"—and Tex needs," Mary Lou added.

The two women fell into each other's arms, hugged, rose, and walked back toward the house.

Suddenly, Lily stopped and nodded. "Perhaps now I understand how much Genevieve means to Mother. I am so thankful for Allena. I don't know where I would be today except for her. But Mary Lou, I just want to care for my baby. Is that so wrong?" she asked wistfully.

"Of course not. I understand how you feel, Lily. But you must also consider something else. Genevieve is Allena's only link to her dead son, regardless of how unruly a son he became. He gave her nothing but shame and heartache when he was alive. Remember, Genevieve is all that is left of her son Doug. That dear, sweet baby girl is the only blessing Doug ever gave her. That could be one reason whey she hovers over Genevieve." In a moment of silence between them, Mary Lou remembered harboring those same feelings toward Allena after her twins were born. She decided to tell Lily to help her understand.

"I remember how wonderful and gracious Mother was to me when Tom brought me home as his wife, sight unseen. To make things worse, I was the second strange new wife. Zack had arrived with Darcy six months or so before Tom brought me. Then Doug came home one morning married to you, a dance-hall girl. Lily, she's had some tough pills to swallow. But Allena is a strong lady with lots of love, and she graciously accepted us all under her roof and calls us her family."

Lily stared wide-eyed at Mary Lou. "I never knew. . ."

Mary Lou laughed. "Well, it isn't exactly dinner-table conversation! Not only that, Lily, but Tom and I lived in the main ranch house when we had the twins. I admit there were times I felt she monopolized them. She was so capable. I had been an only child and hadn't grown my new-mother wings yet. I learned so much from Allena. At that particular time, her loving concern and help were a lifeline for me."

Mary Lou cupped Lily's chin in her hand and looked directly into her misty eyes. "And I harbored some of your same feelings until we moved out of the main ranch into our own house."

Lily's wide eyes softened.

Mary Lou laughed. "Just wait, Lily. After you're married, you will have Genevieve all the time. You probably won't believe this now, but there will be days when you will be eager for Allena to come and take her away so you can get some of your work done in peace and quiet. She will become a blessing in disguise." A calm sigh of release softened the expression in Lily's eyes, and Mary Lou knew she had gotten her message across.

"So," Mary Lou patted Lily's hand, "can't you let your heart loan Genevieve to her grandmother for just a little while longer until you take her home with you and Tex after you are married?"

"I'm sorry." Lily bent her head. "I sound so ungrateful. I'm not—really —but I was afraid Genevieve wouldn't remember that *I'm* her mama. When she wakes every morning I have to fight to be the first one up to get her so I can change and dress her. The only time I get her is nursing time."

Mary Lou suddenly pulled Lily into the comfort of her mothering arms and cradled her as she would one of her twins. *Sometimes mothers have to mother other mamas.* The obvious truth of the thought startled her. Then she remembered Mama had said that.

"We aren't the only ones, Lily. My mama and aunt Tibby knew the agony of hurtful family feelings. They had been ripped away from their mama and disowned by their father's anger for what he called his daughters' disobedience. Their crime? They had chosen to marry the men they loved. Grandfather never accepted either of their marriages. Even their names were never allowed to be mentioned in his presence. I saw Grandmother only once when Mama, Aunt Tibby, and I went to Grandpa's funeral. Mama and Aunt Tibby found all the letters they had written to their mother and father hidden in an old trunk, unopened.

"And, of course, I've told you that my pa didn't approve or accept my marriage to Tom. It was only this past year when we traveled back to Kansas to visit my family that Pa accepted Tom as my husband and the father of his grandchildren. Pa had been a cowboy and had wanted someone better for me, he said. When he recognized what a good husband and father Tom is, and fell in love with his grandchildren, all was forgiven."

The memory of Pa with Beth and Tommy perched on his knees

brought tears to Mary Lou's eyes. How grateful she was for that sweet memory. "So you see, Lily, without Aunt Tibby and Aunt Nelda's blessings I wouldn't be where I am today, the wife of the man I love and the mother of our beautiful twins."

Lily's eyes stared wide with surprise. "I didn't know all that."

Mary Lou reached over, and with a fresh hanky out of her apron pocket, she patted Lily's teary cheek.

"I'm sorry," Lily said softly and sniffed. "I'm crying like a baby."

Mary Lou shook her head. "Nothing to be sorry about. Mama always said that every so often a woman has to have a good cry and doesn't need any reason except that she needs a good cry."

Lily's moist gaze clung to Mary Lou's. "Believe me, I love Mother Allena. If she told me once she has said a dozen times, 'I always wanted a daughter—' "

"And there is nothing wrong with that, Lily. But perhaps you ought to pray to learn to trust your new family. . ."

Lily pulled her own handkerchief out of her apron pocket and daubed her eyes, lifted her chin, and grinned. "I *am* Genevieve's mother and nothing can change that." She slowly shook her head back and forth.

Lily lifted her face toward the sky. "God, please forgive me for my selfishness. Nothing can change the fact that I am Genevieve's mother, but without this family, I would never have had her. Dear Jesus, teach me to give of me and mine as You gave Yourself for me."

"Amen," Mary Lou said softly. Both women rested in the quiet blessing that hung graciously in the air.

Abruptly, Lily squared her shoulders. "Enough of this. I've had my little pity party." She put her arm around Mary Lou. "Thank you for giving me your shoulder to cry on."

Mary Lou grinned and hugged her. "That's what sisters are for."

Lily nodded. Her eyes held a fresh knowing.

The two girls walked slowly back to the ranch house. When they entered the kitchen, Genevieve squealed and toddled toward her mother, arms outstretched, "Ma-ma!"

Lily picked her up and swung her around. "Here's my sweet girl. My, aren't you pretty! Your grandma made you look so beautiful."

Allena turned from dishing up oatmeal and smiled. "Come, breakfast is late, so let's all sit down. Jess fixed breakfast real early for the men so they could get up to your house, and we will all take dinner up in the chuck wagon to eat up there. Hattie and I promised to bring chicken and biscuits and pies."

Mary Lou watched her mother-in-law and Hattie move from stove to table with bowls of oatmeal. Women and children took their places, grace was said, and the new day began.

Before the week was out, Jess drove the ladies to Harness for final supplies for the wedding.

Lily's simple but beautiful wedding dress, covered with a sheet, hung on a hook on Allena's bedroom wall. All was ready. Lily and Tex would be married on the coming Saturday.

Chapter 5

The ranch kitchen door swung wide as Lily and Genevieve greeted the bright morning sun, squinted, and walked toward it hand in hand.

"Fwowers, Ma-ma?" Genevieve asked as she toddled beside her mother. Her curly, brown hair bounced on her shoulders.

"Yes, we will pick flowers. Let's see if we can pick a nice bouquet, for me to carry when I marry Tex tomorrow, and one for you to carry in your basket, and some extra flowers to decorate the house." Lily grinned. *Rare is the bride who goes into the field to pick her own wedding bouquet with her daughter skipping at her side.*

Genevieve suddenly released her mother's hand and ran pell-mell toward a cluster of Texas bluebonnets swaying in the soft morning wind.

"Fwowers, Ma-ma!" The toddler stood poised for her mother's response.

"Yes, they're beautiful. Pick some of those." Lily hugged her shawl around her body to keep out the gusty early morning air that still carried some of its night chill.

It didn't seem to daunt Genevieve's enthusiasm. The delighted child flitted from flower to flower like a selective butterfly, picking some with long stems and roots, others only inches from their blossom.

Lily smiled and squelched a reprimand. How dare she spoil the exuberance of her daughter just because her emotions were on edge? The thought of this being her last day to call the main ranch house "home" sent scary shivers up and down her back and resurrected memories of being passed from pillar to post most of her childhood, depending on who claimed her. The Circle Z was the only place she had ever felt any sense of security.

From that first frightening day when Doug brought her home from the saloon as his wife, her life had taken a new shape. Lily had thanked God for a mother-in-law who with gracious poise had taken all in stride and had accepted Lily as her son's wife regardless of who and what she had been. She knew it hadn't been easy. At first Lily remembered how confused and unhappy she had been, never knowing what to expect from Doug. He had dumped her on his family shortly after they were married, went back to the life he'd always led in town at the saloon, and finally spent little or no time

371

with her or the ranch.

Gradually, surrounded by the love of his family, who had accepted her as Doug's wife, Lily gratefully had relaxed. Allena encouraged her to become her real self. In reality, who was she? Lily hadn't really known.

But it had been the first time in her life Lily had felt what it was like to be safe and loved. Allena had treated her with the same respect she gave her other daughters-in-law. Lily remembered living with her heart in her mouth her first month at the ranch, waiting to be thrown out. Even now, on the day before her wedding, she remained completely overwhelmed by the love of the Langdon family and their loyalty to each other.

Strange, she hadn't thought of Doug for a long time. Today, for some reason her mind kept returning to that horrible morning Doug had brought her home after their hasty marriage by a judge. She would never have gone through with it if she hadn't been so desperate, willing to do anything to escape her life at the brothel. When she finally stood in front of his mother, Hattie, and Mary Lou, their skirts to the ground, she remembered clutching her black fringed shawl around her bare shoulders and arms and wishing her dress had been at least below her knees. Even now she inwardly cringed remembering how uncomfortable and out of place she had felt. But Doug didn't change. She saw very little of him since he spent the same amount of his time at the saloon. At first, Lily couldn't figure out why he seemed to want to hurt his mother so much. It took only a few months of married life to discover that Doug hurt everything he touched and that he had no more consideration of her as his wife than he had for his mother or any other person, man or woman. He had moved in and out of her life as it pleased him, never had considered her feelings, told her where he was going, where he had been, what he was doing, nor when he would return; nor did he leave any money for her needs. His only gifts to her had been to bring her to his home and give her Genevieve.

Lily shook her head. What on earth had prompted her mind to dig up all those unpleasant memories on the day before her wedding? She thought she had deeply buried her old life, but periodically it rose to haunt her.

Allena had helped her with that, too. After a particularly humiliating time with Doug, Mother had told her to bury all her hurts and anger in a grave of forgiveness, then helped her do it. It had been the first time in her life that Lily had known what it was to feel a mother's loving care and concern.

Yet Lily had tossed and turned last night, apprehensive on her next-to-last night under the safe, loving Langdon roof. The old feeling of impermanence and insecurity that had dogged her all her life snuck up and scratched for entrance to shake her present security. Did she really know Tex well enough to trust herself and her daughter into his care? Were most brides as frightened as she was? Her eyes followed her daughter darting here and there as Genevieve carefully picked each flower, ran back, and stuffed another stem into her hand.

A sudden sweet remembrance brought to mind the tenderness of the man she would marry tomorrow, who shyly expressed his love in so many endearing ways. Lily raised her face and heart toward heaven. *Heavenly Father, I'm just learning about You. I want to be a good wife and mother to Tex and Genevieve and the boys. Allena and Mary Lou tell me that You want the best for Your children no matter who they are or how they may have sinned and that's why Jesus died on the cross. Thank You for a good man to care for me and my children. Help us to also give him the love he needs and deserves for marrying us.* Lily looked toward heaven. *But dear God, You'll have to show me how.* Lily wiped her eyes and bowed her head in silence for a moment. *Thank You, Jesus, Amen.*

A sweet peace of acceptance and love soothed the trembling beat of her heart. She opened her eyes. A feeling of peace spread all through her. She glanced around for her daughter, who was nowhere in sight.

Suddenly a mop of curls popped up from the center of a bevy of Texas bluebonnets.

Lily motioned Genevieve to come.

Hair and blossoms flying, Genevieve came running to her mother.

Lily stooped, laid her bouquet on the ground, and spread her arms. Genevieve, tinkling with childish laughter, a spindly bouquet squeezed in her tiny fist, sprayed a trail of escaped flowers as she ran laughing into her mother's arms.

Lily held her close. The Bible verse Allena had read that morning during devotions spoke within: "My cup runneth over." Tears coarsed down Lily's cheeks, tears for happiness she never knew existed. Her cup was running over.

Genevieve backed away, concerned. "Ma-ma cry?"

Lily cupped her child's concerned face. "Something else you'll learn someday, my child. There are tears of hurt and tears of happiness. Grandma calls them happy tears." She smiled broadly as her daughter's troubled face brightened.

Genevieve laughed, "Hap-py 'ears, hap-py 'ears."

Lily kissed her daughter's cheek and took her hand. "I think we have enough flowers, don't you? Let's go home and give some to Grandma."

Genevieve grabbed her mother's outstretched hand and pulled her in the direction of the ranch house.

On the ranch porch Allena stood, her hand shading her eyes, as two small bouncing dots gradually grew into Lily and Genevieve. They were coming. All was ready for Lily's wedding tomorrow. Only a few burlap bags, baskets, and wooden boxes containing the last of Lily's and Genevieve's belongings stood waiting on the porch for transport. This morning Lars and Wilmot's last belongings had been taken by Tex up to their new cabin. Lily's wedding dress hung on a hook in Allena's bedroom, not to be seen until she wore it.

Watching them come, an unwelcome sadness clutched Allena's heart. After Tex and Lily's honeymoon she would lose four members of her family from under her roof. She would miss the children. But there were still six left at the main ranch: she, Nelson and Laura, Zack, Baby Zack, and Hattie.

Allena smiled. But not for long. She clasped her arms around her middle as if to hold and nurture the special secret that Nelson and Laura had been unable to keep so decided to tell only her. She had felt honored, included. They had sworn her to secrecy then told her of the precious child Laura carried within her. They had wanted to keep it to themselves until after Lily's wedding to make the announcement a special moment for the family as well as for them.

Allena had been ecstatic with the news and daily praised God and prayed for a healthy child to be born with two good legs and a strong body. She fought herself to keep from returning to the memories of the years of working with Nelson's legs.

Periodically, when fear swamped her, she immediately prayed to a Father God she knew could deliver a strong, healthy child to Nelson and Laura. Allena asked forgiveness for her weak faith and leaned heavily on her Lord for belief that it could be so.

When she walked back into the house it seemed strangely quiet. *Life keeps alive with each generation.* The words reverberated in the room. Allena swung around almost expecting to see her husband, Zachary, standing at the door. He used to say that. Her heart pounded with the words.

Allena closed her eyes and pictured her husband, tall, stately, handsome, his penetrating eyes searching her very being. "Yes, Zachary," she answered aloud, "just as our children replace us." She pursed her lips and tried to suppress a sudden rush of tears, but they had a mind of their own and cascaded over her cheeks. "Oh my dear husband, I miss you so." She drew her handkerchief from her apron pocket, quickly daubed away her tears, and stood smiling as Lily and Genevieve walked into the ranch yard with their arms full of flowers.

Genevieve toddled toward her grandmother with a fist full of flowers valiantly struggling to hold up their drooping heads. Her little brows frowned when she saw her grandma wiping her eyes. Her little face showed concern. "Gamma cry?"

Allena spread a smile across her face. "I'm so happy to see you that I am crying happy tears."

"Hap-py 'ears!" she called back to her mother. Lily smiled and entered the gate, a large basket of flowers in each hand. As much as she loved this ranch, she was anxious for the time when she, Tex, Lars, Wilmot, and Genevieve would all be neatly settled in their new home, a dream Lily had never dared dream before. For the first time, she thanked God for Doug. Without him realizing it, God had used him to help her dreams come true. Now Tex in his shy, awkward way loved her with a kind of love she never knew existed. Lily felt clean and pure for the first time in her life. She now understood Mary Lou's favorite hymn, "God works in a mysterious way His wonders to perform."

The heavenly Father's current wonders in Lily's life had released a new sense of peace and meaning for Lily. It settled over her like a warm, comforting blanket.

Chapter 6

The morning sun crept through the window and kissed Lily Langdon's eyelids to announce her special day. They raised slowly, drowsily, then opened wide.

My wedding day!

She glanced at her sleeping daughter, quietly folded back the covers so as not to wake Genevieve, slowly slid her bare feet to the floor, and stood up.

Genevieve didn't move.

Lily dressed quickly, slipped out of the room, and hurried to the kitchen.

Allena glanced up from her bowl of oatmeal and smiled. "Good morning, Lily. Happy is the bride the sun shines on, and it's shining brightly today! How'd you sleep?" She patted the chair next to hers. "Come, sit here so Hattie and I can fuss a bit over the bride."

Lily leaned and planted a kiss on Allena's cheek, much to Allena's surprise, then slid onto her chair. "Believe it or not, I had a good night's sleep. All I had to do was lay my head on the pillow! Even Genevieve slept quiet as a mouse all night. Probably exhausted after our running all over yesterday picking flowers!"

Allena nodded. "I remember one time I complained to my mother about being tired and about having to work all the time. Her crisp comment was 'I think God planned it that way, otherwise we'd all be lazier than sin.'"

"Here we are," Hattie hustled from the stove with two breakfast plates, placed one each in front of Allena and Lily, hurried back for her own plate, and took her place.

The three women bowed their heads.

"Good morning, Father," Allena began. "We thank You for this new day and ask Your special blessing upon Lily and Tex as You join them together today as man and wife. We all rejoice with them. Thank You for Your constant provision for our needs, and we ask Your blessing upon us. In Jesus' name, Amen."

The women ate slowly, with none of the usual chatter. They had worked very hard all week to get to this point and relaxed over their breakfast in the assurance they had done their task well.

Allena looked up at Lily. "Do you have any idea how much we are all going to miss you and the children living here?"

Lily laughed. "I should think you would be glad for a breather! It isn't as if we're moving far away. We're about the same distance as Tom and Mary Lou." Lily laughed again. "Don't worry Mother, I think Laura and Nelson being here will keep things stirred up. Especially Laura. She has enough ideas and energy to keep everything and everyone going around in circles."

Allena nodded and laughed. "That she has! Always been that way." Allena harkened back to shortly after she and her husband had purchased the Circle Z, a pretty little eight-year-old neighbor girl began riding her horse to the Circle Z on any pretense. It wasn't long before Allena was enjoying her young visitor and indulged herself by pretending Laura was her own. Now Laura was married to one of her sons. Allena had learned early in life that the Lord always has His own special way of answering His children's prayers.

The women ate quietly, savoring a few rare moments of peace and quiet before everything broke loose.

Lily wasn't the least bit hungry and picked at the breakfast in fear of disturbing the butterflies in her stomach.

Hattie, first one done, began clearing up. "Jess'n the cowboys have had the beeves strung up over the fire since way before daylight. I could smell them early this mornin'. They should be just right by noon. They got them tables all set up in nothin' flat in the ranch yard." Hattie carried dishes to the drainboard and peered out the window. "Looks like the good Lord is going to bless the weddin' with a nice day." Hattie smiled. "In town, yesterday, people were talkin' about the weddin'. From what I hear everybody's lookin' forward to it and said they're comin'."

Lily smiled. "They're very kind. Ruthella sent word with one of the cowboys yesterday that since she lives so close to the church she'll pick some wildflowers and take them to the church early this morning, and she will make sure everything is ready so we won't have to get to the church till half an hour before the wedding. If we leave here at ten that should be enough time, don't you think?"

"Plenty," Allena answered and couldn't contain her smile. She had never seen Lily so nervous or talkative. She thought back to the first time she met Lily, the day Doug brought her home as his bride. How outraged she had been at her son for stooping to marry one of those shameful saloon girls and bringing such disgrace on his family.

Allena now gazed at the lovely young woman beside her. She bore little resemblance to the woman Doug brought home that day. *Why is it we are always surprised at what God can do in the life of one of His children?* He had known Lily's true heart from her beginning and in His mercy had made a way, even through a wayward son, to give her the opportunity to escape her life of sin. A humbling thought settled. *God does that for all of us, if we let Him.*

After a hurried breakfast, the three women brought out their week's work of food preparation, all ready for the planned feast after the wedding. The pungent odor of roast beef began to permeate the air. Pans of fruited wedding cake stood covered on the sideboard. Sawhorses and board tables had been set up in the yard and were covered with white sheets, waiting to hold the special gifts of food brought by neighbors and friends. Every woman in each family would share the best from her kitchen.

After a slow start the early morning hours flew by; then it was suddenly time to get ready for church.

Lily went to her room to dress. Her hands shook as she donned her stockings, white drawers, and chemise. She swung her petticoat and long, blue skirt over her head, buttoning them at the waist and straightening the draped folds in the front of her overskirt. It curved gracefully over her hips. Her white basque had soft lace around the high neck collar with matching lace on the cuffs. She, Hattie, and Allena had worked long hours. They had sent through the mail for sewing patterns from the Butterick Publishing Company in New York. It was the first time they had ever worked with a store-bought, ready-made pattern. The tissue-paper pattern had been folded in an instruction sheet that even showed how to lay the pattern on the material. It had been a great help, and the women decided they would send for other style patterns in their sizes. The cutting and sewing had been much easier than to mold the cloth over the body to cut it to size or to use another dress for a pattern, as they usually did. All three women were pleased at the fine style and fit of the finished dress.

Lily had just slipped the last shell hairpin into her thick chestnut bun, piled high on top of her head, when Mary Lou walked into the room with a wreath of flowers she had made.

"Here, I thought this would look right pretty around your bun."

Lily watched in the mirror as Mary Lou placed it on her head like a crown.

Allena smiled, clasped her hands together, and nodded. "Lily! You are a beautiful bride! Tex is a lucky man."

Lily's eyes filled with tears and she lowered her head. She had always denied herself of the luxury of crying, but determine as she would, her eyes took on a mind of their own, spilling tears in profusion over her cheeks and leaving sprays of damp spots on her wedding dress.

Allena gently folded Lily into her arms. "Cry, Lily, and wash all your former hurts away till you remember them no more. Praise God! He is giving you a chance to be the woman He made you to be."

At ten-thirty, the three women were ready and waiting when Tom and the children drove into the yard in the wagon to pick up Mary Lou and Hattie and take them to church.

Right behind them came Tex, driving a surrey borrowed from a neighbor. He was all dressed up in a brand new pair of black pants, a fancy cowboy shirt, string tie, a shiny new pair of cowboy boots, and his Stetson tipped slightly over one ear.

Tom raised his eyebrows and grinned.

That grin turned Tex's face beet red.

Tex helped Lily into the backseat of the surrey. His eyes brushed past hers like a scared rabbit.

Lily's heart lifted a prayer of thanks to God for His gift of love to her in this shy cowboy who would soon be her husband. He hustled to the other side of the surrey to assist Allena into the seat beside her.

Lily's and Allena's eyes met. Allena reached over and patted Lily's hand for reassurance. To Lily it was a steadying touch of love and acceptance.

The morning sun spread its soft, gentle rays of warm blessing on everyone as the carriages hurried along the road. When they turned into the churchyard it was already more than half fill with horses, buggies, and wagons of smiling neighbors all dressed in their Sunday best. A wedding was a big event in any community. It enabled everyone to take a breather from endless work, giving respite from thankless tasks that never seemed to end and provided the opportunity to socialize with their friends and neighbors.

Tom pulled his wagon around to the side of the church. Tex followed.

Ruthella, all smiles, hurried to meet the bride and groom. "Everything is ready," she assured them and turned to Mary Lou. "Your seats are all up front in your usual place."

Another buggy turned into the churchyard. It was the Reverend Milfield, the only clergyman in the area who could marry them legally. Otherwise they would have had to be married by a judge. After Lily's experience with Doug and a judge, she had made only one request—to be married by a minister. She was now a Christian and had felt it only proper.

Reverend Milfield bowed politely to the ladies, then asked to speak to the bridegroom. Tex, Tom, and the Reverend stepped off to the side and talked a few minutes. Tex nodded his head several times, then Tom walked over, spoke a word to Lily, then went into the church and took his seat next to Mary Lou and his mother on the family bench.

The Reverend took his place.

Finally, the organ pealed a few strong chords, and Ruthella moved into the familiar strains of the wedding march. At the back of the church Lily looked up at Tex and drank in the reassuring caress of love from his warm gaze. He offered her his arm, and they walked down the aisle together and stood before the minister.

The Reverend Milfield began in ponderous tones, "Dearly Beloved, we are assembled here in the presence of God to join this man and this woman in holy marriage which is instituted of God, regulated by His commandments, blessed by our Lord Jesus Christ and to be held in honor among all men. Let us, therefore, reverently remember that God has established and sanctified marriage for the welfare and happiness of mankind.

"Our Savior has declared that a man shall forsake his father and mother and cleave unto his wife. He has instructed those who enter into this relationship to cherish a mutual esteem and love; to bear with each other's infirmities and weaknesses; to comfort each other in sickness, trouble, and sorrow; in honesty and industry to provide for each other and for their household in temporal things; to pray for and encourage each other in the things which pertain to God; and to live together as heirs of the grace of life."

The Reverend turned to Tex and Lily. "Forasmuch as you have come hither to be made one in this blessed estate, I charge you both, that if either of you—" the minister then looked out upon the assembly, "or anyone know any reason why you may not rightly be joined together in marriage, you now acknowledge it. Be well assured that if any persons are joined together otherwise than as God's Word allows, their union is not blessed by Him."

The Reverend Milfield paused and his penetrating eyes slowly moved across the assembly. Even the air seemed to hold its breath.

Mary Lou's thoughts carried her back to her own wedding. God had brought about the fulfillment of her lifelong dream—to be a rancher's wife—Tom's wife.

Now their heavenly Father was answering Lily's dream of a life with a good husband, children, and a home for all of them. Mary Lou bowed her head in grateful thanks for God's special care of each one of His children.

". . .We are gathered here to join together this man and this woman into the state of holy matrimony. Marriage is a holy estate ordained by God our heavenly Father and is not be entered into lightly.

"Who giveth this woman to this man?"

A pregnant hush fell over the congregation.

No one had thought of that.

"I do." The voice was the strong, determined voice of Allena.

Necks craned and a hushed buzz rumbled the room. Reverend Milfield jolted to attention, met Allena's determined gaze, nodded, and continued.

He turned to Tex. "Do you Theodore Williams take this woman, Lillian Langdon, to be your lawful wedded wife, to honor, cherish, protect, and love her, and keep yourself only unto her until death you do part?"

Tex cleared his throat and swallowed. "I do."

The Reverend turned to Lily. "Lillian Langdon, do you take Theodore Williams to be your lawfully wedded husband, to love, honor, and obey, and keep yourself only unto him until death you do part?"

Lily faced Tex, smiled and spoke from her heart. "I do."

The Reverend turned to Tex. "What token do you offer this woman of the sincerity of your intentions?"

Tex fumbled in the breast pocket of his vest, brought forth a plain gold ring, and placed it in the Reverend's outstretched hand. He returned it to Tex.

Tex took Lily's hand and looked into her eyes.

"Repeat after me. With this ring I thee wed—"

Tex slid the ring on her finger, looked up, and poured love from his eyes into hers with the repeated vow.

Mary Lou daubed her eyes, reliving each word of the ceremony.

"Now by the power vested in me, I do pronounce this man and this woman to be husband and wife until death do them part. May our Father God bless this union with His grace and mercy."

The Reverend bowed his head. "Let us pray. Our Father God, you ordained from the creation of this world that man and woman should live in companionship. We now ask Thy holy blessing upon this new union and ask You to guide them to live within Your will and so honor Jesus Christ, our Savior. We pray in the name of the Father, the Son, and the Holy Spirit. Amen."

Reverend Milfield looked up at the young man and woman before him and smiled. "May God bless you." The Reverend glanced at Tex and grinned. "You may kiss your bride now, Son."

Tex put his arms around Lily and kissed her tenderly. They turned and faced a roomful of smiling friends. Tex took Lily's hand and they walked back up the aisle while the organ pumped out "Blest Be the Tie that Binds." They were greeted outside the church by the Circle Z cowboys, who whisked them away.

Inside, Reverend Milfield raised his hand and spoke to the congregation of family and friends. "I have been asked by the Langdon family to invite you all to the Circle Z Ranch for the wedding feast."

Smiles broke across the faces, and the room came alive.

The churchyard emptied quickly. Guests loaded themselves into their own buggies and wagons or mounted their horses and followed the newly-weds' surrey to the Circle Z. Everyone was hungry.

Chapter 7

Shortly after one o'clock, horses, buggies, wagons, and carriages of all kinds streamed into the Circle Z lane and parked anywhere they could find a space. People flowed out of them to join the celebration of Lily and Tex's wedding. The titillating aroma of roasted beeves greeted them and whetted everyone's appetite.

Each woman carried a dish, a pan, or a basket containing her family's special contribution to the wedding feast. Before long, the tables were groaning.

When Reverend Milfield arrived, he moved and chatted among the guests and invited all to come to church. Finally when given the signal, he held up his hand until he got everyone's attention. "Let's ask God's blessing on this special meal." He bowed his head.

A hush descended as all heads bowed. Reverend Milfield called for the grace and blessing of God on the bride and groom, their family, their friends, and the food. His "Amen" drew forth echoes from the bowed heads of the men standing round; then everyone shuffled to the table to find a seat of some kind and began passing their plates. Women filled plates with what was before them and passed them on until everyone was served.

While they were eating, Skinny Adams arrived all dressed up in his big Stetson and fancy shirt, his fiddle tucked under his arm, and gladly accepted the invitation to join the guests for dinner.

Get-togethers of all the neighbors usually happened only at special times like weddings, funerals, harvesting, and barn dances and gave welcome respite from the harsh labors of every day. The women, in particular, enjoyed the company of other womenfolk. Their days were often spent in long, lonely hours and doubly hard work when the men were away on cattle drives or riding the range. It was only at church, weddings, harvest time, quilting parties, or barn dances that they saw much of one another. They relished the rest, the ample variety of food on the table, and the opportunity to talk to other women as the older children played with and cared for the younger ones.

Men seized the opportunity to discuss and compare crop prices, trade, and new improvements made on each farm or ranch and to add their appraisal of the new combine harvester that was making the strenuous work of harvesting a great deal easier.

As soon as Skinny Adams had eaten his fill, he cradled his fiddle under his chin and moved slowly around, softly playing the well-known Civil War love song "Lorena." Everyone joined in singing. He moved into "I'll Take You Home Again, Kathleen" and "My Darling Clementine." When the meal was over, his bow suddenly came alive and bounced into "Goober Peas." That set everyone's feet tapping, and he headed for the barn.

Tom grabbed Mary Lou's hand. They seized the hands of the bride and groom and called, "Everybody out to the barn so we can celebrate with our feet!"

Skinny began playing waltzes as soon as he reached the barn. One by one, the male guests now had the opportunity to take a turn or two with the bride long enough to pin greenbacks to her dress.

Suddenly Skinny picked up the tempo and called, "Ladies in the center, gents round them run, swing yer rope, cowboy, an' git yo' one." Soon feet were stomping and skirts a-twirling as the fiddle enticed everyone into action. The young children held hands, jumped, skipped, and twirled. The older girls waited eagerly to be chosen.

Suddenly the music stopped and Skinny called out to the men, "Now take your pretty partner and we'll have a quadrille!"

Squares were formed.

The fiddle squeaked out "Turkey in the Straw," and soon the barn echoed the rhythmic shuffling of feet as the ladies' skirts swirled high and low through set after set, call after call. Dancing was a favorite pastime of most of the pioneers.

Then came the call "Swing the other gal, now swing yer sweet. Paw dirt, doggies, stomp your feet. Swing and march—first couple lead—clear around the hall an' then stampede."

The "stampede" headed for the pump, where men wet the ladies' handkerchiefs. The women thankfully daubed their warm faces, necks, and wrists. The men splashed their faces, some even stuck their whole heads or hair under the water to cool down. They shook the water off like sheepdogs then led their partners to tables filled with pitchers of water and lemonade, cold tea, and delicious baked goods from the ladies.

Finally, Tex grabbed Lily's elbow. "Come on, let's go," he said quietly and guided her toward the house. With everyone busy, they thought they might be able to sneak out without being seen.

But Mary Lou saw them leave and followed. When she walked into Lily's room, Lily was frantically trying to manage buttons with shaking hands. "Let me help you, Lily," she said. In short order, Lily was securely buttoned into her travel dress and ready to go.

Lily stood for a moment looking at Mary Lou then smiled, walked to her, and put her arms around her. She didn't speak, just clung.

Mary Lou felt her pounding heart, pushed Lily back, and gazed into her swimming eyes. This was a new Lily, the shy bride she had never been allowed to be. Mary Lou cupped her face with her hands. "You're going to be fine, Lily. Tex is going to make you a fine husband."

Lily nodded and smiled. "I know." She dipped her head for a moment then looked into Mary Lou's eyes. "This may sound like a funny thing, coming from me, but this is first time I have ever had the choice of giving myself to a man who loves me."

The words pierced Mary Lou's heart. She thought of Doug and cupped Lily's face in her hands. "That's all past, Lily, forget it. You're not that woman now. You are God's forgiven child, Tex's wife. God and your husband will watch over you. You don't have to be afraid anymore. All you have to do is love them both." Mary Lou suddenly grinned. "I discovered my main duty was to love, be a helpmate and companion to my husband, love and care for our children and be a good neighbor. If I'm doing all those the best I can, God will honor me."

Mary Lou reached into her pocket, withdrew a handkerchief, daubed Lily's swimming eyes, then grabbed her hand. "Come. Knowing husbands, yours is probably impatiently waiting for you and wondering why you are taking so long to get dressed. Men never seem to understand we are just trying to look pretty for them!" Mary Lou pushed Lily at arm's length. "And you look beautiful." She planted a kiss on Lily's cheek, and they walked to the door just as Allena came in.

Allena stood for a moment, studied Lily, then spread her arms.

Lily walked into them.

Life would change for all of them. Enough words had been said. Allena just held Lily, kissed her on the forehead, and released her. "God bless you, my dear daughter. The Lord go with you."

Lily's eyes welled with tears. "Thank you—Mother."

Allena touched Lily's cheek and smiled. "May the good Lord bless you, Child."

Lily nodded and hurried outside.

Tex sat in the surrey, fidgeting with the lines and darting nervous, anxious glances at the door. When Lily appeared, he jumped to the ground to help her into the surrey.

Smiling guests had come from the barn and circled round, waiting to wave them off. Standing beside Allena were Lily's children. Lily gathered the bubbly little Genevieve into her arms and smothered her with loving kisses. "Be a sweetheart for Grandma. I love you so much." Genevieve patted the tears slipping down her mother's cheeks. As Lily handed her baby girl to Allena, she saw that Lars's and Wilmot's eyes displayed fear and confusion.

Lily dropped to her knees, circled them in her arms, and kissed each one on the cheek. "Tex and I will be back in a couple of days; then we all will go back to our new house. You get your things all ready." She wiped Wilmot's tears and smiled at Lars, who was standing very straight with his protective arm around his little brother, fighting to keep his lower lip from trembling.

Lily kissed them both. "We aren't leaving you. You'll be fine with your—" Lily looked up at Allena and smiled, "with your grandma. When we come back, Tex will be your papa, and we'll all go home to live in our new house." Lily stood, kissed each boy's forehead, climbed into the surrey, and blew them a kiss.

Allena moved behind the boys and put her arms around them. Then the bride and groom were off, amid waves and good wishes for happiness and a shower of rice from their neighbors to wish them prosperity.

The wagon rumbled down the ranch lane and turned onto the road toward town. Lily waved and they were gone.

Slowly, neighbors one by one gathered their children and food dishes and headed for their own homes. It was chore time.

Mary Lou watched the last one go, dropped on the nearest bench, and cried.

Tom was at her side immediately. "What's wrong?"

Mary Lou looked at her husband through a veil of tears, reached into her pocket for her hanky, and mopped her tears. "I'm just so happy for Lily and Tex."

Tom grinned and teased, "I thought when you're happy you were supposed to smile!"

She stood up and slid into his waiting arms. "I know, but sometimes when you're the happiest the tears insist on coming."

Tom looked down into her face, grinned, and shook his head. "I don't think we men will ever understand women."

Mary Lou batted her tears with her eyelashes and laughed. "You're not supposed to. That's what makes us so intriguing!"

Tom pulled her back into his arms. "I'm sure the good Lord knew what he was doing, but you ladies sure gives us fellas pause sometimes."

Mary Lou tweaked his nose. "Well, we have to get your attention some way!"

Tom put his arm around her, and laughing, they joined the others in the cleanup.

Chapter 8

Six months later

H ello! Hello!"
    Familiar voices.
    Mary Lou hurried from her bedroom to the kitchen door to greet Allena and Laura. They released Baby Zack, whose sturdy, little legs flew him to the barn calling, "Tommy, I comin'!"

Laura entered the kitchen puffing. "I do believe that road gets steeper and longer every time I travel it." She cupped her hands under her stomach to help ease the weight and sought a chair.

Mary Lou laughed. "It isn't the road that's longer or the grade that's steeper, it's the burden that gets heavier."

Mary Lou turned to her stove. The boiling teakettle rattled and steamed its readiness. She spooned tea leaves into Mama's big, old teapot Aunt Nelda had insisted she take home with her when they visited last year. It had been Mama's favorite.

Laura placed cups and saucers on the table then plopped herself on a chair and took several deep breaths. "Mary Lou, how on earth did you ever carry two?"

"The same way you are carrying one except it was a double load."

The women laughed and withdrew into their own thoughts, remembering.

Mary Lou set a pan of cinnamon biscuits she had made that morning and a small jar of her precious berry jam on the table. The teakettle whistled, she served the tea, snuggled Mama's tea cozy over the pot, and sat down.

"Has anyone seen much of Lily since the wedding?" Mary Lou asked. "Tom told Tex to take a week off for their honeymoon, but they came home after four days. Tom said Tex appeared at our barn right after they got home 'cause he was concerned about the new colt's knee. Then finally he admitted he and Lily got homesick and were eager to get back to their new home and children."

The women laughed.

"Oh, these men pretend to be such tough birds but most are really like old mother hens when it comes to their families and animals," Allena commented. "I remember one day I told my Zachary I thought he loved his horses more than he loved me." Allena grinned at the raised eyebrows and surprised expressions of the younger women.

"What did he say?" Mary Lou asked.

"Being the gallant gentleman he was he said his horses only gave him obedience, loyalty, and money, but I gave him the most important things, love, a wife, and family."

The women nodded and withdrew into their own thoughts.

"Well I don't even keep count anymore of the number of nights Tom spends in the barn, especially when our mares are ready to foal or a horse is sick," Mary Lou admitted. "But he has saved many a colt or filly that might not have made it if he hadn't been there. Tom says he has a big investment in every animal we have."

"He's right. Every birth is special," Allena said quietly. "Birthing is a gift of God," Allena said quietly, "be it animal or human. It's what happens after birth that is important. It has always amazed me how much God allows us to assist Him in His work. I remember a few weak colts who lived only because Zachary rescued them from being trampled in the stall by their own mothers."

Mary Lou caught that wistful, far-off look that usually filled Allena's eyes when she talked about her late husband.

She continued, "Zachary was as concerned about his animals at birth as he was when each one of his sons was born." Allena slowly exhaled a deep breath and smiled at the women around her. "Every so often these men forget they have to be tough and show how tenderhearted they really are."

The young women smiled and nurtured their own personal memories.

"But as you each well know life can be both hard and wonderful at the same time," Allena added softly.

Was Allena allowing them to peek into a deep loneliness Mary Lou had sensed in Allena? If something ever happened to Tom—she shuddered to even think of it. Mary Lou couldn't imagine her life without him. They were as one, and incomplete without the other. Mary Lou restrained herself from getting up, walking over, and putting her arms around her mother-in-law. It would have embarrassed her, so she smiled and prayed instead. *Father, gather Allena into the comfort of Your love and give her the peace and contentment she seems to need right now. You are now not only her God and Father, but her husband, as well.*

Allena glanced across the table at Mary Lou and smiled.

Mary Lou realized Allena had been staring at her. Was it possible to transfer thoughts? Yet, how else could Allena sense she was thinking of her?

Mary Lou was constantly amazed at how much more there was to God's spiritual world and life than she ever realized or understood. She had learned that God expresses His love in and through people and events that happen, even though many times people were not aware of it. *He loved us while we were yet sinners.* Mary Lou sensed she would never fully understand God's love but thanked Jesus for showing His children the great extent of Our Father's love when He died for us on the cross.

The women quietly sipped their tea.

"I talked to Ruthella at church Sunday," Allena commented.

"She said even though it is early she and Anna are already preparing their work plans for the new school year. How fortunate we are that Ruthella is so gracious and includes Anna. Ruthella commented that getting old hasn't erased Anna's knowledge or wisdom nor her teaching ability and that there is still a lot of good teaching left in that spunky woman." Allena paused and laughed. "I remember one time Anna talked to me of a concern she had of what would happen to her when she was too old to teach, since she had no family to go to. I told her that she was a part of God's family and He wouldn't forget her." Allena paused, sipped her tea, and added, "I remember awhile back wondering what was going to happen to me when I got old. Now I know. Whether you're in the human or heavenly family, you have a place in the pasture."

The room was stilled and the women sipped their tea in quiet.

"You have a big pasture, Mother," Mary Lou finally said.

Allena looked into Mary Lou's eyes and nodded. "The *Lord* has a big pasture." She looked around the table and nodded. "I thank God for each one of you every day here in my pasture."

The women sipped their tea.

"Ruthella told me she is planning to have Anna concentrate on reading and numbers in groups, which will enable her to sit while she listens to the children read and drills them on their numbers. And Anna will grade papers, which will free Ruthella to do more individual teaching with each child on the different grade levels. They won't only accomplish twice as much, but each child will have more individual teacher attention. Our children are blessed, and I hope the parents recognize they are getting a real bargain. Two teachers for the price of one!"

"Perhaps we could gather a little extra donation from the parents sometimes," Laura suggested.

"Absolutely not!" Allena stated. "If either one of them thought we were taking up a collection, they would consider it charity and their dignity would be insulted. I think the best way to help is to see to the schoolhouse and their cabin, supply them with the food they need from our ranch gardens as we always have done, and include them with our families on holidays or family gatherings. I'm sure that will mean more than a little extra money which most of the parents cannot afford."

"Could we figure out a way to just raise Ruthella's salary?" Laura asked.

Allena shook her head. "That wouldn't work. Those two women are too smart to fall for that. A raise later or next year, yes, but not now." She laughed. "Anyway, you don't raise a teacher's salary before she starts a new year. Ruthella would catch on to that right away. Anna told me the other day she is so grateful the ranchers and Ruthella are allowing her to stay. To have a home and do what she loves to do is pay enough, she said."

Mary Lou removed the tea cozy and refilled the teacups.

The women sugared their tea, leaned back in their chairs, and sipped, relishing these rare moments of peace and a quiet time together.

Sudden squeals pierced the stillness. The children emerged from the barn and ran toward the house.

Allena and Laura rose together. "I guess it's time we're getting back."

Allena asked, "Is it alright if Tommy and Beth come home with us to play with Baby Za—" She smiled. "By the way, I must inform everyone that Zack says it's time we stopped using the word *baby* in front of little Zack's name. He's not a baby anymore. He said we are to call him Zachary."

The women smiled, and the children surrounding them grinned at Zachary and each other.

Tommy ran over to Baby Zack and hit his chest with his hand. "Yor're Zachary."

Baby Zack grinned. "Me—Zachary, me—Zachary," he said and jumped up and down. "Zachary. . .Zachary. . .Zachary. . .

The children jumped up and down with him and yelled "Zachary. . . Zachary."

Everyone joined their tinkling laughter.

Allena picked up Zachary's hand. "Now I think it is time we all headed for home. . .but—" she turned and looked at Mary Lou, "I'd like to take the twins home with me."

Mary Lou nodded. "Fine. When you're ready to eat dinner, send them home."

"Oh, let them stay," Allena said and smiled down at the children.

Mary Lou's glance met two pairs of upturned, imploring eyes, and she threw her hands up. "Oh, all right, but come home right after supper so we can get our bedtime chores done."

The twins were off and running before her sentence finished. Mary Lou watched everyone go, Laura swaying in that familiar gait. It would be her turn soon. Mary Lou sent a prayer to the Lord to bless Laura and Nelson with a baby of good health. For Nelson's sake. Although she never mentioned it, she knew Allena was concerned. His mother longed for Nelson to have a perfect child to validate himself. They would know soon. Laura's baby was carrying low.

Chapter 9

Mary Lou stepped out her ranch door, took a deep breath of the fresh morning air, and basked in the warm sunshine. A sudden flurry of activity at the main ranch captured her attention. A rider galloped hard toward their barn, halted in a cloud of dust, and called for Tom. It was Lily. She quickly dismounted at the barn door and hurried in.

Mary Lou shaded her eyes. Had something happened? She waited a long moment then decided to walk to the barn. Halfway there, Tom suddenly emerged from the barn, riding Tinder bareback, and galloped hard toward the main ranch.

Tommy ran after his father, then stopped. With a frown on his face he turned and followed Lily and his sister as they walked toward his mother.

"What happened?" Mary Lou called out as they neared her. The serious expression on Lily's face brought fear to her heart. Something terrible must have happened.

"Allena just received a telegraph message from Darcy's father," she gasped between breaths. "Darcy has been in an accident. She was thrown from her horse and is calling for Zack. I guess she's hurt real bad. Her father asked Zack to come immediately and bring Baby Zack with him. Unfortunately, Zack left this morning on the train for the Texas State Legislature. The operator telegraphed back to Darcy's family that as soon as they locate Zack they will have him contact his father-in-law." Lily lowered her head and said softly, "As much as I had a hard time with Darcy, I pray her injuries aren't serious."

Mary Lou nodded in prayerful agreement. She called the twins and sat them together on Lily's horse, and they walked fast to the main ranch.

Hattie and Allena had just finished breakfast cleanup when they entered the ranch kitchen. The twins raced toward Baby Zack and Genevieve.

As the woman talked, Mary Lou's tender heart reached for Darcy. Her confidence in God still encouraged her to hold to the belief that Darcy could have been reached if she had just stayed in Texas longer and tried a little harder to adjust.

"God never gives up on anyone," Mama had often said, "and we shouldn't either." For all Darcy's scornful, tempestuous ways that had driven everyone to distraction, Mary Lou had felt a kinship—perhaps because they had both been new brides in the family. She was sorry she hadn't tried harder to befriend Darcy, to help her make the adjustment to the abrupt change to ranch life. Because Mary Lou had grown up on a ranch, much was familiar to her, but she now realized that for Darcy it must have been like a foreign land with none of the niceties of Boston that she was accustomed to. Yet, perhaps this accident would lay her down long enough to think about what she really wanted, her husband and son or Boston's high society.

Mary Lou remembered Mama saying, "Sometimes God has to set us down hard to get our attention." Mary Lou smiled. *Just as I have to do with Tommy and Beth once in awhile.* "I do hope Darcy isn't hurt too bad," she said.

Allena shook her head. "The telegram said 'serious.'"

Somehow the news had spread to their neighbors. Just before noon, Emily Shepard walked into the kitchen and placed two large baskets filled with bread and meat on the kitchen table. She was followed by her sons Luke and John, who carried in baskets and pans, set them on the table, grinned, and hurried outside to join the men.

Emily walked over to Allena, looked lovingly into her eyes, and patted her shoulder. "When trouble comes, friends need to share the bad as well as the good."

Looks of loving concern passed between the two women as they readied the table. When the coffee and tea were steaming, everyone sat down. Prayers for Zack, Darcy, and her family were expressed along with thanks for the food.

The presence of dear friends and neighbors eased the tension that had held everyone in its iron grip since the news of Darcy had arrived.

In Harness, at the new train station, Tom and Nelson sat enthralled as they watched the telegraph in action. *What an invention! Imagine! Messages sent from one place to another on pieces of wire!* It boggled Tom's mind. *What a help it is to communicate between towns. Between towns? Between states!* The message to Zack had been sent all the way from Boston!

"It's a miracle, that's what it is," Tom said to Jim Johnson, the telegrapher. "Imagine, being able to send words halfway across the country on wire and get an answer the same day! Why, it would have taken weeks to get a message to Zack by stagecoach or even the old pony express."

Jim smiled. "Yep! And have you seen them new phonographs? Tom Edison invented them. It has a flat wheel that goes around and you put these black, flat plates that have grooves cut out in them—they call 'em records. Then there's a swing arm with a needle in it that you put in the grooves on the outside edge of the record. Then you start the thing spinnin' and it plays music or talkin'." He laughed. "I'd like to get me one of those someday. Hey!

Ain't this a great time to be livin'!"

It took two long hours before the telegraph clicked a message from Zack that he was on his way home by train. Tom and Nelson headed for the Circle Z.

The family was in the middle of making hurried plans for Zack's trip to Boston.

Allena had folded Zack a couple of extra clean shirts and packed more underwear and socks to add to what he had taken with him to the capital. As she worked, she grew more uneasy and finally expressed her concern to the family. "It will be very difficult for both Zack and Baby Zack to travel all that way. What about food and someplace to sleep?"

"You just sleep on the train, Mother, in your seat," Nelson answered.

Allena shook her head. "Why they will have to sleep sitting up on the train all night! I should go and help care for Baby Zack." The words were no more out of her mouth the Allena looked over at Laura, who was large with child. She could be due before Zack would return. Allena had planned to deliver the baby. . .and check it. . . She didn't want Nelson or Laura to know how concerned she was, but she figured they were both thinking the same as she but hadn't made any mention of it. Would Nelson's child be whole, hardy, and able to walk? Her concerned thoughts spilled out. "I would go and take care of Baby Zack but—Laura's baby could be born while I am gone and I. . .and. . .Laura had expressly asked me to be with her to birth and inspect the baby." The thought of Nelson's child inheriting his weakness was never voiced, but fear lodged in the house unspoken, and Allena wanted to be there just in case. Early massage and care were especially vital immediately after birth.

During the discussion, Hattie spoke up and flatly stated, "I could go with Zack and take care of Baby Zack."

Her words hung in the air for consideration by surprised family members.

"Oh, Hattie," Allena commented, "that would be a hard trip for you with Baby Zack."

Hattie shook her head and laughed. "It would be like a vacation compared to one day's work around here! Anyway, I've never been on a train."

Eyes moved from one to another as the family digested the idea.

"Well then, Hattie," Allena finally said, "let's sort of gather you together just in case. Then we'll see what Zack wants to do when he gets here."

"I think we ought to meet Zack at the train in Harness," Tom said. "He needs to go as soon as he can if Darcy is hurt as bad as we've been told. He could save a day's ride if we were there to meet him, and he could board the next train going east right away."

The family looked at one another. It made sense.

The women scurried to pack for Hattie and Baby Zack. Tom and Nelson collected what they thought Zack might need for the longer trip.

Finally, all was ready. The whole family climbed into buggies and wagons and drove to the railroad station on the outskirts of Harness to meet the train.

Zack was the first one to swing off the train and spied his family waiting for him. His concerned face widened with a grateful grin.

Allena threw her arms around her tall, distinguished son, then backed away and let him and Tom talk. She walked to Hattie, who stood in the midst of their baggage, all dressed for traveling and awaiting the final decision. Allena reached forward and placed an envelope in Hattie's hand. "I want you to give this to Mrs. Whitney. It's a letter to her as one mother to another and a written prayer that has helped me in my times of trial. I don't know whether she is a Christian or not, but prayers help everybody. Somehow I don't think she will be offended. Zack said she is a sweet, gracious lady."

Hattie nodded and tucked the envelope into her reticule and gave it a pat. "Just from things Zack has said I think I'm going to like that lady."

Zack was outwardly pleased with the arrangements to take Baby Zack with him, doubly pleased that Hattie would go as nursemaid. On the trip home, his legal mind had searched some of the ramifications that might enter into his father-in-law's cagey, legal, maneuvering mind. Zack didn't trust him. He would have preferred to go alone if he hadn't felt it only right to try to let his son see his mother again. Could it be that in her weakness she might discover the joy of having a son? Stranger things had happened. Circumstances change people. His mother had firmly embedded in each one of her boys' hearts and minds that God never runs out of miracles and that Jesus has already paid for everybody's sins on the cross.

So regardless of what his father-in-law thought, Zack felt he was doing the right thing. *If Darcy is as injured as they said in the telegram. . .maybe. . . yet. . .* He'd wait to make any judgments till he got there.

The train going east huffed and puffed into the station and released huge white clouds of steam as it wheezed to a stop.

Amid farewell kisses and hugs, Zack, carrying his son, helped Hattie up the train steps, found some seats, piled their luggage under the seat, sat down, and leaned to the window to wave just as the train began pulling away from the station. His whole family stood outside waving and smiling. Their active, concerned love tugged at his heart. He was proud to be a Langdon.

Hattie settled in her seat, straightened her skirt, took off her Sunday church-meetin' hat, then reached for Baby Zack.

Zack grinned. "Hattie, you just sit back and enjoy the scenery for a while. I'll hold him." He perched his son on his knee and smiled into the child's upturned face.

Wide-eyed, Baby Zack suddenly nestled into the safety of his father's arms and stared up with questioning eyes.

Never in all his growing years had Zack appreciated the meaning of family as he had today. He remembered his strong, steady father, and for the first time in a long time, felt a hollow ache and a longing for his father's presence. He had automatically become the head of the family since he was the oldest son and a lawyer. His chest rose and fell in a deep sigh. He felt as if he could use a big dose of his father's wisdom right now.

Zack was thankful he had been able to delegate most of the decisions about the ranch into Tom's and Nelson's capable hands. When he had left for the East to study law, he had been rather reluctant to turn the office books and keys over to Doug, but being second son in line it was his responsibility. He hadn't trusted Doug then but prayed and hoped Doug would measure up. Now, with Doug gone, he had been able to turn complete management of the ranch over to his two younger brothers, which freed him to pursue his own law business.

Zack glanced over at Hattie and grinned. She sat ramrod straight, chin up, gazing out the window, her face filled with delight. Zack grinned at her obvious pleasure. He fondly remembered the first day she came to the ranch. He had been ten, Doug eight, Tom four, and Nelson just a baby. His father had met her on a westbound stage and brought her home to help in the kitchen at the ranch. Hattie became second mother to all of them and had been a stalwart, sustaining comfort to his mother since the tragedy of his father's death.

A fresh discovery perched in Zack's mind. *Fancy clothes and prestige never make a lady. It begins in the heart and grows by loving.* He had learned that from his mother. Zack caught Hattie's eye and smiled at her.

She returned his smile. The delighted expression on her face told him she was having the time of her life. He was doubly thankful to her for coming with him. Baby Zack was used to her and obeyed her well. He wasn't surprised. As a young boy he knew that she had never said anything twice. If any of them hadn't "listened up," they were left out. Zack grinned. Yep. It was about time Hattie had a vacation. He settled back for the long trip.

Three days later, after changing trains twice as they crossed the mid-eastern states, the engine huffed and puffed its way into Boston and wheezed a sigh of relief.

So did Hattie. Though she had been fascinated watching the country fly by, her bones felt as if every one had been hammered numb. She was already looking forward to a night's rest, laid out flat on a solid bed.

Zack glanced down at his son's sleepy, dreamy eyes staring up at him. He smiled and touched the tip of Baby Zack's nose with his finger. "We're going to see your mama, Son."

Baby Zack perked up and soon started a barrage of innocent questions.

Chapter 10

The train slowed to a stop at the Boston station. Zack rose, allowed Hattie and Baby Zack to move into the aisle, and retrieved the baggage from under the seat.

Hattie flopped the handle of her reticule over her arm, took Baby Zack's hand, and followed Zack quickly to the end of the car.

Zack hopped to the platform, lifted his son to the ground, and grabbed Hattie's outstretched hand as she stepped from the train to the platform. Zack motioned to a waiting cab and helped Hattie into it.

The horses stepped high as they rode through Boston on the cobblestone streets. Hattie's eyes widened at the parade of grand buggies with fancy dressed men and beautiful women in large plumed hats that rode past them. "My, my! This is a big, grand place."

"Yes, it is," Zack answered. In a momentary flash he viewed it fresh through Hattie's eyes, with new understanding of how Darcy must see Texas. Even though the new house he was building in Texas was elegant in its own way, it still smacked of Texas. Boston was a lot more civilized and cultured and still was "home" for Darcy, *because home is where your heart is.* His wife had painfully taught him that.

All the time he had been in Boston studying to become a lawyer, he remembered, his mind and heart periodically longed for the wide open spaces of Texas. At first he had been delighted he had escaped to the East to pursue his dream to be a lawyer, but as he neared the end of his studies, he had found himself longing for the wide open spaces of Texas where a constant wind blew. Summers were often oppressively hot in Boston.

The carriage finally turned and moved through wide, wrought-iron gates and deposited its passengers at the front door of an elegant Tudor mansion. Hattie gratefully clasped the hand of the chauffeur as he helped her and Baby Zack alight.

Zack paid the driver, picked up his son, walked up on the porch, and turned the handle of the doorbell.

The front door opened slowly, then Emery, the butler, smiled in recognition and swung the door wide. "Mr. Langdon! Good to see you, Sir." He stepped aside as the guests entered. "We're mighty glad you're here, Sir." A wan smile crossed his mouth, then his face resumed its dutiful mask. He carried in their luggage and placed it against the hall wall and nodded to Zack. "Hope you had a good trip, Sir."

"Yes, we did, thank you." Zack stopped and turned to Hattie. "Emery, this is Hattie Benson and my son, Baby Zack."

Emery smiled at Hattie and placed his hand on the boy's head. "What a fine big boy you are. I'm glad to meet you, Sir. Your mama has talked a lot about you."

Hattie tried to keep her face composed. Her thoughts went askance at Darcy's concern. She had seemed to find him a hindrance when she was in Texas. Other than playing with him now and then, she had left him to Allena to care for. Hattie immediately chastised herself for such thoughts. Trouble had a way of siftin' and sortin' things out. She hoped maybe Darcy's illness had laid her down long enough to straighten out what was really important. Hattie would continue to pray that Darcy wake up and realize what a blessed woman she was to have such a fine husband and son.

Emery bowed and turned. "This way, Ma'am."

Baby Zack took his father's hand, and they followed Emery and Hattie up the wide stairway. The boy was fascinated with the steps. Rambling ranch houses seldom needed stairs.

Hattie followed Emery. She glanced around at the elegance and remembered the grandeur of a couple of houses in Pennsylvania where she had visited before she went to Texas.

"How is Miss Darcy, Emery?" Zack asked. Funny he should refer to his wife as "Miss Darcy." Probably because that is what the servants always called her.

"She had a bad night, Sir, much pain." He led them down the hall, carrying luggage to the nursery, a large room containing a small bed Darcy had slept in when Baby Zack's age and a larger bed for her nanny. One wall was lined with shelves containing books, toys, and games. They looked as though they were eager and waiting for a child to come play with them.

Sarah Whitney slipped out of Darcy's rooms, closed the door quietly, and met them in the hall with a sigh of relief, hands outstretched in welcome. "You're here!" she called softly and hurried toward them. "Oh, Zack! I'm so glad you are finally here. She's been calling for you."

Zack walked toward his mother-in-law and folded both her hands in his and lifted them to his lips. Her smile was gracious as usual, but Zack read her eyes, which relayed the hurt in her heart. Lines had etched her extreme tiredness in her face. "How is she?"

Sarah squeezed his hands, pursed her lips, shook her head, and tightened her lips to keep from crying.

"The doctors say they have done all they can do for the moment. Her body will have to do its own healing." Tears welled and she shook her head. "Oh, Zack, you'll be shocked when you see her. You won't recognize your beautiful wife." She took several deep breaths before she could continue. "It was an awful accident. All we can figure out is that the team must have spooked, bolted, and raced down the street. The buggy turned completely over, throwing her out, and the team dragged her with it. The doctor said Darcy must have landed on her back, which is broken; plus she has multiple breaks in one arm and both her legs." Sarah's tears traced a fresh wet track over her cheeks, and her lips trembled. "It's a wonder she's alive."

As they entered Darcy's suite, Darcy's soft, pitiful moaning could be heard from the bedroom. The intense agony behind the sounds clutched Zack's heart. He passed through the little sitting room, walked into the familiar bedroom and over to the motionless, moaning body of his wife. Standing there beside her in what used to be their bedroom, he still thought of her as his wife. He perched carefully on the edge of the bed and folded her limp hand into both of his. "Darcy? Darcy, it's Zack, I'm here." He lifted her limp hand to his lips and kissed it.

Slowly, Darcy opened her swollen eyes, stared at him out of two slits for a long moment with wavering, unbelieving eyes, then opened her mouth and emitted an agonized wail that seemed to come from her innermost depth. "Zaa-ack!" she cried and her stare clung to his face.

Zack leaned over her, smitten by the fear that poured from her eyes. He had never, ever seen her so helpless, so dependent, so out of control. He couldn't suppress the thought that even during her contrived temper tantrums she had always been in control and charmingly manipulative. Zack shook his head in sympathy. To have always been in command and now stripped of everything must be sheer terror and devastating to her spirit.

Her wild, blurry gaze clung to his and locked him into her stare. He felt a slight pressure of her fingers in his hand, so he leaned over and kissed her lightly on the cheek. "Darcy—" was all his choked throat would allow.

She kept her intense, terror-filled gaze anchored on Zack's face as if she was trying to tell him something. Her lips quivered in an effort to form words but there was no sound. Her eyes grew desperate, and she fitfully tossed her head back and forth then closed her eyes with a low moan.

Zack ached to help her. He would have gathered her into his arms to calm her obvious fear but was afraid to touch her for fear he would hurt her. She was almost completely wrapped in bandages. He leaned over and gently placed his cheek on hers.

She emitted a whimpering cry, and Zack felt a slight twitching of her fingers. *O God, how can I help her; what can I do?*

Sarah laid her hand on Zack's shoulder, left them alone, but soon returned leading Baby Zack, followed by Hattie. She moved to the other side of the bed and lifted her grandson. "Darcy, I'm holding Baby Zack. Thank you, my daughter, for this sweet child. He's a precious boy."

Darcy's eyes shot open and locked on her mother a moment then moved to her son. Tears flowed in steady streams down the sides of her face and her lips labored over "m—my—s—son."

Sarah daubed her daughter's tears with a handkerchief, then sat Baby Zack on the side of the bed beside his mother.

Darcy stared at her son who stared back at her. He reached his hand and touched her shoulder. "Mama?"

Darcy began to cry and tossed her head from side to side, growing more agitated by the minute.

Sarah picked up Baby Zack. "I'm going to take the boy downstairs. I'm sure it's too hard for him to understand why his mother can't talk to him."

"No!" Zack objected. "He needs to be here with his mother."

Quick surprise in his mother-in-law's face at the tone of his voice made him apologize.

Sarah sat her grandson down gently on the bed beside Darcy and stood motionless at the side of the bed.

Zack leaned forward. "We're here, Darcy, to help you fight and get well. You are going to have to help by resting to allow your body to heal. Everything is being taken care of. You just concentrate on getting well." He leaned over and kissed her, and his heart sank within him. His mind swarmed with confusion. What should he do? The divorce had been Darcy's and her father's doing. He hadn't been given any say in it. But she was the mother of his son! Exactly where did his loyalty lie now? He searched his legal mind, but it gave him no answers.

His heart searched for words to pray. *How much prayer does it take for God to hear you in your need?* Zack had never given a whole lot of serious thought to prayer, although he had prayed all his remembered life as a little boy and a young man. But that had been kid stuff. He secretly admitted he hadn't needed prayer a whole lot as he grew older. In truth, he had always counted on his father and mother to do the real praying in the family.

An old memory took shape in his mind and quickly transported him to a time when as a young boy he had happened upon his father praying aloud in the barn. Zack had heard him pray in church and return thanks at mealtime, but it had been the first time he had heard his father pray alone. It was so passionate Zack had held his breath and stiffened his back against a stall wall so as not to interrupt his father with his loud thumping heart. He had felt as if he were witnessing and hearing something he shouldn't, so private it was wrong to even listen.

Still he had squatted behind the bales of hay, fascinated, scarcely breathing, fearful of being found eavesdropping as he listened to his father bare his soul aloud before God. Suddenly there was silence, a long pause, then a soft "In Jesus' name, Amen." His father's boots thudded across the dirt floor and out of the barn.

The memory of that prayer stunned him more now than when he first heard it and convicted him for his lack of awareness and preparation to pray for his ailing wife. He had been brought up to believe that men should be self-sufficient and learn to handle whatever they came up against. Up to this moment, he had felt completely confident that there wasn't much he couldn't handle. He was wrong.

Darcy tossed her head fitfully back and forth. She opened her mouth as if to speak, but only an agonizing sound came forth. Her eyes fluttered open and moved wildly around the room. She flung one hand in the air. Zack caught it, enclosed it in his, and rested his lips on it. She settled and a slight smile crossed her lips. "Ar—thur" she moaned then closed her eyes.

Zack felt her grip release and his own heart stop. *Arthur? Who is Arthur?* The old familiar wave of helplessness engulfed him, followed by a slow kindling of anger that almost smothered him. He looked across at his son, who sat quietly on the other side of the bed, staring at his mother.

Sarah's smile faded into despair.

Suddenly, Baby Zack scooched off the side of the bed and ran to his father.

Hattie suddenly stepped to the bed, reached for Darcy's wrist and stood head down, brows, knit, and fingered her pulse. She moved her fingers around the woman's wrist then looked at Zack. "You better get the doctor. Her color don't look good, and her pulse is growin' awful weak."

Sarah was out of the room before Hattie finished speaking. "Emery, send for Dr. Corbett! Tell him we need him right away."

Chapter 11

D r. Josiah Corbett hustled up the stairs behind Emery, his medical bag gripped tightly in his hand.

Thomas and Sarah met him with concerned faces at the door of Darcy's bedroom.

"Oh, Doctor, I'm so glad you're here. We've—"

"Hush, Sarah, let the doctor get to his work," Thomas said gruffly.

Sarah stepped aside.

Dr. Corbett pushed past them both to his patient's bedside. "Everyone out of the room, except Sarah," he stated flatly.

"Everyone? I'm her father, Doc," Thomas said.

The doctor raised his eyebrows, grinned, and shook his head. "Fathers and husbands are sometimes the worst. You can come back in after I've examined her." He herded the men to the door, and they dutifully filed into the hall. Dr. Corbett closed the door behind them.

Zack stood with his back to the wall, an uncomfortable place where he seemed to find himself too often lately. He couldn't fight it. Darcy was the mother of his son. Seeing her again, so helpless, his mind kept searching for a way to draw upon that first happy year of their life together. They had been head over heels in love with each other. Or so he had thought. He had even learned to enjoy some of the parties as he became better acquainted with the Boston social set. It was made up mostly of professional men and their wives who were advantageous for Zack and Darcy to know.

Then Thomas gradually enlarged Zack's workload until even Darcy complained. On some evenings when he had come home early, she had already gone to dinner with her friends, so Zack ate his late dinner alone in the dining room served by the maid, Sylvia.

Then young men began coming to escort her. Zack remembered how jealous he had felt toward these stylish young men who were so attentive to his new wife. But Darcy had laughed and calmed his fears by telling him that to be seen with Darcy and Thomas Whitney was advantageous for young men trying to become prominent lawyers in Boston and that it also helped them mingle in the right circles of society.

It was true. At one time he had been one of them. Also, Darcy had reminded him it was not proper in Boston for a lady to go places without an escort and that these nice young men were just friends helping her attend the parties when he couldn't go. Secretly, he had been glad. The parties had grown to be a bore—going to the same places, doing the same things with the same people. Zack remembered how disillusioned he became when he finally admitted to himself that if Darcy and Thomas had their way he would always be just one of the associate firm lawyers and able to go only so far under Thomas.

Back home in Texas, his dream and goal had been to become a lawyer, have his own law firm, and help bring law and order to Texas. There was a growing need for interpretation of the law, since Texas had finally seceded from Mexico, joined the union, and become a state. He had even dreamed of becoming a Texas state legislator. Texas needed him. A slow grin spread across Zack's face as he admitted, "And I need Texas." It was man's country. "Once a Texas boy, always, a Texas boy." Yep. His mother had been right.

Zack remembered he'd had to use all his accumulated courtroom powers of persuasion to get Darcy to agree to leave Boston, including a honeymoon at her sister's home in Georgia. He knew she wasn't happy in Texas when she changed into a petulant, childish woman and the bane of his family. He appreciated their patience as they all tried to help her adjust. Zack knew she missed the concerts, parties, and picnics, yet he had hoped she'd settle and adjust as she got acquainted with the ranchers and their wives and got involved in the general work. He now regretted it had taken him so long to realize that she had no intention of doing any such thing. "I hate ranch life," she spit out finally during one of their almost daily arguments. "It's dirty, smelly, and unrefined, and I hate it here."

After that Darcy had refused to attend any of the rancher's socials and too often rode out alone even when Zack asked her not to. There were wild animals and sometimes unfriendly Indians, treacherous terrain. . . . It bore no resemblance to the Boston Commons.

He remembered the first time Darcy stated she was homesick and insisted she just had to go home for awhile. Naively, he thought it might help her wean herself from Boston. But when he had helped her board the train she had looked into his eyes and flatly stated, "I'm not coming back, Zack. If you want me for your wife it has to be in Boston." At the time, he ignored her comment. It had come from her homesickness. They loved each other. They had a son. She needed him. He needed her. She was his wife.

He should have known but didn't want to accept the fact that she meant it. Now only an agreement upon property settlement lay between Zack and the finality of the divorce. He had refused to sign any final papers till he discussed a number of things with Thomas. Zack hated an inner gut feeling he couldn't shake off—a gnawing suspicion that his father-in-law would wipe him clean if he could. Knowing Thomas, he had thoroughly investigated his family's holdings in Texas and—

The bedroom door opened.

Dr. Corbett walked to the two men. "I've adjusted the brace on her back and her leg to keep it as immobile as possible till she heals. She is in a lot of pain, but I've given her a pain potion, and I'll leave some with Sarah."

"Will she be able to walk again?" Thomas asked abruptly.

"That I don't know. It depends on the way her back and leg bones heal and work—many things. I don't know how much damage has been done to the nerves. I'm sorry she lost the baby. That weakened her body even more."

Zack's mouth dropped open. He stared at Dr. Corbett. "Lost the—baby? What baby?"

From the look on his father-in-law's face, it was as big a surprise to Thomas as it was to Zack.

"The fetus was only about two, maybe three months old. It was a surprise to me, too, gentlemen. Darcy hadn't mentioned anything about it but she must have known."

Two or three months! Zack's stomach churned. Darcy had been in Boston for over a year!

His father-in-law shot a quick glance at Zack, his face a storm cloud. He turned back to the doctor. "Did Sarah know?"

"I don't think so. If she had I'm sure that would have been one of the first questions Sarah would have asked right after the accident, out of concern for both Darcy and the baby." Dr. Corbett turned to Zack and patted his shoulder. "I'm sorry, Son."

Zack nodded stiffly and tried to swallow the awkward lump in his throat. His body was suddenly awash with weariness, and he felt like an out-and-out coward for wishing he, Baby Zack, and Hattie were on a train going west. When one isn't loved or wanted—

Suddenly, Thomas turned on his heel and left the room without a word.

Dr. Corbett slowly put his coat on and closed his bag. He patted Zack on the shoulder again. "I'm sorry I can't give you more hope, but many of her injuries are internal and as yet have given us no signs they are serious."

Zack reached for Dr. Corbett's hand and shook it. "I know you are doing everything possible to help her."

The doctor nodded and smiled. "Thank you. Let me know if she becomes restless. I've left more powder packets on the table if you need them. I'll be back tomorrow." He picked up his bag and left.

Zack's chest ached. He walked into the bedroom, sat down on the chair beside Darcy's bed, reached for her limp hand, and held it in his. He took a deep breath and exhaled it slowly through his lips to relieve the heaviness he felt inside.

Darcy lay quiet.

Zack watched her breast laboriously rise and fall. It seemed to grow more shallow with each labored breath. Every so often, she moved her head slightly and moaned.

A disturbing thought surfaced in Zack's mind. Had Darcy ever at any time in her life accepted the Lord Jesus as her Savior? Sometime in her childhood, perhaps? He'd have to ask Sarah. He knew Sarah was a strong believer who from the beginning of her marriage had courageously faced her petulant husband every Sunday noon at dinner because she had insisted on taking Darcy to Sunday school and church, which made Sunday dinner one-half hour later than Thomas liked.

Zack admired that little woman's spunk.

He remembered right after he and Darcy were married they had joined Sarah and gone to church with her. Then there were Sundays when Darcy complained "she didn't feel well" or some other excuse she could find not to go. Finally she plain refused to get up and go.

The subterfuge would finally end when he and Sarah went to church while Darcy rested in bed without excuse after a Saturday evening festivity. Thomas, as usual, spent Sunday morning riding his horse on the park trail.

One particular Sunday morning rose in his mind. He and Sarah had arrived home from church a few minutes later than usual. Thomas had grumbled all through dinner about their being late and had vehemently expressed his summation of religion in one word. *Foolishness!*

Another Sunday he became more vocal and said he thought that all people who attended church were wasting their time. He had guffawed at how easily they allowed themselves to be bilked out of their hard-earned money. "Anyone who believes in a man who lived centuries ago, supposedly was raised from the dead, and called himself the Son of God is an addle-brained weakling—a crybaby who never has enough gumption to learn to stand on his or her own two feet."

Zack sighed. Unfortunately, early in his marriage, he had reluctantly discovered his beautiful wife believed as her father did. Now, to his chagrin, in his strong desire to become a distinguished Boston lawyer, Zack admitted, he had compromised and pushed aside his own deep, personal beliefs and feelings to accommodate his wife and father-in-law. He could do it no more. He had decided to establish his own law firm in Texas. When Darcy was well, they would buy a house in the state capital and live there.

Suddenly, a memory of his own father surfaced in Zack's mind. He had been fifteen. They were out riding the range during roundup, which was when they did a lot of man-talk.

"When you choose a wife, Son," his father had advised, "be sure she is a Christian woman who knows the Lord Jesus as her Savior. The Bible strongly advises both men and women not to become unequally yoked with unbelievers." Zack now wished he had followed his father's advice.

Darcy moaned, opened her eyes, and stared at him.

He leaned over and kissed her.

Her eyes pleaded with him, then closed, and she seemed to rest.

Early the next morning Zack was summoned by his father-in-law to his law office, hopefully, he said, to get a few things settled. He watched Thomas's well-planned movements. He could read him like a book. This sudden meeting was to hurriedly get holdings settled if—or before Darcy died. If she died, Thomas would be stripped of any legal power in Zack's life. His inheritance in the Circle Z and the custody of his son would belong to him alone. Zack's chest ached. He felt like a sitting duck perched temporarily on an uncomfortable hard rock, waiting for some bad little boy to throw a rock at him.

Chapter 12

The next afternoon Zack sat by Darcy's bed again. She had not responded since the doctor left. He watched her labored breathing grow more shallow with every breath. Her eyelids fluttered open and her glassy eyes stared at Zack for a moment then shut again and she quieted.

Zack inhaled a long, deep sigh and his spirit thought of Darcy's salvation. Had he failed as the spiritual leader of his family that his father had told him every man should be? What's a man to do when his wife refuses or ignores his guidance? Force is not the way. In his practice of law he had seen too much of that and the devastation it heaped on families.

He looked down at the little boy sitting on the chair beside him, who had been very quiet. He stretched forth his arms.

Baby Zack hopped down from the chair, climbed onto his father's lap, and nestled into the crook of his arm. His wide questioning eyes stared up into Zack's face. "Mama sick?"

Zack nodded. "Yes and we are going to pray she'll get well, aren't we?"

As if on cue, Baby Zack bowed his head.

Zack recognized his mother's training and smiled. He picked up Darcy's limp hand lying on top of the quilt and his son's small hand, folded the three together and bowed his head. "Father in heaven, here we are, three of your children who need your help. My son and I ask that you heal his mother and make her well again—" Zack paused and swallowed. "We pray in the name of Jesus, your Son and our Savior." He opened his eyes and found his son's gaze pinned to his face.

"Where is Jesus?"

Zack smiled. "He's everywhere, in heaven, or wherever people need him to be." Zack smoothed away the frown between the pinched brows of his son's forehead. *How do you explain to a child what you do not fully understand yourself?*

The child's eyes spoke questions he wasn't old enough to form into words. "Why doesn't Jesus just come here and make Mama better?"

The innocence of a child. Zack smiled. "Jesus is always here. Don't you remember the story we read in the Bible about Jesus feeding all those people

406

on the mountain when they were hungry, and about Him healing the little cripple boy? Sometimes we have to go where Jesus is."

Darcy moaned. Her breathing labored, and she tossed her head fitfully from side to side.

Baby Zack stared at his mother and snuggled closer to his father.

Zack searched for words that might enable him to explain some of this to his bewildered little son. He found none, so he bowed his head and spoke from his heart. "O Lord Jesus, comfort my little son. Help me to help him understand the hard, confusing things he is facing today. He's so young and I confess, Lord, I don't have all the answers."

Baby Zack stared at his father.

Zack longed for Darcy to get well, if only to be given time to learn to enjoy the son she had not known. Her son needed her.

The door opened. Dr. Corbett and Sarah walked through.

Zack rose, nodded, and took his son out into the hall while the doctor examined his patient.

As they stood together, the boy looked up. His eyes begged for answers.

Zack stooped and picked him up in his arms.

Eyes sparkling with tears, Baby Zack leaned his face on his father's shoulder. "When we go home is Mama coming home, too?"

Zack shook his head. "I hope so. We'll have to wait until the doctor tells us she is well enough to travel that far."

Dr. Corbett came out of the room. "I'd like to speak to you alone, Zack."

Sarah put her arm around Baby Zack. "Come, Dear, let's go down to the kitchen. Cook made fresh cookies this morning. They should be cool enough to eat by now." Baby Zack looked back at his father, grinned, and allowed himself to be led off by his grandmother and the promise of goodies.

Dr. Corbett went back into the room, gathered his instruments into his bag, and came and joined Zack. They stood in the hall.

"I'm glad I have a chance to talk to you alone, Zack, to tell you how serious Darcy's injuries are. I have done all I can do here. She has internal injuries we can only guess at, and it's getting to where I must keep her heavily sedated with powders and potions. She couldn't stand the pain otherwise. But that's not solving the problem. She was badly mangled when the carriage flipped and dragged her with it during the accident." The doctor took hold of Zack's arm and faced him. "The hospital has just received a newly invented machine called an X-ray machine. It takes pictures of what a person looks like on the inside. If we could get those pictures of Darcy, we would be able to see where she is broken. What she has really needed all along is to be in a hospital where she can be watched constantly by trained doctors and nurses but—" Dr. Corbett pursed his lips and shook his head. "But Thomas won't have it. I don't understand that man. I don't know where he gets his information, but his excuse is that too many people die when they go to the hospital and that is why he hired me and private nurses to attend her here at home." He looked Zack straight in the eye. "But that's not enough! She's *not* getting the care she needs. I don't understand him. For such an intelligent man. . ." Dr. Corbett shook his head. "He seems afraid to let her out of his control. Can't he see she needs close watching and the care of a trained private nurse with a hospital doctor on constant call?" The doctor looked directly into Zack's eyes. "As her husband, you could make the decision to send her to the hospital. If it is not already too late, it could save her life."

Zack felt the heavy weight of responsibility slowly settle on his shoulders. He was hung again. He was divorced but he wasn't. Thomas was using his typical tactic of controlling just enough strings to keep everyone off balance and him in charge. What self-serving reason did Thomas have in withholding the finalizing of the divorce papers? Zack had a sneaking suspicion that his father-in-law had been investigating the Circle Z holdings, gearing for a property fight. Zack faced Dr. Corbett and grinned. This time, his little game was going to kick back.

"Thomas hasn't yet given me the final dissolution papers to our divorce, so I feel I can still legally make this decision. If it will help Darcy, I say yes— you have my permission to move her to the hospital for the care she so desperately needs."

Dr. Corbett shook his hand. "Thank you, Son, I'll make arrangements immediately and send the hospital ambulance wagon here as quickly as possible." He picked up his medicine bag, checked his patient, who at the moment was resting quietly, and left the room.

A little face peeked around the door frame.

"Come in, Son."

Baby Zack hustled in, a cookie in each hand, climbed up on a chair beside his father, and nibbled on one. He offered his father a bite.

"Thank you, Son," Zack said and broke a small piece off the cookie and popped it in his mouth. "Mmmmm. Cook makes good cookies, doesn't she?"

Baby Zack nodded then bit off another piece.

A sudden commotion rose from the lower hall. Raised voices and a slamming door brought Zack to attention. He wasn't surprised the noise was followed by angry footsteps on the stairs and a determined walk down the hall. It was Thomas. Zack took a deep breath and prepared to defend himself.

Thomas stormed in like a thunderous cloud. "How dare you make a decision about my daughter with the doctor without consulting me. I am her father!"

Zack grinned. It looked as if Thomas's carefully laid plan had fallen apart. "But because you have dragged your feet on the divorce, I am still legally her husband, therefore, I have the final say. I checked out the papers at the office the other day, Thomas. You are withholding the final papers for some reason you haven't told me yet."

Thomas snorted and ignored him. "You have no right to make such a decision. I told the doctor I will not allow my daughter to be experimented on by some new fly-by-night, crazy medical machine."

Zack faced him. "Thomas, if there is something that will help Darcy get well and Dr. Corbett approves, then I think we should take his advice. He knows a lot more about making people well than you or I do."

Thomas stared a hole through him. "You have no right—"

Zack almost felt guilty at the smug feeling of victory that surged through him. "Yes, I have. You gave me that right by withholding the final divorce papers from being processed in court. The divorce papers I saw at the office were not legally finalized. Darcy is still my legal wife. Therefore as her husband, I have the last say." Zack couldn't suppress his grin. His father-in-law's craftily made plans had backfired.

Thomas's snapping eyes flung daggers. He swung on his heel and stomped out of the room.

Zack inhaled a deep breath and exhaled it slowly to quell the tightness of his chest.

Darcy moaned, suddenly became agitated, and began tossing her head fitfully back and forth.

Zack hurried to her bedside. Could it have been possible she heard them?

She whimpered. Her mouth tried to form words that came out like moans and grunting noises and made no sense. Had she been conscious enough to hear what he and her father had said? Poor girl. She didn't need any more problems.

Baby Zack, face upturned, stared at his father, his little brows pinched together. His lips quivered.

The bewildered look on his little son's face tugged Zack's heart. How frightening and bewildering it must be for a child to see adults argue, particularly members of their own family. Zack had never heard either his mother nor his father argue or even say an unkind word to each other in all his life. He shot a grateful prayer of thanks heavenward for the caring, Christian parents he had been given. The more he lived as a grown man, the more he found something to thank them for every day. Until now, he hadn't realized how blessed he had been to have a God-fearing father and mother who had respected and lived the truth.

Sarah hurried into the room to Darcy's bedside, picked up her daughter's hand, and perched nervously on the side of the bed. Her swollen, teary eyes betrayed her.

Poor Sarah. Zack's heart ached for this good woman. Thomas had vented his anger on her, as usual. Zack had heard his blustering and shouting below. She always seemed to get the blunt end of everything in this family. Sarah glanced nervously toward the door as the thundering boots of her husband pounded up the stairs. She leaned over, kissed her daughter on the cheek, and smoothed her hair.

Zack walked over and patted her shoulder. "Don't be worried, Sarah. Hospitals are not allowed to use new machines unless they are thoroughly tested and approved. Who knows, this may be a healing machine of the future."

Sarah shook her head and said softly, "I don't know about the machines. I want her to go so she'll get better care than we can give her here." She reached into her dress pocket for her handkerchief, daubed her eyes, and wiped her nose.

"Mother," Zack hadn't called her that in a long time. "The hospitals test and test these new machines before they use them on patients." He took her two shaking hands in his and looked intently into her eyes. "Sarah, now is when we test our faith." He looked down into Sarah's pain-filled eyes. "God has a lot of wayward children and still loves them same as he does us. I think he encourages us to try and help them in any and every way available to us."

Sarah looked up, her lips quivering, her eyes swimming with tears.

Zack's heart went out to her. A small woman in stature but all and brave in spirit. He had always admired her courage and the inner strength he knew it must take to live with such a dominating husband.

On impulse, Zack suddenly gathered her into his arms and held her. "You can cry, Sarah, your husband isn't here."

At first, she fought. Finally the dam broke.

Zack held her for a few moments, then she sank into the rocker beside the bed, bent over, buried her face in her hands, and sobbed.

"Mo–ther."

Sarah gasp, bolted upright, and rushed to Darcy's side.

Darcy peeked through tiny open slits in each eye.

"I'm here, Child." Tears streamed down Sarah's face.

"Yesss—" Darcy's voice was a gasping whisper.

Sarah sat on the side of the bed, leaned over, and gently gathered her child in her arms as best she could without hurting her. "I'm here, Dear. I won't leave you."

Darcy strained to pull her eyelids half open then fixed her gaze on her mother. "Moth–er." The sick woman tried to stretch her lips into a smile but only managed to settle a peaceful look on her face. Suddenly, her eyes sprang wide open. She made a feeble effort to rise, gasped, released one long shivering breath, and relaxed into her mother's arms.

Zack rushed to Darcy, grabbed her wrist, and searched for a pulse. He couldn't find it. There was none.

Sarah's face pleaded with Zack. Blinding tears ran down her cheeks. Sarah pulled Darcy into her arms, rocked back and forth, and quietly cried.

Zack leaned over and put his arms around them both. Baby Zack ran to them and stretched forth his little arms. Zack and Sarah gathered him in.

A gruff voice and heavy boots invaded the downstairs hall, stomped up the stairs, and resounded along the hallway. Thomas thundered into the room and boomed, "Darcy is not leaving here. I told the hospital I forbid them to use her to test their new machine—" He stopped abruptly.

Everyone was huddled over Darcy on the bed.

Thomas moved to the bed. "What's going on here?"

Sarah's soft, muffled sobs escaped into the room.

Zack stood and the two men's eyes met. "It's over. Darcy's dead," Zack said in a husky voice. "You lost the case."

Chapter 13

Harness, Texas!" the conductor called as he entered the coach car and walked through. "Harness, Texas!"

Zack rose and pulled the luggage from the hat rack and under the seat.

Baby Zack watched wide-eyed then tried to wiggle free from Hattie's strong hold.

"Sit still, Child, your father will get you in a minute." She tightened her hold and turned to the window. The station came into view. Hattie pointed. "Look! There's your grandma and Uncle Tom and Aunt Mary Lou and the twins. They're here to meet us. They must have received the telegram we sent."

Baby Zack pressed his face against the glass, giggled, and waved and waved until the train slowly jerked to a stop. The twins had run alongside the train, jumping, waving, and calling to him. He squirmed and tried to slide off Hattie's lap.

"Sit still, Son, till the train stops." Zack piled a barricade of luggage on the aisle seat.

The family waiting outside scanned the passengers one by one as they came down the steps. Finally Zack's tall form filled the opening. He stepped down, lifted his eager son and luggage to the ground, and helped Hattie manage the last big step.

Baby Zack immediately raced to Tommy. They stood and grinned at each other. Beth skipped over to them and threw her arms around Baby Zack. He shook her off. The two boys ignored her.

Two Circle Z Ranch wagons waited. Allena grabbed Baby Zack, boarded one, sat him on her lap, and planted a kiss on his cheek. He frowned and wiped it off. She grinned and nodded knowingly. He was growing up. She glanced at Zack. "We're all very sorry about Darcy, but thank God her suffering is over. As I understand she was seriously injured, wasn't she?"

Zack nodded his head.

"Now the Lord has other plans for you, Son, so we bow to them."

Zack smiled. Those words had a familiar ring. It surprised him that he remembered them. His mother had made that same statement when they had returned from his father's funeral. He had been a young twenty-three. They had sounded cruel to him then—like a slap in his father's face. The aching, hollow spot in his heart had resented the way the family brushed its hands and seemed to get on with business as usual. His father's absence had been unbearable for him that first year. Zack had felt, since he was the oldest son, he must assume his father's responsibility to his mother and take the place of his father. He now knew that, if it hadn't been for that concern to take his father's place, his world without his father would have left an unbearable hole. What he understood now he wouldn't have been able to accept just a few years ago. *Death has such a final ring to it. You can't change it. You can't escape it. It's a callous, hard, cold fact of life everyone has to face some time or other.* His lawyer mind now analyzed his feelings. *At first, one is bereft, steps aside from life, and wraps his arms round the hurt and loss to ease the pain. But the time comes when one has to settle his feelings about it, no matter what those feelings are, and move with it.* He remembered it had taken him a long time to feel life had any semblance of normalcy after his father died. His absence had created a desperate, lonely ache in his chest that took a long time to go away, and even yet, as old as he was, he still missed his father.

With Darcy, it was different, somehow. Zack was almost ashamed to admit that the heavy stone he had been carrying in his heart and spirit during the years of their married life had eased. Reflecting back, he had hung in limbo most of the time, never knowing what to expect. He was ashamed to admit the only emotion he felt now was a settling relief. It was over. He could get on with his life. *God forgive me for such selfish feelings.* He took a deep breath. As it released, the burden of unfinished business seemed to ease off his chest.

"—so Tex and Lily are pretty well settled in their new home. Lots of finishing to do, but it's livable."

Zack was suddenly aware his mother had been talking and he hadn't heard a word she had said. He stabbed at an answer. "Good," he said.

The twins giggled and wiggled among the luggage in the back of Tom's wagon ahead of him.

Zack smiled. Watching their bobbing heads and hearing their carefree laughter carried him back to his childhood and the carefree joy he had known then. He almost envied them their carefree life. But a man with family has responsibilities and accepts them. Their day would come. Zack inhaled deeply. His spirit relaxed and settled. He wouldn't want life any other way. Thank God for responsibilities and the joy that hides in the midst of them.

When the wagons rolled under the familiar Circle Z arch, Zack took a deep breath and exhaled slowly. It was time to begin again.

ʊ

The conversation at the dinner table was mostly from Zack and Hattie as they told of the events of the past weeks. At first, Zack shied and would rather have avoided the subject, but as he and Hattie told it from their different views he felt the settling of a warm sense of peace.

"My heart goes out to Sarah," Hattie commented. "What a strong spirit she has to have to live each day. I admire her."

So did Zack. A new thought took root. He turned to Nelson. "Nelson, would you be able to paint a picture of Baby Zack to send to his grandmother, Sarah?"

Nelson grinned. "I don't see why not. I'll need help from someone to keep him still and occupied long enough to pose for a basic outline, and I think I can handle it after that."

Hattie spoke up. "Oh, Sarah would love that. I felt so sorry to part her from her grandson when she handed Baby Zack to me when we left. She adores him. From what I learned about her on our visit she's my kind of strong, unsinkable lady."

Zack nodded. "That she is, and a brave one." No words were said about his father-in-law and no one asked. It was just as well. *Least said is still the soonest mended.* How many times had his mother said that? Again he found his mother had known what she was talking about.

As the daylight waned, Tom and Mary Lou gathered their twins to head for home. As usual, the children begged to play some more. "Tomorrow," Tom said, swooped his son into his arms, sat him up on his shoulders, and headed out the door. Mary Lou and Beth followed him. They waved and turned to the path that led to their house. It was painted with dancing, silvery moonbeams.

"I can't help but feel sad and glad at the same time," Mary Lou said as they walked along. "Perhaps now Zack's life can begin to take shape so he can concentrate and get on with building his law practice.

Tom nodded. Yes, a whole new life stood ready and waiting to open up for his brother. He would be free to seize the opportunities that were now open to him to become a representative or senator for the state of Texas. *He'd be a good one,* Tom mused.

Mary Lou helped her children into their nightclothes, listened to their prayers, kissed them, tucked them into bed, said good night, and walked to the kitchen door. She could see a lantern light bouncing across the doors and windows of the barn as Tom made rounds of his night chores at the barn. She pushed her new screen door open and slid onto her restin' chair just outside the kitchen door, laid her head back against the outside wall, and lifted her face to the gentle, warm, evening breeze that brushed her warm cheeks.

She placed her hand on her stomach. She would tell Tom her special secret tonight. She had wanted to be sure. Three months. The timing was good. The twins were going on three.

Her thoughts soared to Kansas and Pa and Aunt Nelda. In Nelda's last letter Mary Lou almost read between the lines that there might be a chance of her and Pa coming to visit now that the railroads were fanning everywhere across the country and had connected Kansas with Texas.

Mary Lou smiled and hoped they would come. She and Tom had even talked about them getting older, and perhaps the time would come when they would live with them. Pa would like their ranch. That had been his dream at one time before his accident. Dare she ever hope that Pa might consent to their moving to Texas and living with her and Tom? She wanted her father to watch his grandchildren grow. She knew they would be delighted with all the time he could probably spend with them. Mary Lou sighed and raised her eyes to heaven. "Mama, you always said, 'When you dream and pray, do it big, 'cause we have a great, loving Father in heaven Who delights in giving good gifts to his children.'" Mary Lou lowered her eyes, smiled, then looked up again. "Lord, I'm prayin' big tonight!"

Her heart soared. She blushed at her untoward audacity toward her heavenly Father.

"Your heavenly Father has cattle on a thousand hills, plenty for all his children." Mama used to say. "All you have to do is ask Him!"

Mary Lou remembered she and Mama had done a lot of "askin'." For Pa's safety when he traveled. For rain and sunshine. For the vegetable garden to grow a good crop. Even for the little hurt rabbit Mary Lou had found in the field one day and brought home.

Pa had wanted to shoot it, to "put it out of its misery," he said, and have Mama make rabbit stew.

The very thought of the poor, helpless, little thing being shot broke Mary Lou's heart, and she had cried and wailed and pleaded for Pa to let her keep it. Finally, Mama had told Pa that she and Mary Lou would nurse it back to health and care for it, then let it go.

Pa had harrumphed and said, "Don't come to me when it gets into your vegetable garden." But he let Mary Lou keep it.

The rabbit had been Mary Lou's first pet till it was full grown, and then one day, it disappeared.

Mama had held her in her arms to comfort her while she cried. "My child, it is the same with all things. Everything must move on. Things never stay the same. When it's time, it's time. That's how we learn." Mama had cupped Mary Lou's teary face in her hand and smiled. "And someday that rabbit will be a papa and have a family. I'll bet he'll be a proud papa."

That had been a new thought for Mary Lou. She smiled now as she remembered that whenever she saw a rabbit in her yard, she wondered if it was part of "her" papa rabbit's family.

Mary Lou raised her face to the heavens and closed her eyes. "Thank you, Mama, for all my good memories." Her chest ached. If Mama could only see her grandchildren.

And who says she doesn't?

Mary Lou's heart almost burst with joy. Her heartache released and flew upward and she lifted her face to the sky. "I bet you watch us every day, don't you, Mama?" Mary Lou knew it had to be, sometimes Mama seemed so close. . . .

The quiet night whispered its answer with a soft, gentle breeze that blew Mary Lou's hair. No. There were no voices. Just a shower of comforting assurance that bloomed comforting thoughts and snuggled them into her heart.

Warm tears slid down Mary Lou's cheeks and freshened the wings of her thank-you prayer as it ascended to her heavenly Father. She closed her eyes and relaxed.

♘

Tom finished the last of the chores, stuck the pitchfork upright in the hay, and closed the doors of the barn to keep out the wolves. The evening air cooled the perspiration on his brow and his damp shirt. He turned toward the house.

He spotted Mary Lou on her restin' chair and grinned. "Trying to get a breath of fresh air" was the excuse she always gave. As he neared, he slowed down and walked quietly and grinned. She was asleep. He wasn't surprised. It was only when the twins were asleep in bed she could relax. He walked softly and stood looking down into her face. It hadn't changed since the day he married her, only more mature, more lovely.

She was beautiful. His heart swelled within him. He tipped his head from side to side and grinned. Hmmm. She was gaining a bit of matronly weight through her middle. He pursed his lips. He'd better not voice that observation.

Mary Lou slowly opened her eyes, then they popped wide open when she saw Tom standing before her. "Oh! I didn't even hear you come up!"

Tom smiled at her.

"How long have you been here?"

"Just a minute or so. You were sleepin' so peaceful I didn't want to disturb my beautiful wife and took the rare opportunity to just stand and look at her." Tom grinned. "I have to admit I had an awful hard time not bending over and kissing you."

Mary Lou laughed and stood up. "If you open your arms I'll find my way into them."

As his arms folded around her, Mary Lou felt a joyous sense of peace and safety. Tom's strong arms were her haven of rest, her place to release her cares and bask in the love she felt there.

He gave her a long, lingering kiss.

It was the right time. Nestled in his arms she smiled and looked into his blue, blue eyes. "I have some news to tell you."

"Oh?" Tom's eyebrows pinched in question.

"We have a new baby coming to increase our family."

Tom's brows raised and a big smile spread across his face.

Mary Lou nodded. "In about six months or so, we can expect a little bundle from heaven."

Tom threw his head back, laughed, lifted her into his arms, and spun her around before he set her back on her feet. "Best news I've had in a long time. Much better than a new calf or colt!"

"Tom!"

"Just kidding. I'm proud. We could have a dozen and I wouldn't—"

Mary Lou threw horrified hands into the air. "Oh, please. Let's not overdo it."

"Now we sure could use a real house." Tom cupped her face. The love in his eyes melted her heart. "I love you, Mary Lou," he said huskily. "You have far exceeded my highest expectations of how wonderful a wife could be."

Mary Lou nodded. "I feel the same love for you, Tom."

His arms tenderly gathered her to him, and he held her pressed against him—the safest place in her whole world. Her spirit rose in thanksgiving to her heavenly Father for this dear, sweet man He had given her for a husband. *My cup runneth over,* flooded her mind.

Tom kissed her softly, released her, opened the door, and they went inside.

Zillions of stars in a wide, blue-black sky twinkled "Good night!"

Chapter 14

M ary Lou smiled with pride as she watched her energetic twins run down the road to the main ranch, Beth's long curls bouncing, her skirt flapping around her legs. As usual, Beth was trying to keep up with Tommy.

Suddenly, Beth stopped, turned, ran back, took her mother's hand, and walked like a little lady beside her. Mary Lou glanced down into her upturned face and smiled.

"Tommy just wants to hurry and play with the boys, but we walk like ladies, don't we, Mama?"

Mary Lou suppressed a smile. "Yes, we do, Beth."

Beth nodded her head emphatically. "We walk like ladies," she repeated and fell into step with her mother, who narrowed her steps to fit the little tiny lady beside her.

Mary Lou had often wondered what Mama had looked like when she was a little girl. She had no pictures of Mama as a child but could see many of Mama's mannerisms in Beth, and her daughter had Mama's eyes and hair.

For awhile, Mary Lou had despaired that her dainty little Beth would become a tomboy. Considering the fact that most of her playmates were boys, it should have come as no surprise. But lately Beth had quieted some, and she often came into the house by herself to play with her doll, or she brought a book to Mary Lou to read to her, rather than play with the boys. Now Mary Lou had begun to share whatever task she was into, and Beth seemed to enjoy working with her. After supper, Mary Lou and Beth did the supper dishes together while Tom and Tommy went out to the barn to do evening chores.

As they approached the main ranch, Genevieve came running out the door, waved, and ran toward them.

"Geevie, Geevie," Beth called and raced to meet her.

When they met they grabbed hands, giggled, and wandered off into their own little world of fantasy.

Mary Lou walked into an empty kitchen. It was unusual not to find Hattie bustling about her work. All seemed strangely quiet.

"Hello!" Mary Lou called.

"Hello!" The answer came from one of the bedrooms.

She found Nelson in his wheelchair in the hall outside his bedroom door, and a worried look on his face.

A painful moan came from within.

Mary Lou leaned over and patted Nelson's shoulder and smiled. "When did all this start?" she asked.

"About five this morning."

"Mary Lou? That you? Come in here!" Allena called from the bedroom.

Mary Lou hurried in.

Laura lay on her bed, tossing her head and pulling the side of the mattress against the pain. In a relaxed moment, Laura gave Mary Lou a weak smile.

Mary Lou leaned over and gave her a quick kiss on a damp forehead, smoothed her hair back, and smiled. "I'm glad your time is here. I know I'll be glad when mine is. Just keep thinking that the reason for the pain is so that little baby who is giving you so much trouble now will soon be resting in your arms."

Laura's mouth hinted at a smile. She blinked her eyes and nodded agreement. Then another pain began its course.

"Good, Mary Lou, you came just at the right time," Allena said without looking up. "Get washed."

Mary Lou washed her hands and hurried back to the bedside. "What's happening?"

"The baby is in position," Allena said. "It shouldn't be too long now."

Laura held the sides of her stomach, taking short, shallow breaths and blowing them out, then she suddenly moaned, inhaled, and grabbed Mary Lou's arm and pulled as another pain began.

Hattie came in with a fresh basin of hot water and plenty of cloths and set them on the commode, walked to the bedside, and felt Laura's forehead and her stomach. "You've dropped quite a bit, Child. We should have this little tyke in our arms before long."

Laura stretched a weak, thankful smile and drawled, "I'm willin'—anytime!" She relaxed a bit, then another pain started its course.

"When did her pains begin?" Mary Lou asked Allena.

"Early this morning, and the way this baby's moving, it looks like it's in a hurry to get here. I don't think it will be too long now."

Allena was right. One-half hour after those words, she gave a sound smack to the tiny buttocks of a baby boy with two perfect, strong legs, who gasped for his first breath of Texas air and let out a husky squeal.

Mary Lou hurried out to Nelson, sitting right outside the door, grabbed him by the shoulders, and beamed at him. "Nelson! You have a son—a beautiful, perfect baby boy."

Nelson took a deep breath, closed his eyes, and exhaled. "Thank God," he said. "How's Laura?"

"Oh, she's fine and mighty proud to give you a son."

Nelson bent his head over his chest.

Mary Lou put her arms around him. He was trembling. She knew she could never imagine the deep concern he must have had, wondering if his child would be whole and healthy. *Thank You, Father, for Your sweet gracious-ness to Nelson and Laura. Thank You for that whole, healthy baby boy, for a son who will make them proud.*

Shortly, Allena walked out of the bedroom with her new grandson in her arms and gently placed him in Nelson's lap. "You hold your son for a bit while his mother takes a well-earned rest." She opened the blanket and bared a squirming little fellow with two strong, little legs kicking the air. "All right, Papa, what are you going to name him?

Nelson's face beamed. He slowly ran his hands over each perfectly formed limb, then folded the blanket over him and gathered his son into his arms and held his small body against his chest. He looked up with glisten-ing eyes. "His name is Jonathan, 'Jehovah has given.' "

Tears would not stay contained and spilled down Mary Lou's cheeks. "He is a beautiful boy." At last, Nelson had found his fulfillment as a man in his perfect little son. She patted his shoulder and smiled at Allena. "Con-gratulations, Grandma." She knew it was just as big a victory for Allena.

Now it was time for Mary Lou to gather her twins and go home, where chores too numerous to count were awaiting her.

A horse galloped into the yard.

Mary Lou looked out the window. It was Tom on his way to town. He dismounted, ground-reined Tinder, and hurried into the house. She met him at the door and took him immediately to Nelson's bedroom without saying a word.

Tom grinned. "Well, little brother, what have we here?"

Nelson's broad smile sparked a twinkle in his eye. "We have my son— my perfectly healthy son." He leaned over and picked him up from Laura's side, laid him gently on his lap, and unwrapped the blanket to expose two active, jerking little legs. When Nelson looked up at Tom, there were tears in his eyes.

Tom gripped his shoulder, grabbed his hand, and squeezed it hard. "I'm glad, Nelson. I'm happy for you." He glanced at Laura. "For you both."

Mary Lou thought for the thousandth time since she had become a Langdon how wonderful it was to have brothers and sisters. "The Lord supplieth our every need," Mama had often said. He certainly had for her.

She left Tom with Nelson and walked back to the kitchen. She felt her aunt Nelda's letter in her apron pocket, the one she had picked up from the mailbox. Her aunt had mentioned again that they were making plans to visit within the next year and would come by train.

An old thought Mary Lou had nurtured for a long time surfaced again. Maybe after they got there and saw Texas they might consider moving to live with her, Tom, and the children. Pa would love being around all the horses and his grandchildren. . .they could bring all of Mama's things.

She'd talk to Tom.

Chapter 15

Six months later

With the twins at Lily's house, Mary Lou finished her morning chores early and slowly walked to the main ranch mailbox. The sun hung high and hot, but its golden head was shaded by large, cottony clouds that had lingered in the sky for several days, growing heavier and darker. The poor, dry, dusty earth stretched its arm for a drink.

With most of the crops planted and everything moved into the new frame house, Mary Lou felt done in. Her body drooped like a heavy sack, and her back had been aching for a couple days. She was more than ready to have this baby. To have her slim body and energy to work would be wonderful.

She walked slowly. June, their new shepherd collie dog, caught up with her and trotted alongside. Mary Lou patted her head. "Poor pup. You miss your morning romp with the twins, don't you?" Mary Lou laughed. "Sorry, June. I'm not up to much more than a lean over to pat your head."

A sharp pain shot through her back and took her breath. That was the hardest one yet. She had been having pains off and on all morning. Should she turn and go back home? She stopped and took a deep breath. The pain eased so she continued to the main ranch. If she needed help, it was closest.

Hattie stretched and hung a wet shirt on the line and spotted movement on the road to Tom's ranch. She shaded her eyes. Mary Lou was coming. She hung a few more shirts and looked for Mary Lou again. She had stopped and was standing, holding her stomach. Slowly she began to move then stopped again. Hattie turned from her clothesline and hurried into the house.

She emerged as quickly as she went in, followed by Laura, who shaded her eyes and watched Mary Lou walk unsteadily toward the ranch. "Hattie, keep your water boiling. I'm going to get Mary Lou." She ran to the ranch door and called, "Mother, come help me with Mary Lou!"

Laura was barely out the gate when Allena hurried through the kitchen door and followed her.

Mary Lou knew she was in trouble. The pains were stabbing not only her back but down near the bottom of her stomach. Her legs grew unsteady. She looked for something to hang on to. There was nothing. She put one foot in front of the other. She had to keep walking.

Active movement from the ranch put a smile of relief on her face, and she stopped. Laura and Allena were running toward her. She broke out in a cold sweat and staggered forward as best she could.

"We're coming, Mary Lou," Allena called. "Just stand there."

Mary Lou stopped while another pain shot through her body. Ambivalent feelings of fear and joy moved one foot in front of the other, and she staggered forward. She was breathing hard. This baby was coming, ready or not! Laura and Allena were running toward her. She smiled and raised her face to heaven. "Thank You. . . Oh, thank You, Lord." Her knees became unreliable, and she was sinking to the ground when Laura and Allena reached her and caught her before she fell.

Allena and Laura supported her like crutches and nearly carried her toward the house.

Laura called, "Hattie, Hattie, get things ready! Mary Lou's having her baby."

One pain blended into another until Mary Lou felt as if she were being torn apart; then she thankfully sank into oblivion.

When she opened her eyes, she was in Allena's high four-poster bed. Her body was at peace, and Allena was sitting at her side, smiling at her. She felt her stomach. It was flat. She started to rise up. "The baby—"

"Lie back down and rest, my dear, your task is finished," Allena said, rising up and tenderly kissing her forehead. "Thank you, Mary Lou, for giving me another granddaughter."

Mary Lou's smile spread from ear to ear. Inner joy overwhelmed her. God had answered her prayer for a baby sister for Beth. Now her whole being lifted in a wordless prayer of joy and thanksgiving.

Tom sat at the side of the bed, holding one of her hands against his cheek. He leaned over her and touched his warm lips to hers. "Thank you, Darling, for our new daughter."

She nodded and tried to smile, but a wave of weariness washed over her. She had never felt so tired in all her life. Her eyes closed voluntarily, and she had no strength to pry them open while she felt herself slowly sink into nothingness.

An eternity later, Mary Lou opened her eyes and turned her head. Tom sat beside the bed, looking down and smiling at the little bundle in his arms. She saw wisps of soft brown hair on a tiny head surrounded by a blanket. She slowly turned on her side and reached for her daughter.

Tom looked at her and smiled. "You're awake." He placed their new daughter into her mother's arms. "Thank you, dear wife, for another sweet little daughter." He grinned. "She looks like you must have looked at this size."

Mary Lou laughed. "Oh, Tom, how would you know?"

"Remember your mother's locket you keep in your dresser drawer? Isn't that a picture of you?"

Mary Lou had forgotten about that. It was the only picture she had of herself as a child. She'd have to look at it again.

Allena walked up behind Tom and placed her hands on his shoulders. "If I'm any judge of babies, she is a little Mary Lou." She leaned over and kissed her daughter-in-law's forehead. "In my old age, I am going to be surrounded by the little girls I yearned and prayed for half my life, thanks to you and Lily. When am I going to learn that when the Lord blesses, he always blesses abundantly!"

Lily peeked into the room and grinned. "You awake? There are a couple of little people here who would like to see you." She stepped back and pulled Tommy and Beth into the room.

Beth hurried to the bedside with worried eyes and stretched out her arms to her mother who folded her into hers. "You sick, Mama?"

"Just for a little bit. Tomorrow I'll be much better."

For the first time in his young life, Tommy had nothing to say. He stood at the side of the bed and stared at his mama.

Mary Lou reached out her arms for Tommy, who made a jump for the bed but was caught by his father, who sat him gently on the edge.

Mary Lou could barely contain the joy bursting within. She looked from Beth to Tommy. "Did you see your new baby sister?"

Both of them nodded.

"Where the brother baby?" Tommy asked.

There was a breathless pause then everyone laughed.

How could Mary Lou ever explain to him why there was only one baby when he and his sister had been two? Perhaps it was time for Tommy to learn that there are some questions even his parents had no answers for.

After everyone was gone, Mary Lou's soul lifted in praise and thanksgiving to God for their new little daughter, and she sank into a restful sleep.

Later, after Tom had put the twins to bed he slid in beside Mary Lou and took her hand in his and kissed her fingers.

They looked into each other eyes and found a love deeper than either had ever dreamed existed.

"Thank you, Mary Lou, for being the beautiful wife and mother you are," he said in a whisper.

She snuggled into his arms. "Tom, I never knew such happiness existed until I met you. Mama told me once she prayed every night for God to search out a good husband for me and bring us together. God answered her prayers abundantly in you, Tom."

Tom kissed her eyes and the tip of her nose and found her lips. "Sure am glad God found me," he said with of an impish grin.

Mary Lou stretched and kissed him. "Me, too." She relaxed in his arms. Her tired body felt at peace. It had done its job well and now, in its weariness, sank into the blessed peace and safety of her husband's arms.

Chapter 16

Tom finished cleaning the last stall, grabbed the handles of the manure-filled wheelbarrow, wheeled it out, and dumped it on the mound. On his way back into the barn, he saw Mary Lou running toward him, waving something over her head. Had something happened? He dropped the handles and hurried toward her.

"They're coming! They're coming!" she shouted.

Tom opened his arms and caught his breathless wife, whose face radiated a joy he hadn't seen there for awhile. Now her eyes danced in her beaming face.

"Guess what! Pa and Aunt Nelda are coming to visit next month!" She handed Tom the postcard.

Can visit in August. Will telephone details, it said.

Tom looked up and laughed at Mary Lou's beaming face. He was glad for her sake. He knew she had grown homesick to see her aunt and father from little comments she often made about them. Surrounded as he was by his family all the time, he could only imagine what it must be like to seldom see them at all.

Breathless, Mary Lou began, "I'm sure Mother has some extra blankets I could borrow, and she has a—"

"Whoa!" Tom laughed. "Let's take it one step at a time!"

She chattered on, planning where they would sleep.

"They won't believe how big Beth and Tommy have grown. I'm glad Pa and Aunt Nelda will finally get to meet Allena. Pa will be thrilled with the ranch and all the horses—"

Tom let her talk. Her eyes were bright and sparked the plans that germinated in her mind and tumbled out her mouth.

She reached up, threw her arms around him, and kissed him. "Oh, I'm so happy they're coming. I've missed them so." She burst into tears.

Tom held her and let her cry out all the years of yearning he knew had built up inside her.

"Well—" Mary Lou pushed herself from Tom's arms, picked up her apron, dried her tears, and grinned. "Enough of that!" She smoothed down her apron, stretched up, and kissed Tom again, turned, and ran for the house.

Tom grinned and went back to his wheelbarrow, finished the barn work, and walked to the house. He passed the cabin he and Mary Lou had lived in their first few years of married life, while they were building their home. Now they used it for wood and tool storage. It was still a solid three-room cabin and had a good fireplace.

A recurring thought took root. Would Buck ever consider coming to live in Texas? He knew that was what Mary Lou yearned for. Buck and Nelda could live in that cabin, and Mary Lou could have her family with her.

The more Tom thought about it the more pleased he was with the idea. He'd keep mum and feel Buck out first before he said anything to anyone else. Tom would like to know Buck as a friend. He sensed in him a strong pride that his injury had broken. Perhaps if Tom opened the door and invited him to become part of the Circle Z, his injured pride could heal and he would be able to enjoy life instead of resenting it. The more he thought about it, the more Tom liked the idea. He'd wait and talk to Buck and get his thinking on it. No sense stirring up the rest before they were ready for it.

Tom grinned, remembering Nelda's help when he and Mary Lou were married. She had been on his side from the beginning and had finally pulled it off so Mary Lou didn't marry Glenn. He would be ever grateful to both Nelda and Tibby for their meddling. Without those "meddlin' ladies," he would have lost the love of his life. Tom had no doubt in his mind Nelda would be delighted and move without a qualm, but it would be up to Buck to make the final decision. He'd wait. The timing would have to be right.

ひ

Mary Lou sat in her kitchen rocker, nursing little Nellena. She could hardly contain herself. It would be wonderful to see Pa and Aunt Nelda again. Now *her* family could take part in the life of her children. She sighed. *Family is so important.* An old thought resurfaced. *Would it—could it ever be possible for Pa and Aunt Nelda to sell out in Kansas and come to Texas to live on their ranch? Pa could watch his grandchildren grow—Aunt Nelda would be part of a family again…* Mary Lou smiled. Mama always said, "When you think and dream of the things you want, you smooth a path for them to come." Lately, Mary Lou had been thinking a lot about Papa and Aunt Nelda coming to live with her and Tom. Now it was time to talk with Tom.

She looked down at the sweet baby in her arms and smoothed the soft brown hair on her head, so much like the color of her own. For the thousandth time, she wished Mama could have seen her grandchildren. She would have been a proud and wonderful grandmother.

Mary Lou's eyes filled with tears. She laid her head on the back of the chair, slowly rocked, and raised her eyes to heaven. "Oh, Mama," she whispered, "can you see your new granddaughter? We named her *Nellena* after Aunt Nelda, you, and Allena who have all guided me to become the woman I am." She gazed down at her sleeping baby, rose, gently laid her in the cradle, and stood looking at her.

Was it wishing or purely imagination that made her feel Mama's presence so strong? Regardless, she relished the moment and sent a prayer of grateful thanks heavenward.

Chapter 17

The Reverend Milfield folded his hands on the pulpit and bowed his head.

The congregation bowed for his closing prayer.

"Our Father, we thank You for this time of worship on this beautiful Sabbath day and ask Your blessing on all who have gathered here. We thank You for strength and health, for friends and family, and for the bounties of this growing season." He raised his hand in benediction. "Now may His Holy Spirit rest upon you and give you peace today and throughout this week. In Jesus' name, Amen."

Reverend Milfield stepped from the pulpit and walked down the center aisle to stand at the door and shake hands with his congregation as they filed out.

Allena remained in her seat until the congregation had left then walked over to Ruthella as she began to close up the organ. "We would be happy if you and Anna would come home with us and join us for Sunday dinner. We never have a chance to visit at church."

Ruthella nodded. "Oh, thank you, we'd be delighted." She hurried to Anna, who nodded her head and smiled at Allena.

The ride home was pleasant. A recent rain had washed the dust away. As they rode under the Circle Z arch, a horse and rider galloped in from the opposite direction. It was Zack.

They waved. He saluted from the brim of his hat and rode behind them to the ranch house, dismounted, and came to help the ladies from the buggy.

"This is a pleasant surprise," he said as he helped Ruthella down.

"Yes, thank you." Ruthella smiled and mentally scolded her heart for banging its surprised pleasure.

"Didn't see you in church, this morning, young man," Anna said. "Where were you?"

Zack smiled. "It was eleven-thirty when my train got in from the legislature, so I came on home." He escorted the ladies to the ranch house door and opened it.

His observant mother met them and pulled Anna in. "Dinner won't be ready for a bit, Zack. Ruthella has only been here once, so why don't you and

Ruthella take a little walk to show her the ranch and work up an appetite while we finish? We'll send one of the children to let you know when it's ready."

"Sounds like a good idea to me." He turned to Ruthella and cupped her elbow in his hand. "Do you mind?"

"I'd be delighted. I've heard the Circle Z is one of the biggest ranches in Texas."

Zack smiled. "We can thank our father for that. He was a man of great vision."

Ruthella liked a man who spoke well of his father. Her mother had told her to always beware of any man who didn't speak well of his family.

They walked toward the corral.

"May I extend my sympathy to you?" Ruthella said softly. "I heard your wife passed away."

"Thank you. It was a blessing in disguise. She was so badly injured and so ill she would have been a complete invalid all her life, bound to a bed or wheelchair. She couldn't have handled that. She loved life, and it would have been utterly miserable for her to have to live that way."

They walked around the vegetable garden, Zack pointing out the barns and buildings of the ranch. When they reached a corral, several young horses stood hovering over an empty watering trough. Zack casually walked over and pumped water into it.

"My, this is a big ranch," Ruthella said as she surveyed the buildings and land expanse around it.

"Yes, my father envisioned it even larger than it is now." He pointed south toward Tom's ranch. "That is Tom and Mary Lou's ranch house up that road." He pointed to the east. "That is where Lily and Tex live. She was married to my brother, Doug, who died." He pointed west. "And that is my house, half-finished and empty."

"Oh," Ruthella said and felt the hurt she heard in Zack's voice. She looked up and was swallowed in his intense eyes gazing down at her.

"I'd like to take you—and Anna—to look at the house sometime." Zack smiled and gave a big sweep of his arm. "That and a few thousand acres all around and beyond that you can see is the Circle Z Ranch."

"How wonderful! Your family should be very proud of it."

Zack smiled. "We are. My father had a great vision of what this country could be and spent a lot of time instilling it into his sons."

"He sounds like a very wise man, and you must miss him very much."

"Yes, I do." Zack nodded slowly and looked off into the distance. He turned suddenly and looked at her. "And where is your family, Ruthella?"

"I lost my mother, father, and my little brother in a train wreck while I

430

was away at normal school getting my teacher's certificate." She looked up into Zack's blue, blue eyes. "Other than an aunt and uncle back east, I have no other family I know of." Ruthella blushed. *Why am I telling him all this?* Her heart hammered an immediate answer. *Here is a tender man, Ruthella, a gentleman from a loving family which appreciates him. Don't be too proud, he may be the very man God has for you.* She looked up into Zack's eyes, smiled, and turned to walk back to the ranch house.

"Ruthella," Zack said.

The intensity of his voice made Ruthella turn and look at him.

Suddenly Zack stopped, turned toward her, and reached for her hand.

She halted beside him and looked up into his face. His penetrating eyes looked into her soul.

"Is it too soon to have your permission to court you?" His voice was soft and pleading. "I would like to get to know you better—and I'd like you to get to know me."

She opened her mouth but nothing came out. "I—ah—I—"

"I assure you, Ruthella, my intentions are honorable."

Ruthella stood gazing up at him, her heart turning sommersaults, and undeniable joy bubbled within her. "Why—yes, Zack, I would like to know you better."

A big smile spread across Zack's face. He felt like a schoolboy who had just asked for his first date. "Thank you. Perhaps we could go out to dinner this coming Friday."

"Zack, Ruthella, dinner is ready," Allena called.

Chapter 18

Tom, Mary Lou, and the twins watched the passenger cars of the train roll by and come to a clanking stop. The conductor swung off the bottom step with his stepstool and put it in place.

They watched passenger after passenger step down, then finally saw Aunt Nelda reach for the hand of the conductor and step to the ground. She turned and watched as Buck made his careful descent with the conductor's help.

Mary Lou ran to her father and threw herself into his arms. "Oh, Pa. I'm so glad to see you." The feel of his strong, familiar arms around her brought tears to her eyes.

Buck released his daughter, held her back, looked at her, and nodded. "You look well, Child. It's good to see you."

Mary Lou turned, threw her arms around her aunt, and squeezed her hard. "Oh, how many times I have lived this moment in my mind." She sniffed and brushed her tears away and looked from one to the other. "I can't believe you're finally here." She turned to Tom, who stood with a twin on either side of him.

Tom stepped forward and shook Buck's hand. "Glad to see you again, Sir. Welcome to Texas." He hugged Aunt Nelda. "Glad you could come."

Buck stood looking at his grandson then put out his hand.

"Hello, young fella, I'm your grandfather."

Tommy hesitated for a moment and looked up at his father.

Tom nodded and gave him a nudge. "It's true. Shake hands with him, Son, he's your grandfather."

Tommy placed his small hand in his grandfather's huge one, grinned sheepishly, and pumped his hand. "Hello, Grandpa."

Buck turned to Beth. "And this must be little Beth. You're a very pretty young lady and look a lot like your mama when she was a little girl." He leaned over and kissed her cheek.

Beth shied back into her mother's skirts then suddenly stepped forward and threw her arms around his neck. "Hello, Grandpa."

Grandpa. Mary Lou kept fighting a rising tide of tears that threatened to spill. An indescribable feeling of love, mixed with the joy of having her whole family together, filled her soul.

Tom helped Buck and Tommy into the front seat of the buggy and Nelda into the backseat beside Mary Lou and Beth. Each was given a piece of luggage to hold, and they were soon moving through Texas terrain that brought back memories and favorable comments from Buck.

"I was in Texas for awhile when I was a young cowboy and punched cows. Almost stayed here, but my trail boss talked me out of it."

Mary Lou feasted her eyes on her father. His hair was speckling gray, and he was more like she remembered him as a little girl, before the accident. He and Tom were talking as any two men. Aunt Nelda had said in a letter he had changed. She smiled her wonder to Aunt Nelda, who had been watching her reaction to her father.

Nelda nodded her head slowly.

Mary Lou fought tears. Had Aunt Nelda's tender, loving care created a miracle?

Nelda leaned over and whispered, "Your pa has been going to church with me."

Mary Lou couldn't believe her ears. She looked askance at Aunt Nelda, and a couple tears finally refused to be contained and escaped down her cheeks.

The buggy finally rumbled into the main ranch yard. Allena had promised to have dinner all ready for the travelers. She also declared it would be a nice way for everyone to meet Buck and Nelda.

The minute the buggy turned into the lane, the family poured out of the house and warmly welcomed the travelers. Mary Lou took baby Nellena from Allena's arms and proudly held her up for Buck and Nelda to admire. "Here, Grandpa, is your newest grandchild, we named her Nellena."

Buck reached out a finger to touch the soft rosy cheek of the baby. "She is truly a little Mary Lou," Buck observed with pride.

Allena called, "Everybody get washed up. Hattie has dinner all ready."

One by one everyone came to the table with clean hands and took their places. Mary Lou sat between Tom and her pa. Her heart was so filled with happiness she could hardly contain it.

When they were all seated, Allena nodded to Tom.

"Let's bow our heads for prayer," he said. "Our heavenly Father, we gather round this table today with special thanks for our family gathered together. Thank You for a safe trip for Buck and Nelda and for the bounty of our land that is set before us. Help us to remember that all good things come to us through Your loving hand. We are mighty grateful this day, Lord, for all these blessings.

"Now, our Father, we ask You to bless this food to the use of our bodies and us to Thy service. In the name of our Lord and Savior, Jesus Christ, Amen."

Each head raised a smiling face.

Tom lifted a bowl of mashed potatoes, handed it to Nelda, and everybody started talking at once.

After dinner and a short visit, Tom helped Buck, Aunt Nelda, and his family into the buggy to finish their journey to their ranch house.

Mary Lou had borrowed a couple of beds from Allena and Lily and set one up in Tommy's room for Pa and one in Beth's room for Aunt Nelda. As she was settling Aunt Nelda, Mary Lou asked, "Have you and Pa ever considered moving here to Texas?"

Aunt Nelda's mouth dropped open. "Move to Texas?"

"Yes, why not? There is nothing but bare subsistence for you on Pa's land. He could sell it and move here, and you could both be here with your family and let me take care of you for a change. Pa's grandchildren are here. I'd think he would want—to—be—" Mary Lou's tears refused to be contained any longer and spilled down her cheeks.

Aunt Nelda tenderly folded her arms around her niece until her sobs subsided. "I must be honest with you, Child, your father is going to lose his land to back taxes. Your plans and the money to pay for this visit are godsends."

Mary Lou stared at Aunt Nelda in surprise.

"We talked to Tibby, and she said we could move in with them. It was kind of her, but I knew here's where we should be, so Buck can be with his own daughter and watch his grandchildren grow up. Your father is a changed man, Mary Lou, from the last time you saw him."

Mary Lou nodded and smiled. "I can see that, Aunt Nelda."

Nelda bowed her head then looked up and smiled. Her eyes were glistening. "I've been in much prayer about this trip. But the good Lord's timing is always right." Nelda suddenly threw her hands up and covered her face. "Oh, don't let your pa know I told you all this. He'd have a fit."

Mary Lou brushed her tears away with her hands. "Why shouldn't I know? I'm his only child." She nodded. "But I know. He's a proud man, and there's nothing wrong with that. But Mama always said 'pride goeth before a fall.' Thank you, Aunt Nelda. I'm glad you told me. And I thank you for taking care of Pa for me all these years since Mama died. You and I both know that I wouldn't be Tom's wife if it hadn't been for you and Aunt Tibby, who fought to make it possible for me to even marry Tom. We have always been grateful for that."

The two women stared at each other, digesting what had been said.

"Let me talk to Tom and see what he says."

"Oh, I'd be delighted to move here." Nelda's face broke out into a relieved grin that eased some of the new worry lines Mary Lou saw in her face. She heaved a big sigh. "I can't tell you how glad I am we are here. I feel that what Buck needs now is the touch of his daughter and family in his life. He's fought through his anger of the accident that crippled him. What he needs now is to be a grandfather and see his grandchildren grow up. He needs that hope."

"And I need my family here. I *want* my family here." Mary Lou admitted. "I know Tom feels the say way I do. He has always had a kind, defensive word for Pa."

By the time the women and Tom had the beds ready, everyone was ready to fall into them.

As Mary Lou slid into bed beside Tom, she cuddled up to his back.

He turned and took her into his arms and kissed her.

"We have some talking to do," Mary Lou said softly.

"I know, but it can wait until tomorrow. It has been a big day."

Mary Lou sighed and snuggled. "A wonderful day."

The next time Tom kissed her, she was asleep.

Chapter 19

Zack turned the buggy onto the road to his house. He glanced over at Ruthella, who sat prim and proper beside him. When he had gone to get Ruthella and Anna that morning. Anna hadn't been feeling well and had taken to her bed.

Ruthella had said she couldn't go either.

It had taken some convincing talk, with Anna's help, to get Ruthella to agree that it would be all right for her and Zack to visit his house without Anna. They wouldn't be there alone. The carpenters would be there. Zack had had a sudden inspiration to hire workers and finish the house that had stood dormant for numerous months.

He pulled the buggy to a halt, flipped the reins around the whip, hopped out, and helped Ruthella to the ground. "The outside is completely finished, and the inside is coming right along and is ready for paint and wallpaper."

The carpenters were busy at their work.

Zack glanced at Ruthella. "I'm now at the point where I need a woman's opinion about things."

Ruthella smiled and admired the resemblance of the house to some of the Eastern homes she was familiar with. "It looks beautiful from the outside, and I'm impressed with the inside," she said. Her heart did another one of the odd, little flutterings she had been putting up with all morning.

Zack tucked his arm through hers and helped her over the uneven ground and up the wide porch steps. She recognized the touch of the Southern plantation look. She could picture white wicker chairs with flowered cushions in them spread across the porch.

As they stepped into the entry hall Zack led her to the banister of a large, wide, sweeping staircase that led to the second floor. The rail curved up and around, exposing the upstairs walls with four bedroom doors. Zack guided her through the rooms and made comments on how pleased he was that the men had done so well and had finished much more than he realized.

As they walked through the upstairs bedrooms, Ruthella pictured each one in her mind with four-poster beds covered with quilted comforters and long floral draperies at the windows. When they came back downstairs, her mind placed the hall benches and the coat hanging racks. The parlor was big enough to take a large-size sofa, and she imagined lace curtains and brocade draperies at the tall windows. The kitchen wasn't too big—just big enough— with a huge fireplace on one wall. She would put. . . What was she doing? She blushed and realized she was furnishing the house in her mind!

"The kitchen will have a well right outside the back door. Many of the new homes in the East are starting to have water brought right into the home by pipes. I'm looking into that."

"Why, that would be wonderful!" Ruthella answered and felt her cheeks flush warm again.

The circled back to the entryway and walked out on the porch.

Zack stopped, turned to Ruthella, and grinned. "Well, what do you think of it?"

"Oh, Zack, it is elegant! Any woman would be thrilled having—a— home like—this." She felt her face grow warm with a blush.

"I'm glad you like it. But I'm not interested in *any* woman." He picked up her hands and pulled her to face him. "Ruthella—"

Ruthella's heart fluttered. She stared at the buttons on his coat and held her breath.

Zack lifted her chin and gazed down into her eyes. "Ruthella, I'm tired of playing games and trying to be so diplomatic. I have to know. Do you care for me at all?"

The words exploded into the air and sounded like beautiful music to Ruthella's ears. She slowly, bravely released her hold on her feelings and looked up into Zack's eyes and let her love pour through hers. "Yes, Zack, I admire you very much."

Zack shook his head. "I don't mean *admire,* Ruthella. I'm in love with you and wonder if you could ever return that love."

Ruthella had been waiting for a long time to hear those words, the most beautiful words she had ever heard in all her life and until now had begun to wonder if she would ever hear them said to her. She allowed her heart to speak. "Yes, Zack, I've loved you for quite some time, but this is the first time I've had the courage to admit it, even to myself."

Zack swept her into his arms and pressed his lips against hers. He kissed her again and again then held her back and smiled at her, his eyes flashing.

Ruthella lowered her eyelids. She could feel the blush on her face but it didn't matter. She tilted her face again to receive his kiss and clung to him.

They parted, turned, and looked at the house around them. All of a sudden it began to look like home.

Zack put his arm around her waist, and they turned and began a new walk through what would be their home.

Suddenly, Ruthella stopped. "Oh, Anna. . ."

"What about Anna?"

"Oh, Zack, what will she do? She can't live in that little cabin all alone."

"Well, than she'll just have to come and live in one of these rooms. It's a pretty big house. I think we could find one."

Ruthella's eyes glistened as she looked up into his face. "Oh, Zack, thank you. I couldn't have left her alone. I had planned to just have her as my helper even though they could no longer pay her for teaching. If she wasn't teaching, what could she do? She has taught me so much. A country school where you have full charge is a lot different from being a teacher in one of the schools of the East, where you are responsible for only one room." Ruthella laughed. "I've learned what sticks and logs to hunt for to build a good fire, when it's time for the berries to ripen and where they are, to take the children berry picking so they can eat fresh fruit for lunch, I've. . ." Ruthella laughed then suddenly quieted and stared seriously into Zack's eyes. "You will let me keep on teaching. . .won't you?"

"It means that much to you?"

"Oh, yes. Zack, I promise you, I can be a wife and a schoolteacher, too."

Zack pulled her into his arms. "If you want to teach school, then you teach, and I'll help you all I can."

Ruthella threw her arms around his neck and hugged him hard. "Thank you. Thank you."

"And—after we're married—after our honeymoon—" Zack grinned, "we'll move Anna right in with us. I agree she'd never be able to fend for herself in that little cabin. Besides she can keep you company when I have to be away at the legislature for weeks or a month at a time."

The heavy weight on Ruthella's chest changed to a feather and floated away. She threw her arms around Zack's neck and hugged him hard. "Oh, Zack, thank you."

On the way home, they talked and made plans. Zack pulled into the Circle Z and looked at Ruthella. "I want to stop and share our good news with Mother, and we both need to talk to Zachary."

Ruthella agreed.

As they walked into the kitchen, Hattie lifted a pie from the oven.

"No wonder it smells so good in here," Zack said.

"Give it a half an hour and you can have a piece," Hattie said as she set it on a cooling rack.

"I'll wait! Where's Mother?"

"Here I am." Allena beamed as she stepped from the hallway. "Ruthella, how nice to see you." She looked behind her. "Where's Anna?"

Ruthella blushed. "She wasn't feeling well this morning."

"Oh, then, you didn't see Zack's house," Allena's face fell.

Zack smiled. "Yes, we did, Mother, and we have something to tell you. Ruthella not only loves the house, she loves me and has accepted my offer of marriage."

Allena's face first showed shock, then pleasant surprise. "Oh, that is the best news I've had in a long time." She threw her arms around Ruthella. "My Dear, I'm not only happy for you but for me, too."

Hattie was all smiles. "Well now, ain't that grand." She patted Zack on the back and said, "It's about time. I was afraid you were going to let this good girl get away!"

Everyone laughed. Leave it to Hattie. Nothing ever got past her, yet whenever you asked her a question, she never knew a thing. At one time or another everyone in the family had learned that she was the only one in the family who could keep a secret.

Allena suddenly frowned. "Oh, but—but what about Anna?"

"No buts," Zack said. "She'll come and live with us, and she and Ruthella will continue teaching just as they are now."

Allena gazed at her oldest son. He grew more like his father every day.

Chapter 20

Mary Lou grabbed her empty water buckets and went out to the well, filled them, and set them by the door. She was tired, so she decided to seize the rare opportunity to sit down on her restin' chair. It felt good just to sit. She had scrubbed and hung clothes all morning, her baby was finally napping, Pa had ridden out on one of the hay wagons with Tom, and Aunt Nelda and the twins were down visiting Allena. She relished these few rare moments alone.

A faint baby's cry soon brought Mary Lou to her feet, and she went in to check on her baby daughter. She lifted little Nellena into her arms. She was such a tiny thing.

She sat down in the rocker and nursed the baby and thought of all the changes that had come about in the past year. Their family was growing all the time. Mary Lou lifted her heart in praise to God for her pa and aunt Nelda being here. She felt more settled, like a mother hen when all her chicks are safe in the nest. They both seemed happy, and she couldn't get over the change in Pa. He even sang the hymns in church. For the first time in all her life she could now see why Mama fell in love with him, and it made her heart happy to see Tom and Pa talking and working together. She gently laid little Nellena in the cradle so as not to wake her.

She heard men talking and before long Tom and Pa came in.

"Shhhhhh!" She put her finger across her lips to quiet their talking, and their voices dropped to just above a whisper. Mary Lou hurried and dished up three steaming plates of stew and dumplings from the simmering pot on the stove and placed them in front of the men and herself and sat down.

After Tom said grace he turned to her. "What have you been doing today?" Tom asked her.

"We got a letter from Isobel, and she is fine."

"Glad to hear that," Tom nodded and grinned. "Well your pa and I checked out the old cabin, and he says he likes the idea of him and Nelda living there; then it won't make it too crowded here."

"Yep. It's good and sound. It will do fine," Pa said. He grinned. "And that way Nelda can have some of her things out around her. She says it makes her feel more homelike.

"But Pa, it'll need some fixin'," Mary Lou said.

"We and the boys can do that," Tom said.

"Well, you fix it, and Aunt Nelda and I will clean it."

"Good 'nuf," Tom said.

The men finished and went back out to fix one of the wagons.

It did her heart good to see Tom working with her pa. As Mary Lou watched she noticed Pa walked different. He still had his limp that swung his body from side to side, but his head was up, his shoulders straighter. Yep, as Aunt Nelda said, since Pa became a Christian he had become a new and different man—more so than she had ever seen him. Mary Lou's heart sang for the joy of having her family with her. She looked up. *Oh, Mama, Pa is here, and our children are going to have a grandpa. I wish you were here, too.* The tears she shed were for joy unspeakable.

A Letter to Our Readers

Dear Readers:

In order that we might better contribute to your reading enjoyment, we would appreciate you taking a few minutes to respond to the following questions. When completed, please return to the following: Fiction Editor, Barbour Publishing, Inc., P.O. Box 719, Uhrichsville, OH 44683.

1. Did you enjoy reading *Tumbleweeds?*
   ❑ Very much. I would like to see more books like this.
   ❑ Moderately—I would have enjoyed it more if _____
   _____
   _____

2. What influenced your decision to purchase this book?
   (Check those that apply.)
   ❑ Cover   ❑ Back cover copy   ❑ Title   ❑ Price
   ❑ Friends   ❑ Publicity   ❑ Other

3. Which story was your favorite?
   ❑ *Cottonwood Dreams*   ❑ *Pioneer Legacy*
   ❑ *Rainbow Harvest*   ❑ *A Heart for Home*

4. Please check your age range:
   ❑ Under 18   ❑ 18–24   ❑ 25–34
   ❑ 35–45   ❑ 46–55   ❑ Over 55

5. How many hours per week do you read? _____

Name _____

Occupation _____

Address _____

City _____ State _____ Zip _____

Grace Livingston Hill Collections

Readers of quality Christian fiction will love these new novel collections from Grace Livingston Hill, the leading lady of inspirational romance. Each collection features three titles from Grace Livingston Hill and a bonus novel from Isabella Alden, Grace Livingston Hill's aunt and a widely respected author herself.

Collection #7 includes the complete Grace Livingston Hill books *Lo, Michael, The Patch of Blue,* and *The Unknown God,* plus *Stephen Mitchell's Journey* by Isabella Alden.

paperback, 464 pages, 5 ³⁄₁₆" x 8"

♥ ♥ ♥ ♥ ♥ ♥ ♥ ♥ ❤ ♥ ♥ ♥ ♥ ♥ ♥ ♥ ♥

♥ ♥ ♥ ♥ ♥ ♥ ♥ ♥ ❤ ♥ ♥ ♥ ♥ ♥ ♥ ♥ ♥

If you enjoyed

TUMBLEWEEDS

then read:

Prairie BRIDES

Four New Inspirational Love Stories from the North American Prairie

The Bride's Song
The Barefoot Bride
A Homesteader, a Bride, and a Baby
A Vow Unbroken